DETROIT PUBLIC LIBRARY

W9-BXF-642

DAMAGE NOTED

DAMAGE NOTED

Browsing Library
Detroit Public Library
5201 Woodward Ave.
Detroit, MI 48202

AUG 2 2 2001   BL

Praise for *The Little Country* by Charles de Lint

"A milestone in contemporary fantasy. This book sings. You grip the pages till your hands lock in place, or turn them so fast you accidentally tear them out. . . . De Lint's career can no longer be described as promising; he has fulfilled his promise; he has arrived."
—Orson Scott Card

"The author of *Moonheart* . . . asserts his unique ability to weave together a seamless pattern of magic and realism as this story-within-a-story unfolds with unique grace. Highly recommended."
—*Library Journal*

"His ability to fuse the mundane with the strange is certainly very much of a gift. This reminded me of that long-ago book, *Mistress Masham's Repose*, by T. H. White. I was certainly swept into another and very fascinating world page by page and was aware of an unusual and very forceful gift."
—Andre Norton

"Really original: one of the most fascinating books of this decade. No hackneyed werewolves or vampires, but a real sense of wonder."
—Marion Zimmer Bradley

"Excellent . . . Magical, mysterious, mystical. Frighteningly weird."
—*Chicago Sun-Times*

By Charles de Lint from Tom Doherty Associates

The Little Country

Charles de Lint

A Tom Doherty Associates Book
New York

This is a work of fiction. All the characters and events portrayed in this book are either fictitious or are used fictitiously.

THE LITTLE COUNTRY

Copyright © 1991 by Charles de Lint

All rights reserved, including the right to reproduce this book, or portions thereof, in any form.

This book is printed on acid-free paper.

An Orb Edition
Published by Tom Doherty Associates, LLC
175 Fifth Avenue
New York, NY 10010

www.tor.com

Library of Congress Cataloging-in-Publication Data

De Lint, Charles.
    The little country / Charles de Lint.—1st Orb ed.
       p. cm.
    "A Tom Doherty Associates book."
    ISBN 0-312-87649-1
    1. Cornwall (England : County)—Fiction. 2. Fairies—fiction. I.
    Title.
  PR9199.3.D357 L58 2001
  813'.54—dc21

                                              2001016388

First Tor Edition: March 1993
First Orb Edition: April 2001

Printed in the United States of America

0 9 8 7 6 5 4 3 2 1

for
Don Flamanck and Colin Wilson
two wise Cornishmen

and for all those traditional musicians
who, wittingly or unwittingly,
but with great good skill,
still seek to recapture that first music

Acknowledgments

Grateful acknowledgments are made to:

Robin Williamson for permission to use a portion of "Five Denials on Merlin's Grave" from the book of the same title published by Pig's Whisker Music Press; copyright © 1979 by Robin Williamson. For further information on Robin Williamson, write: Pig's Whisker Music Press, P.O. Box 27522, Los Angeles, CA 90027; or Pig's Whisker Music Press, BCM 4797, London WC1N 3XX, England.

James P. Blaylock for the use of the quote from *Land of Dreams,* Arbor House; copyright © 1987 by James P. Blaylock.

Paul Hazel for the use of the quote from *Undersea,* Atlantic, Little, Brown; copyright © 1982 by Paul Hazel.

Carrie Fisher for the use of the quote from *Postcards from the Edge,* Simon and Schuster; copyright © 1987 by Carrie Fisher.

Margaret Mahy for the use of the quote from *Memory,* J. M. Dent & Sons; copyright © 1987 by Margaret Mahy.

Hilbert Schenck for the use of the quote from *Chronosequence,* Tor; copyright © 1988 by Hilbert Schenck.

Tom Robbins for the use of the quote from *Jitterbug Perfume,* Bantam; copyright © 1984 by Tibetan Peach Pie Incorporated.

Susan Palwick for the use of the quote from "*The Last Unicorn*: Magic as Metaphor," which first appeared in *The New York Review of Science Fiction*, February 1989; copyright © 1989 by Dragon Press, reprinted by permission of the author.

Russell Hoban for the use of the quote from *The Medusa Frequency,* Viking; copyright © 1987 by Russell Hoban.

Matt Ruff for the use of the quote from *Fool on the Hill,* Atlantic Monthly Press; copyright © 1988 by Matt Ruff.

Ian Watson for the use of the quote from "The Mole Field," *The Magazine of Fantasy and Science Fiction*, December 1988; copyright © 1988 by Mercury Press Inc., reprinted by permission of the author.

Robert Holdstock for the use of the quote from *Lavondyss*, Victor Gollancz Ltd., 1988; copyright © 1988 by Robert Holdstock.

Colin Wilson for the quote from *Beyond the Occult*, Bantam Press, 1988; copyright © 1988 by Colin Wilson.

Jack Dann for the quote from "Night Meetings," *Velocities: A Magazine of Speculative Poetry* #4, Summer 1984; copyright © 1984 by Jack Dann; all rights reserved; reprinted by permission of the author.

Contents

Coda

Appendices

Author's Note

The novel that follows is a work of fiction. All characters and events in this book are fictitious and any resemblance to actual persons living or dead is purely coincidental.

The tune titles heading each chapter are all traditional, except for "Leppadumdowledum," which was composed by Donal Lunny; "So There I Was," composed by John Kirkpatrick; and "Absurd Good News." Musicians interested in tracking down the tunes should look for them in the usual sources—tunebooks, old and new, but especially in the repertoire of musicians, whether recorded or in live performance and sessions; those tunes credited to Janey Little have been transcribed and can be found in the appendix at the end of the novel for the hopeful enjoyment of interested players.

A work such as this doesn't grow out of a vacuum. *The Little Country* had its origin in sources too exhaustive to list with any real thoroughness, but I can still pinpoint its original spark: many an evening in the early seventies spent listening to my friend Don Flamanck telling stories of Cornwall as he remembered it. When my wife, MaryAnn, and I finally went to Cornwall in October of 1988 to research this book's settings, we found it to be everything Don had promised it would be, and more.

Thanks are due to Don, first and foremost, for that inspiration, and also to Phil and Audrey Wallis of Mousehole for more wonderful stories and their hospitality; to Bernard Evans of Newlyn for filling me in on the local music scene; to Ben Batten, Christopher Bice, Des Hannigan, John Hocking, Robert Hunt, John and Nettie Pender, Derek Tangye, Douglas Tregenza, Ken Ward, G. Pawley White, and a multitude of others too numerous to list here for background material; to Colin Wilson for his logical explorations of those things that defy logic; to those many, many traditional musicians, again too numerous to mention, who keep the music alive and give it new life with each note they play; to those musicians who attend the local music sessions here in Ottawa ("All of a Monday Night") and by their enthusiasm keep my own playing in right good fettle; and last, though not least, to my wife, MaryAnn, a mean mandolin player in her own right, for her support, both musical and literary, and for her love that I could not do without.

—*Charles de Lint*

myself, a brat who . . .
couldn't figure numbers worth a damn
was always a chancer
and given three lines to add I'd put the middle row
down as the answer
but I could read all day if I could get away with it
and all night too with a flashlight under the covers
of that Green Man . . . or of Merlin of the borders. . . .

—ROBIN WILLIAMSON,
from "Five Denials on Merlin's Grave"

He wanted the sort of book that didn't seem to need
a beginning and end, that could be opened at any page
without suffering for it—slow, candlelight reading.

—JAMES P. BLAYLOCK,
from *Land of Dreams*

PART ONE

The Hidden People

Man has closed himself up, till he sees all
things through the narrow chinks of his cavern.

—WILLIAM BLAKE

Underneath the reality in which we live and
have our being, another and altogether
different reality lies concealed.

—FRIEDRICH NIETZSCHE

The Quarrelsome Piper

Like burrs old names get stuck to each other and
to anyone who walks among them.

—PAUL HAZEL, from *Undersea*

There were two things Janey Little loved best in the world: music
and books, and not necessarily in that order.

Her favorite musician was the late Billy Pigg, the Northumbrian
piper from the northeast of England whose playing had inspired her
to take up the small pipes herself as her principal instrument.

Her favorite author was William Dunthorn, and not just because
he and her grandfather had been mates, though she did treasure the
old sepia-toned photograph of the pair of them that she kept sealed
in a plastic folder in her fiddle case. It had been taken just before the
Second World War in their native Mousehole—confusingly pronounced "Mouzel" by the locals—two gangly Cornish lads standing
in front of The Ship Inn, cloth caps in hand, shy grins on their faces.

Dunthorn had written three book-length works of fiction, but until
that day in the Gaffer's attic when Janey was having a dusty time of
it, ferreting through the contents of old boxes and chests, she knew
of only two. The third was a secret book, published in an edition of
just one copy.

The Hidden People was his best-known work, remembered by
most readers with the same fondness that they recalled for *Winnie
the Pooh, The Wind in the Willows,* and other classics of their childhood. It told of a hidden race of mouse-sized people known as the
Smalls, reduced to their diminutive stature in the Middle Ages by a
cranky old witch who died before her curse could be removed. Supposedly the Smalls prospered through the ages, living a hidden life
alongside that of more normal-sized people right up to the present
day. The book was still in print, in numerous illustrated editions, but
Janey's favorite was still the one that contained Ernest Shepard's delightful pen and ink drawings.

The other novel was *The Lost Music,* published two years after
the first. While it didn't have nearly the success of *The Hidden People*—due no doubt to its being less whimsical and the fact that it

dealt with more adult themes—its theories of music being a key to hidden realms and secret states of mind had still made it a classic in the fantasy field. It too remained in print, though there were few children who would find a copy of it under their Christmas tree, illustrated by whichever artist was currently the nadir of children's book illustrating.

Which was really a pity, Janey often thought, because in the long run, *The Lost Music* was the better book. It was the reason that she had taken up with old things. Because of it, she went back to its sources, poring over folktales and myths, discovering traditional music and finding that the references between old lore and old tunes and songs went back and forth between each other. It was a delightful exploration, one that eventually led to her present occupation.

For while she had no interest in writing books, she had discovered, hidden away inside herself, a real flair for the old music. She took to playing the fiddle and went wandering through tunebooks tracked down in secondhand bookshops, the tunes sticking to her like brambles on a walk across a cliff-side field. Old tunes, old names, old stories. So Dunthorn was partially responsible for who she was today—a comment that made the Gaffer laugh when she mentioned it to him once.

"Wouldn't Billy smile to hear you say that now, my robin," her grandfather had said. "That his writings should turn a good Cornish girl to playing Paddy music for a living—not to mention traveling around by her ownsel' with nothing but a fiddle and a set of Scotch small pipes to keep her company."

"*You* like my music."

The Gaffer nodded. "And I don't doubt Bill would have liked it too—just as he liked his own writing. He'd sit up and scribble by the lantern till all hours of the night sometimes—took it all very seriously, didn't he just?—and he'd have admired your getting by with the doing of something you love.

"He always wanted to live by his writing—writing what he pleased, I mean—but all the bookmen wanted was more fairy tales. Bill . . . he had more serious stories to tell by then, so he worked the boats by day to earn his living and did his writing by night—for himself, like. He wouldn't give 'em another book like the one about the Smalls. Didn't want to be writing the same thing over and over again, was what he said."

"*The Lost Music* has fairy-tale bits in it."

"And doesn't it just, my beauty? But to hear him talk, they weren't made-up bits—just the way that history gets mixed up as the years go by. *The Lost Music* was his way of talking about the way he believed that old wives' tales and dance tunes and folktales were just the tangled echoes of something that's not quite of this world . . . something we all knew once, but have forgotten since. That's how he explained it to me, and very serious he was about it too. But then Bill had a way of making anything sound important—that was his gift, I think. For all I know he was serious about the Smalls too."

"You think he really believed in things like that?"

The Gaffer shrugged. "I'm not saying yes or no. He was a sensible lad, was Bill, and a good mate, but he was a bit fey too. Solid as the ground is firm, but ever so once in a while he'd get a funny look about him, like he'd just seen a piskie sticking its little brown head around the doorpost, and he wouldn't talk then for a while—at least he wouldn't say much that made sense. But I never heard a man not make sense so eloquently as Bill Dunthorn could when he was of a mind to do so, and there was more than once he had me half believing in what he was saying."

Dunthorn had also written essays, short stories, travelogues, and poetry, though none of those writings survived in current editions except for two of the short stories, which were constantly being reprinted in storybook collections for children: "The Smalls," which was the original version of *The Hidden People,* and "The Man Who Lived in a Book," a delightful romp about a world that existed inside a book that could be reached by placing a photograph of oneself between its pages. Janey could still remember all the times she'd put pictures of herself between the pages of her favorite books, in the very best parts, and gone to sleep, hoping to wake up in one of those magical realms.

"I could use that trick now," she murmured to herself as she brushed the dust and cobwebs from a chest that was thrust far back under the eaves of the attic.

She still couldn't believe that Alan had left her in the lurch, right on the eve of a new tour of New England and California.

Things had not been going well between them this past summer, which just went to show you that one should pay more attention to the old adages because they were all based on a kernel of good solid common sense.

Never mix business and pleasure.

Well, of course. Except having a relationship with one's sideman seemed too perfect to not take advantage of it. Instead of leaving your lover behind, he went on tour with you. What could be better? No more lonely nights while your sideman went out with some guitar groupie and you were left alone in the hotel room because you just wanted to be *away* from the crowds for a change. Away from strangers. Away from having to put on a smiling face when you just wanted to be silly with a friend, or slouch in a corner and simply do nothing at all, without having to worry about what kind of an impression you made or left behind when you traveled on.

But relationships tended to erode if they weren't worked on, and Alan's and hers had been no exception. They'd become grouchy with each other on their last tour of the Continent. Complaining, not with each other, but about each other. Mostly it was just little things, dissatisfactions and petty differences, but it began to affect the music until it got to the point where they couldn't work up a new arrangement of any sort without a row.

Argumentative was how Alan described her.

Perhaps she was. But she wouldn't see the music compromised. Improvising was fine, but not simply because he couldn't bother to remember an arrangement. And banging his guitar strings like they were horseshoes and his pick the hammer, that was right out. It was still her name on the tour posters. People came to see her play the music, and she meant to give them their money's worth. They hadn't come to see her sideman get soused and have evenings where he made the Pogues sound like brilliant musicians.

And that was the real heart of Alan's problem. They hadn't come to see Alan MacDonald; they'd come to see her.

"Oh, sod him," she said as she dragged the dusty chest out from under the eaves.

Her voice rang hollowly in the attic. She wondered what the Gaffer would think to hear her sitting up here, talking to herself, but she had the house to herself. He was up in Paul, at the King's Arms, having a few pints with his mates. Perhaps she should have gone. Chalkie Fisher would be there and if he'd brought along his box, they could have had a bit of a session. And after a few tunes, Jim Rafferty would take out his wee whistle and ask quietly, "Do you know this one, then?" just before he launched into the version of "Johnny Cope" that was his party piece.

But for once Janey knew she'd find no solace in the music. Not with the tour still looming and her without a sideman. She had an advert in a couple of the papers, but she'd have to go back to Jenny's flat in London for the auditions. *If* anyone even bothered to call. Knowing her luck, she'd end up being stuck with some three-chord wonder that she'd have to teach to play his bloody instrument before they could even start to work on their sets. Because everybody who was decent wasn't available. Unless she wanted to go begging Alan to at least finish this one tour with her.

No thanks.

She creaked open the wooden chest and sneezed at the musty odor that rose from its contents. It appeared to be stacked, from top to bottom, with old journals. She took one out and flipped through the pages, pausing when she came to a familiar byline. "Tom Bawcock's Eve in Mousehole" by William Dunthorn. The article was a brief description of the traditional festivities in Mousehole on December 23rd, when the fishermen gathered to eat "Stargazy Pie"—a pie made with whole fish, their heads sticking out through the crust.

She looked through more of the journals and found brief articles by Dunthorn in each one. Most she'd already seen—the Gaffer had kept all of his mate's writing that he could lay his hands on—but there were one or two she'd never read before, and many of them were in manuscript form as well as published.

Well, this was a find, wasn't it just? Wouldn't it be perfect if down by the bottom there were manuscript pages of some uncompleted novel? Or, better yet, a completed novel, just aching to be read. . . .

Her breath caught in her chest as her scrabbling hands came up with a leather-bound book right at the bottom of the chest.

Be still my heart, she thought.

There was some mildew on the cover, but it came off when she rubbed it with the sleeve of her shirt, leaving only a faint smudge. What made her breath catch, however, was the title of the book.

The Little Country. A novel by William Dunthorn.

Fingers trembling, she opened the book. A folded slip of paper fell out onto her lap, but she ignored it as she flipped quickly through the thick parchment pages.

My God. It *was* a novel. A complete, published Dunthorn novel that she'd never heard of before.

She turned to the copyright page, not quite taking in the phrase "published in an edition of one copy" until she'd read it a number of times.

One copy.

This was the only copy.

What was it *doing* here?

Slowly she put the book down on a stack of journals and manuscripts and picked up the slip of paper that had fallen to her lap.

"My dear friend Tom," the letter began.

Her gaze traveled down to the signature. It was a letter from Dunthorn to her grandfather. Blinking once, she went back to the top of the page and read the letter through.

> *Here is the book you promised to keep for me. Read it if you will, but remember your promise—it must not leave your possession. It must not be published. Not ever!! Its existence must remain secret—not simply the tale told in its pages, but the book itself.*
>
> *I know you think me mad sometimes, and God knows I've given you reason enough (a good solid bloke, am I?—I smile whenever I hear you describe me so), but you have my eternal gratitude if you will humour me this one last time.*
>
> *I have a sense of foreboding for this coming year—yes, that famous Mad Bill Dunthorn Gypsy prescience strikes again!— so it is with great relief that I turn over the possession of this book to you and know that it will remain safe with you.*
>
> *Godspeed, my friend. I wish there was more time.*

Janey reread the letter, then her gaze settled on the date under Dunthorn's signature. He'd written the letter just two months before his death.

Gypsy prescience?

A secret book?

Thoughtfully she folded the letter and stuck it back into the book between the front cover and endpaper. Then, sitting there in the Gaffer's dusty attic, she turned to the first page and began to read. Within the first few paragraphs, all her troubles had melted away and she was caught in the spell of Dunthorn's secret story.

Life Is All Chequered

Sometimes I feel like I've got my nose pressed up
against the window of a bakery, only I'm the bread.

—CARRIE FISHER, from *Postcards from the Edge*

If our lives are all books," Jodi told Denzil Gossip, "then someone's
torn a few pages from mine."

"Tee-ta-taw," the old man replied in a mildly mocking tone. "Listen to her talk."

He was perched on a tall stool at his worktable under the eaves,
tinkering with a scaled-down model of his newest flying machine.
Squinting through his glasses, he adjusted the last tiny nut and bolt
for the third time since Jodi had arrived at his loft that rainy afternoon. Jodi waited patiently as he broke a morsel of Burke cheese
from the piece he kept in the pocket of his tweed vest for the purpose
of enticing the pair of mice who would be powering the odd little
craft—at least they would be if they could be got from their cage
and into the two revolving mechanisms that looked like exercise
wheels attached to either side of the machine.

Denzil was never one to force an issue, especially not on the creatures upon which his experiments depended.

"They've got to want to do it, you," he'd explained to Jodi when
she had asked why he didn't just pick them up and put them in.
"Those mice and I are partners in solving the mystery, not master
and slaves."

The mice, wiser than many would give them credit for, ignored
the bribe and stayed in their cage, peering through its open door,
pink noses quivering. Jodi tried to remember which of the pair had
been riding in the miniature hot-air balloon that was navigating the
length of the loft when she'd dropped by one day last week. She
thought it was the one with the brown spot on his left hind leg.

"I don't see much point in any of it," she said.

"What?" Denzil looked up at her. He pushed his wire rimmed
glasses up to the bridge of his nose. "Well, I go to sea! It's the secret

of flight, we're speaking of here—the last frontier! And you want to just ignore it?"

"Not really, I suppose," Jodi said. "But what use is a flying machine that you have to run like a madman to keep aloft? You'd be quicker taking the train—and better rested to boot."

"Where's your sense of adventure?"

"I think I left it in my other jacket. Shall I go fetch it?"

Denzil hrumphed and went back to coaxing the mice while Jodi settled back in the fat, stuffed armchair that she'd commandeered from its spot near the hearth and dragged over to the workbench so that she could watch him go about his business in comfort.

"Fetch it," the parrot sitting on the back of the chair repeated. Then he walked back and forth along the top of the padded cushion, mimicking Denzil's hrumphing sounds.

Jodi reached back and ruffled his feathers. "Don't you start, Noz," she told him.

Denzil's loft was a curious haphazard mixture of zoo, alchemist's laboratory, and mechanic's workshop.

In cages along one wall were four more mice, two white rats, a fat, black, lop-eared rabbit, a pair of green lizards, and a turtle. There was also a murky aquarium that presently held two sleepy-looking catfish; Noz's perch, currently in use by a black-eyed crow; and an empty cage where Ollie, the pale brown rhesus monkey, was kept when he started to misbehave. At the moment Ollie was asleep on top of a bookshelf, sharing the spot with Rum, an old orange tomcat with one shredded ear.

The workbench was vaguely divided into two sections: one side a bewildering mess of test tubes, beakers, glass pipes, a gas burner, clamps, ring stands, thermometers, jars, a set of scales, a microscope with a messy tray of slides, and other such paraphernalia; the other side where Denzil was now working presented an equally bewildering display of mechanical tools, wiring, bits of metal, clockwork mechanisms, and the like.

The remainder of the large loft had a small sofa that doubled as a bed on the other side of the hearth, dormer windows, a twin to the armchair Jodi now occupied still in its spot by the hearth, a small kitchen area centered around a black iron stove, and bookcases wherever there was room for them, stuffed with books, folders, and loose bits of paper. Everywhere one tried to walk there were little piles of Denzil's belongings: a heap of scrap metal by the door; a bag of feed leaning against a bookcase; a box filled with rolled-up maps in the middle of the room; little stacks of books, periodicals, and papers.

The room was like its owner, who invariably presented a disheveled, half-bemused face to the world, while underneath his worn and patched clothes, bird's-nest hair and beard, and thin, pinched features was secreted a brilliant mind that never ceased to question the world around him. Jodi spent more time with him in his loft, or going on long rambles in the countryside looking for some missing ingredient for his latest experiment, than she did anywhere else in the town of Bodbury.

His company was worth the assault on her nose that the loft always presented—a weird mixture of chemical odors, smells from the cages that she usually ended up cleaning, machine oil, and Denzil's pipe. And though he always appeared totally engrossed in whatever task was at hand, he was still capable of carrying on conversations on the most diverse series of subjects. There were pauses and lags in those conversations, times when a sentence broken off one morning was completed that afternoon, but the conversations were always worthwhile.

"What sort of pages are you missing?" he asked now.

He put the cheese down between the mice's cage and the flying machine and gave her another glance. Up went his hand to push back his glasses.

"Oh, I don't know," Jodi replied. "I'm just at loose ends and I can't seem to remember anything anymore. I suppose that happens when you get old."

Denzil chuckled. "And you're so very old, you. Seventeen, is it now?"

"Eighteen. And I feel ancient."

"Ancient, is it? My gar. You don't look nearly old enough to be ancient yet. I'd give it a few more years, you."

He pushed the bit of cheese closer to the mice's cage.

"I really do need to *do* something," Jodi said. "I need a Purpose in life."

"Come 'pon that," Denzil said, "I suppose you're right. You can't spend the whole of your life puttering around up here with me. That's not half natural."

"I don't putter. I'm your assistant. You told me so yourself."

"Now was that before or after we decided that it was an assistant's duty to clean up after the animals?"

Jodi grinned. "Before. And it was you that decided it—not me."

"Hmm."

Denzil picked up the morsel of cheese and popped it into his mouth. Reaching into his other pocket he took out a small wedge of Tamshire cheese and put a bit of it near the mice's cage. Both mice regarded it with interest, but neither moved.

"A purpose, you say?" Denzil went on. "And missing pages?"

Jodi nodded. "Great blocks of time. Like this spring. Can my whole life be all so much the same that nothing stands out anymore? *What* did I do this spring?"

"When you weren't helping me?"

Jodi nodded.

"I don't remember, you. What does Nettie say?"

Jodi lived with her Aunt Nettie in a small apartment on the top floor of the bordello that her aunt kept at the edge of town. It was her aunt's greatest disappointment that Jodi hadn't followed the family tradition and taken up the "life of leisure" as the other women in their family had.

"There's those that like 'em scrawny and looking like a boy," her aunt would tell her, which did little to further Jodi's interest in the profession.

Besides, she would tell herself, she wasn't scrawny. Thin, perhaps; lean, even. But never scrawny. Cats were scrawny. Or children.

It didn't help that she was just barely five feet tall, kept her blond hair trimmed short, and went about in scruffy trousers and a shirt like some twelve-year-old boy from the Tatters—the poorer area of Bodbury that was little more than a series of ramshackle buildings leaning up against one another for support in a long tottery row that looked out over the Old Quay's harbour.

"Nettie just says that she doesn't know what to make of me," Jodi said. "Of course, Nettie's always saying that."

"Well, if you're asking me, my advice would be to put it from your mind for now, you."

"And do what? Go quietly mad?"

"No. You could help me convince these obstinate mice to do their part in testing my machine before we all die of old age."

"It's the story of my life," Jodi said as she hoisted herself out of her chair and walked over to the workbench. "Even bloody mice get more attention."

"Tension," Noz repeated from the back of the chair, spreading out his wings and hopping down to the spot Jodi had just vacated.

"Taupin says," Jodi went on as she made a trail of crumbled cheese from inside the mice's cage to the flying machine, "that the world is a book that somebody's writing and we're all in it. That's why I was talking about missing pages. I really do think someone's torn some of mine out."

"Taupin is nothing more than a hedgerow philosopher who wouldn't know an original thought if it came up and bit him," Denzil said. "So what could he know?"

"I suppose. Besides, who'd publish a book as boring as our lives?"

"*I* don't find my life boring, you," Denzil said.

" 'Course you don't. *You've* got a Purpose."

"And I've assigned you yours—convince these mice that this experiment is for the betterment of mankind. And mousekind, too, of course."

The mice had eaten all the cheese that Jodi had put in their cage, but were venturing not a step beyond its confines.

"Oh, bother," she said.

Picking them up, she put one in either exercise wheel.

"I hope you realize that that's coercion," Denzil said.

The mice began to run on their wheels. Cables connected to the wheels spun wooden cogs, which in turn spun others until the propeller at the front of the miniature machine began to turn and the machine lurched forward on the worktable.

"That's got it!" Denzil cried. "By gar, it's a proper job now!"

He lifted the machine from the table, holding it aloft until the propeller was turning at such a speed that it was a blur. Giving Jodi a grin, Denzil cocked his arm. The parrot immediately lifted from his perch on the back of the armchair and took sanctuary on the top of a bookcase. When Denzil let go, the little flying machine jerked through the air, staying aloft for half the distance of the long room until it took a nosedive.

Jodi, already running after it, caught it just before it hit the ground. Setting the machine on the floor, she took the mice out and cradled them in her hands, making "there, there" sounds.

"You've scared them half to death!" she said.

"All in the name of science."

"That doesn't change anything. They could have been hurt."

"Exactly, you! Which is why I was calling for volunteers—not coerced subjects. I wouldn't doubt that their sulking helped weigh the machine down."

"That doesn't make any sense."

But Denzil wasn't paying attention to her.

"Oh, dear," he said, picking up the machine. "Look at this. The cogs on this gear have snapped right off."

Jodi sighed. This, she decided, wasn't where she wanted to be today either. Having already been sent forth from the bordello for her long face, then having wandered up and down Market Street and skimmed pebbles over the waves on the beach for an hour, she didn't know what she could do to fill up the rest of the hours that remained until supper.

She replaced the mice in the cage by the wall with the others. A glance out the window showed her that though the sky was still grey, the rain had let up. The cobbles of Peter Street were slick and wet.

"I'm going for a walk," she announced.

"Take Ollie with you, would you? He's been a nuisance all morning."

"He seems fine now," Jodi said, glancing at the monkey.

Denzil shook his head. "I know him, you. He's just storing up energy to wreak havoc in here this evening. I won't get a stitch of work done. Go tire him out so that he'll sleep the night away."

Jodi put on her jacket and called Ollie down from the bookcase. He perched sleepily on her shoulder, one arm around her neck, tail wrapped around her arm.

"If you find those pages I've lost," she said when she reached the door.

Denzil looked up from the workbench where he was fussing with the flying machine again.

"I'll send them straight along," he said.

Jodi grinned as she closed the door and started down the rickety stairs that would let her out onto Peter Street. There was a bit of a damp nip in the air, but rather than going back upstairs to fetch the trousers and sweater that the monkey wore in inclement weather—there was something rather too undignified about dressing animals up as people for her taste—she let Ollie nestle inside her jacket before she stepped out on the cobblestones and headed back in the direction of Market Street.

The monkey snuggled against her chest, radiating as much heat as he absorbed, his small head poking out from the jacket, just below her chin. She got the odd curious stare from passersby, but most people in town knew her too well to be surprised by anything she did. Since she was often out and about with both the monkey in tow and Noz perched on her shoulder, his green feathers iridescent against the grey granite houses and cobblestoned streets, they paid little heed to one pale brown head that appeared to be poking out of her chest.

Come one, come all, she thought as she paused to study their reflection in a store window. See the amazing two-headed woman.

Scratching her second head under his chin, she walked on.

2.

Just beyond the row of weather-beaten buildings in the Tatters that faced the sea, the Old Quay of Bodbury's harbour stretched along the shore in a mile and then some length of crumbling stone and wooden pilings. The pilings were rotting and heavily encrusted with dried salt above the waterline, barnacles below. Abandoned piers thrust seaward at right angles, planks missing, greying wood dotted with the droppings of seabirds. The air was heavy with the smell of salt and dead fish swept up against the quay.

At low tide there could be seen, scattered here and there beyond the quay, the hulls of rotting boats and broken spars—a miniature graveyard for that part of Bodbury's small fishing fleet that had fallen victim to the last great storm to hit the town, twenty years ago.

Bodbury's harbouring business was carried out in New Dock now, situated in that part of the town where Market Street opened onto Market Square, and the Old Quay lay abandoned to all but wharf rats, some few old-timers who strolled the stone walkway in the afternoons, reliving memories of other days, and the children of the Tatters who considered the entire area their own private domain.

When Jodi arrived, Ollie asleep in her jacket, a small gaggle of the latter were busily arguing over a game of Nine Men's Morris that two of their company were playing. They had scratched a board on one of the quay's flagstones and were using pebbles and shells for markers. As Jodi approached, they turned grubby faces in her direction.

"Hey, granny," one red-haired boy said, giving her a lopsided grin.

"Have you come to throw that ugly babe into the sea?"

To them, anyone over the age of twelve was too old and fair game for their teasing.

"Lay off the poor old woman," another said. Jodi glanced in his direction and recognized Peter Moyle, the son of one of her aunt's working girls. "Can't you see she's got enough troubles as it is, all bent over and ancient as she is?"

A chorus of good-natured laughter spread among them.

"You see?" Jodi asked her sleeping burden. "I'm the low rung on every ladder. Denzil's assistant. Black sheep of the family. Too much the girl to be a boy, too much a boy to be a girl. Relegated to carrying beasts around in my jacket instead of breasts."

"You're not so ugly," another boy said.

"Not like your babe."

"Best drown him quick."

"Time was," Jodi continued to Ollie, "I'd thrash the lot of them, but I'm much too dignified for that now."

"Too old you mean."

"Ah, don't you listen to them," Kara Faull said.

She was a thin gamine, barely eleven, dressed in an assortment of raggedy clothes—shirt and trousers with patched sweater and a skirt overtop the trousers. Her feet were bare, her thin features only marginally less dirt-smudged than her companions. Getting to her feet, she ambled over to where Jodi stood, and reached out to pet Ollie.

"Can I hold him?"

Jodi passed the now-awakened monkey over to her, whereupon Ollie immediately began to investigate the pockets of Kara's skirts.

"Fancy a game?" Peter asked.

"What're the stakes?"

"Ha'penny a man."

"Don't think so, no. I don't feel lucky today."

"Too old," someone remarked. "No time for games."

"Is that true, granny?" another asked.

Jodi laughed at the lot of them. They stood in a ragged circle around her and Kara, eyes twinkling merrily in their dirty faces, hands shoved deep into their pockets. She was about to return their quips when the group suddenly fell silent. They backed to the edge of the quay's low stone wall, studiously not looking in the general area behind Jodi, two of them whistling innocently—separate tunes, that were hopelessly off-key, on their own and with each other. Upset by the sudden shift in mood, Ollie pulled free from Kara's grip and jumped into Jodi's arms.

When Jodi glanced casually around and saw who was approaching, her own days of running wild with the children of the Tatters returned in a rush. For no accountable reason, she felt guilty, certain she was about to be accused of some dreadful crime that she hadn't committed, but would suffer for all the same.

The Widow Pender tended to foster such fears in the children of the Tatters. They were all convinced she was a witch and more than one Tatters mother had threatened to punish misbehaving by "sending you to the Widow, just see if I don't."

Silent as the children, Jodi joined their quiet group as the tall, hawk-faced woman dressed all in black went slowly by, walking stick tapping on the quay's stones, back stiff and straight as a board, grey hair pulled behind her head in a severe bun. She gave each of the children a disapproving look, fierce grey gaze skewering each of them in turn, lingering longest on Jodi.

The Widow frowned as Ollie hissed at her. For one long moment Jodi thought the old woman would take her stick to them both, but then the Widow gave her a withering glance and continued on her slow way.

Not until she was well out of hearing did the children relax, loosing held-in breaths in a group sigh. Then they filled the air with whispers of brave talk to take the chill that the Widow had left behind her out of the air.

"Fair gives me the creeps, she does."

"Oh, she doesn't frighten me."

"Didn't see you playing smart with her."

"Someone should give her a shove in."

"Her friends'd just shove her back out again."

It was said that she had caused the storm, twenty years ago, that had drowned the Old Quay and sunk the fishing boats. Called it up because her husband, a fisherman himself, had been gadding about town with a barmaid from the Pintar. Fifteen men were drowned that day, trying to save the boats. The barmaid had left town, though there were those who whispered that she hadn't so much left as been killed by the Widow and buried in a secret grave up on the moor.

Every child in the Tatters knew that the drowned dead were hers to command.

"Ratty Friggens says she's got a Small in that old house of hers—a little wee man that she keeps in a jar."

Jodi turned to the last speaker. "A Small?"

"It's true. Ratty saw it himself—a little man no bigger than a mouse. A Gypsy brought it 'round her house in a wooden wren cage and handed it over right before Ratty's eyes. Told me so himself. Says she'll be using it to creep into people's houses and steal their valuables—once she has it trained."

"She doesn't need valuables," Peter said. "Her whole cellar is loaded with treasure."

Kara nodded. "My da' said that one night, talking to his mates."

"A Small," Jodi repeated.

She looked down the quay to where she could see the Widow, a stiff figure in black, gazing out to sea. Her heart beat quicker. Sensing her excitement, Ollie made a querulous sound. She stroked his head thoughtfully.

Could it be true? If the Widow *did* have a Small, hidden away in that old house of hers . . .

Wouldn't that be something?

And if it *was* true, did she herself have the nerve to sneak in for a look at him?

Not likely.

She didn't have the nerve.

Nor would there really be a Small.

But what if there was?

The Widow turned then and it seemed that, for all the distance between them, her gaze settled directly on Jodi's. The old woman smiled, as though reading her mind.

I know secrets you can't begin to dream of, that smile said. Secrets that will cost you your soul if you'd have them from me. Are you still so willing to learn them?

Jodi shivered. Visions of drowned corpses coming for her flashed through her mind. Bloated white skin, bestranded with wet seaweed. Reeking of death. Dead things lurching into her room while she slept. . . .

Before the Widow returned to walk by them again, Jodi gave the children a vague wave and hurried off, back to Denzil's loft.

The Sailor's Return

I would that I were where I wish,
Out on the sea in a wooden dish;
But if that dish begins to fill—
I'd wish I were on Mousehole Hill.

—OLD CORNISH RHYME, collected from Don Flamanck

The old smuggler's haunt of Mousehole in Paul Parish is in the Deanery and West Division of the Hundred of Penwith in southern Cornwall. Its crooked narrow streets and stone-built cottages climb from the western shore of Mount's Bay up the steep slope of Mousehole Hill at a point approximately a quarter of the way from Penzance to Land's End, following the coastline west.

Janey Little's grandfather loved the village, and delighted in regaling his granddaughter's visitors with snippets of its history and folklore that he'd acquired over the years. The source of its name alone could have him rambling on at the drop of a cloth cap.

Some historians, he'd explain, think the village acquired its curious name from the Mousehole, a gaping cavern—now collapsed—that lies south of the village, or that it's a corruption of Porthenys, the Port of the Island, meaning St. Clement's Island, which lies close to the village. Others cite a reference to an old Cornish manuscript that speaks of "Moeshayle," getting its name from the small river that flows through it—"moes" probably being an abbreviation of "mowes," meaning "young women," and "hayle" meaning "river," for a translation of "Young Women's River."

The most dramatic event in Mousehole's history happened in 1595 when the village was sacked by troops from three Spanish ships; it was a Mousehole man who first spied the Spanish Armada seven years earlier. The only surviving building of that period is the Keigwin Arms, which perches on granite pillars above the courtyard where Squire Keigwin killed six Spaniards defending his home. That event is celebrated annually to this day, every July, with a carnival and festivities that end in a commemorative dinner at the Cairn Dhu Hotel where the names of the various dishes serve to tell the story.

Mousehole's other historical claims to fame are far less dramatic. The same back street that houses the Keigwin Arms was also the birthplace of Dolly Pentreath, the last-known native speaker of Cornish whose tombstone is a part of the stone wall of St. Paul's Church overlooking the village, and whose funeral, it's said, was interrupted for a whiskey break. South of the village, along Raginnis Hill overlooking St. Clement's Island in Mount's Bay, stands the Wild Bird Hospital begun in 1928 by two sisters, Dorothy and Phyllis Yglesias, which manages to survive to this day on private donations. Against a mossy wall is a bell with a sign that reads, "Please ring the bell if you have a bird." Each year the hospital tends to more than a thousand sick wild birds brought in by the public.

Mousehole was once the center of Cornwall's pilchard-fishing industry, but though it still retains the flavour of an old Cornish fishing village and there are still fishing boats to be found in its harbour, its principle industry is now tourism. There are few fishermen left, and the only smugglers who remain are in the memories of the older villagers.

Thomas Little remembered the smugglers, though he wasn't thinking of them as he came down Mousehole Lane from the King's Arms in Paul to the home he shared with his granddaughter on Duck Street. A pint of Hick's bitter sloshed comfortably in his stomach. In a brown paper bag he carried a takeout of two brown ales.

The Gaffer, as everyone referred to him, was thinking of Janey at that moment. He'd wanted to show her off to his mates at the local, but she was in one of her moods and hadn't wanted to come. But tonight . . . well, there was a session up at Charlie Boyd's, at his farm on the road to Lamorna, which was the rambling house of the area where the musicians and storytellers would often gather on a Friday night.

Boyd's farm was on a headland near Lamorna with a good view of the bay. The flat clifftop was bright with the cries of stonechats and gulls that rang above the dull pounding of the surf on the rocks below, the air sharp with a salty tang. The constant pounding of the waves had eaten away at the granite cliffs, but the farm would stand at least a century or two longer before the rock on which it stood completely eroded.

Until then it remained home to Charlie and his family—brother, wife, daughter and two boys, musicians all—and a welcome place to visit on a Friday night for those interested in such entertainments.

There weren't that many anymore, not these days—even with the revival of interest in traditional music in other parts of the country—but they usually had a fair crowd, with folk dropping by from as far away as Lizard's Point, across the bay.

Some fine musicians could be counted on at the session tonight, but, the Gaffer thought with pride, his granddaughter would likely still be the best. Hadn't she made two professional recordings to date? Wasn't she always on tour—on the Continent and in America, if not in England?

He continued up the street, a short, round man with a balding head and the ruddy features of a fisherman, dressed in old corduroy trousers and a tweed jacket patched at the elbows, smiling to himself, a jaunty lift in his step, brown ale bottles clinking in the paper bag he carried at his side.

Oh, yes. He was looking forward to showing her off tonight.

When he reached the door to his house—owned outright, thank you, and maintained with his pension and what money Janey sent him while she was on tour—he was whistling one of Chalkie's tunes in anticipation of the evening to come.

"Janey!" he called as he stepped inside. "Do you have a spot of tea ready for an old man?"

For a long moment there was no answer.

2.

Janey had heard an author describe his writing process once as seeing a hole in the paper that he could step into and watch the story unfold, and that was just how she felt with this new Dunthorn novel. It was like being at a good session when you forgot who you were, where you were, the instrument in your hand, and just disappeared into the music. When the tune finally ended, you sat up and blinked for a moment, the sense of dislocation only momentary, lasting just so long as it took the last echoes of the old tune to fade and a new one to start up.

She looked up from the book now, only vaguely aware of the dusty attic she was sitting in and the book on her lap, her thoughts still wandering the world she'd found within its pages. Then she slipped Dunthorn's letter in between the pages to keep her place and rose from the floor, the book under her arm.

"I'm up here, Gramps!" she called ahead of her as she started down the narrow stairway that would take her to the second floor of the house.

Her grandfather was waiting for her in the small vestibule, the door to the street still open behind him. He looked up to where she came down the stairs. At twenty-two she hadn't yet lost the enthusiasms and energy of a teenager. Her auburn hair hung free to just past her shoulders, except for the bangs in front, and was redder than its natural colour because she'd recently hennaed it. Above her hazel eyes, her brows maintained a slight arch giving her a constant look of questioning surprise that never quite left. Her skin was a good English peaches and cream, nose small and slender, while her smile came so easily and often that it had left dimples in her cheeks.

She was wearing a black leotard under a yellow skirt and a baggy black sweatshirt overtop. Yellow hightop sneakers matched her skirt. Presently the knees of her leotard were dusty and there was a smudge of dirt on her nose. Her cheeks had a healthy ruddy flush of excitement.

"You've got dirt on your nose, my flower," he said as she bounded down the last few steps to join him.

His round Puck's face broke into a smile as she leaned forward to kiss his cheek. But then his gaze alit on what she was carrying under her arm and the smile faltered as he recognized it for what it was.

"Found it then, did you?" he said after a moment.

Janey had the sudden sense of having overstepped her bounds.

"I didn't mean to go prying," she began. She remembered Dunthorn's letter. *Its existence must remain secret.* . . . "You're not cross with me, are you?"

The Gaffer shook his head. "Never with you. It's just . . . ah, well. I meant to give it to you sooner or later, so why not now?"

"It's a marvelous book, isn't it just?"

"Halfway finished it already, are you then?"

"Hardly!"

"Funny you should find it now, though. There was a woman came knocking on our door not three days ago, asking after it. First time that's happened in years. There were lots of crows, circling about when Billy first died, but as the years went by, I'd only see one every year or so, and then not for, what? Five years now? Until this woman came to the door."

"How did she know about the book?"

"Well, she wasn't so much after *it* in particular. She wanted any unpublished writings of Billy's—writings or artifacts. Were hers by right, she said. She was an American woman—about your age—and as unpleasant as Americans can be. Claimed to be the granddaughter of some cousin of Billy's that *I* never heard of before."

"What did you tell her?"

"Well, nothing, my robin. I had a promise to keep, didn't I? Besides, she rubbed me wrong, she did, making some crant the way she was. Offered me money straightway—as though money can buy anything. I sent her packing. Still, it bothered me, her asking like that. It was like she knew there was something. Maybe not so much the book itself, but something, and didn't she just want it?"

"What was her name?"

"She didn't say. Though she did say she'd be in touch—once she'd spoken to her lawyers."

"And you never told me?"

"Janey, my beauty, what was I to tell you? Some daft American comes knocking on my door asking about a book I can't admit to owning. . . . I wasn't ready to tell you about it yet, but I wasn't about to lie to you either. There's no lies between us, am I right?"

Janey nodded.

"Well, there you go."

"And you haven't heard from her since?" Janey asked.

The Gaffer shook his head. "What's to hear? There's nothing she or her lawyers can do. The book doesn't exist."

Janey looked down at the very real book in her hand.

"Yes, well," the Gaffer said. "In a manner of speaking, it doesn't."

"When were you going to tell me about it?" she asked.

"Well, that's the funny thing, my love. I had the feeling the book would choose its own time—and now didn't it just do that very thing?"

She looked for, but couldn't find a teasing twinkle in his eyes.

"Gramps! You don't believe that a book could—"

"Come get your old grandfather his tea and I'll tell you a wee bit more about the Mousehole half of your two Billys."

"Two Billys" was their private joke for her infatuation with the work of Billy Pigg and William Dunthorn. Something very, very good was "almost two Billys' worth of bully."

"I still can't believe you never told me about this," Janey said as she led the way to the kitchen.

"Yes, well"—the Gaffer's gaze settled on the top of Dunthorn's letter marking her place in the book—"I see you've read the letter, too, so you know why I kept it from you."

"I just happened upon it," Janey said, ready to apologize all over again.

"Getting my tea's penance enough, my love," the Gaffer told her.

The center of the Little household was the kitchen—it always had been, especially when Janey's grandmother was still alive and filling it with the tempting smells of her baking and the warmth of her presence.

Janey and the Gaffer had shared equally in the auto accident that had taken the Gaffer's wife and son, Janey's grandmother and father. She was just nudging eight at the time, so that most of her growing up had taken place in this house that she and the Gaffer had made their own special place over the years. Her mother—Constance Little, née Hetherington—had run off with a filmmaker on holiday from New York a few years before the accident and remained unheard from since the day the divorce papers became final. Although Janey's mother had reverted to her maiden name for legal purposes, she kept Connie Little as a stage name. Considering the sort of film work she was involved in, Janey's father Paul had remarked in an odd moment of bitterness before his death, she should have used Lingus as a surname.

The Gaffer didn't like to think of the woman. So far as he was concerned, the day she'd walked out on Paul and Janey, she was no longer to be considered a part of the family. She had no place in the life that he and Janey had made with each other.

No matter where Janey's music took her, nor for how long, Mousehole would always be her home—this house on Duck Street where the Gaffer lived, just a half-minute's walk from the harbour from which he'd once set sail in his boat along with the other fishermen of the village. Though the pilchard shoals had ceased at the turn of the century, there was still work for a fisherman when the Gaffer was a young man. That work declined decade by decade until now it was only a shadow of the industry it once was. Most of the boats leaving Mousehole harbour now carried only a crew of tourists.

The first tune that Janey ever wrote was a simple reel on the fiddle called "The Gaffer's Mouzel," and the front cover of her first album jacket was a photo of the village, taken from the ferry that ran between Penzance and the Scillies, out on Mount's Bay. The village was in her blood as much as in her grandfather's.

The Gaffer sat at the kitchen table, rubbing his hand on the cover of the book, while Janey busied herself at the counter making their tea. She brought sandwiches and steaming mugs of tea over, then sat across from him and put her hand on his.

"I've made you sad, haven't I?" she said. "Made you remember sad things."

The Gaffer shook his head. "I could never forget, my robin. Garm, we were a pair, Billy and I, and isn't that God's own truth? Always into mischief. Born a century earlier and I don't doubt we'd both have been smugglers. We knew all the old places where they landed, you know."

Janey nodded. She never tired of rambling the whole countryside around Mousehole with him, the Gaffer full of old bits of lore and stories. He was always ready to tell a tale about these standing stones, that cliff, this old road, that sandbar, that abandoned tin mine. Everything had a story. Especially the stoneworks that riddled Penwith Peninsula. The Merry Maidens stone circle with the two pipers stones just a field over. The Men-an-Tol holed stone east of Penzance. The Boscawen-Un stone circle with its nineteen stones and tilted center pillar just south of Crows-an-Wra. The old Roman Iron Age village on the Gulval downs.

"This letter," she said. "It's so mysterious. . . ."

"Oh, I know. Billy was a real dog in a tayser sometimes—a gruff fisherman with a streak of the old madness in him a league wide and then some. Where do you think I got half my tales from, my queen? The giants and piskies, the saints and smugglers. It was Billy talked of them all, one as real as the other."

"But what's so wrong with him being like that?" Janey asked. "I've heard the old fellows talk down at the local. They're all half-mad with the same kind of stories themselves."

As you are, she added affectionately to herself.

The Gaffer shrugged. "Self-preservation, I suppose. For both of us. We fought in the War together, you know. The other soldiers made enough fun of our country ways as it was without letting them think we might believe in piskies and the like as well. The simplest things, like gulls being—"

"The spirits of dead sailors," Janey said.

"That's what my own dad told me, and I believe it. But there's those you tell that kind of a thing to and they treat you like a half-wit. Or they'll think you're quaint—like the tourists do. Billy didn't much care, but I did. At least I did then. Became sort of a habit since then, I suppose."

"So Billy really believed in what he wrote?"

The Gaffer laughed. "Oh, I don't know, my robin. He'd *tell* you he believed, and in such a way you'd swear he did, but there was always a gleam in his eye if you knew to look."

Just like there was in the Gaffer's, Janey thought, when he started a similar kind of tale. "Do you see that stone there, Janey, my beauty?" he'd begin. "Time was . . ." And off he'd go on some rambling story. Face solemn, not a twitch of a smile, but the gleam was there in his eyes.

"Why do you think Billy didn't want anybody else to see this book?" she asked. "I'm not far into it, but I can tell it's as good or better than the others. And if it's so important that it be kept a secret, why was it published at all?" She opened the book to the copyright page and read aloud, " 'Published in an edition of one copy.' It seems so . . . odd."

She flipped to the title page and glanced at the bottom where the publisher's name was Goonhilly Downs Press, Market Jew Street, Penzance.

"Odd," the Gaffer agreed. "It is that."

"You never asked him about it?"

The Gaffer shook his head.

"Why not?"

"A man's entitled to his secrets if he wants them. A woman, too."

"I suppose." Janey put her finger on the publisher's name. "Maybe we could ask these people. Goonhilly Downs Press. Do they still exist?"

"I've never heard of them before."

The Goonhilly Downs were out on Lizard's Point, across Mount's Bay. It made Janey wonder why a Penzance publisher would take them for the name of its imprint. Well, she could ask them that as well.

"Think of all the people who would love to read this," she said, thinking aloud.

"You mustn't talk about it," the Gaffer said. "I made a promise— a family promise, my flower. You're held to it as well."

"But . . ." Janey began, but then she nodded. A promise was a promise. "I won't tell anyone," she said.

"Is there more tea?"

Janey rose to get the pot. After first putting a half inch of milk at the bottom of each mug and two spoons of sugar in the Gaffer's, she poured them each another tea.

"Is this book the only secret writing of Billy's?" she asked as she sat down again.

"The only one he had me promise to keep secret. There's some unpublished articles in a folder in the same chest where you found this book—writings about local things—but I never did anything with them. Hadn't the heart, to tell you the truth. It never seemed right to make money from a friend's death. Not to me."

Janey covered his hand with her own again. "Not to me either," she said.

They sat quietly, holding on to the moment of closeness, then the Gaffer shifted in his seat and found a smile.

"Well, then, my beauty," he said. "I think you owe me a favour."

"What did you have in mind?" she asked warily.

"Oh, nothing bad. There's just this session at Charlie Boyd's to-night and—"

"You wanted to show off your granddaughter."

"I only have the one."

Janey smiled with genuine affection. "I'd love to go," she said. "Gives me a chance to show off my granddad."

3.

Felix Gavin walked through London's Victoria Station with the rolling gait of the seaman he was. He was a tall, broad-shouldered man, deeply tanned, with dark brown hair cropped close to his scalp, pale blue eyes, and a small gold hoop in the lobe of his right ear. He drew the gazes of women he passed as he made his way to his platform, not so much for his size, or because he was handsome, as that his were features that instilled an immediate trust.

He radiated a sense of strength and calm; the promise that he was a man who could be counted on. He wore loose flannel trousers, a plain white T-shirt with an unbuttoned pea jacket overtop, and sturdy black workman's shoes. In one hand he carried a navy blue duffel bag, in the other a squarish wooden box, painted black and plastered with decals from the ports where his various ships had docked—mostly European and North American, but others from as far away as Hong Kong and Australia.

He'd been a sailor for a good third of his twenty-eight years, most recently as a crewman of the freighter *La Madeleine,* sailing out of Montreal. He'd left the ship in Madrid when he'd received the letter that was now in the front pocket of his trousers. Taking the first flight he could get to London, he'd arrived at Gatwick early this morning, changed his money to British currency, and immediately boarded a train to Victoria Station.

Now he waited at the platform for another train to take him into the West Country.

He set his baggage down at his feet and leaned against a pillar, hands in his pockets. The fingers of his right hand touched the folded letter.

"Oh, Felix," it began, and went on:

> *I feel terrible writing this. You always send me postcards, when I haven't managed much more than a Christmas card, and it doesn't seem fair. But you said if I ever needed help, I could call on you.*
>
> *I do need help. Can you come to the Gaffer's?*
> *Please don't hate me. I wouldn't ask, but I'm desperate.*
>
> > Love,
> > Janey

The letter was typed, even the signature. The postmark was Mousehole, in Cornwall, where her grandfather lived. Where Felix sent his postcards every few months. The cards were never more than just a few lines from whatever port he happened to be in—brief condensations of the long one-sided conversations he had with her when he was at sea and she couldn't hear him.

Sighing, Felix prodded the letter with his fingers, folding it into an even smaller square.

Hate her? Never.

His feelings were always mixed. He was happy that he'd known her, sad that everything had fallen apart the way it had, frustrated that they hadn't been able to put it back together, that they hadn't really tried. The good history they had—the two and a half years when everything just seemed perfect—couldn't seem to defeat the last few months of pointless arguments when things better left unsaid were aired and then regretted too late. Once spoken, those words had taken on a life of their own and couldn't be recalled.

But he never stopped loving her; never stopped hoping that someday, somehow, they'd be together again. Yet now, now that she was finally asking for him, hope was tempered with the fear of what could have happened that was so bad to make her reach out to him.

Not the Gaffer, he prayed. Don't let anything have happened to that sweet old man.

But what *had* happened? The letter was so vague—so was Janey, in some ways, with her thoughts bouncing every which way.

His train arrived and he thankfully gave up the worry in the bustle of boarding, stowing away his gear, and finding a seat. The carriage was only a quarter full. This time of year—mid-October—the English didn't flock to the West Country for their holidays the way they did in the summer. The area around Penzance was known as the Cornish Riviera, and in the summer, it lived up to its name. Now only the people who lived there, or those who had business there, made the trip out to the Penwith Peninsula.

Settling into his seat, he pulled out a paperback mystery novel and tried to read as the train pulled out of the station. But Janey's features kept intruding on the storyline and he couldn't follow the private eye's narrative for more than a few sentences before he had to go back and begin the paragraph again. Expectations of what he could look forward to were mixing too strongly with an anxiety born of that same anticipation of seeing her again.

Finally, once they left London, he set the book aside and stared out the window, watching the hedgerow-bordered fields flicker by. As memories rose up, one after the other, he simply let them come.

A little more than five hours later, he disembarked at Penzance Station and stood out in the car park, looking over at St. Michael's Mount where it rose like a humpbacked swell from Mount's Bay. It was already dark, the grey skies slating into night. A brisk easterly wind blew in from the water, thick with the tang of salt and the promise of rain.

He turned finally, walking towards a phone booth before changing his mind. He wasn't ready to call her. He didn't want the first contact to be an impersonal communication over a phone line. He thought of taking a taxi to Mousehole—the village lay a few miles west of Penzance, just past Newlyn, the three set all in a row along the shore of Mount's Bay like three gulls on a ship's railing—then decided against that as well.

More memories were waking here. Better to walk through them now, before he reached the Gaffer's old house on Duck Street, he decided, than try to deal with them in the back of a cab.

Swinging the strap of his duffel bag to his shoulder, he hefted his wooden box and set off, taking the Quay Wharf Road to where it met Battery Road, then following the Western Promenade out of the town and into Newlyn.

Even in the dark, Mousehole was just the way he remembered it. Maybe especially in the dark, because he'd rambled through its benighted streets with Janey often enough to know it as well as he did his own hometown of Deschenes, in West Quebec. Both were fronted by water, but there the resemblance ended.

Deschenes, at least when he was growing up there, was a poverty-stricken village on the wrong side of the tracks that fronted that part of the Ottawa River known as Lac Deschenes. The streets were packed dirt, the buildings ramshackle, some of them little better than tarpaulin shacks. The memories he carried away from it centered around the fighting of his alcoholic parents, his brother Barry who wrapped his Harley around a lamppost, killing himself and his girlfriend, their sister Sue who had her first kid when she was fifteen, and a hundred other unhappy events.

Mousehole was an ancient port, an unspoiled fishing village of narrow streets and alleyways that wound through tiers of cottages and tiny flowered courtyards. If there was poverty here, it didn't show the same underbelly to the world that his hometown did.

He entered by the Parade, passing the Old Coastguard Hotel, and made his way to North Cliff. There he stood in front of the newsagent's and looked seaward at the two arms of the quay's seawalls that enfolded the village's harbour in a protective embrace. He'd sat on one or another of those walls with Janey on more than one moonlit night, listening to the waves beat at the stone walls, watching the sea, or sitting with their backs to the water and taking in the picturesque view of the terraced village as it climbed the hill, lights twinkling in the windows of the cottages. Those were good nights. They didn't always need conversation. The darkness simply held them in a companionable embrace as comforting as the arms of the quay's seawalls did the harbour.

Felix turned away from the view. He was dawdling, and he knew

why. This close to seeing Janey again, all his courage was washing
out of him as surely as the tide stole the water from inside the seawalls.

He walked past the newsagent's to where a tiny alleyway separated the buildings on either side of it and walked up its narrow
length. This was Duck Street, starting out no wider than a couple of
yards, but broadening into a one-lane street by the time it reached
Wellington Place, the square just before the Gaffer's cottage on
Chapel Place, across from the Methodist Chapel.

A black and orange cat eyed him curiously from the stone wall as
he opened the wrought-iron gate that led into the Gaffer's tiny courtyard. There were lights on in the two-and-a-half-story stone cottage.

Janey was in there, he thought. Probably sitting around the hearth
with her grandfather. Reading. Or playing a game of dominoes with
the Gaffer. She wasn't playing music, because he couldn't hear either
her pipes or her fiddle.

He hesitated at the door.

Come on, he told himself.

He lifted the brass knocker on the door, rapping it sharply against
the plate screwed into the wood behind it. And suddenly he got a
strange feeling.

There was no one home. He could feel the emptiness that anticipation had hidden from him. Neither Janey nor the Gaffer was in.
But there was somebody. . . .

He knocked again and heard a crash. Without stopping to think,
he let his gear drop to the cobblestoned walk and tried the door. It
was unlocked, opening at his touch. He stepped inside, nerves prickling, and sensed the blow coming before it struck.

That momentary warning was enough to give him time to turn
aside and take the blow on his shoulder. A figure darted by him,
something bulky under his arm. Felix caught his balance and snaked
out a hand, snagging the man by the shoulder of his coat. Before he
could pull him back into the cottage, the man slammed what he was
carrying into Felix's midsection.

Felix lost his grip on the man's shoulder. He buckled over, catching hold of what proved to be a box of papers and magazines. The
man struggled for a moment, trying to regain ownership of the box,
his features still hidden in shadow. Then a door opened in the cottage
next door. At the neighbour's cry, the man shoved the box harder

against Felix and fled. By the time Felix regained his balance once more and stepped out into the courtyard, he could see the man fleeing up Duck Street towards Mousehole Lane.

He set the box down on the doorstep and turned to face the Gaffer's neighbour, struggling for a moment before he remembered the man's name.

"Mr. Bodener?" he asked. His voice was husky as he caught his breath.

George Bodener was a few years the Gaffer's senior, and like the Gaffer, he was a Mousehole native, although he'd never traveled farther than Plymouth in the whole of his life. He was thin and grey-haired, but he had a round piskie's face that was rarely without a smile. That smile was missing just now, however. He had a cane upraised in his hand and peered carefully at Felix before he finally brought it down to his side.

"Felix, isn't it?" he asked. "Janey's musician friend?"

Felix nodded. "I surprised a burglar—"

"A burglar? In Mousehole? La, Jey! But I never." He took a few steps closer. "Did you take a hurt, you?"

"No, I'm fine. Just a bit shook up."

But thinking of the moment of violence, he looked worriedly back into the Gaffer's cottage. Had the man hurt Janey or her grandfather?

"Don't you be worrying about them, you," George said. "Gone out, they have, up to Boyd's farm. It's Friday night, isn't it just?"

Friday night meant a session at Charlie Boyd's, Felix remembered. Some things never changed. But what was Janey doing, going to a session, when she was supposed to be in trouble?

Supposed to be? Felix amended. Then what did he call the burglar he'd just surprised? A houseguest?

"My gar," George said as he joined Felix in the hallway and peered inside. "Made a bit of a mess."

Felix nodded. There was a floor lamp lying on the carpet, its glass shade broken. A scatter of books lay on the floor around the hearth. Pillows were pulled from the sofa and the Gaffer's club chair by the window. He looked down at the box he'd rescued from the burglar. It was filled with papers and what appeared to be a book. Who burgled a house for this kind of thing?

"Would you like some tea, you?" George asked him.

Felix shook his head. "I think I'll try to clean this up before Janey and the Gaffer get back—lessen the shock a bit."

"Now there's a kind thought."

"Been much trouble about here lately?" Felix asked, keeping his voice casual.

George blinked in surprise. "Trouble? In Mousehole? It's not London, you. Not even Penzance."

Felix gave him a smile. "I wasn't thinking," he said.

"No crime in that," George said. He gave a last look around the living room. "Well, it's back to the telly for me, Felix. Come 'round in the morning, why don't you just, and tell me a tale of far-off ports."

"I'll do that."

He collected his belongings from the courtyard and brought them and the box of papers inside as George returned to his home. Then he spent a half hour straightening the room and repairing what damage he could before he put on some tea.

An odd thing to steal, he thought as he took the box into the kitchen. He looked through the papers and saw that they were manuscripts and articles by the Gaffer's old mate, Billy Dunthorn. There was a book, too, with a title that wasn't familiar to Felix, but that was hardly surprising. He'd never had much of a head for authors' names or how many books they'd published. He just read what came to hand and either enjoyed it, or didn't.

But he knew Dunthorn because Janey never tired of talking about the man and his work.

Taking his tea into the now-tidy living room, he sat down in the Gaffer's chair with the book and idly flipped through its pages while he waited for Janey and her grandfather to come home.

The Creeping Mouse

Thumbkin, Pointer, Middleman big,
Sillyman, Weeman, rig-a-jig-jig.

—NURSERY RHYME

Jodi couldn't help herself—she had to know.

Of course there was no such thing as a Small. How could there be? And the Widow Pender wasn't a witch. She had no mysterious powers to wield over the living, nor could she call up the dead. To think otherwise was to live in a fairy tale.

The world was a strange and wonderful place as it was, Denzil never tired of reminding her. What need was there to go prying about, chasing after supernatural oddities that couldn't possibly exist when the mysteries of nature itself were barely understood?

Yes, and of course, and I do agree, Jodi would reply.

But there were always the stories—so many of them. Of ghosts and hauntings and things that went bump in the night. Of fairies and giants and impossible creatures. Where did they come from? Out of our heads, and that was it? Surely something had sparked their authors to imagine the incredible. Surely, somehow, there was some tiny grain of truth to the tale that set it spinning through the author's mind.

What if impossibilities were true marvels?

And what if the moon was made of cheese, Denzil would reply dryly. The question then would be, who ate it, night by night, and how did it come back again, piece by piece, just as good as new?

So Jodi would nod in reluctant agreement, but no matter how sensible she tried to be, she couldn't stop that little voice that whispered in the back of her mind.

What if the marvels were real? What *if*?

She just had to know.

So late that night, when the last of the night's customers was gone and Aunt Nettie and her girls were finally off to bed, Jodi crept out of her window, slid down the drainpipe, and set off through Bodbury's cobblestone streets, heading for the Widow Pender's house.

And it was a night for mystery, wasn't it just? Clouds scudded across the sky, hiding the moon, waking shadows. The sea murmured to itself like an old woman, slapping the pilings of the quay that fronted the Tatters, phosphorus glistening on the tide. There wasn't a light in a single window she passed—not even in Denzil's workshop.

She walked with a swing in her step, breathing in the salty tang of the night air, her soft-soled shoes silent on the cobblestones. She wasn't even a bit nervous—her sense of adventure overriding any such possibility—until she finally reached the outskirts of town and the Widow's cottage came into view. Then she slowed down, pausing when she reached the protective cover of the last cottage before the Widow's.

The two-story stone building that belonged to the Widow Pender rose in gloomy foreboding from its shadowed gardens. A flicker of light came from one ground-floor window. Occasionally a shadow passed the window, as though the Widow were pacing back and forth.

She'd be going out soon, Jodi thought as she settled down by the wall of the neighbouring cottage to wait. In the Tatters it was well known that the Widow went out late each night, when all the town was asleep, and stood on the headland across from her house to watch the sea.

Remembering her husband, the townsfolk said.

Conversing with the sea dead, the children of the Tatters whispered to one another.

The latter seemed all too possible to Jodi as she crouched nervously against the wall, watching the Widow's cottage. The night had changed around her. There was a nasty undercurrent in the murmur of the tide now. The light wind coming in from the water seemed more like breathing than a sea breeze. Trees groaned ominously. Unseen *things* rustled in the hedges.

The warm comfort of her bed seemed very far away, and most appealing, but she chewed at her lower lip and kept to her vigil, refusing to be unnerved. It was a time for bravery, and she was determined to be just that. Yet as she waited there, she couldn't help but think of all the ghostly stories she'd ever heard. Of hummocks, rising from behind hedgerows to frighten travelers with their spectral presence. Of drowned men stumbling from the tide, limbs wrapped with strands of seaweed, water streaming from their rotting clothes. Of the Bagle Wight, a strawlimbed scarecrow of a creature whose head was a large carved turnip; he captured and ate children who snuck out from their houses in the night. . . .

Jodi wished she hadn't thought of him. Now all she could hear was his soft footfall on the street behind her. It was too easy to imagine him creeping towards her, catching her with his knobbly fingers, sharp thorn nails digging into her arms.

She shivered and peered over her shoulder so often that she almost missed the Widow finally leaving her cottage. Jodi watched her go, then rose quickly to her feet. Keeping an eye on the Widow's receding back, afraid to even breathe, she darted over to the lit window and peered in.

And saw nothing out of the ordinary.

She looked in on what appeared to be the Widow's sitting room and what she saw was common enough to make her yawn. A coal fire burned in the hearth. On the mantel above it, two fat white candles sat in silver candlesticks, throwing their flickering light across the room. There were a pair of comfortable chairs by the fire, knitting lying upon the seat of one; a sideboard displaying china plates—mostly with scenes depicting Bodbury and the surrounding country-side; another long table by another wall that reminded her of one of Denzil's worktables as it was littered with various woodworking tools and pieces of wood and cloth; and a bookcase, with as many knickknacks as there were books on its shelves. Paintings and samplers hung on the walls. A cozy thick wool rug lay on the floor.

But nothing magical. None of the paraphernalia associated with witches—no cauldrons bubbling on the fire, no bundles of herbs and odd charms. And of course there wouldn't be, would there? If the Widow was a witch, she'd hide the tools of her trade. In the attic, perhaps. Or the cellar.

Jodi's attention returned to the worktable. At the far end was a square box covered with a piece of velvet. She glanced in the direction that the Widow had taken, but there was no sign of her return yet.

Did she dare? She'd come so far, but to actually enter the woman's house and poke about in her belongings . . .

She hesitated for a long moment, then went 'round by the door and tried the knob. It turned easily under her hand, the door swinging open silently when she gave it a push. She hesitated again on the threshold, before taking a deep breath and stepping in.

She stood there in the hallway, expecting she knew not what. An alarm of some sort, she supposed. A cat to lunge at her, hissing and spitting. A raven to come screeching down the hallway towards her. A black dog to rear up from the floor at her feet, appearing out of a cloud of dense smoke, red-eyed and snarling. But there was noth-ing.

And why should there be? There were no such things as witches. The Widow Pender was merely a lonely old woman, making do with her loneliness and her pension, and here Jodi was, entering her cot-tage uninvited and undoubtedly unwelcome.

Ratty Friggens says she's got a Small in that old house of hers. . . .
But Smalls were no more real than witches, were they?

A little wee man that she keeps in a jar.

She moved down the hall towards the sitting room. It appeared as innocuous from her present vantage point as it had from the window she'd peered through. It could be any old woman's room, the fire cheery, a vague scent of dried flowers in the air.

She stepped inside, running a hand along the smooth wooden surface of the sideboard, and moved towards the worktable. She paused when she reached it, looking curiously at what the Widow had been working on.

Doll's furniture.

A little wee man.

There could be a hundred good reasons she was making doll's furniture.

She's got a Small. . . .

Jodi put her hand on the cloth covering the box at the end of the table and slowly pulled the cloth away to reveal an aquarium. But unlike the ones in Denzil's loft, this one was furnished like a doll's house. There was a small table with two chairs; a miniature hearth with a coal in it, the stovepipe rising up the side of the aquarium and escaping from the back through a circular hole in the glass; a wardrobe and a dresser; a tiny woven rug; a bed, complete with bedclothes and pillow. There was even a doll lying under the covers. But then the doll turned around and looked up at Jodi and her heart rose up into her throat and lodged there.

The Small.

Oh raw we, there truly was a little man.

He was no bigger than a mouse; a miniature man, perfectly formed, blinking up at her from his glass prison. He clutched his bedclothes tightly to his throat, eyes wide and a look of alarm on his tiny features.

She bent closer to the glass side of the aquarium, moving as slow as she could so as not to startle him more, when she felt a draft of cold air on the back of her neck. Still moving slowly, but from fear now, she straightened once more and turned to face the doorway.

The Widow stood there, a look of amusement in her dark eyes. She leaned on her cane, the dark folds of her mantle falling about her to the tops of her high, laced boots.

"What have we here?" she said. "Come spying on me, have you, Jodi Shepherd?"

There was no place to hide—it was too late for that anyway—and no place to flee either, so Jodi held her ground, knees knocking against each other as she faced the Widow.

Something moved in the doorway by the Widow's feet, drawing Jodi's gaze. Half-numbed already—both from the existence of the Small and having been caught by the Widow—she could only stare at the little creature that crouched there.

It was no bigger than a cat, or Denzil's monkey, but its body was hairless. Spindly limbs supported its round-bellied torso. It had a triangular face with a wild thatch of dark red hair above it. Ears like clam shells stuck out at right angles from its head. It clung to the hem of the Widow's mantle, staring back at Jodi from its saucer-wide eyes. The flicker of a grin touched the wide gape of its mouth.

Jodi dragged her gaze back to the Widow's face.

"What—what are you going to do to me?" she managed finally.

"Well, that's the question now, isn't it?" the Widow replied.

Her tone was mild, but there was a look in her eyes that made Jodi shiver.

Oh, how could she have been such a fool to come here and no one knowing where she'd gone?

She was doomed to spend the rest of her life as a toad or a newt or whatever the Widow decided to turn her into for trespassing in her cottage and discovering her secrets.

"I—I didn't mean any . . ."

Harm, she wanted to say, but her throat just closed up on her and she couldn't get the word out.

"My little man's so lonely," the Widow said.

By her feet, the odd little creature began to titter. Jodi tried to back up, but there was only the worktable behind her and she was already pressed up against it.

"Please," Jodi tried.

The Widow spoke a word that seemed to hang in the air between them.

It was in no language that Jodi knew, but still, she could almost understand it. She felt queasy, hearing the repetition of its three syllables, as though her body subconsciously inferred its meaning and shied away from its import.

Then the Widow said Jodi's name. She repeated it, and again. Three times in all.

Now Jodi felt light-headed.

I won't faint, she thought as she reeled away from the table.

A stifling sense of closeness came over her, seeming to rush in at her from all sides. At the same time, the walls sped away in the opposite direction.

Dizzy, staggering, and disoriented, Jodi fought to keep her balance, but the floor rose up to meet her all the same.

The Hunt

Proud Nimrod first the bloody chase began—
A mighty hunter, and his prey was man.

—ALEXANDER POPE, from "Windsor Forest"

West of Mousehole, far west; past the craggy cliffs of Land's End, across the Atlantic Ocean, and farther west still; across the North American continent to the southern tip of Vancouver Island . . . There, in an immaculately kept Tudor-styled house in the residential section of Victoria known as James Bay, an old man woke from a light sleep and sat up in his bed.

In his late eighties, John Madden was still as fit as he'd been in his mid-sixties, and he'd been fit then—enough so that his doctor had remarked at the time, "If you hadn't been my patient for the past twenty years, John, I'd swear you weren't a day over fifty."

It was true that the shock of black hair belonging to the young man he'd been had turned to grey and thinned some. He moved more slowly now, as well, his lean frame feeling the brittleness of his years so that bones ached in inclement weather, muscles were stiff when he rose in the morning, or from a long session at his desk. But he still saw to his own portfolios with all the shrewdness that had made him a very rich man many times over, and his mind was as sharp and discerning as it had ever been.

He was a marvel in the circles in which he moved—always a leader, never a sycophant. His associates wondered at his acumen and his uncommon health for his age, though never in his presence. But he could see it in their eyes, more so as year followed year and he remained essentially unchanged while they fell by the wayside, young turks taking their place—the same questions eventually coming into their eyes.

But the secret to his success rested in neither the quick faculties of his mind, nor in the superb condition of his aging body. The key lay, instead, in the small image of a grey dove that was tattooed on the inside of his left wrist, placed just so that his watchband hid it from a casual glance.

Flicking on the light above his bed, Madden pressed a button on the intercom that sat beside the telephone on his night table.

"Sir?"

The response was almost immediate, crisp and alert, even though the recipient of the call had undoubtedly been asleep when it came to his room on the ground floor of the building.

"I'd like to see you, Michael," Madden said.

"I'll be right up."

Madden leaned back against the headboard and closed his eyes.

Thirty-five years ago he'd matched wits with one of his own countrymen, and lost. That loss rankled still, not the losing itself—even then Madden was long past such negligible concerns—but for the irreplaceable prize that had been forfeit.

He'd almost had it in his hands—a secret that couldn't be measured in secular terms—and it had slipped away, as vague and untouchable as mist burned off by the morning sun. It continued to exist, but his adversary had concealed it too well. It slept in some hidden place, the knowledge of which his rival had taken with him to his watery grave.

Madden had sent agents in pursuit of it, time and again, but sleeping, the secret was invisible. Impenetrable. Lost. He'd been through the house and the surrounding area himself—he, with his knowledge and understanding of what he sought, if not the configuration that it presently inhabited—and found nothing, so how could he hope that others would succeed?

Still he had them keep watch.

And he waited.

Because one day, he knew, it would wake again.

And then the secret would be his.

And he would take it into forever.

A knock at the oak door of his bedroom roused him from his reverie. He opened his eyes.

"Come in, Michael," he said.

The man who entered was another secret—suspected, perhaps, only to the world's hermetic community, but its importance went beyond occult concerns. Michael Bett was—Madden had proved it to his own satisfaction, irrefutably and beyond any doubt—a reincarnation of one of the early twentieth century's greatest sorcerers. Born December 5, 1947, his existence was proof, not only that reincarnation was possible, but that a sorcerer's will was strong enough to give him more than one opportunity to walk the world in corporeal form.

Madden had known Bett well in the man's previous life, so well that he could not fail to recognize him when he met him again in his new identity.

The resemblance was not physical. Bett was a wiry, thin man— unlike the man he'd been. He wore his dark hair fashionably long, his features were angular, his cheekbones pronounced, his forehead high, his too bright eyes somewhat sunken. But he had the same powerful will, the tendency towards excess, the incapacity for natural affection, the egotism, and the brilliant mind.

He had been misunderstood in previous lives, and he was misunderstood now. But not by Madden. Madden had nurtured that brilliance.

He'd found Bett ten years ago, stumbled across him as he stood over the corpse of his latest victim in a windy Chicago alleyway, and had known with a flash of insight whose troubled spirit lay behind the man's bright gaze.

Before Bett could turn on him, Madden invoked the Dove—whose symbol both he and now Bett wore on their wrists—and he took Bett away. Groomed him and quelled his insatiable appetite for the suffering of others. Channeled the man's incredible will towards the doctrines of the Order where—given an intellectual outlet for his excesses—he was weaned from the need to wreak havoc on the flesh of others and surpassed all of Madden's already high expectations.

But knowing who Bett was, how could he truly have been surprised?

There were secrets, and there were secrets. This one belonged to Madden and Michael Bett, and to no one else. It was ten years old, but it still brought a glint of satisfaction to Madden's eyes every time he looked on his colleague.

He waved Bett over to his bedside. Crossing the room, Bett sat on the end of Madden's bed.

"You've felt it again?" he asked.

Madden nodded. "Twice in one day. I think it's time you joined Lena."

Bett frowned.

"I know," Madden added. "If she becomes unreliable, or difficult to manage—"

"I'll rein her in."

"But gently. Her father stands high in the Order."

Bett nodded and rose from the end of the bed.

"I'd best go pack my bags," he said.

He turned to go, pausing in the doorway.

"You can count on me," he told Madden, and then he was gone.

Madden nodded to himself. Count on you to bring it to me, he thought. But once the secret is pried from its present configuration and available for our use? Will I still be able to count on you then?

Madden was wise enough to not let his affection for Bett cloud his awareness of the man's avaricious nature. For all that Madden had done for Bett, his colleague's first loyalty would always be to himself.

But then, Madden thought as he gazed across the room, we're not so different in that, are we?

It was what set them apart from the sheep.

What the Devil Ails You?

It's always good when you come into contact with other players and you discover you're not this *freak*, that there are others . . . playing this strange instrument.

—KATHRYN TICKELL, on playing the Northumbrian pipes; from an interview in *Folk Roots* No. 41, November 1986

It was Manus Boyd—Charlie Boyd's grandfather, a Kerryman from Ballyduff near the Mouth of the Shannon—who first brought the Irish custom of a rambling house to the Penwith Peninsula at the turn of the century. Janey had heard the story so often that, like

Charlie's children, she only rolled her eyes and thought about other things when Charlie decided to tell it again.

Manus had crossed the Celtic Sea with his wife Anne in 1902 and, one way or another, found himself in Cornwall where he became a dairyman on a farm near Sennen that belonged to one of the great Cornish estates. In those days the estates had trouble finding tenants for their farms so an established middleman farmer would rent the unwanted land, stock it with cattle, and lease the holding to a dairyman of his own choosing. This dairyman had no responsibility to the estate; the responsibility of upkeep lay in the hands of the absentee farmer.

By the time Charlie took over the farm, he no longer dealt with the middleman farmer, but leased the farm directly from the estate through a land agent. He was the third generation of Boyds to work that land, and by the beginning of the Second World War, their taciturn neighbours eventually allowed that it was the Boyd Farm, rather than the Dobson Farm, the Dobsons being the tenants before Manus Boyd.

Manus and Anne had passed on, as had Charlie's own father and mother, but there were still Boyds in plenty on that land, what with Charlie, his wife and three children, and his brother Pat. And the music sessions that had made it a rambling house in his grandparents' time were as popular as ever with those who had an ear for a proper old tune or song.

About the only thing that Janey didn't like about the sessions was that there were so many people smoking; she always came away with her clothes and hair smelling of smoke. It was the same when she played in most folk clubs, but while it was irritating, it was only a minor annoyance considering the grand time she invariably had.

A good crowd was already present by the time she and the Gaffer arrived.

Chalkie was there with his melodeon, sitting next to Jim Rafferty who hadn't taken his tin whistle from the inside pocket of his jacket yet. A couple of members of the Newlyn Reelers—a local barn dance band—had come, as well as Bobbie Wright and Lesley Peake, a professional duo who lived on the other side of Penzance and played guitar and fiddle, respectively.

There were others from the surrounding farms, some with instruments, others with simply their voices, and, of course, the Boyds:

Uncle Pat on tenor banjo, Charlie on fiddle, and his wife Molly on piano and Anglo concertina; their daughter Bridget on concert flute and whistle, and their sons, Sean also on fiddle and Dinny who played both the Irish Uillean pipes and the Northumbrian.

It was Dinny who'd tracked down Janey's first set of pipes when she started to talk about wanting to take them up. He taught her both the basics and encouraged her whenever the complexities of the instrument got to be so much that she just wanted to pitch them into Mount's Bay.

Also there that night, sitting beside the two chairs that were waiting for Janey and her grandfather, was Janey's best friend, Clare Mabley. Clare was a dark-haired girl, slender and pale, who worked in a bookstore in Penzance. A blackthorn cane lay on the floor beside her chair. She pulled a small tin whistle from her purse as Janey sat down.

"I got that F whistle," she said. "It came with the post today."

Janey smiled. "And?"

"I'm still getting used to the pitch."

Clare had a good singing voice, but she had always wanted to play an instrument. The trouble was, she couldn't seem to concentrate on learning any one she tried. Finally she took up the whistle and stuck with it when Jim Rafferty assured her it was simple to learn and offered to teach her to play. She was much happier at the sessions now, though whenever her turn came around, she always picked a tune that everyone knew so that she wouldn't have to play it on her own.

As they did every Friday night, they were all gathered in the Boyds' huge kitchen, chairs and stools and crates pulled up into a kind of rough circle around the gas stove and the big kitchen table where was laid out the vast array of cakes, biscuits, and cookies that had been brought along by the various guests. There was always tea steeping in a big ceramic teapot by the stove, though many brought stronger drink, as the Gaffer had with his brown ales, one of which stood under his own chair, the other under Janey's.

The music went 'round the circle. When their turn came up, each person had to offer up something: a tune, a song, a story, a joke— it didn't matter what. If you knew the piece, and it seemed appropriate to do so, you joined in; if you didn't, you merely sat back and enjoyed it.

As always seemed to happen when they arrived, no sooner had

Janey sat down than the turn had come 'round to her. Complaining good-humouredly, she lifted her pipes out of their carrying box and buckled the bellows above the elbow of her left arm. Then she attached the air bag with its drones to it, laying the drones across her body so that they rested on her right arm, and connected the tiny chanter. After a few moments of tuning the drones to the chanter, she gave Dinny a grin and launched into a sprightly version of "Billy Pigg's Hornpipe." The tune was a favorite of hers, having been written by Pigg himself.

Playing in the key of F as she was, most of the other musicians couldn't join in. A peculiarity of the Northumbrian pipes was that they couldn't play in the keys of most standard dance tunes. But Dinny, after letting her go through it once on her own, joined her the next time around on his own pipes, as did Clare on her tiny new F whistle, its high sweet tones cutting pleasantly across the bee-buzz of the pipes' drones and the mellower sound of their chanters.

They ended the tune with a flourish to a round of applause, Clare blushing furiously, and then it was the Gaffer's turn to tell one of his improbable tales. After that Chalkie started up a version of "Johnny Cope" on his melodeon and Janey swapped her pipes for her fiddle. By the time Chalkie switched to "Tipsy Sailor"—an Irish variant of the same tune—everyone with an instrument in hand was playing, those who didn't have one were clapping their hands, and the kitchen rang with the sound of the music.

And so the evening went, with tunes and songs and poetry recitations. Whenever her turn or Dinny's came up, they'd both take up their pipes, enjoying the opportunity of playing together. It was what Janey liked best about the sessions.

It was too bad she couldn't get Dinny to come with her on this upcoming tour, she thought as they were in the middle of a particularly sensitive version of the slow air, "The Flowers of the Forest." They played with the melody line, first one, then the other chanter taking up the lead, harmonizing beautifully against the sweet burring of their drones.

But Dinny had no interest in touring. He loved music, but like all his family preferred sessions to organized gigging. It was only after weeks of persuasion that she'd ever gotten them to play on a few tracks of either one of her albums.

At one point the turn in the circle came 'round to Frank Woolnough who had a farm just outside St. Buryan. He didn't play an instrument or sing, but he loved to spin a tale, the more exaggerated the better. Every so often, he and the Gaffer would spend the night seeing who could outdo the other, and since the Gaffer had told his story about the pair of ghostly hummocks he'd seen one night on a country lane near Sennen, didn't Frank have to top him?

"Well," he said. "I got this from my father and it happened down your way, Gaffer, in Mousehole harbour it was. There was a boat from the Lizard docked there and my father was reeling his way from The Ship after a pint too many—wasn't his habit, understand, but he'd had a bit of luck that day and didn't everyone have to stand him a drink?

"Still, drunk he might have been, but 'ark to what he told me. There he was, standing at the rail and looking at the boats all tipping one side or another, it being low tide, and what does he see but a little man come out of that boat from the Lizard. No bigger than a mouse, he were, stepping his way along the mooring line, balanced just as easy as you please.

"Well, my old dad blinks, then blinks again, and somewhere between the two blinks, didn't that little man just vanish?"

By the stove, Uncle Pat gave a laugh. "Back into the bottle he came from, why!"

"Laugh as you will," Frank said, "but my old dad he went down into the harbour to have himself a closer look and what do you think he saw? Tiny footprints leading away from the mooring line across the sand and away to a great heap of netting that was lying there on the stairs."

Frank nodded sagely, one eye turned gravely to the Gaffer.

"Hummocks is one thing," he said. "But could have been was nothing but a mist you saw, Gaffer. No offense, but that's how I see it. But this little man—it was a piskie my old dad saw and that's God's own truth. The footprints there were proof plain for all to see."

"And who else saw them?" Chalkie asked.

"Oh, well," Frank replied. "Tide came up, didn't it, and washed them away. But he saw them plain and, drunk or sober, my old dad wasn't one to make up a tale like that."

Janey had to smile at the story. It reminded her of Dunthorn's work, and of the new book she'd discovered this afternoon that she'd only barely started. But before she could think too much about it,

Bridget Boyd, sitting beside Frank, struck up a tune and the music took them all away again.

'Round about midnight, the music wound down and people began to drift off to their homes. Janey and the Gaffer were among the last to leave, the Gaffer having an earnest conversation with Uncle Pat about the door-to-door wet fish business that the Gaffer ran from his home, making his deliveries in a beat-up old Austin stationwagon that was painted a bright yellow with the legend "Fresh Local Fish" painted on each side.

Dinny and Janey were caught up in their own discussion, sitting almost head to head, as they discussed the peculiarities of reeds, particular turns of odd tunes, and other piper talk that had Clare and the others—who'd heard this sort of thing all too often when the pair got together—ignoring them for less esoteric conversation.

When finally it was time to leave, Clare joined Janey and the Gaffer so that they could give her a lift home. Janey packed her instruments in the back of her tiny three-wheeled Reliant Robin—which prompted Dinny to make his usual comment about when was she going to get a *real* car?—and they set off for Mousehole along the winding lanes that ran from Lamorna to the village, the hedgerows rising tall on either side of the narrow roads.

They dropped Clare off at the door of the cottage she shared with her mother on Raginnis Hill, just a few doors down from the Mousehole Wild Bird Hospital. After a promise of getting together tomorrow because it was Clare's day off, Janey gave her friend a wave, the Gaffer adding a "Sleep well, now, my blossom," and they headed on down the hill for home.

2.

Felix heard the small Reliant before its lights flickered in the Gaffer's living room as it came 'round the corner from Mousehole Lane and parked beside the Gaffer's stationwagon. He set aside the rescued book he'd been reading and leaned forward in the chair, pulse quickening in anticipation.

It's been three years, he thought.

Had she changed? Had he? Would it be awkward?

He ran a hand across the stubble of his hair, listening to their voices outside. He started to rise from the chair, but then the door was flung open and Janey burst into the room in her usual enthusiastic manner.

And stopped dead in her tracks when she saw him sitting there in the Gaffer's chair.

The Gaffer came in behind her more slowly. He was first to speak.

"Felix, my fortune. How *are* you?"

Felix rose from the chair, but before he could speak, Janey had dumped her instruments onto the couch and literally flew across the room to embrace him.

"Felix!" she cried as she hugged him, small arms tight around his body.

Felix's pulse doubled its tempo again. He put his arms around her, touched the familiar shape of her shoulder blades under her jumper, smelled the cigarette smoke that clung to her clothes and hair, but under it the sweet scent that was her.

He couldn't say a word.

Janey leaned a bit back from him so that she could look up into his face.

"This is such a wonderful surprise," she said. "It's been *ages*."

A surprise? Felix thought.

The Gaffer closed the door to the cottage.

"You should have told us you were coming," he said. "We would have come by and picked you up at the station."

Janey gave him a last hug and stepped away, face still beaming.

"You big galoot," she said, giving his shoulder a soft punch. "Trust you to show up like this all unannounced."

"But . . ." Felix began.

"It's just wonderful to see you," Janey went on before he could finish. She dragged him over to the couch so that they could sit down beside each other. "You have to tell me everything. Where you've been. What you're doing here." She glanced over at his baggage, gaze settling on the wooden box. "I see you brought your accordion. I hope you've brought some new tunes as well."

"There's no beer," the Gaffer said, "but I can put on a kettle."

Felix shook his head. "No thanks. I just had some tea."

Beside him, Janey took his hand and gave it a squeeze. "How long can you stay?" she asked. "Tell me it'll be weeks."

Felix wanted to just bask in her attention and not say anything, but couldn't.

"Janey," he said. "Why are you surprised to see me?"

She blinked. "Why shouldn't I be? You never said you were coming."

"But the letter—"

"You wrote?" She looked over at the Gaffer. "We never got a letter, did we?"

The Gaffer shook his head.

"It must've got lost in the mail," Janey said. "Where did you send it from?"

"I didn't write to you," Felix said. "You wrote to me."

Janey blinked again. "I didn't never," she said.

Felix disengaged his hand from hers and pulled the folded letter from his pocket. He handed it over to her.

"Then what's this?" he asked.

Janey opened the letter and scanned it quickly.

"I didn't send this to you, Felix," she said.

Felix frowned. "It's not funny," he said. "I came a long way. I . . ."

What could he say? That he'd come because he'd promised once and promises were sacred to him? Because he'd told her that he'd always be there for her, no matter what? Because the letter had burned like a bright beacon in his mind, awaking dead hopes?

"I honestly didn't write it," Janey repeated. "And I'm not in any trouble, desperate or otherwise."

"But . . ."

"Well, that's not completely true. I broke up with Alan and I've got a tour coming up and I *am* desperate for a sideman, but it's not the kind of thing I'd write to you about." She poked the letter with a finger. "This sounds so . . . so serious."

"That's why I came."

Janey had gone all earnest now. She reached out and took his hand again.

"It means a lot that you did come after getting this," she said.

"Can I see this letter?" the Gaffer asked.

Janey passed it over to him.

"It's a queer sort of game to be playing on someone," the Gaffer said after he'd read it through.

Felix met the old man's steady gaze and saw in it that the Gaffer knew exactly why he'd come—and that he approved. Of course, he and the Gaffer had always got on well. But much as he liked the old man, it was his granddaughter he wanted to get on well with first.

"Did you travel far?" the Gaffer added.

"I got it in Madrid," Felix said, "and came right away."

"I really didn't write it," Janey said. "I don't even own a type-writer."

He wanted to believe her. But if she hadn't sent it, then who had? Who knew him well enough to know that a letter like this would bring him to her, no matter where he was when it reached him? And why would they bother?

It made no sense.

"It's not Janey's sort of prank," the Gaffer said.

"I know."

At least he thought he did. The Janey he'd known would never have done it for a lark. But who could tell how much she'd changed in three years?

He rubbed the stubble on his scalp again, feeling foolish to have come all this way, to be here, when he wasn't needed.

"It's still *wonderful* to see you," Janey said.

"And better that there is no trouble, don't you think, my robin?" the Gaffer added.

Trouble, Felix thought.

"Well, there has been trouble," he said.

Briefly he described what had happened when he first arrived.

"How could they know?" the Gaffer said when Felix was done.

"Know what?" both Felix and Janey asked at the same time.

The Gaffer glanced at the book where it sat on the arm of his favorite chair. For long moments he said nothing. Then finally he sighed.

"There's a thing about that book," he said. "I don't rightly know what, but there's been people after it for as long as it's been in my possession."

Janey sat forward on the edge of the couch. "That's right! You said some American woman had been asking after it."

"And she's not the first, my gold," the Gaffer said. "When I first got it from Billy. I . . . well, we were mates, Billy and I. Close as brothers, weren't we? I didn't know what it was about the book that made him send it to me, or want me to hide it—I've read it through myself and it's just a tale like the others he's written—but hide it I did.

"First I kept it at Charlie's place, and then later up at Andy Spurr's farm, over near the Reservoir, and a good thing I did, for there were men coming around asking after it, threatening legal action against me—though they didn't have half a leg to stand on—and even coming to the house when neither myself or the missus were home."

"When was this?" Janey asked.

"Oh, years ago—before you were born, my love. But they came and pried and snooped for a few months, never giving me a moment's rest, until one day they were all up and gone. Time to time, I'd get a letter—or a phone call, once we had a line put in—asking after Billy's 'unpublished writings.' They'd be publishers, see, wanting notes or stories that hadn't been published before, or asking after photographs and artifacts, but I could tell the difference between the genuine article and whoever these others were. They weren't publishers, though I can't tell you how I know that, or who they really were. Nor what they really wanted."

Janey shivered. "This is becoming more and more mysterious every moment."

The Gaffer nodded, but he didn't seem very happy about the mystery of it.

"When Andy died last year, his widow had me come take the box of Billy's writings away because she was leaving the farm to live with her son in St. Ives. I put it up in the attic, but I didn't look in it except to see that the book was still there. Didn't open the book."

"Why not?" Felix asked.

The Gaffer shrugged. "Don't know, my gold. It's just a feeling I have that when that book's opened, things start to *happen*."

"But what kinds of things?" Janey wanted to know.

The Gaffer looked as though he was about to say something, then shrugged again and settled on: "That the crows would come sniffing around again."

"I suppose there's money to be made from a previously unknown and unpublished Dunthorn book?" Felix asked.

Neither the Gaffer nor Janey replied.

"Well, wouldn't there be?"

"I suppose," the Gaffer said. "But it wouldn't be right. I made a promise, didn't I?"

"I didn't mean that you should get it published," Felix said. "It's only that it explains why people are coming around looking for it— that they're even willing to steal it. There must be some rumour of the book's existence that gets resurrected every once in a while."

Janey shook her head. "I've got all the biographies on him and I never came across even a hint of *The Little Country,* or *any* unpublished book, until I found it this afternoon."

"It's more than money," the Gaffer agreed. "There's something odd about the book. I can't put it into words, but it's there. Just a feeling I get."

Felix thought about the book. There *was* a certain feel about it, though he wouldn't have called it odd. The word he would have chosen was comfortable. It was the sort of book that no sooner had he opened it than he felt at ease and among friends. Ready to follow the storyline, no matter how fantastic. And he didn't even care much for that kind of book in the first place.

"What will you do now?" he asked the Gaffer. "Hide it again?"

"I suppose."

"But not until I get to finish reading it!" Janey protested.

The Gaffer smiled. "No. We can wait that long, my queen. But we'll have to be careful and hide it well whenever we go out."

Janey gave another little shiver. "Isn't it all kind of, oh, I don't know, sort of eerie?"

"It's queer, all right," the Gaffer agreed.

Though no more strange than the mysterious letter that had brought him here, Felix thought. He looked at it lying forgotten on Janey's lap, then picked it up and refolded it once more.

"Felix," she began as he put it away in his pocket. "I honestly didn't send that."

"It's all right," he said. "I don't mind having come. It's really good to see you—both of you."

"You're not going to run off again, are you?" Janey asked.

Is that how she saw the way their relationship had ended? Felix wondered. That he'd run off on her?

"No," he said. "I'll stay for a day or so, but then I've got to go."

"But you just got here."

How to explain what it meant to him, being here with her, but not *with* her?

"I used almost all the money I had to get here as quickly as I could," he said. "I have to get back to London and see what ships are in port and if I can get a job."

"You can stay with us," Janey said.

"I'll stay tonight."

"There's lots of room," the Gaffer added.

Felix knew what he meant. It could be like it had been before, when he'd lived here with them. But it wouldn't—couldn't—be what it had been before. And while Felix didn't ever not want to be friends with Janey, right now he was feeling too confused to even think about their getting back together again.

There was that letter lying between them. . . .

"Don't blame me for something I didn't do," Janey began, but the Gaffer shushed her before she could go on.

"Give the man a chance to catch his wits, my love." He glanced at Felix. "You remember your old room?"

Felix nodded.

"Nothing much has changed. You can go on up and use it if you like."

Felix turned to Janey. He wanted to explain the confusion, but while he could speak so eloquently to her when she was only present in his imagination, when he was far out to sea on some freighter, sitting here in the Gaffer's house on Duck Street, with her presence all too real, everything was just a jumble in his head.

"I guess I'll go up," he said.

Janey caught his arm as he got up from the couch and he paused, looking at her.

"I . . ." she began, then sighed. "I just wanted to say good night."

Felix gave her a weak smile. "Good night," he said.

Collecting his baggage, he went upstairs.

3.

Janey sat for a long time on the couch after Felix had gone up. As she listened to him moving about in his room, a flood of memories went through her. They were good memories and they made her wonder for the first time in a long time just why their relationship hadn't worked out.

He'd never been jealous of what success she'd found as a musician like Alan, nor had the touring it necessitated troubled him as it did the fellow she'd dated before Alan—probably because Felix's own work took him all over the world. They'd spent weeks together in Mousehole, though, when she wasn't on the road and he was off ship, and when she did tour, he'd often turn up in the oddest places just to spend a few days with her. In New England, once, when his ship had docked in Boston. In California another time, when he took a few months off and hitchhiked across the country to see her. At a festival in Germany. Another in Scotland.

Like Dinny Boyd, he enjoyed playing music, but had absolutely no ambition to turn professional—a fact that constantly irritated her because he was just so bloody good on his box. In the circles that knew about this sort of thing, he was reckoned in the same breath as some of the masters of the instrument—John Kimmel, Paddy O'Brien, Joe Cooley, Tony MacMahon, Joe Burke—and was considered on a par with his contemporaries such as Martin O'Connor, Jackie Daly, and the like. He also played a mean whistle, as well as a little concert flute and guitar. But while he'd sit in with her the odd time, he refused to make the commitment to record or tour.

They used to argue about it—a great deal towards the end of their relationship. In fact, she thought, if she was going to be honest about it, it was the constant pressure she'd put on him about it that had contributed the most to the breakup. They'd start off talking about his reluctance to tour, or about his wanting to settle down—a laugh, since his work took him to the four corners of the world—and somehow that would segue into pointless and often strident arguments that, when she looked back on them, really weren't about anything very important at all.

She could remember his trying to stop them, his calmness in the face of her quarreling, but she had too volatile a temper and his imperturbability just made her more angry. It was silly, really, because five minutes later, she'd forget all about it, but though he wouldn't say anything, he'd still carry the hurt. She could see it in his eyes, or in the cautious way he dealt with her, and that would just set things off again until finally they called it quits one day. Before she was even fully aware of what they were doing, he'd packed up and was gone.

She'd missed him terribly at first and accepted a long tour on the Continent—one that she'd refused when it was first offered to her because she and Felix had had plans to spend a month traveling around Ireland. Without him, she didn't want to go to Ireland anymore. And she didn't want to stay in Mousehole. All she wanted to do was to try to put it all behind her.

So she'd done just that. But seeing him tonight—feeling her heart lift when she saw him and the way she just fit so perfectly into the circle of his arms—she realized that she'd been too effective. What she should have done was not let him go in the first place.

Sighing, she glanced at the Gaffer who was sitting in his chair by the hearth, pretending not to be watching her.

"He doesn't believe me, does he?" she said.

"Well, it's a strange business, my gold."

"I feel funny seeing him again. It's like we never broke up, but at the same time it's like there's a whole ocean lying in between us."

She tugged at a loose thread at the hem of her short skirt, her gaze fixed on what she was doing, though she wasn't thinking about the thread or her skirt at all. Finally she looked over at her grandfather again.

"Do you think second chances are possible?" she asked.

"Well, that depends," the Gaffer said. "We didn't worry much about that kind of thing in my time. Couples tried to make do, to see each other through the rough spots. I'm not saying that way was right or wrong—there's times when a man and a woman just aren't right for each other and no matter of work can make things better between them—but mostly we stuck to it."

"But what about me and Felix?"

"How do you feel about seeing him?" the Gaffer asked.

"All mixed up."

"Well, my robin, first you have to decide what it is that you want."

"I suppose."

The Gaffer nodded. "It's hard, I know. But know what you want first, my love. If you just try to muddle through, you'll only give each other still more heartbreak."

"But how can I convince him that I didn't send that stupid letter?"

"It's not so stupid, really, is it?" the Gaffer said. "It brought him here, didn't it?"

Janey gave him a sudden considering look. "You didn't send it, did you?"

The Gaffer laughed. "Not a chance of that, my flower. I learned long ago to keep my nose in my own business, *especially* when it comes to family."

"Well, then who did?"

"Don't worry about that so much. Worry about your heart, my love. He won't be here long."

"But he doesn't believe me."

"Give him time to believe."

Janey sighed. "You just said he wasn't going to be here long, and now you tell me I should give him time."

The Gaffer rose from his chair. "Now you know why I like to keep to my own business," he said. "In this sort of an affair, no matter what you say, you're wrong."

"I'm sorry. I didn't mean—"

"That's all right, my dear," the Gaffer said. "Your old grandfather knows you better than you think. Now I'm for bed. Are you staying up?"

Janey shook her head.

The Gaffer picked up the Dunthorn book from the arm of the chair and handed it to her.

"Well, don't leave this lying around," he said.

"I won't. Good night, Gramps."

"Good night, my robin. Things will look different in the morning when you see them with fresh eyes."

"I need a fresh brain," Janey muttered, but the Gaffer was already leaving the room and gave no notice that he'd heard her.

Or maybe a fresh heart, she added to herself. Oh, why did things always have to get so complicated?

She slouched on the couch for a while longer, until at last she got up and collected her instruments. Turning off the lights, she went outside to her own room.

The Gaffer's cottage had a small courtyard in front of it—the same place where Felix had struggled with the burglar earlier that evening. A low stone wall, broken by an wrought-iron gate, closed it in from the road. Flower boxes hung from either side of it, while Jabez, the Gaffer's black and white tomcat, could be found lounging upon the top most days and well into the evening.

Turning right from the front door, the stone patio went through a small archway to a smaller courtyard. Directly facing the arch was the entrance to the cellar where the Gaffer kept the freezers for his fish. Turning right again, one could see a narrow set of stairs that led up to where Janey lived.

She had two rooms.

The outer one had the bathroom directly in front of the door as you came in, and two windows, one looking back into the courtyard, the other overlooking the Gaffer's tiny square of lawn in back of his cottage, which was hedged with blackberry bushes. This was Janey's sitting room and where she practiced her music. The walls were covered with festival posters, including her favorite from the Cornwall '86 Folk Festival in Wade-bridge where she'd gotten her first large print billing, as opposed to being lost in among the tiny type or simply listed as "and others." Near the door were two paintings by the Newlyn artist Bernard Evans—one of Mousehole harbour, the other depicting one of the old luggers that used to fish this part of the coast.

The furnishings here consisted of two wooden straightback chairs (Janey couldn't play sitting on a sofa or a chair with arms); a battered sofa that she'd patched with swatches from a pair of Laura Ashley dresses she'd outgrown; a crate under the back window with a hotplate, kettle, and teapot on it; a dresser filled with records that held her stereo on top, along with a jumble of cassettes; a bookcase filled mostly with tunebooks; and of course her instruments. Two other fiddles and a flat-backed mandolin hung from the wall, her first set of pipes sat in its case in a corner, while various whistles, pipe chanters, spare reeds, and the like were scattered across the low table in front of the couch. A bodhran lay on the couch itself.

The other room was her bedroom. In one corner was the Aquatron shower that the Gaffer had installed for her a couple of years ago, saving her from having to throw something decent on to go next door whenever she wanted to take a shower. There was also her bed, an old wooden wardrobe stuffed with clothes—some of which she'd long outgrown but couldn't throw out—another dresser, and a bookcase jammed with more books than it should have been able to hold. The window in this room also looked out on the inner courtyard.

Leaving her instruments in the first room, Janey wandered into her bedroom. She undressed slowly, only half thinking of what she was doing, then curled up under her comforter, the Dunthorn book held against her chest.

Things were going to look different in the morning, the Gaffer had promised. Which was all well and fine, but how was she supposed to stop thinking about them in the meantime?

She lay there for a long while, listening to the wind outside and the patter of rain that it soon brought with it. After a time she opened the book and let Dunthorn take her away from her troubles until she fell asleep, the book dropping onto the bedclothes beside her leg.

Off She Goes!

It's not that I'm afraid to die. It's just that I don't
want to be there when it happens.

—attributed to WOODY ALLEN

Jodi had never fainted before. In the story that was her life she saw
herself as the plucky and brave heroine who—when some moment
of adventurous duress finally arose—Got Things Done and Made A
Difference. She definitely did *not* see herself as a light-headed poppet
who collapsed at the first sign of trouble.

But faint she did.

And when she came around, she almost fainted again.

For she found herself lying on top of a bed with a man sitting
beside her on the coverlets who bore an awfully close resemblance
to the little fellow she'd seen inside the Widow Pender's aquarium,
except that this man was the same size as she. What made her almost
pass out once more was the realization that he hadn't become large.
No. For she could see past the bed, through the glass sides of the
aquarium, to discover that she was with him in the aquarium, set up
on the worktable in the Widow's giant sitting room.

The little man hadn't grown large at all.

She'd been shrunk down to his size.

It was impossible, of course. She was just dreaming. Any minute
now she'd wake up in her aunt's house to find that she'd fallen asleep
and only dreamt the whole affair. Her midnight adventure had yet
to begin, and given the warning wisdom of her dream, she'd do the
sensible thing for a change and just stay in her bed until morning.

"Are you feeling a little better?" the small man asked.

She still thought of him as tiny, even though they were now the
same size. He was a pleasant enough looking individual with a coun-
tryman's rounded features and a sturdy frame; older than she was—
at least in his early twenties—which would make him positively ancient to the children of the Tatters. She gave him a considering
glance, then tried to will the whole scene away.

Wake up, wake up, she told herself.

Her surroundings and size remained uncomfortably unchanged.

"Miss?" the little man tried again.

Jodi sat up on the bed, leaning against the backboard when the inside of the aquarium began to do a slow spin around her. She waited a few long moments for her head to settle down, then focused on the little man's face again.

"I'm dreaming, aren't I?"

He shook his head. "No dream—though it is a nightmare."

Well, of course he wouldn't think it was a dream, not when he was a part of it. She tried to place his accent. It wasn't quite the soft burr predominant around Bodbury; instead it had a clipped property about it, which gave it a bit of a formal ring. She wondered what his name was.

"Edern Gee," he told her when she asked.

And that sounded exactly like something she'd make up—not a proper name at all.

"My name's Jodi," she said. "Jodi Shepherd."

Edern nodded. "I know. I heard it when the witch charmed you."

"I didn't find her very charming at all," Jodi said.

"I meant when she used her magic—when she enchanted you."

Magic. Oh raw we. It made her head ache to think about it.

"And you?" she asked. "I suppose you've been enchanted, too?"

Edern gave her a sour look. "Do you think I was born this size?"

"How would I know? We've only just met."

That earned her a smile.

Jodi looked around their glass prison once more.

"So this is . . . real?" she asked.

"All too."

"Did you come snooping about her house as well?"

Edern shook his head. "I only meant to pass through Bodbury and stopped in here to ask if there was any work that needed doing. I never got any farther into town."

"She didn't like the job you did?"

"Didn't want to pay me. She shrunk me down when I argued about it with her. I've been here three weeks, locked up in this glass box like her pet toad."

"*Three* weeks?"

Edern nodded glumly.

"And you didn't try to escape?"

"You try climbing those glass walls."

"But what about over there?" Jodi asked, pointing to where the tin chimney rose up from the stove and climbed up alongside the glass.

"The tin's too hot."

Jodi laughed. "Well, then put out the fire."

For a long moment Edern just stared at her, then he sighed.

"It's not just getting out of the box," he said. "There's that as well."

Jodi looked in the direction he indicated and began to feel all faint again.

Stop this, she ordered herself.

But it was hard, for sitting there on the high back of a chair was the Widow's odd little creature, all fat-bodied and spindly limbs. When it saw it had her attention, it grinned at her, revealing long rows of wickedly sharp teeth. It had been the size of a cat the last time she'd seen it. Now, with her own reduction in size, it had the relative bulk of an elephant.

"Bother and damn," she said.

Not only was this impossible, it wasn't fair either. She could almost hear her aunt's voice as soon as she had the thought. "Fairness is for those what have the money to pay for it," she liked to tell Jodi. "Not for the likes of us."

"It's almost always about," Edern said. "When you can't see it— just a tap on the glass will bring it scampering back to its post."

"What is it?"

"Her fetch."

"But that's like a hummock, isn't it?" Jodi said. "Just another kind of a ghost?"

"It's also a witch's familiar. She calls it Windle. Witches grow them from their own phalanges—usually the ones from their little toe."

Jodi gave him another considering look. Edern Gee might claim to be a simple traveling man, but he seemed to know an awful lot about witches and magic and the like.

"I don't think you're a traveler at all," she said. "I think you've come from the Barrow World. You're a Small—a little piskie man that she caught out on the moors."

"I could say the same about you."

"Ah, but you saw me big. You saw her shrink me down to mouse size."

She found it easy enough to say, but she was nevertheless hedging her bets, mostly because she was still praying that this *was* all a dream.

"You seem to know all about magic and the like," she added.

Edern just shrugged. "Did you never hear the stories of the traveling people in Bodbury? How we're all spellmen and witchwives?"

"But those are just stories. . . ."

Jodi's voice trailed off. Like Smalls were. Or the fact that a witch could grow an odd little creature from the bones of her baby toe, or shrink someone down to the size of a mole.

"What's she going to do with us?" she asked finally.

"Don't know. Keep us as pets, I suppose. She likes to come in here and talk to me while she makes these tiny furnishings and the like. I don't think she's bad at heart—just lonely."

Jodi couldn't find much sympathy for a lonely witch—at least not for one who'd enchanted her the way the Widow Pender had.

"I can't stay locked up in here," she said. "I'll go mad."

"Does anyone know where you've gone?"

Jodi shook her head. "I'll be missed—sooner or later. Probably later, when either Denzil or my aunt finally goes looking for me at the other's place. But that could take a day or so and they'd never know where to look. How about you?"

"A solitary traveling man? Who's to miss me?"

"Well, I'm not staying," Jodi said.

She got slowly off the bed. Her head still ached, but at least the room stayed in one place. Crossing the aquarium, she leaned against the glass wall and peered out. Windle sat up on the back of its chair and looked at her with interest in its saucer-big eyes.

"Why hasn't she put the cover back on?" she asked Edern.

"She only does that when she goes out."

"And when does she do that?"

Jodi knew about her afternoon walks down by the Old Quay, and her midnight excursions out onto the headland, but that was all.

"Afternoons and late at night—regular as clockwork," Edern replied, adding nothing to what she already knew.

"Then I suppose I'll just have to wait until this afternoon," she said.

She turned from the glass wall to look at her companion.

"Who gets the bed?" she asked.

"It's big enough for two."

"I suppose. But mind you keep yourself to yourself."

Edern laughed. "You're a bit young for me."

Was she now?

"Well, you're far too old for me, geezer," she told him.

Ignoring his smile, she went 'round to the other side of the bed and, not bothering to remove her clothes, crawled under the covers.

Maybe I'll fall asleep and wake up back home, she thought.

Maybe she would. And maybe she'd only dream that she did. How would she ever know?

Thinking about that only made her head ache more, so she tried to think of more pleasant things. But everything merely went around and around in dizzying circles, each of which centered on the impossibility of her present situation.

La, but life could be confusing, she thought as sheer exhaustion finally let her drop off.

2.

Waking provided no relief.

She was still mouse-sized when she opened her eyes, still trapped in an aquarium like one of Denzil's catfish, though happily, unlike theirs, this one wasn't full of murky water. But dryness was little comfort, all things considered. Her situation was so fanciful that she might as well be in the Barrow World of Faerie—a place she'd longed to visit ever since she read her first fairy tale—as in her native Bodbury. Caught up in the uncomfortable reality of her adventure, however—in reduced circumstances, as it were, she thought with a rueful smile—the wonder of it all had lost much of its previous storybook appeal.

I would settle for my old life, she decided. Pages missing and all. There was no question of it. Unfortunately, the decision of what was to become of her life didn't seem to be hers to make anymore.

"Getting up, are you?"

She glanced over to the other side of the aquarium where Edern was sitting at a table, eating.

"Best hurry up," he added, "unless you don't mind eating in the dark."

"What do you mean?"

"It's past noon and she'll be going out in a bit. It's her habit to feed me—us, now, I suppose—before she leaves."

Rubbing sleep from her eyes and feeling rumpled from having slept in her clothes, Jodi swung her feet down from the bed and crossed the aquarium to join him. At the mention of food, her stomach had begun to rumble, but the small platter of crumbled cheese and tiny bits of bread didn't seem very appealing. It reminded her too much of what Denzil fed his mice.

She stood there, combing her short hair with her fingers, until Edern motioned her to sit.

"Is this it?" she asked, waving her hand at the food as she sat down.

"I've had worse."

"Maybe you have, and maybe I have too, but this . . . this is what you feed mice. I'm *not* her pet and I *won't* eat it."

Never mind that she liked both cheese and bread. It was the principle of the thing.

Edern laughed. "But that's all we are to the Widow—her pets."

Jodi said nothing.

"Starving won't solve a thing," Edern added.

At Jodi's frown, he pushed one of two ceramic thimbles across the table towards her.

"Have some tea, at least," he said.

"Well, maybe some tea."

She pulled the thimble over to her and took a deep sip. The tea was good, but its container made her feel like Weeman from the old nursery rhyme. She could make up her own bit of verse now:

> *Now I am small, but once I was big;*
> *I feel like a fool, oh, rig-a-jig-jig.*

Without really thinking about it, she put some cheese between two bits of bread and ate it, washing it down with more tea. It was only when she was on her third sandwich that she realized what she was doing. She gave Edern a quick glance, but he was studiously ignoring her.

So she was eating. Well, who cared? Besides, she needed her strength for her big escape.

She finished the third sandwich, then turned her chair so that she could examine the Widow's sitting room.

Windle didn't seem to be about, which was just as well. The witch's fetch made her feel like the Bagle Wight was breathing right upon her neck. And with neither the witch nor her creature in the room, it was a perfect opportunity to do some scouting.

Leaving her seat, Jodi went over to the stove first. The fire was out, so she cautiously touched the stovepipe and found it only warm, rather than hot. Since she'd been climbing about on gutters and roofs from when she was six years old and on, she knew she'd have no trouble navigating the pipe's length. She could even go inside it, which would save her having to try to pry the thing away from the glass when she got to the top. She could just scoot through, then climb down the cloth the Widow would drape over the aquarium when she went out.

Descending from the worktable was another matter again. But she soon spied a roll of twine. If she could open the window, then tie the twine to its latch, she could simply roll the twine over the side and into the garden. And she'd be away.

Then she thought about Edern and studied the stovepipe again. Would he fit? Two could manage both the window and twine more easily than one. But if he couldn't get through . . .

She looked to where the pipe met the glass. It wasn't glued or anything. If she clung to the cloth and gave it a good kick, she might be able to get it away from the glass. It would be easier done from the outside than the inside, at any rate. She turned to share her plan with him, but just then the sitting-room door opened and the Widow came in.

Humming to herself, the Widow took a small pair of tongs from the worktable and used them to extract a coal from the hearth, which she brought over to the aquarium.

Oh, no, Jodi thought. Don't.

She might as well have wished for the moon to come down from the sky and whisk her away.

"And how are you today, my sweets?" the Widow asked as she removed the glass lid of the aquarium.

Her voice boomed like dull thunder. Jodi glared at the Widow's enormous face looming over her, but Edern merely ignored it.

A huge hand came down into the aquarium and shooed Jodi away from the stove. She moved sullenly, wishing she had a large pin. The Widow opened the door to the stove and placed the coal inside, then closed it up again and withdrew her hands.

"There," she said. "Now you'll be warm and snug."

Back went the glass lid. She took the velvet from where it had been hanging over the back of a chair and draped it over the aquarium.

"Now be good," the Widow said before the cloth hid her and the room from view.

It was immediately gloomy inside the aquarium, the only light coming from where the stovepipe met the glass. The cloth had been cut away there so that it wouldn't touch the tin.

As soon as she heard the sitting-room door close, Jodi turned to her companion.

"I've got a plan," she told him.

"This'll be good."

"Do you want to escape or not?"

Edern held his hands out in front of him in mock surrender. "I'm all ears."

"Well, help me get rid of this coal," Jodi said.

They pushed the rug back from the stove, then used the back of a chair to lift the coal up from inside and topple it to the floor where it fell with a shower of sparks upon the glass.

"That's made a fine mess," Edern said.

"Oh, bother and damn," Jodi said. "Will you be quiet?"

Edern listened to her plan and slowly nodded his head when she was done.

"It might work," he said. "But . . ."

"But what?"

"You're forgetting Windle."

"We'll pick up a nail from the Widow's worktable and stab him with it."

"Um-hmm," Edern said dubiously.

Jodi glared at him for a long moment, then turned her back on him and stuck her head in the stove. It was still warm from the coal, but not uncomfortably so. She turned on her back and then squeezed herself up into the stovepipe.

Plenty of room, she thought.

It was just a few moments' work to shimmy her way up the pipe's length. The corner where it made a right-angle turn to leave the aquarium proved a little tricky, but manageable. Grabbing handfuls of velvet cloth, she pulled herself out. With her feet balanced on the lip of the pipe, her hands keeping her balance, she found herself face-to-face with Edern, only the glass wall of the aquarium separating them.

She raised her eyebrows questioningly. When he nodded that he was ready, she took a firmer grip of the velvet and swung out, coming back to kick the pipe with both feet, the force of all her weight behind her. It came loose on the first kick. Edern swayed on top of it, looking as though he was going to drop with it. He only just managed to get hold of the opening before the pipe fell away, back into their prison. It crashed onto the glass floor beside the bed.

They both held their breath, listening. And heard nothing.

"Come on," Jodi whispered.

She made her way quickly down the cloth, lowering herself hand over hand until her feet touched the surface of the worktable. As Edern started his own descent, she crawled out from under the cloth and cautiously peered about the sitting room.

Their luck held, for there was no sign of the witch's fetch.

While Edern manhandled the roll of twine across the tabletop, Jodi clambered up on the windowsill and gave the latch a try. It wouldn't budge.

"I need a hand," she called softly to her companion.

Edern joined her and with his help they got the latch undone and swung the window open. The sharp tang of a salty wind blew in at them.

"La," Jodi said. "I can already taste freedom."

She tied the twine to the latch with a seaman's knot, then the two of them hoisted the roll of twine up onto the sill and let it tumble out the window where it landed on the ground between the cottage wall and the rosebushes growing up alongside of it.

Edern gave her a flourishing bow. "After you."

Grinning, Jodi scampered down the rope, then held it taut for Edern as he descended.

"Now where to?" he asked when he reached the bottom.

"To Denzil's," Jodi said. At Edern's questioning look, she added, "He's my friend. An inventor."

"An inventor?"

"He's—oh, never mind. You'll see soon enough."

She led the way out from under the rosebush, Edern on her heels. He bumped into her when she came to an abrupt stop.

"What . . . ?" he began, but then he saw what was waiting for them on the Widow's lawn.

Windle was there, saucer eyes laughing, teeth bared in an unpleasant grin. The creature was crouched low and out of sight from a chance passerby on the street beyond the Widow's garden and obviously just waiting for them to move from under the thorny bushes to pounce on them.

"Bother and damn," Jodi muttered. "We forgot our nail."

"Nail?" Edern said softly. "We'd need more than a nail to stop that creature. Look at the size of it!"

He was horribly accurate, of course. Small as mice as they were, the cat-sized fetch appeared to be monstrously huge.

"What are we going to do?" Jodi asked. "The Widow'll be back soon."

Edern nodded glumly, gaze not leaving the creature.

"I'm not going back into her aquarium!" Jodi said.

Brave words. Her legs trembled, knees feeling weak. If only her heartbeat would slow down. The drum of her pulse in her ears made thinking impossible.

"I'm not," she said, as though repeating it would make it true.

Edern nodded again, then touched her arm as the fetch cocked its head and looked towards the low, overgrown stone wall that separated the garden from the street beyond it.

"What's that it hears?"

"The Widow . . . ?"

Edern shook his head.

They could see nothing, but there was a jingling in the air, accompanied by a snuffling sound.

Excitement pushed Jodi's fear aside.

"Edern," she said slowly. "Can you whistle? Whistle really loud and shrill?"

Pull the Knife and Stick It Again

I don't feel guilty for anything. . . . I feel sorry
for people who feel guilt.

—attributed to TED BUNDY

Michael Bett took one of Madden Enterprises' private jets to London's Heathrow, with only one stopover in St. John's for refueling. He didn't leave the plane in St. John's, preferring to keep at his research.

His only true enjoyment in life was discovering what made things work—to cut through all the frivolities and get to the heart of whatever particular business currently absorbed his interest. Sometimes that involved research and study, as he was doing now; sometimes it was a matter of living a certain kind of life, as he did with Madden's Order of the Grey Dove; sometimes all it required was to take a knife and see how deeply and often it could cut before the mystery of life fled.

The first to fall under his knife was the family dog. Body still aching from the beating his latest "Daddy" had given him, he'd taken the old hound out into the vacant lot that stood between two deserted tenements near his mother's house. He stood for a long time looking down at the dog. There was a curiously empty feeling inside him as its trusting eyes looked up into his own. The lolling tongue and the big tail slapping the ground that always made him laugh couldn't even raise a smile today.

Then he took the knife he'd stolen from the kitchen out of his jacket pocket, pulled up the dog's head to expose its neck, and drew the sharp blade across its throat. Blood fountained and he only just stepped back in time to keep it from spraying all over him. Circling around, he came at the dog from behind and brought the knife down again and again, stabbing and hacking away at the poor creature long after it was dead.

He'd been eleven years old at the time.

Other neighbourhood pets followed the first dog's fate. When he was thirteen, he killed his first human—a five-year-old boy whom he kidnapped from a backyard and took away to an empty building where the boy's dying amused him for hours. When he was fifteen, his latest victim—a teenage girl lured away into a deserted tenement with the promise of a party—provided him with a moment of pure epiphany.

Dying, helpless, an inferno of pain flaring in her eyes, she'd croaked out one word: "Why?"

Until then Bett hadn't thought to question what he did, hadn't understood what drove him to such ultimate thievery.

"Because I can," he'd told the girl.

But that wasn't the whole of the truth, just the most obvious part of it. Lying under it was a purpose that, as the years went by, became the focus of his existence: the need to understand, not just the secret of life, but the mystery of its passage into death; how a thing worked, *why* it worked as it did. He never felt a sense of self-recrimination or outrage for his methodology of pursuit for this knowledge. The deaths were only a kind of fuel to feed the curiosity that burned inside him like a smoldering fire.

He lived a kind of controlled autism in the sense that he was always absorbed in one form or another of self-centered subjective mental activity, but he had no difficulty relating to the world around him. The world and what inhabited it fascinated him. He was disciplined to the degree that he could settle his attention single-mindedly on an object or subject for as long as it took him to understand it, or in the case of the subject, for as long as it took his victim to die.

Everything was important—but only in how it related to him.

Sitting in Madden's jet, his undivided attention was fixed upon the puzzle of Janey Little.

He wore a Walkman on which played a tape containing both of her albums. The small cassette machine was turned to its reverse mode so that the tape played over and over again, stopping only when the batteries wore out. Then Bett replaced them, and the music played on once more.

On the empty seat beside him was a leather briefcase, beside it a Toshiba laptop computer. On his lap was a slender folder of press clippings and a private detective's thirty-seven-page report; the subject of both was the same woman whose music sounded in Bett's ear. He was currently absorbed in the profile of her in an old issue of *Folk Roots* magazine. He'd read it so often that he could have quoted the entire article, word for word. Mostly he studied the photos that accompanied the article, comparing them to those that were attached to the detective's report.

With the material at hand, and the video tapes he had—also provided by the detective agency—he knew as much, if not more, about Janey Little as anyone. Perhaps as much as the woman did herself.

Madden knew nothing of this private research Bett had undertaken—undertaken long before Madden sent him to Cornwall earlier this evening. For Bett had seen, as soon as he learned of the interest that the Order had in Thomas Little, that the answer to what they were looking for lay not in him, but in his granddaughter. She would be the doorway to the old man's secrets. But the approach had to be made subtly—far more so than the Order's own previous bumbling attempts to plunder whatever riddle it was that Tom Little kept.

Ah, yes: the riddle. The secret.

What was it?

Madden wouldn't—perhaps couldn't—say, and no one else knew. And that made it infinitely intriguing to Bett.

He smiled, thinking of John Madden. Sitting together with a glass of sherry before them in the library, Madden loved to repeat the story of how the two of them had met. How he, Madden, had immediately recognized the soul of his old friend Aleister Crowley in Bett's eyes. Madden had a mind that was sharp as a razor, but he let his hermetic studies blind that one part of his logic that would reveal all the occult mumbo-jumbo as drivel.

Bett had another impression of that night in Chicago. All Madden had recognized in Bett was a kindred spirit—the difference between them being that Madden only dreamed of picking up the knife, while Bett allowed himself whatever indulgence pleased him at the moment.

Still this reincarnation business had served Bett well. It amused him to keep up the charade. As soon as he'd realized what could be his if he could convince Madden that he really was the sorcerer who'd called himself the Beast, he'd surreptitiously researched Crowley's life. Utilizing the same thoroughness with which he approached every project, he'd come away with enough obscure details of biographical data that Madden wasn't simply convinced; he *believed*.

Naturally, Bett hadn't been fool enough to give it all out at once. He fed it out, tidbit by tidbit. Haltingly. Unsure of himself—allowing Madden, and his excitement, to "convince" both of them.

This weakness of Madden's—his only weakness—was what made the man so fascinating to Bett. That a man with his hard-nosed common sense and acumen should so readily accept what could only be fairy tales . . .

If that was what they were.

Bett was blessed, or cursed, with an open mind. Even with such illogical beliefs as those held by the Order, he was still willing to withhold complete judgment. For there were certain anomalies between what could logically be real and what he perceived to be real among Madden and his peers. There was the matter of Madden's longevity—shared by other old guard members of the Order. Their worldly success that couldn't always be put down to simple business astuteness. The curious way in which they invariably attained what they aimed for.

The will is all, the Order said.

Bett knew about will and what one could accomplish with it. What he wasn't ready to make a decision on was whether one's will allowed one to tap into an outside force or entity to gain its potency— as the Order held—or whether that strength came from within one's own self. Or both.

Until he had resolved that to his own satisfaction, Bett would remain a part of this secret order of old men and women who thought they ruled the world.

2.

A car met him at Heathrow and took him to Victoria Station where he caught the train to Penzance. Madden had been surprised at that decision, arguing against it, but Bett had remained unswayed.

"I need the time to fully assimilate the role I mean to play," he had explained. "Besides, with the time difference, I'll still arrive in plenty of time."

"What role?" Madden asked.

"Allow me to bring you the results first," Bett had countered. "Then I'll explain."

And Madden, the doting mentor, had smiled and nodded. Bett could see the suspicion in the old man's eyes—but it was no more than was always present. He'd yet to fail Madden; so why should he fail him now?

On the train he completed his transformation from Madden's acolyte into his new role. Gone was the businessman's tailored suit, the stiff body language, the expressionless features that gave no inkling as to the thoughts that lay behind them.

He was casually dressed now in corduroys, a light cotton shirt, Nike running shoes, and a dark blue windbreaker. He'd left his briefcase in the jet, bringing only a Nikon camera in a worn case, the laptop computer, and a battered suitcase holding his notes and files and changes of clothing similar in style to what he was wearing.

His body language was relaxed now, his face expressive and open, his whole attitude making him appear ten years younger than the forty-one years he actually was.

When he arrived at Penzance Station, he disembarked looking as fresh as though he hadn't just put in all those many hours of travel. He helped an older woman with her bags, smiling easily with her when she allowed that she wished her own Janet's husband was half as kind with his family, little say a stranger. After he saw her off, a small unsavory-looking individual approached from where Bett had first noticed him sitting outside the bus station.

"Mr. Bett?"

Bett frowned at him. The man was shabbily dressed, his coat patched, shoes worn, a brown cloth cap pulled down low over his ratty features.

"What do you want?"

"Miss Grant sent me to fetch you, uh, sir."

"Give me the address and I'll find my own way."

"But—"

Bett leaned close and his pretense at an easygoing nature fell away as though it had been stripped from him with the blade of a gutting knife.

"Never call me by name," he said. "Never question what I say. Do it again and I'll feed your heart to your mother."

"I—I . . ."

Bett stepped back, smiling pleasantly. "The address?"

Stumbling over his words, the man gave him the name of a hotel on the Western Promenade, overlooking the bay, and a room number. When Bett ascertained that it was within walking distance, he left the man standing there in the station's parking lot and set off on his own.

3.

Lena Grant looked the same as she always did—beautiful, spoiled, and bored. Her dark hair was coiffured and swept back from her brow in a stiff wave. Her makeup was Park Avenue immaculate and out of place in this small Cornish town. As was the perfect cut of her designer blouse and skirt; the blouse unbuttoned far enough to show the lacy top of her bra, the skirt slit so that a long stockinged leg was revealed whenever she took a step.

"The Golden Boy," she said as she opened the door of her room to him.

Bett pushed by her and shut the door.

"Where's Willie?" she asked.

"Can I assume it was 'Willie' who met me at the station?"

Lena nodded. "Willie Keel. He's local."

"I don't doubt that."

"You didn't get along?"

"I never get along with fools."

Lena frowned. "One of my father's security men recommended him. Daddy always says that you should use local talent when you're—"

"The operative word there is talent," Bett said, interrupting her.

The perfect lips began a pout that Bett simply ignored. He wasn't in the mood to listen to the perfection of everything and anything associated with "Daddy." He knew all about Daddies.

"Have there been any new developments since yesterday?" he asked before she could go on.

"I did the best I could," Lena said.

He'd give her that. Playing a long-lost relative of Dunthorn's and demanding his personal effects—that was about the limit of her imagination. Or maybe it had been "Daddy's" plan. Roland—"Call me Rollie"—Grant might be a big wheel on Wall Street, but there his expertise ended . . . along with his sense of propriety and his social graces, so perhaps it wasn't all Lena's fault. But Bett had no time for sympathy. About the only interest he had in Lena was in how long it would take her to die and that, unfortunately, was something he was unlikely to find out.

For now.

While the Order was still of interest to him.

"I had Willie go into their house last night," she told him. "He found a box of Dunthorn's manuscripts."

Bett's eyebrows rose with interest and he looked about the room. "Where is it?"

"Ah . . ." She wouldn't meet his gaze.

"*Where* is it?"

"He got surprised by some thug and only just got away himself."

Wonderful. Now the Littles would be more on their guard than ever.

It was too bad that Madden was so certain that Tom Little would take his friend's secret to the grave, because the simplest solution to all of this would be to just snatch the old man and let Bett have him for a few days. Madden's beliefs notwithstanding, Bett didn't doubt he'd pry the secret from Little. Maybe he could just cut Little's granddaughter in front of him until her bleeding jogged his memory. . . .

He put the pleasant image from his mind.

"A thug, you said?" he asked.

Lena shrugged. "A big man, according to Willie. Arriving with luggage. Looked a bit like a sailor, but then everyone does around here."

"Would he recognize the man from a photo?" Bett tried, but Lena was off on a tangent now.

"I mean, what a dismal place. There's no water pressure in what they call a shower so I can't wash my hair properly. The food's abysmal. There's nothing to do. The air stinks. Everywhere you turn there's—"

"Shut up," Bett said.

He spoke quietly, but with enough force to get an immediate result. She blinked with surprise, then pointed a manicured finger at him.

"If I tell Daddy how you treat me, he'll—"

"Complain to John who'll do nothing. Tell me about this man."

Again the pout. "What's to tell? Maybe they've hired a bodyguard."

Of course she couldn't have taken the initiative to find out who he was and what he was doing at the Littles'. Though if Bett thought about it for a moment, perhaps that was a blessing. Who knew how she'd mess that up.

"You're to have nothing to do with the Littles from now on," he told her. "And you're to act as though you don't know me if we should happen to meet. In fact, it would be better if you simply didn't go out at all."

"I'm *not* staying cooped up in this room."

"Then perhaps you should go home."

She laughed without humour. "I can't. Daddy wants me to do this."

Bett nodded. He'd heard talk among some of the old guard of the Order. They weren't happy with Lena. For all that she carried their mark on her wrist, she was simply too much the debutante to be trusted. Never mind how she lacked the necessary regimen to follow their studies, what they were most afraid of was the possibility of her committing some indiscretion such as having one of her sulks and talking to a tabloid about the Order: revealing what they stood for; who was a member; what they did. With the continuing rise of the Fundamental Christian contingent in business and politics, that could be a disaster.

If her father hadn't been among Madden's oldest confederates— Grant had been one of the founding members of the Order—she probably would have been dealt with a long time ago. As she might still be.

Bett hoped they'd give the job to him.

Until then, he had to deal with her as best he could.

"If you can't go," he said, "then you'll just have to do as I say. I've got the full confidence of the Order behind me and—"

"I know, I know. You're their Golden Boy."

Bett realized that they could continue along this tack forever, so he shifted gears and put on a new mask. He smiled, winningly, charming her despite herself.

"I'm sorry," he said. "I know it's hard for you, all this business. But we're both in the same situation. Do you think I want to be here? Madden insisted that I do it. But if I fail . . . that's it for me."

"What do you mean?"

Her voice was less sulky, betraying her interest.

"You're born to your position," he said. "I have to work at it constantly. If I fail this job, I'm out."

She was unable to resist his false sincerity. "They wouldn't, would they?"

He nodded, eyes downcast. "I don't get a second chance."

"That's horrible. I'll talk to Daddy. . . ."

"That won't do any good."

"No," she said, obviously thinking of the grim old man she knew Bett's mentor to be. "Not with Madden."

Bett glanced at her through lowered lashes. It never ceased to amaze him how easily some people could be manipulated. A moment ago she'd hated him with all her shallow heart. Now they were confederates.

"We could help each other," Bett said. "Let me do this my way— but we'll share the credit. That way we both win out."

"Why would you do that for me?" Lena asked, suspicion finally aroused.

"I'm not just doing it for you—it's for me as well. I can't fail."

Lena sighed. She walked over to him and trailed a hand along the front of his jacket.

"You're such a confusing man," she said. "Sometimes you're just like ice and I'm sure that you hate me, then there are moments like this when you're just so . . . I don't know, vulnerable, I suppose . . . that all I want to do is protect you from the rest of the world."

"This is me," Bett said. "I've got to act cold—that's what Madden wants—but it's hard to do that with you."

"Really?"

He met her gaze, his blue eyes opened wide and guileless. "Really."

She seemed to make a decision and let her hand fall to her side.

"All right," she said. "I'll wait here for you and I won't get in your way. Just promise me one thing."

"What's that?"

"That you won't be mean to me anymore. When it's just us, you don't have to put on a face. I'd like us to be friends."

It was unbelievable, he thought, and so like her. If everyone acted sweet around her, well then, everything was all right, wasn't it? Everyone liked her and would be her friend.

"I'd like that, too," he said.

She leaned forward again and gave him the kind of kiss prevalent among her crowd—bussing the air near his ear.

"I'm glad," she said, then stepped back. "So what do we do?"

Bett straightened his shoulders. "First we get your man Keel to look at some photos to see if he recognizes the man he saw last night."

"And then?"

Bett hesitated.

"I'll stay out of your way," she said. "Honestly. It's just that nobody ever lets me know what's going on."

"All right," Bett said, and he spun her a tale of how he was going to approach the Littles on the pretense that he was a reporter for *Rolling Stone* interested in Dunthorn's work—concentrating his attention not on the old man, but on his granddaughter who was apparently an enthusiast for Dunthorn's work herself.

It was mostly a lie, but Lena was happy with it.

4.

Bored as she was, Lena was still relieved when both Bett and Willie Keel had left.

Bett made her uncomfortable. She never knew where she stood with him. Most of the time he treated her like a bimbo, but then he'd turn around and be so nice that she just *had* to like him—even when she knew she couldn't trust him; knew he disliked her; knew that under the calm mask he turned to the world there lurked something infinitely dangerous. Pressed, she couldn't have explained how she could be so sure. She simply *knew*.

Intuition . . . or maybe it was what Daddy called magic.

As for Willie Keel . . . while Jim Gazo might have recommended him—and she trusted her father's security man implicitly—to put it frankly, Keel was uncouth. He looked like a weasel in his disheveled, ill-fitting coat and trousers. His breath smelled of stale tobacco and garlic. His clothes smelled as though they hadn't been washed since the day they'd been handed down to him. And God help her, his body odor was enough to make her gag.

Just thinking about him made her feel queasy.

So it was with relief that she stood at the window of her hotel room and watched the two men go their separate ways on the street below. Once they were out of view, she returned to her bed and picked up the photograph that Willie had chosen from the half dozen or so that Bett had presented to him.

This was the man who'd interrupted his burglary at the Littles' the previous night, he'd assured them, his gaze darting nervously from Lena to Bett, then back again.

Felix Gavin.

A common merchant sailor, Bett had said. Maybe Gavin was, but she liked the look of him. Comparing him to Bett and Willie, she decided that he'd neither smell, nor make her feel uncomfortable.

She turned the picture so that the light didn't glare on its glossy surface. An old lover of Janey Little's, was he? Come back to rekindle his romance with her? An old friend such as he was, mightn't he know something about any Dunthorn heirlooms that just happened to be lying about the Little household? Maybe, at one time or another in their relationship, the Little girl had confided in him . . . confided secrets that were only shared with a lover. . . .

Lena smiled. Perhaps she'd go slumming and show Daddy that she was as good as Madden's Golden Boy. And wouldn't it make Bett frown if she was to succeed where everyone else, Bett included, had failed?

The thought of Bett angry brought a return of uneasiness to her.

Best not to think of that. Think of the glow of pride on Daddy's face, instead.

And she could do it. Like Bett, like Daddy and his cronies with their little tattooed doves—she rubbed the one on her wrist as she thought of the old men's club that called itself the Order—she had her own secrets. Hadn't she been taking her acting lessons, twice a week, for two years now? Didn't her teacher say she was doing as well, if not better, than any of her previous students?

Lena studied herself in the mirror that took up the length of the room's closet door. She could do it: She could make Felix Gavin tell her anything. But not like this. He'd go for class—his kind always did, because normally a woman such as herself was so unattainable for him—but the way she looked at the moment would just make him nervous.

Still, she could easily fix that.

Humming to herself, she changed into a pair of designer-faded jeans, complete with the appropriate tear in one knee, a tight MIT T-shirt, and a pair of hightops. She removed her makeup, then reapplied it, this time going for a casual look. When she was done, she put on a leather bomber's jacket and regarded herself in the mirror.

Yes, she decided. This would do. This would do very well. Felix Gavin didn't have a chance.

Now all she had to do was find him. *Without* Bett being any the wiser.

She put in a call to the front desk and left a message that she was sleeping and wasn't to be disturbed for the duration of the day. Then, feeling deliciously like a spy, she left her room and went to the ground floor by the stairs, waiting until the foyer was empty for a moment before slipping out the front door.

The salty wind tousled her hair as soon as she stepped outside, but rather than irritating her as it had every other time she'd left her hotel, now it just added to the adventure. The skies were grey, promising rain. She turned up the collar of her jacket.

How to find Gavin?

Willie would know.

The Dogs Among the Bushes

Luck is a very good word if you put a "P" before it.

—MARY ENGELBREIT

The nice thing about animals, Jodi thought, was that their hearing was so much better than that of people.

Unfortunately, the witch's fetch had an acute sense of hearing as well. Its head turned sharply when Jodi and Edern put their fingers to their lips and the shrill squeaks of their whistling rang out—but by then it was too late. Two dogs came bounding into the garden and Jodi recognized them both.

One was a small mixed breed—part terrier, part who knew what—named Kitey. The other was a border collie named Ansum. Both lived within a few doors of Aunt Nettie's house and had gone for many a long ramble by the cliffs with Jodi and Denzil.

Kitey barked shrilly when he caught sight of the fetch and pounced towards it, Ansum hard on his heels. Windle fled at their enthusiastic approach. The fetch leapt over Jodi's and Edern's heads, over the rosebushes, and went straight through the window, landing with an audible crash on the worktable inside. Kitey ran back and forth in front of the bushes, then burrowed into them through a gap and ran up to the window where he stood on his hind legs, yapping cheerfully. Ansum stayed on the lawn side of the bushes and pushed his head in towards the spot where Jodi and Edern stood.

Edern backed nervously away. When he looked as though he was about to bolt himself, Jodi caught hold of his arm.

"They know me," she told him.

Ansum continued to peer curiously at the two mouse-sized people. A few moments later Kitey left off his vigil at the window and joined the border collie, prancing about on the lawn with barely contained excitement.

"They won't hurt us," Jodi said.

I hope, she added to herself.

As Ansum thrust his nose in towards them, obviously puzzled at the familiar scent coming from such an unfamiliar tiny creature, Jodi moved up to him.

"Hello there, old boy," Jodi said.

She put out a hand to touch his muzzle and was shocked at how tiny her fingers were compared to his nose. Ansum backed nervously away and whined.

"Right," Edern said, his voice betraying his own nervousness. "They won't hurt us at all."

"Oh, do be still," Jodi told him, starting to feel cross. "They're just confused by my size."

"It's more like they're trying to decide whether we're worth eating," Edern muttered. "If you ask me, I'd . . ."

His voice trailed away when Jodi glared at him.

"Come on, then, Ansum," she said. "Hey, there, Kitey."

While the terrier continued to rush about the garden, letting off the odd zealous yap, Ansum lay down on the ground and pushed his muzzle forward until his nose was only inches—by a normal-sized person's reckoning—from Jodi. He made a contented throaty sound when Jodi scratched his muzzle.

"Now what?" Edern asked, still keeping his distance.

"Now we make our escape."

"But the dogs—"

"Are here to help us. Did you never hear of good fortune where you came from?"

Edern sighed. "To be sure. But I've also heard of hungry dogs and I don't much care to—"

This time he was interrupted by the sudden change in pitch and volume of Kitey's barking.

"Evil little creatures," cried an all-too-familiar voice.

"It's the bloody witch," Jodi said.

Ansum started to lift his head, but stopped when Jodi called his name.

"It's now or never," she told Edern as she hurried forward.

Edern could only stare at her as she hauled herself up the border collie's neck, then snuggled in behind his collar so that she was braced between it and his fur.

"You're mad," Edern said.

"Then stay and get turned into a toad. No!" she added as Ansum began to rise again. Then to Edern: "Are you coming? Last chance."

"Go away!" the Widow was crying. "Get out of here, you filthy creatures."

"*I'm* mad," Edern said as he hurried forward.

Moments later he too was hanging on to Ansum's collar. The border collie surged to his feet. White-faced, Jodi and Edern held on for dear life as the dog bolted out of the garden, the yapping Kitey running at his side, head turned back to voice his disdain at the Widow. Jodi caught one glimpse of the Widow's fetch glaring at them from the window, then the Widow's house was lost to sight.

It was a mad, jolting journey for the two of them as the dogs raced through Bodbury's narrow streets, making for the harbour. They clung to Ansum's collar, gritting their teeth against the bounce and jolt of their ride.

"Slow down, slow down!" Jodi tried crying, but neither dog heard her.

Finally they came to a panting halt on the cobbles near the wharves. Crates rose like mountains about them on the dock. Foothills of fish netting lay in untidy piles and heaps. Before the dogs could run off again, Jodi gave Ansum a poke with her elbow. The dog shook his head.

The world spun and her stomach lurched. Frowning, she gripped the collar for all she was worth.

"Will you stop that!" Edern cried as she lifted her elbow to poke the dog again.

"We have to get down, don't we?"

Ansum stood very still at the sound of the tiny voices coming from below his chin. He gave his head another experimental shake, pausing when Jodi shouted at him.

"I'm going to be sick," Edern said.

Jodi knew just what he meant. It was disconcerting and altogether unpleasant to be hanging here from the dog's collar in the first place, without having Ansum try to shake them off as well.

"Down!" she cried as loud as she could. "Lie down, Ansum, there's the boy."

The border collie merely stood there with a puzzled look on his face. Kitey gave a quick yap.

"Don't you start, Kitey!" Jodi cried.

She could feel herself losing her voice from having to shout like this.

"Lie down!" she cried again.

And finally he did.

Before he could change his mind, Jodi and Edern crawled out from behind the dog's collar and scrambled down to the ground. They wobbled about unsteadily on the cobblestones, feeling all off-balance from their wild ride. One of Ansum's enormous eyes turned to solemnly regard them. Kitey yipped and yapped happily.

Edern gave the terrier a nervous look.

"I don't much care for the look of his teeth," he said.

Jodi laughed and pushed him towards a nearby gap in the crates. As soon as they were safely inside, she turned to peer out again. Looking one way and another, she decided that no one had taken any notice of the dogs or their curious cargo.

"We weren't spotted," she said over her shoulder.

Edern slouched against a crate, legs sprawled out before him.

"I can't tell you what a relief that is," he said.

"No need to get all huffy," Jodi told him. "I got us out, didn't I?"

Close at hand, both Ansum and Kitey were still directly beside the crates. The terrier sat with his head cocked, looking at her. Ansum whined and scraped a paw on the cobbles.

"Thank you very much," Jodi told them, "but it's time you were off now."

Neither dog moved.

"Shoo!"

She ran a few steps forward as she shouted and the dogs jumped back, only to return to their stations once Jodi had retreated back between the crates.

"Bother and damn," she said. "They won't go away, which means *we* have to before some nosy tar comes along to see what the fuss is."

Edern gave her a weary look. "Don't you ever get tired?"

Jodi shook her head. She walked by him, stopped long enough to look over her shoulder at him, then continued on. Edern got slowly to his feet. He looked at Ansum and the terrier. When Kitey offered him a shrill bark, he rolled his shoulders to get rid of the shiver that settled in his spine whenever he thought of those dogs, then hurried after his companion.

2.

It was gloomy in the small spaces between the mountain of crates. The air was heavy with the smell of fish and salt, and little daylight worked itself into the narrow corridors along which Jodi led Edern. After much backtracking and wandering about they finally reached the far side of the mountain and got a look at the sea.

"Well, I don't suppose we'll be leaving by this way," Jodi said.

The crates were stacked right up to the end of the wharf without space for even their mouse-sized bodies to squeeze by. Below, high tide was lapping at the pilings. Out in the harbour, the fishing luggers floated in a careless array, their crews on shore, cleaning fish and mending nets until the next early morning run. Out beyond the shelter of the harbour they could see a freighter approaching.

"What odds these crates are meant for it?" Edern asked.

Jodi shrugged. "It'll take time for it to dock. Then there's paperwork to be done with the harbourmaster and another tide to wait out. We'll be fine."

"I'd rather be out on the open road."

"You're a bit of a tatchy wam, aren't you just?"

"Speak for yourself."

"Well, I'm not gadding about all grouchy and finicky, am I?"

"I'm just not used to this," Edern said. "Give me the hills to walk any day."

"Where some stoat or weasel would have you for its dinner. Wouldn't that be lovely?"

"You know what I mean."

"I suppose. I'm not exactly having the best time of my life either."

She slouched down, letting her feet dangle over the edge of the wharf, not caring if some fisherman spied her or not.

"Where to now?" Edern asked as he settled down beside her.

Jodi shrugged. "We'll wait here until it gets dark, then we'll go off to Denzil's. He'll know how to help us if anyone does."

"Help us?"

"Get back to our proper size, you ninny. Do you think I want to spend the rest of my life as a mouse?"

"I meant to tell you about that," Edern said.

"Tell me what?"

Edern looked uncomfortable.

"Tell me what?" Jodi repeated.

He turned to look at her. "Did you never think about where the rest of you went?"

Jodi blinked, then gave him a blank look.

"One moment you're full-size, and the next you're the height of a prawn. Surely you've thought about the discrepancy?"

"La," Jodi said. "I never did notice."

Edern shook his head. "When the Widow shrunk you down, part of you stayed you—at your present size—but the rest of you was sort of scattered about, into the air as it were. To get those bits back, you need the third part of you, which the Widow kept for herself."

"I don't know *what* you're talking about," Jodi said, feeling uneasy now.

"It's a kind of code of what makes you properly you. A charm, if you will, that will call back the scattered bits when you're ready to go back to your proper size."

"I'm ready now."

Edern shook his head. "Without the charm, you'll never be restored to your rightful size."

"A charm," Jodi said slowly.

Edern nodded.

"That the Widow has?"

Another nod.

"Bother and damn. Why didn't you say something earlier?"

"You didn't give me time."

"I gave you all the time in the world. More than likely you just wanted to get away yourself, and didn't want my head cluttered up with other concerns."

Edern gave her a wounded look.

"Or maybe not," Jodi said. "So what's this charm look like?"

"It's in the shape of a button and it's sewn to the inside of her cloak."

"And yours? What's your charm?"

"I don't know," he said. "I saw her work the spell on you—that's how I know as much as I do. When she worked it on me, I was in the same state as you were. Unconscious."

"So we have to go back?"

"Only if you want to be your proper size."

Jodi shook her head. "I can't believe it. Here it is, my Big Adventure, and how does it turn out? A quest to look for a bloody button

on some old woman's cloak. If this were in a book, I'd be embarrassed to turn the page."

"It's not my fault."

"I suppose not. But where's the Romance? Where's the Wonder?"

"Well, you are a Small."

"Oh, yes. What a wonder. To be a mouse. Maybe I'll find some
rat prince to rescue the day. Wouldn't that be romantic?"

"There's always me."

"Oh raw we," she said.

"But, of course, I'm too old for you."

"Much too old," Jodi agreed.

And then she sighed—a long, heartfelt exhalation of air that did
nothing to settle her gloomy mood.

"I suppose it's my own fault, really," she said. "I was always
lumping about, waiting to stumble in upon that Big Adventure of
mine. And now that I have—well, it's typical, isn't it?"

Edern looked bewildered.

"That when I *do*," Jodi explained tiredly, "it would be so—oh, I
don't know. So laughable. So pedestrian."

"Maybe all adventures are that way and they only seem exciting
when they're written up," Edern said. "Though," he added, "when
I think of our escape, I could do without any more excitement, thank
you kindly."

"You know what I'm saying. I'd just like it to be a bit more mean-
ingful than scrabbling about Bodbury, being no bigger than a mouse
and on a quest to find a button. It seems so unremarkable."

"A person being reduced to our size is unremarkable?"

"Don't be a poop."

"Now who's being tatchy?"

"And don't be a bore."

Edern glanced at her and she gave him a grin.

"I'm just being sulky," she said. "And I know I am, so don't
lecture. I'll be over it all too soon and then you'll be wishing I was
back to sulking again."

"You're not very good at scowling," Edern told her.

"Can't help it. I don't get enough practice." Her grin widened.
"Tell me what it's like to be a traveling man," she added. "To pass
the time."

"What's to tell? It's walking the roads, up hill and down. . . ."

Jodi pushed her worries to the back of her mind and settled contentedly against the crate, feet still dangling above the steadily rising tide, and closed her eyes. As Edern spoke, she brought up images in her mind to accompany his words—images of roads that wound through wild moorland and down craggy footpaths to the sea, of roads with hedgerows patchworking pastures and fields on either side that wound in and out of stone-cottaged villages in places she'd never been, of roads that were sun-drenched by day and mysterious by night. . . .

It wasn't until the sky darkened beyond their refuge, the long shadows of Bodbury's buildings cast out across the harbour, that she woke up to discover that she'd fallen asleep with her head on Edern's shoulder. He was asleep too, so she stayed where she was, looking out across the water until twilight grew into night. Then she gave Edern a poke with her elbow and sat up.

"Time to go," she said.

"Give me five more minutes."

"I never realized that a traveling man could be so slothful."

"Why do you think we wander about like geese, instead of settling down in one place?"

Jodi merely grinned. She stood up and stretched the kinks out of muscles, then faced him, arms akimbo.

"Ready?"

Edern groaned and made a great pretense of being an old man as he slowly rose to his feet.

"I suppose you have some new amazing plan?" he asked.

Jodi nodded. "We're still off to see Denzil. He might not be able to make us bigger, but I'm sure he'll be able to think of a way for us to get those buttons away from the Widow."

Edern shivered. "Maybe it's not so bad, being a Small."

"Maybe," Jodi agreed cheerfully, "but I don't intend to settle into the life of a mouse until I have to."

The last of her words were thrown over her shoulder as she set off to retrace their path back through the winding maze made by the mountain of crates. Edern followed at a slower pace, wondering how she could move so surefootedly through the dark. It seemed to take forever and he was barely paying attention when she came to a sudden stop ahead of him. He only just stopped himself from bumping into her.

"If you're going to stop like that, the least you could do is warn me so—"

"Whisht!" Jodi said.

"What is it?" he whispered, moving up beside her.

He had time to see the enormous bewhiskered face of a cat staring in at them from beyond the crates, then both he and Jodi were scrabbling back as a clawed paw came shooting in to try to catch them. The cat hissed in frustration, stretching its paw in farther. Jodi and Edern backed up well out of reach.

"Bother and damn," Jodi said. "Now what do we do?"

"Did you never hear of good fortune where you came from?" Edern asked.

Jodi gave him a withering look. "Don't you start," she said.

"You mean you can't charm it?"

The cat made an angry growling sound as it continued to reach for them.

"What do you think?" Jodi asked.

Edern sighed. "I think we'll still be here when the men come to move these crates onto the freighter in the morning."

3.

Denzil Gossip was at his worktable, fussing with a small model steam locomotive, as night fell. He was hunched on a stool, back bowed like a victory arch, as he concentrated. His glasses kept slipping down his nose and he'd have to pause in his minute adjustments of the train's clockwork mechanism to push them back up again. Moments later they'd fall back down once more.

It wasn't until it was almost fully dark and he couldn't see a thing that he sat up and looked around his shadowed loft. Seeing that there was finally a chance to gain his notice, the animals immediately began to vie for his attention.

Rum gave a sharp cry and scratched at the door, working new grooves into the wood to join all those he'd already made in days past. Ollie swung down from the top of a bookcase and landed on his shoulder, startling him so much that he dropped the tiny screwdriver he'd been using.

"Now look what you've done," he said.

"Dumb, dumb," Noz cried from his perch and opened his wings to fan the air.

As though he'd planned it from the start of his leap, Ollie continued down from Denzil's shoulder to land on the floor where he stood innocently picking at his nose.

The mice and rats ran back and forth in their cages, excited by the sudden movements. The lop-eared rabbit pressed its face against the mesh of its cage front. The lizards skittered about, before freezing into new positions. The turtle stuck its head out of its shell and stared. The crow gave a loud caw from where it was perched on the top of the window sash. Only the catfish gave no notice, but then they never did to anything except for when bread bits or something equally edible was sprinkled on the surface of their water.

Was it early morning or evening? Denzil wondered.

He got off his stool to search for his screwdriver, but Ollie already had it and was trying to poke it into his ear.

"Give me that," he said.

"Brat, brat," Noz said.

Across the room, Rum added yet another series of scratches to the door.

Denzil stuck the screwdriver into his pocket, took off his glasses and gave them a perfunctory wipe on his sleeve, then crossed the room to the window where he put them back on.

Early evening, he decided. That meant a day had gone by—only where had it gone? Had he been asked, he would have assured his questioner that he'd only sat down to tinker with the clockwork train a half hour ago. Perhaps an hour, tops. Just after breakfast. . . .

He went to the door and let Rum out, then realized he had to follow the tomcat down the stairs to open the street door. He caught Ollie by the shoulder as the little monkey made to follow Rum out onto the street.

"Don't be bold, you," he said as he swung Ollie up to sit in the crook of his arm.

He took a look up the street, then down it, before closing the door and heading back up the stairs. Ollie squirmed in his arms, but he held on to the monkey until they were inside the loft and he'd closed the loft door behind them.

The vast room seemed very empty for all the animals. Denzil lit a lamp, then another. Very empty. And no wonder.

Jodi hadn't been by yet today.

Now that was odd, he thought. Where could she be?

As he went about cleaning cages and feeding the animals, he tried to remember if she'd said anything about not coming 'round, because it was quite unlike her not to stop in at least once during a day. More often a half dozen times.

All he could remember was talk of missing pages and loose ends and porpoises—no, that had been purposes. Purposes in life. She'd mentioned Taupin again—just to irritate him, he was sure—and then gone out, only to return with some gossip about a Small being spotted at the Widow Pender's. In short, a typical day's worth of her cheeky conversation.

But not a word that she wouldn't be by today.

Was she ill?

Unlikely. She seemed to be blessed with a constitution that didn't know the meaning of the word.

Run off, then?

To where? And from what? For all her talk of boredom and lacking a purpose in life, she loved her Nettie and she'd never go without first saying good-bye to him.

Kidnapped by thuggees, perhaps? A ludicrous thought, Denzil told himself as he stood by the window, looking out at Bodbury's benighted streets. Still, where *was* she?

Frowning, he thrust his hand into his pocket and immediately impaled it on the sharp end of the screwdriver. He pulled his hand out and sucked at the cut, then made up his mind.

If she wasn't coming here, why then, he'd go looking for her.

He put on his jacket, then a stovepipe hat that canted to one side. From a bamboo holder by the door stuffed with canes and umbrellas, he selected a walking stick topped with a silver badger's head.

Because he was worried.

"Be good, you," he told the animals as he closed the door behind himself.

Awfully worried, really.

When he reached the street, he stood there uncertainly.

The trouble was, he didn't know where to begin to look.

The Unfortunate Cup of Tea

Courtship consists of a number of quiet attentions . . . not so
pointed as to alarm, yet not so vague as to be misunderstood.

—LAURENCE STERNE

Janey slept late that morning. By the time she got up and made
her way next door for breakfast, the Gaffer was already back from
his morning's deliveries and sitting down for a cup of tea before
lunch, his copy of *The Cornishman* on the table beside his cup. He
took in her sleepy look and gave her a grin.

"And how are we this fine and sparkling morning, my robin?" he
said.

"Mmm," Janey replied.

She sat down at the table with him. Pouring a half inch of milk
in the bottom of the cup the Gaffer had set out for her when he had
his own breakfast, she pulled the teapot over and filled the cup up
to its lip. The Gaffer went back to his paper until she'd finished that
cup and had poured herself a second.

"Where's Felix?" she asked, eyeing the box of cereal on the sideboard without much enthusiasm.

"Went out early for a walk."

That woke her up. The clock beside the door leading to the kitchen
told her it was nearing half past eleven.

"Did he say where?"

The Gaffer shook his head. "He borrowed a pair of my old gum
boots, so I'd suppose he went up along the coast path."

"Did he say when he'd be back?"

The Gaffer shook his head again. "Give the lad a chance to get
his own thinking done, my love." When she made no reply, he added,
"Made a decision, then, have you?"

"No. Yes. Maybe." Janey sighed. "Oh, I don't know. It was so
good seeing Felix again; I never realized how much I missed him till
he was standing there in front of me. But what's going to change?
He still won't want to go gigging, so where will that leave us?"

"Have you asked him?"

"I haven't had much of a chance yet, have I?"

The Gaffer folded up his paper and laid it on the table. "What is it *you* want, my fortune?"

"If I could have anything at all?"

The Gaffer nodded.

"For us to live here with you—both Felix and I—for most of the year. To make records together. To tour a couple of times a year. Have some babies—but not too soon."

"And Felix? What does he want?"

"I . . ." Janey sighed. "I don't know."

"Well, my love, it seems you know your own mind—at least as well as you ever do. So now it's time you sat down with Felix and found out what he wants. But mind you—"

"Don't quarrel with him. I know."

"I was going to say, mind you really listen to him," the Gaffer said. "Half the quarrels in this world come about because one side or the other simply isn't listening to the other."

Though he didn't come right out and say it, Janey knew he was referring to her. She had the bad habit of being so busy getting her own points across that she didn't pay much attention to what anyone else was saying. That, combined with her unfortunate temper, had made more than one important discussion all too volatile.

Rolling up his paper, the Gaffer stuck it in the inside pocket of his jacket.

"Well, I'm off, my love," he said as he stood up. "I promised Chalkie I'd come 'round and give him a hand mending that old wall in back of his cottage. You'll be all right?"

"Just brill. Don't worry about me."

"And you'll remember what I said when you talk to Felix? Lads like an emperent sort of a woman, my flower, but there's a grand difference between cheekiness and simply being wayward."

Janey had to laugh. "Did you ever think of writing an advice column for the paper?"

Out came the rolled-up newspaper to be tapped on her head.

"I'll tell the world that my old granddad beats me," she warned him.

"Old, is it?"

Up came the paper again, but Janey was out of her chair and had danced away before he could reach her with it.

"And cantankerous," she said from across the room. "Or should I say—what did you call it?—wayward?"

"If I didn't have business elsewhere . . ."

He tried hard to sound serious, but the threat was an empty one. Smiling, he put away his paper.

"Come give this old man a kiss before he goes," he said.

When she came, it was cautiously, but he neither tickled nor pinched her as she'd feared.

"When you do talk to Felix," he said, "don't push too hard. And that's the last unasked-for bit of advice I'll give you, my heart. Leave sparking couples to their own, my dad used to say."

Janey watched him go from the front window, then settled back down at the table to have some toast. She took her time, hoping that Felix would be back soon, but finally returned to her own rooms when it got to be twelve-thirty and he still wasn't back. She tried playing some tunes, but wasn't in the mood for music. Picking up the Dunthorn book, she sat down with it by the window overlooking the backyard, but found she wasn't in the mood to read either.

Instead, she idly flipped the pages of the book and stared out at the yard, watching a stonechat hop from branch to branch in the blackberry bushes that hedged the small square of lawn. After a time, she felt the beginnings of a tune stirring inside her.

Usually when she composed, tunes grew out of a practice session. They were rarely planned. A misplayed phrase from one tune might spark the idea for a new one. Or the lift and lilt of a particular set might wake the first few bars of an original piece. Rarely did the tunes arrive whole cloth as it were. And never did she hear them the way she could hear this one.

It didn't seem to come so much from inside her, as from without, as though she heard someone playing from just over on the other side of a hill, the music drifting across to her, faint, vaguely familiar, but ultimately unknown. And while normally she only needed to hear a tune through once or twice to pick it up, this one remained oddly elusive.

She hummed along with it, her fingers no longer flipping the pages of the book. Setting the book aside, she took her mandolin down from the wall and tried to capture the order of notes. She got one phrase, then another. The third wasn't right. It went more like—

The Gaffer's bell rang next door, breaking her concentration.

Ignore it, she told herself, but when she turned back to her instrument, the music was gone.

"Oh, damn," she muttered as she put the mandolin down.

But then it might be Felix, she thought as she went to see who it was. So don't be cross with him. There was no way he could have known that he'd be interrupting you.

Still, it was a shame. Because the tune had been a good one. Although it *was* odd that she couldn't remember any more than those first two bars of it now.

Keeping a smile firmly in place, she opened the door between her little courtyard and the Gaffer's only to find a stranger standing by the Gaffer's front door.

There was nothing threatening about him. He was slender—no, quite thin rather, she corrected herself—with longish dark hair and that certain kind of pale, but bright eyes that always reminded her of Paul Newman. He wore corduroys and a dark blue windbreaker, had a camera in its case slung over one shoulder, a couple of cases on the ground beside him.

He could have been anybody, he was undoubtedly innocent of any bad intention, but the first thing Janey thought as she looked at him was, he's after Dunthorn's lost book.

It was too late to undo the smile that had been meant for Felix, and there was—for all her premonition—something too infectious about his own smile for her to stop.

"Janey Little?" he asked.

She nodded warily, for all that she was still smiling like a loon.

"I hope I haven't come at a bad time," he went on. "My name's Mike Betcher; I'm with *Rolling Stone*."

"What? The magazine?"

Betcher nodded. "I was hoping I could interview you."

For a long moment Janey didn't know what to say. She looked at him, glanced down at his cases to see that one of them was for a portable computer, then met his gaze again.

"You can't be serious."

Betcher laughed. "We don't just do Madonna and the like."

"I know but . . ."

"If I've come at a bad time, I can come back."

"No, it's just . . ."

Just what? Ludicrous that *Rolling Stone* would want to do a piece on *her*? That was putting it mildly.

"I'm doing a piece on alternative music, you see," Betcher explained. "I'm over here on holiday and thought I'd like to get a few interviews with some British artists who I admire to round out the article. At the moment it's got too much of a Stateside slant."

"Yes, but . . ."

"You can't pretend that you don't know you have a following in the States," he said.

"Well, no. It's just that it's so low-key. . . ."

"And that's exactly what I'm hoping to change with this piece," Betcher said. "There are a lot of artists like you—on small independent labels, doing their own music—who remain relatively unknown to the general record-buying public. And that's not right. Take yourself. You're a headline act in Europe—"

"In small halls."

"Doesn't matter. And didn't your last tour of California sell out?"

"Yes, but I was only playing in small clubs."

Betcher shook his head. "Maybe I'll run that as the headline: 'The Modest Little.' "

Janey couldn't help but laugh. "That sounds redundant."

He shrugged. "So help me come up with a better one. Look, it can't hurt to give it a go, can it? What have you got to lose? At least give me a chance. I've come a long way."

"You said you were on holiday anyway."

"Okay. But it's still a long way from London. I've been almost six hours on the train."

She should just invite him in, she thought, because, as he'd said, she had nothing to lose and everything to gain. To get some coverage in a national paper like *Rolling Stone* . . . it was as good as being on the cover of the *NME* over here. But something still bothered her about his landing on her door just now.

First that American woman looking for the Dunthorn book.

Then Felix showing up.

Now a reporter from *Rolling Stone*. . . .

It all seemed a bit much. So, no. She wouldn't have him in. But she'd be a complete ass to just send him on his way.

"Just let me get a jacket," she said, "and we can go for a cup of tea. Would that be all right?"

"Absolutely."

She left him there and hurried back upstairs.

A reporter from *Rolling Stone*. Right here in Mousehole. To interview *her*. What a laugh. She could hardly wait to tell someone about it.

A quick glance in the mirror stopped her. God, she looked awful. She put on some eye shadow and lipstick, worried over what might be a pimple but proved on closer inspection to be just a bit of dried skin, then brushed her hair. It took her a few moments to dig up her jacket from underneath the clothes she'd dumped on it last night. As she put it on, her gaze fell on the Dunthorn book that lay on the couch by the window.

It wouldn't do to leave that lying about. She had to hide it, only where?

Looking around her rooms, she realized that there really wasn't any foolproof safe place it could be hidden. So taking her cue from Poe, she merely stuck it on her bookshelf beside his other books. Hidden in plain sight, she thought, pleased with her own cleverness.

Catching up her purse, she went back outside, locking the door behind her and pocketing the key.

Now that felt odd, she thought. She couldn't remember the last time she'd locked her door.

Pushing the feeling aside, she rejoined Betcher by the Gaffer's front door.

"Where to?" he asked.

"Pamela's Pantry. They've got the best cream teas in town."

And 'round about this time of year, she thought, just about the only ones as well, but she wasn't about to admit that to him. Let him think that quaint though it was, Mousehole had as much to offer as any place up country—which was what the Cornish called the rest of England.

"Cream tea?" Betcher asked as he hefted his cases. "What's that?"

"You'll see."

2.

The Cornish Coastal Path is 268 miles long and runs from Marshland Mouth on the Devon border, around the coast past Land's End, and all the way on to the shores of Plymouth Sound. It is the central part of the 520-mile South West Way, the longest continuous footpath in England.

Much of the Cornish section is based on the tracks marking out the regular beats walked by Coastguards. In 1947, when a new National Parks Commission first suggested that a continuous pathway 'round the British coast was a possibility, it was seen that Cornwall presented the ideal conditions for it, but it wasn't until May of 1973 that the Cornish Coastal Path was officially opened.

Like the whole of the South West Way, the Cornish Coastal Path is usually walked from north to south, a psychological "downhill" journey that leads the walker southwest from the six-hundred-foot cliffs at Marshland Mouth to the granite shoulders of Land's End, then back east to follow the gentler south coast. When Felix walked it that morning, however, he went the opposite way.

He walked up Raginnis Hill in the west part of Mousehole and past the Wild Bird Hospital and the Carn Du Hotel to where the road turned right. A smaller road continued past a cluster of stone cottages into a narrow lane bordered by blackberry hedges. A handful of cows grazed placidly in the pastures behind the hedges on the left, while beyond them was the sea. When the lane ended, a footpath led on through the fields, heading west to Lamorna.

Felix walked all the way around Kemyel Point and Carn Du to Lamorna's sheltered cove. The path was rugged, climbing up and down the steep cliffs with sometimes no more than two-foot-wide stands of gorse between himself and the drop below. The wind came in from the sea, bringing a salt tang with it. The long grass was bent over, dried and brown from the salt. Gulls wheeled overhead, and except for them, he had the path to himself. As he neared Mousehole on his return, he stopped at a kind of stone armchair that jutted from a granite outcrop just before the Coastguard lookout behind Penzer Point. There he sat and gazed out over Mount's Bay.

Somewhere below him and to the left was the Mousehole Cave that he and Janey had explored on another walk a few years ago. There was a haze in the air so that St. Michael's Mount was only a smudge and the long line of the Lizard coast was completely hidden from view. On a sunny day, and he'd been here on such days, you could see the houses of Marazion and the large dish aerials of the Goonhilly satellite tracking station when the sun caught them just so.

Plucking a long stem of stiff grass, he twisted it between his fingers and thought of Janey, of the letter that had brought him here, and wondered just what he should do. When he thought of how their relationship had ended . . . He didn't want to go through those last few months again.

But what if it *could* be different? He'd never know if he didn't try, and wasn't Janey important enough to him for him to make the effort?

No question there. He just didn't think he could handle it all falling to pieces around him again.

He sighed, dropped the twist of grass, and plucked another stem. Talk it out with her, he told himself.

He looked down the path towards Mousehole, his heart lifting when he saw a figure making its way through the fields towards him. It's Janey, he thought. But then the figure's cane registered and he knew it wasn't her. It was Clare Mabley.

He waited patiently through her slow progress until she'd reached him, then stood up and gave her a hug.

"It's been a long time," he said as he stepped back.

Clare lowered herself onto the seat he'd so recently vacated and gave him a smile.

"Hasn't it, though?" she said. "But I got your letters, so I didn't feel as though you'd simply dropped off the edge of the world. You never did visit though—and you promised."

Felix shrugged. "I wasn't ready yet. How'd you know I was in town?"

That ready smile of Clare's reappeared. "Have you been away that long? Mr. Bodener told Greg Lees—he delivers the milk now that his dad retired—and Greg told my mum. Edna next door also heard it from Mr. Hayle who got it from the Gaffer."

"Some things don't change."

"Well, it's a bit of excitement, isn't it?"

Felix nodded. "I suppose."

He sat down on a nearby rock and plucked another grass stem, which he began to shred.

"I thought I'd find you here," Clare said after a few moments of silence.

Felix looked up.

"Well, it's where you used to come the last time you and Janey were having your rows."

"We haven't had a row."

Not really, he thought. Not yet. But that was because they'd barely had a chance to talk.

"Didn't you? That's good. But I saw you walking past the house earlier this morning—by yourself. It didn't seem a good sign."

Clare had been Felix's confidante when he and Janey were breaking up. She was Janey's best friend, but she'd become Felix's as well. Like the Gaffer, she'd hated to see the two of them making a muddle of their lives, but unlike the Gaffer, she hadn't been shy about giving Felix advice when they'd talked. Unfortunately, while he listened attentively and never seemed to mind her concern—he called her "Mother Clare" when she went on too long—he hadn't taken her advice either.

"We haven't got together enough to break up again," Felix said.

When Clare lifted an eyebrow, he looked away across the bay once more. For long moments he said nothing, then finally he began to tell her how his return to Penwith had come about.

"For God's sake, Felix," she said when he was done. "You have to tell her how you feel."

"I know."

"And if she gets angry, be angry back. I don't mean you should start bullying her, but you know Janey. She only really listens to those who talk louder than she does. She doesn't mean to be so bloody obstinate; it's just her nature."

Felix knew that, too. And he'd always been the sort who was willing to accept a friend's faults. But that didn't change the basic differences that underlay all of his disagreements with Janey.

"But why won't you tour?" Clare asked when he brought that up. "You've never told me and you've probably never told Janey either. You love music, so what's so bad about making your living playing it? It must be better than hauling about cargo on a freighter or whatever it is that you do on those ships of yours."

Felix wouldn't meet her gaze.

"Oh, come on, Felix. If you can't tell me, then how will you ever be able to tell her? Is it like the way Dinny feels? That if he plays for money he's going to lose the crack?"

Again, silence. Still he wouldn't meet her gaze.

"Felix?"

He turned finally.

"It scares me," he said. "It scares me so much that I get sick just thinking about it."

He could see the surprise in her eyes and knew exactly what she was thinking: A great big strapping man like himself—scared of something so trivial?

"But . . . you don't have any trouble playing at sessions," Clare said.

"It's not the same."

"Still, people are watching you just as though you were on stage, aren't they?"

Felix shook his head. "It really isn't the same. Believe me, I've tried to get over it. I don't know how many times I've gone to a club on a floor singer's night and given it a go, only to freeze up. Then I can't even get the first note out of my box."

"Well, it's not the end of the world," Clare said.

"Maybe not. But how can I tell Janey about that?"

"She'll understand."

"Do you think so? She thrives on being in the spotlight—that's when her music really comes alive. How could she understand?"

"You believe she'll think the less of you because of it?"

"I know she will," Felix said. "Remember when Ted Praed used to get up to play at The Swan in Truro?"

Clare nodded. "He never got through one song without his voice going all quavery and then he'd leave the stage. . . ." She paused, then went on. "And when we drove home Janey'd have us in stitches mimicking how his voice went."

"Carrying it over with little scenarios of what it must be like to go into a bank or a shop and have his voice break up and then he'd go running out. . . ."

"But we all laughed—you did, too. And we all made jokes about it."

"I couldn't stand her laughing at me like that, Clare."

She nodded. "It wasn't very nice of us, was it?"

"I used to feel like a heel, thinking about it."

"But Ted never knew."

"That still didn't make it right."

"I suppose not."

Felix sighed. "I'd rather have her angry at me than have her laugh at me."

Neither said anything more for a time. They watched gulls circling the ferry that was heading out towards the Scilly Islands. Felix shredded a few more grass stems while Clare poked the end of her cane into the dirt by her feet.

"You'll still have to tell her," she said finally.

"I told you, I couldn't stand to have her—"

"Give her more credit than that, Felix. Maybe she will understand. If she cares about you at all, I *know* she will."

"But when I think of Ted . . ."

"Oh, Ted. He was such a silly ass anyway. So full of himself. The real reason we made fun of him was because he was always going on about what a smashing singer he was and then as soon as he got up on stage, he'd fall apart. It's not the same thing, Felix. If we hadn't laughed at him about that, it would've been something else. It's true," she added before Felix could interrupt, "that it wasn't a nice thing to do, but you have to admit, he did bring it on himself."

"But Janey—"

"Was no worse than the rest of us. If Ted hadn't been such a poppet, she would have been the first to help him get over his stage fright."

She tapped Felix's leg with the end of her cane until he looked at her.

"So you will tell her?"

"If it comes up."

Clare shook her head. "If it comes up! What is it about men that they all feel they have to live up to this silly macho image? I thought you were more liberated than that."

"It's not that," he protested. "It's just . . . well, do *you* like looking like a fool?"

"Of course not."

"Neither do I. It's got nothing about being macho or not."

"But looking like a fool still happens to all of us," she said. "Whether we like it or not. Anyway, we're not talking about me, we're talking about you and Janey. You have to tell her."

"Yes, Mother Clare."

"No, really."

"I will."

"Good. Now you can see me home, like a good gentleman would, and tomorrow you can come by to tell me how it all went."

Felix had to laugh. "Yes, Mother Clare. Will there be an exam?"

She whacked his leg with her cane, then offered him her hand so that he could help her up. She kept her hand in the nook of his arm and chattered about inconsequential things as they made their way back to her house, bringing Felix up-to-date on all the local gossip that might interest him.

Enjoying her company, Felix wondered, and not for the first time, what would have happened if he'd met Clare before he'd met Janey. She was attractive, smart, and they got along famously. She should have been perfect, but she just wasn't Janey. There could only be the one Janey—to which the Gaffer would add, "And thank God for that," if she was in one of her moods.

"Tomorrow, now—don't forget," Clare said as Felix left her at her door.

"I won't. Wish me luck."

"You don't need luck—just be yourself. Nobody could want more than that from you. And *don't* you 'Mother Clare' me again today, or I'll give you such a whack with this cane that you'll be too busy healing to even think about sparking."

Felix gave her a wave, then continued on down Raginnis Hill. Clare was probably right, he thought as he walked. Janey wouldn't laugh—not if she really did care. But how he was ever going to get up the courage to tell her, he really didn't—

He paused in mid-step and stared ahead to where he could see Janey walking in the company of a man Felix had never met. It was hard to tell the man's age, but it was obvious from his cases that he'd only just arrived in Mousehole. Oblivious to Felix, they laughed with each other and went into Pamela's Pantry.

The first thought that came to Felix's mind when he saw the man's cases was, had Janey sent out more than one letter?

He put his hand in his pocket to touch the folded paper that was still there.

But no. She'd denied ever sending it, hadn't she? And he believed her, didn't he?

He had no claim to her, but he couldn't help feeling a little hurt.

You're the one that went off for a walk, he told himself. She didn't. Why should she have to sit around waiting for you?

Because—because . . .

Oh, bloody hell, he thought and went on down the street.

When he reached the harbour, instead of turning up Duck Street to the Gaffer's house, he continued on up Parade Hill until it took him out of Mousehole and onto the coastal road that led to Newlyn.

3.

Janey found it easy to relax in the reporter's company—so much so that she had to keep reminding herself that he *was* a reporter and making her feel at ease was part of his job. Because she tended to just talk off the top of her head, she'd had to learn her lesson the hard way when her first interviews appeared and some of her more outrageous, and sometimes unkind, statements lay there on the page, all too accurately quoted. She'd been thoroughly embarrassed by some of the things she'd said in the past and wasn't about to let it happen again.

She'd also made sure that Mike Betcher really was the reporter he said he was.

As soon as they'd sat down at a table in Pamela's and placed their order with the waitress, she'd asked him if he had any ID, whereupon he produced a press card, sealed in plastic.

How hard would it be to get something like that? she wondered.

She had no idea. But his looked official enough and she realized that questioning him any further would just make her look like an ass. She knew that there was no conspiracy. The American woman looking for Dunthorn's book, Felix's arrival, and this reporter had no logical connection.

Deliberately, she put it all out of her mind and concentrated on the business at hand. She was determined to be on her best behavior. Did *Rolling Stone* have a million readers? More? If just five percent of them were interested enough to buy her records and come to her gigs, she'd be doing very well indeed.

"This is great," Betcher said after the waitress brought their order.

Janey had always loved the Pantry's cream teas—two scones with jam and thick Cornish clotted cream, served with a pot of steaming tea on the side—but she didn't allow herself the luxury of having them often. If they did, she'd kidded Clare one day, they'd turn into the Amazing Balloon Women.

"I thought you'd like it," she said.

He didn't bring up Dunthorn or his books, lost or otherwise. Instead, he talked about the music, with enough authority that Janey knew that his enthusiasm had to be genuine. She didn't always agree with him, but she made a point of disagreeing diplomatically—not an easy undertaking for her, but good practice, she thought.

"Why do you think there's so many young pipe players on the scene?" he asked at one point.

"Young players? You're forgetting Alistair Anderson, Joe Hutton, Jim Hall—"

"From the Ranters, yes," he said. "I'm not forgetting him, or any of those others, but they don't seem to have the same popularity as the younger players such as yourself, Kathryn Tickell, Martyn Bennet—"

"He plays the Scottish small pipes."

"For the purposes of this piece," he said, "there isn't really enough distinction between the two to make a difference."

"There is when you consider the kind Hamish Moore plays."

"What do you mean?"

Like any piping enthusiast, Janey immediately warmed to her subject.

"Well, there's three kinds of Cauld Wind Pipes," she said. "The Scottish small pipes that we're talking about are related to the Northumbrian, but they use a Scottish style of fingering and tend to be pitched in lower keys. Then there's also the lowland or border pipes, which are more related to the highland pipes, although they're a lot quieter because of the conical bore of their chanter. Nobody much cares for them these days."

"Yes, but—"

"And lastly," Janey broke in, "there's the pastoral pipes, which have a long extended foot joint at the end of the chanter. They also have a regulator and looped bass drone one octave below normal, which gives them a sound that's very much like that of the Irish Uillean pipes." She paused to give him a look. "You're not taking any notes," she added.

Betcher laughed. "That's because you're getting far too esoteric for my readers. Why don't we just stick to the instrument you play?"

"I suppose." She thought for a moment. "You didn't mention Becky Taylor. I did a workshop with her at the Sidmouth Festival in Devon this past summer."

He dutifully wrote that down, then returned to his earlier question. As the interview went on, Janey was surprised at how much he knew of her career, and couldn't help but feel pleased. He avoided all the usual questions, concentrating on the kinds of things that she felt were important but that no one in the press ever seemed to cover in an interview.

"Now what about some of these tunes you wrote yourself?" he asked. " 'The Gaffer's Mouzel' is self-explanatory, now that you've told me about your grandfather. But what about some of these others?"

"Which ones?"

" 'The Stoness Barn'?"

"It's named after an old barn on a farm in Canada where I stayed for a weekend."

" 'The Nine Blind Harpers'?"

Janey laughed. "I've no idea where that title came from. Probably from Felix."

"That's the Felix in 'Felix Gavin's Reel'?"

Janey nodded.

"And the Billy in 'Billy's Own Jig'—that would be Billy Pigg?"

"No," she said. "That one was for Billy Dunthorn."

He wrote that down in his notepad. "Did he play the pipes as well?"

"Not likely. He was a local writer. William Dunthorn. He's the one who wrote *The Hidden People*."

Betcher frowned, as though trying to catch a thought, then his face lit up.

"Really?" he said. "The one about the Smalls? I read that as a kid and loved it. It's funny he never wrote anything else—or was it just that he was like Grahame or Carroll and we only remember him for the one piece?"

"You never read *The Lost Music*?"

Betcher shook his head.

"But that's his best book—*better* than *The Hidden People* by far. It's all about what I do—traditional music and its magical qualities."

Betcher's eyebrows lifted in exaggerated surprise. "Magic?"

"Oh, you know what I mean. Not witches and things like that— though he's got that in it—but the way the music makes you feel. The magical way it connects you to history. To everything that's gone before. He's one of the main reasons I got into music in the first place."

"Well, I'll have to track down a copy of the book then. Is it still available?"

"They've got it down at the newsagent's on North Cliff—after all, he was born here."

"I'll make sure to pick one up after we're done, then." He referred back to his notes. "So it was Dunthorn who got you interested in music—was that your fiddle playing?"

Janey nodded.

"What brought you to take up the Northumbrian pipes? They're not exactly a traditional Cornish instrument."

"I'll say. It's mostly all choir singing here, like in Wales. Something to do with all the mining, I suppose." Janey grinned suddenly. "Here's an old joke of the Gaffer's: What's the definition of a Cornishman?"

"I don't know."

"A man at the bottom of a mine, singing."

Betcher smiled, then brought the conversation back to its original topic. "What started you on the pipes?"

"Well, that was Dinny's doing—I told you about Dinny?"

Betcher nodded. "He plays on the albums."

"He got me interested in the pipes, but the only spare set he had at first were these Northumbrian small pipes, so . . ."

The next two hours went by very quickly and all too soon Betcher was putting away his pen and notepad.

"I want to put this in some kind of order," he said, "but would it be all right to come by—say, tomorrow—if I've missed anything?"

"Call first," Janey said, and she gave him the Gaffer's phone number.

"And now . . . two last requests. I'd love to hear you play in person. Do you have any gigs lined up in the next few days?"

Janey shook her head.

"That's too bad."

"I'm on holiday. What's the other thing?"

"I need some pictures. A few of you around your house—wherever it is that you practice, say—and one or two of you somewhere around the village."

Remembering the face that had looked back at her from the mirror this morning, she shook her head again.

"Not today," she said.

She needed to wash her hair, find some decent clothes to wear. . . .

"Tomorrow?"

She sighed. It also meant cleaning up the jumble of her room.

"If you have to. . . ."

Betcher laughed. " 'The Modest Little'—I think I'll stick with that as a title."

"Don't you dare!"

He held his hands up placatingly. "Your wish is my command. Tomorrow it is for the pictures—and maybe a few tunes?"

He looked so earnest that Janey finally had to give in.

"Oh, why not," she said. "But mind you don't ring up too early.

I really am on holiday so I'm in my usual slothful state—and don't quote me on that."

"Wouldn't dream of it."

"Where are you staying?" Janey asked. "Maybe I can get a bit of a session together for tonight. If I do I'll ring you up."

"I'm open to suggestions."

"Would a bed and breakfast be all right?"

"Perfect."

Janey put on her jacket and gathered up her purse. "Come on, then, and I'll walk you over to one that's nearby. But after that you're on your own. I've got a friend visiting and here I've gone and spent the whole day ignoring him."

The fact that she'd only just thought of Felix made her feel guilty, but surely he'd realize what this article could do for her career?

Betcher rose with her. He paid their bill, then gathered together his own belongings.

"I hope there won't be a problem," he said. "With your friend, I mean."

"I don't think so. Felix is very understanding."

She hoped.

"This is the Felix Gavin you wrote the tune for? Is he a musician as well?"

She nodded. "And a very good one. But don't try to write him up in an article. He can't stand the business side of things. All he loves is the music."

"You seem very fond of him."

Was that a touch of regret she heard in Betcher's voice? It gave her pause when she realized that she might have been missing the signals. But, now that she stopped to think about it, the signals had been there all along. She just hadn't seen them. It was too bad. He seemed a very likable sort of a fellow, and if Felix weren't here, maybe she would have followed up on this interest of his that apparently went further than the interview.

But Felix *was* here.

"Very fond," she said.

Yes, he was a bit keen on her. She could see his disappointment, for all that he tried to hide it.

Best to just pretend she didn't see it, she decided. Her love life was complicated enough as it was.

"Come on," she said. "If we wait too long, all the rooms'll be gone."

"At this time of year? I thought the tourist season was over."

"It is. But that doesn't mean the B and Bs close down. There's all sorts of folks still traveling about. Hardy hikers. Salesmen. Reporters from American pop papers. . . ."

"I get the picture," he said as he allowed himself to be led away.

4.

It never ceased to amaze Michael Bett at how easy it was to manipulate an individual. All one needed to know were the right buttons to push.

Madden liked to think of it as magic, but while Bett agreed it had to do with the strength of one's will, and how able one was to use it to overpower the natural defenses of a subject—the "sheep" as Madden and the other members of the Order liked to call the uninitiated—Bett himself believed it to be simply a form of mesmerism.

He preferred that old term—based on the techniques and theories of Franz Mesmer, which, in turn, had interested Jean Charcot and his peers in the possibilities of "animal magnetism"—to the more contemporary perceptions of hypnotism. For Bett's use of his will *was* a form of animal magnetism, utilizing the same unspoken domination that an alpha wolf held over its pack, the same hypnotic control a snake practiced upon its prey. The difference lay in the fact that Bett's victims were never aware of the control he held over them.

Take Janey Little.

Yes, perhaps he would. But not now. Not yet. Not until she'd given him what he'd come for.

She was a perfect example. Headstrong and bright, she would never dream that she was being manipulated. She was the sort who dominated a group by the sheer exuberance and vitality of her personality, yet by approaching her as he had—offering her a chance at fame, concentrating on her music, feigning a wistful, unspoken attraction for her, in short, giving her what she wanted—she was as easy for Bett to manage as would be the most simpleminded of Madden's sheep.

Given time, he would have her doing anything he told her to do.

Anything.

His will—his "magic," as Madden would put it—was simply that strong.

She would not reveal Dunthorn's secret today. But reveal it to him she would. It was inevitable.

He let her take him to the newsagent's where he bought a paperback edition of *The Lost Music,* then she took him to a bed and breakfast on the east edge of the village. When they'd determined that there was a room for him, he followed her back to the front door where she gave him her easy smile.

"Well, I'm off then," she said.

"Thanks for everything," he told her. "You've been just great. If you—no, never mind."

"If I what?" she had to know.

"I was just going to say, if you do get a session together tonight, or even if you just find you have nothing to do, I'd . . . you know. Love to hear from you."

"I'll see about the session, but I've got—"

"Your friend staying with you. Right. I forgot. Well, maybe the two of you . . . ?"

She laughed. "We'll see. But don't hold your breath. Felix and I have a lot of catching up to do."

"I understand. Well, thanks again for everything."

He saw her off, then went inside to use the phone. When he was connected with Lena's room, a man answered.

"Hello?"

Bett hung up without replying and stared at the receiver.

He'd told her to stay in, but he hadn't told her not to have anyone in, now had he? The stupid cow. Did he have to spell everything out for her?

He needed her now, to get Felix Gavin out of the way. Not to be having a little tête-à-tête with some busboy in her room. He considered calling Willie Keel to have him go around and straighten things out, but then realized it was probably Keel who had set her up with someone in the first place.

He'd just have to do it himself.

5.

North of Mousehole, about halfway between the village and neighbouring Newlyn, is the old Penlee Quarry. Though not nearly so busy as it was in its heyday, the quarry's silos still stored the blue alvin stone that was once shipped out in great quantities to many ports, but now only went to Germany. As Felix approached the quarry by the road, he was a little taken aback—as he always was—by the faulted land that presented itself on his left. In picturesque Penwith, with its pleasant winding lanes and hedges and its magnificent sweeps of cliff and moor, the heaps of raw dirt and old scars of the quarry seemed much too out of place.

He stood in the shadow of the silos that loomed over him on the sea-side of the road, and looked at the quarry. There was no activity at the moment. Just an old Land Rover parked by a decrepit building, the ruins of other buildings beyond it, and the scarred land. Behind him, enormous disused storage pits were housed beside the silos, stone-walled and metal-roofed, their broad entrances fenced off from the road. Above him, the skies were smudged with grey, promising rain.

It was the perfect place for a murder, Felix thought.

He wasn't in a good mood.

He wasn't angry with anyone—except for himself. Though he loved this part of England, and had a number of friends in and about Mousehole that he'd met through Janey, he hadn't been back since they'd broken up a few years ago. At this moment he wished he hadn't returned.

As the sky so surely promised rain, so his return had seemed to promise something as well. But now he'd found that Janey had never sent the letter that had brought him here. It was all too plain that while she was happy to see him, she had her own life to lead now—one that didn't include him—and he wondered how he could ever have been so stupid as to think it would be otherwise.

It didn't matter who the man was that she'd accompanied to Pamela's Pantry. He could be a boyfriend, an agent, her bloody solicitor—it made no difference. Seeing her with someone else just brought home the undeniable fact that no matter what he wanted, no matter what Clare said, things hadn't changed. And wouldn't change. Why should they? Janey owed him nothing. She had a right to her own life. Just because a mistake had brought him here, didn't mean she had to drop everything and try to take things up again with him.

She fancied him—but as a friend. So grow up, he told himself. Accept her on the same terms and stop mooning about like some lovesick teenager.

You have to tell her, he could hear Clare saying.

But what was the point when he already knew the answer? Why make things uncomfortable? It was better to just spend a couple of days in the village. Better to hang about with her, play some tunes, see Clare again—but not alone, or she'd nag him—maybe go up to the farm and visit with Dinny and his family. . . . Make no waves. Just try to have a pleasant time, and then go.

Say nothing, and just go.

You have to tell her how you feel.

No he didn't. He had his own life to live as well. And if he chose to live it without Janey—well that'd be *his* choice, wouldn't it?

Without her.

With only that ghostly memory of her to talk to at night on the rolling deck of some freighter going from who-cares to what-does-it-matter. Killing time on the ocean.

God, he hated this side of himself.

In most matters he was the sort of person who knew what he wanted to do and then went and did it. He got things done. He didn't have problems with indecision or soul-searching.

Except when it came to Janey.

He picked up a stone by the roadside and flung it into the fenced-off storage pits beside the silos. Time to head back, he thought, irritated with himself for the way his stomach tightened at the idea. Maybe he should go down into Newlyn and find a pub where he could get something to eat before he returned. Except he didn't feel like eating.

Looking down the road, his attention was caught by the figure of an unsteady bicyclist making her way up the graded hill towards the quarry. She wobbled on the narrow shoulder of the road, visibly flinching when a car went rushing by.

A late-season tourist, Felix thought. Not used to these roads. He wondered if she'd been on any of the B-roads yet, because compared to those narrow little lanes, this road was like a four-lane highway.

He started to turn away, but then another car went by the cyclist. Her unsteadiness grew more pronounced in the wake of that car and he could see her wheel catch a stone and the bicycle start to fall almost before it happened. She landed badly, twisting her leg under her. Felix jogged towards her.

"Shit, shit, shit," she was saying when he reached her side.

"Don't try to move yet," Felix told her.

She looked up. Tears made her eye shadow run and her mouth twisted with pain, but neither hid the fact that she was a very attractive woman. Her hair was short and swept back. The leather of her bomber's jacket was scuffed and there was a tear in one knee of her jeans, but the latter appeared to be more a matter of style than caused by her fall. From the MIT T-shirt she was wearing, Felix knew she was an American even before her accent registered.

"Where does it hurt?" he asked.

"My—my ankle. . . ."

"Okay. Just take it easy now."

Gently he helped her disentangle herself from the bike. Once he'd set the bike aside, he helped her up.

"Can you put any weight on it?" he asked.

She gave it a try.

"I think—no!"

She jerked from the sudden pain, trembling as she leaned against him. Felix helped her sit down, then studied her ankle. It was swelling a bit, but was it sprained or broken? He couldn't tell. Lying on the ground nearby was a watch, the links of its bracelet broken.

"Is this yours?" he asked, picking it up.

She put a hand to her wrist, then nodded. As Felix handed it over he noticed what he first took to be a smudge of dirt on her wrist. Then he realized, just before she tugged down the sleeve of her jacket, that it was a tattoo of a small grey bird.

Curious, he thought. When she was wearing the watch, it would be completely hidden. So what was the point of it?

Sitting back, he found her regarding him.

"Hi," she said.

He smiled. "Hi, yourself."

She seemed to be recovering somewhat, now that her weight was off the ankle again and the initial shock of her fall had faded.

"Guess that was a pretty stupid thing to do," she said.

"Accidents happen. Where are you staying?"

"In Penzance. My name's Lena."

She held out her hand.

"Felix Gavin," Felix said as he took her hand to shake.

Lena laughed. "God, we must look silly."

Felix smiled. She gave his hand a quick squeeze, then let go—reluctantly, it seemed.

"Thanks for coming to the rescue," she said.

"You should get that looked after," Felix said, nodding to her ankle. "There was a Land Rover parked back at the quarry. Do you want me to see if they'll give you a lift to the hospital?"

"Oh, it just needs some ice, I think."

"Okay. I'll see about that lift."

She caught his arm as he was about to stand.

"I don't want a big fuss made over me," she said. "Maybe you could just wheel me on the bike? It's mostly downhill."

"You're sure?"

"I feel dumb enough as it is without having a bunch of strangers all gawking at me."

"And we're not strangers?"

"Not anymore—we introduced ourselves, remember?"

Felix couldn't help but return her smile.

"Okay," he said. "I'll give it a go. But if it hurts too much, just let me know."

He retrieved the bike and brought it near to where she was sitting, then leaning it against himself, he reached down and gave her a hand up so that she didn't put any weight on her ankle. It was a man's bike, so he lifted her up onto the crossbar, then wheeled the bike over to the road.

"You sure you'll be all right?" he asked as she grimaced.

She nodded.

When Felix got on the bike, she turned towards him, steadying herself with her arms around his waist, and leaned against him. Feeling awkward, but resigned, Felix started the bike freewheeling down towards Newlyn. The traffic was light and he didn't have to start pedaling until he was down by the harbour, crossing the boundary between Newlyn and Penzance.

6.

The Gaffer and Chalkie were having lunch in the Smuggler's Restaurant in Newlyn, after taking a break from the wall mending that they hadn't actually got around to starting yet. They had stood about in Chalkie's backyard in their wellies, studying the broken-down wall from a number of different angles, but then Chalkie had announced that he was hungry and insisted they eat out, his treat.

"Why dirty dishes, when someone else can do your cooking for you?" he asked the Gaffer.

The truth was, Chalkie always ate out. The highest his culinary skills aimed for was to make the odd bit of porridge or toast for himself in the mornings. And didn't he brew a mean cup of tea?

So they were sitting at a window table in the restaurant at the time that Felix rode by on the bicycle with Lena snuggled against his chest. The Gaffer had to look twice, to make sure he was really seeing what he was seeing. The pair went by so quickly that he could almost doubt who they were—almost, but not enough. He'd recognized them both and it gave him a knotty feeling in the center of his chest.

Poor Janey, he thought.

"Does my heart good to see that," Chalkie said. "A couple out on a single bike like that. Remember when we used to go sparking with our bikes, up Kerris way? What were the names of those sisters again?"

The Gaffer gave him a blank look, then nodded.

"Feena and April," he said.

Chalkie grinned. "That's right. And Feena rode with me on my bike, but April"—his grin grew broader—"she had her own, didn't she just? Had her own bike and you were the loser."

"Wasn't I just," the Gaffer said.

And he was the loser again, he and Janey both. For that woman he'd seen in Felix's arms was the same one who'd come by the house demanding Billy's unpublished writings not four days ago. He would never have thought it of Felix, but now it made sense, his showing up the way he had with that letter of his. Of course Janey hadn't written it—he'd written it himself.

When he thought of how much he'd always liked Felix—he'd been the best of any lad Janey brought home—it made his heart break.

"Have you gone deaf?"

The Gaffer lifted his head to find Chalkie looking at him, a puzzled look creasing his brow. He hadn't heard a word that Chalkie had said.

"What's that, my beauty?" he asked.

"I said, have you gone deaf?" Chalkie repeated. "Garm, you were lost at sea just now, you."

The Gaffer sighed. "I was thinking."

"Bad thoughts?"

"Well, they weren't good ones," the Gaffer said.

"Comes from getting old," Chalkie assured him. "Always think of the good times, Tom. Makes it easier."

"I suppose."

The good times. Lost times. No, they weren't good to dwell upon. But what did you do when you found out that some of them were lies?

Oh, how was he going to tell Janey?

7.

Everything works out in the end, Lena thought, and she hadn't even needed Willie's directions. She had a sprained ankle, and that wasn't fun, but she couldn't have found a better way to meet Felix Gavin than if she'd planned that tumble from the bike herself.

He'd actually carried her upstairs to her room, then seen about getting a pack of ice, which he was now applying to her foot, which was propped up on the bed before her. While he'd gone down to the lobby to get the ice, she'd changed into a big floppy sweatshirt that covered her to her knees. The strained white look on her face from the pain that the change in clothing had cost her hadn't been put on. Just that small effort had almost completely worn her out. And kind-hearted hunk that he was, her rescuer had immediately insisted that she lie down when he returned.

He was an interesting man—strong and gentle and she could easily understand what the Little girl had seen in him. What she couldn't understand was why Janey Little had dumped him.

Oh, well, Lena thought philosophically. Her loss, my gain.

She was on her best behavior with him, utilizing everything she'd ever learned in her acting classes. The image she projected was a rather appealing mix, even if she did say so herself.

Demure, but not naive. Hurting, but being brave about it. Open and friendly, a bit lonely, but no hard come on. In short, she was charming the pants off him, without coming off as a tart.

And she could tell that it was working. It wasn't in anything he said or did—he was being the complete gentleman, which rather surprised her, considering his background—but she could tell she was having an effect upon him all the same. It was the way he studied her without really looking. The way he was having an increasingly hard time making ordinary conversation.

"Boy," she said, wriggling a bit as she adjusted her position against the headboard. "What a dumb thing to have done. You'd think I'd never ridden a bike before."

"Do you do a lot of cycling?" Felix asked.

She nodded. "I love it. But I'm not used to these roads and the crossbar on the bike made me feel a bit weird, too. Why do they have those things on men's bikes, anyway? You'd think it'd make guys even more nervous."

Whoops, she thought as he raised an eyebrow. Tone it down. You don't want to scare him off.

"Anyway," she added quickly, "I was lucky to have you be so close to give me a hand. You've been a real angel."

"It was no big deal."

"Not to you maybe."

Felix shrugged and looked about the room.

"Are you here on holiday?" he asked.

A wry smile touched Lena's lips. "You don't really want to hear the whole sorry story of what I'm doing here on my own, do you?"

"I'm a good listener."

I'll just bet you are, Lena thought. And since she wanted to keep him around for as long as possible, she spun out a story of how she was a secretary in Boston, with aspirations to be an actress, and how she'd come here on a sort of business holiday with her new boyfriend—"ex-boyfriend, let me tell you"—who'd claimed he was a film director checking out some locations and did she want to come along just for the fun of it?

"So like a dummy, I agreed," she finished up, "and we're here one day and he dumps me because I wouldn't, you know. Show him a good time."

"What was the film supposed to be about?" Felix asked.

"What film? Everything about it was a big secret before we left and now I know why: There was no film. What I can't figure out is why he brought me all the way over here with him if all he wanted from me was sex, you know? Seems to me that there's cheaper ways to get yourself a girl."

She was tempted to tell him that this "boyfriend" of hers was going around pretending to be a reporter from *Rolling Stone,* but all she had to do was think of what Bett's reaction would be to quickly squelch that idea.

"Maybe there really is a film," Felix said.

Lena nodded slowly. "You're probably right. And since I wouldn't come across, he's found some local bimbo to take my place."

"Don't be so hard on yourself."

"Why not? This whole trip was a mistake from the start and I have to have been a bimbo to fall for it at all." She shook her head. "And I've *still* got nine days before my flight home." She inserted a well-timed sigh. "It's not that there's anything wrong with Cornwall—I *love* it around here—it's just not a whole lot of fun when you're on your own."

"I know what you mean."

Lena gave him a quick smile. "Sounds like you've got your own hard-luck story. Want to talk about it? I know I feel better already."

"I don't think so," Felix said.

"It's a woman—right?"

Felix looked up with surprise to find Lena looking sympathetic.

"It's always something like that," she said. "I think we're cursed to never really find the right partner in life and then, to make things worse, we screw up our lives even more in an endless chase for that perfect someone who's usually not out there in the first place. And when they *are* out there, they're married or won't give us the time of day, or *something*."

"I can tell you're coming out of the wrong side of a bad relationship," Felix said.

Lena shrugged. "Maybe. I'm not usually so maudlin about this kind of thing—I mean, *he* sure doesn't deserve my spending the time thinking about him—but it starts to wear on you after a while, don't you think?"

"I suppose."

He looked uncomfortable and Lena decided she'd better pull back when he changed the conversation himself.

"That tattoo on your wrist," he began.

"Oh, that old thing. . . ." Self-consciously, she covered it up with her free hand. "I got that done when I was a teenager—one of those things that you regret about ten minutes too late."

Felix laughed. He'd already taken off his jacket earlier. Now he rolled up the sleeve of his T-shirt to show the tattoo he had on his left biceps. It was a full-colour rendition of an old man, sitting on a crate playing an accordion.

"Now that one I like," Lena said. "Do you play one of those things yourself?"

Felix nodded.

"Professionally?"

"Not likely."

"Oh, I bet you're really good at it."

"I get by." Felix indicated her left wrist. "So why a dove?"

"It's the symbol . . . that is, it's supposed to be the symbol of an old . . ."

Now she'd gone too far. If Bett was to hear her now. If her *father* was to hear her now . . .

"An old what?"

"Oh, you know. Peace, love, and flowers, and all that stuff. I was enamoured with the sixties when I was a kid—mostly because I just missed out on them. So when I decided to get the tattoo, I thought I'd get a peace symbol, but I never really liked that circle thing, so when I saw the dove in the tattoo guy's catalogue, I picked it instead."

Was he buying it?

She had no chance to find out because just then the phone rang. Before she could think of a way to stop him, Felix had reached over and picked up the receiver.

"Hello? Hello?"

He gave her a puzzled look.

"There's nobody there," he said as he hung up.

"That's weird."

The actress in her wanted to add, maybe it was my boyfriend checking up on me, just for the drama, but she thought better of it. Felix glanced at his watch.

"I should get going," he said. "Are you going to be okay? Can I get you some takeout or something for dinner before I go?"

She decided not to push it any more today. There'd be another day. She was sure enough of herself to know that. And besides, if that *had* been the Golden Boy on the phone, the sooner Felix was out of here the better.

"No. I can just call room service."

He stood up and retrieved his jacket from the chair where he'd tossed it earlier.

"There is one thing, though," she said. "If it's not too much trouble. . . ."

"What's that?"

"Well, I'm going to need a cane to hobble around with for the next few days. Is there any chance you could pick one up for me?" As he hesitated, she added, "I'd pay for it, of course."

"It's not that. It's just—" He hesitated a moment longer, then nodded. "Sure. I can do that."

"I know the stores are closed now, so you'd have to go tomorrow."

"No problem. What time will you be getting up?"

"Nine-thirtyish?"

"I'll be by around ten."

She put on an apologetic look. "There's one more thing. I'll take whatever kind you can get, but if there's a choice, could you maybe find something a little funky? Maybe an old one?"

Felix smiled. "No problem. There's some antique shops over on Chapel Street. I don't know what time they're open, though."

"Whatever. I really appreciate this—everything you've done. You've been really great."

Felix nodded. "See you tomorrow, then. And try to stay off that foot."

"Yes, *sir*."

Laughing, Felix let himself out.

Lena settled back on the bed and smiled to herself. The hooks were in and sinking deep. And if he really was coming off a second rebound with the Little girl, well, that'd just make her job all that much easier, wouldn't it?

So why did what she was doing make her feel a little dirty?

It was an hour later that Bett came by, railing at her. He obviously didn't believe her story about stumbling over the corner of the rug and spraining her ankle, but there wasn't a whole lot he could do except glare at her—that awful promise that if she wasn't protected by her father just simmering in the pale depths of his eyes.

When he gave her his instructions concerning Felix Gavin, she wanted to rail right back at him. Trust him to take her own idea so that he could get the credit for it. But she said nothing, and did nothing, until he finally left, that unpleasant promise of his still burning in his eyes. Then she picked up the phone and had the operator give her an overseas connection.

"Hello, Daddy?" she said when she got through. She put on her best little-girl voice. "I don't want to sound like a baby or anything, but Mike's beginning to act a little strange. . . . No, he hasn't been threatening me or anything, at least he hasn't *said* anything, but he did give me a push and I fell down and kind of sprained my ankle. . . . No, it's okay; just sore. Oh, would you? Could you send Jim? Have him book into a room here, but he should wait for me to contact him."

Slowly she'd been letting the little-girl voice change to that of a capable woman.

"I think you'll be happy with some developments I've been making on my own, Daddy. There's this man who's very close to the Little girl—no, their surname is Little, remember? She's quite grown up. Anyway, I'm *this* close to having him bring me whatever this secret thing of Dunthorn's is. I thought you'd be pleased. Of course I'll take care. I love you too, Daddy."

There, she thought as she cradled the phone. Her father would tell the other members of the Order that working through Gavin had been her idea and soon she'd have some protection against Bett. Everything was falling neatly into place.

But when she thought of how she was using Felix, she still felt dirty.

Don't be stupid, she told herself. He's just a dumb sailor.

True. But he was a nice dumb sailor, and maybe not so dumb as that. And he'd certainly treated her better than most people in her own social circles did. How many of them would have even stopped if they saw a woman—attractive or not—take a fall from her bike?

She stared across her room. Her ankle was aching again.

"Shit," she said to no one in particular.

Why did everything always have to be so complicated?

8.

There was no one in when Janey got back home. She put on water for tea and went next door to her own rooms to get a sweater. After she'd put it on and checked her mirror to make sure that that thing she'd seen this morning really *hadn't* been a pimple, she went over to the bookcase to make sure that The Little Country was still there.

It was right where it was supposed to be.

Taking the book down from the shelf, she flipped idly through a few pages, pausing for a moment when she thought she could hear that music again. But no sooner did she listen for it, than it was gone. Sighing, she closed the book with a snap and went back to the Gaffer's with the book under her arm to call Clare.

"I'm so sorry I didn't ring up earlier," she began when she had her friend on the line, "but the most amazing thing happened." Whereupon she launched into an account of the reporter coming by late that morning and how they'd gone over to the Pantry for the interview.

"What was he like?" Clare wanted to know.

"Oh, very nice. American. I'm not quite sure how old, but not *too* old. He's got Paul Newman eyes and he knows about as much about the music as anyone I've met, so I'm sure the article will be good."

"Because of his eyes?"

"Clare!"

Her friend laughed. "Just teasing. You must be pleased."

"Aren't I just."

"When's it coming out?"

"He didn't say. It probably won't be for a while, though. You know how these magazines work—they're buying Christmas stories in June."

"Have you seen Felix yet?" Clare asked.

"No. I was just going to ask you the same thing."

"I met him up by the Coastguard lookout about midmorning. When he left, he was going back to your place. That was only a bit past twelve."

"I must have just missed him. I wonder where he's gone off to now?"

"How do you feel about seeing him again?"

"I'm not sure," Janey said. "Both happy and scared, I suppose."

"But you still fancy him?"

"Oh, yes," Janey said before she really thought about what she was saying, but then she realized it was true.

"He's a wonderful bloke," Clare said. "Make sure you hang on to him this time."

"I'm planning to have a talk with him when he gets back," Janey said. "And this time I won't be the least bit emperent, as the Gaffer'd say."

"Maybe he likes you cheeky."

"Maybe he does. I hear someone at the door, so I've got to run. It might be Felix."

"Call me tomorrow."

"I will."

Janey cradled the phone just as the door opened, but it was the Gaffer. Much as she loved her grandfather, right then Janey wished it had been Felix instead.

"Not had a good day, Gramps?" she asked when she saw the grim set to his features.

The Gaffer sighed. "Oh, I've some bad news to tell you, my gold, and I don't know where to begin."

"Chalkie isn't hurt, is he?"

She could imagine the two old codgers messing about with that stone wall of Chalkie's and one of them dropping a great big hunk of granite on the other's foot.

"No," the Gaffer said. "Nothing like that."

He looked so sad.

"Well, what is it?" Janey asked.

The Gaffer sat down at the kitchen table, moving stiffly as though he'd begun to feel the weight of his years for the first time. Seeing that made Janey feel even more concerned.

"It's about Felix, my robin. He's betrayed our trust."

As the Gaffer told her what he'd seen in Newlyn that afternoon, who Felix had been so cozy with on his bicycle, all the blood drained out of Janey's features.

"It's not true," she said in a small voice. "Tell me it's not true."

"I wish it weren't, my love, but I saw what I saw."

All Janey could do then was look at him, her eyes brimming with tears.

The Wheels of the World

This was the machinery of life, not a clean, clinical well-oiled engine, monitored by a thousand meticulous dials, but a crazy, stumbling contraption made up of strange things roughly fitted together.

—MARGARET MAHY, from *Memory*

Nettie Shepherd opened her front door to find Denzil standing on her stoop. He leaned on his silver-headed cane and peered at her through his hazy glasses that were fogging up due to the heat escaping from the house.

Ample was the best description that came to mind whenever Denzil met Jodi's aunt. She was a large woman, but her largeness was proportionate. She had enormous thighs, and equally bounteous breasts, broad shoulders, a generous face, a waterfall of red-gold hair—in short, everything about her was larger than life. The grin that touched her lips at the sight of him was wide and expansive as well, touched with a cat's knowing satisfaction.

"Well, now," she said. "I never thought to see you here."

"I'm not here for business, you, I'm here . . ." Denzil's voice trailed off as he realized what he was saying.

"For pleasure? They're one and the same under this roof, Master Gossip."

"Ahem. Yes, well. Actually, I've come 'round about Jodi. Is she in?"

"You mean she's not been with you?"

Denzil shook his head, "I haven't seen her all day."

Nettie pursed her lips, then opened the door wider.

"You'd better come in," she said.

Denzil hesitated for a moment, looking up and down the street before he followed her inside. Though he hadn't thought it possible, Nettie's grin actually widened.

"Afraid someone would see you entering this den of iniquity?"

"It *is* a bawdy house," Denzil replied somewhat huffily.

"Yes, we do have bodies."

"Please."

Abruptly Nettie looked serious. "You're quite right," she said.

She took his cane and hat, leaning the one against the wall, hanging the other by the door. Denzil snatched the opportunity of having both his hands free to wipe his glasses.

"This isn't much of an evening for bantering," Nettie added.

Denzil soon found out why.

Ushered into her sitting room, he discovered that he wasn't Nettie's only non-paying visitor of the evening. Sitting each to a chair by the window were Cadan Tremeer, Bodbury's chief constable, and the Widow Pender. Tremeer lifted his bulk from his chair and offered Denzil a pudgy hand. The constable smelled vaguely of perfume, which made Denzil wonder if he hadn't been called to duty from one of the rooms upstairs. Once Denzil had shaken the man's hand, Tremeer settled back into his chair with obvious relief.

The Widow merely nodded at Denzil.

"Some tea?" Nettie asked.

Denzil shook his head. He took off his glasses, cleaned them again on the sleeve of his jacket, then set them back upon the bridge of his nose where they promptly fogged up once more. Nettie indicated a chair, but he remained standing.

"Has Jodi got herself mixed up in some sort of misadventure?" he asked.

The Widow hrumphed.

"It's serious this time," Nettie said.

Tremeer nodded, trying to fit a grim look to his jolly features without much success.

"She broke into the Widow's house and stole an heirloom," he said.

He pronounced the word "hair-loom," as though what had been stolen was a tool on which one could weave hair.

Denzil shook his head. "Jodi wouldn't steal a farthing, you."

"The Widow saw her leaving through a window herself. I've been 'round, Master Gossip, and there's a fearsome mess there. Glass broken. Geegaws scattered every which way. It doesn't look good."

Denzil looked to Nettie. "What does Jodi have to say about this?"

"Well, that's what makes it look so bad," the constable said before she could reply. "Young Miss Shepherd's not to be found."

Denzil finally took the chair Nettie had offered him earlier.

Now this was a fine how-to-do, wasn't it just? he thought. It was the last thing he would have expected to discover when he first decided that Nettie's place was where he should begin his inquiries.

"When was the last time you saw her?" he asked Nettie.

"When she went to bed—early for her. Before midnight."

"And?" Denzil prompted her, perceiving that she hadn't told all yet.

Nettie sighed. "Her bed hadn't been slept in and her window was open. Time to time, she thinks she's like your monkey, Master Gossip, and goes climbing about on the drainpipes. Gets her to the ground quickly and without being seen, and then she's off on some kitey lark or another."

"Such as robbing an old woman of her memories," the Widow said, speaking up for the first time.

Her voice was quavery and she was wearing a hangdog expression that Denzil didn't believe for a moment. He'd seen her jaunting about often enough to know that she was as spry as a woman half her years, and as mean as the most curmudgeonly old salt. He'd believe her capable of any nastiness—knowing she'd do it for the pure spite of the deed. What he didn't subscribe to was the so-called magical curses she supposedly could command—no matter what the children of the Tatters claimed.

"How do you know it was Jodi?" he asked. "It was at night, wasn't it? Couldn't you have been mistaken, you?"

"I know that girl," the Widow said. "She eggs on the other children to lampoon me."

Now *that* Denzil could believe.

"Why did you wait so long to report it?" he asked. He glanced at the constable. "I take it she has only just made her complaint?"

Tremeer looked guilty and shot a glance roofward before catching himself.

"I . . . uh," he began. "That is, she . . ."

"It's hard for a woman my age to get about easily," the Widow said. "It's the arthritis."

Now the lies began again, Denzil thought.

Tremeer had recovered his officiousness in the meantime. He took up a notepad and pen from the table beside him.

"And when was the last time you saw her, Master Denzil?"

"Yesterday. When she didn't come 'round today, I got worried." Denzil sighed. "Jodi's not the sort to be involved in this kind of mischief," he added.

Nettie nodded, glad of his support.

"She's a child, isn't she?" the Widow said. "And aren't all children an annoying nuisance?"

Not so much as you are, Denzil thought, but he didn't bother to reply. Rising to his feet, he nodded to Tremeer and the Widow before turning to Nettie.

"Call me if I can help in any way," he told her.

"Thank you. I will."

"And if you should happen to find her . . ." Tremeer began.

"I'll be sure to notify you straightaway," Denzil said.

He waved Nettie back into her chair as she rose to see him out.

"I can find the way," he said.

Once he was out in the hall, he collected his hat and cane by the door and quickly made his escape. Outside, his glasses immediately fogged up again, but he ignored the discomfort. Sometimes it seemed that he spent half his life peering through murky lenses and the other half cleaning them, so he was well used to the burden by now.

Something odd was going on, he thought, and he meant to get to the bottom of it. But first he needed a good stiff drink to take away the taste of the Widow's poor playacting and Tremeer's toadying up to her.

He gave Nettie's house a last considering look, then headed towards the harbour and made his way to the nearest pub, which in this case happened to be The Ship's Inn.

Naturally, to make the night a perfect loss, he found Taupin sitting there with a look about him as though the hedgerow philosopher had been waiting just for him. Or at least waiting for someone to buy him a drink.

He almost turned and walked out again, but Taupin hailed him cheerily and Denzil didn't have the heart to walk the ten blocks or so to The Tuck-Net & Caboleen.

Besides, he thought, the children all liked the old fool. Maybe he'd know where Jodi was.

2.

It was no use just sitting here, Jodi decided after a half hour had passed and the cat still wouldn't go away. Getting up, she dusted off her trousers and set off to find another way out of the maze of crates. But at each exit they found that the cat, drawn by the whispering sound of their tiny footfalls—and Jodi's running commentary on the dubious ancestry of cats, this one mangy cat in particular—was waiting for them.

"Bother and damn!" Jodi cried.

Picking up a stone, she threw it at the cat, but it had no visible effect. The largest one she could find that she could throw with any accuracy was no bigger than a peppercorn. Still, she kept up a steady barrage until her arm got sore. Then she returned to slouch down beside Edern.

"Why do cats have to be so bloody patient?" she wanted to know.

Edern shrugged. "This friend of yours," he said. "What was his name? Dazzle?"

"Denzil."

"He's a magician?"

Jodi laughed. "Denzil's about as logical a man as you're likely to find, which means he doesn't believe in magic. If it can't be explained by logic, he'd say, then we simply haven't found the proper parameters and reference points."

"Then he won't be much help to us, will he?"

"He's also wise and clever and my best friend."

"Yes, but if he doesn't know anything about magic, there won't be anything he can do for us."

"Do you have a better idea?"

"I think so," Edern said. "What do you know about the stoneworks 'round about the countryside?"

"Bloody little, except they make me feel tingly and sort of—oh, I don't know, touched by mystery, I suppose."

"Did you ever hear that they're supposed to be the places where our world meets the Barrow World?"

Jodi laughed. "Oh raw we. Now you want to call up hummocks and piskies to give us a hand?"

"If a witch can shrink us, then why can't the Little People exist?"

"That's your plan?"

When Edern nodded, Jodi started to laugh again, but she caught herself. Fine, she thought. Let's think this through—logically, as Denzil would have her do it. Magic worked. It obviously existed—they were proof positive of that. So why *not* Smalls?

"Why would they help us?" she wanted to know.

"Maybe we could trade them for their help."

Jodi stuck a hand in her pocket and came out with a piece of twine, some dried pieces of biscuit left over from dinner that she'd meant to give to the first stray dog she ran across, three glass marbles, two copper pennies, a piece of sea-polished wood that had no discernible purpose, two small geared wheels that obviously did have a purpose, though Jodi didn't know what kind of a mechanism they'd come from, a small penknife, and some lint. She gave it all a critical look, then held out her hand to Edern.

"What would they like from this?" she asked.

"We could trade services," Edern said patiently.

"What sort of services?"

"We'd have to ask them that, wouldn't we?"

Jodi sighed. "I don't know." She glanced at the cat who continued to eye them with unabated interest. "Besides, first we have to get away."

"But when we *do* . . ."

Jodi stored the detritus from her pocket back where it had all come from, only keeping out the bits of broken biscuit. She offered Edern a piece and chewed on another herself.

"Stoneworks," she said, mumbling the word as she chewed. She swallowed, wishing she had a drink. "Like the stone crosses and such?"

Edern nodded.

"What if God sends down an angel to see what we're about? I don't think He'd be ready to help me because I rather doubt that I'm in His good books."

"It's unlikely that would happen," Edern said.

"If piskies can exist, then why not God?"

"I was thinking more of a place like the Merry Maidens."

"Oh, I know the story behind them. Some girls were dancing on a Sunday, weren't they? Thirteen of them. And God turned them to stone. There were two pipers playing for the girls and they ran off, but they got turned to stone all the same and stand a few fields over."

"Why all this sudden talk of God?" Edern asked.

"Well, you brought it up."

"The story I know of the Merry Maidens is that they're mermaids who got caught dancing when the sun came up, so they were turned to stone."

"You're thinking of trolls."

"The point is," Edern went on as though she hadn't interrupted, "that there's a sea wisdom in those stones. The sea's full of powerful magic and lore. If we could get Her help . . ."

"I don't think I'm in Her good books either," Jodi said. "At least my family isn't."

Both her father and uncle had been taken by the sea. A year later her mother died of a broken heart, which amounted to the sea being responsible for her death as well. Jodi was quiet for a long moment, thinking of the parents she only knew from the fuzzy memories of the toddler she'd been at the time of their deaths.

"Jodi?"

She shook off the gloom that had started to settle upon her.

"I'm fine," she said. "I was just thinking."

"About the stoneworks?"

She nodded. "I don't think I'm quite ready to accept that the sea could have a bit of a chat with us."

"There's also the Men-an-Tol stone, though that's farther away."

"I've been through its hole the nine times it's supposed to take to wake the charm, but nothing ever happened."

"At moonrise?"

"Not at moonrise. But then—" She gave him a sudden rueful grin. "I can't *believe* we're having this conversation."

"You didn't believe in magic before the Widow enchanted you."

Jodi nodded. "I suppose we could try this stone of yours, but first we have to get the button charms from the Widow's house."

"Better we go to the stone first to find out *how* the spell works. That way, when we do retrieve the charm, we can work it there on the spot."

"And have her shrink us right back down again in the next moment."

"Not if we go when she's not about."

"I suppose. . . ."

"Perhaps the Little People can give us some protection against her magic," Edern said.

Jodi banged the back of her head against the crate in frustration.

"And perhaps," she said, "we can fly away on a leaf and save ourselves the long walk to the stone. Bother and damn! I'm *tired* of perhapses and maybes."

She stood up, chose another stone, and flung it at the cat.

"Get away, you!"

Surprisingly, this time it worked. The cat backed away, looked once to its right, then fled.

Jodi turned to her companion with a grin. "That showed him, didn't it just?"

But Edern didn't look in the least bit pleased. He sat very pale and still, just staring at the gap between the crates through which the cat had been peering at them. With a sinking feeling in the pit of her stomach, Jodi turned to see what it was that he was looking at.

Windle, the Widow's fetch, stared back at her. It had chased off the cat merely to take up the watch itself. And there it would stay, Jodi knew, until the Widow arrived with some new kind of spell to snatch them willy-nilly from their hiding place.

"Found something then have you, my sweet?" a too familiar voice called out.

Or maybe the Widow was already here.

3.

It was smoky inside The Ship's Inn, thick enough to be a fog. Those who weren't puffing away on pipes and cigars had cigarettes dangling from their mouths, each exhalation adding to the general haze. Blinking behind his glasses, Denzil navigated his way through to the bar where he resignedly took a stool beside Taupin.

Brengy Taupin looked the part of the hedgerow philosopher he claimed to be. He was thin as a rake and wore an odd collection of raggedy clothes that hung from his frame with about the same sense of style as could be expected from a scarecrow—in other words, it was all angles and tatters. The gauntness of his features was eased by a pair of cheerful and too bright eyes. His hair was an unruly brown thatch in which bits of leaves and twigs were invariably caught. Denzil often caught himself staring at it, waiting for a bird's head to pop up out of its untidy hedgery.

"Can I buy you a drink, you?" he asked.

He signaled to the barman to bring them two pints of bitter without waiting for Taupin's reply.

"This is a kindness," Taupin said after a long appreciative swallow of his bitter, which left a foamy moustache on his upper lip.

"Not to be confused with a habit," Denzil said, still wishing he'd chosen to walk the extra few blocks to the Tuck.

However, if the truth was to be told, for all Denzil's gruffness towards his companion, he and Taupin got on rather well, for they both loved a good philosophical discussion—a rarity in temperate Bodbury—and were each capable of keeping one going for weeks on end.

"Naturally," Taupin replied.

He dug about in one of the enormous pockets of his overcoat as he spoke.

"I've got something for you here," he added as he came up with an odd mechanism that he set on the bartop between them.

Denzil couldn't help but be intrigued.

Taupin knew his weakness for inexplicable machinery and the like. If it was odd, if it appeared useful but couldn't be readily explained, then it became an object of the utmost fascination to the inventor.

What lay on the bartop was most intriguing. It was obviously a clockwork mechanism of some sort, but Denzil could see no way in which it could be wound up. Nor what it would do even if it were wound up.

"What is it?" he asked.

"I haven't the faintest idea," Taupin replied. "But watch."

He gave the thing a shake, then set it back down upon the top of the bar. For a moment nothing happened. Then a cog went rolling down a slight incline, caught another, which made the second cog turn. A small metal shaft rose, returning the first cog to its starting point while the gears of the second turned yet another cog, which in turn set a whole series in motion until a shaft at the far side of the machine began to turn. In the meantime, the first cog had rolled back down its incline to engage the second once more.

Denzil leaned closer, utterly captivated.

"How long does it run?" he asked.

Taupin grinned. "Well, it's not the perpetual motion machine you're always on about, but it'll go for a good hour."

"With only the one shake to get it started?"

Taupin nodded.

"Where did you get it?"

"In a junk shop in Praed. Fascinating, isn't it? You can keep it if you like."

"How much?"

"Fah," Taupin said, waving aside the offer of monetary return. "You can have me over for dinner some night—but when Jodi's cooking, mind you. I won't eat your idea of a meal."

Regretfully, Denzil pulled his gaze away from the machine that went merrily on about its incomprehensible business. Pushing up his glasses, he turned to Taupin.

"I meant to talk to you about her," he said.

"Who?" Taupin asked. "Jodi? A delightful girl. Quite clever and quick to learn. And oddly enough, considering how the greater part of what she's learned has come from you or my own self, a remarkable cook."

Denzil nodded. "I just wish you'd stop filling her head with fairy tales."

"Why ever for? What can it possibly harm?"

"Her intellect. The logical progression of her reasoning."

Taupin laughed. "Look," he said. "This"—he pointed to the mechanism—"is how you see the world. Everything has its place. It all moves like clockwork, one event logically following the other.

When something doesn't fit, it's merely because we haven't understood it yet."

"So?"

Now Taupin reached into one of his voluminous pockets and
dumped its contents on the table. Geegaws and trinkets lay helter-
skelter upon one another. A small tatty book lay entangled with a
length of netting. A tin whistle had a feather sticking out of its mouth
hole and what appeared to be a dried rat's tail protruding from its
other end. A square of cloth with buttons sewn to it, each oddly
connected to the other with startlingly bright embroidery that almost,
but not quite, had a discernible pattern. A crab's pincer with a hole
in it through which had been pulled a piece of string. Two stones—
one with the fossil of a shell upon it, the other with what might be
faded hieroglyphics or simply scratches.

There was more, but it was all too much for Denzil to easily catalogue.

"This is how the world really is," Taupin said. "A confusion in
which some things make perfect sense"—he shook the whistle free
of its encumbrances and rolled it back and forth on the palm of his
hand—"while others may never be explained."

Now he plucked up the stone with its curious markings and offered it to his companion. Denzil took it gingerly, as though afraid
it might bite, and gave it a cursory glance. The markings did appear
to be some sort of language—though not one he could recognize.
And it was very old.

"I found that around by the point," Taupin said. "Washed in from
the sea, it was." He pointed back to the bartop. "*That's* the true face
of the world, Denzil—all jumbled up with no distinguishable pattern
except that, *somehow*, it's all connected to itself and the whole thing
muddles through in the end."

"A pretty analogy," Denzil said as he handed the stone back, "but
a mistaken one."

"Still, we're not so different, you and I. We both pursue Truth."

"We *are* different," Denzil assured him. "I go about my search for
Truth in a rational, scientific manner. You hope to stumble over it
through blind luck and tomfoolery."

Taupin raised his glass to him. "Here's to Wisdom, wherever it
may be found."

"What I need to find at the moment is Jodi," Denzil said.

"Misplaced her, have you?"

"This isn't a joke, you."

Taupin's grin faltered, his features growing increasingly grave as Denzil explained the situation.

"It makes no sense," Denzil said as he finished up.

"Not a smidgen," Taupin agreed.

"Jodi's simply not like that."

"Not at all."

"And I don't know where to begin to look for her."

Taupin said nothing for a long moment. Brow wrinkled with thought, he slowly moved the contents from his pocket from the top of the bar back into his pocket, then finished the last inch of his bitter.

"There's two ways we can go about this," he said finally.

"And they are?"

"We begin with the Gossip method of logic, whereby we search the town from top to bottom, leaving word with the Tatters children and the like as we make our way."

"And the second method?"

"Well," Taupin said, "once we've exhausted the logical route, we'll take the illogical one and start to consider the impossible."

Denzil shook his head. "I haven't the faintest idea what you're on about."

"I smell magic in the air," Taupin said simply.

Denzil snorted. "What a pile of nonsense!"

"It may well be. But I smell it all the same. And after all, rumour has it that the Widow *is* a witch." He held up a hand before Denzil could argue further. "But first we'll take a turn around the town, a-foot and with our eyes peeled for mischief—yes?"

Denzil gave a reluctant nod, which made his glasses skid down to the end of his nose. He pushed them back up again, thinking of Taupin's offer. Denzil knew he needed help. He just wished he could have found it in a more practical corner. Still, a man took what he was offered.

Finishing his own bitter, he pocketed the mechanism that Taupin had given him and got off his stool.

"Let's be on our way," he said.

The Piper's Despair

If you live close enough to the edge of the land and the edge of the sea, if you listen hard and watch close, you can get some sense of places that are different from what most people see and hear.

—HILBERT SCHENCK, from *Chronosequence*

Felix thought about Lena as he walked back to Mousehole from Penzance. She seemed like a decent sort of person, yet he couldn't help but feel uncomfortable about her obvious interest in him. It wasn't that she was unattractive, or that she'd thrown herself at him. He just didn't need or want any more complications in his life at the moment.

He had enough on his mind already.

But the trouble was, he felt sorry for her. Dumped by her boyfriend in a strange place, unable to even tour about now because of her accident, and then he showed up. . . .

Was it the Japanese who believed that if you saved someone's life you became responsible for that person? His helping her hadn't exactly been a rescue from a life-threatening plight, but he couldn't deny that—now that he knew of her and the unhappy situation she was in—he did feel just a bit responsible for her.

It was probably a case of empathy, because he knew exactly how she had to be feeling. But there was also something else that troubled him about her, some subtext underlying the time he'd spent in her company that had nothing to do with her attraction to him, or his feeling sorry and just a bit responsible for her. Whatever it was, he couldn't put his finger on it. He didn't really want to think about it or her.

He just wished he hadn't met her in the first place. And having met her, he wished he weren't seeing her tomorrow, because that only complicated things more.

Was nothing simple anymore?

At North Cliff he turned up Duck Street towards the Gaffer's house. When he got to Chapel Place and found his bags sitting outside the garden wall, he realized that he hadn't known what complication was yet.

Now what was going on?

Pulse quickening uncomfortably, he left his luggage sitting there, both duffel and accordion case, and knocked upon the door. The grim face of the Gaffer as he answered did little to allay his growing distress.

"Hello, Tom," he began. "What's—"

"Get away, you," the Gaffer said.

"Don't I even get some sort of explan—"

"Is that him?" he heard Janey ask from inside.

"He's not worth your time, my gold," the Gaffer said, but Janey pushed by him in the doorway.

Felix was shocked at her tear-stained face, the hurt in her eyes that grew rapidly into anger the longer she stood there looking at him.

"I hate you for what you've done," she began, her voice deadly calm.

Felix could feel his heart turn to stone at her words. A foggy numbness settled over him, making everything appear to be happening at half speed.

"What—what is it that I'm supposed to have done?"

His own voice, when he spoke, seemed to drone on forever just to get those few words out.

"We know all about you and your—" Her voice cracked, tears welling up anew in her eyes. "You and your little tart."

She meant Lena, he realized.

"But—"

"Don't start lying again!" she shouted. "Gramps *saw* you with her."

Quickly now, Felix told himself. Explain the innocence of your meeting with the woman because this was already getting far too out of hand as it was.

But his voice was still trapped behind the growing numbness that was fogging him. The coldness in his chest deepened. When he spoke, his words seemed distant—unreal even to himself.

"I don't know what he saw, but—"

"And that's not the worst. That stupid lying letter of yours—you wrote it yourself, didn't you? Or did *she* do it for you? You knew— you *knew* how much the book meant to me . . . and the promise . . . the promise Gramps made Billy. . . ."

She couldn't go on. Tears streaming down her cheeks, she turned to the Gaffer who enfolded her in his arms.

"Get away from us," the Gaffer said.

"But—"

He could feel his world collapsing around him like a house made of cards knocked apart by the uncaring sweep of a giant hand.

"Get away," the Gaffer repeated, adding, "or I'll call the law on you."

He turned away, pulling Janey with him, and slammed the door in Felix's face.

Felix stood there, numbly staring at the door. Deep in the pit of his stomach a knot, hard as a rock, was forming. His chest felt tight, heart drumming a wild tattoo.

This couldn't be happening, he thought. They weren't going to shut him out of their lives like this without even giving him a chance to explain that he'd done nothing wrong, were they?

He lifted his hand to knock again, then simply let it fall to his side.

Madness: This whole trip out here had been nothing but madness.

He thought of the letter that had brought him to Mousehole.

Janey claimed she hadn't sent it.

He thought of the odd stories the Gaffer had told about strangers trying to steal his old mate's writings.

What had turned such kind and gentle people as the Littles into a pair of raving paranoids?

Those stories—were any of them even true? There was the theft he'd stopped. . . .

He lifted his hand a second time, then slowly turned away. What was the use? They weren't going to listen to him.

His own eyes were burning now. He let the tears fall as he collected his bags and stumbled off to the only sanctuary he might still have in the village.

"Oh, no," Clare said when she opened the door. "It didn't go well, did it?"

"It went bloody awful," Felix said. "It didn't go at all."

His head had cleared a little on the walk over to her place, but the coldness was still there inside him. He didn't know if it would ever go away. He could think a little more clearly again; he just couldn't believe that the scene that had played itself out on the Gaffer's doorstep had actually happened. He kept wanting to go back, to prove to himself that it had all been a mistake, something he had only imagined, but then he'd see Janey's face again, the hurt and the anger in it, he'd see the Gaffer's rage, and know it had all taken place.

Clare ushered him inside. Her mother was already in bed, but Clare had been sitting up reading. She took him back into the kitchen and poured him a cup of tea from the pot she'd just made for herself. Felix accepted it gratefully, almost gulping the scalding liquid down. He was trying to warm the coldness that had lodged inside him, but the tea didn't help. Maybe nothing ever would.

"Do you want to talk about it?" Clare asked.

Felix lifted his head slowly from the whorls of wood grain on the kitchen table that he'd been staring at.

"There's nothing really to tell," he said. "I never got to say a thing. I got back from Penzance to find my cases sitting outside by the wall and when I knocked on the door, all she did was yell at me. She was crying and shouting all at the same time. The Gaffer said he was going to call the cops if I didn't leave."

Clare listened with mounting horror. "What did you *do*?" she asked.

Felix laughed bitterly in response. It was an ugly sound that grated even on his own ears.

"That's just it," he said. "I didn't do anything except . . ."

Slowly he told her of what he'd done since he'd seen her to her door earlier in the day.

"I swear there was nothing going on between us," he said, finishing up. "I mean, what was I supposed to do? Leave her lying there by the side of the road?"

"Of course not. You did the decent thing."

"Maybe it looked bad, when I was taking her back to her hotel on her bike, but, Jesus, shouldn't I at least get the chance to tell my side of it?"

Clare nodded. "There's got to be more to it than just that."

"She thinks I wrote this letter she sent," Felix said. He pulled the crumpled paper from his pocket and tossed it onto the table. "Or that Lena wrote it for me," he added.

"Oh, no," Clare said. "She's wrong. That's not at all what—"

"And then there's all the Gaffer's crap about people coming around trying to steal William bloody Dunthorn's precious writing."

Felix shot her an anguished look. "They've gone off the deep end—both of them."

He shoved his seat away from the table and stood up.

"I can't stay here," he said.

There was a wild look in his eyes, like that of a caged animal.

"Felix, you can't just go."

"You're wrong. I can and I will. I've *got* to."

"At least stay here for the night."

Felix shook his head. "I'll find a place in Penzance, get the stupid cane for Lena, then I'm going to hitch back to London and find myself another job. I spent almost everything I had just to get here as quickly as I did. If Janey wants to talk to me, she can just show up at whatever dock my next ship happens to land in."

Clare caught his hand before he could walk away.

"The stores are closed tomorrow," she said. "It's Sunday."

"The antique shops . . . ?"

"It's not the tourist season anymore."

"Shit."

"I can lend her one of my canes. There's some business cards beside the typewriter in the study with the store's address on them. You can tell her to drop it off there when she's done with it. No sense in spending the money on a new one."

She let go of his hand and Felix moved to the doorway, pausing on its threshold.

"You believe me, don't you?"

Clare nodded. "I just wish I'd known earlier you fancied girls with canes." She obviously regretted saying that as soon as it was out of her mouth. "I'm sorry. This isn't a time for teasing."

"That's okay," Felix said. "I know you mean well. I'll keep in touch with you. And I'll come visit. I should have sooner, but I . . . ." He sighed. "I shouldn't forget what friends I *do* have."

"Don't write Janey off so quickly," Clare told him. "Things can still work out."

Felix merely shook his head. The coldness hadn't left him. He was still numb and shaken, but reality had settled in.

"There was never anything to work out," he said. "I see that now."

"You can't believe that."

"If there *had* been," Felix said, "she'd have heard me out."

"But that's just her temper. You know Janey, she's—"

"That's right. I do know Janey. Or at least I know her now. I . . ." He shivered. "I have to go, Clare. I just have to get out into the air. I feel like my head's going to explode if I don't. Where's that cane?"

"Beside my desk."

She followed him out of the kitchen into the study where he picked up the cane and a business card.

"Felix," she began when they were by the front door. "About that letter."

He shook his head. "I don't want to talk anymore. I'll call you before I leave Penzance tomorrow, okay?"

"But—"

"Thanks for the cane." He bent down and gave her a kiss. "I love you, Clare. Always have. You were always there for me. I'll try to make it up to you sometime."

He saw the tears starting up in her eyes. Before she could say anything more, he gave her a quick hug, then collected his luggage and went out the door.

2.

That's what you get for meddling, Clare thought as she watched Felix head back down Raginnis Hill towards the harbour.

She sighed and looked out over the rooftops to where Mount's Bay lay dark and brooding in the Cornish night. There were no stars visible over the water tonight, the sky being overhung with a cloud cover that promised rain. She looked back down the road, but Felix was gone now. The street was empty, except for the inevitable Mousehole cat. This one was the small calico female that lived a few doors down. She was prowling along the side of the road, stalking who knew what.

Clare watched her for a few moments longer, remembering the old story about the red cats of Zennor.

Between the two World Wars, a woman came to the village of Zennor, which lay on the north coast of Penwith Peninsula, and announced that she was going to breed tigers. The local authorities, needless to say, forbade her to do so, whereupon the woman promptly announced that if she couldn't breed tigers, then she would breed a red cat as fierce as a tiger. Now, if one was to go anywhere from St. Ives to Zennor, it was the oddest thing, but nearly every cat one would see would have a tinge of red about it.

When the calico disappeared into a garden across from the Wild Bird Hospital, Clare went back inside her own house and closed the door.

Meddling, she thought.

She'd always been a meddler.

It dated from when she was very young—just after her accident down by the cave—when the doctors told her parents that she'd never walk again. She'd been playing above Mousehole Cave and followed some older children who were clambering down the rocky fields to where the cave lay; only where their longer limbs took them easily down, with her smaller size, it was all she could do just to keep them in sight. She scrambled after them and one misjudged step later, she was tumbling straight down a twenty-foot drop.

She'd been lucky to come out of it alive, though that wasn't how she viewed things in the first bleak months of her convalescence.

The bones of one leg sustained multiple fractures, and to this day that leg remained thinner and weaker than the other as it had never healed properly. She could sense the weather in it, as an old sailor could in his bones. But there had been damage done to her spinal column as well.

For two years she'd had no use of her lower limbs. But she was determined to walk again and whether it was through the sheer persistence of her will—"Never seen a child with such heart," the doctor told her parents when, after an initial depression, she simply refused to give up her dream of walking again—or whether it was a miracle, eventually the nerves and muscles healed. She was in a wheelchair for three years after that, a walker for another six months, the crutches for far too long, but finally she could get about with a cane as she still did to this day.

The muscles never fully recovered, and she still had her bad days when her leg gave her such trouble she could only walk after taking a painkiller against the hurt, but what did she care about that? Compared to being a bedridden invalid for the rest of her life, her present mobility was a gift from heaven.

Janey had been her best friend before the accident, and stayed her friend after. While Clare was still bedridden, she came by after school to share her lessons, or just to gossip, and once Clare was mobile again—if only in her wheelchair—Janey pushed her about all over the village, struggling up the steep roads, hanging on the back as they played daredevil in places where the inclines weren't too steep.

Still, for all Janey's companionship, Clare had far too much time on her own. It was during this period that she began a lifelong love affair with the written word. And it was also then, when it appeared that she would only be able to sample a great deal of life vicariously, that she began her meddling.

It was Clare who convinced her mother to go back to school when Father died. She was the one who pushed Jack Treffry into trying out for the local rugby team where he did so well that he eventually turned professional. She, along with Dinny, kept after Janey when she was first starting up the pipes because Clare understood long before any of them that, while a fiddler was welcome at any session or barn dance, one needed something a bit more exotic to make a mark for oneself in the folk circuit where fiddlers were a penny a dozen.

It became such a habit that when she *could* take up the reins of her own life again, she continued to meddle in the affairs of others all the same. As she had with Janey and Felix.

But how, she asked herself, could she do anything but meddle when it came to them? They were the two friends she loved most in the world. And she *knew* they were right for each other. They were just each too thick-headed in their own way to put what was needed into their relationship to keep it together.

So she'd done what she could, only now it had backfired on them all.

Clare sighed.

She'd do anything for Janey. And when it came to Felix . . .

Her only real regret with Felix was that she hadn't met him before Janey had, but she knew she'd kept her feelings well hidden about that over the years—except for the stupid remark she'd blurted out to him just before he left.

Fancying girls with canes.

She wished.

But he and Janey were never to know and she could only hope that feeling as he had, Felix would simply forget her momentary lapse.

Time to set matters right, she thought as she put on a jumper her mum had knit for her last winter. Over that, she wore a yellow nor'wester against the coming rain and stuck a matching yellow rain hat in its pocket.

Leaving a note for her mum, in case she should wake up and

wonder where her daughter had gone off to when she said she was staying in for the evening, Clare let herself quietly out the front door and set off down the hill towards the Gaffer's house, her cane tap-tapping on the road by her side.

3.

Felix wished he were back at sea.

Mousehole, the closeness of its cottages and houses, its narrow streets and its sense of close-knit community, had none of its usual charm for him tonight. The lit windows behind which families went about their business were only reminders of what he didn't have. The buildings appeared to lean towards him, making him feel claustrophobic. The noisy revelry inside The Ship's Inn when he went by, the cheerful faces of its patrons, laughing and chatting as they kept one another company, was something he felt he'd never share.

And in his loneliness, the sea called to him. As it always did. It was what had kept him sane the last time he and Janey had broken up.

He walked past the harbour, listening to the tide murmuring, but even over its calming sound, all he could hear were Janey's accusations, the grim set to the Gaffer's voice, and Clare. Trying to explain it all away again.

Clare.

I just wish I'd known earlier you fancied girls with canes. . . .

Oh, Clare, he thought. I never knew.

He'd never seen past the friendship, past her warmth and gentle teasing, that he might have meant more to her than just a friend. But lost in his own anguish as he'd been, heart open and hurting, he'd been privy to her innermost longings in that one moment before she realized what she'd said and quickly covered it up.

Why couldn't he be like everyone else? Felix wondered, and not for the first time.

It wasn't just his stage fright that stood between Janey's and his happiness. He knew that, subconsciously, a part of him sabotaged their relationship for fear that it would be no different from that of his own parents. That was why he never opened himself up completely—it wasn't just the fear of ridicule.

He'd never even told Clare that.

And how kind had he been to her? How much of a friend? Writing, oh, yes, lots of long letters, but—never mind what he'd discovered tonight—all he seemed to do was lean on her, borrowing her strength because his love life wasn't going well, and all the time she'd loved him. From afar, as it were. Talking him through his problems with no hope of her own needs being fulfilled. . . .

He was outside of the village now, on the road to Newlyn and nearing the quarry. The sea still spoke to him and he made his way down the stairs by the old silos to the concrete wharf below by the sea where the ships used to dock to collect their loads of blue alvin stone. He put down his cases and Clare's cane. Sitting on the edge of the wharf, he looked out across the water.

What was he going to do with himself?

Run away again? Because that was what he *had* done the last time. Never mind that he and Janey had called it quits. He'd been as much a part of their quarreling as Janey had, but the old adage was true. It took two to argue. And for all that he'd tried to see things through, to stay calm and keep the dialogue going, had he really tried hard enough? Or had he simply given up, leaned on Clare until even her support could no longer sustain him, then simply run away?

He just didn't know anymore.

Why couldn't he just fit into a normal nine-to-five slot, instead of traipsing all over the world, looking for a heart's peace he was never going to find anyway? Marry, raise some kids, have friends in one place instead of scattered halfway across the planet. Not worry about whether he was going to turn out to be the same kind of a shit as his parents had been, just carry on with life. Not worry about playing on stage, just keep the music as a hobby. . . .

But, of course, it wasn't that simple. Nothing was. And no one's life was free of complications.

How many times hadn't he listened to friends, tied down to some office job by their mortgages and families, thinking he was such a lucky stiff for being footloose and free? How many times hadn't he heard about lost loves, and might-have-beens and if-onlys from them? What was so different between them and him? It was only details.

The woman he loved hated him, as did her grandfather.

He had some secretary-cum-struggling-actress interested in him because her boyfriend had dumped her and she was bored.

A woman he'd thought of as his best friend had been hiding romantic feelings for all these years.

The one thing he did well—playing music—was denied him as a career because he was too much of a chickenshit to fight a little stage fright.

He worked in a thankless job with no future, because the freedom of movement it gave him kept him from making too many lasting ties and the sea was the only thing that kept him sane. . . .

He was no more screwed up than anybody. He just hadn't learned how to deal with it properly. Other people's problems? He was always willing to listen and was all too good at handing out advice that could solve them if they only gave what he offered a try. His own? Don't think about them seemed to be his motto, and maybe they'll just go away.

But they never did.

They just got worse.

They got so bad that no matter where you turned, something was screwing up.

Felix watched the lights of a boat go by across the bay.

That was him, alone in the darkness. But didn't it only take his coming out into the light to make all his troubles go away? Wouldn't that at least be a start?

He just couldn't think about it anymore. Not right now.

He couldn't go back to Mousehole, to either the Gaffer's where he wasn't welcome anyway, or to Clare's where he was perhaps too welcome. Neither did he want to go into Penzance where Lena was sitting bored and alone in her hotel room.

Instead, he tried to give the sea an opportunity to calm the turmoil in him. That's what worked best. When he had the late watch on ship, or when he was in a place like this—that secret territory between sea and shore—he could almost step outside of himself and become part of some hidden otherworld where time moved differently and the familiar became strange. Then he understood how the sailors of old could have seen mermaids and sea serpents and ghost ships, how they could hear a music in the waves that could only be the beckoning of sirens.

For there was a music in the sea that Felix could hear at times like this. Not the obvious music of wave on shore, rattling stones on shingle beaches, waves lapping quietly against wharf and pilings, breakers thundering in desolate coves. But another, more exotic music that went deeper. That had its source in the hidden lands undersea and came to the ears of men from how it echoed with the movement of their heart's blood, rather than by physically vibrating against their eardrums. A music that called up tunes from his own fingers, to join its singular measures.

He reached behind him and took his button accordion from its case, setting it on his knee while he undid the bellows straps. It was a vintage three-row Hohner that he'd bought in a little shop in the old part of Quebec City. Its grillwork was battered, the instrument's casing scratched and worn, the bellows repaired so often they probably didn't have a bit of original material left to them. But the action on the buttons was still perfect, the reeds were true, and he'd yet to run across an instrument he fancied more, though the opportunity had come up often enough.

Felix loved rummaging about in old music shops, loved tracing the history of a particular box, or even just the instrument in general. Its origin was fascinatingly peculiar, coming about by happenstance rather than design.

A cousin to the mouth organ, the accordion was a free-reed instrument that was invented by a German named Christian Buschmann in the course of his development of the mouth-blown instrument. He produced a device that had twenty reeds on a brass table, powered by a leather bellows, which he called a "handaeoline." Further improvements were made by Demian of Vienna in 1892, who coined the name "accordion," but the first serious commercial production of diatonic accordions, or melodeons, was the work of the M. Hohner harmonica factory, situated in the Black Forest's Trossingen some fifty years later.

Felix had often suffered the ignorance of those unfamiliar with the instrument to whom the word "accordion" conjured up painful versions of "Lady of Spain"—a far cry from the music that Felix and his peers played. Those same souls, once they heard what could be done with both the piano and button accordion in traditional music, were, more often than not, won over with only a few tunes. And they were surprised at the instrument's heritage.

For before zydeco and rock 'n' roll, before Lawrence Welk and Astor Piazzolla, the "squeeze box" was being used in traditional music—to accompany Morris dancers in England and clog dancers in Quebec and on the Continent, and to give an unmistakable lift to the jigs and reels of Ireland and Scotland. Without the pedigree of the harp, the flute, the fiddle, or the various kinds of bagpipes, it had still developed a surprisingly large number of virtuoso players who were only just beginning to be acknowledged as some of the finest proponents of the folk tradition.

Their music could make the heart lift, the foot tap, and, as Felix had found so often, bring consolation to him when he was feeling depressed. The only thing better than listening was playing.

He slipped one shoulder strap over his right shoulder; the other went over the biceps of his left arm. Thumbing down the air-release button, he opened the bellows and ran through an arpeggio of notes, fingers dancing from one row to another as he went up and down the three-row fingerboard. He didn't touch the accompaniment buttons, just played a freeform music with his right hand to loosen up his fingers.

Then, still looking out across the choppy waters of the bay, he let the secret music hidden in its dark water mingle with the jumble and confusion inside him and he began to play.

It was a plaintive, disconsolate music that he called up that night. It neither cheered him nor eased his problems. All it did was allow him the expression of his sorrow and cluttered thoughts so that he could at least face them with a clearer mind.

The wounds of his heart ran too deep for an easy cure; healing would take more than music.

Two hours later, he finally set his instrument aside. A surreal calm touched him as he stored the accordion back into its case and then slowly rose to his feet.

He knew what he had to do now.

He would drop the cane off with Lena, but that was as far as he'd let her complicate his life. Then he'd go. He needed money, needed a job. But this time when he worked the ships, he'd save his money. He wouldn't moon over what was lost, or what couldn't be. He'd look ahead to what could be. He'd finally do something with himself; face life, rather than avoiding it.

Thinking of Janey still hurt—would always hurt, because it was impossible to simply put her aside as if she'd never had any importance—but he couldn't let his need for her continue to steer the course of his life.

And he would come back.

To Penwith. To Mousehole. Because he wouldn't let what couldn't be with her affect his friendship with Clare and Dinny and the others he knew in the area.

Not anymore.

Easy to say, he thought as he gathered up his duffel bag and slung it to his shoulder.

He picked up his accordion case and Clare's cane and started back up the stairs to the road that would take him into Penzance. He paused at the top to look back towards Mousehole. The village was mostly dark now. Above him the clouds let fall the first misty sheet of a drizzle that would probably continue throughout the night. His chest was tight again as he turned from the village and started to walk away.

His hard-won resolutions clotted like cold porridge inside him, sticking to one another in a tangle that no longer made the sense he'd thought he'd resolved them into only a few moments ago. It was all he could do to not turn around and go back.

Goddamn it, Janey, he thought. Why couldn't you have just *listened* for a change?

There was a wet sheen on his cheeks as he steeled himself to continue down to Penzance. Most of it was due to the light drizzle that accompanied him on his way.

But not all.

4.

All Janey wanted to do after the Gaffer had sent Felix off was crawl away and die. A numb, sick feeling settled over her. She sat slumped in an easy chair by the hearth, her arms wrapped around the Dunthorn book as though it were a life ring that would keep her from drowning. She stared at Jabez washing himself on the throw rug by her feet, not really seeing the cat, not really aware of anything except for the emptiness that had lodged inside her.

It was really true, she thought. You never knew what you wanted until you lost it.

She started when the Gaffer laid his hand on her shoulder.

"Don't blame yourself, my gold," he said. "It was none of your fault."

She nodded, not trusting herself to speak.

The Gaffer sighed. Giving her shoulder a squeeze, he went over to his own chair and sat down, the same unhappy look in his features.

"But who would have thought," the Gaffer began. He shook his head. "He seemed the best of men. . . ."

"He—he wasn't always . . . like this. . . ." She couldn't go on.

"No, my love," the Gaffer agreed. "I do suppose what hurts the most is being three scats behind to find out just what sort of a man he'd become since last we saw him."

Janey nodded again. There should have been some hint, shouldn't there? she thought. Surely a bloke couldn't change that much without it showing somehow? But he'd been just the same old Felix—the little she'd seen of him.

Bloody hell. Why did he have to go and do it?

To be fair, she had no claim on his heart. What he did with his love life was his own business, for all that it hurt. But to betray their trust by siding with those who were basically trying to rob Billy's grave. . . .

"We'll have to hide that book again," the Gaffer said, as though he were reading her mind.

"I—I just want . . ."

The Gaffer nodded. "You go ahead and finish it, my queen. But then it has to go away."

Trust things to go all awful like this, Janey thought. It had just been too perfect to last. Finding the book, Felix coming back, the reporter from *Rolling Stone* wanting to do a piece on her. . . . Trust it to turn all horrible. It was the story of her life. Surely she should have learned by now: Don't get too happy, or someone would come along and pull the carpet out from under her. Like bloody Alan making a mess of their upcoming tour. Like Felix arriving to wake a promise in her heart, only to stab her in the back.

She just wished she could feel angry instead of so lost.

"I have to go to bed," she said.

"Sleep in my room," the Gaffer said. "I don't want you next door on your own."

"I . . . I'll be all right. . . ."

"It's not your heart I'm thinking of, my gold; it's these bloody vultures out to pick Billy's bones. Best we stick together, you and I."

"All right," Janey said.

Still clutching the book, she went up to his room. She didn't bother to undress, just crawled under the comforter where she curled up in a fetal position and tried not to think. When Mike called a little later, she asked the Gaffer to tell him that she was sick and couldn't speak to him.

"Maybe you should see him," the Gaffer said. "It might take your mind off things."

"I—I can't see anyone, Gramps."

"Perhaps it's too soon," he agreed.

Any time, period, was going to be too soon, Janey thought as he went back downstairs. Oh, Felix, why did you have come back? I was doing just fine not remembering you until I saw you again yesterday.

She tried sleeping, to no avail. All she could do, when she wasn't crying, was lie there in the dark and stare up at ceiling. When she heard the doorbell ring downstairs, she up in bed, half hoping it was Felix, half dreading it. But when the visitor spoke, asking for her, she recognized Clare's voice and let out a breath she hadn't been aware she was holding. A pang of disappointment cut across her relief.

"She's not feeling well, my heart," she heard her grandfather say.

"She's still going to see me," Clare replied, "and you're both going to listen to me. Pardon my rudeness, Mr. Little, but you and Janey have been acting like a pair of twits tonight and I'm not leaving until I talk some sense into the both of you."

Janey burrowed back under the comforter. She couldn't face Clare's well-meaning, but this time misguided, attempts at getting her and Felix to reconcile. Not tonight.

"Now see here, you," the Gaffer began.

"No," Clare interrupted him. "You *will* listen to me." Louder, she called up the stairs: "Janey! I know you're here. Will you come down on your own or do I have to go up and drag you down here?"

Couldn't she be left alone with her grief?

"Janey!"

"I don't know rightly what's got into you, Clare Mabley," the Gaffer said, "but if you don't leave off your shouting, I'll—"

"You'll what? Call the police to come take me away? Go on and do it then, but I'll still have my say before they arrive."

"You don't understand," the Gaffer tried to explain. "What happened with Felix was—"

"No, you don't understand." Again a loud cry up the stairs: "Janey!"

Was the whole world going mad? Janey wondered. First Felix betraying them, now Clare carrying on, sounding angrier than Janey had ever heard her before.

"Janey!"

"You'll stop that shouting!" the Gaffer cried back.

Janey dragged herself out of bed. Still hugging the Dunthorn book to her chest, she shuffled out into the hall and stood at the head of the stairs, looking down at the pair of them. The Gaffer had gone all red in the face. Clare stood by the door, an equally angry look in her own features.

"Please don't fight," Janey said.

They turned like guilty children, then they both tried to speak at once.

"It's about time—"

"She wouldn't go—"

Janey held up her hands. She looked from Clare to the Gaffer, loving them both, wondering how things could have deteriorated to the point that they should all be at one another's throats.

"Why don't we make a pot of tea, Gramps," she said, "and then we can see what Clare wanted to talk to us about."

It felt decidedly odd to Janey to be acting as a mediator—especially between the Gaffer and Clare. Her grandfather was so good-natured that he was everybody's mate, and Clare was normally so even-tempered that Janey felt she could count on the fingers of one hand the number of times she'd seen her friend angry. But mediating helped keep at bay the bleak feeling that was inside her and she wanted to hear what Clare had to say—hoping, she had to admit to herself, that Clare would somehow be able to defend Felix's behavior, however unlikely that seemed.

It took a while, but when Janey and the Gaffer had heard her out, the three of them sitting in the kitchen with a pot of tea, Clare's story did exactly that. At the first mention of Lena, the Gaffer interrupted to explain who the woman was—that she'd come around earlier, sniffing after Dunthorn's secrets.

"I never knew," she said. "And neither did Felix."

Before the Gaffer could take the conversation off on a tangent, she went on with her story, refusing to be interrupted again until she was done. Then she let them speak.

"But I *saw* him and that American woman," the Gaffer said. "The two of them together on that bike, looking for all the world like a pair of lovers."

"And how else was he supposed to get her back to her hotel?"

"Did he never think of an ambulance?"

"And did you ever give him a chance to explain?" Clare shot back.

"He'd only *just* met her. Would you rather he'd left her there by the side of the road?"

Janey found herself nodding, then realized how spiteful she was being. Besides, if what Clare was saying was true, then Felix couldn't have known who this Lena was in the first place.

"That's well and fine," the Gaffer said, "but it still all rests on our taking Felix at his word."

"And did he ever lie to you before?" Clare demanded.

Janey shook her head. But the Gaffer nodded.

"There was that letter," he said. "Janey never sent it. I *believe* her."

"Of course she didn't send it," Clare replied. "I did."

Janey's eyes went wide. "You?"

Clare nodded. "Someone had to get the two of you back together again."

"So—so Felix had nothing to do with—with any of it . . . ?"

Janey felt about an inch tall. She turned to the Gaffer, the anguish plain in her eyes. The Gaffer looked as mortified as she felt.

"Of course he didn't! For God's sake, how could you even *think* Felix would be involved in anything that would hurt you?"

He wouldn't, Janey realized. And if she'd given it even a half moment's thought, instead of going off half cocked the way she had, she would have seen that.

Oh, Felix. Talk about betraying a trust. . . .

"I'm awful," Janey said. "I'm an awful, horrible person. How—how could I have treated him like that?"

"We both did," the Gaffer said bleakly.

"Well, it's partly my fault," Clare said. "I shouldn't have sent that letter. It just seemed like such a good idea at the time. . . ."

"It was a very good idea," Janey said.

Because seeing Felix again had made the world seem better. She'd been a little confused about her feelings at first, but that was only natural. Once she'd had a chance to think things through, she'd realized just how much she'd missed him. Yet now . . .

"Is he—is he at your place?" she asked.

Clare shook her head. "I lent him a cane that he was going to drop off with that Lena woman—I wonder if she even *did* sprain her ankle—and then he was going to hitch to London to get a job."

"How long ago did he leave?" the Gaffer asked.

Clare looked at the clock. "It took me a half hour to get here, and we've been talking for almost two hours. . . . I'm not sure. Say three hours all told?"

"What hotel was she staying at?"

"Felix never said."

"He'll be gone now," Janey said. Tears were welling up in her eyes again. "Bloody hell! Why couldn't I have listened to him?"

"You didn't know," the Gaffer began, reaching over the table to pat her arm.

She refused to be comforted.

"That's right," she said. "But I should have."

She rose from the table.

"Where are you going?" the Gaffer asked.

"To look for him—what do you think?"

"I'll come with you."

Janey shook her head. "This is something I have to do myself, Gramps." She turned to her friend. "Thanks, Clare. I mean that."

"If I hadn't sent that—"

"I'm *glad* you did," Janey said fiercely. "Now I have to see if I can't salvage something from what you started for me."

She went next door to get a jacket and her car keys and came back to find Clare and the Gaffer outside. Clare was just buttoning up her nor'wester. She was wearing a matching yellow hat against the light drizzle that had started up. The whole outfit made her look like one of the lifeboat Coastguards.

"Do you want a ride?" Janey asked her.

Clare shook her head. "You just go on and find Felix. I'll be fine."

"Clare, my gold," the Gaffer said. "I don't know how to say I'm sorry."

"We've all got things to be sorry about tonight," she told him. "Go on, Janey. I'll talk to you both tomorrow."

Janey waited a few heartbeats. Clare gave her a small smile, then started off for home. The Gaffer waved Janey to her car.

"Bring him back," he said.

Janey nodded. "I will, Gramps."

5.

Chapel Place, the small square on which the Gaffer's house stood, took its name from the old Methodist Chapel on its northeast corner. The chapel had a small yard, separated from the square by a low stone wall, the base of which was slightly raised from the street, for the village still climbed the hill towards Paul, here, where Duck Street became Mousehole Lane.

Sitting behind the wall, hidden from view and apparently listening to a Walkman, was Michael Bett. He wore a low-brimmed hat that hid his features and what appeared to be a pair of sunglasses but were, in fact, specially treated infrared lenses that served the double duty of both disguising him further from a chance glance and allowing him better night vision. He was bundled against the night's damp chill with a heavy sweater under his lined raincoat, thick denim trousers, and rubber shoes with a thick sheepskin insulation.

Removing the earplugs from his ears, he waited to hear the Gaffer's door close and for Clare's footsteps to fade. Not until the sound of Janey's three-wheeled Reliant Robin had died away as well, did he finally sit up.

When he'd hired the private eye Sam Dennison, part of Dennison's surveillance had included the installation of a state-of-the-art microphone/transmitter remote eavesdropping system. Four miniature wireless transmitter microphones had been placed in the Gaffer's house—one each in the kitchen, living room, and main bedroom upstairs, the fourth in Janey's rooms. At Bett's request, Dennison had left the microphones in place when he'd completed his surveillance.

The microphones had a transmission range of fifteen hundred feet—far more than Bett required in his present position, though he would have appreciated a greater range so that he could have remained in the comfort of his B and B, instead of crouching here in the drizzle. But then, he thought, he wouldn't be in such a perfect position to take immediate action, now would he?

Storing the receiver in the inner pocket of his coat, he hopped over the wall to the street below and made his way to the red box of a telephone booth he'd noted near the post office when he'd explored the village earlier. Fishing coins from his pocket, he put through a call. Lena answered on the second ring.

"Did anyone ever tell you that you have a beautiful telephone voice?" he asked her.

"What do you want?"

"Well, it's an odd thing, but I was listening in on a conversation that the Littles were having earlier with their good friend Clare Mabley, and what do you think I found out?"

"I'm not in the mood for games, Bett."

"Neither am I. I told you to *stay* in your hotel room this afternoon."

There was a momentary pause that Bett didn't fill. Let her think about it, he decided.

"I can explain," she began.

"Don't bother. Surprisingly enough, you didn't screw up." He filled her in on what he felt she needed to know about what he had recently learned, then finished up with, "He's going to be showing up at your room any minute now."

"Oh, shit."

"Do I detect a certain reluctance in your voice, dear Lena?"

"No. I . . ."

She was just regretting the trouble she'd brought into Gavin's life, Bett realized with surprise. Now there was one for the books. The Ice Queen was worrying about somebody else for a change. That was just what he didn't need now—to have the Ice Queen turn into a soft-hearted cow. Bad enough she was so stupid.

"Here's what's going to happen," he told her in a voice that would brook no further discussion. "He's going to show up at the hotel and you're going to keep him there, in your room, and you're not going to let him leave."

"But—"

"I don't care how you do it, just make sure that you don't screw it up. You see," he added, "if I find him wandering around the streets tonight, the next time he shows up in public will be when the tide washes his body in. Am I making myself clear?"

"What are you planning?"

"I've got some business with another of Janey Little's friends. Like you, she's been sticking her nose into what doesn't concern her. Unlike you, she's not going to get a second chance."

There was another moment of stiff silence as Lena digested that.

"Daddy said this was supposed to be a low-key operation," she finally said.

Bett laughed into the receiver. A low-key operation. Christ, she had the terminology down pat, but she didn't have the first clue as to what she was really talking about.

"This isn't some spy novel," he told her.

"But Daddy—"

"*I'm* in charge here. Just do it." He hung up before she could whine any more.

She was seriously getting on his nerves.

Opening the door to the telephone booth, he stepped out into the drizzle and took a few steadying breaths, hands opening and closing at his sides. It had been a long time since he'd taken someone apart to see how they worked, and the more he listened to her whiny voice, the more he wondered just how long she'd last under the knife.

She'd squeal. She'd beg and plead. She'd—

Forget it, he told himself.

He couldn't touch her. Not without Madden's okay. Just as he couldn't touch the Littles—at least not until they'd coughed up what the Order was looking for.

Fine. He could handle that. But no one had said anything about the Littles' friends.

Take the Mabley woman.

Yes, thank you. I do believe I will.

She was an interfering whore who couldn't be allowed to go around making everything hunky-dory anymore. He wasn't going to have the time to do her right, but he'd still get a little satisfaction out of throwing her off a cliff. He didn't like meddlers. And he didn't like cripples.

According to the file Dennison had compiled on her, she'd taken a fall once when she was a kid. Those cliffs out past her house were dangerous places for a crip. It'd be a real shame if she took another fall.

Poor Clare Mabley.

And poor Janey Little, losing a friend like that, hard on the heels of screwing up things with Gavin who—if Lena knew what was good for her—would soon be found in a compromising position with the "enemy."

Janey was going to need a friend. She was going to need comforting. And he knew just the man for her—Mike Betcher, ace reporter for *Rolling Stone*.

Bett felt calmer now, enough so that he cracked a smile as he set off to find the Mabley woman before she hobbled her way back to the supposed safety of her home.

He'd do her inside, if he had to.

It'd just make things that much easier if he could save himself the trouble of having to break in.

Lonely streets. Dark streets. Anything could happen on them. Even in a quiet little village like this.

6.

The Gaffer returned inside and shut the door behind him. He looked slowly about the room, feeling a constriction that he'd never experienced before in its cozy limits.

Came from doing the wrong thing, he thought. Clare had been correct in that much. They'd never given Felix a chance to explain himself at all. They'd treated him unfairly, as though he'd proved himself unworthy of their trust long before today's incident, and the Gaffer knew that he himself was the most to blame for that.

He wondered if Felix would forgive them. Wondered if they would be allowed the chance to find out. He could be anywhere, and the Gaffer didn't hold much hope that Janey would simply run across him. That smacked too much of chance, and chance, of late, had proved to be working against them.

His gaze settled on the copy of *The Little Country* that Janey had brought downstairs with her, but then left on the sofa when they had all gone into the kitchen to have their talk with Clare.

Whether Felix was innocent or not—and the Gaffer was inclined now to give Felix the benefit of the doubt—he still couldn't shake the feeling that Billy's book was at the center of the web in which all the events of the past few days had become entangled.

He picked up the book and took it to his chair by the hearth. He didn't have to open it to remember the story—for all that he hadn't dipped into its pages since that time, years ago, when he'd first read it. A time when, he recalled, another series of baffling events had made their presence felt in the Little household. It hadn't just been the vultures, out scavenging for anything that had belonged to Billy. There'd been other occurrences, less easily explained, but evident all the same.

Music heard, when it had no visible source.

Movement sensed from the corner of one's eye, but nothing being there when one turned to look.

An uncommon restlessness in himself and his young wife, Adeline, that was even less easily explained.

And their son Paul—starting and crying with night-fears late at night, when normally he slept through the dark hours and had no fear of the shadows under his bed, or in his closet.

All gone when the book was safely hidden once more.

"What did you do, my robin?" he asked the ghost of his old friend whom he could sense hovering near. "What did you hide in this book?"

Nothing that the Gaffer could see.

True, it was odd that it should have been published in an edition of only one, but that explained little. And the story—while told in Billy's remarkable prose—was no more remarkable than that of either of his previous books, though the Gaffer had liked it the best of the three.

He had particularly appreciated one of the lead characters who was the captain of a fishing lugger called *The Talisman,* back before the end of the pilchard industry. He became the best friend of the book's heroine, an emperent young orphan who had disguised herself as a boy and worked on *The Talisman* until she was found out. And wasn't there a row about that, for having a woman on board ship was bad luck, as any fisherman knew—nearly as bad as having a dog, or worse, a rabbit or a hare. The fishermen wouldn't even use the common names of animals while at sea, calling them two-deckers instead.

Billy had set their story in an imaginary town, but it had been easily recognizable to the Gaffer as a combination of Penzance, Newlyn, and Mousehole—the three rolled up together into one fanciful harbour town. There was a bit of the familiar Dunthorn magic in the book as well: the Smalls, whose miniature craft was found in the harbour one morning at low tide, and the hidden music that could grant any one wish, could one but remember its odd phrasing and repeat it. Both were details that Billy had used in his previous two books.

That had surprised the Gaffer some, for Billy hadn't been one to repeat himself, but the story itself had been a new one, and a good one. A story that the Gaffer had felt spoke directly to him when he was reading it, and became more so as he grew older and he could find parallels between his own life and that of *The Talisman*'s captain in the book.

Still, none of that explained why it should be of such interest to this Lena woman and her friends. Nor why they'd been searching for it for so long, for the Gaffer was convinced that this new interest was merely a renewed interest, though why he thought so, he couldn't have explained.

Thirty-five years it had been, now, since the crows had first come 'round looking for it.

He flipped through its pages, trying to fathom what it was about the book that made it more than merely a literary curiosity, but still nothing came to mind.

He paused for a moment, head cocked and listening, thinking he had heard something. Janey returning perhaps, or . . . he didn't know what. It was gone now.

Just the wind, he thought. Or a scatter of earnest rain, in among the drizzle.

He glanced at the clock to find that Janey had only been gone twenty minutes. He was tired, but knew he couldn't sleep until she returned—with Felix, or without him. He had to know.

Opening the book again, he decided to reread it while he waited. He smiled at the opening lines and was soon caught up in the familiar story, humming an old, half-familiar tune under his breath as he read.

The Moving Bog

From ghoulies and ghosties and long leggety beasties,
And things that go bump in the night, Good Lord, deliver us.

—CORNISH PRAYER

Don't look into her eyes!" Edern cried as the fetch moved aside to allow the Widow to bend down and peer in between the crates to where he and Jodi were hiding.

But his warning came too late.

That one enormous eye of the Widow's, staring at her with its unblinking magnetic gaze, had already pinned Jodi to the spot where she stood. It mesmerized her, called to her.

Come to me, come to me. . . .

Jodi took a step forward.

"Jodi, don't!" Edern called.

He might just as well have tried to catch water in a sieve, for the Widow's spell was already taking root in Jodi's mind. All she could hear was that warm, friendly voice, beckoning her to its promised safety.

Come to me, my pretty. . . .

As Jodi took a second step, Edern grabbed her by the arm and

shoved her roughly against the side of a crate. The jolting movement
was enough to momentarily break the Widow's spell.

"What . . . ?" Jodi began.

Edern's face was inches from her own.

"*Don't* look into her eyes," he warned again, "and don't listen to
what she says."

Before Jodi could argue, he caught her arm again and hauled her
deeper into the labyrinth between the crates. Freed now from the
Widow's mesmerizing gaze, Jodi shivered. Behind them, the Widow
called after them, her words dripping honey, promising them their
heart's desire if they would only return. Will she, nill she, Jodi found
herself starting to turn back until Edern gripped her arm again and
began to sing. His clear tenor voice cut through the Widow's enchantment leaving her words to lie bare and be revealed for the lies
they were.

But if she didn't listen to Edern's voice, it was so easy to just
believe. . . .

Edern, as though sensing how she was weakening again, sang
louder as he reached the chorus:

> "*Hal-an-tow,*
> *Jolly rumble-o,*
> *We were up, long before the day-o—*"

"Sing with me !" Edern cried.

Jodi hesitated for a heartbeat, then joined in on the familiar song.

> "*To welcome in the summer,*
> *To welcome in the May-o,*
> *For summer is a-coming in*
> *And winter's gone away-o.*"

Forgoing a verse that she might not know, Edern launched straight
into a repeat of the chorus. He kept a hand on Jodi's arm, pulling
her along when she seemed to falter in her step.

Singing at the top of their lungs, they retreated to where the wharf
ended and they could go no farther. They could still hear the
Widow's voice, but now the stretch of the massed crates between
them and the sound of the tide as it washed the pilings below stole
away its enchantment.

Finally, the Widow gave up and fell silent.

Jodi slumped against a crate. "Oh raw we," she said. "Wasn't that close?"

"Too close," Edern agreed.

"How can she do that with her voice? She must be able to get anything she wants from anybody."

Edern shook his head. "She needs to have a piece of you, first. Your name called three times, or a pinch of your soul, the way she's got that one of yours sewn up in her cloak. Can you imagine having a conversation with someone who, just before they ask you something, calls you by your full name three times? It wouldn't be long before they knew her for what she was and brought out all the old charms to ward off her spells."

"Still, we're safe for now, aren't we?"

"Not for long. And don't forget, they'll be loading these crates soon and then where will we hide?"

"Maybe we can get inside one of them?" Jodi tried.

"And end up where?"

She nodded glumly. "Bother and damn. You'd think—" She paused to lift her head, smelling at the air. "What's that awful pong in the air?"

She couldn't really make out Edern's features in the gloom, but she could sense his sudden tension.

"Edern," she said. "What's the matter?"

"She has more power than I gave her credit for," he replied.

"*What* are you talking about?"

Jodi stood up as she spoke because the wood planking of the wharf under her was becoming damp. The smell grew worse: It was like the stink raised from disturbing stagnant waters. Standing, she wiped at the seat of her trousers and wrinkled her nose. The planking underfoot was acquiring a definite spongy feel to it.

"Have you ever heard of a sloch?" Edern asked.

"No," she said, shaking her head. The motion was lost in the darkness. "Why do I get a bad feeling about what you're going to tell me?" she added.

"Because they're terrible creatures—especially to folk our size."

Jodi could hear something approaching now—more than one something, each moving with a wet, sucking sound.

"Normally a witch will use them like a fetch," Edern explained, "but they are only temporary fabrications. They rarely live out the night in which they were created."

Jodi stared back the way they had come, into the shadows. In the distance she could make out a dull green glow, but that was all. The reek was truly awful now and there was a chill in the air that had nothing to do with the normal damp of an autumn night in Bodbury.

"What *are* they, Edern?"

"They're made from materials collected in a bog—fouled mud and rotting twigs, bound together with decaying reeds and rushes. Stagnant water runs in their makeshift veins like muddy blood. Their eyes glow with the marsh gas that the witch combines with a spark of her own soul when she animates them."

Jodi could see the ghostly pinprick glow of those eyes as he spoke—small malevolent sparks that shone brightly in the sickly green glow that preceded the creatures. The stench was so bad now that she had to breathe through her mouth.

"What are they going to do to us?" she asked. "What *can* they do?"

By the glow that seemed to emanate from their skin, she could see the shape of them now as the sloch shuffled wetly forward. Stick-thin limbs attached to fat-bellied torsos, squat heads atop, connected without the benefit of necks. Jodi gagged, nausea roiling in her stomach, as a new wave of their stench rolled towards her. Underfoot, the wharf's planking had become as soggy as the soft ground of a bog.

"They can take us back to the Widow," Edern replied bleakly.

"No," Jodi said. "I won't go back."

"They can pull us to pieces, those things," Edern said. "They're far stronger than their origins would lead you to believe."

"There must be something we can do."

But there was nowhere left to go, no place to turn. They were backed up to the edge of the wharf now. Below lay the sea. On either side, crates blocked their way. And in front of them, approaching slowly but inexorably, came the Widow's reeking creatures.

"There's nothing," Edern said. "Unless. . . ." He turned to look at the dark waters below. "Can you swim?" he added.

"Yes, but the size we are . . . How would we ever make it all the way to shore?"

"It's the chance you'll have to take—the only one left to you. The brine of the sea will protect you."

"What do you mean, protect *me*?"

"Witches are like hummocks in that way," Edern said. "Neither can abide the touch of salt. That's something the travelers know, if others have forgotten it."

"I meant," she said, "the way you just said me. What about you?"

The sloch were close enough so that their faces could be made out in the feeble light that their bodies cast. Jodi wished they had stayed in the shadows. They had heads like turnips, featureless except for leering grins that split the bottom parts of their faces and those ghastly glowing eyes. The very lack of other features made them that much more horrible to her. This close, their reek was unbearable.

"I can't swim," Edern told her.

"I'll help you—Taupin showed me how to swim while towing someone along with you. It's not so hard."

"You don't understand—it's not just that I can't swim. I would sink to the bottom of the ocean as soon as I touched the waves."

"That's nonsense. Why would you—"

"Trust me in this."

"I'm not going without you."

Edern took a step away from her, towards the horrible creatures.

"You must," he said. "Remember the Men-an-Tol. Go nine times through it at moonrise."

"I'm not—"

But she had no more chance to argue. Edern ran at the creatures, ramming into them as though he were a living battering ram. The foremost sloch went tumbling down, falling into the ones behind. A weird hissing arose in the air that sounded like an angry hive of bees.

"I want them alive!" Jodi could hear the Widow faintly cry from beyond the crates.

Jodi danced nearby the struggling figures, trying to get a kick in, but Edern was blocking her way. The passage between the crates was so narrow that only a pair of the creatures could get at him at one time.

"Let me help!" Jodi cried.

But "Go!" was Edern's only response, made without his turning his head towards her.

He grabbed the arm of the closest creature and pulled it from its torso. Black, muddy blood sprayed about. A drop splattered against the back of Jodi's hand, stinging like a nettle. And Edern, who took the brunt of the spray—

Jodi started to gag.

His features seemed to be melting. Where once had been his somewhat handsome face, now there were runnels of dripping skin, like wax going down the side of a candle.

"Y-you—" she began.

He pulled the limb from another of the sloch and a new spray of the stinging blood erupted. The bee-buzz of the creatures grew higher pitched and angrier now. The sloch in the rear began to clamber over their fallen comrades to get at Edern.

"No!" Jodi heard the witch cry. "You'll ruin them!"

Jodi nodded dumbly in agreement.

"Don't hurt him . . ." she said in a small voice.

Him? she thought. Was he even a person?

She took a hesitant step forward. Edern turned towards her, his face melted now to show metal, not bone, under the skin. The polished steel gleamed in the light that came from the creatures' bodies. Jodi put a hand to her mouth, too shocked to even speak. A sloch punched a hole in the little man's chest. When it withdrew its arm, clockwork mechanisms spilled forth, gears and little wheels and ratchets rolling across the soggy planks of the wharf.

Frozen in place, Jodi stared at what Edern was revealed to be: a clockwork man.

Like something she might find on Denzil's worktable.

But he'd walked and talked like a real person. Clockwork mechanisms moved with stiff, jerky motions. They couldn't speak. They couldn't feel. They . . .

"You . . ." she began. "You can't. . . ."

This couldn't be real.

The sloch pushed him aside. More cogs and tiny geared wheels spilled from his chest as he hit the soggy wharf planking.

None of this was real.

But he looked up at her, life still impossibly there in his eyes.

"Remember," he said. "The stone. Nine times through its hole. . . ."

His voice had a hollow ring to it now.

"Remember," he repeated.

She nodded numbly. At moonrise.

"You fools!" she heard the Widow cry.

She backed away from the shuffling creatures, gaze still locked on

Edern's ruined face. When the light finally died in his eyes—no, the eyes simply changed from a real person's eyes to ones made of glass—she turned and ran towards the edge of the wharf.

The creatures followed. The air was filled with their bee-buzz anger. Their reek was almost a physical presence in the air. She could hear the Widow shouting, caught a glimpse above her of Windle peering down at her through a crack in the crates, then she reached the edge and launched herself out into the air.

Moments later, the dark waves of the sea closed in over her head.

2.

Denzil and Taupin traveled back and forth through Bodbury for hours, but could find no trace of Jodi. It was as though she had simply vanished into thin air.

Early in their search, Taupin had enlisted the help of Kara Faull, one of the Tatters children, by the simple method of tossing pebbles at her window until she came down to see what they wanted. Once the situation had been explained to her, she set off on her bicycle and soon there was a whole gaggle of Tatters children scouring the town as well. From time to time, one of them would pedal up to wherever Denzil and Taupin were to give a report.

"She hasn't been seen on the Hill."

"No sign of her in old town."

"We've been up and down New Dock, but didn't see a thing except for the Widow walking with what looked to be the ugliest cat I ever did see."

"It had no fur, I'll swear."

"Garm, yes. And such a pong there near the wharves."

Well past midnight, the children had all returned to their beds and only Denzil and Taupin remained to continue the search, neither of them knowing how to proceed now.

"Well," Taupin said finally, sitting on a low stone wall by the Old Quay. "We've done it logical, haven't we?"

"Why do I not want to hear what you're going to tell me next?" Denzil asked.

Taupin smiled. "All the same, it's time we considered the impossible now." At Denzil's frown, he added, "We did agree to that."

"You decided that."

"Have you got a better idea?"

"We could take another turn around by . . ." Denzil's voice trailed off as Taupin shook his head.

"To what purpose?"

"To find Jodi, you!"

"Will you give me a chance to explain?"

Denzil sighed. "All right. But I'm worried, Brengy."

"I am, too."

"What did you have in mind?"

Taupin pointed with his chin over to the far side of the Tatters where a number of old warehouses stood.

"We'll go ask Henkie."

"Now I know you're mad," Denzil said.

Hedrik Whale was the town reprobate. As his surname hinted, he was an enormous man, standing six-foot-three and weighing some three hundred pounds. He had a beard that came down to his waist, portions of which he wore in tiny braids, and hair cropped so short he might as well have simply shaved his scalp. He gadded about town in paint-stained dungarees and old workboots, a knee-length jersey and an ever-present scarf.

Years ago, when the pilchard died out, he had used the immense inheritance left him by his father—Rawlyn Whale, of Whale Fisheries—to buy up a few of the old Tatters warehouses, which he peopled with the derelicts of the town. One he kept for his own use and in it he stored an immense library and the enormous canvases upon which he worked. His paintings were invariably of beautiful women—who for some unknown reason were attracted to him in droves for all that he almost always smelled as though he hadn't washed in a week—and his style was stunning. His canvases seemed to literally breathe—not just with life, however, but with lewdness and debauchery as well.

His real notoriety—if one discounted the mural of the town council depicted in various states of inebriation and undress that he'd painted on the side of one of his warehouses—was the curious case of a missing corpse. When one of his derelict friends, a certain John Briello of no fixed age nor address, died a few years ago, Henkie, rather than giving the fellow a proper funeral, had followed Briello's instructions and had his friend stuffed.

He'd kept the body propped up in a corner of his studio until the authorities got wind of its existence, but when the constables arrived en masse at the studio, the body wasn't to be found. Nor was it ever heard of again, save in rumour.

For all Denzil's admiration of the man's craft—or at least the stylistic excellence of his craft, for Denzil, if the truth be told, was somewhat of a prude—he'd never been able to spend more than a few minutes in the man's company. Henkie smelled bad and, for all his artistic ability, was himself an obese eyesore. He was brash, unreasonable, crude, offensive, belligerent . . . in short, not an easy man to like.

"You only have to get to know him," Taupin argued.

"That," Denzil said, "is what I'd be most afraid of, you."

"He can help us," Taupin insisted.

"Tee-ta-taw. About as much as the Widow could."

"No," Taupin said. "But he has some of her rumoured talents."

Denzil rolled his eyes. "I suppose he can scry with a glass ball?"

"Better. He can speak with the dead."

"You really are mad, you."

Taupin stood up from the wall and made a great show of dusting some nonexistent lint from the sleeve of his coat.

"It makes no sense," Denzil said.

Taupin studied his nails, then dug into his pocket until he came up with a penknife that he used to clean one.

"It would be a complete waste of time," Denzil tried, obviously weakening.

Taupin began to whistle a bawdy pub song and turned to look out at the harbour.

Denzil sighed. "I know I'll regret this," he said.

Turning to face him again, Taupin gave Denzil a hearty clap on the back.

"That's the spirit, old sport," he said. "Optimism. One can do wonders with optimism. Bottle it up and serve it as a tonic, I wouldn't doubt, if we could only find a way to distill its particular—"

Denzil straightened his glasses, which had gone all askew on the end of his nose, and pushed them back until they were settled in their proper place once more.

"Can we just get this over with?" he asked.

"—healing properties." Taupin gave him a grin. "You won't regret this."

"I already regret it," Denzil assured him as they set off along the Old Quay towards Henkie's warehouse.

The woman who answered their knock was a breathtaking brunette whose only clothing was a sheet that she'd obviously only just half-heartedly wrapped about herself for the express purpose of answering the door, for it was also obvious, from the light that shone behind her, that she wore nothing underneath it. Denzil recognized her and couldn't help being surprised to find her in this place.

Her name was Lizzie Snell, and by day, she was the mayor's secretary.

"Hello, Brengy," she said. "And Mr. Gossip. What brings you by at this time of night?"

"Is Henkie still up?" Taupin asked.

Lizzie blushed. "Well, he was when I left him."

"I meant, can he see us?"

"Oh. I'll see. Do you want to wait inside?"

She closed the door behind them once they'd come in, then wandered off into a labyrinth of bookcases leaving them in the company of a fifteen-foot-high painting of herself in which she wore no sheet to disguise her undeniably generous charms.

"Beautiful," Taupin said.

"Yes," Denzil said after one quick eye-popping look. He turned away and studiously looked at a pamphlet that he picked up from the table by the door. "He's a gifted artist."

Taupin laughed. "I meant Lizzie."

Denzil read the title of the pamphlet—"The Care and Spiritual Welfare of the Penis: A Study by Hedrik Whale"—and hastily returned it to the table.

This night was proving far too long, he thought.

"Perhaps we should go," he said to his companion. "It's obvious we're rousing him from his, ah, bed, and—"

"Go?" a deep voice boomed out. "Bloody hell. But you've only just arrived."

Denzil blinked for a moment as he turned, thinking a bear had come trundling out from between the bookcases where Lizzie had disappeared earlier, but then he realized it was only their host—all three hundred pounds of him, wrapped in a bearskin. His own hairy legs protruded from underneath, appearing oddly thin. Lizzie came up behind him, dressed now in a loose Arab-styled robe.

"Tea for everyone?" she asked.

"Or something stronger?" Henkie boomed.

His voice, Denzil remembered as he fought the impulse to rub his ears, was always this loud.

"Tea would be fine," Denzil said. "Wonderful, really."

"I'll have the something stronger," Taupin said.

A half hour later they sat around a potbellied coal stove that stood in a corner of the warehouse given over to be a makeshift sort of kitchen. Lizzie and Denzil were both on their second cups of tea. Denzil had lost track of how much whiskey Taupin and their host had consumed. Amenities had taken up most of that half hour as Henkie and Taupin brought each other up-to-date on what they'd been up to since the last time they'd gotten together, but finally Taupin got around to relating the reason behind their visit.

"Oh, I never liked that Widow," Lizzie said. "She's always about his lordship's office, complaining of this, wanting that."

"Not to mention what a pissant Tremeer is," Henkie added. "Bloody stupid constables."

"Had another run-in with them?" Taupin asked.

Henkie nodded. "Don't start me on it."

Yes, Denzil thought. Don't.

Happily, after a moment of dark brooding, Henkie turned to Denzil.

"Brengy's got the right of it," he said. "There's the stink of magic in the air tonight."

Not to mention the odor of unwashed bodies, Denzil thought. He stole a glance at Lizzie. How could she sleep with the man?

"But I think we can help you," Henkie added.

"You see?" Taupin put in.

"How can you help?" Denzil asked.

"Well, it won't be me, directly," Henkie said. "We'll have to ask Briello."

Denzil could only stare at him. "Pardon?"

"My mate, John Briello."

"The *dead* John Briello?"

"Who else?"

Denzil turned to Taupin. "I really think we should go, you."

"Don't be so hasty to judge what you don't bloody well understand," Henkie told him.

"Dead men don't talk," Denzil said flatly. "But whiskey does."

Henkie's eyes went hard. "Are you calling me a liar?"

All of Denzil's instincts told him to back down, but that simply wasn't his way. He pushed up his glasses with a stiff finger and met Henkie's gaze, glare for glare.

"If you tell me that I can get advice from a dead man," he said, "then yes, I'm calling you a liar."

Henkie glared at him, then burst into a sudden laugh. "Oh, I like you, Denzil Gossip. You've a dry wit, and that's rare in bloody brain-dead Bodbury, isn't it just?" Turning to Taupin, he added, "But we'll have to blindfold him."

"Denzil won't mind," Taupin replied. "After tonight he'll realize he's been going all through his life with blinders on."

Denzil shot him a hard stare and got to his feet. "I've got a friend to find and I don't have time to—"

"Oh, do sit down," Henkie boomed.

"Don't take it so hard," Lizzie said. "They're just teasing you."

"I'm not in the mood for jokes tonight," Denzil said stiffly.

"Oh, but it's no joke," she assured him. "Briello really will be able to help you. I've heard him talk myself."

"But—"

"I know it doesn't make sense, but then not much does in this world, does it?"

"No more talk," Henkie said. "Lizzie, get us a scarf to blindfold our friend here—you will allow yourself to be blindfolded?"

"Well, I don't—"

"Good."

"Don't worry," Lizzie said as she came up behind him. She took off his glasses and stuck them in the breast pocket of his jacket, then drew the scarf across his eyes. "I'll make sure you don't take a tumble."

She took him by the arm and then led him off before he could frame another protest.

They walked across wood first—Denzil could hear their footsteps on the planking—then, after the creak of a door of some sort, they were outside, on cobblestones. Denzil could smell the sea in the air. The wind tousled his hair. Moments later they were in another building, then descending a stone stairway. Many stairs and turns later, he heard the creak of another door, and then the scarf was removed. He stood blinking in lantern light, feeling a little disoriented as he fished his glasses from his pocket.

He found himself in a cellar of some sort, only it had been fashioned after a Victorian sitting room. Taupin held the lantern, which cast a bright glow over the furnishings. The walls, not surprisingly, were festooned with Henkie's artwork. Lizzie stood beside him, the scarf hanging from her hands, a reassuring smile on her lips. And Henkie—Henkie stood, still barefoot and wrapped in his bearskin, beside the preserved corpse of a derelict that was leaning up against the far wall.

Except for a somewhat withered look about its skin, and the stiff posture of its limbs, the corpse could almost pass as a living man, Denzil thought. Except a living man didn't have a silver coin in each eye.

Denzil swallowed dryly, sure now that he'd got himself caught up in the clutches of a group of Bedlamites. He gave the door behind him a surreptitious glance, but while it didn't appear to be locked or barred, he doubted he'd be able to get it open and flee before one or another of his captors brought him down.

He turned to Taupin, an admonishment taking shape on his tongue, but before he could speak, Henkie, who had been explaining Denzil's problem to the corpse all this while, was just finishing up.

"So, old mate. Can you tell us where she's gone and bloody well lost herself?"

Denzil, unable to help himself, had to look at the corpse. And then his jaw fell slack.

For the corpse moved. The coins in its eyes blinked eerily in the lantern light as the dead man slowly turned its head towards him. The jaw creaked as it opened and the sound that issued forth was like the wind from an open grave.

But it *was* a voice.

The corpse *could* speak.

"I can see her," it said. "She seems very small."

"La, Jey," Denzil murmured in a hoarse voice. He felt decidedly faint.

"I do believe the sea has her in its grip," the corpse went on. "Out by New Dock. But she's very small. The size of a mouse, seems, but that can't be, can it?"

It turned its head towards Henkie, silver-coin eyes flashing again, and gave a dusty-sounding laugh.

"I'm one to talk about what can or can't be—aren't I just, Henkie?"

It was done with mirrors, Denzil was trying to convince himself. Or they'd drugged him. Hypnotized him. Driven him bloody mad. . . .

"You're sure about that?" Henkie was asking. "She's the size of a bloody wee mouse and floating in the sea?"

"Oh, yes," that dry voice replied.

"In a boat?"

"No, she's wet and shivering and won't last long."

Ventriloquism, Denzil decided. That's how it was being done. And there was someone behind the wall, manipulating the corpse in some manner to make it look as though it could move.

"Thank you," Henkie was saying.

"Do you have something for me?" the corpse asked.

"A new painting—it's almost done."

Now those dry lips actually smiled. Denzil couldn't tear his gaze away from the sight.

"That will be wonderful," the corpse said.

And then it went still.

"We'll have to hurry if you want to rescue your friend," Henkie said.

Lizzie started towards Denzil with the scarf, but he shook his head and crossed the room until he stood directly in front of the corpse.

"Rubbish," he said, lifting a hand towards its face. "The thing's not real. The dead can't—"

Suddenly the corpse's arm lifted up and dead fingers gripped his wrist.

"The size of a mouse," it said, blowing a grave-cold breath in his face. "Now how do you suppose *that* came about?"

Denzil shrieked and jumped back. His glasses flew from his nose. He tripped over a table and would have fallen, except that Henkie caught and steadied him. In that moment of confusion, the corpse returned to its initial position. Denzil stared at it.

Lizzie, who had caught his glasses, handed them to him. With trembling fingers, Denzil got them back into place. He couldn't seem to stop his hands from shaking, so he stuck them in his pockets.

"Come along," Henkie said. "We don't have long to help your friend."

"But—but . . ."

The scarf came over his eyes, blessedly removing the corpse from his sight. Moments later they were leaving the room and beginning the trek up the series of stairways once more.

"It just couldn't be," Denzil kept muttering as he let himself be led along. "*How* could it be?"

It couldn't. It was that simple. He'd imagined—been made to imagine—the whole ridiculous affair. There was no other logical explanation.

But he could still feel the grip of those dead fingers on his wrist.

Four Bare Legs Together

And, after all, what is a lie? 'Tis but
The truth in masquerade.

—LORD BYRON, from *Don Juan, canto XI*

Lena listened to the dead phone for a few moments after Bett had cut the connection, then slowly cradled the receiver.

This wasn't the way things were supposed to go, she thought.

She got up and hobbled over to the window to look outside. A misting rain was sprinkling on the Promenade, giving the surface of the street a shiny wet sheen under the streetlights. Beyond the stone wall separating the sidewalk from the rocky beach below, the waters of Mount's Bay swelled and dropped on the timeless wheel of the tides.

Daddy had made a mistake, she realized. She really shouldn't be here.

It wasn't that she didn't think she could get the job done. And for all her lack of success so far, not to mention the stupid accident with the bike, it was kind of fun. Just *like* a spy novel, never mind what Bett had to say about it.

But to be a part of a murder . . . to have foreknowledge, and not do anything about it. . . .

That didn't sit right.

She didn't know Clare Mabley, except from the files she'd read on the woman. She owed Mabley nothing. But that didn't make a shred of difference to the way she felt at the moment. The woman didn't deserve to die—not simply because she was Janey Little's friend and she was interfering with Bett's plans for Little.

She wondered if Daddy even knew what Bett was up to here. It was one thing to be ruthless in business. She could even condone a little strong-arming, if it became necessary and there was no other option, but not when it was directed at an innocent party. And it made her a little sick to understand just how much Bett would enjoy it.

Because he *would* enjoy it. She knew that much. Whenever she was in his presence, she could sense that core of controlled violence that lay just below the surface in him, straining to get loose. She knew enough about men to recognize that aspect in them when it was present. There were those who talked the tough talk, and then there were those who just did it, and they were the ones you really had to look out for. Because their violent impulses owed nothing to common anger. Instead they were born out of either an amoral view of the world, or worse, a sick need to hurt others.

In Bett, it was probably both.

Maybe the Order, through Madden, had made a mistake in sending him here.

She could still remember the night that her father had initiated her into the secrets of the Order. She was seventeen and had thought the whole idea of this secret group of old men and women who wanted to rule the world to be both goofy and terrifying. But it hadn't just been old men and women waiting for her the night that the Order of the Grey Dove welcomed her into their ranks.

There were three generations represented in that church in upstate New York where they had gathered, men and women both. People old enough to be her grandparents—though her own, from both sides of the family, were dead and Daddy would never tell her which of them, if any, had been members. Then there was her father's generation. And lastly, teenagers, only one of them younger than she was herself.

They were all masked—costumed, she'd thought at the time, like the members of some Elk Lodge getting ready for a parade, though if the Order was a lodge, then it was a sinister one. There had been blood, and she still didn't know if it had been human as one of the other younger initiates had told her later, and there had been a ritual. And there had been the tattoo.

It would all have seemed ridiculous if it hadn't been so deadly serious. And then, as years went by and she was initiated into the deeper mysteries, when she found that you could get anything—*any-thing*—you wanted, just through the use of your will, it hadn't seemed frivolous at all anymore.

Did you want to live forever?

The Order claimed it was possible. Many of the older members avowed to be well over a hundred, though not one of them seemed more than sixty.

Was it prosperity you desired?

They were all wealthy and even though Lena had been born into wealth herself, who didn't want more?

Did you want to wield power over others?

Through the proper use of your will, the Order's secrets taught you how to control the sheep. And if sometimes more physical manipulations—such as the surreptitious use of drugs or other external machinations—were necessary, there was a kind of magic needed to utilize them to their fullest potential as well.

Lena had thrived in that environment, for all that she maintained a somewhat distant and decadent attitude towards the Order. Why give them the satisfaction of thinking they controlled her as well? For she saw that as another aspect of the Order, how the elder members lorded it over the younger; viewed them, in fact, as another kind of sheep.

In many ways the Order was no different than society at large. One rose through its ranks the same as one did in the business world, or in the whirl of society.

Lena preferred to take what she could use, but played their game as little as possible. She had other uses for the knowledge that she'd acquired. Rather than being on the Order's lower rungs, she elected to create her own little circles of power, making sure only that they didn't interfere with any of the Order's.

It only backfired at times like these, when her father, frustrated at his lack of control over his own daughter—and undoubtedly embarrassed when in the company of other members of the Order because of that same lack of control—sent her off on a chore such as this to prove that he could still govern her.

Usually she made the best of it, getting through the task as quickly as possible so that she could return to the social rounds of Boston in which she was a leader, rather than a sycophant. Unfortunately, this time Felix Gavin had to come along to complicate matters.

In some way that she still didn't quite understand, he'd cut through the shield of debutante bullshit by which she held the world at bay, and walked straight into her heart, making her actually care what happened to someone else for a change. And the worst of it was, it didn't feel bad. Except for the hopeless feelings she had for him.

So what was she supposed to do?

Sighing, she took her gaze from the world outside her window and looked down at her wrist. The grey dove, symbol of her father's precious Order. Were those old men and women at all aware of the dark malicious streak that ran through Bett?

Probably.

But she still felt she should call her father.

She limped back to the bed and had the receiver raised in her hand, before she cradled it once more, the call unmade. Another realization had come to her.

Daddy was sending Jim Gazo over to serve as her bodyguard, but there was no way Jim would make it here before tomorrow morning at the earliest. Until then, she was on her own. If she called her father, and Daddy got Madden to call Bett off, Bett would come by to take it out on her. He'd probably go ahead and kill Mabley anyway, then come back and hurt her, and damn the consequences. Just like he really would kill Felix if she didn't find a way to keep him here tonight.

Michael Bett was just that kind of man.

Until tomorrow, she was on her own. Neither Daddy nor the Order could help her until then. Which brought her circling back to that same question: Just what the hell did she do now?

Self-preservation came first. No question there. But the Mabley woman . . . Could she really just stand by and let Bett kill her? And what about Felix? She was having very weird feelings when it came to him. She found she didn't want to lie to him. God help her, she wanted a chance to win him away from Janey Little, honestly and without subterfuge.

It wasn't going to work. None of it was. So she was going to have to settle for a trade-off. Mabley's life in exchange for the lie that would keep Felix here. And maybe, when it all came out in the end, he'd understand. Because Mabley was Felix's friend as well, wasn't she?

She picked up the phone again.

"Hello, Willie?" she said when the connection was made. "No, don't worry. He's not around. Yeah, I don't much care for him either. Listen, this is important. Remember that friend of Janey Little's that Gavin was with this morning? That's right, the Mabley woman. Someone's going to try to kill her tonight.

"No, I don't know who," she lied. "It's just important that she isn't hurt. Can you call that friend of yours in Mousehole and have him deal with it? No, right now. The last I heard, she was on her way home from the Little house. There's a thousand dollars in it for you"—let him figure out the exchange rate—"if she makes it through the night—the same again for your friend.

"Thanks, Willie. I kind of thought you'd be interested. Just make sure you don't screw this up, because—"

There was a knock at her door.

"I'll talk to you later, Willie," she said and hung up.

She ran a hand through her hair and looked nervously across the room.

"Who's there?" she called.

"Felix."

Okay, she thought. I've done my part, now it's up to you to do yours, Felix. Because if you blow it, we're both screwed.

"Just a sec," she called.

She gave herself a quick look in the mirror as she hobbled over to the door, wincing when she put too much weight on the bad ankle. The pained look on her face when she opened the door owed nothing to acting.

"I'm sorry to be coming by so late," Felix began, "but—"

"God," she said, interrupting him. "You look terrible."

He gave her a faint smile, but she didn't miss the pain that was lodged there in his eyes. He was soaking wet, short hair plastered to his scalp, clothing drenched. He had a duffel bag over one shoulder, a square black box on the floor by his side. In his hand he held a cane.

Got it from Clare Mabley, she thought, with a twinge of uneasiness. Willie, you'd better come through for me.

"Come on in," she added.

"I can't stay. . . ."

"That's okay. Just come in for a moment. What did you do, go for a swim?"

"No. It's just that it's raining—"

"I can see that." She took the cane from him and used it to step back from the door. "That's better. You're an angel, Felix. Really. Where did you find it? Come in," she added when he hesitated out in the hall.

"I really can't stay." He dug about in his pocket and handed her a business card. "The cane belongs to a friend of mine—"

"*The* friend?"

He shook his head, the pain deepening in his eyes. "No. But I saw her tonight. She—that is we . . . I don't really want to talk about it."

"So don't. It's okay. You don't have to do anything you don't want to, Felix."

"I just came by to give you the cane. I got it from the woman whose name is on the card. If you could just drop it by the shop when you're done."

"No problem. It was kind of her to lend it."

"Yeah, well, Clare's a good person."

"I'll look forward to meeting her."

Don't screw up, Willie, she thought.

"I'm heading on to London," Felix added. "I just have to get away."

Lena nodded. "Sometimes that's all you can do." She gave him a sympathetic look, then added, "Will you *come* in? Just long enough to dry off a bit, at least. You look like—well, now I know what they mean about something the cat dragged in."

"I don't think—"

"I won't bite."

When he still hesitated, she moved forward—putting on a good show of how much the movement hurt her—and reached for the black case by his foot.

"Okay," he said, picking it up for himself. "But just for a moment."

Lena moved back to clear the doorway. "Why don't you hang your coat on the chair by the window where the heater can dry it off a bit? I'll put on some tea. It's nice the way English hotels have a kettle and the makings in each room, don't you think?"

She kept up a cheerful chatter as he hung up his coat and then lowered himself onto the sofa. Little puddles formed on the carpet around his shoes. Outside, the drizzle had turned into a real downpour. A gust of wind drove a splatter of rain against the window.

"Listen," Lena said after she'd put on the water and sat down on the edge of the bed. "It looks to me like you're on the road because you don't have a place to stay."

"I'll be all right."

"I'm sure you will, but why don't you stay here tonight? No strings. You take the couch, I get the bed. The trains aren't running at this time of night anyway, are they?"

Felix shook his head. "I just have to get out of town."

Would that be enough? Lena wondered. She ran Bett's conversation back.

You're going to keep him there, in your room, and you're not going to let him leave. . . .

No, she realized. It wasn't going to be enough. Because when it came to Bett, she didn't trust what could happen.

She glanced at Felix who was staring at his shoes, shoulders drooped.

Shit. And *he* wasn't going to stay.

That didn't leave her any other choice.

She wore a ring on either hand. Each had a small storage space under the gem. The settings were fixed in such a manner that only using the one hand, it was just a moment's work to twist the ring around, open the secret compartment, and spill its contents into a drink. The powder in each was completely tasteless. The one in the right was a knockout drug. The one in the left was something a little more special. It was based on a variation of thiopentone that had been developed by a member of the Order, and worked not only as a general muscle relaxant and reflex suppressor, but simultaneously broke down the will, leaving the target utterly susceptible to suggestion.

Lena considered which to use. The new feelings that Felix had woken in her told her that rendering him unconscious was all she needed to do to fulfill her bargain with Bett. But considering that she wasn't going to have another chance—not like this, not ever with him. . . .

If he'd only loosen up.

But he wouldn't.

She felt both guilt and excitement as she made her decision. With her back to him, she emptied the contents from the ring on her left hand into a teacup, then poured the tea over it.

"Milk? Sugar?" she asked.

"A little of both."

She added the two and stirred vigorously. Felix appeared at her shoulder, startling her, but he'd only come over to save her the awkward trip back to where he was sitting.

They talked some more, Lena eyeing him surreptitiously, waiting for the drug to take effect. She didn't have that long to wait. Very soon Felix began slurring his words. His movements grew more languid, until finally he just sat there with a glazed look in his eyes.

"Felix?" Lena said.

"Mmm . . . ?"

"How are you doing?"

"Uhmm. . . ."

"You must be feeling a little uncomfortable in those wet clothes. Why don't we hang them there with your jacket and let them dry out."

She got up and, using the cane to keep the weight off her ankle, went over to help him stand. She started him on the buttons of his shirt, and soon he was removing it, and the rest of his clothes, on his own.

"You've got a very nice body," Lena said. "Have you ever done any weight lifting?"

"Uhmm. . . ."

The drug didn't do much for conversation, but Lena wasn't in the mood for conversation anyway. It had been developed for one of the Order's rituals that she wasn't yet privy to, but she knew it was of a sexual nature—something dreamed up by one of the elder members, no doubt, who used it to get their rocks off with some sweet young things that they couldn't otherwise get close to. Sex magic wasn't an aspect of the Order's teachings that Lena had explored to any great extent, preferring to keep that aspect of her life as entertainment.

And she was being entertained now; the last of her guilty feelings fled as she led Felix to the bed. Removing her own clothes, she got up beside him and ran her hands up and down the hard length of his body.

How much was he even going to remember of this? she wondered as she began to stroke his penis and felt it stiffen under her manipulations. Not much, if her previous experiences with the drug were anything to go by.

But she'd remember.

And he'd have such dreams, never imagining their source. . . .

2.

It was a dark and stormy night, Clare said to herself as she made her slow way home. Not a creature was stirring, not even a mouse; but hark, what light through yonder window shines . . . ?

A faint smile touched her lips.

You do read too much, Mabley, she thought.

The trouble really was that she remembered everything she read—especially clichés and homilies and the like. She liked to string them together into nonsense sentences and paragraphs—a habit picked up from too much time spent on her own when she was young. Other similar amusements included taking the top thirty songs from the current music charts, or the headlines from the various newspapers in the newsagent's while she was queued up to be served, or titles from a row of books on one of the shelves in the shop, and seeing how they read, all bunched and tumbled together.

Take Thomas Hardy.

Under the greenwood tree, far from the madding crowd, a pair of blue eyes. . . .

Did what? Juded the obscure?

She shook her head. Adding the "D"—that wasn't quite fair.

Perhaps if she included poem titles.

Under the greenwood tree, far from the madding crowd, the ghost of the past, god-forgotten, weathers the return of the native.

Not bad. There was almost a kind of poetry in the way it—

She paused and peered back down the steep incline of Raginnis Hill, aware of the sudden sensation that she was no longer alone. But there was no one there. Turning, she had the wind in her face. She wiped the rain from her eyes and cheeks with the back of her hand and continued up the hill, the titles of Thomas Hardy's books and poems forgotten.

The night's damp chill had got under her nor'wester and jumper, but that didn't account for the unexpected chill she felt. There was an odd feeling in the air—an electricity that owed nothing to what lightning there might be lurking in the storm clouds above her. Everything seemed a bit on edge—or it had ever since this whole business with Felix and Janey and the Gaffer had come about. People skulking around Mousehole, looking for old William Dunthorn manuscripts. The burglary.

Shakespeare, she thought, trying to take her mind from the peculiar turn it had taken.

Much ado about nothing . . . the tempest. . . .

Bloody hell.

She looked back again, the skin on her back crawling, but could still see nothing out of the ordinary. Just peaceful Mousehole, mostly dark now because it was getting late and no one stayed up much past closing time anyway—even on a Saturday night. The narrow dark street, unwinding steeply behind her between the houses, slick with rain. The shadows thick in the alleyways. . . .

She was spooking herself and she knew it, but couldn't stop herself because nothing felt right.

Don't be a silly goose, she told herself.

Chiding didn't help either.

She tried to hurry, but with the damp in her bones and the steepness of the road, she could only go so fast. A turtle could walk faster. A slug could crawl more quickly. She simply wasn't an efficient walking machine, and that was all there was to it.

The wind quickened, buffeting the rain against her with such force that she had to bend her head, her free hand pulling the neck of the nor'wester more closely to her chin. Under her hat, the skin of her neck was prickling in unhappy anticipation of something horrible— the feeling growing so strong that she finally had to turn again only to find—

She jumped, she was so startled, and nearly lost her balance.

"My God," she said to the muffled figure who had come up behind her. "You gave me quite a turn, coming up on me like . . ."

Her voice trailed off as she took in the long raincoat, the hat with the goggles peering at her from just below its low brim, the scarf pulled across the lower part of the face, effectively hiding all features. Her heart jumped into a double-time rhythm as the stranger took his left hand from his pocket and brought out a large folded knife. As though by magic, the knife's blade came out of its handle with a quick snap of the man's wrist.

"N-no," Clare said. "Please. . . ."

"We're going for a walk, you and I," the man said, his voice muffled by his scarf. "Up by the cliffs, I think."

Cold fear paralyzed Clare's muscles for long moments, then she gathered her wits about her and swung her cane. The man dodged the blow easily. Clare wasn't so lucky when he struck her with his free hand. The blow knocked her cane from her grip and sent her down to the road where she scraped her hands on the pavement. Her bad leg offered up a protesting flare of pain at its mistreatment.

Before she could scrabble away, the man was down beside her, right hand on her shoulder, forcing her down, the knife held up near her face.

"We can do this pleasantly," he said. "A stroll up by the cliffs and no pain. Or I can drag you up there by your hair and we'll see if the rain can wash away the blood as quickly as I can make it flow."

The goggles stared at her, soulless bug-eyes that offered up no hope.

"It could take some time," he added.

Clare opened her mouth to scream, then closed it with a snap as the point of the knife touched her cheek just below her left eye. The rain streamed onto her face, making her vision blur.

"No cries." The voice was so damned conversational. "No screams. Wouldn't do you any good, anyway. There's no one to hear you—not tonight."

The knife pulled back a bit, floating in the air between them. The man held it with a casual familiarity. Clare stared at its menacing point. Dimly she took in the nightmarish image of the man—just a shadowy bulk, featureless with his hat, goggles, and scarf. She had an odd moment of total objectivity. She noticed the crease in the brim of the hat, as though it had been folded in a pocket for too long. The missing button at the top of the raincoat's right lapel. The odd little tattoo on the man's left wrist.

Then he hauled her to her feet and gave her a shove in the direction of the coast path. He closed the knife and returned it to his pocket.

"My—my cane. . . ."

"Do without it," the man said.

"But—"

The knife appeared again, the blade flicking open with a snap.

"You're beginning to bore me," the man said. "Don't bore me. You wouldn't like me when I'm bored."

The knife moved back and forth in front of her face. She took a staggering step back, but he closed the distance again easily.

"You wouldn't like me at all," he said softly.

3.

Janey was having a miserable time of it. The wipers of her little Reliant Robin had decided to work only at half power, which left them less than effective in clearing the heavy rain from her windshield. The defrost wasn't working properly either, so she had to drive with the driver's side window open. By the time she was halfway to Newlyn, her left shoulder and arm were soaked.

And then there was the reason she was out on the road tonight in the first place. . . .

She drove through Newlyn and Penzance, going too fast, but not really caring. Her attention was divided between keeping the Robin on the road, trying to spot Felix on either side of the verge, and roundly cursing herself for the fool she'd been when he'd come by the Gaffer's house earlier. Why couldn't she have *listened* to him, instead of going off half cocked the way she had?

It was her bloody temper.

She banged her fist on the steering wheel in frustration by the time she was on the far side of Penzance. The buses and trains weren't running at this time of night, but what if he'd been hitching? He might have already gotten a ride. . . .

She cruised back through Penzance, crisscrossing through the town and going slower now, without any better luck. Finally, she pulled over to the side of the street just before she reached the Newlyn Bridge at the end of the North Pier. She stared morosely out the windshield. The wipers went feebly back and forth, pushing the rain about more than clearing the window.

This was pointless. He could be anywhere.

Then she remembered Clare saying something about Felix planning to drop off a cane to that Lena woman before he left. On a night like this, he'd be mad to try hitching out of town. Maybe he was still in the woman's room.

Janey's spirits lifted slightly. The American would be staying in a hotel.

She made a U-turn and started east again on the Promenade.

A hotel. Of course. Then her spirits sagged again. Only which one?

She got lucky at the third hotel she tried. Ron Hollinshead, an old schoolmate of hers, was behind the counter. He looked up from the magazine he was reading as she came in. Pushing back his dark hair from his brow, he stood up, a smile crinkling his features. On his feet he only topped Janey by a few inches.

"Hello there, Janey," he said, peering past her to where her car was pulled up to the curb. "Car giving you a bit of agro?"

"Don't talk to me about that car."

Ron came around the counter. "Want me to take a look at it?"

"No. It's not that. I just—do you have an American woman staying here? All I know is her first name: Lena."

Ron nodded. "Lena Grant. She's been here a few days. Thinks she's a bloody princess. What do you want with her?"

"Has she had any visitors this evening?" Janey asked.

"About a half hour or so ago—rough-looking bloke. Looked like he'd been swimming in the bay."

"Did he have any baggage?"

"A duffel and a case of some sort. What's this all about, Janey?"

"What room's she in?"

"I can't tell you that."

"It's important."

Ron looked uncomfortable. "But it's privileged information. I could lose my job if I let people go about bothering the guests. Be fair, Janey."

"I'm not going to bother anyone," Janey said. "Honestly. I just want to talk to the fellow who's visiting her."

"I don't think so," Ron said. "This time of night, there's not much guesswork needed to know what they're up to."

Janey did an admirable job of keeping down the sudden flare of anger that rose up in her.

I sent him away, she told herself. If he's in bed with her, it's my fault. I'm going to stay calm. I'm just going to talk to him. And maybe tear out all of *her* bloody hair. . . .

"I'm sorry, Janey," Ron said. "But there's rules and I've got to stick to them."

Janey sighed. "You won't tell me?"

"Not won't—can't."

"Then I'll just have to find out for myself."

Ron caught her arm as she started for the stairs. "For Christ's sake, Janey. Don't cause a scene."

"I won't. Just tell me what room they're in." She found a disarming smile to charm him with. "Come on, Ron. It's really very important."

"Bloody hell."

"No one has to know who told me," she assured him.

"You won't start shouting and carrying on?"

"Promise," she said and crossed her heart.

I'll kill her quietly, she added to herself.

"If I lose my job . . ."

"You won't, Ron. I'll be up to have a quick bit of a chat and out again, quiet as a mouse. No one'll even know I was here."

He sighed heavily and looked around the lobby as though expecting to find his employer lurking about, just waiting for him to break the rules before she booted him out and then he'd be on the dole again.

"All right," he said. "Room five—top of the stairs on your right. But mind you don't—"

Janey nodded. "I'll be quiet as a ghost."

A ghost of retribution, she thought, then forced that thought away. She was going to stay calm—no matter what she found in the bloody woman's room. She was *not* going to cause a scene.

"Thanks, Ron," she said.

She gave his arm a quick squeeze, then hurried up the stairs before he could change his mind. She looked back down when she reached the first landing to find him staring up at her, obviously still distressed. She put a finger to her lips and tiptoed exaggeratedly on up until she was out of his sight.

I'm going to be calm, she reminded herself as she reached the door with the brass plate that read "Number Five."

Easy to say. Her pulse was drumming wildly as she reached up to rap on the door with her knuckles and the last thing she felt was calm. She paused before knocking and put her ear to the wood paneling. She could hear an odd sound, but the thickness of the door made it impossible to identify.

Maybe they were asleep. Together in the same bed. Exhausted after a frenzied bout of lovemaking. . . .

She was going to kill that woman. She was going to tear out her—

Calm, she warned herself. Be calm.

She knocked, and got no response. But she could sense that they were in there. Empty rooms had a different feel about them. And there was that faint, rhythmical sound.

She knocked a second time, then tried the handle when there was still no answer. It turned easily under her hand. She flung the door open and stepped into the room where her worst fears were realized.

A naked woman was astride Felix on the bed, riding him as though he was some thoroughbred stallion, hands on his shoulders, breasts bobbing as her hips went up and down. She turned wide, startled eyes to Janey, pausing in midmotion with Felix's penis still halfway inside her. Felix never moved, never turned.

"What the hell are *you* doing here?" the woman demanded.

Janey looked around the room for the nearest thing with which to hit her.

4.

Davie Rowe buttoned his shirt across his broad chest and stepped into his trousers, right leg first.

Two bloody hundred quid, he thought as he tucked in his shirttails and then zipped up his trousers. And for doing something legal in the bargain. Wasn't that just something.

"Is that you, Davie?"

Davie glanced at the wall separating his bedroom from his mother's.

"Yes, Mum."

"Who was that on the phone, then?"

Her voice was closer now.

Oh, do stay in bed, Davie thought. But there wasn't much chance of that.

"Just a mate," he said.

His mother appeared in his doorway, a worn, old flowered housecoat wrapped around her thin body.

"Not that Willie Keel, was it?"

Davie shook his head. "It was Darren Spencer. He got himself a flat up by the quarry and needs a hand."

"Because I don't like that Keel chap," his mother went on as though she hadn't heard him. "He's the one what got you in trouble before and he'll do it again, give him half a chance. You mark my words, Davie, he's a bad sort and—"

Davie cut her off with a quick kiss on the cheek.

"I really must go, Mum. Darren's waiting."

"Yes, well. It's important to stand by your friends," his mother said. "Not that I saw Darren stand by you when you went to prison. Where was he then, I ask you? But now, when he needs himself a spot of help at—what time *is* it?"

"Time for me to go. You get back to bed, Mum. I won't be long."

His mother nodded. "Mind you take a coat and hat, now. It's a proper flood out there tonight."

"I will."

He found his boots by the door where he'd dropped them when he came in earlier and quickly laced them up. His mother continued to prattle as he shrugged into a thick raincoat and pushed a fisherman's cap down over his unruly brown curls.

"A big lad like you," his mother said as he opened the front door, "can still catch his death of cold."

"I'll be careful, Mum."

He closed the door and stepped gratefully into the street, preferring the physical discomfort of the rain to his mother's nagging. She meant well, he knew, but her incessant nattering got on his nerves something fierce. Of course it was his own fault, wasn't it? Almost thirty and still living at home with his mum. And didn't that give Willie a laugh, just? Still, what else could he do? He couldn't afford his own lodgings and if he didn't look after the old woman, then who would? Not his father—God rest his soul—and they had no other family since the cousins moved to Canada.

A fine how-do it was when the only Rowes left in Mousehole were a grumbling old woman and her half-arsed crook of a son. Such times. Things were better when Dad was alive, bringing in the odd bit of contraband to augment the family's poor fishing income. And in his grandfather's day . . . time was the Rowes were the best smugglers this side of up country.

But that was in days long past, when the pilchard still ran and men used the wind, not motors, to propel their ships. This was now. At the moment his only concern was the two hundred quid he had riding on finding Clare Mabley and keeping her alive.

Two hundred quid!

As he hurried across the village through the rain to Raginnis Hill, Davie wondered how much Willie was keeping for himself. And he wondered as well about who would want to hurt Clare. He'd done some bad things in his own time, and would undoubtedly do more, but he could honestly say that he'd ever hurt a disabled person, nor stolen from one either.

He couldn't understand a man who would.

Because of the heavy rain, Davie was almost upon the two figures before he saw them. Clare was hobbling painfully up the hill without her cane, while the man with her kept shoving her when she slowed down.

"Here!" Davie cried. "Lay off her, you!"

The man turned. His left hand dipped into the pocket of his overcoat and came back with a knife. Davie took in the man's odd muffled appearance and the knife with a touch of uneasiness. Bugger was decked out like the villain in some bad American movie, he thought. But the knife was no joke. Nor the assured way the man held it, cutting edge up.

Davie couldn't help but picture that blade plunging into his belly and then tearing up his chest until it was stopped by his breastbone. . . .

Still he held his ground.

Two hundred quid, he thought.

And besides, he rather liked Clare.

"Got yourself a knife, have you?" he said. "Makes you feel grandly brave, I'll wager."

The man's only reply was a sudden lunge forward. The knife cut through Davie's coat, but missed the skin as Davie side-stepped the attack. Before the man could swing about, Davie struck him squarely in the side of the head with one meaty fist and dropped his attacker in his tracks.

Those knuckles were going to hurt come morning, Davie thought as he moved in to make sure the man stayed down.

Shaking his head, the man made it to his feet before Davie could reach him. He held the knife between them, effectively keeping Davie at bay. Then Davie spied Clare's cane lying where it had fallen on the wet pavement earlier.

Right, he thought. We'll end this quickly now.

He feinted towards the man, dodged the sweeping blow of the knife, and kicked the man's feet from under him. As Clare's attacker went tumbling to the pavement, Davie stepped quickly over to where the cane lay. He turned with it in hand, just as the man was rising.

"Fun's over, mate," Davie said. "Why don't you bugger off before you get seriously hurt."

The man roared inarticulately and charged. Davie swung the cane twice. One blow knocked the knife from the man's hand. Sidestepping out of the way, Davie delivered the second blow to the man's shoulder as he went by. The man stumbled against a low garden wall, turning quickly. His right arm now hung loosely at his side.

Broken, Davie thought. Or maybe the nerves had simply been struck numb. Either way, the man was in no shape to continue the fight.

Davie raised the cane again.

"I'm serious, mate," he said. "Bugger off or there'll be some real pain."

He could feel the man's hatred burning from the eyes hidden behind those odd goggles. It was a venomous rage that had no need for words to express itself. Davie had lost his cap in their brief struggle and the rain was plastering his curls to his head, running into his eyes. But he didn't move, didn't even blink, until the figure by the wall slowly sidled towards the left, then fled off down the hill.

Davie bent down and retrieved the man's knife, which he pitched off into the darkness behind the nearest house below the road. He collected his sodden hat and shoved it into his pocket, then went to where Clare was crouching wide-eyed on the road.

"Oh, God, Davie," she said as he came near. "He was going to kill me."

Davie didn't quite know what to do now. He helped Clare to her feet, feeling stupid and awkward once she was standing on her own, holding her cane again.

"Yes, well . . ." he started, then he ran out of words.

"You saved my life, Davie."

"It's just, uh, lucky I happened by when I, uh, did."

Clare stepped a little closer and leaned against his arm. He could feel her trembling.

"I've never been so frightened before in all my life," she said.

"Well, he's, uh, gone now."

A new tremor went through Clare. "What if he comes back?"

"I doubt that."

It was getting a little easier to talk to her now.

"But if he does?" she asked. "We'd better call the police."

"No police," Davie said.

"But . . ." Clare turned to look up into his face. She blinked away rain, and then nodded. "Of course," she said. "You don't exactly get along with them, do you?"

Davie sucked on his bruised knuckles. "Not exactly. Did he hurt you?"

"No, I'm just a little shaken still—that's all."

"I'll walk you home," Davie said.

"This is very kind of you."

"You could call the police from your house," Davie went on. "Just don't mention me, that's all."

Clare nodded, letting herself be led on up the hill, past the bird hospital, to her front door.

"What could they do anyway?" she asked. "He's long gone now."

"Long gone," Davie agreed.

"But I should report it all the same, just so he doesn't attack someone else. Unless . . ." Her voice trailed off.

"Unless what?" Davie asked.

Clare shivered. Her fingers shook as she tried to fit her key to its lock. Davie took it from her and unlocked the door for her.

"I had the oddest feeling that he was after me in particular."

"Why would anyone want to hurt you?" Davie asked.

But he was thinking about two hundred quid as he spoke, and of Willie Keel. Someone had told Willie that this attack was going to happen. Someone who was willing to pay at least two hundred quid—probably double that when you took in Willie's share—to make sure that it didn't happen.

The only person Davie could think that would fit that bill was the American woman who was staying in Penzance. But why? And why Clare?

"I don't know," Clare said. "But someone does."

She stepped inside, then looked back at him.

"Will you come in for a bit?" she asked. "You've gotten all drenched. I could put on some tea."

"I suppose I could," Davie said. "Just so long as you don't phone the police while I'm here."

She gave him an odd look. "What've you been up to, Davie?"

"Nothing. I swear. I was just out walking, that's all. But if I'm here when the police come, they'll take me in all the same."

"Well, I can't have that happen," Clare said. "Not after you've helped me. But walking in the rain?"

"It helps clear my mind."

"There's a lot of that needed around here," Clare said.

"Pardon?"

"Nothing. Would you like that tea?"

"Please."

"I'll put the kettle on."

She hung up her coat by the door and started off down the hall to the kitchen. Davie hung up his own gear, then stood awkwardly by the coat rack until she called him into the kitchen.

"I feel better with you here," she said. "Safer. Did you see his face?"

"Not much to see, what with the goggles and scarf and all."

"That's just it. It fairly gives me the creeps just thinking about him."

Davie nodded and took a seat at the kitchen table. It *had* been creepy. And hurt or not, the man was still out there. He could come back. If he did, and Davie wasn't there to stop him, then Davie knew he could just kiss away his two hundred quid. Not to mention that Clare would be dead. . . .

"Do you have a phone I could use?" he asked.

Clare raised her eyebrows. "Are *you* going to phone the police now?"

"Not likely. I just wanted to call a mate I was supposed to be seeing to tell him I won't be by." The questioning look remained in her eyes. "I thought I should, uh, stay a bit," he added. "In case the bloke who attacked you decides to come back. The police wouldn't leave a man here with you, you see."

"That's a kind thought."

"Unless you'd rather I went . . . ?"

"No. I could make up a bed for you on the couch, if you like."

"I don't need much." He paused, then added, "The phone?"

"It's in the study," she said, pointing the way.

"Thanks."

As soon as he got to the telephone, Davie rang up Willie's number.

"You were spot on the money about that attack," he said when Willie answered.

"You had no trouble?"

"None to speak of. Do you know who he was?"

"No."

"Do you think he'll be back?"

"I hadn't thought of that," Willie said. "Is there a place nearby where you can watch Mabley's house?" He was quiet for a moment, obviously thinking, then added before Davie could speak, "Of course there's this bloody weather, isn't there?"

"It's all right," Davie said. "I'm in Clare's house at the moment. She invited me in when I rescued her."

"Can you stay?"

"That's not a problem. What I want to know, Willie, is, what's this all about?"

"Haven't the faintest idea, mate. I just take the money and do the job. That's how you get ahead in this world."

"I'll remember that," Davie said, and then he rang off.

He looked around the room, at the books lining the walls, and wondered if Clare had actually read them all. He remembered her in school. She was still in primary when he was taking his exams to go to the comprehensive school in Penzance—exams that he'd failed. But he could remember how after the accident she'd been home for so long, and then going to school in her wheelchair, Janey Little always at her side.

She would have had plenty of time to have read all of these and more, he decided. He pulled a book at random from the shelves and flipped through its pages. He wondered what it was like to read something like this. As a boy, reading the weekly *Beano* was about the most he could manage. The most he ever read now were the soccer scores—and that was only after he'd had a good eyeful of the page-three girl. But books . . . give him a good film anytime—preferably one of the old ones where black was black and white was white and a man didn't get confused between the two the way it was so easy to in real life.

He hefted a volume, enjoying the feel of it in his hand. Films were all well and fine, but something like this. It had a good weight in your hand.

Clare was clever—had to be after reading all these books. And pretty, too. Funny how he'd never really thought of that before. You saw the cane and then that was as far as you looked.

"Ready for that tea?" Clare called from the kitchen.

"I'm on my way," he said.

Clever and pretty and easy to be with. And now someone was trying to kill her.

He put the book back.

Well, not if he had his say about the matter.

5.

"Felix, how *could* you?" Janey cried.

To find him in bed with this woman was the final slap in the face. The ultimate betrayal. Because she'd been willing to listen to him.

She'd *believed* Clare when she had argued for his innocence. But to find him like this . . . to know that all the time he really had been playing her for a fool. . . .

The red tide of her anger lashed against the false calm that she'd held desperately in place for the past few hours.

"Felix!" she cried again. "Will you at least *look* at me?"

You drove him to this, a part of her protested, so why are you so angry? You sent him away into her arms.

That was bloody rubbish.

She'd sent him away—that much was true enough—but if he was really so innocent would he have rushed here to the American's bed?

"Felix!" she cried a third time, her voice going shrill.

Lena was very cool. She rose from her awkward position—Felix's penis slapping against his stomach as she got off him—and calmly covered her nakedness with a bathrobe.

"Get out of here," she told Janey as she belted the robe.

Her voice was pitched low, but there was iron behind it. It was a voice used to being obeyed. A voice reserved for servants.

Janey ignored her, all her attention on Felix.

He never moved. He never turned his head towards her. He just lay there on the bed, staring at the ceiling, his penis shrinking and soft. He looked ridiculous, but Janey could feel her heart breaking all over.

She took a step towards him. Lena moved forward, favouring her hurt leg, and stood between the bed and Janey.

"I said—" she began.

The woman's movement broke the spell that Janey had been under. Without even thinking about what she was doing, she shaped a fist and hit Lena in the stomach as hard as she could. She stepped aside as Lena buckled over, gasping. Lena's leg gave way under her and she fell to the carpet. Janey closed the distance that separated her from the bed. She moved her hand back and forth in front of Felix's face, waiting for his gaze to track the motion, but all he did was continue to stare at the ceiling.

Comprehension dawned on Janey, if not understanding.

"You've drugged him," she said, turning from the bed.

Realizing that, her anger didn't so much flee as it was redirected. But riding above it now was an awful fear for Felix. What had the woman given him? Would he recover?

Lena was recovering. Using the side of the bed for leverage, she pulled herself up from the floor and leaned against the bed. She flinched when Janey took a step towards her.

"Don't think . . . you can get away with this," Lena said. "I'll have you charged with assault, you stupid little—"

"You drugged him!" Janey cried, overriding the threat. "What did you give him?"

As she stepped closer still, Lena took a swing at her, fingers spread like a claw, long polished nails arching towards Janey's face. Janey dodged the feeble attack and slapped Lena, her hand leaving its imprint behind on the woman's cheek—sharp red against the pale skin. Lena winced. She put up her own hand to cover the stinging cheek, her own attack forgotten.

"*What* did you give him?" Janey demanded.

She made another threatening gesture with her hand when Lena didn't reply that quickly had the woman talking.

"He'll be fine. It's just a drug to leave him open to suggestion. It'll wear off in a few hours."

Her voice was surly, angry, but Janey didn't much care. She'd bully the woman right out of Cornwall if she could.

Keeping half an eye on Lena, she returned to the side of the bed. "Felix?" she said. "Can you hear me?"

"Uuuh. . . ."

She caught up his hand and gave his arm a pull, which brought him sitting up in bed like a robot that could move stiffly on its own, but couldn't generate the locomotion without prompting. Janey glanced around the room until she spied his clothes lying on the floor. She gathered them up and gave them to him.

"Put these on," she said.

He held them on his lap, but stared numbly into some unseen distance.

Janey looked at Lena. All the fight seemed to have gone out of her except for a dark spark of anger that flashed deep in her eyes. Satisfied that she wouldn't complicate matters, Janey helped Felix dress. It wasn't much different from how she thought it would be clothing a mannequin. But she finally had him standing by the door, his duffel and accordion case standing out in the hall. Janey picked up Clare's cane as well. Let the woman crawl around on her knees.

"You're going to be sorry," Lena said suddenly.

"Oh, really?"

Janey was quite proud of the way she was keeping her temper in check.

"You don't have any idea of who I—"

"That's where you're wrong," Janey said. "I know exactly what kind of a person you are, *and* what you're here for."

She smiled coldly as Lena registered surprise.

"That's right," she added. "And maybe you can get anything you want with a snap of your fingers wherever it is that you come from, but it's different here. Here we take care of our own. The best thing you can do is hop on the first train to London and fly back home, because if you come 'round bothering us again, you'll have more than just me to deal with. I have a lot of friends in this area, Lena Grant, and we really do take care of our own."

"You don't—"

But Janey just shut the door on whatever the woman was about to say. She gave Felix a push down the hall, then lugging his duffel and accordion case, Clare's cane awkwardly stuck under her arm, she followed him to where he'd stopped at the top of the stairs.

"Down we go," she said and gave him another little nudge to get him mobile once more.

Ron met them at the bottom of the stairs, his anxiety almost comical. He looked closely at Felix who had paused once more, standing as still as a machine that had been switched off, then turned his questioning gaze towards Janey.

"I heard shouting," he began.

Janey nodded wearily. "Sorry about that. Did we wake anybody up?"

"No. It's just . . ." He looked at Felix again. "What's wrong with him?"

"She drugged him. Nice clientele you have staying in this place, Ron."

"We don't exactly pick and choose. Are you taking him to the hospital?"

Janey shook her head. "I'm taking him home."

"But—"

"About now," she said firmly, "it's the best place for him to be. I don't want him waking up in some hospital room not knowing how he got there."

Ron looked as though he had more to say, but then he just shrugged.

"Here," he said, taking the duffel and case from her. "Give me those."

He stowed them in the car while Janey led Felix out into the rain and got him to fold his bulk into the Reliant's small passenger seat.

"There's nothing more I can do?" Ron asked.

"No," Janey told him. She started up the car. "Thanks ever so much. You'd better get in out of the rain."

She flicked on the headlights and wipers. The latter were still misbehaving and pushed the water halfheartedly about on the windshield. Sighing, Janey rolled down her window and the rain came in. Ron stood watching them in the open door of the hotel. Giving him a wave, Janey turned the car about once more and headed back towards Mousehole.

If she'd ever had a more miserable night, she couldn't think of when it had been.

6.

Lena watched the door close behind them. She lifted a hand to her cheek, which was still stinging. Her stomach hurt too. Opening her robe, she looked down to see a bruise forming.

She was not in good shape.

Slowly she rose to her feet and hobbled over to the window where she watched Janey Little's bizarre three-wheeled car pull away from in front of the hotel. She held a hand across her stomach, gently stroking the soreness, not caring that she stood with her robe open in the window where anyone passing by outside could see. But finally she belted it closed once more and sat down in a chair.

It was karma, she thought. She had been trying to do the right thing, but because she hadn't gone about it properly, it had all fallen apart. There had been a singular lack of focus. She hadn't drawn on the clean sharp strength of her will, but had let her body's pleasure centers rule her mind.

"Never think with your groin," Daddy had told her more than once. "That's the first rule of business and it goes for women as well as men—don't you forget it. Use your logic, not your libido. I've seen more comedowns brought about by business associates thinking with

their brains in their groins instead of in their heads where they belong. . . ."

It made sense. It was good advice.

But she'd gone and broken that rule. She'd let her libido drag her
into a situation where common sense would never have taken her. If
she had just given Felix the knockout drug . . . rolled him up on the
couch and then gone to bed . . . none of this unpleasantness would
have happened.

But now that it had . . .

And when she thought of that little bitch waltzing in here like she
owned the world . . .

Anger didn't solve anything either, but she indulged herself in it
for a few moments all the same until she finally sighed. With an
effort, she put it aside.

Don't get mad, get even.

But that just meant losing him forever. Not that she had a ghost of
a chance in patching things up with him in the first place. Not that she
even wanted to. He was just some big dumb sailor, wasn't he?

Except and but and damn it all . . .

She considered the alien sensibility that had brought her to this
present situation and realized, with a maudlin regard that was also
unfamiliar, that her feelings for Felix Gavin hadn't changed. Not one
little bit. He'd put a crack in the walls that she had raised so pro-
tectively around herself, squeezed his way through, into her heart
and head, and now he wouldn't leave.

It wasn't just the way he'd dropped everything to help her this
afternoon, where anyone in her own circle would have nodded sym-
pathetically and just gone on, if they even bothered to notice in the
first place. Nor was it the simple honesty that just seemed to shine
out of his pores, or the attentiveness with which he'd listened to her
blather on. Nor was it the fact that he had a terrific bod . . .

She didn't know what it was. And what she didn't understand,
upset her. Because it left her open to weakness. Because it had her
sitting here feeling lost and lonely like all the rest of the stupid sheep
in the world who couldn't have what they wanted. . . .

She remembered the feel of his skin against hers. The gentle
strength of his hands. How she'd drawn his hardness deep inside her.
Because of the drug, he hadn't been very energetic without prompting, it was true. If you stopped to think about it, it was almost a
kind of necrophilia . . . but it had all felt so good . . .

Her hand dropped between her legs and she leaned her head against the back of the chair, closing her eyes as she imagined that it was his fingers, rubbing back and forth, his touch, his caring for her that fueled the hot flash that grew deep in her belly and began to spread through her in a wave.

But then she remembered Janey Little. And Felix's disconsolate face when he'd come by to drop off the cane. . . .

Her hand stilled. The desire fled, if not the need.

She opened her eyes and stared across the room. Pulling her robe closed, she wrapped her arms tightly around herself.

Don't get mad, get even.

There had to be a way that she could make good for Daddy and the Order and *still* get everything that *she* wanted at the same time. She just hadn't worked it all through yet.

This isn't over, Janey Little, she thought. Not by a long shot, it isn't.

7.

For Clare, it was a matter of control.

When her assailant first attacked her, out there in the rain, just the two of them, she'd been afraid. Of being hurt. And then of dying. But underlying it all, reaching right to the heart of the primordial core that made her who she was—that differentiated her from the billions of other souls with whom she shared the planet—was the fear of losing control.

What her assailant took from her at that moment violated her very essence. He had stolen what had kept her sane through the bedridden years and the years of physical therapy.

Control.

She had been dealt a bad hand—or dealt it for herself, some might say, though it was hard to think in those terms considering how young she'd been at the time she'd taken her fall. She had lost motor command of her body and fought with all the inner strength and will she could summon to regain it. And regain it she did. She didn't recover it all, but she'd been far more successful than the doctors had allowed she ever would be.

What was the secret?

Control.

When she was finally mobile once more, she swore she'd never give it up again. Not over any aspect of her life.

So when her assailant stole it away—as casually as some horrible little child pulling the wings from a fly, simply plucking it from her with his brute strength and a knife—it undermined everything that had kept her strong through the years. Just like that. And even now, sitting in the kitchen sharing a pot of tea with Davie Rowe, the memory of that theft entangled her like a swimmer caught in a snarl of seaweed, caught and dragged down from the surface of the ocean, down into the depths, losing air, losing strength, losing control. . . .

Control.

What frightened her the most was how easily her assailant had stripped it away.

She glanced across the table at her companion who was trying manfully not to slurp his tea. Davie Rowe. With his severe acne scars, pug nose, and oversize chin; the one large ear and his basically kind eyes that were unfortunately too small and set too closely together; the purple blotch of a birthmark that smeared the left side of his brow . . .

It was a face only a mother could love, and from what Clare knew, only his mother did.

Like Clare herself, Davie Rowe had been dealt a bad hand as well, one over which he could never have had any influence. Based on his looks, he'd never had many friends. When he looked for employment, the doors closed in his face. He'd had little schooling and his only virtue, if it could be called such, was that he could handle himself well in a fight—he'd had a whole childhood and adolescence perfecting that skill. Unfortunately it wasn't marketable. Was it any wonder that he'd taken up nicking wallets and the like from the rooms of the tourists who flocked to Penwith every summer? What else was he supposed to do?

Everyone knew him in the village. He wasn't so much Mousehole's village idiot as its black sheep, and locally he was viewed with a certain amount of wary affection, though no one cared to spend much time in his company.

But never mind his looks, or his history. At this moment Clare felt a pronounced fondness for him. And an odd sense of affinity.

She considered—as a way of taking her mind away from that bleak feeling that had settled deep inside her and refused, point-blank, to be dislodged—what it must be like to be him.

He wasn't crippled, because physically his body performed all its functions in the manner they were supposed to, but he was disabled all the same. Because where people looked no further than her limp and her cane when they met her, with him they looked no further than his face. The principle difference between them was that she'd forced herself to overcome the limitations that society put on her while he either hadn't been able, or been given the opportunity, to try to do the same for himself.

"Have you read all those books?" Davie asked suddenly.

Clare blinked and brought her thoughts back to earth.

"What did you say?"

"Those books in your study," Davie said, nodding with his head down the hall. "Have you read them all?"

Clare smiled. "Not likely. But I've read a lot of them. Why do you ask?"

"I just wondered what it was like."

"What, reading that many books?"

"No. Reading a book. All the way through, like, from start to finish. One without pictures."

"You've never read a book?" Clare asked, trying to keep the incredulity out of her voice.

Davie shrugged. "Never really had the time. . . ."

"But what do you do with your time?" She regretted what she had said the moment the words were out of her mouth. "I'm sorry," she added quickly. "It's really none of my business."

"I don't mind your asking. I like to walk. I go for long walks. And I have a bicycle now that I got from Willie. Sometimes I'll pedal all the way up to St. Ives and back in a day. I listen to the radio a lot and in the evenings Mum and I watch the telly. And I love to go to the cinema. But I look at all those books in your study and I get to thinking that you can't half help being clever after you've read so many of them."

"It takes more than reading to be clever," Clare said.

Lord knew, she saw that every day in the shop where they sold more romances and bestsellers than anything that had a bit more literary worth or insight. She couldn't remember the last time they'd sold a copy of Joyce that wasn't to a student.

"It's understanding what you read," she added. "And it's challenging your mind. I've no quarrel with entertainment, but I like to mix my reading about so that I get a bit of everything."

Davie nodded, but she saw that he was only going through the motion of understanding.

"You play music, too," he said. "Up at Charlie Boyd's, don't you?"

"Most Friday nights," Clare said. "I haven't seen you there, though."

Davie shrugged. "Sometimes when I'm walking by, I hear the music and I stop outside for a bit of a listen."

"Why don't you come in?"

"I can't play an instrument or carry a tune."

"You could tell a story, then, like some of the old gaffers."

"Don't know any stories. I . . ." He shifted uncomfortably in his chair. "It's just that everything changes when I come in a room. Goes all quiet like and then people are always looking at me. When I go 'round to the local, the only way I can get any company is by playing the fool. Then I can have a crowd around me, buying drinks or letting me play billiards with them, but . . ." His voice trailed off.

Clare was at a loss as to what to say.

"I just get tired of it sometimes," he added after a few moments.

Clare nodded. "It's not easy being . . . different. I know that well enough."

"You're not that different," Davie said. "You're pretty and clever and—"

He broke off suddenly and finished his tea in one long swallow.

"It's getting late," he said, standing up from the table. "If you could bring me a blanket and pillow, I can make my own bed on the sofa."

Clare started to say something commiserating, but then left it unsaid. If he was anything like she was, it would just sound like pity, and she hated to be pitied.

"I'll just go get them," she said.

Later she looked in on her sleeping mother—as she had when she'd first come home—but her mother was still sleeping. She left a note on her mother's night table briefly explaining Davie Rowe's presence downstairs, then went into her own room. She changed for bed, but then found she couldn't sleep. Instead she spent the remaining hours of the night staring out the window, watching the rain die to a drizzle, then give away altogether until only an overcast sky remained as a reminder of the night just past.

The gulls were wheeling about the roof of the house when she finally fell asleep in the chair where she was sitting. She dreamed of a masked man stalking her down narrow, winding streets where she could only flee by crawling painfully along the cobblestones because she'd lost her cane. Rain made the cobblestones slick and hard to grip. The goggled face of her pursuer loomed over her. He held a long shining blade upraised in his hand, the incongruously peaceful image of a dove tattooed on his wrist. Laughter spilled from behind the scarf that hid his features.

She woke with that hideous laughter in her ears, then realized it was only the raucous cries of the gulls. Feeling stiff, she limped over to her bed and crawled under the covers where she immediately fell asleep once more, this time without dreams.

8.

The Gaffer awoke with a start when the front door banged open. The Dunthorn book fell from his lap and he only just caught it before it tumbled to the floor. He looked over, then quickly rose to his feet as his much bedraggled granddaughter came in bringing with her an equally bedraggled Felix who also appeared to be in a somewhat somnambulant state.

"You found him!" he said. "Felix, I can't tell you how sorry I am about—"

"Doesn't do any good to talk to him, Gramps," Janey said.

The Gaffer peered closer and saw that while Felix's eyes were open, he saw nothing. The only reason he was moving at all was because Janey was nudging him along.

"What's happened?" the Gaffer asked. "Was he in an accident?"

Janey shook her head. "No. I'd say this was brought about very deliberately. Will you help me get him to bed?"

It took a while to get Felix upstairs, undressed, and in bed. Some more time was spent in fetching his gear from the Reliant, but finally everything was done. Janey and the Gaffer sat down in the living room, sitting together on the sofa, and it was then, as she started to explain what had happened, that the finely held control Janey had kept in place all evening unraveled. She burst into tears and buried her face against the Gaffer's shoulder.

It took him a while to get the story out of her. Then he merely held her, close to him, stroking her hair and murmuring in her ear.

What he said made no real sense. There were promises of everything getting better, and that they'd get to the bottom of things, just you wait and see, my robin, and the mystery would soon be solved, wouldn't it just, when they all put their minds to it together, and how she wasn't to worry.

But it was all just words.

He looked across the room as he spoke, at the Dunthorn book where it lay on the chair.

It was uncomfortably apparent that whatever they had become involved in was just beginning, though the Gaffer couldn't have said how he knew that. It was just a feeling he got.

When he looked at the book.

When he listened to the wind outside the house, rattling the shutters as it went hurrying up the street.

When he remembered the last time the strangeness had come into his home.

He knew it was only beginning.

And that this time it would be worse.

Silly Old Man

Philosophers have argued for centuries about how many angels can dance on the head of a pin, but materialists have known all along that it depends on whether they are jitterbugging or dancing cheek to cheek.

—TOM ROBBINS, from *Jitterbug Perfume*

The water of the harbour punched Jodi like a fist. Stunned, she sank deep into its shadows, propelled down by the momentum of her long drop. Moments later she bobbed back to the surface, brought up by the natural buoyancy of the salt water. The shock of its coldness immediately numbed her. Already suffering from the trauma of discovering that Edern had been no more than some enchanted clockwork man, this second shock on her system left her barely aware of her predicament.

The sea ran cold around Bodbury in late autumn. More than one fisherman had died in its waters as the cold seeped into their muscles, stealing away the sweet heat of life. Then the undertow would pull them under.

If they were washed ashore, their grieving families would have their swollen blue corpses to bury. A small comfort, but comfort nonetheless, for most were dragged out to sea, their bodies never seen again. For all their closeness to the sea—day in and day out upon its waters—given a choice, most fisher-folk would choose to leave their bones on land, buried deep in the solid earth, rather than know that they'd become nothing more than the playthings of the tide and currents.

Jodi was only dimly aware of the cold and the heat it was stealing from her body. She kept herself afloat with haphazard flutterings of her arms and legs, but her mind was locked on a stark impossible image:

Edern Gee. . . .

The spraying blood of the bog creatures as it melted his skin and made it flow like hot candle wax. . . .

The hole punched in his chest and the bewildering spill of cogs and gears and spoked wheels rolling across the boggy planking of the wharf. . . .

The memory stuck in her mind like a waterwheel snagged on a branch and locked in place. Movement frozen. The moment captured and held fast, looped like a cat's cradle string, so that no matter how much you turned it, there was no beginning and no end. Just the endless parade of that one instant, splayed across her mind, that she couldn't escape.

Until her head fell forward and a trickle of salt water exploded in her lungs. She lifted her face, choking and coughing. And then the first shivers began.

Swim, she told herself. Swim or you'll drown here.

But the shivers turned to trembling, which in turn became an uncontrollable shaking. Her head dipped into the water again, too heavy to keep aloft, but she managed to raise her face before she took another breath of water.

The current had already taken her some distance from the pier. She could see its dark bulk towering up behind her. Perched on a crate was Windle, the witch's fetch, gibbering angrily at her. There was no sign of the Widow herself. Farther away still was the length of the Old Quay—the distance between it and her multiplied a thousand times because of her present diminutive size.

She closed her eyes—

. . . and there was Edern, his face melting, his torso burst open, spilling out its clockwork mechanisms. . . .

—and opened them quickly again.

Swim, she told herself again.

But her arms and legs had grown too heavy. They felt so thick— cold and prickling with numbness. Her face sank into the water again and she had barely the strength to lift it. The current turned her so that she was no longer facing shore. When a wave lifted her to its crest, she could see out across the endless wash of its dark waters, then she dropped into another trough.

Hope died in her. Her movements were no more than minimal now.

Why fight the cold? she asked herself. Why fight the waves?

The sea had never been her friend, stealing Mother and Father as it was now stealing her life as well. But she could sense a kind of peacefulness waiting for her deep beneath the waves. A promise of warmth and solace if she just let herself sink. . . .

The wave crest lifted her again, but this time there was more than the never-ending vista of dark water to be seen. Something darker still was moving through the water towards her, leaving a V-shaped wake behind it.

Shark, Jodi thought, a new surge of panic hurling adrenaline through her body. It had to be one of the small blue sharks that the fishermen caught with their baited lines of mackerel and pilchard just outside the harbour.

A moment or so ago she'd been ready to give up, to simply allow herself to sink and let the waves claim her. But self-preservation— kicked awake by the immediate threat of being some shark's late-night snack—had her struggling to live once more.

She splashed frantically in the water, trying to get away, then realized that she was just going to draw it to her all the more quickly with her thrashing about. The swell of the waves drew her down into a trough.

It wasn't fair, she thought, and never mind what Aunt Nettie had to say about fairness. There weren't even supposed to *be* sharks about at this time of year.

Back she rose on the crest of another wave, to find her assailant had vanished.

Oh raw we, she thought with relief, then screamed as something came up from the waters underneath her.

She pounded her tiny fists against the thing, shrieking all the while, until she realized that she wasn't inside a shark's mouth, nor was it a shark's smooth skin that she was pummeling, but rather the wet-slicked fur of a seal's head. Her cries died and she grasped the fur with both hands.

"Oh, thank you, thank you, thank you," she mumbled against the fur.

Her teeth started to chatter against one another again. Her limbs shook as though palsied. She held on tightly, fingers wound into the short fur, as the seal streamed through the waves, bearing her shore-ward. And then, improbably as it might seem, she immediately fell into a comalike stupor, still clinging to the seal as she slept.

Exhaustion and trauma had finally taken their inevitable toll.

2.

An hour or so after he was led blindfolded from the hidden under-ground room that housed John Briello's animated corpse, Denzil still couldn't be sure if the odd turn that the night had taken was all a part of some incomprehensible hoax or not. If it was a hoax, it had been most elaborately planned. And was being most elaborately maintained. For here they were now, the four of them, an incongru-ous grouping if ever there was, out on the harbour in a rowboat, scouring the dark water with lanterns at bow and stern.

Henkie Whale put his bulk to good use, sitting amidships and bending his back to the oars as they rowed back and forth across the harbour. The big man had forsaken his bearskin for dungarees and jersey, the inevitable scarf wrapped about his neck and fluttering in the wind. Taupin sat in the bow, hanging over the hull with one lan-tern as he studied the water before them, both to look for Jodi and to call out warnings against the various abandoned ship masts and hulls they might otherwise run into. Denzil had the other lantern and sat in the stern with Lizzie Snell.

Lizzie had changed her clothes as well, decking herself out like a pirate of old from one of the costume chests Henkie maintained for his models—when he had them wear anything at all. She leaned into the starboard quarter, a long bangled sleeve trailing in their wake as she peered out at the water behind them. Denzil sat in the port quarter.

They were looking for Jodi.

Who had supposedly been enchanted and shrunk down to the size of a Weeman from the old nursery rhyme and was now helplessly adrift in the harbour.

According to a dead man.

Not bloody likely, Denzil thought.

The whole affair was absurd from start to finish. Except Jodi *was* missing. And he could still feel the touch of the cadaver's hands on him, could still hear Briello's ghostly voice, issuing forth from between his dead lips with its cold, raspy tones. . . .

"What's that?" Lizzie cried, pointing off to one side where the light from Denzil's lantern had momentarily illuminated something floating on the swell of the waves.

Taupin shone his own lantern in that direction. Henkie paused in his rowing to have a closer look, then took up the oars once more.

"It's too big," Taupin said.

"Just a seal," Henkie agreed.

"Maybe we should ask it to help us, you," Denzil said, unable to keep the sarcasm from his voice.

But Henkie appeared to give the idea serious consideration.

"Oh, no," Denzil said. "Now you go too far. . . ."

The seamen around Bodbury—fishermen in their pilchard luggers and sharking boats, sailors and Coastguard, smugglers and crabmen, anyone who worked the water—were a superstitious lot. And their notions were a motley and dizzying collection of nonsense and old wives' tales.

They disliked anything being stolen from their vessels—not only for the obvious reasons, but because they believed that a part of the ship's luck had gone with it. Strong steps were taken, or high prices paid, to get it back. For the same reason, anything lent from one ship to the other detracted from the lender's luck, unless the object was first damaged a little, however slightly, before being handed over.

They considered it unlucky to have a clergyman on board, or even to mention a minister, so "fore and after," with its reference to the clerical collar, was used. Another substitute, used by others, was "white choker."

Once on board ship, it was unlucky to return home to fetch some forgotten thing.

Women aboard brought bad luck.

To eat a pilchard by starting from the head was the same as driving away the shoals of fish.

And a hundred other strange and illogical assertions that the fisher-folk clung firmly to, for all that many of them were deeply religious.

Such as their beliefs when it came to the souls of the dead.

Never mind heaven and hell. They said that gulls embodied the souls of dead fishermen and sailors, while seals embodied the souls of dead piskies. The small became large; the large, small, was how they put it. And they firmly believed that to harm either would bring on such an incursion of bad luck as to make a broken mirror a joke.

So the gulls raided the fishermen's wharves and wheeled and spun freely above Bodbury. And the local colony of seals, whose rookery was by the Yolen Rock south of the town, could swim directly into the harbour with impunity, for who would dare harm them? And didn't they help the fishermen—steering them to pilchard shoals, or guiding their luggers back to harbour in deep fog?

There were no tales of selchies in Bodbury—those creatures who were seals in the water and men on the land. Such stories were saved for those who lived farther north. No, here the seals were ancestrally akin to the Good Neighbours, and treated with the same cautious respect as the country-folk extended to the piskies.

It was all superstitious poppycock, of course, Denzil thought. A great load of rubbish, pure and simple.

But Henkie paused in his rowing once more. He cupped his hands together and called out across the water to where the seal rose from a trough to the crest of another wave.

"It's got something on its head," Lizzie said.

"A hat, I don't doubt," Denzil muttered. "Is it a bull or a cow? I hear you can tell by the kind of headgear they assume when they take a turn about the harbour at night."

"It's a cow," Henkie said in the kind of voice that stated a plain fact.

And of course, Denzil thought, being the philanderer he was, Henkie would know.

"Keep that light on her," Henkie said as he started to turn the boat and row towards the seal.

Denzil rolled his eyes and glanced back at shore. His gaze caught and then focused on a figure that stood on the wharf of New Dock, watching them. Because of the distance and the dark, it was hard to make out more than a silhouette framed by a light in the market behind it, but that silhouette bore an uncanny likeness to the Widow Pender.

A shiver went through Denzil and he couldn't have said why. He looked away, then back again, but the figure was now gone.

"My soul and body!" he heard Taupin exclaim.

Feeling tired and irritable, and more than a little put upon with the night's strange goings on, Denzil turned once more to see what had excited Taupin. And then his jaw went slack for the second time that night.

3.

Jodi was having the oddest sort of a dream.

It was a late summer's afternoon and the sea was quiet. She was in the bay near Yolen Rock, floating on the gentle waves in a carker—one of those little boats that the boys in the Tatters made from cork with a piece of slate or hoop-iron for a keel. When you were a Small, a carker was just the right size.

All around her, in the sea and on the rocks about the craggy island of blue alvin stone that was the rookery, were the seals of Yolen Rock. Better than a hundred of them. Mated bulls and cows, bachelors and young females and pups. Sunning themselves. Floating as dreamily in the water as she did in her carker. And making such a racket. Barks and yelps filled the air—a kind of conversation that Jodi almost felt she could understand if she tried a little harder.

She'd often come here when she was her proper size, Ollie snuggled in her jacket when it was cool, perched on her shoulder or rambling about on the ground in front, behind and on all sides when the summer sun shone warm. Sometimes she'd come here with Denzil, and they'd talk the hours away, or with Taupin, and they would sit up on the headland across from the Rock, sit there for hours, not saying a word, while they watched the herd.

She'd never been this close to them before.

A pod of the young pups had a slide near the water and were playing on it like otters—carrying on like a pack of Tatters children as they filled the air with their squeals and shouts. Her carker drifted closer to them, but then was intercepted by a bachelor. His sleek fur streamed water as he lifted his head to look at her.

The stone, he said.

When he spoke, the words sounded in Jodi's ears—a sweet bell-like sound as unlike a seal's vocal barking as a forest is lit by the sun and then the moon. It seemed familiar as well, as though she'd heard just that particular cadence before, that country burr—but with her ears, not in her mind.

Trailing a hand lazily in the water, she looked at Yolen Rock where it rose from the water.

"What about it?" she asked.

Don't forget the holed stone.

An uncomfortable sensation awoke in the pit of her stomach. A dark memory stirred under the stimuli of sun and fair weather that had been warming her.

"No," she said.

Nine times through.

The feeling grew, spreading up to constrict her chest, bringing a shiver that traveled the length of her body. The memory expanded as well . . . something to do with the inner workings of clocks. . . .

"Don't talk like that."

At moonrise.

A dull throbbing started up behind her eyes, a pinprick of pain that whistled into a shriek between her temples.

"Please, don't. . . ."

But it was too late. Already she was remembering. The Widow and her creatures and what they'd done to Edern. What the little man was. A clockwork mechanism that had been smashed to pieces. Cogs and gears scattered all about while she plunged into dark water and drowned. . . .

When you wake, the seal said, his huge liquid eyes engulfing her. *Don't forget the stone.*

"I don't want to wake up."

Because being a Small here was lovely, but waking meant she'd be in a place where everything was horrible. Witches and their fetches. Bog creatures and little clockwork men who got torn to pieces. And the sea, always the dark waters of the sea, closing over her head the way they'd closed over her father's. . . .

"You can't make me wake up."

But her surroundings were already smearing as though they'd only been so much condensation on glass and a huge hand was now wiping the glass clean.

"I won't!" she cried.

But we need you.

Now she recognized the voice's familiarity.

She floated in darkness—not the sea, but in a place where there was no up and no down, just that sensation of floating. And the darkness. But these shadows held no menace.

I need you.

She remembered the old seamen's tales then—how seals carried in them the souls of dead piskies.

She remembered a small man.

Her clockwork man.

Dead now.

All too dead—if he'd ever even been alive in the first place.

"Edern?"

There was no reply.

"Edern?" she tried again. "Were you real?"

Too late now, for she was waking up in earnest and now even the floating sensation and the darkness were going away and she was waking to a bruised and aching body, and a light that shone so bright it stung her eyes and made them tear.

4.

"She's so tiny," Lizzie said, her eyes wide with astonishment. "Like a doll."

Henkie only grunted. He'd had a quick look himself, but now he concentrated more on keeping the boat steady to allow the seal with its odd little burden an easier approach than on the burden itself.

Beside Lizzie, Denzil could only stare at the tiny figure carried through the waves on the seal's head—tiny, but recognizable, God help him—and consider how either he had gone entirely mad, or else he needed to reconsider his complete outlook on the world. He took off his glasses to dry the salt spray that had splashed onto them from a particularly enthusiastic wave and set them back on the bridge of his nose.

Everything had changed.

What could be and what couldn't. What was, what was probable, and what was impossible.

Absolutely nothing made sense anymore and he no longer knew *what* to think. Relief at Jodi's safety—no matter her size—warred with utter bewilderment at how she could be such a size in the first place. And he felt like a fool. Like such a silly, foolish old man. He could hear his own mocking "tee-ta-taw" at every mention of what he considered a scientifically unsound principle.

How completely mortifying to know he'd been wrong all this time. But at the same time, an indefinable excitement was rising up inside him.

That such a thing could be. It opened whole new worlds of possibilities and study.

Denzil's only consolation was that—except for Henkie, who seemed to grow grumpily taciturn whenever he was in the middle of something delicate and obviously approached any wonder in a matter-of-fact fashion—he wasn't alone in his astonishment. Taupin and Lizzie seemed just as dumbfounded as he was himself.

Dumbfounded and enchanted.

For what could be so enchanting as the perfect tiny size that Jodi had become?

Lizzie lifted her carefully from the seal's head. Wrapping the tiny shivering body in a kerchief, she held her close to the lantern, murmuring cooing sounds that, Denzil knew, would drive Jodi mad if she were awake to hear them.

Denzil leaned closer to have a look.

"Is she . . . ?"

"She's had a terrible soaking," Lizzie said, "and the poor little thing is trembling from the cold, but I think she'll be all right. What do you think, Henkie?"

The big man, working the oars again as he rowed them back towards his warehouse at the end of the Old Quay, gave yet another grunt that could have meant anything. Denzil decided to take it as an affirmative. He was just as happy that Henkie kept his mind on the business at hand. It was a tricky business, navigating a way through the graveyard of ship masts and hulls that protruded from the water all along the Old Quay.

Taupin was shining his lantern towards Lizzie, half standing to try to get a better look himself. The boat rocked back and forth.

"Will you sit!" Henkie said.

Taupin sat.

Denzil tore his gaze away from the tiny figure and looked for the seal, but it was gone.

"What an amazing thing," he said softly. "You've my thanks, you!" he added, calling out over the water.

Henkie gave him a look and a smile, but said nothing. The muscles of his arms rolled under his jersey as he rowed them across the harbour with long steady strokes. Denzil turned back in his seat and returned his attention to Jodi.

There was a bump as they reached the shore. Denzil glanced up, surprised that they'd made the trip so quickly.

"Changed your mind then, have you?" Henkie asked him as he stowed the oars.

"About what?"

"About everything."

"I suppose I have."

"Oh, look," Lizzie said, her voice rising in pitch a few notes. "She's coming around."

They all leaned forward to see the tiny eyelids fluttering open.

"It's a bloody miracle," Henkie said. "Pity she doesn't have wings, though. I'd love to see how real working wings would look."

"She's not some Victorian fairy, you," Denzil said.

"But she's a bit of magic all the same, isn't she?"

"Will you be *quiet*," Lizzie hissed.

They looked to see Jodi's tiny features scrunched up, her hands over her ears.

"Let's bring her inside," Henkie said as he moored the rowboat.

He tried speaking quietly, but even his whispering had a booming quality about it.

"Softly," Lizzie said.

Henkie nodded, muttering, "Bloody hell," under his breath as he led the way into the warehouse.

The others trooped in after him. Denzil was last and paused in the doorway to look down the dark stone walkway that spilled the length of the Old Quay all the way to New Dock. He looked for the Widow and saw no sign of her, but he couldn't shake the feeling that something out in the night was watching them all the same. There was a perplexing scent in the air, which he likened to disturbed bog water, but he could find no source for it either.

He stood there for a few moments longer, then finally shook his head and followed the others inside.

5.

Once she got over the initial shock of having all those huge faces peering at her where she sat on the tabletop, and was warmed with a set of dry clothes taken from a doll that Henkie dragged out from somewhere in the vast confusion of boxes and shelves and crates that filled his warehouse, Jodi sipped from a thimbleful of tea and told her story. She was hoarse by the time she was done, even with the tea—laced with rum added to it a careful bead at a time from an eyedropper—to soothe her throat. Thankfully, the giants—which was how she'd come to think of her rescuers—spoke only in whispers so her ears had mostly stopped their ringing.

"Makes me feel like we're a band of conspirators," Taupin remarked.

"I suppose we are, in a way," Henkie said.

Of the four of them, his was the only voice that still made her ears ache. His idea of whispering was a dull, low-pitched growl that rumbled like distant thunder. Whenever he spoke, Jodi could feel the bones in her chest resonating with his deep bass tones.

Like anyone who grew up in the Tatters, she was familiar with the eccentric painter, though this was the first time that she'd actually been inside his warehouse. It was everything that it had promised it would be from the spying glances that she and the other Tatters children had stolen through its dirty windows. She could easily spend hours in its cavernous depths—its immensity magnified still more due to her own present size.

Which reminded her of the first problem at hand.

"How can I get back to my own size?" she squeaked hoarsely.

"First off," Henkie said, "we'll march straight over to the bloody Widow's place and get that button."

"That won't necessarily be so easy, you," Denzil said.

"And why would that be?" Henkie asked.

"Because when we were out in the harbour, I saw her spying on us from New Dock. She'll be warned and have the button well hidden by now."

"And she's such an old grouch," Lizzie added, "that she'll never tell us where she's gone and hidden it."

"Then we'll bloody well beat the secret from her," Henkie growled.

"La," Taupin said. "And won't the constables take that in stride?"

Denzil nodded. "Some of us aren't exactly the most respected members of this community."

"Tremeer would jump at any chance to run you in," Lizzie said.

"There must be *something* we can do," Henkie said.

Jodi winced as the volume of his voice rose.

"What about the stone?" she piped up. "The Men-an-Tol?"

"That's just a fairy tale," Denzil said. "There's about as much magic in a piece of stone, carved by the ancients or not, as there is in—in . . ."

"In what?" Taupin asked with a grin.

"Never you mind, you," Denzil told him grumpily.

Even Jodi had to laugh, though she put her hands over her ears when Henkie joined in.

"Henkie," Lizzie warned.

He glanced at her, then at Jodi, and broke off immediately. Though he said nothing, Jodi saw his lips mouth the words, "Bloody hell." It appeared to be his favorite expression.

"This little man," Taupin said. "You say he was actually a clock-work mechanism?"

Jodi's good humour drained away as she nodded.

"And then you dreamed his spirit was in the body of a seal?"

Another nod.

"I thought only gods and angels spoke to one in a dream," Denzil said, still unable to keep the sardonic tone from his voice.

"Only if it's a true dream," Henkie said.

"Perhaps that's a potential of the piskies that we've not heard of before," Taupin said thoughtfully.

"What is?" Henkie asked. "Speaking in dreams?"

"That, and the fact that they can slip their minds out of their own bodies and into the minds of others—borrowing the bodies of animals and inanimate objects when the need arises and their own bodies can't fulfill the necessary task."

Denzil hrumphed, but said nothing.

Taupin gave him a smile and added, "Surely, every time one turns about, the world proves to be a more marvelous place than it was the moment before."

Lizzie nodded. "Did you ever think of the way a cat just sits there sometimes, looking for all the world as though it was hanging on to your every word?"

Taupin nodded. "It makes you think, doesn't it just?"

"So," Denzil said a little wearily, "you think we should take Jodi to the stone and pass her nine times through its hole?"

"At moonrise," Jodi said.

Denzil sighed. "But what will it *do*?"

"There's only one way to find out, isn't there?" Henkie said.

"But we'll have to be careful of the Widow," Jodi added. "She's got that Windle to spy on us. Who knows what would happen if she followed us out to the stone."

"Now that fetch creature is something I'd like to paint," Henkie said. He glanced at Jodi. "And you as well, all tiny as you are. I never knew Nettie had a daughter in the first place, little say one so pretty."

"I'm her niece," Jodi said.

"And she doesn't want to be painted, you," Denzil added.

He shot a glance at the full-length portrait of Lizzie that was still on the artist's easel, then quickly looked away. The movement earned him another of Henkie's laughs.

"I didn't say in the buff," the big man said.

"It might be kind of fun," Jodi said. "No one's ever painted me before."

"And best it remain that way," Denzil said. "What would your aunt say if—"

"That creature," Lizzie broke in. She'd been looking nervously around the warehouse. "Could it be spying on us at the moment?"

They all fell silent and peered into the shadows that lay beyond their little circle of light.

"Well, we've been whispering," Henkie said, "so I doubt it's heard anything."

"There's also those sloch," Jodi said. "The bog creatures. But Edern said that they won't last out the night, and besides, we would have smelled them by now."

"Smelled them . . . ?" Denzil sat up straighter in his chair and adjusted his glasses, which had gone a little askew. "I did smell a terrible stink when we were coming inside. . . ."

Henkie stood up so quickly that his chair fell to the floor behind him. The loud crash it made brought Jodi's hands back to her ears once more. In a few long strides, the artist had crossed the open space to the door and flung it wide. He stood there for a long moment, taking in the grey dawn that was breaking over the town, then bent down to look at something that lay on the ground near the door.

"What is it?" Taupin asked.

"See for yourself."

They trooped over, Denzil carrying Jodi carefully in his cupped hands, to see the small puddles of marsh mud and vegetation that Henkie was crouched over.

To Jodi, the smell was unmistakable. The horrible memory of Edern's dying reared up in her mind and she turned away, holding tightly on to Denzil's thumb.

"How much do you think they heard?" Lizzie asked.

"Depends," Henkie replied, straightening up, "on how keen their hearing is."

He shooed them all back inside and closed the door firmly behind them.

"What we need is a plan," he said, his voice pitched so low that they all had to lean in close to hear him, "and I've got just the one to leave that bloody witch's mind reeling in confusion. And it won't"—he glanced at Lizzie—"get us in trouble with the law, either."

"And this plan is?" Denzil asked in a voice that made it apparent that he'd just as soon not know.

"Consider Tatters children on their bicycles," Henkie began. "A whole pack of them, wheeling about like so many hornets. . . ."

The Conundrum

Now o'er the one half-world
Nature seems dead; and wicked dreams abuse
The curtained sleep. . . .

—WILLIAM SHAKESPEARE, from *Macbeth*

If the Order of the Grey Dove was a pool of secret water, hidden deep in the forest of the world, then John Madden could be likened to the dropped stone that causes waves of consequence to flow in concentric circles from the center of its influence.

The line of authority was simple to follow to its source, if one knew how and where to look: There was the world, there was the Order, there were the various branches of the Order's Council of

Elder Adepts, there was the Inner Circle, and finally, at the center of it all, there was Madden himself, tugging the strands of his spider-webbed will to govern them all. Like the dropped stone in water, his influence caused a ripple effect that spread, first through the various levels of the Order, then out into the world of the sheep that he knew he had been born to rule.

What he wanted, he invariably got. And he was patient.

He had only known one failure—one absolute failure—and the ripples of *its* effect were still being felt. Such as tonight, when the Inner Circle of the Order met and he was reminded of it yet again.

The theatrics invoked for other aspects of the Order were not present in this suite where they had gathered. There were no masks nor robes nor candles nor rituals. It was a Spartan yet tastefully furnished boardroom, thirty stories above the streets of Manhattan. It gleamed of glass and steel, teak and burnished leather. Five seats, each occupied, were set at one end of a long wooden table. There were no notepads, nor pens with which to write upon them; no recording devices, nor secretaries to transcribe the proceedings. The walls were unadorned, except for a tapestry depicting the grey dove of the Order that hung behind Madden's chair at the head of the table.

To Madden's right sat Roland Grant who *Forbes,* the American business weekly, said was the world's seventh richest non-monarch. He was a large, burly man, a Paul Bunyan of the North American business world, tamed in a three-piece tailored suit, still dark-haired for his years, and trim for all his weight. His assets were a who's who of major corporations and he sat on more boards than a Monopoly game had squares.

If he had one weakness, it was his daughter, Lena.

Beside Grant was James Kelly "J. K." Hale, a slender, tanned man with the lean features of a hawk who was the Hong Kong legal counsel for a number of Western corporations. Madden was presently grooming Hale to enter the American political arena in an advisory capacity, though if Hale had been asked about his planned career change, he would have thought the idea to be his own.

To Madden's left sat Eva Diesel, the West German author and political rights activist who used her considerable reputation as one of Europe's great humanitarians to influence public and government to the aims of the Order. She was a formidable woman, both in appearance and temperament, and Madden had yet to decide how much of her propaganda was actual conviction and how much was simple rhetoric to further the Order's aims when it required the nature of public and state support that she could gain for them.

Beside her, completing the inner circle, was Armand Monette, the French business magnate whose head offices were based in Paris. Like Grant, his world-scale corporate holdings were centered primarily in the fields of shipping, transport, fuels, and various media. Giving lie to the image of a suave Frenchman, he invariably appeared in rumpled suits, tie askew and hair mussed, red-eyed and in need of a shave, but his mind was as sharp as his appearance was disheveled and if his businesses were not as prosperous as Grant's, it was only because Madden didn't trust the man as much and therefore kept a careful—if surreptitious—curb on his successes.

Of the five, not one was under sixty, though that information would have surprised more than one gossip columnist.

They met once a month to assess the viability of the Order's ongoing strategies and ventures, and to discuss private projects—undertakings that only they were privy to in their entirety. General endeavors were reported, in turn, to the branch leaders of the Council of Elder Adepts by the member of the Inner Circle responsible for that particular branch, but the Adepts were told only enough to keep them compliant. The Order as a whole knew little or nothing of the Inner Circle's long-term goals, except in the vaguest of terms.

That was how it should be, Madden had realized long ago, because for all their dedication to his doctrines, the general members of the Order were still just another kind of sheep, subject, in the end, to his will, not their own.

And sometimes he thought—especially on a night like tonight—that the Inner Circle also required a lesson in who ruled and who was ruled. It was important, at least in terms of their continued usefulness to him, to allow them a sense of free will, so he was subtle in his manipulations, but the bottom line remained: He was in charge.

No other.

The Order of the Grey Dove had been created through *his* vision and perseverance. All the others—members of the Inner Circle and of the Council of Elder Adepts alike—were Johnny-come-latelies. Without him, the Order simply would not exist.

So he let them question him tonight; he let them bring him to task for his failure to acquire Dunthorn's secret. But he waited until the end of the meeting to give them their opportunity, and he allowed them only a few moments before he broke the discussion off.

He ruled them.

The underlying vision of the Order was his vision.

"*Bien,*" Armand Monette began—and of course it would be him, Madden thought. "We have yet to discuss the matter of this secret of yours, John. *Le mystère* in Cornwall. How is it progressing?"

"We have two of our best agents working on it now."

Madden was aware of Grant's grateful look for his including Lena in such a positive light, but he gave no indication of his observation.

"But it has been the better part of two weeks," Monette continued. "Surely you have some results?"

"Yes," Eva Diesel said in her clipped, formal English. "You have tantalized us with it for years. Has anything new been learned?"

How to explain that there was a bond between himself and the hidden power that Dunthorn had guarded, that he knew each time it woke and stretched its influence, but that he could gain no sense of what shape it wore, or what it actually was, only that it was a power beyond imagining.

Better yet, he thought, *why* should he explain?

He had long ago regretted ever mentioning its existence in the first place.

"We know only that it has finally surfaced again," he said. "And that we are very close to acquiring it."

J. K. Hale straightened in his seat. "I have to ask you again, John: Why all this pussyfooting around? Why don't we just walk in and take it?"

"We had Dunthorn for two days," Madden said. "He told us nothing. If we move too soon, we're just as liable to lose it for another thirty-five years."

"We have better interrogation methods now," Hale said. "The tongs have been developing some very interesting drugs over the past few years—"

"Not to mention your own government," Monette broke in.

Hale shot him an irritated look. "We could make them talk," he said. "Give my people just one day with them."

"I'm well aware of the pharmaceutical advances made in both America—which is *not* my country, Armand—and abroad," Madden said. "But I know these people. They have a stubborn streak that

goes beyond the reach of the most sophisticated methods of interrogation that we could bring to bear on them. And remember, they
might well not even *be* aware of what we are looking for."

"But you said the secret has been woken," Diesel said. "Surely,
then, someone must have woken it?"

All Madden needed to do was still that inner conversation that all
men and women carry on inside themselves and he could feel Dunthorn's hidden legacy, awake and powerful, reaching out across the
vast range of the Atlantic to speak to him. And this time, more than
ever before, he was realizing a sense of the thing that offered him a
far clearer understanding of just exactly what it was that he had
pursued for so long.

"It might even not be an object," he said softly. "It might be a . . .
place. All we need is the key that will unlock its secret. And soon. . . ."

"A place?" Monette asked.

Madden frowned, annoyed with himself for having said as much
as he had, and with Monette for pressing him. But he couldn't help
himself. More and more he found Dunthorn's legacy whispering to
him, waking odd longings, undermining the usual clarity of his
thought process.

"What do you mean?" Diesel asked as well, her eyes bright with
interest.

Hale nodded, his own eagerness apparent. "You've learned something?"

Only Grant remained silent and for that Madden was grateful.

Madden stood up. "If you can't feel what I feel," he said, falling
back on the mystical to end the probing questions, "then perhaps
you aren't yet ready for the secret's gift. It will be a gift, yes, but one
that must be earned."

He held up a hand to forestall any further conversation.

"Think about it," he added, then left the boardroom.

2.

Madden was sitting in his private office when Grant joined him
a little later. Here thick shag carpeting lay underfoot and the
leather furniture was thickly padded, built more for comfort than
appearance. A ceiling-to-floor bookcase lined one wall; another was
completely given over to one enormous window. The drapes were
open and the New York skyline lay outside, dark and lit with jew-

eled lights. His desk was an antique rolltop, polished until the wood glowed. Original paintings by three different Impressionists hung on another wall. In one corner was a small bar; in another a computer system tied by modem into Madden's own commercial empire.

He looked out the window to the Manhattan skyline, but was seeing past it, away beyond the man-made mountains and their constant hurly-burly of lights and glitter; away beyond the dark reaches of the Atlantic to a small peninsula, its shores rocked by waves, its land cloaked in a darkness that New York City might once have known, but would never know again; away to that place where Dunthorn's legacy hummed and throbbed with a power that Madden yearned to hold in his grip and that had never seemed so close within his reach as it did now.

Grant said nothing when he entered the office. He poured himself a neat whiskey, added two ice cubes from the small bar fridge, then sat down on the leather sofa by the bar and sipped thoughtfully at his drink, patiently waiting until Madden finally turned to face him.

"They don't understand, Rollie," he said.

"I don't understand either."

Madden nodded. "I know. But you're willing to wait for enlightenment and that's what sets you apart from the rest of them. If we didn't need them . . ."

Grant set his drink down on the glass table in front of the sofa.

"They could be replaced," he began.

Madden smiled. "And then we'd have to train a new group and that's something neither of us has the time to do. Nor do we have the time to assume their responsibilities. Besides, at least we *know* these wolves."

"Too true."

Grant picked up his drink again and took another sip before replacing the glass exactly on the outlined ring of condensation it had made earlier on the table's clear surface.

"What do you see, John?" he asked. "When you look out at the night, what is it that you see that we can't?"

From another, Madden might consider this prying. But Rollie Grant wasn't only his oldest business partner: He was also the closest Madden had to what others might call a friend.

"More than power and glory," Madden said. "I see a mystery, a kind of mystical purpose that grows more obscure the further you follow it, but each step you take, the more your spirit grows. Swells. Enlarges until one day, you feel as though it will encompass the whole of the world. But best of all, even then you know the mystery will go on, unexplained, and you can keep following it forever. Past life. Past death. Past whatever lies beyond death."

He looked out the window again, a half smile touching his lips, the distance thrumming in his eyes when he turned to Grant once more. Wild energy and a monumental peace, commingled, played there in Madden's gaze until he blinked.

"True immortality," he said, his voice soft.

"In Dunthorn's legacy?" Grant asked.

Madden nodded. "Enough for us all, but it will only be offered to those we know are worthy. To those who earn it."

He saw anxiety rest fleetingly in Grant's eyes, then it fled before his searching gaze.

"I wouldn't worry, Rollie," he said. "You're on the right road. You've earned the right to taste the secret."

"That's not what's important," Grant said. "Not so much as your achieving it."

If it had been anyone else, Madden would have considered the man to be just toadying up to him, but he knew Grant well enough to know that he sincerely meant what he said. If history was to prove Madden an avatar—as eventually Madden knew it must—then Grant would be ranked foremost among his disciples. Even above Michael Bett, for Bett's present body housed the soul of the Beast, and the Beast, for all his expertise and wisdom, could never be trusted. Not in his past incarnations; not in his present one.

Grant was his John. Simple and steadfast, and he would remain true to the last.

"Whatever Dunthorn's legacy is," Madden said, "it has finally broken free of its constraints once more. Now I can feel its presence in the air, wherever I turn. There isn't a moment when it isn't present."

"Could you track it down?"

"I think so," Madden said with a nod. Then, firmer: "Yes. I'm sure I can."

Grant rubbed his hands together. "So when do we leave for Cornwall?"

Madden laughed. "Just like that?"

His laughter died when Grant didn't join in with it.

"What's wrong, Rollie?"

Grant hesitated.

"No secrets between us," Madden lied. "Remember?"

Grant nodded. "It's Michael," he said. "I spoke to Lena earlier this evening. From what she tells me, I think Bett is losing it."

"Ah, Lena. . . ."

"I know what you think of her, John, but she can be competent when she sets her mind to the task."

"She's just so easily detoured," Madden said.

He held up a placating hand before Grant could defend his daughter.

"I spoke to Michael before the Circle met," he said. "He seemed . . . distraught. I think, that in this case, Lena is very close to the mark. I don't think Michael's out of control—not yet, at any rate. But if we leave him there on his own, he soon will be."

"So we are going?"

Madden smiled. "Of course we are, Rollie. This close to finally putting our hands on Dunthorn's legacy, how could we not?"

"I sent one of my security people over to look after Lena," Grant added. "I was worried about her. Bett—apparently he threatened her. The trouble is, Gazo won't get there until morning at the earliest."

"You did the right thing," Madden said, "if only to set your own mind at ease. But Michael won't trouble her again tonight. Tonight he discovered that not only do sheep have teeth, but sometimes they bite with them as well."

"He's been hurt?"

"Bruised," Madden replied. "And mostly just his pride." He looked out the window again; felt the mystery calling to him, whispering. . . .

"See about our flight, would you, Rollie?" he said, his voice gone soft once more.

He didn't hear Grant's reply, nor did he hear the man leave. His head thrummed with the promise hidden in Dunthorn's lost legacy: lost once, and now awake again. Almost found. Calling to him; calling and calling. . . .

Madden had never heard such a sweet sound before.

3.

Madden wasn't alone in feeling the presence of William Dunthorn's legacy. Like a fog creeping up from the sea, that same presence

touched those sleeping in Mousehole and Paul, in Lamorna and Newlyn, and as far as Penzance.

To some it was merely a feeling of something brighter or darker
in their dreams. It called up memories of those who had emigrated
or moved up country, or merely to another part of the West Division
of the Hundred of Penwith; called up those who had died and gone
on—a beloved wife, a missed friend, a cherished child, a husband or
brother or cousin stolen by the sea; called up hopes and fears and
all the tangled emotions in between; called up the absent and the
dead and walked them through the sleepers' dreams.

Some greeted their spectral visitors with awe and joy and love.

Some were merely confused.

Others could know nothing but dread. . . .

Clare Mabley relived her experience from earlier in the evening, only
this time there was no Davie Rowe present to help her.

In a heavy rain, she crawled down Mousehole's narrow, twisting
streets, relentlessly pursued by her masked assailant, his switchblade
transformed into a butcher's knife that would have done Jack the
Ripper proud. Its blade glowed with its own inner fire and sparked
and sizzled when the raindrops hit its polished steel. He finally caught
her up by the Millpool, his blade lifting high, his face behind its
goggles and scarf more than ever like some monstrous bug, but before the knife could plunge down, she clawed away his mask to
find—

She woke, shivering in her chair, and shook her head.

"No," she whispered. "Never Felix."

One room over, Lilith Mabley met her husband in her dreams.

They sat, the two of them, as they had sat so many times before,
on the stone stoop of their cottage, Mount's Bay spread out before
them in the mist. He draped his hand over her shoulders and if there
was a briny scent about him, Clare's mother didn't mind, for she had
so much to tell him, and he to tell her. . . .

Davie Rowe was in a place where everyone was more disfigured than
he was, their faces swollen until they seemed more like children's
drawings come to life than humans. But it was also a place of miracles—a grotto, hidden away under the granite cliffs near the village.

The sea pounded outside, but inside, the water was as still as a sheet of glass and glowed with phosphorus. Beside a mirror set into the stone above the ledge that ran along the far side of the grotto, there was a candle that gave off more light than a candle should. One by one, in an orderly queue, the people approached it for their share of the miracle.

For in its light, their disfigurements fell away and their inner selves were revealed. That monstrous child, now an angel. That man suffering from neurofibromatosis, now as handsome as a matinee idol. That woman with her deformed facial bones and the grey tumors that spread like a blight across her features, now a beauty. . . .

And finally it was his turn.

He trembled with eagerness as he approached, legs barely sturdy enough to support his massive frame. But the weakness didn't matter, because it was finally his turn.

His turn to bathe in the candle's light and then look into the burnished mirror with its brass frame, only to find that his true self—

(No! he howled.)

—was even more monstrous than the face he presently turned towards the world.

He woke on the sofa in Clare's study and sat up, tangled in blankets and hyperventilating, disoriented by his surroundings until he remembered where he was and how he'd come to be here.

He'd rescued Clare. He'd proved he was really a good person, just like Bogart and Eastwood and the hundred other cinema idols whose exploits filled his waking thoughts.

(Never mind the two hundred quid, hey, Davie?)

He would have done it anyway.

(Of course you would have. But only so you'd have a chance to get into her knickers. . . .)

It wasn't like that.

(And a fine bloody pair the two of you will make—the cripple and the freak. . . .)

He shook his head. It wasn't like that at all.

(A cripple and a freak. . . .)

She's not a cripple.

(And you're not a freak, are you, Davie boy? Not bloody much, you aren't. When was the last time someone looked you in the face without gagging?)

Clare. She—

(Is a bloody cripple.)

Davie shook his head again, trying to shake the voice out from between his ears.

(When was the last time you didn't have to pay for it, Davie boy? Do you think Cary Grant had to pay for it, then? Or does Redford?)

"Stop," he whispered.

(And even then you can see it in their eyes: For all your money, they still wished you'd put a bag on your head. . . .)

Davie rocked back and forth on the sofa, moaning softly, refusing to listen to any more. When the dawn came, smudging grey across the eastern skies, he stole out of the house and away to home, but the voice followed him.

He couldn't escape it.

It was always there in his head.

Sometimes it was just harder to ignore.

Down Raginnis Hill, in the village proper, the Gaffer lay sleeping in his house on Duck Street.

His dream took him out past the protective arms of Mousehole harbour in a rowboat. He sat in the stern with Adeline—sweet, gentle Addie, her arm nestled comfortably into the crook of his arm from where it should never have strayed—while their son Paul rowed them out past Shag Rock and St. Clement's Isle, his back bent easily to the task, that familiar smile of his that lit his whole face, beaming and shining.

On the island, hidden at first by the rocks, the Gaffer's old mate Billy sat up from where he'd been reading and waved to them as they went by, his book tucked under his arm. The oddest thing was that Dunthorn wasn't the young man now that the Gaffer remembered from old photos and his memories, but rather he appeared as he would have had he lived to this day.

"Billy!" the Gaffer cried.

"Did a proper job 'mazing you, didn't I just?" Billy called back. "Thought I was dead, did you?"

The Gaffer turned in his seat. "Wait a bit, Paul," he said.

But Paul kept rowing and the island fell away, Billy still waving on its rocky shore.

"Don't fuss so," Addie told the Gaffer. "Now tell me, how's it been with our Janey?"

"Our Janey . . . ?"

Anxiety rode high and wild through the Gaffer until he looked

into Addie's gently smiling face, and then the turmoil washed away
and he settled back in his seat.

"Our Janey's a musician now," he began, smiling to see how Paul
leaned forward to catch every word as well.

Janey Little's dream was of neither her grandmother nor her father,
but it did involve a member of her immediate family—the forgotten
lost soul that was her mother.

Janey found herself walking at night through an enormous city
that she'd never been in before, but she immediately recognized it as
New York when the thoroughfare she was on dropped her into the
mad hubbub bustle of Times Square. Neon screamed, passersby
pushed her aside in ever-increasing numbers; she was offered drugs,
sex, to be bought, to be sold, all in the space of a half-dozen moments. Her senses were assaulted with the hurly-burly and felt like
they were going to overload until she finally found a quieter side
street to duck into.

There she stood, leaning against the dirty wall, the stink of garbage
and urine making her stomach queasy, the end of the street still spitting its noise and confusion at her. But at least it was quieter. She
pushed off the wall and moved farther down the street, starting when
something stirred in a nest of newspapers near her feet. Light from
a window above fell down on the dirty face that looked up at her.
Through the grime, looking past the multiple layers of filthy clothes
and the greasy hair, she realized with a shock that this was her
mother, lying there, looking up at her.

"Didsha never shink I *wandud* chew come hum?" her mother
asked.

Her voice was thick and alien, muffled from the night's drinking
and her missing teeth.

"I mished muh baby. . . ."

The grubby fingers reached for her—skeletal, like a bird's claws—
and Janey backed away.

"Pleash. . . ."

Guilt reared up in Janey, but she continued to back away from
the woman. Her mother staggered to her feet. As she stood and stumbled after Janey, hanging on to the wall to keep her balance, urine
leaked down one leg. Unheeding of it, she continued after Janey who
turned tail and ran back the way she'd come.

She was pushed back and forth between the angry pedestrians until sheer desperation brought her out of sleep and gasping for air. She sat up in bed, shivering from the chill as her damp body met the cool night air, and tried to slow her breathing. She looked down at Felix who was moving back and forth, caught in his own dream. She started to reach for him—to comfort, to be comforted—but then a final memory from her own nightmare rose up in her mind, staying her hand.

It was her mother's voice, clear and sober, that had followed her out of the grey reaches of sleep.

"Forgive me," she'd said, just as Janey was waking.

Her final words had been . . .

Forgive me.

With a kind of sick uneasiness, Janey realized that she never thought of the woman—couldn't even remember her. Could barely put the word "mother" to her.

The woman had abandoned them; it was like she was dead. But what if she'd realized that it was all a mistake? What if years ago she realized the mistake she'd made, and regretted it, but by then it was too late?

Forgive me.

Hadn't Janey made her own mistakes in the past? Mistakes that seemed just as final, decisions made in the heat of the moment that could almost never be recalled?

She looked down at Felix, still stirring restlessly beside her in the bed.

Forgive me.

She shook her head. It was just a dream, that was all. A bad dream.

Forgive me.

She owed her mother nothing. Her mother owed her nothing.

Forgive me.

Tears welled in her eyes as she shook her head again, but neither helped to dislodge the memory of the New York City bag lady from her dream. Nor did it quiet the echoing refrain of her voice that whispered on and on through Janey's mind.

Forgive me.

"I don't know if I want to," Janey said.

Forgive me.

"I don't know if I even can. . . ."

•   •   •

Felix Gavin had been hanged.

He didn't know what his crime had been, nor who had judged him, but they had put the noose around his neck and he'd dropped the long drop, his neck broken, his limbs twitching, and now he was dead. Still in his body, but it was no longer his to command. He was a passenger now, on a trip that went to nowhere. He merely swung back and forth in the rain, hanging from the makeshift gallows—a huge old tree on a crossroads.

He became aware of a woman approaching him through the rain, cloaked and hooded against the weather. Holding a knife in her teeth, she hoisted her skirts and climbed the oak. When she could reach the rope, she cut him down and he fell into the mud, but he didn't feel the impact.

His nerve ends were all dead. He was dead. A ghost, jailed in its own corpse, dispassionately observing what became of the shell he'd worn while still alive.

Death wasn't what the church had taught him it would be, but he was used to being lied to by figures of authority. The world he'd left with his death was full of lies. But he discovered that one thing he'd heard about hangings was true: You did get a hard-on when the rope hit its limit and your neck was broken—a finger to the world, as it were. A final "Screw you all."

How he knew this to be true was that after the woman had stripped his clothes off, she hoisted her skirts again and rode him there in the mud and rain, drawing his last inadvertent statement to the world deep inside herself, closing her warmth around its dead, cold length.

This was wrong, Felix thought. It was sick. Perverted.

She began to make small noises in the back of her throat and moved faster, moaning and twitching, which struck Felix—in his curious dispassionate state—as odd. So far as he could see this brutal bouncing up and down held about the same amount of excitement as butter being churned.

But then what did he know? He was dead. While she—

Her hood fell back as she arched her back. If Felix had had a throat at that moment, his breath would have caught in it.

She . . .

That dark hair . . .

Those familiar features . . .

She shuddered as she reached her climax, her entire body shaking and trembling. She lay down across his chest, still holding him inside her, and brushed his cold cheek with her lips.

Physically, he felt nothing. But in his heart, in the spirit that lived on, he could feel something dying.

"I'll do anything for you," she said. "Anything it takes to make you mine."

She bit at his lip, hands cupped on either side of his face, then slipped her tongue into his mouth.

No, he wanted to shout at her. But he had no voice. Could feel nothing.

"And if I can't have you when you're alive . . ."

She ground her hips against his.

No, he cried soundlessly again. This is wrong.

He struggled to be heard, to move the dead limbs that had once been his, to push her from him.

". . . then I'll have you when you're dead."

She pushed up, hands against his chest, and began to move up and down once more.

This time when Felix fought to be heard—

—he woke instead.

He felt flushed and cold, all at once. A headache whined like a dentist's drill behind his eyes. The contents of his stomach roiled acidly around and he knew he was going to throw up, but he still couldn't move.

That was because he was dead. . . .

But he could feel his body again, the sheets against his skin, someone in bed beside him. So he wasn't dead. He just couldn't move. All he could do was open his eyes and stare at a shadowed ceiling that seemed vaguely familiar and make a kind of strangled noise.

"N-nuh . . ."

The bedsprings gave as that someone in bed with him shifted position. He tried to turn his head to see who it was, but even that simple motion was denied him. Vomit came burning up his throat.

I'm going to choke on my own puke, he thought. I'm going to—

But whoever it was who was beside him lifted, then turned his head. He had a momentary glimpse of Janey's worried features above him before his body hurled up the contents of his stomach into the wastepaper basket that she had brought up from the side of the bed.

He heaved until his stomach was empty, then heaved some more, a rancid taste in his throat, his chest hurting. But finally it was over.

Finally, he could lay his head weakly on the pillow and take small shallow breaths that didn't make his chest ache. But he still felt queasy. The dentist's drill was still whining inside his head.

He tried to concentrate on Janey, on what she was saying, but for a long time all he could hear was just the wordless soothing sound of her voice as she brought him water to rinse his mouth and wiped his face with a damp cloth.

He tried to understand what he was doing back here—for now he could recognize the bedroom as the one he'd been staying in at the Gaffer's house—and why Janey was taking care of him.

The last thing he remembered . . .

He was a hanged man, being cut down from an oak tree and then—

No. That had been a dream.

The last thing that he could remember was . . .

But that, too, seemed to involve a woman sitting astride him, his hardness drawn deep inside her. . . .

Another dream.

The last real thing he could remember, he decided, was the Gaffer and Janey sending him off. Playing music by the old quarry—a duet with the tide. The storm. Lena. Drinking tea. . . .

"Felix, can you hear me?"

Finally something Janey said registered.

He tried to speak, then settled for nodding his head.

"You're going to be all right," she said. "You were drugged, by that woman—"

Lena. The tea. So that much was real. But drugged? She'd drugged him?

"H-h-how . . . ?" he managed.

"I came and got you. Oh, Felix. . . ."

A flickering image came into his mind. A naked woman. Riding him. Not in the rain and mud. But in a bed. . . .

A dream?

"Can you remember what happened to you?"

The whine in his head grew sharper. He squinted, tried to push past the pain to where his memories lay tangled up with dreams, to sort through which were real, and which were not. But he couldn't get past the pain.

"N-nuh . . ." he tried. "Nuh . . . ing. . . ."

Janey bent down and wrapped her arms around him.

"I'm so sorry I didn't give you a chance to explain," she said. "I'm an awful person sometimes."

No, he wanted to tell her, but it only came out, "N-nuh . . ."

"I love you, Felix."

"Luuv . . . too. . . ."

She gave him a squeeze. He could see the tears in her eyes. His own vision blurred. As she started to draw away, he tried to move his hand to stop her, but couldn't.

Don't go, he wanted to say. Don't leave.

"Nuh . . . nah . . ." was all he could say.

But she understood and lay down beside him once more. The whining ache in his head wound into a dart that sped deep into the back of his mind and he followed it down, leaving Janey to hold his sleeping body until she finally fell asleep again herself.

Felix didn't dream again. But Janey. . . .

This time her dreams took her into a more familiar setting.

She found herself standing at the bottom of the stairs in the Gaffer's house, looking across the room to where William Dunthorn's *The Little Country* lay on the Gaffer's favorite chair. It remained there as the Gaffer had left it earlier, its leather covers sealing in the magic of its words, the light behind the chair spilling a soft halo of light upon it as though the chair were a stage, the book a thespian.

And as though Janey's presence had signaled the opening of the curtains for the first act, the book's bindings made a faint crackling sound and the cover flipped open. The pages rustled as if they were being turned, one by one, ruffled as though by the breath of a wind, or an invisible hand flipping through them.

She took a step forward, then paused as music rose up around her—a wash of mysterious notes that played a tune both familiar and strange. It spoke of hidden places, secrets long lost that waited to be found. Her fingers twitched at her sides, searching for the fingerboard or air holes of an instrument that wasn't at hand.

The pages stopped moving as the music grew stronger. Figurines on the mantel, picture frames on the wall, and glasses and dinnerware in the kitchen cupboards trembled, then clattered as deep bass resonances echoed through the small house. She could feel the floor trembling underfoot, and swayed slightly, moving in time to the curious rhythm.

She took another step forward, then a third, pausing again when she saw something moving on top of the book.

No, she realized. Not moving on top of it. Rising from it. A Lilliputian man stepping from its pages to lift his head and look about the room, his gaze tracking the giant furnishings until it caught, then rested, on Janey's own gaze.

He was no bigger than the little mice or moles that Jabez occasionally deposited on the Gaffer's back doorstep with that smug pride of his species. Janey could have held the man in the palm of her hand—the whole of him, from toe tip to the top of his head.

She found she couldn't breathe as the light behind those tiny eyes locked on her own.

The music continued, a kind of slow reel, but played on instruments she couldn't recognize. They had a certain familiarity with ones that she knew, but something remained odd about them all the same, differences that made their pitch alien, for all their familiarity. There were plucked string sounds and bowed string sounds. An underlying drumming rhythm like that woken from the skin of a crowdy crawn—the Cornish equivalent of a bodhran. Free reed instruments and others with oboe-like tones. A kind of psaltry or harpsichord and distant piping that sounded like a chorus of Cornish pibcorns—the ancient native instrument that had a single reed and two cow's horns at the end of a cedarwood pipe and was much like a Breton bombarde.

She knew this music—knew it down to the very core of her being—but she had never heard it before. Unfamiliar, it had still always been there inside her, waiting to be woken. It grew from the core of mystery that gives a secret its special delight, religion its awe. It demanded to be accepted by simple faith, not dissected or questioned, and at the same time, it begged to be doubted and probed.

There was wonder in its strains, and bright flares of joy that set the heart on fire, but there was a darkness in it as well, a shadow that could reach into the soul and cloud all one's perceptions with a bleak grey shroud. The path between the two was narrow and treacherous, like the winding track that old folk songs claimed led one into Faerie.

Janey knew those songs, knew the lessons of the hard road to Heaven, the broad easy road to Hell, and the dangers of Faerie that lay in between, onion-layered with the world of the here and now into which she had been born, now lived, and would one day die. Given a choice, she would always take the winding road to Faerie, because Heaven was too bright. There were no secrets there, for none could withstand the judgmental glare of its light. And Hell was too dark.

But Faerie . . .

This music seemed to show the way to reach that realm. It led into secret glens where hidden wonders lay waiting for those brave enough to dare to follow it home.

Janey couldn't help herself. She had to go.

The key to where she should put her first foot forward lay there in the music, but it was tantalizingly just out of reach at the same time.

"How can I . . . ?" she began.

A new wash of the music, a sudden swell, rising to a crescendo, made her lose her train of thought, and then died down again.

If you must ask, it seemed to say, *then you will never find the way.* . . .

"But . . . ?"

She looked to the little man on Dunthorn's book for help.

Dark is best, the music whispered. *Dark is all.*

The tiny man looked back at her with a sense of alarm that she shared.

The music had settled into a deep drone. The entire house vibrated with its bass tones, wooden beams cracking, foundation stones shifting against one another. Heaven's awe, Faerie's wonder, faded from its strains.

Janey took another step forward all the same.

An eerie wail rose out of the drone, shrieking across the back of the music like a fingernail drawn across a blackboard. The little man sank back into the book—flailing his arms as though he were being drawn into the quickening mire of a bog.

Janey moved quickly closer, but this time a scratching at the window stopped her. She looked out to see a hundred tiny leering goblin faces staring in at her. The creatures clawed at the glass, slit eyes burning with a yellow light.

The music was a horror soundtrack now.

She caught movement from the corner of her eyes and turned to look back at the book. Its pages were flipping once more, rapidly turned by invisible hands. When they stopped this time, the music shrieked to another crescendo and a dark mist rose from the open pages of the book.

There were monstrous shapes in the mist. The stench of old graves dug open and corpse breath haunted the air. Childhood night terrors came to life: a Pandora's box of horrors and fears; specters of death and pestilence—visited on friends and family.

Her grandfather, stumbling out of the dark fog like a corpse, animated, but the soul was long fled, mouth full of squirming maggots, the eyes dead. . . .

Felix, reduced to a skeletal frame and covered with running sores, reaching for her with bleeding hands. . . .

Clare, dragging herself across the carpet towards her with fingers transformed into eagle's talons, her body ending at the waist, her mouth a horror of barracuda teeth, dripping blood from its corners. . . .

The *Rolling Stone* reporter shuffling forward, eyes milky and unseeing, trailing a ragged stream of his own entrails behind him. . . .

And more, so many more, all converging on her.

All reaching for her. . . .

Hands upon her now, a hundred hands, clawing at her arms and legs and torso, tearing long runnels of bleeding skin from her flesh, dragging her back into the heart of that dark mist where worse horrors waited for their chance to feed on her. . . .

At the windows outside, the goblins screeching their nails on the glass. . . .

The room stinking like an abattoir, reeking of blood and excrement, of burning hair and open graves. . . .

The music a rhythmical electronic drone on which rode the sounds of grinding teeth. . . .

And wet burbling.

Hateful whispers.

And a long pitiful moan that she—when she finally woke—realized was crawling up from her own throat. . . .

It was a very long time before, emotionally exhausted, she finally fell asleep again.

In his small room in the bed and breakfast, just a hop, skip, and a jump away from the Gaffer's house on Duck Street, Michael Bett lay alone, brooding.

He'd dreamt as well—of sunlit fields that were thick with the sweet scent of violets and anemones, and the hum of bees. Steep hillsides that ran down to a cove below where the surf washed against ancient granite. The sky was clear and there was a gentle music in the air—the soft sound of a set of Northumbrian pipes playing a tune that was familiar to him because it was on Janey Little's second album.

Bett had never been in such a peaceful place before.

It sickened him, enraged him.

This wasn't the way the world was. The world was all sharp edges and looking out for number one and take what you can get while you can.

Not this lie.

He took up a stick and began hacking at the flowers, cutting the heads from them with vast sweeps of his arm, but his one shoulder felt as though it had almost been dislocated and the bee-buzz/bird chorus sound of the pipes was getting under his skin until he could barely think and all he wanted was to kill whoever was playing them.

Janey Little.

He wanted to rip her lungs out of her chest.

He spun in a circle, flailing with the stick, trying to find the source of the music, a primordial howl building up in his chest, wailing for release.

He woke with that howl in his throat and only just muffled it in the nest of bedclothes in which his limbs had become entangled. His shoulder throbbed with pain.

He remembered his failure with Clare Mabley earlier this evening.

He remembered Lena Grant's newfound independence.

He remembered having to explain to Madden how things had become unraveled.

He wanted to lash out at something, someone, anything, but all he could do was lie there in the dark room, his shoulder aching, and stare up at the ceiling.

Patience, he told himself. Be patient. Everything's going to come together. And then the hurting was going to start. He was going to find out how they worked, every one of them. What arteries were connected to what veins. How long they could breathe with a hole in their lungs. How loud they could scream as he peeled away their skin. . . .

He could be patient.

But he wasn't going to try to sleep again tonight.

•   •   •

In her hotel room in Penzance, Lena Grant was also awake.

Her dream had been mundane compared to those that had visited others on the Penwith Peninsula tonight. She had simply been confronted by an angered Felix and had tried to explain herself to him. But he wouldn't listen. And her heart was breaking. And she wondered why she was even concerned about explaining anything to him, but she went on trying all the same, over and over again. And still her heart was breaking. Until she finally woke, alone in her room, to find her cheeks wet with tears and an emptiness lying there inside her that she'd never experienced before.

She didn't try to go back to sleep. Instead, she sat up, knees drawn to her chin, rocking back and forth against the headboard, and tried not to let the emptiness overcome her. She turned her mind back to Boston, to what the peers of her social circles would be up to this weekend, but her thoughts came continually spiraling back to Penzance.

Sitting alone in this hotel room, heart breaking.

Wishing . . . wishing. . . .

Trying not to think. . . .

Of Felix and of Janey Little and of what they were thinking of her right now. Of how she could ease this ache inside. She wondered if Willie had got to Clare Mabley before Bett had. She thought of her father's call that she'd just taken, how he and Madden would be arriving in England on one of Madden's private jets first thing tomorrow morning.

Like Michael Bett, she also felt that everything had come apart, but she lay the blame solely on herself. She was the one who was changing. Who had changed. And she couldn't understand why.

How could one brawny sailor do this to her?

But failing her father, and indirectly the Order, and worrying about Bett—these were all secondary concerns at the moment. What she wanted to know was what had happened inside her to turn her world upside down.

If this was love, she'd rather do without, thank you very much.

Unfortunately, no one was asking her for her preference in the matter.

She was finally learning a truth that her father and Madden had yet to learn: For some things, you didn't get a choice.

And so the long night wound on, and those gifted or cursed with the influence of William Dunthorn's legacy journeyed through its seemingly endless hours, with joy and with sorrow, with fear and with anger.

For some the morning came too soon.

For many it seemed as though it would never come.

PART TWO

The Lost Music

Music is the one incorporeal entrance into the higher worlds of
knowledge which comprehends mankind, but which mankind cannot
comprehend.

—attributed to
LUDWIG VAN BEETHOVEN

Originally, the function of songs was devotional. Then in the
balladeering centuries, they became a vehicle for the spreading of
information, stories and opinions. Now in the 20th century, they
have become a way of making money and achieving fame. I think the
other two purposes were better.

—MIKE SCOTT;
from an interview in *Jamming*, 1985

When Sick Is It Tea You Want?

I do not know how I may appear to the world, but to myself I seem to have been only a boy playing on the sea-shore, and diverting myself in now and then finding a smoother pebble or a prettier shell than ordinary, whilst the great ocean of truth lay all undiscovered before me.

—attributed to
SIR ISAAC NEWTON, In Brewster's *Life of Newton* (1831)

Morning came to the Cornish Riviera, blustery and heavy with dark grey skies when it reached Mount's Bay. It was what the locals called black eastly weather—bad, but not storming. In the fishing days, the men would take extra care to watch for the sudden storms that the Atlantic could throw up at them, seemingly from nowhere. But now the trade was mostly tourism, and the season over, so the weather was something one remarked on sitting over the morning's tea, rather than a force that could affect their livelihood.

And if this morning many were quieter than usual, or spoke in subdued voices of their unusual dreams the night before, out-of-doors the tide still rumbled against the shore, the wind still rattled the shutters and spun weather vanes around in dizzying circles as it shifted from one quarter to another, and there were the gulls, sailing like kites and filling the air with their rowdy cries from the first promise of light in the eastern skies.

They were still swooping and diving above the houses on Raginnis Hill when Lilith Mabley came into her daughter's bedroom, the note Clare had left for her late the previous night held in one hand. Once she'd had Clare's same dark hair, but now it was turning to grey; she didn't believe in touching it up or in dyes. The grey added to her stately bearing—straight-backed and head always held high. She carried herself with the pride of a duchess, but then to the people of Penwith, a fisherman's widow was no less the lady than one born to a manor.

"Clare?" she called softly from the door.

Clare woke, heartbeat quickening, then calmed herself when she saw it was only her mother.

"Hello, Mum."

"This note . . . ?"

"I can explain."

"But there's no one downstairs."

Clare sat up and combed her hair with her fingers. Her mind was still muddy from the poor bit of sleep that she'd managed to steal from the first few hours of the morning.

"No one . . . ?" she repeated.

Had it all just been part and parcel of the night's awful dreams?

"Well now," her mother said. "There's a blanket and pillow folded up on the sofa in your study, but no one sleeping on it."

No, it hadn't been a dream, Clare thought as she swung her feet to the floor. For her leg ached something fierce. As did her head. And she had only to close her eyes to see that bug-face with its goggle eyes and scarf.

And the knife. . . .

"Davie's gone?" she said.

Her mother nodded. "Davie Rowe," she said in a tone that showed her surprise. "Whatever were you thinking, bringing the likes of him into our home?"

"I . . ."

Clare tried to remember what she'd said in the note. Nothing more than a vague explanation. Her mother obviously wanted more now.

"I took a fall out in the rain last night," she said, "and Davie happened along to give me a hand home. The rain was so bad by then that I made him up a bed on the sofa. I suppose he left as soon as the weather cleared."

"The last I remember, before going up to my bed," her mother said, "was you sitting in your study, reading."

Yes, but then Felix came by, and she'd gone to Janey's, and some madman had come after her with a knife. . . . But she couldn't tell her mother all of that, not and have anything of the day left to herself. Had Janey found Felix? Had anyone else been attacked?

"I got tired of my book," she said, "so I went 'round by Janey's."

"So late," her mother said, shaking her head. "You were lucky that the Rowe boy came along when he did."

It was obvious from her tone of voice that for all his help she still disapproved of any commerce with Davie Rowe.

"He's not so bad," Clare said.

Her mother nodded. "Of course not. That's why they sent him to prison—because he's such a decent sort of a chap."

"You know what I meant."

"Janey should have given you a lift home," her mother said to change the subject.

"Janey had an errand to run."

"At that time of night?" Her mother shook her head. "What *is* the world coming to?"

Clare wondered that herself.

"I'd better get dressed," she said.

"You're going out?"

"I promised Janey I'd go 'round again this morning."

"I was hoping we could work on that puzzle. . . ."

Her mother loved jigsaw puzzles, the more complicated the better. After they were done, she glued the finished puzzle to a stiff piece of cardboard and displayed it on the mantel until the next one was done. At the back of her closet, there was a stack of mounted puzzles some four feet high. The latest one was a particularly daunting project—a bewildering landscape reproduction of a small lugger with a grey-blue sail, adrift on blue-grey water, the skies blue-grey above, the cliffs grey-blue behind, all the similar shades running confusingly into one another.

Sometimes in the weekday evenings after Clare got home from the shop, and almost invariably on Sunday mornings, they'd sit together at the table in the parlour where the puzzles were laid out, and work together on them. Clare enjoyed that time, for they would bend their heads together, ostensibly concentrating on the task at hand, but more simply enjoying the relaxed conversation that neither of them seemed to have as much occasion for during other times of the week.

"I'm sorry, Mum," she said. "Really I am. But it's important."

Her mother smiled, hiding her disappointment well.

"It's that Felix, isn't it?" she asked. "The pair of them need you to referee another of their arguments, I don't doubt."

"Something like that," Clare allowed.

Her mother tched. "And he back for no more than a day. You think they'd learn. Well, get yourself dressed, Clare. You'd best get over there quickly before there's nothing left to be saved."

"It's not so bad as all that."

"Perhaps it wasn't so bad last night, but you've told me enough of how that pair carried on the last time they had troubles to know you can't leave them alone for long." She shook her head and stuffed

Clare's note into her pocket. "Though what they'll do when they get married," she added, "well, I *don't* know. We'll let that be their worry."

All Clare could do was laugh, but that was enough to clear the last cobwebbed distress of the previous night from her mind. She was finally beginning to feel more like her normal self. Now if only Janey had been able to find Felix. . . .

"Do get dressed, Clare," her mother repeated as she left the room. "Your breakfast will be ready in just a minute or so."

"I love you, too!" Clare called after her.

2.

Felix awoke alone in bed, his headache gone. The experiences of the previous night, real events and dreams alike, tumbled through his mind in a confusing muddle, but clearest of all was the memory of Janey and the Gaffer sending him off.

He thought for one moment that it had all been a dream—for here he was, back in the Gaffer's spare bedroom as though he were just waking on his first morning back in the village—but no, they *had* sent him away. That had been real. The memory was too sharp, and too painful, to have been a dream.

And last night, waking to find Janey beside him again?

He looked around the room. If he was here—though not entirely sure how he came to *be* here—then that hadn't been a dream either.

He sat up, feeling a little groggy, though otherwise no worse for the wear.

So how had he come to return?

His duffel and accordion case stood near the door, Clare's cane leaning against them. His jacket was hanging from the back of a chair, his clothes in an untidy hoard on its seat.

He tried to remember what he could. After the argument, he'd gone up to Clare's. Then there'd been the walk from her house; playing his accordion by the sea; the storm; going to Lena's hotel room to lend her Clare's cane. And then . . . then it all became confusing. Nightmare images. He'd been dead—executed. Cut down from the oak tree to lie in the mud where the woman—

That had been a dream.

He shivered, remembering her features.

She'd been making love to his corpse. And superimposed over that memory was the image of Lena also making love to him, but on the bed in her hotel room. The similarities were shrill—from the symmetry of the two women's positions to his own forced immobility. It had been as though he were an outsider sitting inside the shell of his own body. . . .

Had that been real, or was it the trace memory of yet another dream?

Last night, Janey had said something about him having been drugged.

Lena drugging him.

Try though he did, Felix couldn't remember any of it. Not clearly. Only as vague troubling images that flickered behind his eyelids whenever he closed his eyes.

Sighing, he got out of bed and put on his clothes. He started to wash up in the bathroom, but his legs began to feel weak, his stomach queasy, and he got no further than washing the sour, cottony taste from his mouth before he had to go lie down again.

But not back in his room. He felt sick, but not sick enough to forgo some answers.

He made it downstairs where he found both Janey and the Gaffer sitting at the kitchen table having their breakfast. They shot him identical looks of worry mixed with guilt. If he hadn't been feeling so nauseated, he might have teased the pair of them, but it was all he could do to make his way back out to the living room and lie down on the couch before his legs gave way from under him. He lay there, waiting for the room to stop spinning, hoping he wouldn't throw up.

Janey followed him out and sat down on the couch, the movement of her weight on the cushions making his stomach lurch.

"Felix?" she asked.

"I . . . I'll be okay. . . ."

"You don't look okay."

He tried to find a smile without success.

"Actually," he said, "I feel awful."

"Perhaps we should take you into Penzance," the Gaffer said. "To the hospital."

He'd followed Janey into the living room and now stood near the stairs, leaning against the banister, obviously hesitant to come much closer.

Felix shook his head—and immediately wished he hadn't. Every movement made him want to hurl.

"No hospital," he managed.

If he hated being sick, he hated hospitals more. As far as he was concerned, they were designed solely to make you feel worse than you already did, though how he could feel any worse than he did at the moment, he couldn't imagine.

"It might be a good idea," Janey said. "We've no idea what kind of drug that woman fed you."

"She *did* drug me?"

Janey nodded.

"And you brought me . . . here?"

"All on her own she did, my robin," the Gaffer said.

Felix looked from one to the other, moving only his eyes.

"You both believe me now?" he asked. "That I had nothing to do with these people. . . ."

Janey laid a hand on his shoulder. "Of course we believe you. We were rotten not to have given you the chance to explain."

"We went a bit mad, I suppose," the Gaffer added. "I'm sorry, Felix. Sorrier than I could ever say."

For all his nausea, that made Felix feel a hundred times better. Deep in his chest, a tightness eased. An ailing part of his spirit began to heal.

"That's okay," he said. "We all screw up."

"But not this badly," Janey said.

"It's okay," Felix repeated. "Really it is."

"About that hospital," the Gaffer began.

Felix shook his head again, sending up a new wave of nausea.

The Gaffer eyed him for a long moment. Some of the heaviness that had been lodged behind his eyes had faded while they spoke. He straightened his back and nodded.

"Then you'll be wanting some tea," he said.

That brought a real smile momentarily to Felix's lips. Trust Tom Little. If it needed a cure, why then, it was tea that would cure whatever the ailment. The Cornishman's answer to chicken soup.

"Tea would be great," he allowed.

"You should just rest now," Janey said as the Gaffer went to put a new pot on.

Felix closed his hand about hers as she started to get up to leave as well.

"I don't want to be anywhere but here," he said.

Smiling, Janey remained sitting on the couch beside him.

3.

Willie Keel appeared at Lena's door, bright and early. He stood out in the hallway, cap in one hand, the other hand extended towards her.

"Got the job done," he said. "Just like you wanted."

The sleepless night had left Lena in a foul mood, but she kept a rein on her temper. Depending on how things went, she might still need Willie's help again.

"I don't have cash," she said. "Can I give you traveler's cheques?"

"Are they in sterling?"

"Of course."

Lena looked in her purse to see how much she had left in traveler's cheques. Just a little under six hundred pounds.

"How about if I give you five hundred today and we can go together to the bank for the rest on Monday morning?"

Keel considered that for a moment.

"Well, now," he said with a frown. "That wasn't our bargain, as I recall it. You were the one who called me up in the middle of the bloody—"

"Are you having some trouble, miss?"

Lena looked up to find Jim Gazo standing in the hallway no more than a few steps away—not a flicker of recognition in his eyes, just as she'd asked. He'd come upon them so quietly that neither she nor Keel had been aware of his approach.

If Keel reminded Lena of a weasel, then Gazo was a grey-eyed bull. He was broad-shouldered and tall, his features handsomely chiseled except for a nose that had been broken once and never set properly. He kept his dark hair short, and with the care he took of his physique, whatever he wore looked good on him. Considering his size, his ability to be unobtrusive and next to silent on his feet was one of his major assets. No one wanted a bodyguard's presence constantly screaming protection—unless that was a necessary part of the job, and then Gazo could handle that equally well.

Lena glanced at Keel who was trying to surreptitiously place the newcomer without being obvious about it. He wasn't having a great deal of success.

"I . . ." she began.

"There's no problem," Keel said quickly. "Traveler's cheques would be perfect."

With Keel's back to him, Gazo allowed a flicker of a smile to touch his lips before he gave Lena a nod and continued on down the hall to his room. Keel followed her back into her room where she sat down by the dresser. She dug about in her purse for a pen, then signed over the required number of cheques and handed them to him.

"I'll ring you tomorrow morning," he said as he stuffed them quickly in the pocket of his jacket. "Unless you've got other work for me today?"

"Tomorrow will be fine," Lena told him.

She hobbled back to the door with him and closed it firmly behind him. She started to lock it, then reconsidered. She hadn't asked Willie *how* he'd managed his success with the Mabley woman, but it *had* been done, and knowing Bett, she knew that Bett would be in a worse mood than ever after having been thwarted. She waited a few moments to give the hallway time to be cleared, then limped painfully down to Gazo's room. He opened it on the first knock, gaze shifting quickly left and right, down either length of the hall, before it settled on her.

"Bad move?" he asked.

Lena shook her head. "No, it was just the right one."

Gazo glanced down at her leg and noted the swelling. "Did Bett do that to you?"

"Would you believe I fell off a bike?"

"Coming from you? Yes. You don't know the meaning of doing things halfway. Do you want to come in?"

Lena nodded. "I got in Bett's way last night and though I'm not sure if he knows it or not, I'd just as soon be somewhere he can't find me."

When Gazo offered her his arm to lead her into the room, Lena couldn't help but remember Felix and all of his small kindnesses. She could feel her eyes start to well up with tears, and blinked fiercely.

Damn him.

Damn this whole situation.

When Gazo showed concern, she pretended more pain in her ankle than she actually felt as an excuse for the shiny glisten that thinking of Felix had brought to her eyes.

"Daddy's flying in today," she said once she was sitting and had her emotions under a little better control. "With John Madden."

Gazo, moving like a panther for all his bulk, sat down on the bed. "So what's going on?" he asked. "Or do I even want to know?"

Lena shook her head. "You don't want to know."

This is what it's like to have no friends, Lena thought, astonished at the realization. She'd never really thought of it before. She had employees, from Jim Gazo here to her maids and gardeners at home. She had every kind of person willing to spend time in her company, trying to impress or waiting to be impressed, but no friends. Not one.

Right now she would give anything to have someone with whom she could share the turmoil that tore at her heart. Someone who would understand. Unfortunately, the only person she could think of who fit the bill was Felix Gavin, and she'd closed the book on his ever giving her a moment of his time again.

Last night's bad dreams came roiling back through her mind.

Put them aside, Lena, she told herself. Put it all aside. It was time to carry on. Get that mask in place and don't let it slip again.

Imagine Bett sniffing out her present weakness. . . .

"So tell me, Jim," she said. "What's new in Boston?"

"Other than the Celtics being in top form?"

4.

Like Felix, Janey had her own troubling memories to deal with— both real and dreamed—but unlike him, there was no vagueness in her sense of recall. It wasn't something for which she felt grateful. Images circled around and around in her mind, as though they were spliced together on a tape loop. . . .

The scene outside on Chapel Place, when she and the Gaffer had sent Felix off.

Driving through the rain.

Felix in the American woman's bed.

Her mother as an alcoholic bag lady.

Forgive me.

And the secret Dunthorn book, spilling out its music, so magical at first, until the shadows closed in and then it turned so very, very dark. . . .

She was happy to be with Felix, sitting on the couch with him to keep him company, but she didn't like the silence. Because it gave her too much time to think. It made it too easy to start the tape loop spinning its captured images through her mind and then all she wanted to do was just hit something . . . anything, but preferably the woman who'd drugged Felix, because—

She jumped when the doorbell rang.

Now who . . . ? she started to think, but then she remembered the *Rolling Stone* reporter who was supposed to be by today and thought for one horrible moment that it was him coming to take his photos, and here she was, looking like death warmed over. But when the front door opened, it was Clare who stepped inside.

"Who's that then?" the Gaffer asked, coming out of the kitchen. Seeing Clare, he smiled.

"Decided to forgive me?" Clare asked.

"You were right and we were wrong, my flower," he replied. "*We* should be the ones asking for your pardon. If you hadn't . . ."

His voice trailed off as Clare waved a hand at him.

"It's done," she said. "Let's not worry over it anymore."

She turned to step into the living room, her gaze sliding past Janey to where Felix lay on the sofa. Relief settled over her features. It wasn't until that moment that Janey realized just how anxious Clare had been. As Clare looked at Felix, a tightness eased from around her eyes and the corners of her mouth.

"You *did* find him," Clare said.

She came farther into the room to have a closer look at him and some of her worry returned.

"Is he all right?" she asked.

"Well, the woman did drug him," Janey began, but then Felix cracked open an eye and looked at the pair of them.

"I wish you wouldn't talk about me like I wasn't here," he said.

"Feeling better then, are we?"

Her tone was teasing, for all that the question was serious. She gave his hand a squeeze.

Clare sat down on an ottoman that she pulled over closer to the couch. The Gaffer came into the room as well and, after moving the Dunthorn book, settled into his own chair.

"A bit," Felix replied. "I'm not ready to go body surfing out on the bay or anything."

Janey didn't hear him for a moment. She stared at the book that the Gaffer had moved, the memory of its music—both the glad and the dark—moving through her mind before she turned back to Felix and found a smile to offer up.

"No," she said. "There's been quite enough excitement around here as it is, without us having to call out the lifeboat to rescue some daft sailor who's decided he's in Hawaii instead of Cornwall."

"Excitement?" Clare asked.

So Janey launched into an account of what had happened last night, editing out just what sort of a compromising position she'd found Felix and the woman in. If Felix couldn't remember, well then she bloody well wasn't going to drag it up herself.

"I had a bit of excitement myself on the way home," Clare said when Janey was done.

And then it was her turn to relate how a simple walk up Raginnis Hill had turned into a scene from one of those slasher films that the tabloids liked to dwell on when there isn't any real news for them to either uncover or make up.

"Oh, that must have been awful," Janey said.

Felix looked grim.

"Did you call the constables, then, my love?" the Gaffer asked.

Clare shook her head. "Davie doesn't get along well with them and—"

"No surprises there," Janey interrupted.

"And by the time I got up this morning," Clare went on, "well, I just felt sort of stupid. I mean, what would I say when they asked why I'd waited so long to report it?"

"The truth," the Gaffer said.

Clare shook her head. "That wouldn't be fair to Davie."

"He was probably out looking for someone to rob himself," Janey said.

"And that's not fair either," Clare said. "If it weren't for him, I wouldn't be here talking to you right now."

"I suppose. But Davie Rowe." Janey shook her head. "And then you invited him *in* to your house?"

"What should I have done? Sent him off, back into the rain, without so much as a thank you? Besides, I was still scared. At least with him there, I felt safe."

"But Davie Rowe. . . ."

"I think she gets the picture," Felix said.

Janey turned to him. "I suppose. But you don't know him, Felix. He's been to prison and everything."

"What she means," Clare said, "is that he's not the most handsome bloke you're likely to meet."

"What difference does that make?" Felix asked.

"It shouldn't make any," Clare said.

Janey threw up her hands. "I give up. You know what I meant, Clare. I don't have anything against Davie Rowe."

Clare nodded. "I know."

Janey looked at her friend, sitting there on the ottoman, as unruffled as though she hadn't almost been killed the previous night. How did she do it? How did she stop her own tape loop from replaying its images through her mind?

"You seem so calm," Janey said to her. "If it had happened to me, I'd still have the jitters."

Clare nodded. "I do have them—but they're hidden away, deep down inside me. Sort of locked up and secreted because I feel that if I let them out, then I'll lose control and I won't be able to ever stop shivering. So I act calm, and somehow acting calm makes me feel calm."

"Did you get much of a look at the man?" Felix asked.

"Not really. It's all sort of blurry, and then he was wearing those goggles and the scarf. . . ." She paused as though remembering something. "But there was something. He had this tattoo, right about here—" She lifted her wrist and pointed.

"What kind of a tattoo?" Felix asked.

Janey gave him an odd look. His tone had been sharp, almost cross. He'd raised himself up on one elbow and was staring at Clare with an intensity that was disturbing.

"A dove," Clare said.

Felix sank back against the sofa, seeming to shrink like a deflating balloon.

"A dove," he repeated slowly.

Clare nodded. "Well, it was a stylized kind of a thing. I thought of a dove when I saw it, but I only saw it for a moment. It was definitely a bird."

"Do you have a pencil and some paper?" Felix asked Janey.

The Gaffer got up and fetched some. He started to hand them to Clare, but Felix shook his head.

"No," he said. "Let me see them."

He lay on his side when he had them and made a quick drawing that he held up to show to Clare.

"Did it look like that?" he asked.

Clare went white. "How did you . . . ?"

"I've seen that tattoo before."

"You *know* the man who attacked Clare?" Janey asked.

Felix shook his head. "Lena Grant has a tattoo just like it on her own wrist."

Janey's eyes widened. If Lena and the man who had attacked Clare last night were connected . . .

"It's the book," she said.

The Gaffer picked up *The Little Country,* three pairs of eyes tracking the movement.

"Lena Grant was after the book," Janey went on. "There was the burglary, then she tried to drug Felix while her friend went after Clare. . . ."

She closed her eyes, trying to follow it all through, but her train of thought ran up into a tangled knot that wouldn't unravel.

"Why?" she said. "What could drugging Felix or trying to hurt Clare have to do with that book?"

"Better yet," Felix said, "what is it about the book that's so important?"

Janey nodded. "They can't just want to publish it."

"There'll be more to it than that, my queen," the Gaffer said. "There's something odd about this book of Billy's."

Clare held up a hand. "Everybody wait a minute. You've lost me. I know that there are people trying to get hold of some of Dunthorn's unpublished writings, but what is this book you're all talking about? You don't mean to tell me that there's an unpublished novel . . . ?"

The Gaffer handed it over to her. Clare read the spine, gave Janey a questioning glance, then turned back and opened the book before anyone could speak. She read the title page, flipped to the copyright page. Janey could see her fingers trembling.

"An edition of one," Clare said wonderingly.

She flipped a few pages, read a few lines, flipped a few more pages. As though she was back in her dream, Janey heard a faint trace of music that was abruptly cut off when Clare closed the book. She blinked to find Clare regarding her with an unfamiliar look in her eyes. It took Janey a few moments to realize that it was anger. A sad kind of anger, but anger all the same.

"You know how much I love Dunthorn's work," Clare said. Disappointment lay heavy in her voice. "I'm as mad for it as you are,

Janey—maybe more. How could you keep this from me?"

"It's not what you think."

"I thought we were friends."

"We *are* friends," Janey said. "But I only just found it and—and . . ."

"And what? You couldn't trust me to keep the secret?" Clare shook her head. "I don't understand any of this. *Why* is it a secret?"

"You can't blame Janey, my robin," the Gaffer said. "She was only keeping a promise that I made to Billy when he first gave me the book."

"But . . ." Clare was holding the book close to her, one hand lying possessively over it, the fingers of the other running along the top of the binding. She looked at Felix.

"You knew?"

"Only since yesterday," he replied. "I found it when I was waiting for Janey and Tom to come home from the session. Then they told me it was a secret—their secret. It wasn't mine to tell."

"It was my secret to keep," the Gaffer said. "The book's been hidden for years, but recently I had to store it in the attic and then Janey found it. . . ."

He looked as uncomfortable as Janey was feeling. She'd been so caught up in finding the book, and then there'd been all those curious events since she'd found it, that she'd never thought about how much Clare loved Billy's writing. It hadn't been her secret to share, but she felt awful for not asking her grandfather to let Clare in on it. They both knew that Clare would never break a trust.

"Everything's been so mad lately," Janey said. "I never thought to ask Gramps if you could see it."

"I made a promise to Billy," the Gaffer repeated.

"A promise?" Clare asked.

Janey glanced at her grandfather, who nodded.

"It's in the letter there that I'm using for a bookmark," she said. "Go ahead—read it."

Clare took out the letter, leaving a finger to mark the place, and read Dunthorn's brief note.

"This only makes things *more* mysterious," she said when she'd read it.

Janey nodded. "That's exactly what I felt when I read it."

"Did Dunthorn really have any paranormal abilities?" Clare asked, looking over at the Gaffer.

The Gaffer blinked. "What do you mean?"

" 'That famous Mad Bill Dunthorn Gypsy prescience strikes again,' " she read from the letter. "That makes it sound as though he had fore-told the future on more than one occasion, and foretold it correctly, I'd assume, or why bring it up at all?"

"Well, Billy had a way about him," the Gaffer began.

Janey glanced at him. He was obviously feeling uneasy discussing this sort of thing. She shot him an encouraging look when he turned her way for a moment.

"What sort of a way?" Clare asked.

"Well, my flower, he seemed to *know* things, that's all. Not the marvels he wrote about in his stories, but odd things all the same. Unlucky ships, good times coming, and bad. He didn't talk about it much—for who'd listen to a young lad like he was, spouting off that sort of nonsense?—but he talked to me, and I listened."

The Gaffer hesitated again.

"And?" Janey asked.

The Gaffer sighed. "And he was right more often than not."

"And the book?" Clare asked. "What is it about the book that makes it so important?"

The Gaffer shook his head. "Billy never said, my flower. But things—odd things—seem to just *happen* whenever it's not hidden away. I can't rightly explain what I mean. It's not so much that the book makes these things happen as that it gives them a push to get them started."

"You mean it's like a catalyst?" Clare asked.

"That's the word."

"But why? What could possibly be the purpose in that?"

"Does it need a purpose?" Felix asked. "Maybe it's just enough to know that there's something marvelous still in the world, that all the mystery hasn't been drained out of it by those who like to take a thing apart to understand it, then stand back all surprised because it doesn't work anymore."

That made Janey think for a moment—both about what Felix had said and the fact that he'd said it. She'd always considered Felix to be a very practical, down-to-earth sort of a person—but then that's how her grandfather described Dunthorn as well. She supposed a person could be practical and still have a fey streak.

That was what music was like, she'd always thought. You'd see some old lad like Chalkie Fisher, about as commonsensical a man as you'd care to meet, all plain talk and plain facts, but when he brought out his box and woke a tune from the buttons and bellows, well then it was just a kind of magic, wasn't it?

You didn't try to understand it. You just appreciated it.

Music.

Magic.

The tape loop of her memories brought up that moment in her dream when the book lay open and the music first started to spill out of it. A music so similar to what she'd thought she'd heard when Clare had been flipping through its pages. . . .

"What kind of things happen?" Clare asked, bringing Janey's concentration back to the conversation at hand.

The Gaffer shrugged. "Just . . . odd things, my gold. Sounds and noises where there shouldn't be any. Movement caught from the corner of your eye when there's nothing there. Everyone filled with a certain unexplained restlessness. The village getting a . . . haunted feeling to it. And then the dreams. . . ."

Janey thought she heard a catch in his voice as his words trailed off, but then she was remembering her own odd dreams of the previous night. When she looked about the room, everyone appeared thoughtful, and she wondered what kind of dreams they'd had. If theirs had been anything like her own. . . .

The Gaffer shifted in his chair and cleared his throat.

"But that's neither here nor there," he said.

Felix nodded. "We've got a more basic problem to deal with."

"But where do we begin with it?" Janey asked.

"I think it's time we called in the constables, my love," the Gaffer said.

Janey nodded.

"And tell them what?" Clare asked.

"That you were attacked for one thing," Janey said. "And the house was burgled."

"And that we believe it's all part of some conspiracy by a secret society that's looking for a hidden talisman that just happens to be this old book?" Clare tapped *The Little Country* with a short fingernail. "They'd think we'd all gone bonkers."

Janey leaned forward. "That's it, isn't it?" she said. "That dove tattoo—it must be the symbol of a secret society, like the Freemasons or something like that."

"Could be," Felix said. "Though it seems a little farfetched."

Janey ignored him. "So how do we find out what society uses that symbol?"

"Would it even be possible to find out?" the Gaffer asked.

"What do you mean?" Janey asked.

"Well, if they're known, my treasure, then they wouldn't be very secret, would they?"

"There's people that study that kind of thing," Felix said. "I've got a friend in California who's made a life's study of the weird and the wonderful. The odder the better; the more secret, the more he wants to know about it."

"We have someone like that right around here," Clare said. "Peter Goninan. He's forever putting the strangest books on order—all kinds of obscure historical and hermetic texts—and I don't doubt that he does as much or more by private mail order."

"I know him," the Gaffer said. "He still lives on the family farm out by St. Levan. Billy and I went to school with him when we were all boys and he was an odd bird then."

Janey shivered. "I've run into him along the coast path a few times," she said. "He gives me the creeps."

"I've never met him," Clare said. "He usually makes his orders by phone, then has a neighbour fetch the books for him. At least I suppose she's his neighbour—she's a tall, gangly woman who always rides about on an old boy's bike."

"I've seen her about," Janey said.

The Gaffer nodded. "Chalkie's met her. Her name's Helen something or other and I think she rents a cottage from Goninan."

"Then she's been doing it for a few years," Clare said, "because Tommy knew her from when he worked at W. H. Smith's—before he opened his own shop."

"Do you really think Peter Goninan could help?" Janey asked.

She was reluctant about going out to Goninan's place, but then she realized that just as Davie Rowe's looks gave her one impression, Peter Goninan's gave her another. He was tall and ungainly, skeletal thin and bald, with a way of looking at a person that a medieval peasant would have put down as the evil eye. He dressed in tattered clothing, usually black, so that he looked like some odd sort of crane hopping about the fields whenever she'd seen him.

But since looks weren't everything, as Clare had so recently reminded her, he was probably the kindest of souls.

She smiled to herself. Right. And bloody Davie Rowe had never been to prison. . . .

"It's worth a try," Clare said.

"There's this to think about if you go to talk to him," Felix said. "If there is some secret society that uses a dove as their symbol, who's to say he's not one of their members?"

Clare grinned. "Well, we'll just have to have ourselves a quick look at his wrist before we tell him anything, then won't we?"

Felix smiled back. "Fair enough. So let's go talk to him."

He started to sit up, but immediately lay back down again, his face pale.

"Felix?" Janey began.

He shook his head, then grimaced at the movement.

"I can't go," he said. "Not unless you promise to stop every few feet along the way so that I can throw up. I'm fine when I lie down, but as soon as I sit up, or move at all . . ."

"Janey and I'll go," Clare said.

Janey nodded. She wasn't enamoured with the idea, but Clare couldn't go on her own.

"Will you stay with Felix, Gramps?" she asked.

"I don't like it," the Gaffer said.

"We'll be fine," Clare assured him.

"Fine," the Gaffer replied in a voice that plainly said he thought they'd be anything but. "With madmen running about, attacking people with knives, and who knows what other mischief brewing? Who's to say you won't be attacked on the way? Come 'pon that, who's to say that when you get there, it won't be as Felix said and you'll find Goninan himself in the thick of it?"

"We'll be very careful," Clare said.

"Unless you want to drive Clare over and I'll stay with Felix," Janey said.

She could see her grandfather weighing the danger between the two. The house was in the village, but that hadn't stopped the enemy before. Here, they knew where to find her. Down the coast, they might not be able to find her as quickly. . . .

"Go on, then," he said. "But don't be too long about it."

Janey leaned down to give Felix a kiss.

"You'll be careful?" he asked.

"Very," she promised.

"Can I take this?" Clare asked, picking up the rough drawing of the dove that Felix had made.

Felix nodded.

Janey fetched her jacket and just got to the door where Clare was waiting for her when the phone rang.

"It's for you, my gold," the Gaffer said, holding it out towards her.

Janey sighed, and went back into the room to take the call.

5.

Michael Bett's lack of sleep the previous night left him clearheaded and alert when morning finally came.

The deprivation made little difference to him. He hated sleep anyway, normally allowing himself only the bare minimum amount that his body required. To his mind, sleep bred complacency. It took you away from the edge where everything was clear-cut and precise; that edge where you could make an instantaneous decision and not have to second-guess the consequences. The mind automatically correlated all available data and spat it up so that you could concentrate on getting the job done, not worrying about whether or not you could pull it off or if it was the right thing to do.

On the edge, you just *knew*.

And that was something that Madden's sheep would never experience. Because they were soft-bellied and slothful, their heads stuffed with cotton. When he walked the edge, he was more than a wolf to them; he was an alien species. A man such as he knew himself to be could do anything—so long as he was operating on the edge.

With a man like him, the sheep didn't stand a chance.

Take Janey Little and whatever secret of Dunthorn's it was that she and her grandfather were hiding from the world.

He'd been approaching the problem like a sheep would, soft-stepping around them, playing by the rules. Madden's orders: Don't make waves. But there were no rules—not on the edge—and standing there, with the world in sharp focus all around him, his mind honed as keen as the cutting edge of a razor, he knew exactly how to handle her now.

Madden was still important to him. Bett hadn't finished with the Order and Madden remained his link to it. So he'd accommodate

Madden's wishes for the moment. He wouldn't take the knife to either of the Littles. He wouldn't even hurt their friends. There were other ways to cut their world off from under them.

Leaving his room, Bett went downstairs. He'd heard the owner of the B and B go out a few minutes ago, then watched him head off down the street from his window. With the place to himself, he sat down in the man's sitting room and pulled the phone over onto the fat arm of his chair. It took a few minutes before the operator could make his overseas connection, but finally he could hear the phone ringing on the other end of the line in New York.

"Dennison Investigations," a voice answered.

"Sam? Michael Bett here."

"What can I do for you, Mr. Bett?"

"I'm in Cornwall and things are winding up to a head. It's time for you to work off the final part of our contract."

"Let me get a pen. Okay, shoot."

"First thing you do is contact a man named Ted Grimes." He gave Dennison the particulars of an Upper West Side address and the phone number of Grimes's office there. "Then you're to pick up the woman and the three of you are going to take the first flight over here. I want you all in Penzance, ASAP."

"The woman's coming voluntarily?"

"She's on salary, the same as you."

"I'll get right on to it, Mr. Bett."

Bett cut the connection and stared at the phone for a moment before calling the operator again. He made a half-dozen other long-distance calls, then finally dialed a local number. Tom Little answered and put his granddaughter on the line.

"Janey? Mike Betcher here."

"Oh, hello, Mike. Did you sleep well?"

Bett put a smile in his voice. "Sure. I slept great. Listen, about our getting together today . . ."

"Something's come up and I was just on my way out. Can I ring you up a little later in the day?"

"I wanted to cancel myself," Bett said. "Actually, I didn't want to so much as I have to."

"Is something wrong? Are you all right?"

"It's not me—I'm fine. It's . . . Christ, I don't know how to tell you this, Janey. It's the strangest thing. I got a call from my editor canceling your participation in the article. He wouldn't talk to me about it, he just said he didn't want you in the piece, period."

There was a moment's silence on the other end of the line, then Janey asked, "But . . . why?"

"That's what I want to find out. I'm heading back to London today to see if I can't straighten this all out. You haven't been making any enemies lately, have you?"

"What?"

"The thing is, he seemed pretty pissed—my editor, that is. The last time I heard him in a mood like this was when he got a lawsuit thrown at him by that guy in—well, never mind who. It got settled out of court. But he's not happy with you, Janey, and I can't figure out why. I'm kind of pissed off myself—not at you, naturally—and I'm going to go to bat for you, but if there's anything you can tell me about what's going on that could help . . . ?"

"I—I don't know anything about this."

"Yeah. I didn't think you did. Look, I'm going to straighten this out, but it might take a few days. Can I call you when I get back in town?"

"Of course. But—"

"I have to get going, Janey. I'm sorry to hit you with all of this, but I figured that if you didn't know, then you should."

"I appreciate that, Mike. Only could you—"

"That's the thing I hate about this business," Bett went on. "All these feuds and vendettas and crap. You'd think people could carry on their business with a little maturity, but it's worse than dealing with toddlers in a day care sometimes, you know what I mean?"

"Not really. I—"

"I've really got to run. I'll call you in two days—three at the max. Don't worry, Janey. We'll get this all straightened out. In the meantime, you take care of yourself, okay? And try not to worry."

"But—"

Bett cradled the receiver and thought about what he'd said.

Try not to worry.

He smiled to himself.

Like she was just going to forget about this call. And when the other pieces of the puzzle started to fall into place and she found out just how easy it could be to lose it all . . .

A mind, he thought, was almost as much fun to take apart as a body.

Replacing the phone where he'd found it, he went back up to his room to get dressed.

Time to pay a little social call on the Ice Princess, he thought. Maybe play a few games with the tiny excuse for a mind that she had. Apologize for last night. Come on all sweetness and light. Vow to help her get back together with her sailor, if that was what she really wanted.

By the time he was done with her, she'd be telling him how sorry she was that *she'd* screwed things up. And when Madden and "Daddy" showed up, well Lena and he'd just be the best of pals, now wouldn't they?

Sure they would.

Everything was going to go his way again because he was back on the edge.

Back on the edge and looking good.

6.

Janey slowly cradled the telephone receiver, her face paling as what Betcher had told her sank in.

It made no sense.

Not a smidgen.

"What is it, my robin?" the Gaffer asked.

"That was Mike—Mike Betcher," she replied.

"The *Rolling Stone* writer?" Clare asked.

Janey nodded. "He said that his editor canceled the article. No, that's not right. He just canceled my part of it. Mike asked me if I have any enemies; he said that the editor was mad at me. . . ." She looked from her grandfather to Clare and Felix. "I don't even *know* the man."

"There must be some sort of a mistake," the Gaffer said.

"Or maybe it's just the opposite," Clare said.

"What do you mean?"

"Maybe it was deliberate. If we're postulating conspiracies . . ."

Janey gave a halfhearted laugh, but no one else joined in.

"Oh, come *on*," she said. "Think about what you're saying. It doesn't make any sense."

"I don't know," Felix said. "Maybe Clare's got something there. So far they've already tried to alienate you from me and to kill Clare.

That sounds to me like they're trying to cut you off from your friends. Now they're working on your career. . . ."

"I can't believe Mike's involved in it as well," she said. "He just told me that he's going up to London to argue my side of it with his editor."

"His editor's in London?" Clare asked.

"Well . . . I don't know. That's just what he said. Maybe they have a branch office or something there." She shook her head. "It doesn't make sense that he'd be involved. Or his paper."

"People can be bought," Felix said.

"But . . . ?"

Clare took her arm. "The sooner we see if we can find out something about these people, the better, Janey."

Janey looked at Felix.

"She's right," he said.

"I don't know what Peter Goninan can do to help," the Gaffer added, "but we'd best get to the bottom of this quickly, my gold."

"I suppose. Gramps, would you ring up Kit and ask her if she's heard anything?"

Kit Angelina was Janey's booking agent who worked out of London.

"Her number's in my little red phone book," she added.

"I'll ring her straightway," he replied.

"Ta."

Janey hesitated a moment longer, but then Clare took her arm again, so she followed her friend out to the car.

As she got in behind the wheel, she looked around at the familiar sight of Chapel Place—her grandfather's garden, the Methodist Chapel, the friendly houses all leaning close to the street. Suddenly everything seemed distant, strange. As though they were all part of one world, and she was in another.

It was a horrible, lost feeling.

"Janey?" Clare asked.

She looked at her companion, not seeing her for a moment, then slowly nodded and started up the car.

But as she pulled away, she couldn't help but wonder, why was this all happening to *her*?

7.

Davie Rowe was sitting in the King's Arms, waiting for Willie Keel
to arrive. The pub was in Paul, across Mousehole Lane from St.
Paul's Church. Silver-haired Harry was in his usual spot behind the
bar, talking to a pair of old lads who farmed up Trungle way. Their
gum boots were still muddy, but both men were wearing their Sunday
best—cloth caps and clean jackets and trousers, ties knotted under
their chins. Other than them, Davie had the pub to himself, although
the dining room next door was rapidly filling up. Snatches of conversation and laughter spilled through the open partition behind the
bar that led to the other bar in the dining room.

But on this side it was still quiet. The inevitable Fruit machine was
silent for a change. Davie was tempted to play it for a while, but he
never won much with the gambling machines and he was low on
cash, with no more than the price of another half in his pocket until
Willie came 'round with his money. So he sat on a bench by the
billiards table and nursed his pint.

And waited another half hour.

Willie showed up just after Davie had finally finished his pint and
ordered a half of Hicks bitter from the barman. He was returning to
his table when Willie came in, grinning expansively. Keel got himself
a pint of bitter from the bar and brought it over to where Davie was
sitting. He took a long swig from his pint, draining the glass by a
third, then set it down on the table between them.

"How's the lad, then?" he asked.

"I've been better."

"Well, this'll cheer you up."

Keel glanced towards the bar, then drew a folded sheaf of ten-
pound notes from his pocket that he handed over to Davie. Davie
pocketed them quickly, not bothering to count them. Whatever extra
Willie might have made on the deal himself—taken out of Davie's
share, to be sure—Willie wasn't one to go back on a deal. If he'd
promised Davie two hundred quid, then the bills he'd just handed
over would amount to two hundred quid, not a farthing more nor
less.

"Not bad for a quick spot of work, eh?" Keel said.

"Not bad at all," Davie agreed.

It was very good money.

"And I don't doubt that there'll be still more where that came
from," Keel added.

Davie leaned forward on the table. "What's this all about, Willie?"

"Well, now, you know my feeling on that. You do the job and you collect your pay, but you don't ask questions."

"I know that," Davie said. He'd learned that and a great deal more from the time he'd spent in prison. "But this woman—what could she want with Janey and Clare?"

"What do we care? Just so long as she pays."

"Yes, but—"

"I'll tell you this." Keel leaned closer as well. "Our Miss Grant isn't alone in this business. There's not just money behind her, but more manpower as well. Now we have the in, Davie my lad. It's our backyard, as it were, and the Americans can't move about as freely as we can. But"—he tapped the table with a finger for emphasis— "I'll tell you this. If we go about talking out of turn and shoving our noses in where they don't belong, they'll step in themselves, and then how will we profit?"

"But you just said that they can't get about the way we can."

"And it's true. But there's others'd like a cut of this easy money, Davie. And come nightfall, who can tell the difference between a local man and some American? They may want to step easy, but they're not above doing a little dirty work their own selves. And maybe, the first bit of work they'd take on would be to quiet a flapping gob, if you get my meaning."

Davie shook his head. "I'm not looking for trouble. It's just that . . . well, Clare. Why would anyone want to harm her?"

"There's a thing you need to learn," Keel said, "and that's the plain and simple truth that everyone has their secrets. Some are darker than others, but we all have them. You might have known Clare Mabley all your life—"

"I have."

"But that doesn't mean that you *know* her. I could tell you tales . . ."

"What? About Clare?"

Keel laughed and shook his head. "Not about her. But there's many a fine and upstanding citizen in these parts that's done worse than either you or I could even think of, Davie. I tell you, I know a secret or two."

"Like what?"

"Now that would be telling and then what sort of secrets would they be?"

"That's easy to say."

"Then think of this: Why is it that I've never been sent up to prison, my lad?" Keel patted his upper arm. "That's because I *know* things that important people would rather not see made public."

Davie was still curious, but he let his questions ride. It was true that the law never seemed much interested in Willie Keel, but he doubted that it was due to any hold the little man held over various and sundry important citizenry. Who'd listen to, little say believe, tale-telling when it came from the likes of him? It was far more likely that Keel was simply an informer.

Keel finished his bitter and stood up.

"Well, Davie," he said. "I've work still to do."

"Anything for me?"

"Maybe, maybe not. Stay near a phone and I'll give you a ring if something comes up."

Davie didn't want to leave it at that. He wanted to know more about the American woman—how she could know that Clare was in danger and, more important, *who* the threat was coming from. If Willie wouldn't tell him, straight out, then tagging along with him would have been the next best thing. Because Willie liked to talk and sooner or later, over the course of the afternoon, he'd let some tidbit or another slip. But he also knew he couldn't push.

"Fair enough," he said. "I've got an errand or two to run myself, but then I'll be at home."

Keel gave him a broad wink. "Here's to Americans and their money," he said and made for the door.

Davie watched him leave the pub, then settled back on his bench. He finished his half. Fingering the money in his pocket, he thought of buying another, then decided against it.

It felt wrong to spend this money. Wrong to even have it.

Oh, he'd earned it, no doubt about that. He'd saved Clare and sent her attacker running. He'd done his job.

His job: That was exactly what bothered him. Clare had never been unkind to him—not like some others he could name. Helping her shouldn't have been a job. It should have been something he'd do simply because it needed doing. Because she was in trouble and needed help. Not because there was money to be made.

It was an odd thought, he realized, coming as it did from a man who made his living nicking what he could from the tourists who flocked into the area every summer. But they were different. They were rich, or at least richer than he was. They weren't anybody he knew. They . . .

They weren't Clare.

A couple of local lads came in then and started up a game of billiards. He watched them play until the one who was losing began to complain in a loud voice that he was missing his shots because a certain ugly face was throwing off his concentration. His friend grinned and Davie could feel the red anger come rising up inside himself when he looked into their smirking faces.

He stood up and both lads backed up a little at his size, holding their pool cues more tightly. Davie's hands formed meaty fists at his sides and his eyes narrowed. He started to take a step towards them, but then he glanced at the barman, he thought of Clare, and he let his fists unclench. Nodding stiffly to Harry, he left the pub, laughter ringing in his ears.

They knew he wouldn't fight. Once he had—every time they sniggered or called him names—but not anymore. He couldn't. Not if he didn't want the law on him again. And not fighting made him feel better than them. But it didn't stop the hurt, nor the anger.

As he walked back down the lane towards Mousehole, hands thrust deep in his pockets, he allowed himself the pleasure of imagining how it would feel to smash those smug grins of theirs, but that only made him feel worse.

Think of something cheerful, Davie, he told himself.

The first thing that came to mind was sitting with Clare at her kitchen table. He wondered what it would be like to hold her. If they made love. . . .

What kind of strength did she have in that lame leg of hers? Was it strong enough to wrap around him, holding him tight against her, drawing him in deeper?

You'll never find out, he told himself.

But that didn't mean they couldn't be friends. Perhaps he could go over and borrow a book from her.

He fingered the wad of ten-pound notes in his pocket.

Or he could just talk to her. About what he knew. Perhaps she was in trouble and she could use his help. It would be the two of them against her enemies—just like in the films. He'd be Dennis Quaid and she'd be his Ellen Barkin. And when her enemies were defeated, she would be so grateful. . . .

He could feel himself get hard, his penis pressing painfully against his trousers.

No, he told himself. You'd only be friends.

But that would still be something, wouldn't it? To have a real friend?

He thought of what Willie had said, back in the King's Arms.

Everyone has their secrets.

What were hers?

Some are darker than others....

How dark could hers be?

What did it matter? He knew that however dark her secrets might be, they would never be so black that they would make him turn away from her.

Bloody hell, he thought. The whole thing was hopeless.

But when he got to Regent Terrace, he took the right-hand turn all the same—the one that would lead him across the back of the village to Raginnis Hill where Clare lived.

Touch Me If You Dare

Yield not to evils, but attack all the more boldly.

—VIRGIL, from *Aeneid, Book VI*

The Tatters children began to arrive while Henkie, Taupin, and Lizzie were blocking off the windows of the warehouse. The three of them took turns standing on a rickety ladder, covering the panes with squares of cardboard that they then taped into place. Window by darkened window, the warehouse took on a gloomy air as the only light inside now came from the handful of oil lamps that Henkie had hung about the cavernous room.

Taupin had gone out earlier to leave word with Kara Faul about how they needed the help of the Tatters children and she was now the first to arrive, flinging the door open without so much as a knock and marching inside. Sunlight streamed in through the door, cutting a bright swath of light down the center of the warehouse while deepening shadows beyond.

"Hello!" she cried, blinking in the doorway. "Shall I bring in my bike?"

"Shut the bloody door!"

Henkie's voice boomed from the far side of the warehouse—loud enough to make Jodi wince. She sat on Denzil's right shoulder, because that was the best way for her to stay out of the way, yet still make herself heard to at least one of her co-conspirators. She hung on to his collar to keep her perch, grumbling whenever Denzil bent too far over the table to work on the task that Henkie had assigned to him.

"Does he always have to shout so?" she asked Denzil.

"Actually," he replied, "I rather feel he's been on his best behavior."

"I can't believe that."

"Well, from all I've heard—"

"Will you shut the door!" Henkie repeated, his voice booming louder.

Kara merely smiled at him, now that she could make him out in the gloom.

"The others are just coming," she said, "so we might as well keep it open. What about my bike?"

"Toss it in the bay for all I care."

Kara's lips shaped a practiced moue. "You're not being very friendly," she announced. "*Especially* seeing as how we're here to help *you*."

Henkie glared down at her from the top of the ladder.

"Well, it's true," she added.

"Fine," Henkie told her. "Leave the bloody door open. *Let* the witch's creatures in so they can spy out all our secrets. We've only spent the last bloody hour blocking off these windows so that they can't peer in, so naturally we're delighted that you plan to leave the door wide open so that they can simply waltz in. Shall I put on some tea for them, do you think?"

"What's he on about, then?" Kara asked Taupin.

"Never mind him. We're happy to see you. Just do keep an eye on that doorway and make sure nothing comes in."

"What sorts of nothing?"

Taupin shrugged. "I'm not sure. To be safe, how about nothing larger than a fly?"

Kara's gaze panned from him to Henkie and Lizzie, then to where Denzil was sitting at a table, sewing doll's clothes.

"Nothing larger than a fly?" she repeated.

Taupin nodded. "Just to be safe."

"*Will* you send up another square of cardboard?" Henkie asked from above.

Taupin reached down to the stack by his foot and passed another piece up to Lizzie who stood on a rung about halfway up the ladder. She handed it on to Henkie.

"You've all gone mad, haven't you?" Kara said.

"Not really," Taupin said. "It just seems odd. Give us a few moments to finish up with this here and we'll explain the whole business to you."

"That's all right," she told him. "I like things when they get a bit mad."

"Who's mad?" a new voice asked.

Peter Moyle had come up behind Kara. He peered into the warehouse, over her shoulder.

"Hello there, Denzil," he called. "What's that you've got there on your shoulder—a new kind of monkey?"

"I'm going to give him such a thump," Jodi said. "Once I'm a bit bigger, that is."

"That's not a monkey," Kara said, her voice suddenly all aglow with wonder. "It's a Small."

They both stepped closer.

"No, it isn't," Peter said. "It's Jodi!"

"The door!" Henkie shouted.

Peter glanced up at him. "It's still there," he called back.

"Shut. It."

But neither of the children paid him any mind. They approached the table where Denzil was working, mouths open to form wondering O's.

"However did you turn her into a Small?" Kara asked.

"Can you do me next?" Peter added.

"Bloody hell," Henkie muttered. "See to the door, would you, Brengy?"

"But the ladder . . . ?"

"We'll be fine."

As Henkie turned back to lay the new sheet of cardboard over the window, Taupin went to shut the door only to be confronted by a gaggle of Tatters children who trooped in, all in a group, and were soon clustered around the table where Denzil was now holding court, speaking as though he'd known magic was real all his life and not in the least embarrassed by his abrupt about-face.

Taupin gave a quick glance outside. The children's bicycles lay in a litter of metal and wheels all around the door, but that was all he could see. Or at least it was, until he turned his gaze a bit farther from the area directly in front of the warehouse. Then he caught a glimpse of someone in a black mantle ducking out of sight behind the seawall—there one moment, gone the next.

"She's still out there," he called inside.

It was quieter now, Denzil having admonished the children for their excited cries by explaining how their loud voices were hurting Jodi's ears.

"Any sign of her wee beastie?" Henkie asked. "What's its bloody name? Willow? Whimple?"

"Windle," Lizzie supplied.

"Nothing that I can see," Taupin called back.

"Then shut the bloody door!"

"Henkie," Lizzie said. "Must you shout so?"

He looked down at her.

"Now don't you start in on me," he began, wagging a finger at her. "Ever since Brengy dragged us into this, it's been nothing but 'Henkie, don't do this,' and 'Henkie, don't do that'—"

He broke off as the ladder began to sway.

"Steady now," he cried. "Steady."

But it was his shifting his weight that was making it wobble and as he tried to compensate for the sway, he leaned too far over in the other direction. The ladder tottered for a moment, then pitched to one side. Lizzie jumped and landed on an old mattress that lay nearby, but Henkie was on the top and all he could do was hold on and ride the ladder down.

All conversation stopped in the warehouse as they watched him topple into a stack of paintings. The ladder skidded out across the floor, bouncing once or twice before coming to a stop. Henkie plunged into the paintings and the whole stack tumbled down in a cloud of dust. When the air finally cleared, it was to show Henkie sitting stunned amid the paintings.

He'd poked his hand through one, his foot through two others, but what made the Tatters children hoot with laughter was the paint-

ing that his head had gone through. It was a nude of a busty woman
and hung before him like an apron, his head having gone through
exactly where the model's head had initially been painted.

He tugged it off with a steady stream of curses and lumbered to
his feet, whereupon everyone fell still. There was something more
than a little intimidating about an angry man his size.

"Right," he said. "You and you"—he pointed to a pair of the
children—"finish blocking off the windows. You"—his finger jabbed
the air again—"listen by the door. The rest of you can help Denzil—
you *do* know how to sew, don't you?"

"I can."

A gamine half the size of Kara stuck up a dirty little hand as she
answered. She couldn't have been older than seven. Her face was
round and her hair a mop of tightly wound curls.

Henkie's glare softened. "Can you now?"

The small girl nodded.

"And what's your name?"

"Ethy."

"Well, then, Ethy, you'll be Denzil's special helper."

Her little face beamed.

"As for the rest of you," Henkie went on.

"Wait up a minute," Peter said. "We came to help—not to be
ordered about like you were the law or something. We can get
enough of that at home."

"If you came to bloody help," Henkie started, "then you can
bloody well begin by listening to what I have to bloody tell you, or
you can just bloody well bugger off and leave us to our . . ."

His voice trailed off as Lizzie gave him a kick in the shin.

"Have you gone mad, woman?" he demanded.

"They're all mad," Kara confided to the other children.

"Listen to yourself," Lizzie said.

A rumbling growl began deep in Henkie's chest.

"Listen," Lizzie repeated.

For a moment it looked as though he was going to smash something. Everyone, except for Lizzie, took a step back. But then he
sighed and nodded.

"I'm going to sit down in that chair over there," he said, pointing
to a corner, "and I'm going to quietly drink a great bloody big glass
of whiskey. Call me when the planning can begin."

Lizzie stepped up on her tiptoes and bussed him lightly on the cheek before he went off.

"Ta," she said.

The children parted like the Red Sea before Moses as Henkie stalked towards them, closing up again when he'd gone by. They watched him pour a full glass of whiskey and then sit down in the chair where he swallowed half the whiskey without so much as his eyes watering. Having tried the foul liquid themselves at various times—as children will—they were suitably impressed and more than a little awed.

When they turned their grimy faces back to Lizzie, she faced them and smiled.

"We're very grateful to have your help," she told them, "and though some of what needs to be done is boring, there'll still be some fun at the end of it all."

"What needs to be done?" Peter asked, obviously as charmed by her as he'd been put off by Henkie's attempt at ordering them about.

Lizzie explained how they needed to finish blocking off the windows. There were any number of identical doll-sized outfits to be sewn. Wigs needed to be cut and pasted to dolls' heads. A watch had to be kept against spying eyes and ears.

"What's it all about?" another of the children asked.

Glancing over from her perch on Denzil's shoulder, Jodi identified the speaker—Harvey Ross. He was a big, strapping boy who'd give Henkie a run for his money when he finally stopped growing. At twelve years old, he was already getting odd jobs on the fishing luggers, working side by side with the men.

"Do you know the Widow Pender?" Taupin asked.

"She's a witch," a boy replied.

Jodi didn't have to look to recognize Ratty Friggens's voice. As big as Harvey was for his age, Ratty was small. He was a year younger than Jodi, but topped tiny Ethy by no more than a pair of inches. His real name was Richard, but because of his twitchy nose, pointed features, and the way he liked to skulk about using his size to its best advantage, he'd been dubbed "Ratty" years ago and the name stuck.

"Exactly," Taupin said to a chorus of in-drawn breaths from the children.

It was one thing to suppose there were such things as witches and

Smalls, but quite another to find that they truly *were* more than tales.

"What we have to do is hide Jodi from her long enough to get her to the Men-an-Tol without the Widow being aware of what we're up to."

"What if she turns us all into Smalls for helping you?" Kara asked.

"She needs to know your name and repeat it three times before she can work her spells," Taupin explained. "Surely you could run away from her in that time? Or at least block your ears?"

"And it has to be your true name, doesn't it?" Ratty asked.

"The one that makes you who you are," Taupin agreed. "The one that, in your mind, encompasses all that you see yourself to be. So if she was to try to enspell you, Ratty, she'd have to call you Ratty Richard Friggens, because I'm guessing that's how you think of yourself."

Ratty nodded.

"She can't possibly know all your names," Taupin said.

"But she could learn them, couldn't she?" Ethy asked.

"I . . ."

Taupin looked helplessly at Lizzie who then took over once more. She went on to explain the rest of Henkie's plan. By the time she was done, the children were grinning from ear to ear.

"This *will* be fun," Kara said.

Then it was a matter of setting everyone to their task. All the children wanted to volunteer to help Denzil, because then they could look at the tiny Jodi perched on his shoulder and listen wide-eyed to her story, not to mention giggle at her high-pitched squeaky voice. There were a number of arguments—along the lines of "I had first dibs" and "She couldn't sew if her life depended on it" and "Sod you, too"—but soon it was all sorted out fairly by the simple expediency of allowing everyone to have their turn at the sewing.

By the time everything was prepared—the plans laid out and every contingency that they could foresee argued out to a suitable solution—it was midafternoon and time to begin.

"Remember," Taupin told the children as they all gathered by the door. "If worse comes to worst, you can always jump in the bay and neither she nor her creatures can touch you."

"What about the drowned dead?" Ratty asked.

Various children nodded nervously.

Taupin glanced at Jodi. "Do you know anything about this?"

Jodi shook her head, fed up with how the children all giggled whenever she spoke. She was going to thump more than one of them when she was finally her own size again.

"It's just what I've heard," Ratty said. "That she can call up the dead from the sea and they come shambling out, dripping water and seaweed, to chew on the flesh of the living."

"We have it from a very good source," Taupin said, "that witches can't abide the touch of salt."

"Yes, but the sea dead won't be touching *her,*" Ratty said.

Henkie rose from his chair like a bear leaving its den in the spring.

"If you don't want to go, boy," he said, "just bloody come out and say so."

"I'm not scared," Ratty said.

"Me either," Ethy added. "I'm not scared at all."

"Then let's see what we can do," Henkie said.

Kara was closest to the door. At a nod from Lizzie, she turned the knob, threw it open, and went outside to where her bicycle lay in the dirt.

2.

The Widow Pender wasn't always a widow, nor a Pender.

She was born at that exact moment that lies equidistant between the last sliver of the old moon and the first sliver of the new. Her birthing took place in the bed of a donkey-pulled cart drawn up in back of a hawthorn hedge when the first winds of winter were shivering the trees and the hoarfrost lay black on the frozen ground.

It was an auspicious time for a birth—at least, it was deemed auspicious by her people, for they believed that it was by hardship that a spirit was tempered and made strong.

Her mother's midwife had been a witch, and she was born into a family of witches, the third and last of three daughters to bear the surname of Scorce. Her people were considered travelers by those who knew no better; the traveling people themselves, however, knew exactly what the Scorces were and avoided them when they could, leaving their secret signs scratched into the dirt to warn the other traveling clans of the Scorces' whereabouts.

The new babe was named Hedra in a curious ceremony a few weeks later, for that was the old word for October, the name of the month in which she was born. Her family gathered about a tall, craggy standing stone set high on a cliff overlooking the sea, and had there been observers to view the proceedings, they would have seen much gadding about in the raw, wordless chanting and mad dancing, the burning of small straw figures and charms in fires made of bones, and the crafting of fetishes that were each bound to the new babe's name and her future. Each participant in the ceremony left with one such fetish that they would keep safe through the years to preserve the newly named child's luck.

Under her stiff blouse, the Widow Pender still wore her fetish in a tiny leather pouch. She wore it to remind herself of those days when she had been Hedra Scorce and the world was a merry place of bright wonder, when shadows were only shadows and she had no knowledge of what hid behind their darkness, watching her every move, glittering eyes heavily lidded with cobwebs.

But she didn't wear it for luck, because all her luck had long since fled.

The Scorces had traveled the country for many years—mother, aunt, and grandmother riding in the donkey cart, the girls walking alongside. Like other traveling people, they did odd jobs and mending, picking potatoes and other vegetables in season, selling the besom brooms and baskets that they made and the charms that, unlike those of the other travelers, were potent in and of themselves, requiring no belief to work their magic. They loved the road, the long road that unwound underfoot that had no beginning and no end, carrying them from one town to another, through one village and beyond, up into the lonely places, the moors and rock-strewn clifftops that were anything but lonely to those who lived as close to the earth as they did.

But times changed. They grew harder for all the traveling people as the constables shifted them from town and village green, until only the moors and cliffs were theirs; but they could gain no sustenance from those desolate reaches. The natural beauty and wonder sustained the spirit, but the body required more secular nourishment, and that they could only earn in the villages and towns.

Hard times.

Sometimes now, she could see those eyes, watching her from the shadows. And she'd hear a voice, whispering. And then a whole chorus of them.

"Don't listen," her grandmother told her when she asked about what lay in the shadows. "The mischiefs and evils of the world wait

in the shadows to prey on children innocent as you. They will promise you anything. Follow their advice, accept their gifts, and your
soul will grow bitter. It will shrivel and wither until you can no
longer feel the Mother's presence. When you leave her light, all that
will remain for you is the shadows and I'd wish that on no one, not
friend, not enemy."

"But they say they can help us."

"The sweeter the promise," Grandmother replied, "the surer the
lie."

"But—"

"Remember the lesson that the Christians have forgotten: When
Adam and Eve made their choice in Eden, it concerned neither blind
obedience nor righteous piety. It was a choice of self over God, ar-
rogance over faith."

"We aren't Christians," Hedra objected.

"True. But our Mother of Light and their Christ are not so different—in our hearts we both follow the light; only the names differ.
What speaks to you from the shadows is that same Eden serpent,
child."

"I like snakes."

Her grandmother smiled. "So do I. But there's a world of difference between the small cousin we can catch in the grass and the one
whose voice tempts us from the shadows. Promise me you won't
listen to it."

She had never seen her grandmother so serious, so solemn.

"I promise," she said.

And she did try to follow her grandmother's advice, to keep her
promise, but it was hard not to listen when the world was as it was,
when the light seemed to die, no matter where you turned, and all
that was left was shadows.

Hard times.

Kerra was the first to leave, marrying a shoemaker in Peatyturk.
Grandmother died. Aunt married into another traveling family.
Mother took sick, but recovered. Gonetta stayed on until they passed
through Rosevear, marrying the son of a shopkeeper.

Then there was only herself and Mother left, following the road
with their donkey and their cart.

Hard times.

The whispers in the shadows grew stronger and she couldn't help but listen. But she remembered her promise to her grandmother and did nothing with the secret knowledge that they breathed into her ear.

Not when the constables sent them from town before they could buy a few meager provisions and they were reduced to grubbing for roots and scavenging along the shore.

Not when they were jeered at by those who went to church, those fine upstanding townsfolk who listened piously to the teachings of the light spoken of within the holy stone halls, but left with less charity in their hearts than the cold winter winds.

Not when the children pelted them with stones, or the dogs were set on their heels. For fun.

Hard times.

Mother died on a night as cold and lonely as the one on which Hedra had been born. They were camped in back of a different hedge, but the hoarfrost lay as black on the ground, the wind was as cold. Fifteen years old, Hedra sat up all night, rocking her mother's corpse in her arms. Come morning, she buried the unfamiliar object that her mother had become. It was an empty thing, its soul fled, and bore no more resemblance to her mother than did a stone.

But she could remember comforting arms, a sweet high voice that sang lullabies to the counterpoint of the wind outside their canvas tent, a smile as warm as sunlight in summer.

The shadows drew close to her, whispering, whispering.

She huddled by her mother's grave, arms wrapped around her chilled body, shivering and trying not to listen, but it was hard, hard. As hard as the times. She crooned one of her mother's lullabies, closing her ears to the voices, rocking back and forth again, but this time the burden was in her heart, not in her arms.

And that was how Edwin Pender found her.

He brought her home. He made her his wife. He gave her order and love and comfort and kept the shadows at bay. The donkey grew old and lived out its life in content. The cart stood behind the Pender cottage, its bright paint fading in the rough weather, grass entwined in the spokes of its wheels, its bed home now to leaves and debris while sleepy cats lay on its driver's seat when the sun was warm on the wooden slats.

But Hedra didn't mind, for Edwin Pender had driven the hard times away and filled the emptiness inside her. He worked the sea and she kept their home. If he was disappointed that she never gave him a child, he never once mentioned it. They went to church together and Hedra was content to exchange her Mother of Light for their Christ, because hadn't Grandmother said they were one and the same—that only the names differed?

Hard times fled.

Until she learned of her husband's mistress.

He laughed when she confronted him with her knowledge. A man such as he needed more than one woman, he told her, but she wasn't to worry. Her home was here and he had more than enough love still left over for her, didn't he just? So come to his arms now. . . .

She had backed away from him, but she hadn't said a word.

Her rage was a silent storm.

For as her world went dark, the shadows came back in a rush, eyes glittering in the dark corners of the room where they hid, voices whispering, and she remembered all the secret knowledge that they had ever told her.

When her husband went to sea, she called up a storm. If it drowned the Old Quay and sank the fishing boats, if fifteen men had lost their lives, what did it matter, so long as Edwin Pender was in their number?

Her husband's mistress she gave to the shadows. High on a cliff-top, on a moonless night, she fed the barmaid a length of steel, then buried the corpse in an unmarked grave where its moldering bones remained to this day.

She felt no regret.

She felt no regret because her spirit belonged to the shadows now and they bled all such softness from her spirit, embittering and withering it. In return, they gave her yet more of their secret knowledge.

She spent the years toying with the folk of Bodbury, working small unpleasantries that could never be traced back to her, setting into motion complex patterns of bad luck that took years to be fully realized and were all the more appealing to her for the invisible machinations of her own hand in their intricate making.

She created the approximation of a child for herself, from herself, giving it birth as surely as other women nurtured children from their womb. Her fetch. She named it Windle. Together they lived in the borderland between the world as common folk knew it and the secret world that hid in the shadows. Spying and playing their games, they were like a pair of spiders who made an invisible web encompassing the lives of every man, woman, and child in Bodbury.

And she was content.

The bright child she had once been was as forgotten as though she had never existed.

Hedra Scorce? Who was she? There was only the Widow Pender now.

And the years went by.

Twenty years since the storm, since she accepted the shadows.

Those years stole the lives of fishermen on sea. Others died on land, men and women both. Children were born. The wheels of the world turned. And the Widow Pender grew older, her spirit no more than a smear of darkness inside her, as black as the hearts of the shadows.

But as she grew older, she found herself remembering a time when the world was a brighter place, when she bore a different name and the shadows didn't rule her. The memories came first as small nagging thoughts that she simply ignored. But as time passed, she'd see faces.

Her sisters; her aunt. What had become of them?

Her mother. Her grandmother.

Edwin Pender.

How could so much good have gone wrong? she would find herself wondering. Had there been another manipulator—one such as she was now—who had pulled the marionette-stringed web that was the heart of her life and that of her family?

The shadows hissed and spat when she thought such thoughts. Windle grew distant.

She found her birth fetish lying in the back of a drawer, and took to wearing it again. She thought of luck, bad and good, found and lost.

She remembered an old song she had heard once, verses of which returned to haunt her at odd times of the night or day:

> *You took what's before me and what's behind me,*
> *You took east and west when you wouldn't mind me;*
> *Sun, moon, and stars from my sky have been taken,*
> *And God as well, or I'm much mistaken.*

Her husband had given her everything, and then taken it all away again. She would have done anything for him, but even that had not been enough.

> O black as a sloe is the heart that's in you;
> Black as a coal is the grief that binds me;
> Black as a bootprint in shining hallway—
> 'Twas you that blackened it, forever and always.

That dark, shriveled stain that was her spirit began to ache, deep in her chest. She thought more and more of what her grandmother had told her, of how the shadows lied, of how they could manipulate the innocent. . . .

She tried hard to remember, but she couldn't imagine what it would be like to be any way other than how she was now. Considered so, how could she know if she'd made the right choice in her life? How could she know that the choice hadn't been made *for* her?

To find out, she needed to be free of the shadows and they wouldn't let her go. Not unless she could give them a secret that they didn't hold themselves. That was the price—a simple, impossible price.

Until she remembered the child she had been and the tales her grandmother and mother both had told her of the Barrow World— the otherworld of the piskies. The shadows had no hold there. If she could give them its key . . .

She bought a mechanical toy man and, with wax and charms, made it appear so lifelike that one would expect it to sit up and talk at any moment. Then she woke the one spell concerning piskies that the shadows knew. The enchantment sped through the air one moonless night like a fisherman's hook and line, whirring through the darkness until it snagged and caught the dreaming mind of a little moor man and brought it back to her cottage.

Animated now, her mechanical toy man would still not speak. Would reveal no secrets.

The shadows laughed.

Windle watched, an unfamiliar grin on its lips.

But the Widow was undaunted. Like a child with a new toy, she made a home for her captive in an old aquarium and became engrossed in fashioning furniture and clothing to his size. While she worked, she considered and put aside a hundred plans on how to wrest the little man's secret from him, thought until her head hurt and she began to realize that she was defeated. She would never discover his secrets. She would never be free of the shadows.

In the end, it was the arrival of the snooping Tatters child that gave her a workable plan. She had meant to let Jodi stew for a few days—just long enough for despair at never regaining her own size to settle in—then she would strike a bargain with the girl. If Jodi stole the necessary secret from the little man, then the Widow would set her free.

It was that simple.

Except the miserable girl and piskie both had escaped and now she was back where she'd begun, with only one hope left—that the little man had told the girl something useful while they were together.

It was clutching at straws, but clutching at straws was all that the Widow had left. The pain in her chest ached fiercely. And the whispering laughter from the shadows was driving her mad. Worse still, understanding had come—riding on the back of those selfsame memories that tormented her so—that when she died, she would join the shadows.

If truth be told, she had always known. But it hadn't seemed so important once. Now she grew old, and with age came a fuller realization of what being part of the shadows meant.

Never being free of pain.

Never knowing peace.

Never joining her family in the beyond.

Losing all that was hers not simply once or twice, but forevermore without any hope of reprieve. . . .

The irony of what she was doing—attempting to regain lost innocence through tormenting another—simply never occurred to her at all. She was blind to all but her own need. Had she stopped to consider, she would have understood exactly what it was that made the shadows laugh as they did.

But her strength was her single-mindedness and it was for that reason that she crouched by the seawall of the Old Quay, spying on Hedrik Whale's warehouse, while her fetch scurried about its roof and walls, attempting a closer look. She cared nothing of what the townsfolk would think of her behavior. She wanted only to understand what Whale and the others were up to. She knew they had Jodi in there with them. But what were they going to *do* with her?

They were such an improbable collection of individuals that they made an impossible group to second-guess. Each on his or her own could be odd enough, but collected together, they were literally capable of any mad scheme. And when one added the gaggle of Tatters children that had arrived earlier . . .

The Widow was sure that certain disaster lay ahead.

She shifted uncomfortably from foot to foot, utterly sick of staring at the weather-beaten side of the warehouse. Then she saw a small spidery shape swing down from the roof to come scuttling along the base of the seawall towards her.

Something was up. She could feel it brewing in the air.

Windle began chittering away to her, so fast that she could barely make out a word of the creature's odd language. She finally realized that it was merely telling her what she already felt—that the waiting had ended.

As though on cue, the door to the warehouse was flung open and the whole crowd, adults and Tatters children, came streaming out. The Widow closed her eyes and reached out with her witch-sight— a kind of seeing that looked beyond what could be seen by the naked eye, for it stripped the world down to its basic components.

Blood called to blood.

The Widow had taken the precaution of taking a few drops of blood from Jodi when she was unconscious and swallowing them. The taste of them fired sharply against her palate now as her witch-sight reached for, found, and locked on the first child to come through the door.

That little Tatters girl. She was carrying Jodi, the Widow knew. She could taste Jodi's blood so near the girl that she had to be carrying her.

She started to straighten up and open her eyes, but then she realized that the second child was carrying Jodi as well. As was the third and fourth—they were all carrying her, children and adults alike.

Which was impossible.

She focused her witch-sight more sharply and her head began to ache from the effort.

She felt old and tired.

The bright sun made pockets of shadow at the base of the seawall and she could hear sniggering laughter coming from those dark patches.

Fine, she thought. They've either cut her up and they're all carrying a bit of her, or they've managed some other trick, but it won't help them. She'd merely track them all down, each and every one of them. One way or another, she meant to regain hold of the Small she'd created.

The sniggering of the shadows grew louder.

Laugh all you want, she told them. You'll still not have me in your ranks.

At that, the laughter came long and sharp.

Not ever, the Widow said.

In front of the warehouse, the children were all on their bicycles now. They sped off in a dozen directions, little legs pumping the pedals for all they were worth. The adults also took different directions, only they moved more slowly. The Widow sent Windle after one of the children, then marked and set off after another herself.

Not ever, she repeated.

There was no reply from the shadows, but that was only because she had stepped out into the sunlight where they couldn't follow her.

3.

When she heard her parents complaining, when she saw what it was like to be even a few years older than she was, Kara Faull would think that there couldn't be a grander age to be than eleven. She hated the idea of growing any older. There was the odd adult like Denzil and Taupin who might as well still be children for the way they carried on, or those like Jodi and Ratty who were still in that undefined stage between being normal and adult, but mostly, growing old just seemed to be a steady progression of doors being shut.

On magic.

On wonder.

On just plain having fun.

She was thinking about that as she pedaled away from Henkie's warehouse. If you couldn't go off on a mad lark like this, any which time you pleased, then really, what was the point?

For this *was* a lark. And more, it pointed true to all those things that adults said couldn't be real. For when you saw it with your own two eyes, how could you doubt it? The old stories weren't lies. There truly *were* witches and Smalls and every manner of wonderful thing.

They were *real*. And if that wasn't the best thing she'd learned in weeks, she didn't know what was.

Her legs pumped furiously to maintain her speed up the incline that was Weaver Street. When she reached its crest, she grinned as she coasted down the far side of the hill—fat bicycle wheels humming on the cobblestones, the wind in her face, the skirt of her sundress flapping against her thighs, laughter bubbling up inside her.

Tucked away in a pocket of her dress was one of the dolls that they had made in the warehouse. Not one of them looked anything like Jodi, but that wasn't the point, Taupin had told them. It was the size, and the flash of hair colour, and all the clothing being alike. And it was the tiny drop of Jodi's blood that was carefully dripped onto the head of each doll, the blood that was immediately absorbed by the thirsty cloth.

Kara hadn't liked that part—and neither had Jodi, judging by the grimace on her miniature face when she had to prick her finger with a pin and then give a bit of herself to each doll.

Privately, Kara was sure that even a witch couldn't be so stupid as to mistake any of these dolls for the genuine article, but Taupin had insisted, quoting tales of enchantment and witcheries where just that sort of trick was not only considered clever, but proved to be successful as well.

We'll see, she thought, as she leaned into the corner at the bottom of the hill where Weaver Street briefly met Tinway Walk, crossing over and changing its name to Redruth Steep as it climbed another rise.

She chanced a glance behind as she turned the corner, but the way was clear. Still grinning, and only narrowly avoiding a collision with a pedestrian who shouted angrily after her, she stood up on her pedals at the bottom of Redruth Steep and began the new ascent. Half-way up the hill, she shot into the mouth of Penzern Way—a crooked narrow alley that would take her back to the harbour by a circuitous route as it wound its way between the backs of the close-set stone buildings that clustered in this part of the town.

Well, I'm away, she thought, slowing her pace to avoid a run-in with someone's untidily stacked garbage. The witch and her fetch— whatever *that* was—had chosen someone else to follow, which only proved her point.

The dolls simply weren't the clever trick that Taupin had made them out to be. Now if he'd only listened to her plan of borrowing a fisherman's net with which they could catch the witch and then toss her into the bay, why then they'd all be laughing by now, because—

Something the size of a cat landed on her back and dug its claws into her shoulders.

Kara shrieked and lost control of her bicycle. Its front wheel turned awkwardly on a cobblestone and she was tossed over the handlebars. All that saved her from a terrible collision with an all-too-rapidly approaching wall was that the hem of her skirt caught on the end of a handlebar. The thin cloth ripped, but its momentary hold had been enough to break the momentum of her flight so that she landed in a pile of refuse—winded and shaken—rather than cracking her head on the wall.

But she had no time to consider her good fortune. The thing on her back was clawing at her skin and all she could do was to continue shrieking as she rolled about in the garbage, trying to dislodge it. When she succeeded, it immediately scampered around in front of her and swiped at her face with its talons. Kara jerked her head back so quickly that she pulled a muscle in her neck.

"If," Taupin had told them, "you feel that you're in any sort of danger at all, for God's sake, *give* up your doll. That's what they're after. Give it up, and when they see what it is they've been chasing, they'll hurry off after another one of us."

Taupin's words rang in Kara's mind as she stared with horrified fascination at the creature that was perched so near her face.

Jodi's description had been all too accurate. It looked like a hairless caricature of Denzil's monkey, but there the resemblance ended, for Ollie didn't have claws like the fetch's, nor those rows of sharp teeth that would do a shark proud. Nor did Ollie's throat produce the awful chittering sound that escaped from the creature—akin to drawing a fingernail across a chalkboard.

Kara's earlier curiosity about the creature had utterly vanished. All she wanted to do now was to escape its presence, but the fetch crouched too closely by her. There wasn't a move she could make that would allow her to avoid those sharp teeth and claws.

The fetch's saucer-wide eyes glared with malevolence and she shivered as the creature's gaze locked onto her own. There was a brutal rage in those eyes—and also the promise that the fetch would enjoy the violence that would ensue when that rage was released.

Kara didn't want to hang about to see that happen.

She scrabbled in her pocket for the doll. Trembling fingers took a moment to get a grip on the thing, but then finally she was pulling it free and offering it up to the little monster facing her.

It tore the doll from her hand, rage glittering sharper as it saw what it was. Its chittering rose into a high-pitched crescendo that made Kara's eardrums feel as though they would burst at any moment.

"Th-that's all I've g-got," she managed.

Her throat felt thick and dry and she could barely croak the words out.

The fetch glared at her. It opened its mouth wide and bit off the head of the doll, chewing the cloth and fabric stuffing, throat working as it swallowed the mess down.

Kara could only continue to stare, fascinated and repulsed by its every motion.

When it had finished swallowing the doll's head, it tossed the body away and leaned closer to Kara, grin widening. It swung its paw at her and panic loosened her throat's constriction to let wail another shriek. The creature snickered as she fell back in the garbage in her attempt to get away, then it swung onto a drainpipe and scrambled quickly up to the roof. Two breaths later, it had disappeared.

For a long moment Kara simply lay where she'd fallen. Her every muscle ached. She felt as though she were bruised from head to foot. The stench of the garbage made her stomach queasy and she wanted to throw up.

But she was alive.

The creature hadn't killed her.

She sat up slowly, wincing at the pain the movement brought her. A nervous look at the rooftops surrounding her showed no saucer-eyed face peering down at her still. It was gone now—after one of the others.

Well, that was their problem, she thought. She was just happy to be alive. As far as she was concerned, all the fun had gone out of the day's lark.

But then she thought of Ethy. Little Ethy, with her own doll hidden under her shirt. If the fetch went after her . . .

We were all bloody fools, Kara thought as she hobbled over to

where her bicycle lay. We should have stood up against them together, sitting in great vats of seawater, armed with salt-water balloon bombs. . . .

Balloon bombs. Now that was absolutely brill.

She opened the little purse attached to her belt and counted her
pennies. She had barely enough to buy what was needed—but it was
enough.

She righted her bicycle and got on. Setting off down Penzern Way
towards the market, she couldn't help but groan as every bump she
hit reminded her poor body of the recent abuse it had undergone.
Tears of pain sparkled in her eyes, but she kept on, her mouth set in
a tight line, and ignored the way the bumps made her want to lie
down in a corner somewhere and not move for weeks.

She was determined to give back as good as she'd gotten.

And then some.

4.

It was the Widow who tracked down Ratty Friggens.

Like the others, he'd left Henkie's warehouse on his bicycle, but
he went on afoot as soon as he reached Market Square. Hiding his
bicycle behind a stack of crates that he knew wouldn't be shipped
out for a few days, he continued on through the maze of warehouses
and shipping docks until he reached the beginning of one of New
Dock's long piers. There he swung down to where the storm drains
emptied into the sea. He gave a last quick look out across the bay,
then slipped inside and began to make his way back through town—
underground.

Find me here, he thought with a happy grin. If you can.

Ratty knew every hidden nook and secret cranny to be found, in
and around and under Bodbury. Like his namesake he could squeeze
into the tiniest openings, wriggling his way through narrow drains
that others would swear were too narrow for a cat, little say a boy
from the Tatters, no matter how small he might be. But if Ratty could
get his head in, then it was just a matter of drawing his shoulders in
close to his body until they appeared to be folded across his chest.
And then he would simply slither his way along.

Today he kept to the larger drains. Once his eyes adjusted to the
poor light, it was easy for him to walk along at a steady pace. The
only illumination came from the odd grating that opened up onto

the streets above, but it was enough for him to make do. He kicked at pebbles and the odd bit of debris, pausing to unstop the more complex entanglements that might otherwise dam up a drain.

Ratty kept his underground passages clear for his own convenience, but he was also providing an unknown service to those above whose homes might otherwise be flooded out during a big enough storm. They didn't know and he didn't care if they did or didn't. Below, it was his kingdom.

His plan was to follow the drains right up to the top of the town. From there he meant to go across country for as far as he got before it became dark. He'd been nervous when Taupin first talked about the witch, but then he had made his own plan of what he'd do and where he'd go, and his nervousness had fled. No one was going to follow him down here.

He took his time to reach the far end of the last drain, emerging from it cautiously, but there was no one about. This high above the town he could look out across the rooftops, all the way across the bay. It was one of his favorite places. He could spend hours sitting up here, just watching the boats out on the water, the gulls wheeling above them.

He settled the grating back into place and went to sit on a low wall that backed onto a hedge for a bit of a rest before he continued.

It was amazing really, when he thought about it. He'd spread about the tale that the Widow Pender had got herself a Small just for the fun of it, never dreaming there was any truth in the matter. How could there be? Smalls and witches were part and parcel of fairy tales and had no part in the real world. If there was magic, if there was wonder, then it remained well hidden. So well hidden that it might as well not even exist in the first place. But now . . . oh, yes, now. . . .

Well, he'd seen the miniature Jodi Shepherd with his own two eyes, hadn't he just? *She* was real. There was no denying that. And if she was real, then—

"Ratty Richard Friggens."

His heart stopped cold in his chest at the sound of the Widow's voice. He turned slowly to find that she'd crept up on him as if from out of nowhere—stepping now from the shadows by Kember Cottage, the last building in Bodbury before the hedge-bordered fields began their walk across the hills. She was no more than the length of a half lane from where he was sitting.

She regarded him with an amused smile on her tight lips, dark eyes flashing dangerously.

How could she . . . ? he thought in panic, but the answer came before he could even complete the question.

She was a witch, wasn't she?

"Ratty Richard Friggens," she said again.

He started at the repetition of his name. Remembering what Taupin and Jodi both had told him about witch's spells needing a name spoken three times to work, he hastily pulled the doll he was carrying from his pocket and offered it to her.

"H-here," he said.

Just don't turn me into a toad, he added to himself.

"I don't want that," the Widow said.

"But . . ."

"I want the girl. The Small."

"I—I don't have her."

"Then who does? Who carried her out?"

Ratty swallowed dryly. He couldn't tell because there was no knowing what the witch would do to Jodi when she had her in her power once again. But if he didn't tell, there was no knowing what she'd do to him either.

He just knew it would be something horrible.

"Come, boy. I don't have all day."

"I—I . . ."

The name was on the tip of his tongue, burning to be set free into the air, but he couldn't do it. He just couldn't break faith. Not and still live with himself after.

He straightened his shoulders and met the Widow's gaze with his own, trying to stay steady, though his legs were trembling so much that if he hadn't been sitting down, he would have fallen down.

"I won't tell you."

"Ratty Richard Friggens," the Widow repeated for the third time. "Are you so brave, then, boy?"

Brave? He was frightened out of his wits. But by now his throat was so constricted that he couldn't have given her the name if he'd wanted to.

He shook his head.

"Bah," the Widow said.

She added some words in a language that Ratty couldn't understand and the world went all fuzzy on him.

She's turning *me* into a Small, he thought.

His panic lessened somewhat. That wouldn't be so bad. He could prowl about in places that he'd never been able to reach before. He could . . .

It was growing hard to think. Dizziness rose up in waves. There was a metallic taste on his tongue and he realized that he'd bitten his own cheek. That was his own blood he tasted.

His own blood.

He thought of Jodi pricking her finger, putting a drop of blood onto the head of each doll.

Jodi who was the size of a mouse.

But he didn't seem to be shrinking. Instead, he seemed to be fading away. He was . . .

His thoughts grew too fragile to hold on to anymore. They flitted about through his head like flies, humming and buzzing, but he couldn't snag even one of them.

What—

He looked down at his hand. It had grown so gossamer that he could see right through it.

—was she—

The doll fell from his grip—no, fell *through* his grip to land splay-limbed on the road.

—doing—

Terrified now, he stared at his hand. It was coming apart like smoke. A breeze touched him, took away a finger in a wreath of pink mist.

—to . . .

He never did get to finish the thought.

5.

The Widow smiled humourlessly as the last parts of Ratty Friggens were dissipated by the wind. All that remained was a small bone button on the wall where he'd been sitting. That, and a distant fading cry that sounded very much like his voice, before it too was taken away by the wind.

He'd thought she was going to change him into a Small as well, she had realized towards the end. She'd seen it in his eyes.

Instead, she'd simply unmade him.

Because that had been his real fear. He was the sort who could find fortune in any size he might be. But to be nothing . . .

She smiled and scooped up the button. Needle and thread appeared from her pocket and she quickly sewed it to her cloak where it joined a dozen or so others already sewn there. With the button in place, needle and thread returned to her pocket. She stooped and picked up the doll he'd dropped, her smile fading.

Clever.

Which of them had thought of this?

She lifted the doll to her mouth and licked the spot stained with Jodi's blood.

Too clever.

But she'd have the miserable girl yet. And she'd have gifts as well for the whole gaggle of fools who'd tried to help her. She would change them and unmake them. She would . . .

She sighed. Closing her mind, she reached out with her witch-sight until she found and marked the presence of another one of the carriers. Did this one bear another doll, or the girl herself? The bothersome thing was that there was only one way to find out. She might well waste the entire day tracking them all down.

Unless . . .

She glanced skyward. The early afternoon was aging, the day steadily wearing into the evening. Night would be here soon. She could call up helpers then.

From the marshes.

From under cairns.

From sea graves.

Wrapping her cloak more closely about her, she fingered the newest addition to her collection and set off after the next Tatters child whose position she had noted moments ago.

Behind her, where the shadows were thickening at the base of the wall, shadows laughed softly to themselves. The Widow heard them, as they knew she would, but she paid them no mind.

6.

The animals went mad when Denzil finally returned home in the early afternoon.

Ollie flung himself onto his shoulders as soon as he opened the door, and happily hugged him. Noz gave a complaining squawk from his perch and ruffled his feathers, while the raven swooped down to circle once around Denzil's head, before flying back to its own perch on the bookshelf. The mice scurried about in their cages and Rum wound back and forth in between his legs, tripping him up as he tried to close the door, deal with Ollie, and get into the room.

"That's enough, you!" he cried, straightening his glasses with an angry shove of his thumb and forefinger.

Silence descended. Movement stopped.

"I'm sorry I left you so long, but there were important matters to attend to."

"End to," Noz repeated gravely.

Denzil had to laugh.

He propped up his own Jodi doll by the flying machine on his workbench and spent the next half hour grumbling good-naturedly as he set about feeding them all, then cleaned cages and the mess in the box of sand in one corner where the birds, Ollie, and Rum had been trained to relieve themselves.

Rum scratched to go outside as soon as he was fed, but the other animals followed him about—Noz and the raven with their unblinking gazes, Ollie tagging along like an errant child, making more of a mess in trying to help Denzil clean up than if he'd left well enough alone. But finally order was restored, routines brought back onto track, and Denzil could sit by the window and stare out at Peter Street to consider the past night's odd occurrences.

"Utter madness," he told Ollie, who cuddled close to him on the chair. "That's what it is. All the world gone topsy-turvy."

His gaze traveled across the room to where the Jodi doll was sprawled on his workbench.

Nothing was the same anymore. New equations had entered into the calm, if complex, natural world he thought he had come to somewhat understand. Not well, mind you. He'd barely scratched its surface in the better part of the lifetime that he'd spent attempting to unravel its mysteries. But he'd had the basic tools necessary for the task, the scientific demeanor that told him how to best go about his studies, the understanding of the underlying logic that bound the unknown to the known.

And now everything was changed.

Smalls and witches and dead men who could still move and speak. . . .

Tee-ta-taw. *Utter* madness.

His gaze shifted from the Jodi doll to his bookshelves where the raven was now grooming its feathers. He had a wealth of scientific texts, research notes—those of his own, and of colleagues—and every manner of useful tract on every manner of useful subject, from mechanics to astronomy, philosophy to natural history. But not the one of them was of any use in his present situation. He would have to go down to the library and pore through their collections of folklore and myth to learn what he now needed to know. To understand it all. Understand, and correlate it to what he already knew so that he could fashion some kind of a working plan as to what he would do when this immediate crisis was over.

He sighed.

Correlating madness to what he already knew.

Bother and damn, as Jodi would say.

How could he know what to keep and what to throw out? Piskies were real, but did that mean dragons were as well? The dead could walk and talk, but did that prove the existence of demons? Witches could shrink people down to the size of a mouse, but could they fly through the air on a broomstick?

It made his head hurt to think of it all.

And then there was Jodi.

It made sense that he couldn't bring her home with him. This was perhaps the first place the Widow would look for her. But he didn't much care for her to be out of his sight. To have to sit here and wait and wonder until it grew close enough to moonrise so that they could make their way out to the holed stone on which Jodi, Henkie, and Taupin all put so much faith.

Too much faith, if you asked him.

Yes, he told himself, but come 'pon that, twenty-four hours ago you didn't believe there was such a thing as a Small, either, you.

Another sigh escaped him and Ollie reached up to touch his cheek, trying to comfort him.

"I just don't know," Denzil said aloud.

He had his misgivings about this plan that had been concocted in Henkie Whale's warehouse. For all that he could no longer deny the existence of magic, the reality of myth, he still found it difficult to accept that someone like Henkie carried the kind of wisdom they needed. The only sensible one of the lot of them—himself included, he had to admit—was Lizzie Snell.

She was a clever, down-to-earth, practical jewel of a woman. And utterly wasted on the likes of Henkie. What did she see in him? It was easy to see what he saw in her. . . .

Now don't start that kind of thinking, you, he told himself. You're too old a man to think about sparking with the ladies.

But he hadn't always been so old. There'd been a time, when he was a young man—

He shook his head. No, he'd made a choice then and it was far too late to change his mind about it now. He had his studies and nothing had really altered from the time he had made his decision to the present day. What woman would put up with the likes of him anyway—what with his odd hours and animals, the studies that swallowed his life, and he so set in his ways?

A woman like Lizzie Snell.

Or the woman that Jodi would grow up to be.

It was his own fault that he'd given up any hope of finding such a companion for himself.

Too late, too late, the past whispered.

The present agreed.

Fair enough. He would just have to make do with the surrogate daughter that Jodi had become. He'd done so for years, loved her as though she really *were* his daughter. But that didn't stop regrets bittering up against the corners of his mind.

He shook his head again, trying to dislodge this train of thought. Think of something different, he told himself. But then only worries arose—for Jodi; for the Tatters children that they'd involved in their troubles. If anything happened to them . . .

The afternoon leaked slowly away as he sat there, staring out at Peter Street, at the folk who went about their business below him without any concern or care for the hidden world that he'd discovered lying all about them, all about each and every one of them. He stroked Ollie's fur, smiling vaguely as the monkey fell asleep in his arms, and waited for the time to pass.

7.

Ethy Welet was really too young for the task at hand, but she would never have admitted it, and no one was about to deny her her chance to take up her part in the trick they meant to play on the Widow. In the Tatters, it simply wasn't done. The children accepted one another for what they were, for what they said they could and would do, and judged one another only on how they kept their word and how well they accomplished the promised task.

So Ethy left with the others, her own Jodi doll tucked under her shirt, and pedaled her small bicycle away, a brave grin on her grimy face, waving cheerfully to the others. But once they were out of sight and she was on her own, the nervousness came.

She thought of the Widow. Even without magic, the old woman was a towering fearsome figure—at least four times Ethy's size and easily capable of far more strength than was hidden in her tiny frame. Whatever would she *do* if the Widow confronted her? And then there was this fetch creature that Jodi had described. It sounded as though it was even more awful.

Maybe they wouldn't come after her. Maybe they'd chase one of the others instead.

She could hope. . . .

But that wasn't a kind thought.

Ethy lived with her father in a small shabby room deep in the Tatters. Caswal Welet was an absolutely brilliant darts and billiards champion. Unfortunately, after Ethy, they were his only loves, so while they had any number of trophies neatly lined up, row upon row, in their room, there was rarely much to eat because Caswal couldn't keep a job if his life depended on it, and one change of clothes each was all they had. When Ethy outgrew what she owned, it was the other children in the Tatters who helped her find new garb. Her father simply couldn't muster enough interest in any job to keep it for more than a week.

Ethy's mother had left them because of that and the people of Bodbury considered him, as they did so many who made the Tatters their home, to be nothing more than a lazy layabout. Caswal, in moments of honesty, would have been the first to agree with them. But Ethy didn't see him like that at all.

The man she knew was kind and thoughtful, if a bit silly. But he always made sure that she had enough to eat, even if he didn't, and they had time to walk about together and he taught her how to play both darts and billiards—moving the crate she had to stand upon around the table when it was her turn for a shot. But best of all were his stories.

He knew any number of them. Wise and wonderful stories. Funny ones and sad. And the heroes—they were always brave and strong, yes, but they were kind as well.

"Kindness is important, my little wren," he would tell her. "Doesn't matter how poor you are, you can still be kind. Doesn't cost a tuppence, and maybe those you're kind to won't be kind back, but at least you'll have the satisfaction of knowing that you tried to leave the world a bit of a better place, even if all you had to spare was a smile."

She wasn't that strong, Ethy thought as she pedaled along, but at least she could try to be brave and kind. But the former was easier thought than done. As she took a shortcut through an alley 'round back of the butcher's on Weaver Street, the Widow's fetch dropped on her back and knocked her from her bicycle.

She stared horrified at the creature, trying not to cry from the bumps she'd taken in her fall, and clutched the Jodi doll under her shirt tight against her skin.

The fetch was ever so much worse than Jodi had described it—all teeth and claws and those huge evil eyes. It made a chittering sound that rose *click-clicking* from the back of its throat, a sound like the same harsh words being repeated over and over again. Ethy knew she wasn't really understanding them, but she couldn't help but hear them as—

Killyoukillyoukillyoukillyou . . .

Taupin had said to hand over the doll if she was in danger, but that didn't seem to be a very brave thing to do, no matter how badly she wanted to do it right at this very moment. Because if she handed over the doll, then the fetch would just go after one of the others.

And maybe kill her anyway, just for fun.

She trembled as it advanced on her, and hugged the doll more tightly.

Killyoukillyoukillyou . . .

"D-daddy . . ." she cried.

The fetch's grin widened.

Ethy didn't want to look, but couldn't unlock her gaze from that of the horrible little creature. It crouched low, gathering its muscles to spring at her. A voice stopped it before it could attack.

"Hey, you!"

Ethy looked up and relief went through her. It was Kara.

The fetch turned to look as well and hissed as though it recognized the older girl.

The Little Country

"Come on, you little bugger," Kara said. "You and I, we haven't finished our own dance yet."

Ethy stared wide-eyed at her friend. Kara was scratched, her sundress torn, but she stood as tall as a heroine from one of her daddy's stories, eyes shining, voice firm, just like some knight all in armour, holding up a great heavy sword. Except that Kara didn't have any armour or a sword. All she had was a balloon full of water.

The fetch shrieked and flung itself towards Kara, who promptly let fly her water bomb. Neither of the girls was prepared for what next ensued.

The balloon burst, soaking the fetch with water.

That'll never stop it, Ethy thought.

But the water had been drawn up from the bay, salty seawater filling not only the balloon that Kara had just thrown, but the half-dozen others that she was lugging about in the satchel at her side.

The fetch howled. Steam hissed up from its skin, like water dropped onto a hot griddle. The creature fell to the ground, howling and wailing.

Ethy's fingers went up to her mouth. A moment ago she would have given anything to be able to fend off the creature. Now she felt pity for its pain. Her gaze went to Kara's face to find her own shock mirrored there.

The fetch stopped its thrashing, only to lie still. It whimpered, saucer-eyes filled with pain, its malevolence fled. Its limbs twitched. Its skin was the red of a lobster, steam still hissing from it.

Kara walked slowly around it, never taking her eyes from the creature. She helped Ethy to her feet.

"G-get your bike," she said.

Ethy blinked. "But it's so hurt. . . ."

"It got only what it deserved," Kara replied, but she seemed none too sure of that herself as she spoke. "We have to go."

"We can't leave it," Ethy said. "The poor thing."

She approached it cautiously, holding out one nervous hand. The fetch snapped its teeth feebly at her, but didn't seem to be able to move much otherwise. Ethy looked back at Kara.

"We can't."

Kara hesitated. "What will we do with it?"

"Take it to the Widow's house."

"While she's off attacking our friends?" Kara said, her perspective on the situation returning. She patted the satchel at her side. "We have to help *them* with these."

"You go, then," Ethy said. "I'll take it 'round."

"I . . ." Kara began, then she sighed. "Oh, bother."

She looked about in the refuse that littered the alleyway until she found a relatively dry newspaper. Moving gingerly, she wrapped the fetch in it, her own heart going out to the little creature as it whimpered in pain at the touch of the paper. The fetch tried to bite her, but it had no strength in its jaws. Its whimpering was enough to bring tears to Ethy's eyes.

"Oh, be careful," she said, hovering nearby.

"I am being careful."

Kara lifted the fetch. It made a tiny bundle, easy enough to carry in the crook of her arm. Ethy got her bicycle for her, then the two set off for the Widow's house, Kara walking her bike and carrying the Widow's creature, Ethy fluttering along beside her pushing her own bicycle.

8.

The Widow Pender had Peter Moyle backed up against the wall of an alleyway in another part of Bodbury. She had just repeated his name for the second time when she suddenly doubled over, a sharp cry of pain escaping from between her lips. Her missing toe—the one from which she'd taken the bone to grow Windle—came ablaze with pain.

Gasping, she stumbled forward. Peter ducked away to one side and dashed for his bike. He was on it and wheeling for the end of the alley when he stopped to peer back. The Widow was hunched against the wall, moaning, the tears streaming from her eyes.

Shivering, Peter pedaled quickly off, his Jodi doll still tucked safely away in his belt.

The Widow remained behind in the alley. Once the pain struck, she had been no more aware of his presence when he'd been there than she was of his departure when he left. All she knew was Windle's pain.

Burning as though he'd been boiled alive.

His agony was hers, the pain so sharp, so anguished.

So *raw*. . . .

What had they *done* to him?

She was slow in straightening up from the wall. Her leg could scarcely support her weight, the pain in her missing toe was so fierce. Every inch of her skin felt burned and raw. Cramps threatened to buckle her over again, but she stayed upright. She closed her eyes, not against the pain—there could be no surcease from its fire—but to use her witch-sight to track the position of her fetch.

The agony stretched like a wire between them, making it child's play to place him.

It took a moment longer for her to judge her own position in relation to his, but then she hobbled off, a fire burning in her heart as fiercely as the pain wracked her body.

They would pay, she vowed. Every last one of the monsters would pay for what they had done.

Border Spirit

No magic can change something into something it is not; the imaginative transformation at the heart of magic is recognition, not creation. . . .

—SUSAN PALWICK, from *"The Last Unicorn*: Magic as Metaphor," in *The New York Review of Science Fiction*, February 1989

Janey's Reliant Robin was admirably suited to the narrow back lanes of Penwith Peninsula—lanes so confining that in most places they were only wide enough to allow one car egress at a time. But the Reliant's tiny three-wheeled body took to them like a ferret, low-slung and quick, whizzing along at a happy putter between the tall hedgerows that rose on either side, darting by other vehicles, even where the road hadn't been widened for passing.

While Clare had ridden with Janey more times than she could possibly begin to count, she could never help but feel just a bit nervous on a trek like this. As far as she was concerned, the little Reliant was simply too small, its three wheels much too precarious, and Janey's driving, especially when she was in a mood like this, far too impetuous. Any moment she expected them to come smack upon a lorry, or to have the car tip over on some particularly sharp corner that she was certain Janey took far too fast.

It didn't help today that ever since they'd set off from the Gaffer's house, neither of them had spoken so much as a word to each other. It made Clare feel somewhat put upon. After all, none of this was her fault. She hadn't found some rare book that a gang of thugs were bent upon stealing. When it came right down to it, if it weren't for the Littles, she herself would never have been attacked last night. She was the innocent in all of this. All she'd been trying to do was help.

She shot a sidelong glance at Janey and was surprised to see un-shed tears glistening in her friend's eyes. She immediately felt guilty for the turn her thoughts had taken. She really wasn't being very fair.

It wasn't Janey's fault either.

"Janey," she began, but then was at a loss as to what to say next.

Janey slowed the Reliant's headlong pace and gave Clare a quick sad look.

"It's all gone so awful," she said. "Finding that book . . . having Felix come back. . . . Everything should have been all wonderful and happy, but it's not. It's horrible."

Clare stifled a sigh. Trust Janey to simply feel sorry for herself. But the next thing Janey said made her realize that she'd misjudged her friend once again.

"I never meant to hide the book from you," Janey said. "I would have asked Gramps if you could borrow it. But everything went so odd, all of a sudden, and I never had a chance to even think about it in the first place." She shot Clare another quick glance. "I'm really sorry that I never told you, Clare. Honestly I am."

"That's all right," Clare said, feeling somewhat chagrined.

"I only found it on Friday," Janey went on, "and there's been ever so much going on since then. . . ."

"I really do understand," Clare said.

And she did. Janey had a mind like a sieve and it wasn't because she didn't care that she'd let something like telling Clare about the Dunthorn book slip her mind. It was just that as soon as something new came up, whatever Janey had been thinking of earlier would find itself put away into a little box and then stored off somewhere in the muddle that was her mind, haphazardly stacked up with all the other boxes of ragtag odds and ends by which Janey compart-mentalized her memories.

"I wish I had a brain that worked like a normal person's does," Janey said as though she'd been reading Clare's mind.

"Who's to say what's normal?" Clare replied.

"You know what I mean."

"I do. But if you were any different, then you wouldn't be you."

"Sometimes," Janey said, "I think that might not be such a bad thing."

Clare shook her head. "Don't start."

Every once in a while, Janey would decide that everything in her life was wrong and after long soul-searching talks with Clare would attempt to set it all straight. It never worked. Her intentions were good, but as Clare endlessly pointed out, why try to be someone she wasn't?

Janey's personality was so strong that she simply couldn't change. She had strong views on everyone and everything—not always informed ones, unfortunately—and she could easily rub a person the wrong way. But the other side of that coin was that the very strength of her convictions was part and parcel of her charm. She could wax eloquent on any number of passions, which was far more entertaining than listening to gossip along the lines of who so-and-so's sister was dating, or have you heard about the Hayles taking in a boarder?

She envied Janey's easy geniality and, if not her quick temper, then at least her ability to forgive just as quickly. The envy that was hardest to deal with was how Janey always seemed to come out ahead, no matter what the situation.

Sometimes Clare wondered why she didn't hate Janey for that. Janey always got what she wanted, and got it first.

Got the music.

Got the new Dunthorn book.

Got Felix. . . .

Best not to think of that, she told herself. She glanced at Janey again and stifled yet another sigh. For all the times Janey drove her mad, there were a hundred others when she'd rather not be with anyone else. Hating Janey would be like hating a part of herself.

"We turn here," she said.

Janey steered them through a gap in the hedgerows onto a narrow bumpy track that drifted down to Peter Goninan's cottage. It had been a lane once, but now it barely held back the encroaching woods on one side, or the fields on the other, most of which had grown over into moorland since the land had stopped being farmed. No more than a quarter kilometer along, the track gave out completely, ending at a jumble of rock that had once been a stone fence. A gate in it led over a stream that had dammed into a pool a few yards down the slope because the density of the weeds blocked its flow.

Two paths led from the stream. One wandered down to the cliffs that dropped in a jungle of thorns, gorse, elderberry trees, and thick couch grass that formed a series of broad steps to the small bay below. The other led across an unkempt field to the cottage. Around the cottage, which was itself in good repair, were a scattering of roofless outbuildings and tumbled-down stone walls covered with brambles. Blackthorn grew in abandon; brushwood and gorse bushes littered the fields in unruly tangles.

"It looks abandoned," Janey said, gazing out at the rampaging vegetation.

Clare merely pointed to the thin tendril of smoke that rose from the cottage's stone chimney.

As they crossed the stream, stepping from stone to stone, an orange and black cat rose suddenly from the grass. Clare, having to move more slowly for fear her cane would slip off a stone, brought up the rear. She paused when the cat appeared. The cat watched them with an unblinking gaze for a long moment, apparently fascinated by their crossing, then vanished into the woods. It had no tail.

Another of that Zennor woman's Cornish tigers, Clare thought with a smile as she continued on across the stones.

No sooner had they both set foot on the dry ground than a chorus of barking started up. They looked nervously at each other as a pack of five or so tattery dogs came bounding towards them from the outbuildings.

"Do we stay or run?" Janey asked.

"I can't run," Clare said needlessly.

"They won't hurt you."

At the sound of a stranger's voice, both women started and turned so quickly they almost lost their balance. The newcomer had appeared out of the woods as silently as the cat had disappeared into them. So sudden and quiet was her appearance that Clare had the odd fleeting thought that the cat had merely changed into a woman once it was out of their sight.

Clare recovered before Janey, recognizing Helen Bray from her visits to the bookshop The Penzance. She was a gangly, coltish woman in her mid-twenties, at least six feet in height and slender as a rail. Her red hair was as tangled as the gorse thickets about them, her cheeks flushed from the weather. Her clothes were those of a man and bore the look of many mendings—tweed sports jacket, blue jeans that were worn and had a tear in the right knee, and a navy blue beret that did little to tame her unruly hair. On her feet were green gum boots, besmirched with mud.

As Janey and Clare looked at the woman they realized that the dogs were almost upon them and showed no sign of stopping their charge. Helen gave a shrill whistle, just as the lead dog—a terrier-collie cross—seemed ready to fling himself upon Janey. The dogs stopped in their tracks and all sat down in a half circle, tongues lolling, eyes fixed on the two newcomers.

"The dogs won't hurt you," Helen repeated. "Not if you leave straightway."

Clare cleared her throat. "We're here to see Mr. Goninan."

"He doesn't much care for visitors."

"Yes, well," Clare began, but Janey broke in.

"Why don't you let him decide for himself?" she asked.

Helen had odd pale eyes that were each a different colour—one grey, the other blue. At the question, she turned her intense gaze on Janey.

"That's not really the point," she said.

"Well, what *is* the point?" Janey asked. "It's not as if we could call ahead—he doesn't have a phone."

"He doesn't like to be bothered by people."

"We're not here to bother him," Janey said. "We're here to ask his advice about something."

Helen got a feline look of curiosity in her eyes.

"What kind of something?" she asked.

Janey smiled. "Never you mind." She turned to look at the dogs. "I'm going to walk to the cottage and knock on the door. If one of those dogs bites me, you're going to be very sorry."

Oh, Janey, Clare thought. Don't push so.

But as Janey set off, a determined set to her shoulders, Helen finally gave another sharp whistle and the dogs streamed back towards the cottage and disappeared behind the outbuildings. By the time the three women reached its door, there wasn't an animal to be seen except for an old great black-backed gull that was pecking at something by the stones of the chimney, up on the cottage roof.

Giving Helen one of her patented fierce looks, Janey rapped sharply on the door with her knuckles.

"It's open," a voice called from within.

2.

By the time he reached Clare's house, Davie Rowe knew just what he was going to do. He had his hands in his pockets and fingered the roll of ten-pound notes that Willie had given him.

He couldn't very well hand over a portion of the money to Clare, for all that it would make him feel better. She'd just ask where it had come from and he wasn't about to lie to her about it. That would make the whole exercise pointless. But so that she would get a share of it, he'd decided that he would offer to take her out for dinner tonight.

Just the two of them.

They could go to the Smuggler's Restaurant over in Newlyn for the special Sunday night Feast—a roast-beef dinner with Yorkshire pudding and all the trimmings. They could even have some wine with their dinner, just as the posh folk in the films did.

Davie was pleased with himself for the idea and looked forward to the evening. There was always the chance, he realized, that she wouldn't want to go. Perhaps she and her mother did something special for themselves on Sunday nights. Well, then. He'd invite Clare's mum and his own too. Surely she wouldn't say no to that?

What he hadn't considered was that she might not even be home to say yes or no in the first place.

"I'm sorry," her mother said when she answered the door, "but Clare's gone out for the day."

There was a look in the woman's eye that plainly said, and what makes you think she'd be so blind as to go out with the likes of you? My daughter may be crippled, but she's not daft.

"Do you—ah—can you tell me when she'll be back?"

"She didn't say. Would you like to leave a message?"

"No. I . . . Just tell her I was 'round."

"I'll tell her when she gets in."

The door closed on him before he could say anything more.

Bloody hell, he thought as he trudged off. They were all the same—the lads up at the King's Arms or this woman here in the village. They never gave a bloke a chance. Lilith Mabley would probably have a good laugh about this with Clare when she came home.

He clenched his fists at the thought of Clare laughing at him.

No, she wouldn't do that. She'd ring him up and ask him what he'd wanted, and then he could still ask her out for dinner.

He hurried off home to wait for her call, but when he got there, he found a stranger sitting outside on the front stoop. The man rose up at Davie's approach.

"The name's Bett," he said, not offering his hand. "Michael Bett."

The American accent registered.

"Uh . . ."

"I want to have a word with you, Davie. Is there somewhere private where we can talk?"

There was something familiar about the man, but Davie couldn't pin it down.

"There's the pub," he said, vaguely waving in the general direction of Mousehole harbour.

"I was thinking of somewhere even more private," Bett said. "Isn't there some kind of scenic walk along the coast nearby?"

Davie nodded.

"Why don't we go take in its sights?" Bett said. "I'm in the mood for a nice walk, and I think you will be too, once you hear the proposition I have for you."

"I really can't go," Davie began. "I'm expecting a call. . . ."

Bett pulled a hundred-dollar bill from his pocket and stuffed it into the breast pocket of Davie's shirt.

"All I'm asking for is an hour of your time," he said.

Davie glanced at his house. Should he tell his mother that he was expecting a call from Clare? No. That would just take too long to explain. Clare might not even ring him up. She probably *wouldn't*. But if she should and he wasn't here to take the call . . .

"I . . ."

"C'mon," Bett said. "What've you got to lose?"

"An hour, you said?"

"Tops. Guaranteed."

"All right," Davie agreed. "But that's all the time I have."

"I understand," Bett said. "Time's a precious commodity—especially for a busy guy like yourself."

Was the American making fun of him? Davie wondered.

"Which way do we go?" Bett went on.

Davie pointed back the way he'd just come and the two set off, the American chatting on about how pretty the village was and had Davie lived here all his life and what did a fellow do around here for excitement?

Long before they reached the beginning of the Coastal Path, Davie was sorry that he'd ever agreed to listen to what the man had to say. But he was curious. It was Americans that had something to do with the trouble plaguing the Littles, the trouble that had spilled over onto Clare. Reckoning it so, there might be something useful he could learn from this Bett—if the man ever came out with something even remotely worth listening to.

Davie stopped when they reached the Coastguard lookout and turned to his companion. They had the place to themselves. Bett scraped some mud from his shoe and looked around.

"Nice place," he said.

Now Davie knew he was being mocked. The path itself was beautiful, even in this season. But the same couldn't be said for the station. On its weather-beaten white walls the paint was peeling. In places, flat stones held loose shingles down on its level roof. A ratty chicken-wire fence encircled the building. There was a wrought-iron porch facing the bay, its metalwork rusting. Leaves floated in the rain barrel by its door. Dried ferns crouched against the side of the building, sheltering from the sea winds.

"What do you want with me?" he demanded of the American.

"Well now."

Bett reached into his pocket. When his hand came out again, it held a small automatic pistol, muzzle pointed at Davie.

"You and me," he said. "We've got some unfinished business left over from last night. . . ."

Now Davie understood why the man had seemed vaguely familiar.

The trouble was, as had happened so often in his life, the knowledge came too late.

3.

Peter Goninan's cottage, Janey discovered, was surprisingly bright— the extra light coming from a skylight that had been built into the roof facing the ocean. The interior was all one large room with a kitchen area on one side and stairs leading up to a small sleeping loft on the other. A potbellied cast-iron coal stove sat by one of the many support beams that islanded the ground floor. Set near to it was an old sofa and a pair of club chairs with tattered upholstery.

Goninan sat in one of those chairs. He stood up when they entered, a tall, gaunt man with a bald head that gleamed in the sunlight. While Helen Bray reminded Janey and Clare of a cat, Goninan was more like a bird. His eyes were small and set close to a narrow nose. His cheeks were hollow. His age was indefinable—somewhere between late forties and early seventies, if Janey had to hazard a guess. As it was, he radiated a sense of timelessness.

His birdishness was accentuated by the avian motif that filled the cottage. There were paintings and sculptures of hawks and kestrels. And masks—a dozen or more, from crudely carved wooden ones to one that was ornately decorated with hundreds of tiny feathers. There was a stuffed owl on one bookcase, a raven on another, a pair of stonechats on a third. A heron stood in one corner. An egret and two gulls were by the window. Hanging from the support beams like shamanistic fetishes were dozens of bundles of feathers and birds' feet tied together with leather thongs.

There were books everywhere—on shelves, in boxes and crates, stacked in unruly piles wherever there was space. But what fascinated Janey more were all the oak and glass display cases filled with odd old coins, fossils, ancient clay whistles in the shape of birds and flint artifacts, pieces of bone and tiny wooden dolls with feather skirts, clay pot shards and things that she couldn't readily recognize. Each piece was meticulously identified by a little square of white card set near the appropriate item, the information written on the card in a tidy neat hand.

He really is like a bird, Janey decided, sitting here in his nest with everything he's collected over the years like some kind of magpie.

"They wouldn't go away," Helen said.

Goninan smiled. "That's all right. I've been expecting a visit from Janey Little."

Janey blinked with surprise. "You were?"

"I've seen you any number of times out on the cliffs by the bay—toodling your tunes, piping, and pennywhistling. You make fine music. I believe I even have copies of your recordings . . . somewhere in here."

He waved a hand negligently about the cluttered room. Except for the display cases with their neatly organized contents, Janey could easily see how something could get lost in this room. Lost forever.

"Sooner or later I knew you would come 'round for a visit."

Janey had trouble following the logic of that statement.

"Would you like some tea?" Goninan added.

"Ah . . ."

"Would you put the water on, Helen?"

The tall woman nodded and moved gracefully through the clutter to the kitchen area where she filled a kettle.

"Do take a seat," Goninan said, ushering them both to the sofa facing his chair.

None of this was going as Janey had expected it to, but then again, she hadn't known what to expect.

"And you are?" Goninan asked Clare.

At least he doesn't know everything, Janey thought as Clare introduced herself.

They made their way carefully to the sofa and sat down. Janey perched on the edge of the cushion, unable to stop herself from staring around the room. No matter which way she turned, something odd or wonderful caught her eye.

She could spend weeks in here, she thought.

Goninan smiled at her as he took his own chair again.

"We were wondering if you could help us," Clare said. "You're considered an expert in . . . I guess you could call it arcane subjects. . . ."

"I prefer to call myself a theurgist."

"What's that?" Janey asked.

"A magician," Clare said.

Goninan smiled. "Of a sort."

Janey stifled an urge to roll her eyes.

"Theurgy," Helen said, sitting down in the other club chair. She leaned forward a bit, her disconcerting gaze fixed on Janey. "From the Latin, *theurgia,* meaning a miracle worker. A theurgist is one who is intimate with the spirits that oversee our world."

"And I guess you're his apprentice, right?" Janey said, refusing to let the other woman daunt her.

Clare jabbed Janey with her elbow, the meaning clear: Behave.

"We were more interested in your knowledge of secret societies," Clare said.

Goninan's eyebrows rose questioningly, but he said nothing, so she went on.

"We were wondering if you could identify a symbol we have, if you could perhaps tell us if it's a motif associated with any particular society."

Janey thought about Felix's rough sketch of the dove, then looked around at all the avian material in the cottage and wondered how good an idea this was. The old homily drifted through her mind—*Birds of a feather . . .* —but by then it was too late because Clare had already taken out the sketch and passed it over to their host.

"Ah," he said.

"Is there anything in your library that can tell us something about the people who use this for their symbol?" Clare asked. "They wear it on their wrists—tattooed there."

"Yes. I know. And there's no need for me to look it up. I'm quite familiar with these people."

Bloody hell, Janey thought. We're doomed.

"They call themselves the Order of the Grey Dove, dedicating themselves to hermetic principles, something along the lines of the Golden Dawn and their like. I've followed their growth over the years with considerable interest." He smiled. "Not least because of the symbol they have chosen for their motif."

"Their bird and your birds?" Clare asked.

Goninan nodded. "Mine—if I can use a possessive term such as that for such things—are my personal key to the invisible world of the spirits that surrounds us. My totem if you will."

"And that's what this Order does?" Janey asked. "They . . . ah . . . talk to spirits through a dove?"

"They seek knowledge—as do we all—but their methodology has been known to employ, at times, activities that could be considered to be, shall we say, questionable?"

"What kinds of knowledge?"

Goninan smiled again. "Oh, the usual: Longevity. Power. Even understanding, though that's somewhat rarer among this particular Order's membership."

"That's not all they're looking for," Janey mumbled, forgetting herself.

"How so?" Goninan asked.

Janey gave Clare a glance, but Clare only shrugged as if to say, we're here to get information.

"They seem to think we have something that they want," Janey said finally, "but it's nothing very important. It's not something that can let you live forever or give you power. At least it doesn't seem like that kind of a thing."

Except she remembered what her grandfather had told her about the odd occurrences that had come about the last time the book had been read. And then there was the music.

And her dream.

"The most innocent thing can hold immense power," Goninan said. "To those who know how to use it."

"What do you mean?" Janey asked.

"It's all got to do with magic," Goninan explained.

"Magic?"

Janey wanted to roll her eyes again, but stopped herself in time.

"Oh, not spells and incantations and that sort of thing. More like the beliefs of, say, George Gurdjieff—the Russian philosopher."

Clare nodded. "I know him," she said. "Well, not personally," she added when Janey shot her a curious look, "but I know his work. We've carried his books in the shop—*Beelzebub's Tales to His Grandson* and things like that."

Now it was Goninan's turn for curiosity.

"Shop?" he asked.

"I work at The Penzance Bookshop on Chapel Street."

"Ah, yes. That new one. Your people have acquired a text or two for me."

Clare glanced at where Helen was getting the tea ready.

"That's where I've seen Helen before," she said.

Goninan nodded. "Yes, she's usually kind enough to fetch the books for me. I don't get into town much anymore."

"You were talking about magic," Janey said.

"No, I was talking about Gurdjieff. He says that there are three levels of consciousness. There is sleeping"—he counted them off on his fingers—"there is sleeping wakefulness; and then there is aware-ness. Sleeping is just that. Sleeping wakefulness is when you walk around—" He suddenly pointed at Janey's hand where it was tap-tapping against her knee. "You didn't even realize you were doing that just now, did you?"

Janey looked down at her hand, which now lay still, and shook her head.

"That is sleeping wakefulness. We all walk through the world barely aware of what our bodies do, or what goes on around us.

Awareness is when you are informed—utterly *aware*—of it all. Yourself and your environment. It's akin to being an avatar—the sort of awareness of a Christ or a Buddha.

"For most of us, those moments of true awareness are very rare. They come at high points in our lives, such as the moment before one pronounces one's wedding vows, or just before death—brief moments of complete awareness that encapsulate everything that we are in relation to, everything that is. Do you understand what I mean?"

Janey and Clare nodded slowly.

"Now imagine that you are always in such a state. To constantly recognize everything for what it truly is, and then to have such absolute control over your will that you aren't capable so much of transforming your surroundings or the wills of those around you, but you *can* influence them to such extent that it might as well be considered magic.

"We humans have so much untapped potential that it literally boggles the mind. Consider the amazing things of which we are already capable in moments of need or duress—such as the woman whose child has been run over by a car and she goes over and lifts that immense weight so that the child can escape.

"People will explain this away as being the result of adrenaline, or psychic phenomena, or some such thing. What they don't say is that the basic underlying truth of any such incident is the fact that in our moments of utter awareness, we are capable of things that defy our understanding of our accepted range of capabilities.

"We can literally do anything."

"That . . ." Janey began. "That's what the people of this Order are like?"

"No—but it is what they strive for; it is their magic. And many of them are, if not fully aware all of the time, at least in such a state far more than the rest of the world's population. They have acquired great talents—woken gifts that are inherently present in each one of us—but they have twisted them to dark uses. Selfish uses."

"And . . . this thing they're looking for?" Janey asked. "The thing that they think we've got?"

"It will be a talisman of some sort. A catalyst. For see: Although we are all capable of waking from the sleep through which we live our lives—through perseverance and study and much practice and labour—there have always been objects of power that will facilitate the waking. In the Western tradition they center around relics such as the Spear that pierced Christ's side, or the Fisher King's Grail; there are others less familiar and also less powerful, though no less effective. The trouble with taking such a route is that one acquires the 'magic,' but not the wisdom to use it with any moral enlightenment. Following such a practice—the left-hand path, if you will—results in amorality."

"And this thing we have—is it one of those artifacts?"

"I would have to see it to make that judgment."

"Ah . . ."

Right, Janey thought. All sorts of weird people had been after the Dunthorn book for years, and they were supposed to simply bring it by to show it to Goninan as though it were some old ring that they wanted appraised. She had that done with a piece of jewelry once and the old lady in the shop had tut-tutted over the piece, telling her, "I'm afraid it's not gold, love. More like pinchbeck—what the poor people used in place of gold in Victorian times. It was invented by a Mr. Pinchbeck, but the secret died with him."

So they could pop by with the book and Goninan would pooh-pooh its value and offer to take it off their hands for a tiny sum—as the old shoplady had done—and then later they'd find out that it had been worth a fortune—as her pinchbeck pendant had been.

Not bloody likely she'd fall for that a second time.

Except Goninan surprised her again.

"But I don't think that I *have* to see it," he said. "Not to know what it is."

Janey just looked at him, feeling nervous all over again.

"What do you mean?" Clare asked.

"I knew Bill Dunthorn as well as Tom Little ever did—in some respects better, for we shared a common interest that"—he glanced at Janey—"your grandfather never did."

"Gramps always says that Billy was a practical kind of a bloke," Janey said. "He didn't belong to any mystical orders."

"Absolutely. But he did seek after hidden knowledge. And he found it."

The line from that letter that Janey had found in Dunthorn's *The Little Country* returned to her.

That famous Mad Bill Dunthorn Gypsy prescience . . .

"Magic?" Janey said slowly. "Is that what you're saying he found?"

Goninan nodded. "Though I think he would have preferred to

describe it as a kind of enchantment. He found it and put it in a book. Not the books he had published, but a special book of which only one copy has ever existed. And that, I believe, is what the Order of the Grey Dove seeks from you."

"You know about the book?"

"Of course. Bill and I talked about it a great deal."

"Then how come you never wanted it for yourself?" she asked.

"There are as many different paths to enlightenment as there are people in this world. The path Bill took wasn't mine. I already knew my path. I had, and have, no interest in following another."

"And your path is . . . talking to bird spirits?"

"That is one way of putting it, yes."

"What does the book do?" Clare asked.

"You might call it a gate to knowledge. To understanding. To the invisible world of the spirits."

"Well, how does it work?" Janey asked.

"And where does it take you?" Clare added.

"To both questions, I must reply: I don't know. It was Bill's path, not mine, and though we spoke of our studies to each other, there are always elements to such work that cannot be understood without first being experienced. I had no wish to dilute my own work by testing another's and Bill felt the same way about my studies. We compared results—not tangible results, but spiritual ones."

Janey sighed. "This is making my head hurt," she said.

Helen came over with a tray at that moment, laden with mugs of tea, a plate of scones, and small clay jars of clotted cream and jam. When she put it on a crate of books that stood between the sofa and club chairs, Goninan motioned to the tray.

"We'll break for tea," he said, "and give your subconscious minds a chance to assimilate what I've told you. After we've eaten, I'll tell you about John Madden."

"Who's he?"

"The leader of the Order of the Grey Dove and a very dangerous man."

Janey thought of how Clare had been attacked and Felix had been drugged and nodded.

"I'll say he is."

A somber look touched Goninan's features.

"I hesitate to say this, for fear of spoiling your appetites," he said, "but I must warn you that whatever unpleasantness has already fallen your way, I'm afraid that things will only get worse."

"Don't say that," Janey groaned.

"Why?" Clare asked Goninan.

"Because you've opened the book. I've felt its enchantment working these past few days. And if I can feel it, then you can rest assured that Madden feels it as well. He's been searching for that book for the better part of his life."

"But there's nothing magical *in* it," Janey protested. "It's just a story. There's no secret knowledge—at least there isn't so far. I'm not quite done reading it yet."

Goninan indicated the tray again. "Drink," he said. "Eat. We'll talk again later. But this time we'll talk outside."

"Why outside?" Janey wanted to know.

But Goninan only smiled and helped himself to a scone.

4.

When the knock came at Jim Gazo's door, Lena started to rise from her chair until Gazo waved her back to her seat. He took a small revolver from his pocket and, holding it at his side, out of sight, stood to one side of the door.

"Come on in," he said.

The door swung open and Willie Keel stepped inside.

"Miss Grant," he began when he saw Lena. "I've just come 'round to—"

Gazo stepped from the side of the door. He closed the door with his foot and lifted the revolver until the muzzle was touching the back of Willie's neck. The small man froze.

"Th-there's no need for this," he said.

"How did you know to find Ms. Grant in here?" Gazo demanded.

"That's all right, Jim," Lena said. "You can put away the gun."

Willie relaxed visibly when the muzzle was removed from his skin. Gazo replaced the revolver in his pocket and leaned against the wall.

"I still want to know how you knew," Gazo said.

"Do you mind if I sit?"

Willie directed the question to Lena who nodded in acquiescence.

"I'd like to know, too, Willie," she said.

"Well, now," Willie said once he was seated. "The game of strangers you two played this morning didn't wash with me, so when there was no reply at the door to your room, I just came down here to the room your friend went into this morning."

Lena nodded. That seemed reasonable enough.

"What did you want, Willie?" she asked.

"It's about my money. . . ."

"I told you we'd get it to you tomorrow. Don't you trust me?"

Though why he should, Lena didn't know.

"It's not that," Willie assured her. "It's just that things have changed." He glanced at Gazo, who still stood by the door, arms folded across his chest. "Your other, ah, associate—the one I met at the station for you?"

Lena nodded.

"Well, he was by my flat this morning. Threatened to kill me unless I told him who it was that stopped him from hurting the Mabley woman last night."

"And you just told him?" Gazo asked.

Willie tugged his shirt from his trousers and pulled it up so that they both could see the welter of blue-black bruises that covered his sides and chest. Lena's eyes widened.

"Take a look at this, mate," Willie said to Gazo. "Your friend doesn't have much patience, and I wasn't getting enough money to risk my life, I'll tell you that straight up and no word of a lie. The man would've killed me"—he turned back to look at Lena—"I could see it in his eyes."

He tucked his shirt back in, wincing as he brushed against a bruise. Lena grimaced in sympathy.

"You did the right thing," she said. "Did you warn your friend?"

Willie shook his head. "There was no answer at Davie's place— both he and his mum were out."

Lena indicated the telephone. "Do you want to try him again?"

"No time. I've got a ride waiting for me outside. This time tomorrow I'll be so far from the West Country that your friend will never find me. And it's there I'm staying until he's gone."

"So you want the rest of your money," Lena said.

"If you have any you can give me."

He started to reach into his pocket, stopping when Gazo stepped away from the wall.

"I'm just getting a wee slip of paper with an address on it," he said. His gaze went to Lena. "Is that all right?"

When she nodded, he extracted a folded piece of paper and handed it over to her.

"That's where you can send what you owe me," he said. "I won't be there, and the lad whose address it is doesn't know where I'll be either, but you can leave the money or a message with him and be sure I'll get them."

"I'm sorry about this," Lena said. "Jim, do you have any money?"

"Only traveler's cheques."

"Will you sign some over to Willie?"

Gazo nodded, obviously unhappy about the situation, but not willing to argue with his employer—especially not in front of a third party.

"There . . . there's one more thing," Willie said when Gazo had signed over the cheques.

Willie stood by the door, ready to go.

"What's that?" Lena asked.

"He also made me tell him who'd hired us to protect Clare Mabley—'confirm' was the word he used. He wanted it confirmed. I'm sorry, Miss Grant."

Before either she or Gazo could move, he slipped out the door and was gone.

"That little weasel," Gazo muttered.

He started for the door, pausing at Lena's call.

"At least he came by and warned us," she said. "He didn't have to do that."

"He just wanted his money."

"I suppose."

Why hadn't she thought of that? Lena wondered. Normally, cynic that she was, it would have been her first thought.

"Bett was going to find out anyway," she added. "One way or another."

"No denying that."

Lena glanced at the clock. The afternoon was winding down.

"Daddy'll be here soon. He'll get Madden to call off Bett."

Gazo had crossed the room and was looking out the window, watching Willie Keel's car pull away from in front of the hotel. Once the car was gone, his gaze shifted to the bay where the afternoon sun was gleaming on the water.

"I wouldn't mind dealing with Bett before either of them arrive," he said.

Lena shook her head. "Only if he comes here."

"I know. I was just wishing aloud."

You and me both, Lena thought, but she knew enough not to try to take on Bett—even with Gazo at her side. That was a last resort, because the trouble with Bett was that he was crazy. She could see that now. And how did you deal with a madman?

"What really makes me feel bad," she said, "is thinking about that friend of Willie's that Bett's gone after."

Gazo gave her a curious glance, caught what he was doing, and quickly looked away again. But Lena knew what he'd been thinking.

The Ice Queen was getting a heart.

And it was true. Felix had opened the gap in her walls and now she couldn't seem to close it up again. She found herself worrying about Willie's friend, about what might happen to Jim if Bett showed up here, about all the people whose lives had gotten tangled up with Michael Bett's viciousness.

There was no stopping it, no matter how much she tried.

And oddly enough, she wasn't even sure that she wanted to try.

It hurt. And she didn't like the pain. But she did find herself wondering why she would want to build up those walls again. She couldn't deny the aching, deep hurt that she felt at the moment. It cut so deeply through her that it felt as though it would never go away again. But there was something else as well. Something unfamiliar.

It was what people called compassion.

And she found that it gave her hope. That caring for what happened to others actually made her feel better about herself. It went against everything that the Order had taught her, it might prove to be only a false promise, a momentary aberration in her character, but she found herself growing more and more determined to not go back to being the kind of person she'd been before.

It wouldn't help her with Felix.

But it might bring her peace—something that she'd never even realized she was looking for until she'd tasted it in Felix's company.

"Can people change?" she asked Gazo.

He turned with a puzzled look.

"I mean, can they really change," she said. "Not just their appearance, or the face they turn to the world, but in here"—she touched her chest—"where it really counts?"

Gazo looked uncomfortable. "I don't think I'm sure what you mean. . . ."

"Just be honest," Lena said. "Forget the employer/employee business for just a few minutes and tell me what you think."

Gazo didn't say anything for a long moment, but then finally he nodded.

"It depends on how big a change it is that we're talking about," he began. He was couching it in vague terms, but they both knew he was talking about her. "But if it was a big one—a major change in someone's personality—well, I don't think it'd be easy, and it'd take time and a lot of patience, but I think people can do anything they want—so long as they really set their minds to it."

Which, Lena realized, was a kind of paraphrase of the Order's basic tenets.

And then something sparked in her mind.

This was what enlightenment must feel like, she thought. A moment like this when everything falls neatly into place in one's mind and there's nothing, not one little thing, that's out of place or misunderstood.

It wasn't the Order's teachings that were at fault. It was what one did with them.

"Thank you, Jim," she said.

5.

"John Madden is a very powerful man," Goninan said.

After they'd had their tea, he took Janey and Clare out into the fields overlooking the small cove below his property. They were far from the cottage and its outbuildings—far from any man-made object. Here the unruly vegetation had been given free rein and returned to its natural wild state. They all sat on stone outcrops, the rocks weathered smooth and grey like old bones.

"His magical abilities aside, Madden has enormous business interests. His own fortune is vast enough to deny easy calculation. Other members of the Inner Circle of his Order are also in high positions of influence and power—together they have formed a global network that encompasses the entire sphere of international commerce and politics."

"Why is it," Janey interrupted, "that the current villains in the world are always businessmen or politicians?"

Goninan smiled. "That has never changed. What else can they do but acquire power? And power has always lain in the fields of politics and commerce."

"And religion," Clare said.

"And religion," Goninan agreed. "Hence Madden's Order of the Grey Dove."

"What do they worship?" Janey wanted to know. "This grey dove? Madden?"

"Religion involves worship," Goninan said, "but like anything concerned with spiritual matters, its strictures vary according to how its followers approach it. Some seek solace, others a promise of hope in the hereafter; some enter into it as a means to enlightenment, still others view it as a road to power. It need not necessarily involve worship. A better word for it, perhaps, would be Way. And the Ways of our world are as varied as the road taken by a Taoist, or that followed by a man such as, say, Aleister Crowley."

"Who's he?" Janey asked.

"A Cornishman, actually—originally from Plymouth—who is re-viled or exalted, depending on the person who is discussing him."

"He was evil," Clare said. "Anybody who'd follow his teachings would have to be as bad or worse."

Goninan shook his head. "That is like condemning all Christians for the Inquisition or the Crusades—or for present-day Fundamen-talism. Crowley himself was certainly somewhat depraved, but as in all teachings, there are truths and insights in his work that are rele-vant to all people. L. Ron Hubbard is an excellent contemporary example."

"And who's he?" Janey asked.

"The founder of Scientology."

Janey had heard of Scientologists before. They'd often stopped her on the street in London, asking her if she wanted to take a personality test—whatever that meant.

"I never heard of Hubbard being depraved," Clare said.

"I didn't mean to imply that he was," Goninan said. "I use his teachings as an example of how a body of work can be reviled—mostly by those who have no knowledge of its workings—and yet still carry elements of what can only be considered eternal truths. What Hubbard merely did was couch them in more contemporary terms—not a particularly innovative methodology, I might add. A part of every religion's genesis is the modernizing of old truisms."

"So what you're saying," Janey said, "is that it's not the work or the personality of the founder of a religion that's important, but what its followers do with what they learn?"

"Exactly. Which brings us back to John Madden and his Order of the Grey Dove. The underlying tenets of the Order deal with many of the same universal truths as do other orders and religions, but it is the personality of its followers, *particularly* its founder, Madden in this case, that makes it an extremely dangerous sect."

"What makes these people go bad?" Janey asked. "Not just this Order, but all the people you were talking about."

"Human nature, I'm afraid. We seem cursed with the need to acquire control over each other and our environment. To rule. To change everything we can possibly meddle with."

"Yes," Clare said, "but if we didn't do that, we'd still be living in caves and chewing on bones."

Goninan laughed. "I'm no Luddite," he said. "I agree with you completely. The advances we make in technology and the sciences are very important to our development as a race. But, like religion, science depends on what one brings to it. Were we only seeking cures for cancer and world hunger and the like, I would have no complaints. What I condemn is this narrow-minded quest for the most devastating weapon or the years of research that go into a better deodorant or shampoo. It's madness. It has no heart—no care for the spirit, be it ours, or that of the earth itself. Thousands of acres of rain forests are destroyed every day—*every* single day—the ozone layer is being rapidly worn away, yet our world leaders are more content to argue about how many weapons they can stockpile.

"They remind me of primary school bullies, vying for dominion of the school yard, while an entire world—a real world—lies just beyond its confines. A world of far more sacred importance that they cannot see for their blindness."

As he spoke, his face had reddened, his voice growing cross, eyes flashing. He paused suddenly and looked away, over across the bay, silently watching the dip and wheel of seabirds over the water until the timeless image had calmed him enough to continue.

"Your pardon," he said when he finally looked back at Janey and Clare. "I've lived through one World War only to watch the world grow worse instead of better when we finally put down that madman's Reich."

He laid a hand on the stone beside him, stroking its smooth surface with his fingers.

"I love this world," he added. "That is what rules my life. When I die, I want to have done all in my power to leave it in a better state than it was when I found it. At the same time I know that this can never be. The world has grown so complex that one voice can do little to alter it any longer. That doesn't stop me from doing what I can, but it makes the task hard. The successes are so small, the failures so large and many. It's like trying to stem a storm with one's bare hands."

Janey felt a little embarrassed listening to him. It wasn't that she didn't agree with what Goninan was saying; it was more because she did agree, only she never did anything about it except for the odd benefit gig.

"My quarrel with Madden," Goninan went on, "is that he has the opportunity to make a difference, yet he does nothing with it. His entire life is channeled towards self-gain."

"You seem to know as much as he does," Janey said. "Why didn't you start your own Order?"

"I thought of that," Goninan said. "When I was young. But to acquire the position of power that Madden presently holds, I would have to become as ruthless as he. And then I would be no better than he."

"But if you could make a difference . . . ?"

Goninan shook his head. "I expect that once I reached such a position of influence, I'd no more care for the world than does Madden himself. It may sound trite, but using the weapons of the enemy, no matter how good one's intentions, makes one the enemy."

He spoke then at length of Madden's rise from obscurity and the forming of the Order, sketching in a fuller, if still incomplete, picture of the man.

"So his magic," Janey said. "It's a sham? It's just manipulating people and knowing when to make the best deal?"

"No. The magic is real."

"But . . . ?"

"Consider legend and myth," Goninan said.

"You mean how they're all based on some kernel of truth, no matter how obscure?" Clare asked.

"In part. Legend and myth are what we use to describe what we don't comprehend. They are our attempts to make the impossible,

possible—at least insofar as our spirits interact with the spirit of the world, or if that's too animistic for you, then let us use Jung's terminology and call it our racial subconscious. No matter the semantics, they are of a kind and it is legend and myth that binds us all together.

"Through them, through their retellings, and through those new versions that are called religion while they are current, we are taught Truth and we attempt to understand Mystery. How many brave or chivalrous deeds have come about through a young boy's fascination with childhood stories of King Arthur and his Knights of the Round Table? Or how many injustices were attacked by those who learned of right and wrong from tales of Robin Hood?

"Teaching a child the correct moral choices he or she should make is simple, but not always effective. The young rebel—not because they're amoral, but because it is in their nature to do so. The words of an elder are always suspect—especially here in what is traditionally called Western society. It is through legend and myth, through the young spirit's connection with the old spirit that lies at the heart of this matter, that the lessons are learned without being deliberately taught.

"The lessons lie in the subtext of the stories, as it were.

"Today, children are given toys to look up to as heroic figures. Rock performers and movie stars form their pantheon—an amoral pantheon where the performer who eloquently speaks out against drugs is arrested two weeks later for possession of heroin. Where the stalwart heroic figure from the silver screen is discovered to be a wife beater.

"The subtext here is that one may do anything one wishes—one need only make certain not to get caught."

"And the magic?" Janey asked when Goninan fell silent.

She'd been having trouble making the connection with what he was saying to what she had supposed they were talking about.

"Is real," he said. "It is your perception of it that makes it true—our recognition of the true shape or spirit of a thing. But like legend and myth, magic fades when it is unused—hence all the old tales of elfin kingdoms moving further and further away from our world, or that magical beings require our faith, our *belief* in their existence, to survive.

"That is a lie. All they require is our recognition."

"And the book?" Clare asked. "Where does it fit in?"

"I spoke of totems before we had our tea—do you remember?"
Janey and Clare both nodded.

"Your birds," Clare said.

"Yes. They are a symbol—a talisman, if you like, but a personal one, which is what a totem is. A symbol that sets one in the proper frame of mind to work one's magic. How such totems differ from Bill's book is that they require sacrifice and much study for one to acquire one's appropriate symbology.

"Bill did that study, he made the sacrifices of time and ostracism that such work requires—hence the book's magic worked for him. It was his totem. But, unknowingly, he also created a talisman when he crafted it—a universal symbol so that it is now a catalyst as well as the personal totem it was for him.

"The artifact he created now has a twofold existence."

"I'm not sure I know what you mean," Janey said.

"Every book tells a different story to the person who reads it," Goninan explained. "How they perceive that book will depend on *who* they are. A good book reflects the reader, as much as it illuminates the author's text."

Clare nodded in understanding.

"Now," Goninan said, "imagine a book that literally *is* different for each person who reads it."

Janey frowned. "Do you mean that the story I'm reading in *The Little Country*—I'm the only person who will read that particular story?"

"Exactly."

"But that's not possible."

Goninan smiled. "No, of course it isn't. It's magic."

"But Gramps has read it and he never said . . ."

Janey's voice trailed off as she realized that she'd never actually talked to anyone about the story that was in the book—not her grandfather nor Felix—while Clare hadn't read it yet.

"So," Goninan said, "the book's first purpose is to reflect the reader's spirit—somewhat along the lines of an oracle."

"Would it be the same every time I read it?" Janey asked.

"I can't say for certain. But it's not likely. For see, as you change, so will the story that reflects your spirit change with you."

"But it's following logically along at the moment," Janey said. "The plot's following a logical progression."

"For this story," Goninan said.

"Are they Dunthorn's words that we're reading?" Clare asked.

"It's not likely—although there will be a part of Bill in each story, because it was his creation."

Janey found this a bit much to swallow. But then, everything she was hearing today seemed farfetched. None of it could be possible.

Of course it's not, she could hear Goninan saying again. *It's magic.*

Magic.

Legend and myth.

Her heart wanted to believe. Her logic told her it was poppycock.

The kinds of things that Goninan was talking about simply couldn't fit into the real world—the world she knew. But at the same time, his words awoke resonances inside her that were naggingly familiar, as though when he spoke she was remembering, rather than hearing.

"And the second purpose?" Clare asked.

"Is as a talisman," Goninan said. "An artifact. And I would warn you that to wield such an object, one must be very, very careful. It is a grave responsibility. Every time one uses it, the world changes. One can hide an artifact, but one can't hide one's responsibility to it. The only way that can be done is if the artifact is willingly passed on to another."

"The world . . . changes?" Janey said.

"The more such a talisman is employed, the more pronounced its effects become. Eventually, if it is used long enough, it will remake the world."

"How?" Janey asked.

"Into what?" Clare added.

"Into whatever is possible."

Janey thought again of the little that her grandfather had told her of what had happened when he first got the book, before he hid it away—of the ghosts and odd sounds and how people changed. . . . She remembered her own dream last night. Of the music that came from the book. How it changed.

She thought of that lost tune that she'd been trying to recover and realized she had only heard it when she had the book open, on her lap. . . .

"Does it change forever?" Clare asked.

"That depends on how long it is used. And by whom. Wielded by its proper guardian, it can only do good. Wielded for the sake of personal gain—as Madden plans—it could eventually destroy the world."

"How do we know who its proper guardian is?" Janey asked. "Is it my grandfather? Is it me?"

"I don't know," Goninan said. "But it's not likely. Neither of you follow a Way. You don't have the background, nor the knowledge."

"But you do?" Janey said, suddenly suspicious again.

Goninan only laughed. "I have both," he agreed, "but it's too late for me to take a new road. My birds have brought me as far as I can go and now I stand in a borderland—half in this world, half in the otherworld. Sooner, rather than later, I will be crossing over."

"What do you mean?" Clare asked.

But Janey knew. In the same way that Goninan's words seemed more memory than new.

"You're dying," she said.

Goninan nodded.

"I'm sorry. I . . ." She didn't know what to say.

"Don't be," Goninan said. "I've had a long full life and I have seen where I am going next. My only regret is what I told you before—that I won't be leaving the world a better place than it was when I entered it."

They were quiet for a time then, until Janey stirred. She took her gaze from the small stonechat that she'd been watching as it hopped from thorn branch to thorn branch in the field above them and turned to Goninan.

"And Helen's your . . . nurse?" she asked.

"Great-niece. A kindred spirit. She has long had a similar bent of mind to mine, so I've been teaching her, while she takes care of me."

"And that's why you can't guard the book."

"Exactly."

Janey frowned, thinking.

"What I don't understand is . . . we haven't done anything with the book. We haven't"—she looked a little embarrassed—"you know, chanted above it or lit candles around it or anything. All we've done is read it."

"That's all it requires to come awake—to be opened."

"Well, I'm going to hide it away," Janey said. "Someplace far and safe where no one will ever find it."

"If you can find such a place."

"And I won't read another word."

Goninan shook his head. "You must finish the story," he said. "If you leave it incomplete, the book will remain open—not much, but enough so that someone like Madden will be able to track it down and find it."

"Why didn't Billy *warn* Gramps?"

"I don't think he knew."

"Why didn't you tell him? You seem to know a lot more about it than you said you did back in the cottage."

"I've just been thinking about it these past few days," Goninan said. "Since I first felt it wake. And I didn't speak more of it then, because I was waiting to speak of it now."

"Oh."

Janey picked at a frayed bit of her jeans and sighed.

"What can I do?" she asked finally.

"Finish reading the book," Goninan said. "Your subconscious already knows what you must do. Perhaps you'll find that answer reflected in the book as you read on."

"Why can't you just tell me?"

"Because I don't know."

Goninan rose stiffly to his feet.

"I should go back," he said. "It's time for my medicine and Helen will have my hide if I'm much later."

Janey and Clare rose with him.

"Why did we have to talk about all of this outside?" Clare asked as they walked back towards the cottage.

"As my totems are my birds," Goninan replied. "So Madden's lie in shadows—the shadows cast by man-made objects. He can see through them, hear through them, speak through them . . . perhaps even move through them. They give him his health; they feed on his magic."

"Can't your birds help you?" Janey asked.

"How so?"

"You know—to cure you."

Goninan smiled. "Why should I ask them to? Dying is a part of living—a natural progression. Should I ignore the natural order of my life, twist it to *my* liking and thereby become something I was not meant to be?"

"That sounds so fatalistic—" She put her hand across her mouth the moment she spoke. "I'm sorry," she added quickly. "I didn't mean . . ."

"I know what you meant," Goninan said. "You feel that such a way of living lacks free will."

Janey nodded.

"You forget that I made the *choice* to live in such a way."

There was nothing more that could be added to that. When they reached the cottage door, Helen was waiting for them, a frown vying with worry in her features.

"Thank you for your time," Clare said.

"For everything," Janey added.

Goninan nodded. "I enjoyed the chance to meet and talk with you both."

"Peter," Helen said. "You have to come in."

She motioned for him to enter the cottage. Goninan gave Janey and Clare a wink.

"She's ever so strict."

"We won't take any more of your time," Janey said.

Goninan caught her arm before she could turn away.

"One more word of warning," he said. "Madden has arrived in this country. I can *feel* his step on the land."

"We'll be careful," Janey assured him.

"I hope you will be. Especially of what you say when shadows can hear you speak. Godspeed and good luck."

Janey smiled. She looked at him, seeing the birdishness still in his stock-thin frame and his shining eyes, but seeing the illness now as well.

"You *are* leaving the world a better place," she said.

Before he could reply she hurried off, leaving Clare to follow at a slower pace.

6.

"I guess you're wondering how I tracked you down," Bett said.

A thin smile touched his lips as he watched Davie Rowe. The big man stood as still as the stone outcrops that dotted the clifftop around them, his own gaze not meeting Bett's, but fixed rather on the muzzle of the automatic that Bett held.

Christ, he was an ugly one, Bett thought. Killing him was doing the world a favour.

"I . . ." Rowe began.

Walking on the edge as he was, Bett felt he could see right down into the big man's soul and taste the fear that cowered there. He knew there was no mercy in his own features. All Rowe would see in Bett's eyes was his death. Old Mr. D., staring right back at him, a big death's-head grin laughing in the face of the man's terror.

Bett shrugged.

"Guess you'll just have to take that question down to your grave," he said.

And pulled the trigger.

The automatic's report was loud in the still air. Rowe jerked back as the bullet punched his chest. He went tumbling from the path into the long couch grass at the lip of the cliff. Bett stepped closer, the muzzle of his revolver tracking the man's fall for a second shot. His finger tightened on the trigger.

"Hey!"

Bett turned as sharply as though he'd been shot himself at the sound of the new voice. Coming around the corner where the Coastal Path dipped past an outcrop of rocks that had the appearance of a stone armchair was a young, blond-haired man in jeans and a windbreaker, a small knapsack on his back.

Shit, Bett thought. Just what I needed. A hiker.

He ducked away into the undergrowth, worming his way deep into its thickets on his stomach, pulling himself along on his elbows.

"What is the matter here?" the stranger cried.

German, Bett realized from the accent. And he was no dummy.

The man had stopped near the stone armchair. Keeping a cautious distance, he peered in the direction where Bett had first disappeared into the thick vegetation. But Bett had already worked himself parallel to the path so that he was well away from the spot where he'd disappeared.

Bett smiled.

The man was no dummy, but he didn't have a chance.

He wasn't walking the edge.

The hiker took a few more tentative steps forward, pausing again to rake the landscape with his gaze. Bett ducked as the man's gaze tracked past his own hiding place. He waited for a count of five, then crawled farther along the route he'd chosen, still parallel to the path, but above it now, for here the land rose steeply above the outcropping of rocks of which the stone armchair was a part.

When he chanced another look, it was to find himself behind and above the hiker who was now gingerly approaching the place where

Davie Rowe had fallen. The stranger paused again before reaching the Coastguard lookout and called out once more.

Bett shoved the revolver back into his jacket pocket and rose as silently as a ghost from his hiding place. He crept forward and was about to jump down upon the stranger when the man turned and saw him.

Too late.

Bett landed like a cat beside him and gave him a shove. The hiker went over the edge of the path with a scream, pinwheeling his arms as he fell to the rocks some two hundred feet below. When Bett bent over the lip of the cliff to look down at him, all he could see was the hiker's splayed figure lying still—a splash of colour against the grey. Waves lashed the rocks. The hiker didn't move.

"You picked a bad time to drop by," Bett said.

A shame, really. Walking along this treacherous path all by yourself. One misstep and—

Well, it was a long fall.

Dusting off the dirt from his clothes, he pulled out his revolver again and went over to where Rowe had fallen.

The body was gone.

Frowning, Bett looked over the edge of the cliff here, but there were no rocks below to catch the body. Just the sea, washing against the face of the cliff, ragged waves breaking into white foam as they hit the rocks. If the body had fallen all the way down, Bett knew that he wasn't going to spot it now.

He crouched down and studied the place where Rowe had first dropped. Bett wasn't any kind of a tracker—at least not outside the city. Hunting humans was a game he liked to play in a forest of steel and concrete. The only kind of tracking it involved was some detective work in picking a victim. Then it was just the stalk and, if he had time, a little knife work to see what made the sucker tick. If there wasn't time, then the skinning knife could be used just as effectively for the kill.

Rowe had stolen his knife last night, but it wasn't like Bett didn't have another couple of blades stashed away in his luggage. But he hadn't wanted to use the knife today. Rowe was just too big and Bett's shoulder still hurt from their encounter the previous night. So he used the gun, but he didn't like it.

It wasn't personal enough. A gun didn't let you get up close and see the life-light die.

But you made do.

When time was tight, you just made do with whatever came to hand. But you liked to have a chance to check out the results. You liked the opportunity to stand back and admire your own handiwork.

You liked to make sure the sucker was dead.

So he looked for clues as to what had happened to the body. He'd never had much experience or inclination to play Davy Crockett. But he spotted Rowe's blood where it stained the dirt and grass. And he'd seen the big man take a hit, right in the chest.

He spent a few more moments, combing the undergrowth nearby, then put away his automatic once more and headed back towards the village.

Rowe had fallen over the edge and the sea had taken him. It was as simple as that.

And if last night's failure hadn't exactly been remedied yet, Bett had at least been compensated for it. Now it was time to get on with the rest of the day's projects.

He still had a lot of other business to take care of before his work here was done. Next on the agenda was finding a nice out-of-the-way place, something with four walls that was remote, but not so remote that he couldn't get away from it easily. And thinking back on his walk from Mousehole to where he'd run down Lena's slimy little friend, Willie Keel, he thought he knew of just the place.

He'd go check it out now.

Staying on the edge.

Letting it all fall into place.

Doing it for himself, because if whatever it was that the Littles had stashed away was important enough for Madden to actually make the trip over here today, then it was worth Bett's keeping it for himself. If he couldn't figure it out, if he couldn't get the girl or her grandfather to show him how it worked . . . well, he'd always liked puzzles.

He liked taking things apart just to see how they worked.

It was what he did best.

7.

Janey waited for Clare at the first stile. She leaned against the tumbled-down stone wall beside it, looking off into the woods on their left.

"Why did you run on ahead like that . . . ?" Clare began.

She broke off when she saw the tears glistening in Janey's eyes.

"It's just so sad," Janey said. "He seems like such a dear old man and it's so sad that he's going to die."

Clare nodded. "I know."

"And what makes me feel worse," Janey said, "is all those times I've seen him up on the cliffs and either laughed at the way he looked, or ran off scared. I could have *known* him all this time. . . ."

She looked about in her pockets for a handkerchief, then wiped her eyes on her sleeve. Clare dug about in her own pockets and came up with a tissue that Janey accepted with a nod of thanks. She blew her nose.

"He had such . . . odd things to say," she said finally, still sniffling a bit.

"Very odd."

"Did you believe him?"

Clare sighed. "I don't know. Logically, I know that a lot of it can't be true—not the bits about Gurdjieff or how you can use your will and that sort of thing. I've heard of all that before. But those other things. . . ."

"The *real* magic," Janey said.

Clare nodded.

"There's only one way to find out," Janey said.

"Compare what you've read in the book to what Felix and your grandfather have read," Clare said.

"Because," Janey agreed, "if that's true, then maybe the rest of it is, too."

They started to walk slowly back to where they had left the car. The tailless cat wasn't near the stream when they crossed over. The whole of their surroundings, fields and wood, seemed still, as though the land were holding its breath. Even the babble of the stream was muted.

"You know what Mr. Goninan didn't talk about?" Janey said.

"What's that?"

"Music. That's part of the old legends as well, but it's not something that got written down until during the last century or so. And it's probably never been written down the way it *really* was. Every transcriber you hear about prettied it up, took the modal keys and fit them into minor ones—that kind of thing."

"But it doesn't pass on the same sorts of things that Mr. Goninan was telling us about," Clare said.

"It just doesn't teach it in words," Janey replied. "But you can still find traces of it in things like old mummers' plays and Morris dancing. The Hobby Horse Fool—he's really the trickster. The antlered man—he's Robin Hood. Not the storybook Robin Hood, but the Robin in the Wood. The Green Man."

"I suppose."

"No, really," Janey said. "Think about it. We remember ancient rituals in mumming and dancing. It's like Mr. Goninan said: We don't forget anything."

Clare nodded slowly. "We just forget why."

"I really think that's true. We go through the motions, and it stirs something in us and we feel good, but we don't know why it does. I think that's a real kind of magic—how nothing is ever really lost. Just hidden."

She smiled. "That's what draws us to the old tunes, I think. That's why we always want to learn as many as we can and why they've survived for as long as they have the way they are. Not the tunes in books, but the ones we get from memory, the ones we learn from the living tradition. And that's why we don't change them. We do new twiddles here, and arrange them with any number of modern instruments, but the bones of the tunes, the heart of the music—we keep *it* the same."

When they reached the car, she leaned on its hood and looked back the way they'd come. The sadness came back to her, riding an intangible breeze that washed through her without touching a hair on her head. It went to the heart, ignoring secular concerns. It wasn't the ache she'd felt last night when she'd thought that Felix had betrayed her, but a gentle sadness, like the breath expended into the mouthpiece of a whistle as it called up the bittersweet notes of a slow air.

Her fingers itched for an instrument, but there was none at hand. And this was neither the time nor the place. They had so much still to do. But she still wished she could play a music, something that would carry across the fields to the cottage where Peter Goninan nested with his bird totems and niece, something that he would hear and know by it that she had understood what he'd been trying to tell them. Understood not with her mind, but with her heart. She wanted to show her gratitude to him and knew that the best thanks the old man would ever ask for was the knowledge of that understanding.

She hoped there'd be time to come back.

She glanced at Clare, wanting to share the feeling with her, but Clare, she believed, for all her interest in the old tunes, didn't see them, didn't *feel* them in the same way.

But Felix would understand. She'd bring him to meet Peter Goninan, she decided. The two of them would get along famously. If they all only lived long enough. . . .

Sighing, she got into the car where Clare was already waiting.

"Felix would like that old man," she said as she started up the Reliant.

Clare nodded. "In a way, they're of a kind."

Maybe she'd been wrong, Janey thought. Maybe Clare did understand.

"What do you mean?" she asked.

"They both follow the road that their own hearts tell them to follow and give never a mind to what the rest of the world thinks about it."

"I never thought of it like that."

The track was too narrow to turn around in, so Janey carefully backed the car out onto the lane. Shifting into first, she set off for home at a far more sedate pace than they had left at earlier that day.

"I wanted to talk to you about Felix," Clare said.

"I think we'll be okay," Janey said. "I'm going to try really hard to make it work."

"I know you will. It's just that—"

She broke off and looked out through the side window at the hedges blurring past.

"Just what?" Janey prompted her.

"It's something he should probably tell you himself, but knowing him, he'll never get around to it. And it's important."

Janey's heart sank. What was she going to learn *now*?

"It's about how you want Felix to play with you on stage."

Janey's relief came as suddenly as her worry had.

"I won't push him," she said. "I think I've learned my lesson about trying to do that. If he doesn't want to, then he doesn't want to."

"That's good. Not that it's my business, really. . . ."

Janey laughed. "We're all mates, Clare. And we've always appreciated the way you've made us your business."

"That's nice to know," Clare said.

Janey heard a wistfulness in her friend's voice, but before she could think of a way to ask what was bothering her, Clare was speaking again.

"But I think it's important that you know *why* he won't do it."

"I know why," Janey said. "He just doesn't like it."

Clare shook her head. "He's scared to death of the idea."

All Janey could do was laugh at the very notion.

"Scared?" she said. "That big lug? I doubt he's scared of anything. And besides, I've seen him play in front of people a thousand times. At sessions, on street corners, backstage at festivals. . . ."

"But not *on* stage."

"No," Janey agreed. "Not on stage. Still, what's the difference?"

"I don't know. But I've been reading up on phobias since he first told me about this a few days ago, and while there's usually some hidden root to the problem that can be dealt with, very often there simply *is* no reasonable answer. What he suffers from is called topophobia—stage fright."

"But—"

"I know what you're going to say: Why doesn't he just deal with it? Get on stage a few times and simply work *through* his problem."

Janey nodded. "Well, isn't that how you deal with that kind of thing?"

"Unfortunately, it doesn't seem to be that simple. What happens is a panic syndrome sets in and if you've ever had a panic attack, you'll know it's not fun."

"I guess. . . ."

"I can still remember that last operation I had for my leg," Clare said. "I was panicking so badly—and it's a *horrible* feeling—that I fainted before they could give me the anesthetic."

"Saved them having to give it to you, I suppose."

Clare shook her head. "No, they can't do that. It's too dangerous. Your heartbeat and blood pressure go all irregular and none of their equipment can monitor you properly. They had to bring me around again first, and then give me the needle."

"So you're saying that Felix could faint if he got up on stage?"

"I was reading about the symptoms and they're really odd. You

start off feeling sick, then your heartbeat becomes very fast and er-
ratic; your chest gets tight and you start to breathe too fast. The
rapid breathing actually causes chemical changes inside you that
make your hands and feet feel numb—that awful tingling when
they've fallen asleep, you know?"

Janey nodded.

"The nausea then gets worse and is followed by headaches and
cramps. And those are just the physical symptoms. Your brain also
goes a bit mad. Everything begins to seem unreal. Apparently there
can be the sensation of an out-of-body experience, or peculiar
changes in the quality of light so that you lose your sense of depth
and perspective. . . ."

"It sounds horrible," Janey said. "Is that what happened to you?"

"No. I just fainted, straightway."

"Lovely."

"And if all of that isn't bad enough," Clare went on, "there's also
something called anticipatory anxiety that comes from just thinking
about a panic attack. It apparently brings on a lot of the same symptoms as the actual attack. I saw a bit of that in Felix when he was
telling me about it."

Janey was quiet for a long moment.

"I wish he'd told me this when we used to argue about him touring
with me," she said.

"He was too scared to."

"Scared? Of me?"

Clare nodded. "Of your laughing at him—as you did when I
started telling you about this a few moments ago."

"Well, I didn't really mean to laugh. It's just . . ."

"I know. It's hard to imagine Felix being frightened of anything.
But he didn't want you to laugh at him and he also thought that you
wouldn't think as much of him if you knew about his fear. A male
ego thing, I suppose, since stage fright isn't something that many
people take very seriously. It's always an 'Oh, get on up there; you'll
feel better before you know it' sort of a thing, isn't it?"

"I suppose."

Janey was thinking about all the times she'd bullied people to get
up and play on a stage and began to feel horrible about it.

"He thought you'd think he was like Ted Praed," Clare said. "Remember him?"

Janey started to giggle at the thought of Ted and his quavery voice, but then she realized what she was doing.

"We weren't very nice to him, were we?"

"Well, as I told Felix, Ted wasn't exactly the nicest person himself to begin with."

"But still. . . ."

"But still," Clare agreed. "Think of all the jokes—and Felix was there to hear them all."

"But he used to laugh, too."

Clare nodded. "He laughed, but if you think back, he was never the one who started the jokes, or told any himself."

"I could never think of Felix as being anything like Ted Praed—stage fright or no stage fright."

"Neither can I," Clare said. "But I did want to tell you so that you'd know why he feels the way he does, *before* you brought it up."

"I won't bring it up unless he does," Janey said, "and then I'll certainly not press him to get up on stage."

"That's good."

They were very near the village now, just coming on the south side of Raginnis Hill.

"How did you get him to tell *you*?" Janey asked.

Clare smiled. "I don't have the same things at stake as do the two of you, so I just browbeat it from him."

Janey laughed.

"Trust you," she said as she pulled the car up in front of Clare's house. "Did you want to be let off here," she added, "or are you coming on down to the house?"

"I'd like a chance to see the book," Clare said. "Before it's hidden away forever."

Janey smiled. "We'll read it together," she said.

Taking her foot from the brake, she steered the car on down into the village proper.

The Bargain Is Over

Power without abuse loses its charm.

—PAUL VALÉRY

As their train crossed the Tamar River at Plymouth, John Madden sat up straighter in his seat. This was why he'd opted to return to the land of his birth by train, rather than by one of the more expedient methods of transportation that he could so easily have afforded.

The same *clackety-clack* rattle of the carriage's wheels against the tracks that had helped put him into a half-waking, half-dreaming state now rang with the heartbeat of the land for him and set his pulse drumming to ancient rhythms. A music sang inside him. A native music—that of crowdy crawn and pibcorn. He felt more alert, more *awake* than he had all day, and he knew it was due to the enchantment of the venerable countryside through which they journeyed.

This was Arthur's land.

Tintagel lay to the north, craggy and majestic; Arthur's birthplace, standing now in ruins above the mysterious depths of Merlin's cave. Dozmary Pool was on Bodmin Moor, where the Lady of the Lake had reclaimed Excalibur from Bedivere's hand. There was an Arthur's Chair, where the king was said to have sat and watched the sea. An Arthur's Cave, where he and his knights still slept. . . . The Once and Future King had been a West Country man—Madden had always believed that and over the past few decades the work of modern archaeologists supported that claim.

But there were older mysteries than Arthur hidden in this countryside.

Lyonesse, the drowned land, once stood between Land's End and the Isles of Scilly. The Scillies, and St. Michael's Mount near Penzance, were all that remained of that land today, though one could still hear the tolling of its bells beneath the sea.

And older still . . .

The land was riddled with Bronze Age stone circles, standing stones and other prehistoric relics.

There were the Merry Maidens near St. Buryans.

One tale held that the stones of its circle, and the two solitary menhir standing nearby, were dancers and musicians turned to stone for dancing on a Sunday. An older tale held that they were mermaids, caught by the sun one dawn and turned to stone like trolls, "merry maiden" being an old sailor's name for the women of the sea.

And Gwennap Pit between Redruth and St. Day.

The Methodists claimed it was an irregular mining sink that John Wesley was instrumental in having remodeled into its present form in 1806, but folklore told another story: Of how when Mervin the harper of Tollvaddon cracked his skull, he played his harp until his fingers were worn to the bone. The harp god Larga showed pity on him then, removing his wound and transferring it to the earth. So those who preferred the folktales called that great pit "the hole in the harper's head."

And the Men-an-Tol near Morvah.

The largest tolmen in the British Isles, archaeologists believed that it could be all that remained of the entrance to an ancient barrow or tomb. But tradition had it that passage through the holed stone brought healing to those who were ill and that it marked not the entrance to a barrow, but to the Barrow World, the land of the *muryan,* or piskies.

But beyond legend, beyond stone relics, Madden knew that the land itself was enchanted.

He was not alone in this understanding. Crowley, a native son, had known it. Dylan Thomas had been drawn to this countryside, living in Newlyn and Mousehole, a poet rather than a magician, but then again, at one time there was no difference perceived between the two. Dennis Wheatley had lived in the West Country as well.

And others, modern as well as the old:

Colin Wilson, whose career Madden had been following since his remarkable theories were first aired in *The Outsider,* now lived in Gorran Haven where he continued to study the Mysteries with a scientist's precise documentation. And Peter Goninan, the reclusive theurgist with whom Madden had crossed swords on occasion.

The land gave them birth, or drew them to it. Its hold ran deep, far beyond its simple pastoral beauties or coastal splendors. It ran as profound as the ancient granite backbone of the land, as instinctive as the inexplicable urges that first drew a man or a woman into the Mysteries, so that there was no choice involved, only inevitability.

An untapped wealth remained in the heartbeat of this land and every time Madden returned, he wondered anew why he had ever left in the first place. The secular concerns that drove him to live in other parts of the world seemed insignificant whenever he again set foot here.

"Kernow," he breathed.

Rollie Grant turned to him when he spoke. "What's that?"

Madden smiled. "The ancient name of an ancient country—this country."

"What, Cornwall?"

Madden nodded.

"I thought it was just like a state of the U.K.—you know, like Rhode Island or Connecticut."

"It's a state of mind," Madden said, remaining deliberately oblique.

Grant looked past him out the window for a long moment, then shrugged and returned to the business papers he was reading. They didn't speak again until they reached Penzance where Grant wanted to call a cab to take them from the train station to the hotel.

Madden laughed. "This isn't New York," he said. "We can walk."

"Walk?"

"Yes, walk," Madden said, still chuckling. "It's not far."

He glanced at a couple who were arguing a few carriages down from where they had disembarked, then hefted the small overnight case he'd brought and set off along the ocean front. Grant collected his own bags and hurried after him.

It was a fifteen-minute walk at Madden's slow pace to where the Queen's Hotel stood at the corner of Morrab Road and the Western Promenade Road, but it took them longer because Madden kept stopping along the way. Near Battery Rocks, he stood at the site of the old gun battery and looked out across the bay for a long time, breathing in the salt tang of the sea air, watching the waves spray against the rocks below, listening for the sound of bells. Across the road, he admired the St. Anthony Gardens and dawdled in front of the shop windows along the way, for all that most of them were closed and only carried tourist souvenirs anyway.

When they finally reached the Queen's Hotel, Grant looked up at it and sighed.

"This is the best the town's got?" he asked.

"No, but it's charming, don't you think?"

Grant smiled. "You're really in your element here, aren't you?"

"I've come home."

"I thought it was your father—John Madden Sr.—who was born in Cornwall."

"It was," Madden lied. "And my grandfather as well—in the 1850s." Another lie. "But it still feels like coming home."

Grant nodded and gave the hotel another look. "Well, I did tell Lena to keep a low profile. Looks like she's actually been listening to me for a change."

"When you come to another country," Madden said, "even one that in many ways is similar to your own, what's the point of staying in a Holiday Inn?"

"Comfort. Security. You know what you're getting."

Madden shook his head. "What you're speaking of is complacency, Rollie, and that will simply put you to sleep." He led the way towards the door. "Shall we register?"

They went to their own rooms after registering, meeting a few minutes later in Madden's when they had both had a chance to freshen up. There was a little confusion in reaching Lena, for she didn't answer her door when they knocked, but a request to the desk had their call transferred to where she was, and soon they had joined her in Jim Gazo's room. Madden settled into one of the chairs by the window, Grant in the other. Lena perched on the edge of the bed after giving her father a welcoming hug. Gazo stood by the door.

"Do you want me to go for a walk, Mr. Grant?" he asked.

Grant glanced at Madden who shook his head. As Gazo started to lean against the doorjamb, Madden indicated the head of the bed.

"You might as well be comfortable, Jim," he said. "It *is* your room."

Madden could read Gazo's thoughts easily. Sure, it was his room, but Grant was paying for it. Gazo was just on the payroll and being in Madden's company made him nervous, though if Gazo had been pressed he wouldn't have been able to say why he felt that way.

Which was how it should be, Madden thought. The nervousness of sheep was something that he cultivated. It kept them alert—or at least as alert as sheep could be—and stopped them from having too many thoughts of their own because they were so busy trying to stay in Madden's favour.

"Why don't you tell us how things have gone?" Madden said to Lena.

She spoke for some time, obviously choosing her words carefully because she knew that Michael Bett was Madden's protégé, but laying out all the facts. Madden was impressed with her delivery. He felt she was holding something back—something to do with this Felix Gavin—but it didn't appear to have any bearing on his own immediate concerns, so he didn't press her on it. But while she was tactful in how she spoke of Bett—making no judgments, but rather allowing Madden to make up his own mind from what she had to report— her father had no such reservations.

"He's out of control," Grant said when Lena was done.

"Perhaps," Madden said.

"I'm sorry, John, but we've got to face the facts. He's working on something for himself."

Madden nodded slowly. "I expected this," he said.

Only not so soon. He'd known all along that the reincarnated spirit of Crowley would eventually turn against him. Crowley had always been a leader, as witness his altercations with MacGregor Mathers and the like, but Madden had still expected to have some time before it was necessary to deal more firmly with Bett. He had thought to squeeze a few more years of service out of the man and then, depending on his loyalty, decide whether he would be discarded or rewarded.

He had half imagined Michael as a son. . . .

"What are we going to do about Michael?" Grant asked.

"That will require some thought," Madden replied. "First we must discover exactly what it is that he is up to."

"That's simple," Grant said. "He wants what you want. He wants whatever it is that Dunthorn hid from us."

Madden nodded. "If that is true, then I'm afraid we will just have to deal with him before he has the chance to find it."

But what a waste that would be. Michael had such potential.

His mistake, Madden realized, was in thinking of Michael as a kind of tabula rasa—as though he could create whatever he wanted from the blank slate of Michael's spirit, when all along that spirit had already been formed and shaped and fired in an iron will of its own—not through merely one lifetime, but through many. It was easy to forget that he wasn't teaching Michael; he was helping him remember.

The danger had been in allowing him to remember too much.

Madden wasn't terribly worried about that, however. Mistakes were unfortunate, but if caught in time, they were only temporary setbacks. They could be corrected. Not always easily, not necessarily without regret, but they could be corrected.

And Madden had no compunction about seeing that it was done. None whatsoever.

His only loyalty had always been to himself.

2.

Sam Dennison was in a foul mood.

He was feeling punchy and red-eyed from a lack of sleep and wished, not for the first time that day, that he'd known Bett was going to call him this morning. He wouldn't have had quite so many drinks the night before if he had. Hell, he wouldn't have had any. He would've turned in early and been all bright-eyed and bushy-tailed for this gig. As it was, his patience level was right on the edge and he had to catch himself from wanting to hit someone just to ease the tension.

It wasn't so much the flight over, nor the wait for their train and the subsequent five-and-some-hour journey to the West Country, as the traveling companions with whom he'd been thrown together on this job. The woman was bad enough.

Connie Hetherington was a good-looking woman—at least Dennison thought she was, somewhere under all that makeup and the teased peroxide hair. She had an hourglass figure that would do a college kid half her own age proud, and legs that just didn't stop, but she carried herself like a tramp. Not to mention dressing to fit the role: skimpy skirt and high-heeled pumps, low-cut blouse and cheap fur jacket.

She was a looker, but Dennison was embarrassed to be in her company. And not just because of the way she dressed and came on to just about anything wearing trousers that got within talking distance of her. She chewed gum with her mouth open, chain-smoked, and hadn't stopped whining since they'd left Kennedy Airport first thing that morning. Baby-sitting her was like being trapped in the opening frames of a porn flick—unending hours of inane conversation and double entendres that had him gritting his teeth by the time they finally arrived at Penzance Station.

Ted Grimes was the opposite end of the spectrum.

He was dressed in a tailored dark suit and didn't look in the least bit rumpled from the hours of travel. His black hair and dark complexion placed the source of his genes in the Mediterranean, but Dennison didn't figure him for a wise guy, never mind the way that Grimes moved with the ice-cool, easy cruising style of one of the Cerone Family's enforcers. He didn't have the size—coming in a half head under Dennison's own six-one—but there was something of a shark about him all the same and Dennison could tell, the moment he laid eyes on the man, that if Grimes wasn't a hitman, he'd still done his share of killing for hire.

He might not be connected, but he had the flat, dead eyes of the type, and Dennison figured that his own baby-sitting duties didn't include looking after Grimes. They hadn't exchanged more than two words since Dennison had collected him. Grimes had ignored Connie as well after giving her one cool look when they picked her up. He hadn't even batted an eye when she pointed to his prosthetic hand and asked him, "Hey, you got a vibrator attachment to go with that thing?"

Dennison had wondered about the hand, too, but hadn't said a thing about it. Wasn't his business. He'd learned that long ago. Never mind the white knight PI crap that TV and paperbacks foisted off on the public, the only way you got ahead in this business was by sticking strictly to the job. Leave the crusades for those who didn't have to make a living.

What he didn't like about having Grimes tagging along was that if Grimes *was* setting up a hit, then that left Dennison himself as an accessory. Maybe he wasn't a white knight, but Dennison still had drawn lines between what was kosher and what wasn't, and being involved in a hit was definitely stepping way over the line.

As soon as they left the train, Grimes vanished.

"We'd better be getting a hotel room soon," Connie complained. "I'm sick of traveling. I feel like shit, you know what I'm saying? I need to wash up and get beautiful, pal."

Dennison ignored her and took care of getting their luggage out on the platform.

"Hey, where's poker-face?" she went on. "I thought we were, like, a big happy family."

Dennison was wondering that as well. He scanned the platform, but except for some French hikers with their knapsacks, a family of four with luggage enough for twice that number who were obviously also tourists, and a pair of older gentlemen—probably businessmen—they had the area to themselves.

"You know I'm getting kind of sick of the silent treatment from you guys," Connie said. "It'd be nice if you acted like I was here. I mean, just because you've got a pickle up your—"

"Shut up," Dennison told her.

The few people present were all staring at her. He threw his raincoat at her, which she caught awkwardly.

"And put this on," he added.

She started to throw it back at him. "Hey, don't go getting all prissy on me, Mr. Big Shot Private Det—"

She broke off at the glare in his eyes. He didn't say a word, just continued to give her a long hard stare until she slowly put the coat on. It was far too big for her and made her look like a bit of a clown with her high heels and stockinged calves underneath it and her teased blond hair and painted face above, but it also made her look the best she had since he'd first collected her at her Lower East Side apartment, where she'd met him at the door dressed in a baby-doll nightie right out of the pages of a Fredricks of Hollywood catalogue.

He stepped over to her and spoke in a voice pitched just loud enough for her to hear.

"Let's get something straight," he told her. "We're both on a payroll. You screw up, and it looks bad on me, and I don't like looking bad, got it?"

"Sure, I—"

"I don't know what the hell Mr. Bett has got planned for you, but you can be damn sure it doesn't include parading your ass all over town so that everybody who happens to be within a hundred yards of you will never forget you. So keep a lip on it and keep that coat on until we get a hotel room and then you're going to change into something a little less—well, let's be polite and only call it trashy."

"C'mon," Connie said. "Give me a break. It's not like—"

"If Mr. Bett is paying you anything like he's paying me, you owe him this much." He lifted a fist between them. "I'm sick of your whining and I'm not one of those candyasses who wouldn't lay a hand on a woman—not if that's what it takes to shut 'em up."

Her lip curled, but Dennison spoke before she could get a word out.

"I'm not jiving you, lady."

Connie shrugged. "Screw you, too," she said, but there was no force behind her words.

She lit up a cigarette and studiously ignored him.

Dennison sighed. He didn't feel particularly proud about threatening her, but he was way beyond his usual limit of patience.

What the hell made her tick? He could see kids getting into the skin trade because it looked like a fast track to the good life, but surely a woman her age would have seen through the lie by now? What the hell made her still play out the party-girl image?

Getting old doesn't mean you get smart, he answered himself. She probably just didn't know any better.

Happily, Grimes chose that moment to reappear.

The guy moved like a ghost, Dennison thought, as Grimes collected his small traveling case from where Dennison had placed it on the platform.

"You missed our PI here playing the tough guy," Connie said.

Grimes gave Dennison a glance. For a moment Dennison thought he saw a trace of humour behind the man's flat gaze, but it was gone before he could be sure.

"What happened to you?" Dennison asked him.

"Saw someone I'm not ready to do business with yet," Grimes replied.

So it was a hit, Dennison thought. He'd have to talk to Bett about this. No way he was going to be a part of this kind of a thing.

"Ready to find a hotel?" he asked.

Grimes shook his head. "Bett knows how to get in touch with me when the time's right."

"Do you need to know where we're staying?"

"Can't see why."

Maybe things were going to work out after all, Dennison thought. With Grimes on his own track and if he could keep Hetherington quiet until Bett needed her, maybe he could salvage a little something for himself out of all of this. He'd enjoyed his previous trip here, but he'd only been playing the tourist then. Maybe he could fit in some real sight-seeing time before he had to head back to the States.

"Well, good luck," he said.

Grimes smiled. "I've been waiting a long time to settle some unfinished business and I'll tell you right now, it's going to be a real pleasure finally getting the job done, but luck's not going to have anything to do with it. Just patience."

Dennison didn't look at the prosthetic hand, but he knew that whatever Grimes was talking about had something to do with it. He gave Grimes a nod, then handed Connie her overnight case and picked up their other two cases.

"Let's go, sunshine," he said.

Connie butted her cigarette under the toe of her shoe and followed him with unfeigned reluctance.

Yeah, me, too, lady, Dennison thought. But we're stuck with each other for the moment. He wasn't going to say let's make the best of it. All he wanted to do was get this crummy job over with.

Leppadumdowledum

For the moon's shining high
and the dew is wet;
and on mossy moor,
they're dancing yet.

—CORNISH RHYME

Jodi had suffered through her fair share of long, boring afternoons before, but she couldn't remember one as tedious as this one that she spent tucked away for the most part in the pocket of the mayor of Bodbury's secretary.

It made sense, of course, for her to go with Lizzie. Of all the conspirators to gather in Henkie Whale's warehouse earlier that morning, Lizzie was the most likely candidate to take on the responsibility of hiding the Small that Jodi had become from the Widow Pender. It seemed logical that the Widow would pursue Denzil or Taupin, or any of the Tatters children, before she would think to confront Lizzie in her tiny office at the back of the town hall.

The logic was impeccable, everyone had agreed—especially Taupin, whose idea it had been. But logic didn't make the hours go by any more quickly; nor did it relieve the boredom.

When they first arrived, Jodi had insisted that she be given the freedom of the desktop at the very least. As Lizzie rattled away on her typewriter, Jodi had wandered about the oversize desk, investigating common objects made strange by her new size: giant pens, a wooden letter opener as large as an oar, enormous sheets of paper as large as bedsheets and the like. She walked up and down the mayor's correspondence, amused at reading words composed of letters that were each as big as her hand, and played soccer with a wadded-up bit of paper and two erasers as goalposts, but the novelty of it all soon palled.

She ended up sitting on Lizzie's thesaurus, swinging her heels against its leather spine and wishing she were anywhere but where she was—until she was nearly caught by one of Lizzie's coworkers, and Lizzie insisted that she remain out of sight. Then Jodi spent a half hour in a drawer, which was too dark, even with the slat of light that came through the crack that Lizzie had left open, and even more boring.

Eventually she went back into Lizzie's pocket where she divided her time between dozing and peeking up over the edge of the pocket to look at the clock on the wall and gauge how much time had passed since the last time she'd looked. It was invariably less than ten minutes.

"Bother and damn," she muttered. "What's the point of being magical if this is all it gets you? Where's the glamour and romance? Where's the adventure?"

But then she thought of Edern—her Small who had turned out to be a clockwork man when he died, and then, in a dream, spoke to her from the mind of a seal. . . .

Oh, Edern. Why did you have to go and die? Were you ever even real in the first place?

That line of thought just made her feel depressed. And it brought back memories of the Widow, and the creatures at the witch's command. Adventure? She realized that she could do without the adventure, thank you all the same.

But this endless monotony . . .

"I wish I could *do* something," she said and kicked out against the fabric of the pocket in frustration.

"What are you doing?" Lizzie whispered.

Jodi stuck her head out of the pocket and stared up at Lizzie's enormous face.

This is the world as a mouse sees it, she thought. Oh raw we. What if she was stuck like this forever?

"I'm going all kitey," she shouted back in her high piping voice. "Desperately kitey."

"Well do try to keep it down," Lizzie replied, still whispering. "What if someone hears you?"

"Tell them it's your stomach rumbling and you must go home for an early supper."

Lizzie shook her head, which was a disconcerting gesture. It was like the top of a mountain moving back and forth. Her blond hair cascaded about her shoulders like a waterfall unable to make up its mind as to which course it would follow. It made Jodi's head ache to watch.

"Stomach squeaking, rather," Lizzie said.

"It's not my fault I sound like this. Are you almost done for the day?"

Again the mountaintop moved back and forth. "We agreed it was best for us to stay here where the Widow won't dare start a row—remember?"

All too bloody well, Jodi thought.

"I really am going mad," she told Lizzie.

"You'll survive."

"Yes, but without a brain. It'll have all turned to porridge in another few hours—truly it will. How can you stand to work here, day in, day out?"

"I like it. It gives me a chance to—"

"Who are you talking to, Lizzie?"

Jodi dropped back into the pocket as Lizzie started nervously and looked to the doorway where one of her coworkers stood.

"Just thinking aloud," Lizzie replied.

The woman in the doorway smiled and shook her head. "That's the first sign of madness," she said, "talking to yourself."

"I thought it was when you answered yourself," Lizzie said.

"That, too."

The woman went on to her own office and Lizzie looked down at her pocket.

"Do you see what I mean about keeping hidden?" she hissed. "You almost gave it all away."

Jodi peeped above the top of Lizzie's pocket again.

"I'm ever so frightened," she said sulkily.

"Be good," Lizzie said, "and I'll leave early. We can get some ices and walk along the Old Quay before we meet the others."

"Don't . . ." Jodi began, then sighed.

Don't talk to me as though I'm a child, she had been about to say, but she realized that Lizzie was only treating her like a child because she was acting like one. Lizzie was using the same tone of voice that Jodi did when she talked to Denzil's monkey.

Bother and damn.

I'm even smaller than Ollie, she thought. And not nearly so well behaved.

"I think I'll have another nap," she said and dropped back into the pocket.

Lizzie went back to her typing.

Ten minutes later Jodi popped her head up to check the time once more. Only six minutes had passed.

Bother and damn, she thought as she sank back down into the pocket again.

2.

This was utter foolishness, Kara thought as she and Ethy approached the Widow's cottage. They were supposed to be avoiding the Widow and her creatures, yet here they were bringing the wounded home to be tended. The Widow would probably work a spell with the snap of her fingers to heal the little beastie and then they'd simply have to deal with the fetch all over again.

That was if they didn't run into the Widow at her home first. . . .

When Kara glanced at her companion, she could see that Ethy was having second thoughts as well, now that they were so close. What they should do was just drop the fetch right here within sight of the Widow's cottage, lay it on the cobblestones, bundled up and all, and pedal off while they still had a chance.

That was the sensible thing to do.

Windle moved in her arm and made a piteous sound.

Kara sighed. Unfortunately, she wasn't so hardhearted as to be able to do it. Not now, after having come this far. Not with the little creature so helpless. They'd given up the opportunity to be sensible from the moment they first set off with the wounded fetch in hand.

When they reached the last cottage before the Widow's, Kara leaned her bicycle up against its garden wall and turned to Ethy.

"Wait for me here," she said.

"What are you going to do?"

"Lay it on her doorstep."

"I can help."

"There's nothing for you to do," Kara explained.

She left unsaid the fact that there was no need for them both to be at risk when one could do the task as well as two.

"But—" Ethy began.

"You can watch our bikes," Kara said.

Keeping a careful grip on the fetch in its newspaper bundle, she crossed the road and darted into the Widow's garden. From there it was only a few steps to the cottage stoop where she knelt and laid down the fetch.

Was that a sound from inside the cottage? she wondered nervously.

No. Just a shutter rattling somewhere.

She gave Windle a comforting pat and the fetch snapped feebly at her hand.

Wonderfully grateful creature, she thought. Wasn't it just?

She straightened up and began to back away when she heard Ethy's warning shout.

"Kara!"

She turned to see the Widow in the road, Ethy cowering near the garden wall where their bicycles were leaning.

"Monsters!" the Widow cried. "Murderers!"

"Get away!" Kara shouted to Ethy, but the little girl was too frightened to move.

"I'll fry you both," the Widow said, her voice dropping to a menacing growl. "I'll cook you in a pie and feed you to the crows. I'll pull off your fingers, one by one, and make a necklace of them that I'll hang about my neck."

"W-we—we brought him back," Kara stuttered.

The Widow was standing directly by her gate now, blocking Kara's escape. Kara glanced at Ethy, willing her friend to flee, then looked about the garden for another gate, but there was none. Still, the hedgerow wasn't that thick. Perhaps she could squeeze through and give the Widow the slip. Only that left Ethy, frozen by their bicycles . . .

The Widow was still cataloging the terrible fates she had for the pair of them.

"I'll pop your eyes and boil them in a soup. I'll make shoes of your skin and laugh as I dance in them."

Kara was so frightened that she almost forgot the satchel hanging at her side. But when she took a nervous step towards the hedge, the satchel banged against her knee. With trembling fingers she took out a balloon and held it up in her hand.

"You—you just keep back," she said, advancing towards the gate.

The Widow's eyes narrowed. "What have you got there girl?"

"Keep back or I'll throw this," Kara replied.

"What have you *got*?"

But Kara could tell that the Widow already knew. She backed up as Kara continued to move forward, gaze fixed on the balloon filled with seawater that Kara held in her hand.

When she reached the road, Kara edged around so that she was still facing the Widow, but each step brought her closer to where Ethy was standing near their bicycles.

"Kara Faull," the Widow said.

Kara shivered. Three times named was what it took for the witch to work her spells—that's what Taupin had told them this morning. So the Widow had just spoken the first third of a spell.

"You shut your gob," Kara cried, hoisting the balloon higher "or I *will* throw it."

"I have you marked," the Widow said. "You, and Ethy Welet, there, and all your miserable friends. Don't think that I haven't."

Kara had reached the bicycles now. She nudged Ethy with her foot, but got no response, so she gave the smaller girl a light kick on the shin with her toe.

Ethy blinked and shivered.

"Get on your bike," Kara told her.

"I'll bake you in an oven until your heads pop open and your brains spill out," the Widow said. "I'll crack your bones and suck out their marrow."

Kara got on her own bike.

"Go," she told Ethy. "I'll be right behind you. She won't harm you."

"Harm her?" the Widow cried. "I'll unarm her. I'll pull off her legs and use them to stir a stew."

"Go," Kara repeated.

Straddling her own bicycle, she held it upright with her knees and gave Ethy a push with her free hand. Ethy's bike wobbled as she set off down the hill, but soon picked up speed. With the balloon still in one hand, her other gripping the handlebar of her own bicycle, Kara backed up, wheeled her bike farther away from the Widow.

"I'll have you all," the Widow told her. "There'll be no escape."

Shuddering, Kara quickly turned her bicycle about and whizzed off down the hill herself. She dropped the balloon back into its satchel and bent low over her handlebars, trying to catch up to Ethy who was still far ahead of her. Behind her she could hear the trailing fade of the Widow's curses. She heard her name a second time, but before she could hear it repeated for the third time that Taupin had said would give the spell its potency, she was beyond hearing distance and safe.

Safe.

Her pulse drummed with fear. How could she ever be safe again when she knew that from now until forever she was carrying a witch's enmity along with her wherever she went? She and Ethy might have escaped for the moment, but sooner or later the Widow would track them down, each and every one of them—just as she'd promised—and then what would they do?

What *could* they do?

They would have to push her into the sea, Kara realized. They would have to become murderers in truth.

The day had begun as a lark. Now it felt so grim that Kara wondered if she'd ever feel lighthearted again.

She finally caught up with Ethy and the two of them pedaled on across town until they reached Peter Street. There they threw their bicycles by the door that led up to Denzil's loft and pelted up the stairs to tell him what had happened.

3.

The Widow stood in the middle of the road until the two girls were out of sight. She saw a curtain move in the window of a neighbouring house and turned in its direction. Whoever had been watching from the window had now ducked out of sight.

"You, too," the Widow said. "I'll ruin you all. I'll bring down such a storm on this town that there won't be anyone left after its tempest and roar to remember it."

But first she would deal with this ragtag gaggle of miserable urchins and the like who thought they could prove any sort of a match for her.

Faint laughter spilled from the shadows alongside the hedge as she entered her garden, but she ignored it. She knelt down by the stoop and unfolded the newspapers from around her fetch. Her eyes teared as she took in the damage that the small creature had sustained.

"There, there," she crooned, gently lifting Windle from the papers. "Mother will have you well again, my sweet."

Her heart broke at the pitiful whimpers that even her gentle handling drew out of the fetch.

This would be redressed, she swore.

"On the graves of my mother and grandmother," she said, looking into the shadows where they collected against the side of the cottage. "Do you hear me? Let them never know rest if I fail to keep my vow."

We hear, the shadows whispered.

"Will you lend me what I need?"

Whatever you need.

And then the shadows rang again with that too familiar laughter, hollow and mocking.

The Widow merely regarded them for a long moment, then opened the door to her cottage and carried Windle inside.

4.

High on Mabe Hill, overlooking the town of Bodbury, were the ruins of an old church called Creak-a-vose after the ancient barrow mound upon which it had been built. A rambling affair, its bell tower had fallen in on itself and one of its walls had tumbled down. Its roof was open to the air. The remaining three walls were covered with vines and ivy and home to birds and one owl. It was there that the conspirators met as evening fell, straggling into the ruins by ones and twos until all, except Ratty Friggens, were gathered.

"I fear the worst," Denzil said when another half hour had dragged by and the Tatters boy still hadn't made an appearance. "After what the girls told me . . ."

Henkie nodded grimly. "The bloody Widow must have got to him."

Jodi's happiness at finally being freed from the confines of Lizzie's office had taken a downward turn as she learned of the narrow escapes made by Kara and Ethy. Ratty's absence simply made her feel worse.

It was still an hour's walk across farmers' pastures and moorland to the field where the Men-an-Tol stood with its two outriding standing stones, one on either side of its hole. Taupin had reckoned that if they left Creak-a-vose come dusk, they would reach the tolmen just as the moon was rising. The argument now was as to who would go.

"The children must be sent back to town," Denzil said. "We can't be responsible for harm coming to any more of them, you."

The other adults nodded in agreement, but Kara shook her head.

"We're coming," she said.

"Don't start," Henkie told her.

But Kara stood her ground.

"It will be too dangerous," Lizzie said. "You've done your share already—more than your share."

Taupin had also reckoned that they'd had such an easy time of it for the later part of the afternoon because the Widow had been lying low, seeing to the wounds of her fetch.

"We're not scared," Ethy said, though even in the dim light they could all see her trembling.

"You don't understand," Kara added. "It's not that we *want* to come; we just don't have any other choice."

Ethy nodded.

"We have to stick together," Peter said.

"None of us wants to be on our own when the Widow sends her creatures out to hunt us down," Kara said.

"I hadn't thought of that," Taupin said.

But Denzil still disagreed. "She'll be too concerned with us to trouble anyone else tonight," he said.

"How can you be sure?" Kara asked.

"I . . ." Denzil looked to the others for help, but no one could offer any. "I can't," he finished lamely.

"So there you have it," Kara said firmly. "We all go."

"If we're going," Taupin put in, "then it'll have to be quickly. If we're to make it to the stone by moonrise, that is."

Denzil looked around one last time at the other adults, hoping that someone could think of a better solution than bringing the children along with them, but there was still no help to be found. Lizzie sighed and shook her head. Taupin shrugged. Henkie grumbled into his beard.

"No other way about it that I can see," the big man said.

"Maybe we shouldn't go at all," Jodi piped up. "Any of us. We could sit out the night in a boat, out on the bay where she can't get near us."

"Sea dead," Peter muttered.

"She didn't call up any sea dead last night," Jodi said.

"It was probably too late at night," Kara said, "or it all happened too quickly for her. Perhaps it takes time to call them up."

"Perhaps there's no such thing," Denzil offered.

Taupin smiled. "Still begrudging what lies at the end of your nose?"

"Just because one mad thing is true, it doesn't mean it all is," Denzil replied.

"How can you look at Jodi and not accept—"

"I accept she's a Small, you," Denzil said. "But the secret to science is that one should be able to arrive at the same set of results every time one has set up a specific experiment or set of conditions. It has to be repeatable—nothing else will do. I can see Jodi is a Small, and she remains a Small, therefore such a thing can be."

"And the Widow's magics?"

"I can accept that she's capable of turning a normal-sized being into a Small and I will remain open to her other powers for safety's sake, but that doesn't necessarily mean she can do all that a witch from the folktales can."

"Like raising the dead?" Henkie asked.

"Exactly."

"Can't be done?"

Denzil nodded firmly.

"Then what do you have to say about my mate Briello who you were gabbing with last night?"

"I . . ."

"It grows late," Lizzie interrupted.

Denzil blinked at her for a moment, then nodded. "We should go."

They trooped outside and stood in a bunch.

"Seawater works against the Widow and the creatures she makes,"

Henkie said, "but what about these sea dead? What'll we do if we run into them?"

They each had satchels carrying balloons filled with salt water, or watersacks filled with the same. They were heavy, but no one complained.

"We'll have to hope that we're going too far inland for them to come," Taupin said. "Come along now, and watch your step."

With the moon still below the horizon, it was dark out in the fields. Henkie complained about the lack of light. He had a big hammer stuck in his belt and had also carried up an oil lamp.

"It's not like she won't track us down," he said.

"Only why make it easier for her?" Lizzie asked him.

The big man's reply was a wordless sound that rumbled deep in his chest.

"If we should get separated," Denzil said, always the worrier, "should we plan to meet back here—at the church?"

With that agreed upon, they finally set off.

Taupin led the way cross country, following trails that only he knew, acquiring his knowledge of them from his constant traveling about the countryside that surrounded the town. He knew which fields had boggy patches that needed to be avoided, which hedgerows could be slipped through with the least amount of effort, where there were nettles and where there weren't.

The fields opened up into ragged moorland as they neared the Men-an-Tol. Sweeps of heather, dried ferns, and prickly gorse spread out on all sides of them, but were soon lost to easy view as ragged mists rose up from the ground with the cooling of the night air.

"Good weather for hummocks," Peter whispered.

"Don't even mention anything to do with ghosts," Denzil warned him.

He was holding Ethy's hand and could feel her trembling beside him at the very thought of some ethereal hummock rising up from the gorse to pluck at her clothing.

They reached the holed stone just as the moon was peeking over the horizon, giving the mists an even ghostlier air. Photographs and etchings gave the tolmen a height and majesty that it didn't have in real life. The circular stone came to just barely above Henkie's waist, but the hole was large enough for even Peter to crawl through, and there remained an air of mystery and ancient riddles about it despite its small size. The rising mists added to its sense of otherworldly glamour.

Shivering, they all gathered about the stone and looked at one another.

"What do we do now?" Kara asked.

"I have to go nine times through the hole in the stone," Jodi piped.

Her throat was getting sore again from constantly having to shout to be heard.

"Do the rest of us do anything?" Peter asked as Lizzie stepped towards the stone with Jodi cupped in her hands.

"Watch, I suppose," Jodi said.

"Should we make a circle of seawater around the stone to protect us from the witch's creatures?" Henkie asked.

"That would kill the vegetation," Taupin said.

"Who's to mind?"

"Maybe what we're calling up from the stone?"

"There's that," Henkie agreed.

He set his oil lamp down on the ground at his feet and fingered the haft of his hammer.

"Are you ready?" Lizzie asked Jodi.

"What's to do?" she replied, sounding cockier than Denzil knew she must be feeling.

Lizzie passed her through the hole in the stone.

"That's one," Henkie said.

Nothing happened, except that the mists continued to deepen, hanging low to the moors, while the moon climbed steadily up in the sky. As Lizzie continued to pass Jodi through the hole in the Men-an-Tol, one voice, then another, joined Henkie's counting until they were all counting with him.

"Seven."

Denzil cocked his ear, thinking that he had heard something. He sensed something approaching, *felt* it deep in his bones. It wasn't the Widow, or any of her creatures. It was more a sound. A strange sort of music, distant and eerie. Unfamiliar, but he felt as though he'd known it all his life.

"Eight."

The music grew until he could begin to pick out the instruments. He could hear harping in it and fiddle, the hollow drumbeat of a crowdy crawn and a breathy flute. But there were no musicians, just the moor.

He could tell that the others also heard it now as they lifted their heads and tried to peer through the mists that surrounded them. A faint light caught Denzil's eye. He turned back to look at the tolmen where a glow like the last ember of a fire hovered in the center of the stone's hole.

Lizzie brought Jodi through the hole and around the outside of the stone again. As she started to put her through for the final time, the music swelled around them.

"Nine," Henkie breathed, his voice alone, the others all hushed.

Light flared from the hole, piercing and bright. The music had risen to a crescendo with the flare, then faded to dying echoes as the light died, winked out, was gone.

Henkie fumbled with a match, muttering to himself until he finally got his oil lamp lit. The lamp's light cast a dim glow over the stone where Lizzie stood staring down at her empty palms.

"She's gone," Lizzie said. "She simply vanished. . . ."

With the light, Denzil thought. With the music.

Deep in his chest he felt a pang of loss.

"Jodi . . ." he whispered.

Would he ever see her again?

"Oh, bloody hell," Henkie said.

Denzil looked up to see what had agitated the artist this time and his own heart sank. Coming out of the mists on all sides of them were shambling man-shapes. A bog-reek was in the air, low and cloying. Cutting above it came the sharp scent of the sea: salt and brine; the smell of wet seaweed and rotting fish.

Why did he have to be wrong again? Denzil asked.

But wrong he was.

For these were drowned men that encircled the stone, drowned men called up from the sea graves that marched across the moors and fields to confront them here in this place.

The Widow *could* call up the sea dead.

5.

From the dark night on the moors outside Bodbury, the ninth passage through the stone's hole plunged Jodi into a world of bright light.

Daylight, she realized as her eyes adjusted to the glare.

A sunny day.

In a different world.

Oh raw we. . . .

She found herself to be the same tiny size she'd been in the other world. She was sitting in a bed of dried ferns and looking straight at the Men-an-Tol, which had either come with her to this world, or existed here as well. The sunlight gleamed on its stone.

How could this be real?

And that made her want to laugh—hysterically, perhaps, but laugh all the same. For here she'd just spent the better part of two days the size of a mouse and she was thinking that magical otherworlds were impossible?

But still. . . .

"Jodi."

She turned at the sound of that familiar voice to find a stranger facing her—but a stranger with eyes she knew, whose body, for all its physical unfamiliarity, stood in the same stance that someone else's body had often stood, who stepped towards her with a step that was also familiar.

And she had never seen him before in her life.

He was small, just as she was, which made him exactly the right size, she supposed. His ears tapered to small points at their tops, small gold hoops in each lobe; his hair was curly and golden and also swirled up to form a bit of a point at the top of his head. His eyes were familiar, his face merry, his body slender in a shirt, jacket, and trousers of mottled moorland colours. He was barefoot.

She knew him. She didn't know him.

"Edern . . . ?" she asked.

The stranger nodded.

"I'm grateful for your coming," he said.

Constant Billy

The stories are always waiting, always listening for names;
when they hear the names they're listening for
they swallow the people up.

—RUSSELL HOBAN, from *The Medusa Frequency*

Janey wasn't ready for more bad news, but that was what was waiting for her when she and Clare finally got back to the house on Duck Street.

"I'm sorry, my fortune," the Gaffer said. "I rang up Kit as you asked me to do and she told me she was about to call you herself. It's about your American tour."

Janey could feel her heart sinking.

"What about it?" she asked.

"It's been canceled."

"Canceled? But . . . ?"

She looked to Felix for help, but found only sympathy.

"Oh, Janey," Clare said, laying a hand on her arm. "That's awful."

"How can it be canceled?" Janey asked. "Did she say why?"

The Gaffer shook his head. "She had no idea. She said she would look into it, but couldn't expect to have any word back until tomorrow, it being Sunday and all. I'm sorry, my love. I know you were looking forward to it."

"It's not just that. It . . ."

First that odd message from the *Rolling Stone* reporter this morning about how his editor had canceled her participation in his article, and now this. It wasn't coincidence. Someone was out to make her life as miserable as they possibly could. And now, after the talk she and Clare had had with Peter Goninan, she could make an educated guess as to who that someone was.

"It's Madden," she said. "It's that John Madden."

Clare nodded in slow agreement. "If what Mr. Goninan told us about him is true, then I think you're right. He's set upon getting the book from you and until you give it to him, he's going to keep after you until you don't feel you have any choice *but* to give it to him."

"I think we're missing something here," Felix said.

Janey looked at the confusion on his and her grandfather's features. Sighing, she plunked herself down on the sofa beside Felix.

"We learned an awful lot from Peter Goninan," she said.

The Gaffer hrumphed. "I hope you listened with a grain of salt. The man *is* half-daft."

"But the other half," Clare said with a smile as she took a seat, "is fascinating."

"I like him," Janey added. "I like him an awful lot."

The Gaffer shook his head. "Now that do belong," he said. "Peter Goninan charming anyone, little say you."

"I'm easy to get along with," Janey protested. At the raised eyebrows that statement called up from everyone in the room, she added, "Well, in a manner of speaking."

"I wasn't thinking of you so much, my love," the Gaffer said, "as I was of Peter. He's such an odd bird"—Janey couldn't stop a little smile at that description of Goninan—"sticking to himself up on that farm of his the way he does. Gives new meaning to the word recluse, doesn't he just? I'm surprised he even spoke to you at all."

"He's dying," Janey said.

The Gaffer fell silent, considering that.

"Maybe the reason he keeps to himself is because there's never been anyone else interested in the kinds of things he is," Janey added. "That doesn't make him bad—just eccentric. He probably got into the habit of being alone when he was younger and now he just prefers it that way."

"I never thought of it quite like that," the Gaffer said. "He was always—standoffish. Seemed to hold himself to be better than the rest of us. Didn't care for games or fishing or anything that the rest of us did, just his books and his birds. The only ones of us who had any time for him were Billy and Morley Jenkin—but the Jenkins moved up country just before we all took our O levels and Billy never seemed to spend that much time with him—not that I ever saw."

"Maybe he just seemed standoffish," Clare said. "It's not easy to be mates when you don't think you have anything in common with the rest of the blokes."

The Gaffer nodded.

"That woman," Janey said. "Her name's Helen Bray and she's his niece. She's nursing him."

"And he's dying, you say?"

Janey nodded.

"Makes me feel a bit of a rotter."

"I know exactly what you mean, Gramps. When I think of how I used to laugh at his stick figure out by the cliffs, I just feel awful."

"You couldn't know," Felix said.

The Gaffer nodded. "But we should have been more charitable." Janey sighed, then sat up a little straighter.

"Anyway," she said, "he knew all about the tattoo. It belongs to a hermetic order called the Order of the Grey Dove and the head of it is this John Madden who's so mad keen to get his hands on Billy's book."

She and Clare went on to relate what Goninan had told them of Madden's background, of the different states of consciousness, and how an artifact or talisman like *The Little Country* was a kind of shortcut to attaining higher planes of being and the subsequent power that came with them.

"The years of study are what prepares a person to be responsible when they finally attain those higher states," Clare finished up. "Without it, they have power, but not the wisdom to use it properly. Responsibly."

Neither Felix nor the Gaffer had much to say and Janey knew exactly why. It all sounded a bit mad. Laid out as they had just presented it, she wasn't all that sure herself anymore as to how true any of it was. It made a kind of sense—but first you needed to take that quantum leap forward that accepted the fact that paranormal abilities were possible in the first place.

"He also told us about Lena," Janey said. "Apparently her father, Roland Grant, is a big-shot American businessman who also just happens to be a member of the Order's Inner Circle."

She went on to name the other three.

"I've heard of Eva Diesel," Felix said. "She doesn't seem to fit in with what you're telling us. So far as I can tell, from what I've read by her, she's heavily into humanist causes and environmental concerns."

"It's supposed to be a facade," Clare said. "Mr. Goninan said that if you took the time to thoroughly document all the various causes she's supported, together with the eventual ramifications of those that were implemented, you'd find that her hands are just as dirty as the rest of them."

Felix shook his head. "You know what this sounds like? One of those nutty conspiracy fantasies. Paranoia running out of control. It doesn't seem to fit the real world."

"I can't help that," Janey said.

She could feel her back getting up and tried hard to stay calm.

"What about things like the Christine Keeler affair or the American Watergate?" Clare asked. "They seemed just as Byzantine and improbable when news of them first surfaced."

Felix smiled. "But they didn't involve magic."

"You're just being obstinate," Janey said.

"No, I'm not. I'm just trying to put it into perspective, that's all. I mean, it's like seriously considering Elvis still being alive."

"It's not like that at all," Clare told him, "and you know it."

"Okay," Felix said. "I stand corrected. But how's this Goninan, living way out in the sticks the way he does, supposed to have the inside line on all this stuff?"

Maybe his birds tell him, Janey thought.

"That's not really the point, my gold," the Gaffer said.

Felix turned to him. "What do you mean?"

"Well, there's the book itself."

Janey nodded. "We can prove it with the book. You've read it, Gramps. What's it about?"

"I was just looking at it again last night," he replied, "but I remember the story well enough that I didn't need to read it again. It takes place in an imaginary town, very much like Penzance, but set around the turn of the century, or perhaps even a bit before that."

Janey and Felix both nodded in agreement, but their features grew increasingly more puzzled as the Gaffer went on to relate his version of *The Little Country,* of the captain of a fishing lugger called *The Talisman* and the orphan girl who'd disguised herself as a boy to work on the boat with him.

Clare, not having read the book herself, could make no comment, but Janey and Felix were both shaking their heads when the Gaffer was finally done outlining the novel for them.

"That's not the story I'm reading," Janey said finally.

"And it's not the one I'm reading either," Felix said. "Mine's about a sailor, all right, but he works on a freighter. He comes to the same town, and he meets a girl with the same name, but she's older than your orphan, Tom, and it looks to me like the book's going to be a romance as much as it is an adventure story."

Janey felt an odd tingle start up in the base of her neck and travel down her spine.

"There aren't any sailors in the one I'm reading," she said, "but there's lots of magic. The story's just thick with it."

Clare looked at them one by one. "This is weird," she said.

"Very weird," Felix agreed. "I think I'm ready to listen to what your Peter Goninan had to say about all of this."

"Can I see the book?" Clare asked.

Janey fetched the copy of *The Little Country* and brought it over to where Clare was sitting. She perched on the arm of the chair as Clare opened the book to the first page of text and started to read.

"What's the first line say?" Janey asked.

" 'She hadn't always been crippled, but she might as well have been,' " Clare read.

Janey shook her head. "That's not what I see."

She read out the opening line that was there for her, then looked up at the others. It wasn't even remotely the same. Her version opened with a line of dialogue.

The tingle in her spine grew stronger.

"It isn't possible—is it?" she asked.

The Gaffer only shrugged helplessly. Felix crossed the room to where the two women were sitting and, looking over Janey's shoulder, read the opening line of his own version aloud.

"It's really true," Clare said in a voice as quiet as a whisper. "It really *is* different for everyone. . . ."

"Listen," Janey said suddenly. "Can you hear it?"

As shadows sometimes seemed to move when viewed from the corner of one's eye, so she could hear—from the corner of her ear, as it were—a faint hint of music. She couldn't pick out either the melody line or the instrumentation. It was too vaguely defined for that. But she could hear it. She knew it was there.

And she'd heard it before. It was that same music that she'd been trying to pick out yesterday afternoon when the *Rolling Stone* reporter had come 'round and interrupted her.

"Music," the Gaffer said. "It's like music. . . ."

Janey reached over to Clare's lap and gently shut the book.

The sound disappeared as soon as the cover was closed, vanishing as though a turntable arm had been lifted from the spiraling matrix of a record's grooves. But the tingling sensation that Janey felt was still with her.

"Magic," she said.

The others nodded in agreement. For a long time none of them could speak, each lost in the wonder of the moment.

Janey hugged the reality of the book's enchantment to her like the precious secret it was.

Magic was real.

Smalls and . . . that music . . . the hidden music that was the title of Billy's second book . . . the music that she'd always wanted to hear. To be able to play it. . . .

It was all real.

And then another reality pressed to the fore of her mind. If the magic was real, then so was John Madden's Order of the Grey Dove. And the danger they presented lay on more levels than simply the physical world.

"Mr. Goninan said the book is a talisman," she said. "A talisman that should only be wielded by its proper guardian. And that if none of us was that guardian, then we should hide it—keep it safely in trust for when that guardian would come for it."

"That guardian won't be John Madden," Clare said.

Janey shook her head. "And I don't think it's any one of us, either, except . . ." Her voice trailed off.

"Except what, my flower?" the Gaffer asked.

"I feel so close to its music. . . ."

"Where can we hide the book?" Clare asked, ever practical.

"I don't know. I . . ." Janey looked around the room. "I can't think of *any* place that would be safe."

"Mr. Goninan said the book would tell us," Clare reminded her.

Janey nodded. "That's right. He did. Only if it does, I haven't got to that bit in it yet."

"We should hide it quickly," the Gaffer said.

"We have to finish reading it first," Janey said.

"Now is that wise, my robin?"

"That's what Mr. Goninan said. Until we finish reading it, a crack of its magic will stay open and Madden will be able to use it to track the book down."

"Tom's already finished it," Felix said. "That leaves the three of us. We could sit together on the couch."

"Ta," Clare said.

Felix's eyebrows rose quizzically. "What for?"

"For including me."

"There was never any question," Janey said. "It's just . . ." She shook her head at the look that came over her friend's features. "Oh, no," she added. "I wasn't changing my mind about your reading it. I was just wondering if we shouldn't go through the rest of Billy's manuscripts and the like first. He might have made notes on the book—written something that would explain things to us better."

"Want me to get them?" Felix asked.

Janey nodded. "There's the box in the kitchen that we almost lost to that burglar, and then more in the open chest in the attic."

She went to help him bring down the chest. The Gaffer set about making some tea while Clare prepared a plate of sandwiches. By the time it was all ready, the living room of the Gaffer's house looked as though a bomb had hit it with manuscripts, papers, magazines, and the like piled every which way one turned.

It was Clare who found the second piece of magic, hidden away in Dunthorn's chest.

"Look at this," she said, holding up an old photograph.

It was tinted in sepia tones, the image area fading near the edges. The surface of the photo was wrinkled from having been bent sometime in the past, but the image was still easy to make out.

"That's my Addie when she was a girl," the Gaffer said.

"Can I see?" Janey asked, reaching for it.

The photo showed a young girl of about eleven sitting in an old fat-armed easy chair. She was dressed in an old-fashioned dress and brown lace-up shoes and her hair hung in ringlets. There was a cheerful smile on her face and her gaze was fixed on something just over what must have been the photographer's shoulder—probably her father, making a face at her to get her to smile, Janey thought.

Most of the rest of the photo was blurry, but she could make out curtains and a picture on the wall behind the chair, a door directly to the right of it, while on the left—

Janey's breath went short.

There on the left arm of the chair was the ghostly image of a little man. He was dressed in a white shirt and dark trousers. His head was bald, but he had a full, trimmed beard. And he was playing a fiddle, hunched over the instrument that was in the crook of his shoulder.

A Small.

Janey's tingling sensation intensified as she looked at the little man. She could almost hear the music he was playing.

"What is it?" Felix asked.

"There," Janey said. "On the left arm of the chair."

"Looks like a smudge of light—there was probably a window open behind the chair and the light coming through it reflected on the camera's lens. They didn't exactly have the best equipment in those days."

But Janey was shaking her head. "*Look* at it," she said. "Take a *really* close look at it."

So Felix did, with Clare and the Gaffer peering over his shoulder.

"What am I supposed to be seeing?" Felix asked.

Janey pointed. "If that's an arm . . ."

"It's a little man!" Clare cried. "Oh, my God. There's a little man sitting there, playing a fiddle."

Felix started to laugh, but then both he and the Gaffer saw the Small as well.

"Garm," the Gaffer said. "I never."

"That's unbelievable," Felix added. "Even if it's just a trick of the light, it's just fabulous."

"It's a Small," Janey said. "That's where 'The Smalls' and *The Hidden People* came from. *That* picture."

"Or maybe," Clare said with a mischievous gleam in her eye, "it only confirmed something he already knew."

"I'll bet you're right," Janey said.

"I've seen that photo a hundred times," the Gaffer said, "but I never noticed the little man in it before."

"You've got another copy?" Felix asked.

The Gaffer nodded.

"Can we see it?" Janey asked.

"I'll see if I can find it, my love."

He rummaged about through some photo albums in the bottom of the bookshelf near the hearth until he finally found the one he was looking for.

"Here it is," he said, holding the album open so they could all see it.

"And the Small's there as well," Janey said. "I wonder if he's in any more photos?"

She started to reach for the album, but Felix touched her shoulder.

"It's starting to get on," he said. "Maybe we should get to the book. If Madden's already in town as your friend Goninan said he was, we probably don't have a whole lot of time."

Clare nodded. "I'm a fast reader so I'll be able to catch up with the rest of you quickly."

"And in the meantime," the Gaffer said, "I'll continue to look through all of this."

He waved his hand at Dunthorn's papers and manuscripts that were littering the room. True to his word, he sat himself down in his reading chair and picked up another sheaf of papers. The others made themselves comfortable on the sofa, Felix in the middle, Janey and Clare on either side of him, and started to read.

"It's not his usual style of writing, is it?" Clare said as she turned the page to the second chapter. "It's not as well written as his other books."

"I thought that, too," Janey said. "I suppose it's because *we're* telling the story to ourselves."

Felix tapped the book with his finger.

"Let's just read and save the critiques for later," he said.

"Spoilsport," Clare said.

"Bully," Janey added.

Felix smiled at the pair of them and shook his head.

"Just read," he said.

2.

John Madden sat quietly in the chair by the window in Gazo's hotel room and watched the movement of the waves on Mount's Bay, his mind far from the view that his eyes took in. Behind him, Gazo was still sitting on the bed, reading a magazine. Grant, was in the other chair, his daughter sitting by his knee. They had been conversing with each other in soft voices for a time, but now the only sound in the room was that of Gazo turning the pages of his magazine.

Madden appreciated the quiet. It let him still his own thoughts. It let him put to rest all the inner conversation that the mind will always amuse itself with if given free rein, allowing the antiquity of the land to soak into his soul.

From the westernmost tip of Land's End to where the Tamar River followed the Devon-Cornwall border, almost making an island of Cornwall, the familiar spirit of the countryside spoke to him. Its quiet murmur filled him with its presence, whispering ancient stories and secrets, unlocking riddles, replenishing his store of its hidden wisdoms that had slowly leaked away since he had last walked its shores.

Time stole all—even from one such as Madden who hoarded these secret resources as a miser might his gold. So now he filled the holes in his memory, renewed his bond with the past and the unaging mysteries that history carried into the present. This was the real magic to which he was heir: the understanding that neither logic nor emotion on its own was enough to keep a man's soul pure, and thereby at the peak of its power. The mind narrowed and blocked the world into understandable packages with which it could deal, but the soul required a broader view, one that encompassed both the microcosm of the mind's perceptions as well as the macrocosm of

the world as a whole with which it must interact. Less than a perfect
harmony of the two left one crippled.

So Madden drank in the sweet secret that was the underlying
heartbeat of the land. He let the rhythm of his own pulse join with
its ancient rhythm until the two hearts beat as one.

The one dissonance was the trail of his protégé as he walked heed-
lessly across the land's mystery, disturbing and unraveling its harmony with his unconsidered intrigues and scheming.

Heavy footsteps; a thoughtless tread.

From the vantage point of perception that he now inhabited, Madden could read every irresponsible move Michael had made, every
tenet of the Order that he had set aside.

For, Madden realized now, Michael had forgotten the first rule of
dealing with the sheep. The trick to ruling them was to not let them
know that they were being ruled. Treat them well, and they were as
happy as their wool-bearing cousins in the fields, contented with their
lot. One needed to cull the odd dissident, or firmly yet subtly deal
with the odd disguised wolf that might creep in among the innocents.

It was plain common sense. Happy sheep were sheep that did what
they were told and caused no disharmony or inconvenience. They let
the gears that run the world turn freely, without need for repair.
Sometimes patience was necessary, for subtle control required equally
subtle solutions to problems that did arise, but the rewards were
proportionate to the effort one expended.

Michael's present methods gained immediate results, but they also
required far too great an expenditure in time and resources *after* the
fact to tie up the loose ends. The point Michael missed was that,
certainly, he could remove an interference such as the Mabley woman
had proven to be, but then he had to deal with the ramifications of
that act as well as continue with his principal course of action. Too
many such deviations from the central project and one lost one's
control of the situation.

As witness the present state of affairs.

Madden sighed.

A great deal of work lay ahead in bringing some semblance of
order back to what Michael had mismanaged. For at the heart of it
all lay the secret that Dunthorn had hidden away: the key.

Madden was still undecided as to whether or not it was an artifact
of some sort, a physical talisman that would unlock a mystery of
which he still lacked a full understanding, but he knew he must have

it. He had also come to realize that the key must be acquired with the least amount of coercion. It could be stolen, but the cost must not be in blood.

He had fallen victim to that same erroneous mismanagement when first confronting Dunthorn; and he had paid for that mistake. Paid with decades of lost time—years in which, if he had had the key, he would have been that much further along in his ambitions.

The lost time nagged at him, like a heartache that came and went, and had no cure. But it had taught him patience, and he wouldn't make the same error twice.

He doubted that the key would ever be willingly handed over to him—which would be the optimum method of acquisition. But he could see to it that when it finally came into his possession, it did so with the least amount of harm to its present guardian.

To do that, he must first deal with Michael.

There was no indication on his features as to what went through his mind. To all intents and purposes, it appeared as though he was merely watching the view from the window. But that was another part of Madden's magic: control. He was aware of every thread of movement about him, yet gave no sign that he was even paying attention in the first place. So it was that he could sense the almost imperceptible movement of Lena shifting her position slightly and knew that she was about to speak before she ever said a word.

"I've been thinking about the Littles, Daddy," she said.

Madden glanced over at her.

"What about them?" he asked before her father could reply.

"Well, shouldn't we warn them—about Bett, I mean?"

"And what do we tell them about *how* we know?" Madden shook his head. "No. Much as I will regret it if any harm comes to them, we must play this out without warning them."

But he looked more carefully at Lena, and wondered. It was odd how her question had cut so close to the turn his own thoughts had taken, but then he realized that her concern grew not from the same source as his own. He worried about despoiling the key by acquiring it through violence. She worried for the Littles themselves; and their friends. Most of her worry was probably for this Felix Gavin.

And that was odd as well, he thought. In all the years he'd known her—watching her grow from the child she had been to the woman she was today—he had never sensed in her an interest for anything other than a fulfillment of her own desires and amusements. Her trip here had softened her, made her care for others—and it wasn't simply her libido driving that concern; her compassion was selfless.

Had the land touched her?

But if that was so, then why had it not left its mark on Michael as well? The reincarnated soul that his body carried had its roots in this countryside from a previous life. Surely the ancient mysteries the land carried, the heartbeat that Madden's own pulse still twinned, would have spoken to Michael as well.

Perhaps they had.

And Michael had heard only the darker tones in its music.

"We could say Bett and we represent rival publishers," Lena was saying. "You know. We've heard a rumour of a rare manuscript and each company would consider it a coup to be the first to acquire . . ." Her voice trailed off as she took in Madden's sudden intent interest in her proposal.

"A manuscript," Madden said. "Of course."

That was where the secret lay—in an unpublished manuscript. What better place to hide it than somewhere in among Dunthorn's papers and manuscripts? And to think he'd only wanted that paperwork for the clues it might afford him.

He had spent years trying to guess the key's secret—its physical shape, did it even have one. He had thought it would be small, and something that could be easily carried—a coin, an earring, a tie pin. And it would have something of the land in it—tin was his best guess, considering how much the tin mines had once been a part of Cornwall's economy. But it could have been bone, too, from one of the animals indigenous to the area; a simple fishbone. Or even a pebble. A chip of granite. A sliver of blue alvin stone.

The years of frustration had finally led him to consider his current pet theory: that it might not even be something tangible at all. It might be a phrase. A snatch of music.

And he knew now—absolutely *knew*—that he'd been partially right. The key was hidden in a manuscript. But it was only by reading it aloud that the key would be activated, the door unlocked. . . .

"Why did I never think of that before?" he murmured.

He probably had. But the concept, the idea, had simply evaded him. Was that another part of its enchantment? That the very *idea* of it would be hidden, so that just thinking about the talisman's shape or its whereabouts made it all the more secret?

"Think of what?" Grant asked.

But as Madden was deciding how much he cared to tell his associate, Lena was already replying.

"It's hidden in a manuscript," she said. She glanced at Madden.
"That's it, isn't it?"

"It seems likely," Madden admitted. "All things considered."

Lena sighed. "And I almost had my hands on a whole box of
them. . . ."

"Maybe it's just the directions to find the thing that are in a manuscript," Grant said.

"Either way, we need to acquire them," Madden said.

But he already knew that somewhere in Dunthorn's paperwork
the key itself lay hidden, or else how could the Littles—knowingly
or unknowingly—have woken it? How else could he sense its call?

"So what do we do?" Grant asked. "Do we still wait for Bett to
show up, or do we go after the papers ourselves?"

Madden wished it were that simple.

"Let me think about it," he said.

3.

Although they still had a handful of chapters left to read, they all
decided to take a break around five. Felix stood up to stretch while
Janey sat down on the floor beside the Gaffer to look at the other
photos he'd found scattered in among the manuscripts and magazines. She studied each one carefully, but there was no little man in
any of them. Nor anything else remarkable either. They were just
old sepia photographs, fascinating in their own right for the windows
they opened onto Mousehole's past, but of no more help than any
of the manuscripts that the Gaffer had skimmed through proved
to be.

Clare remained on the couch, holding *The Little Country,* rubbing
her thumb against its leather cover.

"Did you find anything useful in the storylines you read?" she
asked the others.

Felix shook his head. "Not really. Mine's turned into a murder
mystery. Hasn't got any magic in it at all."

"That's probably because you don't go for that kind of thing in
the first place," Clare said.

"I read his other books—and enjoyed them both."

"But you don't normally go for that kind of a book, do you?"

"Not really."

Clare turned to Janey. "How about you?"

"I'm not sure," Janey said. "Is the Men-an-Tol in either of yours?"

Clare and Felix both nodded.

"But I don't think it's in the same spot as it is in our world," Felix said. "At least in respect to Penzance, if the town in the book is even supposed to be Penzance."

"Is the stone closer?" Janey asked.

"Just an hour's walk."

"It's the same in mine," Clare said.

"And is there a high hill behind the town with a ruined church on it?"

Again Clare and Felix nodded.

"They were both in the story I read as well, my treasure," the Gaffer said.

"How did he do it?" Clare asked. "How could all the stories have the same elements, the same characters and settings, and still be so different?"

"It's like one of those books you hate," Janey said with a grin. "What are they called again?"

"Interactive fiction," Clare replied with a look of distaste.

"Maybe the book's really a magical computer," Janey said. "We all open the same program, but we each use it differently."

"Why were you asking about the Men-an-Tol?" Felix wanted to know.

"Because it gave me an idea," Janey said. "A daft sort of an idea, but then again the whole situation's a bit mad, isn't it?"

"I don't think I'd blink at anything anymore," the Gaffer said.

Janey nodded. "Did you ever hear of the Men-an-Tol being the entrance to a prehistoric barrow?"

"Of course," her grandfather replied.

Clare nodded in agreement.

"Well, what if it's not?" Janey said. "What if it's the entrance to the Barrow *World*?"

"Do you mean a different world entirely?"

"Where the piskies live," Janey agreed, smiling.

"That's just a story . . ." the Gaffer began, then he slowly shook his head. "What am I saying?"

"Nine times through the hole," Janey said. "Folklore says that will cure your ills. But my version of the book says that if you do it when the moon's rising, it will open a door to the Barrow World."

"And then what?" Felix asked.

"We put the book in and close the door."

Clare laughed. "You're right, Little. That is a daft idea."

"Maybe not," Felix said. "The rules have all changed now. Magic works."

Clare nodded. "Yes, but . . ." She looked from one to the other and then sighed. "It just seems too much."

"There've always been odd tales about moorland," the Gaffer said. "Hummocks and piskies and old barrow mounds. If enchantments are real, then it stands to reason that there would be a whole unseen world waiting to be discovered."

"I've sometimes felt that long before we learned about the book," Felix said.

"I know exactly what you mean," Janey said. "There've been times when I've been out toodling tunes by the cliffs when I've had the uncanniest feeling that there was more listening to me than the rocks and the grass, only there's never anyone, or *anything,* to be seen."

Felix nodded. "I've had that feeling, too. Especially when I'm playing near water."

"Music's magic anyway," Janey said. "Always has been. Why wouldn't it call to Smalls and the like if there really are such things?"

There came a knock at the door just then, interrupting their conversation.

"Tonight," Janey said as she went to get the door. "After we've finished the book, we'll go to the Men-an-Tol tonight and see. Oh, hello, Dinny," she added as she opened the door.

Dinny Boyd gave her an awkward smile. "Didn't know you had company, Janey. Maybe I should come back another time?"

But Janey was already pulling him inside. One look at him had told her that something was up, and considering how odd the past few days had been, she didn't doubt for a moment that it had something to do with all the other mad goings-on that had already disrupted her life.

"Hello, then," Dinny said, nodding to the others as Janey closed the door. "Lovely day it's been, hasn't it just?"

He looked, Janey thought, as though it had been anything but. She'd never seen him in such a sad state.

Tucking her arm in his, she walked him to a vacant chair where she sat him down.

"What's happened, Dinny?" she asked.

"I . . ." His gaze shifted from hers, returned as quickly. "Is it that obvious?"

" 'Fraid so."

"It's just—I don't know where to begin."

"I'll put on some tea," the Gaffer said.

Janey sat on the arm of the chair and took Dinny's hand. He looked up at her and gave her a vague smile that never quite reached his eyes.

"We've lost the farm," he said.

"Oh, no!" Clare cried.

Dinny nodded. "Dad got the oddest call from a man who said he'd bought out our lease and was evicting us."

"But they can't do that, can they?" Janey asked.

"I don't know. Dad rang up our solicitor, but he said there was nothing he could do until Monday morning. He's going to ring us back first thing."

Janey could feel her heart sinking. This had an uncomfortably familiar ring about it. First her participation in the *Rolling Stone* article, then her tour. . . .

"But if your solicitor can't do anything until Monday," Clare said, "than neither can this man, I should think."

Dinny sighed. "That's what Mum said. But this man—he never did give us his name—seemed very knowledgeable and sure of himself. He knew all the details of our lease and . . ."

He glanced at Janey.

Here it came now, she thought.

"He said it was because of you, Janey. He said you could stop the whole thing from being finalized. What did he mean?"

This was awful, Janey thought. How could she begin to explain?

"I've made myself an enemy," she said finally. "A very powerful one, it seems."

"I don't understand."

"Neither do I—not really. I . . ." She glanced at Clare. "I think you should ring up your mum," she said. "And, Gramps," she added to the Gaffer who'd just come in from the kitchen where he'd put on the kettle, "when Clare's done, perhaps you should ring up Chalkie and some of your other mates."

As Clare nodded, Janey gave Dinny a much edited version of the past few days. She left out any reference to the paranormal, concentrating instead on Madden and the apparent wide sphere of his influence.

"It doesn't make any sense," Dinny said. "What would this man want with an old book?"

"I think he stands to make a great deal of money from it," Janey replied.

It wasn't wholly a lie. Because money was power—an unpleasant reality that they were now having driven home to them. She just didn't know what else to say that wouldn't make Dinny think they'd all gone a bit bonkers. She certainly wasn't going to let anyone else start reading the book—not at this late date.

"Though Lord knows why he would need more," she said. "Any luck, Clare?" she added as her friend put down the receiver.

Clare shook her head. "Mum's fine. But there were two messages for me. Davie Rowe was by the house earlier today and Owen from the bookstore left a message for me to call him. I'm going to ring them both up now."

The others went back to their discussion as she picked up the receiver once more. The first call was short, the second longer.

"Well?" Janey asked.

Clare gave the Gaffer her seat by the phone so that he could make his own calls and returned to the sofa.

"Davie's mum hasn't seen him since he left the house late last night," she said. "And that doesn't bode well."

"Didn't know you were mates with him," Dinny said.

"Don't start her on him," Janey said.

Dinny shrugged. "Seems like a nice enough bloke to me."

"What about Owen?" Janey asked.

"Well, Owen," Clare said. "A man called him and told him that if he didn't give me the sack, he'd make sure that there wasn't a publisher that would supply him with a single other book until he did."

"How can they *do* this?" Janey cried. "Where's the bloody justice in it? I don't doubt that first thing Monday morning, we can call up the bank to find that the bloody bastards have managed to do something to our bank accounts as well."

She started to pace back and forth across the room, kicking a stack of manuscript pages across the carpet before Felix got her to sit down. By then the Gaffer was off the phone, his face grim. Janey buried her face in her hands.

"I don't want to know," she said, her voice muffled.

"That was Chalkie," the Gaffer said. "Someone killed Sara—his cat"—he added for Felix's sake—"and nailed her body to the tree 'round back of his house."

"Oh, no!" Janey cried. "What if they've got Jabez?"

She jumped from her seat and ran to the door. Flinging it open, she called out for the Gaffer's cat who came sauntering in after a few anxious moments and gave Janey an uncomprehending look as she swept him up into her arms to give him a hug. Janey kicked the door shut with her foot and returned to her seat on the sofa, still holding the cat.

"What do we *do*?" she asked.

Felix took charge. "There's not much *anyone* can do until Monday morning," he said, "so as I see it, we have to go on with our plan. We finish the book, then we hide it."

"But what's the point?" Janey said. "Even if we hide it so well that no one could ever find it, that still won't stop them from ruining our lives and that of every one of our friends."

"We'll fight them," Felix said.

The Gaffer shook his head. "That will cost money, my beauty. They'll take it to the courts and solicitors cost money—money that none of us have to spare. We're not rich folk like this John Madden."

"If the book's gone—gone forever," Felix said, "then there'll be nothing left to fight about, will there?"

"Unless they just want revenge," Janey said morosely.

"I still don't understand," Dinny said. "What's so special about this book? Why would a man want to ruin the lives of people he has never met, just for a book?"

"Greed," Clare said.

"Spite," Janey added.

"We'll stand up to him," Dinny said. "All the Boyds will. And our friends will stand by us, just as we'll stand by you."

"We appreciate that," the Gaffer said.

Dinny nodded, looking grimmer by the moment. "We should go to the police as well. There must be laws to protect us."

"But we can't prove anything against these people," Clare said. "We don't even know what they look like—except for that Grant woman in Penzance."

Janey glared. "And *don't* start me on her, either," she said.

"Then we'll just have to maneuver them into a position where we can prove it," Felix said.

"What do you mean?" Dinny asked.

Felix started to explain, but Janey shook her head.

"Don't talk," she said.

"Why not?"

She pointed to the shadows that had been growing in the corners of the room as the day drew to its end.

"Remember what we told you about what Mr. Goninan had to say about Madden and the shadows cast by man-made objects?" She shook her head. "We've been bloody fools. He'll have heard everything we've already talked about."

"What's old Peter have to do with this?" Dinny asked.

"It's too long to explain just now," Janey said. She turned back to Felix. "Maybe it's not true, this thing about the shadows and Madden; maybe it's impossible, but the magic in the book's real, isn't it?"

Dinny looked from one to the other in confusion. "Magic?" he said.

"It's a mad sort of a story," Janey told him.

Dinny stood up, obviously ill at ease.

"Perhaps I should be going," he said.

Janey nodded and saw him to the door. "I'm sorry that any of this had to come on you and your family."

"It wasn't your fault."

"We'll try to get things sussed out," she told him. "Don't worry about the farm. We'll think of something to stop this man before anything else happens."

"If you need any help . . ."

"We'll make sure to call you straightway," Janey said.

When she returned to the living room, the others were still arguing about magic and shadows and the like.

"If Mr. Goninan wouldn't talk about it in his house," Clare said, "and this Madden isn't even looking for *him* . . ."

The Gaffer pointed to a spot just above the front door where a small brass figurine of a piskie stood on the door frame—placed there for luck.

"Jan Penalurick will keep us safe from any kind of magical spying and harm," he said. "So long as we stay in the house."

"It's not really the same thing," Clare said, but the Gaffer merely shushed her.

"If you can accept unkind magics, my love," he said, "then you'll have to accept kindly ones as well."

Felix looked at Janey who simply nodded.

"I suppose," she said.

She picked up a worn photo of William Dunthorn and looked at those familiar features that she knew only through other photos.

It all centered around him.

Oh, Billy, she thought. Didn't you think about what you were doing when you magicked your book?

The Man Who Died and Rose Again

Christ's image is just the perfect symbol for our civilization. It's a perfect event for us—you have to die to survive. Because the personality is crucified in our society. That's why so many people collapse, why the mental hospitals are full. No one can survive the personality that they want, which is the hero of their own drama. That hero dies, is massacred, and the self that is reborn remembers that crucifixion.

—LEONARD COHEN, from an interview in *Musician*, July 1988

When Bett pulled the trigger of his automatic, the normal flow of time ceased to have meaning for Davie Rowe. He could almost see the bullet leave the muzzle of the revolver, the spark of light deep in the bore that had ignited the propulsion, the bullet's passage through the air that left a streaming trail of afterimages in its wake. The report of the shot was like a clap of thunder.

And then the bullet hit him, dead in the chest.

The pain started—sharp and central, first just above his heart where the bullet impacted, then in his shoulder, then in a wave that exploded through the remainder of his body.

He knew he was dead.

The fall to the ground took an age to complete—time enough for a thousand regrets to flood his mind, riding the pain.

That he'd never had a real friend.

That he'd never had a sweetheart.

That he'd never once looked in a mirror without cursing God or fate or whoever it was who was responsible for the ravaged features that looked back at him from his reflection.

That he'd never had the strength of will to make something of himself, never mind the hand that fate had dealt him.

That he'd never be the hero he'd imagined he could be, if he was just given half a bloody chance; a hero like those larger-than-life celluloid idols of his who stalked across the screen in the cinema down in Penzance.

That he'd die and not be missed, not be grieved for.

Except by his mother. And would she miss *him,* or merely the body that brought in what money it could to support them, the heart that was there for her to wound with her nagging and thoughtless words?

"If you didn't have such an evil mind, Davie," she would tell him, "God wouldn't have punished you with that face."

Davie Rowe didn't believe in God.

But he couldn't help but wonder if what she said was true. For he did have evil thoughts. Ugly thoughts of hurting those who mocked him. Of simply taking what he wanted because the world bloody well *owed* him, didn't it? Of having his will with someone like Clare. . . .

They weren't the thoughts of a hero.

There was no bravery in them. No decency.

He had lived in a constant state of rage. All that let him suppress the worst of his impulses was the knowledge that giving free rein to them would put him right back in prison. Locked in a cage like the animal he was in the eyes of the world.

It hadn't been compassion that stayed his hand; it had been the simple fear of returning to that cage.

And now he was dying.

He lay here dying as meaningless a death as his life had been with no chance to make good. Shot down like a dog, lying here in his own pooling blood. Unable to move, unable to feel anything but the pain and the wash of regret that was drowning him.

Like a dog; not a hero.

Every dog has its day. . . .

But, like all else in this world, he'd soon realized that the old homily was a lie as well, for this hound never got his day.

Last night he'd done the one good and important thing he'd ever accomplished in his life—saving Clare from Michael Bett—and his only reward was this: lying here with Bett's bullet in him, helplessly watching Bett approach to finish off.

Because of the odd change in Davie's sense of perception, Bett appeared almost comical as he moved closer. It was as though the air had turned to honey and Bett could barely make his way through the cloying thickness of it that impeded his progress.

But there was nothing humourous about the weapon in Bett's hand.

And dying was no joke—though maybe God, sitting up there in his great sky and looking down, was having a good laugh.

Bett leveled his weapon—slowly, slowly—and Davie braced himself for the second bullet.

It never came.

Bett turned away, distracted, and then through that same endless drag of time, like a slow-motion sequence in a cinema, moved off, away and out of Davie's range of vision.

Relief came in a flood that washed away the regrets and pain. Davie felt as though he were floating. The blue of the sky had never seemed so sharp. His ears had never been so attuned to sound—the waves lashing the rocks below, the rustle of the ferns and couch grass in the wind, a bird's call . . . all came to him with a clarity he had never experienced before.

He glanced at a dried fern and knew that the fern was a part of the clifftop moor, which was in turn a part of the land, which was part of Britain, which crouched in the sea, a part of the earth, which was part of the sky, and beyond, beyond . . . the stars, the galaxies, the universes . . . all connected . . . each an integral part of the other. . . .

And he was a part of it all as well. No better or worse than that singular frond of dried fern. As important as the queen in Buckingham Palace, as important as a vole rooting about at the base of a hedgerow.

Dying, he had never felt more alive.

And then he realized that he wasn't dying.

He lifted a hand to his chest and winced at the pain. But his searching fingers found no open wound. Instead, they connected with the small silver flask he carried in his inside jacket pocket. He had nicked it from a tourist at Land's End this summer just past and, when he could afford to, liked to fill it with the dark rum he so loved.

He wasn't a tippler, nor a drunk, but there were times when he would sit out on the rocks, overlooking the bay, and have a swig or two, imagining himself to be one of those old smugglers who once haunted the coast, tippling a bit of his swag. The flask had been empty today—it often was—but he still liked to carry it about with him. And now it had saved his life.

He could feel the dent in the metal from where the bullet had struck it and then careened off, leaving his chest bruised, but the skin unbroken.

Then where did all the blood come from . . . ?

He winced again as his fingers explored farther and found where the bullet had ricocheted up from the flask and gone through his shoulder.

He could have shrieked with agony as his probing finger touched the wound—but the pain was sweet, for it carried a message that made his heart sing.

He was going to live.

But Bett . . . where was Bett and his revolver? Surely the man wouldn't leave him here, still alive, with the possibility that he would survive to tell the tale?

He reached for Bett's presence—thinking that he was lifting his head—but then the oddest thing of all occurred, for he realized that it was his mind that was reaching out to Bett, not his physical senses. As he'd felt the connection with the whole of the world and the stars that lay beyond, a connection that he could not retain because it was simply too vast for one mind to encompass, he now felt a connection with his would-be murderer. He still lay there on the ground, but he knew exactly what Bett was about. It was as though he sat on the man's shoulder, or rode along in the back of his mind.

He followed Bett, crawling through the thick undergrowth, stalking . . . stalking . . . a hiker.

He wanted to shout a warning to the unsuspecting man, but couldn't get his throat to work properly. And then his own sense of self-preservation cut in.

Get away, it told him. Get away while you can.

So he crawled into the undergrowth on his own side of the path, burrowing deeply into its tangles, his mind still connected to Bett. The pain, as he moved, was so fierce that he fell in and out of consciousness. But the odd flow of time continued so that what he thought of as long minutes were only the briefest of seconds. He swept feebly at the trail he was leaving behind him with a stiff bit of brush that he managed to pull from a dead thorn thicket.

And on he went, nesting deeper into the wild jungle of vegetation that ran riotously along the clifftop. He paused when Bett pushed the hiker from the cliff. His connection to Bett widened suddenly, encompassing the hiker as well so that he followed the man in his plummet to the rocks below. He almost shrieked when the hiker hit the rocks; he was left shivering afterward.

His mind was slow in returning to his own head. His strength was waning. It took most of what remained to tear a strip from the bottom of his shirt, using his good arm and his teeth, and then awkwardly binding it about his wound.

The bullet had gone straight through. If he could keep the wound clean and have it properly looked after . . .

He sensed Bett looking for him and lay very still. Through his connection to the man, he could sense Bett's puzzlement. Bett searched for a while, but his heart didn't seem to be in the task. His mind was on other matters that Davie could sense—seething there in the turmoil that was Bett's mind—if not quite grasp. But the connection remained, even when Bett finally walked back along the Coastal Path towards Mousehole.

The connection remained.

He followed Bett through the village, and out again along the road to Newlyn.

I can find you, Davie thought as he laid his head wearily in the grass, too exhausted to move anymore. Wherever you go, I can find you now.

And when he did . . .

Every dog has its day.

Willie had a stash in a crib that was part of a farm up back of the village. Davie had been up there with Willie often enough, and knew exactly under which floorboard Willie had hidden his spare handgun, wrapped up in plastic and oilskin to protect it from the weather.

Davie would make his way up there and then he'd do his second good deed in as many days. He'd rid the world of one Michael Bett and bugger the consequences.

Unconsciousness rose in a wave to cloud his mind and drag him down into its dark depths. Davie let himself go, but there was a smile on his lips when he finally let the darkness swallow him.

So There I Was

Under the earth I go,
On the oak-leaf I stand,
I ride on the filly that never was foaled,
And I carry the dead in my hand.

—SCOTS TRADITIONAL, collected by Hamish Henderson

We can't leave our land anymore," Edern said, "except in dreams—our dreams, your dreams. . . ."

"Seal dreams?" Jodi asked.

Edern smiled and nodded. "Even seal dreams." Then he sighed. "But dreams are not enough."

His smile and body language, like his voice, remained familiar. But it was odd for Jodi to see what she thought of as Edern's mannerisms being used by a stranger. A familiar stranger, but a stranger all the same.

They sat, the two of them, in the shade of the tolmen in the world to which the hole in the Men-an-Tol had carried her. Edern leaned against the stone, legs stretched out in front of him, crossed at the ankles. Jodi was perched on another stone across from him where she sat swinging her legs lightly, kicking her heels against the rough granite.

Edern had brought out a kind of old-fashioned leather knapsack from which he drew bread and a spread made from crushed nuts to go on it, sticky buns and cheese. For afters, there were candied fruits and something that tasted remarkably like chocolate, though Edern told her that it was actually made from another kind of nut. Completing the meal was a waterskin full of cold tea with which they washed it all down.

"There was commerce once between our worlds," Edern went on when they'd finished eating. "An interchange of poetry and song, of art and ideas. We were almost one world, divided only by a thin onion-skin thickness of wall. Passing through it was like stepping through a thick mist—a clammy feeling, but not unpleasant.

"Still, that was long ago."

"What happened?" Jodi asked.

"Cold iron."

She shook her head. "I don't understand."

"Your world took to metalwork in a fierce fashion. The soft metals were no longer enough—gold and silver, copper, bronze and tin. You needed iron, for its strength. But iron was anathema to us, and remains so up to the present day.

"That soft onion-skin border thickened. Layer upon layer was added to it until now only a poet's dreams can cross from one to the other."

"Are you a poet?" Jodi asked. "I met one once—in the Tatters. His rhymes were fine, even if the lines didn't scan as well as they might. But they were funny poems. What kind do you write?"

"I use the word in its old sense," Edern said. "Words have power, and power is the realm of magic."

"I thought magic lay in names."

"It does," Edern said. "And what are names, but words. They are the first words—the ones we learn as babes to make sense of the world around us. They lose their power as most of us grow older; only for poets do they retain their potency."

"Are you a poet? I mean *that* kind of a poet. Are you a . . . magician?"

"Of a sort."

"Then how come you didn't magic your way out of the Widow's place when she caught you?"

"Because she bound me in a body constructed of metal."

"And there was iron in the alloy?"

Edern nodded.

"She caught my dreaming mind," he said. "Caught it and pulled it from my world to yours, then confined it in that body with its iron bindings so that I could not escape back home again to where my body lay sleeping."

"So you were never a traveling man? She never turned you into a Small—like she did to me?"

"No."

"Why did you lie to me?"

"I didn't know if I could trust you."

"But you trust me now?"

"I would trust you with my life," he said.

Jodi shook her head. "I don't understand. What changed?"

"I came to *know* you," he replied simply. "Had we more time together in your world, I would have told you there."

Easy to say now, Jodi thought. But then she realized that she believed him. She couldn't have explained why that was. Maybe she'd just come to *know* him, whatever that entailed. Or maybe it was just that she wanted to trust him.

"Why did you want me to come here?" she asked finally.

"Our worlds need each other," Edern said. "They grow too far apart now and we suffer for it—both our worlds suffer. Their separation makes for a disharmony that reflects in each of them. Your world grows ever more regimented and orderly; soon it will lose all of its ability to imagine, to know enchantment, to be joyful for no other reason than that its people perceive the wonder of the world they are blessed to live in. Everything is put in boxes and compartmentalized and a grey pall hangs over the minds of its people. Your world will eventually become so drab and drear that its people will eventually destroy it through sheer blindness and ignorance."

"And your world?"

"Grows too fey. Magics run amuck. Anything that can be imagined, is, and if left unchecked, my world will simply dissolve into chaos."

"This sounds like Denzil's two-minds theory," Jodi said with a smile.

"How so?"

"Well, he says that each side of our brain has a different"—she paused to search for the word—"physiology. The left side is sort of like the captain of a lugger. It handles all the day-to-day aspects of our lives." Her voice took on the cadences of Denzil's theorizing as she spoke. "It sees everything up close, like through a microscope. The right side holds the hidden self. It's nondominant and that's where our feelings and instincts come from. It gives a wide view of the world, connects everything instantly, instead of you having to figure it out through trial and error; it does it intuitively. The trouble is, you can't just call on it like you can the left side—that's why Denzil calls it the hidden half. But if you *don't* use it, it gets lazy.

"We need to use both, Denzil says, because both are necessary for a fully rounded personality."

"That's exactly it," Edern said. "Your world is becoming a place without light—an opaque and joyless place that is almost no longer real—while my world has too much light, so much so that it will eventually consume us. We both—the peoples of your world as well as my own—have knots in our minds that need to be untied and the only way we can do that is by bringing the worlds closer together again."

"But what you're saying isn't true," Jodi said. "There's people in my world who make the most beautiful things—painters and sculptors and artists and musicians. . . . If they don't have any of this light of yours, then how can they do that?"

"Are there many of them—in relation to the rest of your population, I mean?"

Jodi shook her head.

"It's the same in my world. We have our logicians and theorists, but they are few in number and while they are respected by the general populace, no one truly understands them. Not what motivates them, nor exactly what it is that they are sharing with us."

Jodi nodded slowly. "I suppose it's the same thing with the artists in my world," she said. "Sometimes I think that *they* don't even know what they're doing, they're just driven to do it."

"They are reaching out for the Barrow World," Edern said, "just as my people reach for the Iron World—your world."

This, Jodi thought, seemed a perfect opportunity to find out something that she'd been curious about ever since she'd arrived in the Barrow World.

"Where *are* your people?" she asked.

"They knew you would be arriving soon, so they stayed away," Edern explained. "They didn't want to meet you."

Jodi scowled. "That's not very nice."

"No, no," Edern said. "Don't think ill of them. It's for a very good reason that they stay away and it doesn't reflect on you personally. The danger with meeting an Iron Worlder for us is that we can never forget that meeting. Forever after we yearn for that other half of ourselves. That sense of wanting something more—of reaching to your world—is always present in us, but it becomes unbearable once we have had the actual experience.

"It can drive us mad."

"Like mortals crossing over into Faerie," Jodi said.

Edern nodded.

"Our folktales say the same thing," she added. "That the experience leaves a man mad . . . or a poet." She looked more closely at Edern. "Is that what happened to you?" she asked.

Edern nodded again. "I dreamed too long in your world."

"Oh raw we. Is it going to happen to me?"

"I don't know. I'm hoping we can do something about it—you and I."

"But I don't have any magic," Jodi protested. "I'm nobody important."

"It doesn't require either importance or magic," Edern explained. "Only sympathy . . . and music."

Jodi laughed. "You certainly picked the wrong person then. I don't know the first thing about playing an instrument and whenever I try to sing, people applaud—but only because I've stopped."

"You don't need to know how to play an instrument or sing," Edern said. "You just have to be able to take the music into your heart and carry it back into your world with you."

"But how?"

"We all carry that music inside us," Edern said. "Here"—he tapped his chest—"in our hearts. It's the pulse of our heartbeat."

"If it's already there, then why do I have to carry it back with me?"

"Because you have to learn to recognize it—and then teach others to do the same. It's not difficult. That's the real magic of the world— its truths are far simpler than we make them out to be."

"Yes, but—"

"Let me explain. How much do you know about music?"

"I know a good tune when I hear it."

Edern smiled. "People composing music—and I speak of the true artists now—are only trying to recapture the strains of a first music— the primal music that shaped the world and gave it its magic. That is what drives them. The closer they get, the more they are driven to seek further. Then there's the old music—the jigs and reels that have always seemed to be around. Are you familiar with them?"

Jodi nodded. "I like them best."

"Most people do; it's because they set up a resonance—an echo to things lost—in the listener. The reason those old tunes retain that resonance is that they haven't been tampered with as much, they haven't really been changed. The musicians who play them retain the heart of the music, layering new instrumentation or arrangements over them, but the bones are always there.

"Those tunes are played now as they were played then—a hundred years ago. A hundred hundred years ago. They come very close to that first music, but they're still wrong. They still remain only echoes of the first song that the snake taught Adam and Eve—an old dance, the oldest dance of all.

"What I want to teach you is that first music. I want you to learn how to recognize it in yourself, in others, in your own world. Wake it, and the borders will grow thin once more."

Jodi shook her head. "I don't understand. If you know it, then why don't you do all of that?"

"We all know it in this world," Edern said. "We know it too well. It's the underpinning to the magic that runs rampant in the Barrow World. Where it *isn't* remembered is in *your* world. It must sound in both."

"But I told you—I can't carry a tune."

"If you'll let me," he said, "I will teach you how."

"Will it be hard or . . . hurt?"

Jodi didn't know why she was asking that. She supposed it was just because it seemed that it couldn't be that simple—never mind what Edern said about that being the magic of the world.

Its truths are far simpler than we make them out to be.

"It will hurt some," Edern said. "It's an old magic. Remembering calls up both sides of the coin—the storm and the sunny day."

"And will it help me get back to my own size?"

Edern shook his head. "That you must accomplish as I told you. The Widow has a part of you that you need to regain from her. But the music will help you once you have done so."

"Why is it that her magic still works in my world? I thought you said it was all gone."

"I didn't say it was gone," Edern replied. "Only that it was going. But most of it *is* gone. Will you help me, Jodi?"

"I . . ."

She was frightened now. And again, she couldn't have said of what. But there was a hollow feeling deep inside her. Her throat was dry and felt like sandpaper. Her chest felt too tight; an enormous stone had settled in the pit of her stomach.

Bother and damn, she thought. Wasn't this what she'd been aching for? Hadn't she been complaining about just this sort of thing to

Denzil not two days ago? How she wanted to do something that was important. Something that had meaning.

She swallowed dryly.

"I . . . I'll try," she said.

She thought she'd feel better with the decision made, but the hollow feeling only grew worse.

"But I'm scared," she added.

"I'll be by you," Edern assured her.

And that brought some comfort.

She wondered if what she was feeling—all these instinctual trusts and suspicions, the sudden fluctuation of her emotions—had something to do with the Barrow World itself. If it was like Denzil's two-minds theory, and this world was her world's subconscious, then didn't it stand to reason that it would have her own intuition working at full tilt? Except then, why didn't she already *know* this first music that Edern was talking about? *Know* it the way she *knew* him . . . ?

Her head started to ache the more she tried to think it all through.

"When do we start?" she asked.

"As soon as you're ready."

Jodi took a deep breath. She looked around at the sunny moorland about her—the sweeps of heather and dried ferns, the gorse all still in bloom, yellow flowers bobbing on their prickly stems.

She'd stepped from night in her world to this.

From the Iron World into the Barrow World.

By magic.

And hadn't there been a music playing, just before the light took her away and brought her here? A wonderful, heart-stopping music that brought tiny chills mouse-pawing up her spine when all she did was just think about it? A music that when you heard it, you realized you'd been sleeping through your life, because what it did was it woke you up. Suddenly and completely.

If that was the music he was going to teach her . . .

If he was going to show her how to always know it . . .

She smiled at Edern. He smiled in return, his unfamiliar features growing more familiar the longer she sat with him here. Not because she was growing used to them, she realized, but because she was learning to *know* him.

"I'm ready," she said.

2.

Denzil's first thought was for the children. He should never have let himself be talked into allowing the children to accompany them here. They'd been mad to let them come.

But then the whole affair was mad, wasn't it?

Witches and bogies and walking dead men.

Jodi vanishing in a wash of music and light. . . .

Despair stalked his heart and he turned to his companions, but they were more concerned with practical matters.

"Bugger them," Henkie grumbled. "The seawater won't do us any good with this bloody bunch, will it?"

"Not likely," Taupin said. "They'll be mostly seawater themselves—corpse flesh and bone, seawater and weed."

"I thought the bloody Widow couldn't abide the stuff," Henkie said.

"Maybe she can't," Kara said. "But these things can."

Ethy huddled near Denzil, her small hand creeping up to clasp his.

"I am scared now," she said in a small voice.

Denzil nodded. "No less than I, you."

For they were monstrous figures, these sea dead. Their eyes were flat, swallowing the light that spilled from Henkie's oil lamp, rather than reflecting it. Their pale flesh gleamed wetly, seaweed hanging from their tattered clothing in long, damp streamers. Behind them, other shapes moved in the darkness that lay beyond the circle of light cast by the lamp—long, thin shadowy figures that seemed to caper and prance with glee.

They moved, not as might normal shadows cast by some flickering light, but with a movement all their own. Their dance mesmerized Denzil, sending new shivers through him to join the fear that was already lodged deep in his chest.

There was a boggy smell in the air—that same unpleasant odor that Denzil had smelled last night when the Widow's spies were near. But they had been just tiny things, hadn't they? That was what Jodi had told them. The sloch that she and Edern had faced had been tiny and about as swift-moving as these slow drowned men with their shuffling gait.

But these shadowy creatures . . .

What new deviltry had the Widow called up with her witcheries?

Nowhere could Denzil spy the Widow herself, but then what need was there for her to make the trek out here? She wanted them all

dead, but it need not be by her own hand. Her drowned dead and
giant sloch would be more than up to completing the task on their
own and the end result would be as final.

At least Jodi was safe from them.

It was small comfort, but it would have to be enough.

"What can we do?" Lizzie said.

The Tatters children were clustered near the tolmen, all except for
Peter and Kara who stood their ground with the adults.

"Well, now," Henkie said. "Mostly made of seawater, are they?"
He turned to grin at Taupin, teeth flashing white. "What is it you
do when you get a soaking?"

The dead men came shuffling closer. Denzil looked for something
he could use as a weapon, but nothing lay at hand. Their only weapons were the hammer in Henkie's belt and the small penknife that
Peter had produced from his pocket and was now holding, blade
outward, in a trembling hand.

"Why, you dry yourself off," Henkie went on, answering his own
question. "You sit near the fire and steam the bloody damp from
you, don't you just?"

He stepped suddenly forward and, opening the top of the lamp,
swept it in a half circle in front of him. The oil caught fire as it
sprayed outward, splashing over the nearest creatures. In moments
their clothing was afire and patches of oil burned on white flesh, set
thatches of limp hair aflame. The night air, already fouled with the
boggy smell of the sloch that capered beyond the sea dead, now filled
with the stench of burning hair and cooked flesh.

A dull wet roar gurgled and spat from the drowned men as they
burned. Henkie howled and tossed his lantern at another pair. The
only light now came from the oil burning on the flesh of the sea
dead.

"Have at them!" Henkie roared.

He charged forward, brandishing his hammer. The first blow
struck one of the sea dead square in the chest and the drowned man's
flesh literally exploded from the blow. Salt water sprayed from the
wound and the monster collapsed into a limp, shapeless bundle to
the moor.

Denzil stared, aghast. He held Ethy's head against his side so that
she couldn't see. All that remained of the drowned man were his
bones and the pale white folds of his skin that had covered them.

"They can die!" Henkie cried, attacking another.

A second fell, then a third.

Now there was an opening in their ranks.

"Come along," Denzil cried, pulling Ethy and another of the children in Henkie's wake.

"Get your balloons ready," Taupin said.

He and Lizzie ushered the rest of the children ahead of them and then took up the rear. Kara took a saltwater bomb from her satchel.

"What good will they do?" she asked. "They *come* from the sea."

"It's not for the sea dead," Lizzie said. "But for *them*."

She pointed to where the thin shadowy figures of the sloch were gathering to attack Henkie ahead of them.

Kara nodded and flung her balloon. Her arm was strong, her aim true. The saltwater bomb flew over Henkie's head and burst against the foremost sloch. Salt water sprayed over it and its nearest companions. Wails and shrieks filled the air. As Kara reached for another balloon, the other children began to throw theirs as well.

"That's it!" Henkie cried. "Drown the buggers!"

The stench in the air was something awful. Moans and shrieks and a terrible caterwauling rose in a deafening cacophony. Sea dead and sloch both gave way to the little company as it forged forward.

"I think we might actually have a chance," Denzil muttered.

He looked down at what was left of the first sloch that Kara had dropped with her bomb. The stink was worse here than it had been so far. The thing was a little taller than Ethy, which made it almost four feet tall. It seemed to be made of equal parts bog mud, rotting weeds, thin twisted bits of wood and shadow. Luminous eyes stared up at Denzil as he stepped around it, the light dying in them.

"Don't look," he told Ethy.

"Come along then," Henkie called from up ahead. "Quick march, unless you want to be dinner for the bloody things."

They hurried after him, holding their water bombs ready. The sloch kept their distance for the moment, merely pacing them, keeping them hemmed in on either side. And while their quick pace was leaving the sea dead behind, the drowned men were still following.

"Where's the Widow?" Lizzie said worriedly.

"That's what I want to know," Taupin muttered.

Denzil didn't even want to think about her.

"Hedrik Henkie Whale," a sharp voice called from out of the night ahead of them.

With the moon at her back, the Widow stood on the moor, her

arms raised as though she meant to enfold the sky with them.

"Shut her gob!" Taupin cried.

Denzil nodded. Three times named and the Widow would be able to enchant the strongest member of their small company. And then what would they do? But how could they hope to stop her?

She had magic—and powerful magic it had proved to be. And the bogies she had called up from bog and sea easily outnumbered them. Her sloch rose in a wave from the moorland around her, more than they could ever hope to combat with their rapidly diminishing supply of saltwater bombs.

"Don't listen to her," Lizzie said. "Stop your ears."

There was no chance to retreat, Denzil realized, for the sea dead were rapidly closing in on them from behind. No chance to go forward. And how could one not listen to the Widow? How could they *not* hear what she cried?

But then Denzil remembered Jodi's story—how the Small had stopped the Widow from enspelling her by singing.

He started to sing then, as loudly as he could—that same old song that Edern had sung with Jodi.

> *"Hal-an-tow,*
> *Jolly rumble-o,*
> *We were up, long before the day-o;*
> *To welcome in the summer,*
> *To welcome in the May-o,*
> *For summer is a-coming in,*
> *And winter's gone away-o. . . ."*

His was not a marvelous voice, but it was enough to carry a tune, and he put volume behind it to make up for his lack of skill. The others joined in, a ragged chorus, but surely loud enough to drown out the Widow's voice?

The Witch merely laughed—a cackling sound that brought an answering clap of thunder from the sky above. The singers faltered over their words and the Widow called out Henkie's name for the second time.

Again she laughed. Clouds came rolling in on the heels of the Widow's laughter, rapidly hiding the moon and stars. Darkness deepened on the moor. Lightning licked the sky, followed by more thunder. Above it and their tattered voices, they could still hear the

Widow's voice as she cried out Henkie's name for the third and last time.

The singing faltered again and this time Denzil couldn't save it from dying out completely.

"Be stone," the Widow told Henkie.

And stone he became.

Denzil saw Henkie stiffen. His hands fell to his side, the hammer dropped from numbed fingers to the ground. His neck arched back, his head turned to the sky, and then he was gone. All that remained was a tall, fat standing stone where once he had stood.

"No!" Lizzie cried.

Peter flung a balloon at the Widow, but the distance was too great and it fell short. The balloon burst uselessly on the moor. Lizzie started forward to where the stone now stood, but Taupin caught her arm. One of the children began to wail in fear. Denzil bundled Ethy up in his arms.

"Run!" he told them all. "Run as best you can."

But it was too late, he realized.

It had been too late from the first moment that the Widow's drowned men had encircled them at the Men-an-Tol. For while the Widow had transformed Henkie from man to stone, the sea dead had approached them silently from the rear. Before the small company could scatter, the dead were in among them—the dead drowned men, reeking of weed and salt, catching hold of them with their pale corpse hands, gripping them hard so that no matter how they might struggle, they couldn't break free.

Only Kara evaded their first onslaught. She dodged in between them and caught up the hammer where it had fallen from Henkie's grip. She swung it wildly against the knee of a drowned man. His skin burst, gushering seawater, and then he collapsed in an untidy heap of bones and skin and rotted clothing. Before Kara could swing the hammer again, another of the sea dead had wrested it from her hands and held her in a grip she couldn't escape.

The Widow named her three times and turned her into stone—a small menhir to stand beside the larger bulk of the stone that had once been Henkie.

"No!" Denzil cried. "Leave the children alone. They've done no harm."

"No harm?" the Widow said. "Ask my Windle how harmless they are."

Ethy whimpered in Denzil's arms as one of the sea dead tore her from his grip. He fought the iron grip of his own captor with a desperate fury as the Widow spoke the child's name three times and transformed her into a tiny standing stone as well.

Denzil went limp in his captor's arms and despaired. He remembered the small hand in his, the trusting face turned to his for protection. Now she was stone. All her vibrant life stolen from her while he had been helpless to do a thing to stop the change.

One by one the Widow transformed first the other children, then Taupin and Lizzie, until only Denzil was left. He cursed her with an eloquence that would have put Henkie to shame, but she only laughed. Above them, the storm grumbled and shot the thick clouds with streaks of lightning.

The Widow stepped close to Denzil. He looked from her features to those of the evil little fetch that clung to her shoulder. There was no difference between them. The same hate lived in each of their eyes. Behind them the sloch pressed near—dozens of the creatures, filling the air with their bog reek and chittering voices.

"I can still spare you," the Widow said. "Who knows, perhaps you can find a cure for your stony friends. All I require is the girl. Give me the Small and you can live."

Denzil knew she lied. And even if she didn't, he still would never give her Jodi.

"Fool," she said, and she spoke his name.

Once, then twice.

"Bravery doesn't become you, Denzil Gossip," she said, completing the charm with the third voicing of his name. "You won't reconsider?"

He spat in her face.

She never moved, gave no indication of her anger except that the coals that were eyes glimmered a touch more brightly. The spittle ran down her cheek touching the corner of her mouth as she smiled.

"Be stone," she said.

And Denzil felt the greyness of granite come over his limbs.

3.

Above the moor, the clouds grew thicker still. Thunder cracked, lightning spat. But the Widow Pender was calm. She surveyed her handiwork—the new scattering of standing stones that littered this part of the moor—and was partly content. Had Jodi Shepherd been in their company, the moment would have been perfect, but as it was, she was as satisfied as might be expected.

She sought the missing Small with her witch-sight, but it was as though the diminutive girl had been spirited away from the world itself. Turning to look at the Men-an-Tol, she couldn't help but wonder what it was that the girl's friends had hoped to accomplish out here on the moors tonight. Had she come just a few moments earlier, she would have known.

Now she must continue her search again.

The shadows would help her. Just as they had lent her their strength for the large sloch that she had called up from the bogs, for the drowned dead that had marched up from their sea graves for the storm that had grown from the red fire of her rage to cloud the sky with her anger so that her own mind would remain calm.

She would find the girl.

But first she would deal with Bodbury.

She had only this one night of borrowed power and she didn't mean to waste it. The shadows were generous, but the cost was dear. If she failed them, it was very dear.

But she wouldn't fail them.

She would give them Bodbury, just as she had given them the girl's miserable friends.

Darkness stirred at the bases of the newly made longstones.

We want more, they told her.

"I will give you the Barrow World," the Widow said. "But first Bodbury."

Give us more.

"Oh, you will feed well tonight, never fear."

Open the door between the worlds for us.

The Widow glanced back at the Men-an-Tol once more and wondered what part it had played in the girl's disappearance. She had walked this moorland in day and in night, searching for the Barrow World's entrance. She had poked and pried into every hollow and dip of the land, dug around the bases of the stoneworks, tipped one or two over on their sides, but all in vain. She'd never found so much as a hint of a gate to that otherworld.

She looked at the Men-an-Tol once more. She had searched long and hard, coming back time and again to that holed stone, for around it, the mystery seemed to lie thickest. The very air resonated with it.

But the stone never gave up its riddles. Not before—

The tolmen mocked her with its silent mystery.

—not now.

What *had* the girl's friends been up to?

We want, we want, we want, the shadows chanted.

The Widow nodded. "I know what you want."

She thought she could see eyes flickering in their depths, vague disembodied smiles.

We want it all. . . .

The first pinprick of uneasiness went through the Widow at that. They wanted it all?

"First Bodbury," she said.

She turned to face the sea where it lay hidden by moor and hill. Putting the mystery of the Men-an-Tol at her back, she set off for the town, the sea dead shuffling in her wake, the sloch capering along either side.

What did they mean by *all?* she couldn't help but wonder.

As though reading her thoughts, behind her, on all sides and before her, the shadows laughed in response.

4.

"So what do I do?" Jodi asked.

Edern pointed to the hole in the Men-an-Tol. "That would be a good place to sit."

Jodi looked up. If she'd been her normal size, getting up to the hole would have presented no difficulty. All she'd have had to do was bend over and scrunch herself in. But mouse-sized as she was . . .

"Here," Edern said.

He lifted his lanky frame from the ground and stood underneath the stone, cupping his hands to give her a step up. Jodi gave him a dubious look.

"I don't know," she said.

"There are handholds."

And so there were, she realized, as she gave the stone a closer scrutiny. It was only the first bit that looked hard.

"All right," she said.

She stepped into his cupped hands and gave a startled little gasp as he lifted her up, up, above his shoulders. She held on to the stone to keep her balance, wondering at his strength.

More magic, she supposed.

"I can't hold you up all day," he said.

She found a handhold, then another. A few moments later she had scrambled the rest of the way up and could sit down in the Men-an-Tol's hole. With an enviable skill that would have put Ollie to shame, Edern made his own quick way up until he had joined her. He sat at her side and gave her a reassuring smile.

"Now what?" she asked.

"Empty your mind."

Jodi laughed. "Do you think it's so full of wise thoughts? It's empty most of the time, I'm afraid."

Edern shook his head. "I mean, stop thinking. Let your mind clear until all you can feel is quiet, until you are drifting, without thought, without that constant burr of conversation that murmurs in your mind, day and night."

"Are you going to hypnotize me?"

Again he shook his head. "Just try."

So Jodi did.

She sat there, looking out over the moorland, enjoying the feel of the sun and the rare clear skies. She wondered what it was going to feel like to find this secret music—this first music. What would it sound like? She thought of all the old tunes she could, wondering which came the closest.

"What are you thinking of?" Edern said.

"Of music," Jodi replied.

"Well, don't. Think of nothing. *Don't* think at all. Just be."

Jodi found that it was harder to do than she had expected. The more she tried, the more quickly this thought or that popped into mind. One led to another, then to another, to yet more until her head was filled with a long connected parade of observations and memories and little commentaries, all tangled together in a noisy confusion in her head.

And suddenly she'd be aware of them, and remember what she was *supposed* to be doing. She'd sigh, and start all over again.

And back would come the parade.

"I can't do it," she said finally.

Edern smiled. "You've hardly tried."

"I've been trying for ages."

"You've been trying for ten minutes."

"Honestly?"

He nodded.

"Bother and damn. I'll never be able to do it."

"Try listening to your heartbeat. Don't think about listening to it, just focus on it, on its rhythm, on how it moves the blood through your arteries and veins. If some extraneous thought comes to mind, don't worry at it, don't be impatient with it; just set it gently aside and return to your contemplation of that steady rhythm of your heartbeat."

This was a little easier, Jodi discovered after a few moments of following his advice.

Whoops, she realized. That was a thought.

Back she went to concentrating.

Dhumm-dum. Dhumm-dum.

Odd bits of memory and the like continued to float up from the pool of her mind, but she found it easier and easier to set them aside. She did it gently—as Edern had told her to. She didn't allow herself to become frustrated by them. Didn't worry about how she was doing, whether she was doing well or poorly.

She just listened.

Dhumm-dum.

And drifted.

Dhumm-dum.

Until she felt as though she were floating away, out of her body.

Dhumm-dum.

Away and away—or was it deeper and deeper within herself? It didn't matter. She just followed that steady rhythm . . .

Dhumm-dum. Dhumm-dum.

. . . away and down . . .

Dhumm-dum.

. . . deeper and farther. . . .

Dhumm-dum.

At some point she passed between awareness of what she was doing and simply doing. At that moment, in that place, she found the first music waiting for her.

It was born of harp string and flute breath, fiddle note and drumbeat.

Dhumm-dum.

But it had no sound.

It was a place where lives end, where lives begin. Where lost things could be found, where found things could be lost. A forbidden place, fueled by that forgotten music. A place of shadows and echoes. A place that encompassed every landscape that she had ever viewed or imagined.

But it had no physical presence.

Dhumm-dum.

It consisted of pure logic. It showed her how everything that existed in the world, no matter how large, no matter how small, was all connected to each other, could not exist without each other.

At the same time, it made no sense whatsoever.

Dhumm-dum.

The individual disappeared into its vastness, into the greater whole, linked together so that there was no division between where one began and the other left off.

The whole was divided into individuals, each so separate and distinct from the other that their unity was incomprehensible.

Impossibility abounded.

It all made perfect sense.

It was a mystery, and all the more revered for that.

An old magic.

She knew such unthinkable joy at discovering it that she thought her heart would burst. No. Not at discovering it, but at *rediscovering* it, for she knew now that it had always been there. In the world around her. Inside her. . . .

And then that part of her that was still her recalled what Edern had said about the music. How remembering called up both the storm and the sunny day.

And she wept.

For all the things that were lost because of the segmentation in the world, the divide that had created an Iron World and a Barrow World. Species extinct. Hopes extinguished. Heartlands ravaged. Wastelands and barren lands that lay both in the world and in the hearts of its inhabitants.

Some could be found again—just as she had found the music. Some would be found again.

But there were so many that could never again be reclaimed.

Lost forever. . . .

•   •   •

She was still weeping when she returned to Edern's side in the hole of the Men-an-Tol. He was shaking her—not hard, but firmly.

"Stop," he was saying. "Let the music be still."

She regarded him through eyes blurred with tears.

"But all that's lost . . ."

"Would you lose the rest as well?"

He pointed then, beyond their vantage point in the tolmen. She saw the moorland heaving and moving like an angry tide. Waves of heathered hills rose in crests to cascade down again. There was a roaring in the air, a shrillness of grinding stone, a thunder of rumbling earth.

The peaceful calm of the Barrow World had changed into a place of mad chaos.

"I—I . . ."

She was doing this, she realized. Here in the Barrow World where magic ran rampant. Her calling up the first music had let it run free, pulling the world into chaos.

But she didn't know how to stop it.

The tolmen shook and she clutched at Edern for balance. He braced himself so that they wouldn't topple over into that seething mass of earth, but the effort to do so grew rapidly more difficult with each buffeting wave of earth that rocked the stone.

A heaviness lay inside her—a deep sorrow that even the remembered joy that the music had also brought could not take away.

"H-help me," she asked Edern.

Braced against the stone, holding her firm, he gave her a grave, considering look—the worry plain in his features.

"Please. I—I can't stop it. . . ."

And he tickled her.

Her first thought was that he'd gone mad. They were going to fall into the roiling flood of earth that lashed and beat against the tolmen.

"Stop it!" she cried.

But then her body betrayed her and she couldn't help but squirm. And giggle. Try to push his hands away, but he wouldn't stop until she almost fell from their perch and then finally lay still. Exhausted. And became aware of the silence.

She lifted her head weakly to see that the world had returned to what it had been. There were no waves of earth, washing across the moorland. No thunder under the ground. No shrieking of stone.

Only stillness.

Quiet. And—

Dhumm-dum.

—the sound of her heartbeat, echoing on inside her.

She remembered her experience, but already it was fading into a vague, disconnected series of images and emotions that she would be hard put to frame into coherent thought, little say words. But the joy was remembered. And the sorrow.

Both were bearable now.

"What—what happened?" she asked.

"It was my fault," Edern said. "I hadn't realized what your Iron World blood would call up when you remembered the music."

"I almost destroyed your world, didn't I?"

Edern shook his head. "I told you, the magic is too thick here. All you did—with the sorrow the music woke in you—was give it something to focus through."

"I can't call it up again," she told him. "I can't chance it."

"It won't be the same in your world," he said. "There it will be a quiet murmur of mystery that will set hearts beating to the old remembered dance—but gently."

"There's so much lost," she said. "So much gone forever."

"But there's still much we can reclaim," Edern said. "So much that is now in peril that we can yet rescue."

"And . . . and that's all I do?" Jodi asked. "I just follow my heartbeat down to the music when I'm back in my own world?"

Edern nodded.

"It seems too easy."

"The magics of the world," he began.

"Are far simpler than we make them out to be," Jodi finished for him. "I remember." She was quiet for a moment, then asked, "Why do you call it music?"

"What would you call it?"

Jodi thought about that and realized music was as close a word as could come to describing it. Except for perhaps—

"What about mystery?"

"Or magic. It has a hundred thousand names and is sought after in a hundred thousand ways, but it can't be named. That is its magic. Men have borrowed pieces of it for their own use, but they can't tame *it,* only those pieces that they steal away, and the cost of doing so is dear. What's saddest of all is that they didn't need to take or steal those pieces in the first place—they had their own echoes of it inside themselves all along."

"Could an instrument play that music?" Jodi asked.

Edern shook his head. "But it can come so close as to almost make no difference. It can come so close that the resonances it sets up call the first music to it."

Jodi said nothing for a long time, then. She just sat, thinking. Remembering. Until Edern finally spoke.

"You should go," he said.

Jodi nodded. "How do I get back?"

Edern stood up and called through the hole in the stone, called something in a language that Jodi didn't recognize, though she did hear a phrase that was repeated three times. She gave a little start as a cool draft of air wafted over her and she could see the night of her own world from where she stood.

It made for a very disconcerting experience. Looking one way, she could see the sunlit moorland of the Barrow World; the other, and she was looking into the benighted moors of her own world.

Edern clasped her shoulder and gave it a squeeze, but Jodi wasn't going to leave it at that. She stepped close to him and hugged him fiercely for a long moment.

"Thank you," he murmured into her hair.

"No. Thank you."

She moved from his arms and took a step across the odd border, pausing when she stood with one foot in her own world, one in his.

"Will I see you again?" she asked.

"If we can thin the borders, we'll see each other whenever we choose."

"And if we don't? If it takes a long time to work—longer than we have years to live, or at least than I do. I suppose you live forever."

"For a long time," Edern agreed.

"Well?"

"Then we'll see each other in dreams."

Jodi sighed. Dreams weren't going to be nearly enough.

She started to step through once more, then paused for a second time.

"Edern," she asked. "Will the music stop the Widow's magics? Can I use it to get back to my proper size?"

He shook his head.

"Only salt will work against her," he said.

"Like seawater?" Jodi asked, remembering Kara's saltwater bombs.

Edern nodded. "But tears work best."

She had more she wanted to ask him. A dozen more things, a hundred. She knew she could stay here forever, just talking, but also knew she shouldn't. Her friends were waiting for her, back in her own world. They might be in danger. And she had a message to bring, as well—a secret song to sing in the quiet places that would hopefully ripple away through the world and bring it closer to its cousin, here on the other side of the Men-an-Tol.

So she smiled, gave Edern a wave that was far jauntier than she felt, and stepped all the way through.

She shivered at the chill in the night air of her own world, blinking as her eyes adjusted to the darker light. When she turned to look back, Edern and the Barrow World were gone. She saw only the moorland of her own world through the hole in the stone where once they'd been.

Oh raw we, she thought. What a tale I have to tell.

But when she looked for her friends, she found herself alone here. The area around the Men-an-Tol was deserted.

She had a sudden fear. She found herself remembering all those tales of mortals straying off into Faerie—gone for an hour or a day or a week, only to find that years had passed in their own world while they were gone.

Had this happened to her?

She wrapped her arms around herself, shivering at the thought. And then she caught the boggy smell in the air and another kind of fear overrode the first.

The Widow's creatures had been here.

Had they harmed Denzil or any of the others?

Thunder rumbled and she turned in the direction of the town. The skies were beclouded here, but a true storm hung over Bodbury. Lightning flickered in the dark clouds above it. And then Jodi's gaze fell on something that lay in between the town and the tolmen. Standing stones.

They hadn't been there before, she thought.

Had years and years passed since she stepped from one world to another?

But there was something familiar about their number. And their heights. Their stone surfaces, even viewed from a distance, seemed too unweathered. Too new. She counted them off. The one large stone. Three more almost as tall, but not so thick. All the small ones. . . .

And then she knew.

Clearly, immediately, with an intuition that echoed the magic of her experience in the Barrow World when she touched the hidden music.

They were her friends. Turned to stone by the Widow.

And that storm hanging over Bodbury . . . She remembered the stories of the Widow and the storm she was said to have brought some twenty years ago.

That storm was also her doing.

She had to get to town. She had to stop the Widow. She had to rescue her friends, regain her size. . . . But it was so far and she was so small. The journey would take her *days* at her present size.

What was she going to *do*?

The answer was taken out of her hands.

Fingers closed around her, tightly, fiercely.

Jodi shrieked with alarmed surprise.

She was hoisted into the air and found herself face-to-face with Windle, the Widow's fetch, left behind to watch the holed stone. Chittering with pride, the evil little creature clutched her to its breast and bounded from the tolmen, heading for Bodbury, ignoring the blows that Jodi rained on it with her tiny fists.

Those blows, she soon realized, had about as much of a chance of hurting the fetch as a man might have trying to swab out his boat with a piece of netting.

But she kept hitting it all the same—all the way across the moorland and into the town. And once in town, she began to shriek for help. But her voice was a tiny piping thing, barely audible at any distance in normal times. It was utterly useless now with the winds of the storm whistling down the streets and the thunder rumbling above.

Tottering Hame

You must understand that our lives were raw, red bleeding meat.

—CAITLIN THOMAS, from an Interview in *People*, June 1987

So how do I look?"

Connie stood in the doorway of Sam Dennison's room, leaning casually against the doorjamb as she tried to gauge a reaction from the private investigator's taciturn features. He gave back nothing, just sat by the small desk in his room, tapping an envelope against his knee.

She wondered why she bothered looking for his approval—she didn't even like the man. But looking for approval was a habit. She couldn't come near a man without trying to get a reaction. It had always been that way, getting worse instead of better as the years went by. If she didn't get what she was looking for the first time, then all she did was keep shifting gears until she did. It was the unfortunate story of her life—she saw her own worth only in how it was reflected in a man's eyes.

She didn't want them, but she needed them. Needed the confirmation.

So she'd done what Dennison had asked—toned down the makeup and hair and squeezed her bod into some sucky threads that she'd brought along at Bett's request: a narrow tweed skirt with a hem that fell just below the knee, a white blouse with only the top button undone, and, yessir Mr. Uptight, a bra underneath so we don't go too bouncy-bouncy. Completing the look was a snappy little businesswoman's jacket worn overtop, sensible stockings, and flat-heeled shoes. What more did he want?

Personally, she thought she'd have a lot more effect on the Gaffer and her kid looking the way she usually did. But what the hell. When you took the money, you played the gig their way. The least Dennison could do was appreciate the effort.

"C'mon," she said, pouring on the charm. "You've made your

point. Everybody knows you're a hard case, so why don't you lighten up a bit."

Dennison nodded. "Okay. You look good."

"Yeah, but do I look great? I feel like I've got a pickle up my ass in this getup."

A smile touched his eyes, there and gone, and she knew that was all she was going to get. But it was enough. She had him figured now. It wasn't that he didn't like women, he just liked the packaging to hide more of the product, that was all. He wanted to imagine, before he got to see.

Well, lookee but no touchee, big guy.

Knowing now that she could turn him on, she lost interest in him and settled down on the edge of his bed. He handed her the envelope he was holding.

"Mr. Bett dropped this by for you," he said.

The envelope wasn't sealed. Connie slid its contents out onto her lap and found herself looking at a photocopy of a legal document, the last will and testament of one Paul Little.

"I still can't figure out why Bett flew me all the way in to hand this over to them," she said. "Don't they have lawyers over here?"

"You tell me—you're the native."

Connie shook her head. "That was a whole other person, pal. I'm not from here anymore. When you live in a city like New York, it doesn't matter where you come from, *that's* where you belong."

"I know the feeling," Dennison said.

She didn't doubt that for a moment. Born and bred in the Bronx, this was probably the first time he'd ever been away from home in his life.

She tapped the papers again. "Seems to me having a lawyer deliver these would make it more official. Save Bett some dough, too. I don't come cheap and then there's expenses. . . ." She looked around the room. "Not that Bett's going all out on us. Economy class tickets and this dump. I've met bigger spenders in my time, let me tell you."

"I think Mr. Bett is pushing for the psychological edge."

Connie thought about what her reappearance might mean to her father-in-law and daughter. How long had it been since they'd seen each other? Fifteen, twenty years?

Never bothering to think about it, she'd lost count long ago.

"I'm not really looking forward to it," she said.

She'd spoken before she really thought about what she was saying, but it was true. She was surprised at the realization. It was going to be unpleasant—she'd known that from the first time Bett had approached her with his proposition—but she'd been sure she could handle it. She was still sure. But when she thought about how this was going to hurt the old man and Jane . . . She might never see the kid, but she was still *her* kid.

"Then why are you doing it?" Dennison asked.

Connie put her uneasiness aside, her tough mask slipping easily back into place.

Screw 'em both. It wasn't like they'd ever had time for her either.

"For the ten grand Bett's paying me," she said. "What did you think—that I'd be doing it for charity?"

Dennison didn't say anything, but she read disapproval in his silence.

"It's not like you're doing this just for your health," she added.

"Didn't say I was."

No, he was just sitting there thinking that he was better than she was because it wasn't so up close and personal for him. Like he'd never done a sleazy thing in his life.

Asshole.

Connie sighed. Why did guys like Dennison always rub her the wrong way?

"So what do you think?" she asked finally. She held up the will. "Is this thing legit?"

Dennison shrugged. "Beats me."

"The way I figure it, Paul would've changed his will as soon as the divorce went final."

"Doesn't much matter whether it's legal or not," Dennison said. "Not for Mr. Bett's purposes. Like I said, he's playing head games with them and you can bet that this is just one more move on the board. Mr. Bett doesn't strike me as the kind of guy who'd do anything halfway."

Connie nodded. "He's got money to burn, all right."

She stuffed the will back into its envelope and stood up, hiding a smile when she caught Dennison staring at her legs.

"What is it?" she said. "About dinnertime? I'm so screwed up with these time changes."

Dennison checked his watch. "Just going on six-thirty, English time."

"Well, then. I guess we might as well get this over with."

How did that old Shangri-las' song go? Something about how you could never go home again?

Well, it wasn't true, she thought as she rode in the back of the cab with Dennison.

You could go back—there just wasn't much point in it. When you left for the reasons she had, because you wanted to see the frigging world instead of being caged up in the past, coming back was just putting yourself back into the cage again and shutting the door.

She didn't need this.

The familiar sights of her childhood flooded her mind with memories; some bad, some good. There'd been changes, but not so many as she had expected. She'd rarely thought of her ex-husband, because there was nothing in her life to remind her of him. But here, where they'd both lived, where they'd gone through the whole shmear—growing up together, falling in love, getting married, having a kid—it was hard not to remember him.

He'd never understood what she needed.

They'd talked of leaving—Paul just as eager as she was—of seeing more than what Penwith had to offer, but it never happened. The past hooked Paul, just like it had God knew how many generations of Littles. Whenever she brought up the idea of moving—to London, say, or anyplace where the twentieth century had a stronger hold—it kept getting put off. When the farthest you went was a day-trip to Plymouth, you just lost patience after a while. Hooked on to the first ride out you could get—in her case, a sleazebag film producer—and made your escape.

She had to smile at the idea of calling Eddie Booth a film producer. That was like calling herself an actress. But what the hell. She was up there on the screen, and she made good dough, and she couldn't really complain. She'd known what she was getting into as soon as Eddie came on to her in the pub where they'd first met.

He was her way out of the cage—and that was it. He set it up so that she got her green card without a hassle, got her some dancing gigs, and then the film work. Sure he was connected, but then who in the industry wasn't? And it wasn't so bad. You could make out fine. Just stay clean—no drugs, no booze—and they didn't have a hold on you. You could walk, anytime you wanted to.

The time just hadn't come for her yet.

She was in her late forties now, but so long as her bod held out, she was going to hang right in there. Because she liked the action. She liked the idea of all those little weenie men sitting in dark theatres or renting video cassettes, getting hot because of what she could put out. If they only knew what went into those films. Like making them was anything but a chore.

She had to work a little harder than all the fresh young talent the sleazebags like Eddie "discovered," but then she had the experience. She could do more in five minutes on the screen than most of those kids could in a whole reel.

Maybe she was an actress after all.

She watched Mousehole approach through the front window of the cab.

Not like anybody here would understand—or even care.

She wondered what Bett's game was. What the hell could the Littles of Mousehole have that was so important? About the most they had going for them was the ability to bore you to tears without half trying. Still it had to be something, something big, because Bett was throwing around an awful lot of money to get it.

There was a bonus waiting for her and Dennison if they could get it themselves. Whatever "it" was. Kinda hard to imagine them collecting that bonus when they didn't even know what it was that Bett was looking for in the first place. She got the idea that he didn't know either, but that just made it more interesting.

The cab pulled up in front of the newsagent on North Cliff. Connie got out, leaving Dennison to handle the cabbie, and looked out at the harbour.

Now this hadn't changed a bit. It gave her the creeps to think of how she might have spent the whole of her life in this dead-end hole.

Thank you, Eddie, she thought. Maybe I owe you more than I thought I did.

"Ready?" Dennison asked as the cab pulled away.

Connie nodded. "The sooner we get this over with and I can get out of this place, the happier I'll be."

"What's wrong with the town?"

"Village," Connie corrected him. "Over here, they're very set on what's a village and what's a town and get insulted when you screw it up."

"That still doesn't tell me what's wrong with it."

"*Look* at it. The place hasn't changed for five hundred years, I'll bet. It's got nothing going for it."

"I think it's pretty."

Connie sneered. "Or quaint?"

"Yeah, that too."

"Christ. You should try living here." She laughed. "Wouldn't that be something? Mousehole with its own hotshot private dick. Be a lot of work for you here, I'll bet."

"You don't much care for the place, I take it."

Connie gave him a hard stare. "You wouldn't understand," she said.

"Try me."

She shook her head. "Let's just get the job done, okay? We can socialize later."

Her humour returned at the frown that settled on his features. That was supposed to be his line. She licked a finger and made a mark in the air with it.

"Score one for the gal," she said.

2.

So far, Ted Grimes had no complaints about the way Bett had handled things. It showed he was serious, and Grimes appreciated that in a man.

Bett had booked him into the kind of room he wanted, away from the tourist areas—although at this time of year that wasn't hard to manage. With the tourist season over, it looked like everything was away from where the sightseers liked to hang out. The package was waiting for him on his dresser, as well. After stowing his bag in the closet, Grimes cut the string and unwrapped the brown paper from the parcel to find a nice snub-nosed Colt .38 Detective Special and a box of shells.

Grimes didn't much care how Bett had gotten hold of the goods. All that was important was that they were here. One-handedly, he took the gun apart, cleaned and oiled it in record time, then loaded it up with one shell. He snapped the cylinder back into place and gave it a spin with his prosthetic hand.

The Colt had a comfortable heft in his left hand as he held it, weighing in at a clean seventeen ounces. Six shots. More than enough for the job.

If there was a job.

Everything else Bett had promised had turned out just the way he said it would, but Grimes wasn't sure about the job itself. It didn't figure that Madden would head over here without a single member of his security force in tow—not when you considered the way he lived at home. His house in Victoria might not look it, but the damn place was a fortress.

Grimes knew.

His missing hand ached with the memory.

Of course the thing about Madden was that maybe he never needed guards. He sure hadn't needed them that night.

The ache in his missing hand deepened.

Wasn't that a thing? Frigging hand had been gone now for the better part of two years, but he could still feel the sucker sitting there on the end of his stump.

Grimes gave the cylinder another spin.

It's *Wheel of Fortune* time, he thought. Round and round and round she goes, and where she stops, nobody knows.

He spun it again, then lifted the gun to press its muzzle up against his temple.

Okay, Madden, he thought. Here's your chance. Work your hoo-doo. Finish what you did to me—just like you should have done before.

Adrenaline pumped through him as he slowly squeezed the trigger. The world turned sharp—every object in the room going suddenly into a deeper focus than it had been moments ago.

The hammer clicked against an empty chamber.

No go.

Grimes brought the gun down again and snapped open the cylinder. Holding the gun between his prosthetic hand and his chest, he loaded the chambers until all six carried a load.

You had your chance, Madden. Now it's my turn.

He laid the gun on the table within easy reach and tucked the box with its remaining shells into his jacket pocket. Then he sat and waited for the phone to ring, heartbeat still quick-stepping from the adrenaline charge he'd given it a moment ago.

Russian roulette: the game of champions.

He'd been playing it with Madden ever since that night Madden had stepped inside Grimes's head with those hoodoo eyes of his and made Grimes cut off his own hand.

Madden didn't know about the game, but he was going to find out. Real soon now.

It was that, or Michael Bett was going to be one sorry sucker before this night was through.

Fortune My Foe

One of the bugbears of modern life is too much rationalism, too little easy interplay between the world of the unconscious and the unseen.

—ROBERTSON DAVIES, from an interview in *Maclean's*, October 1987

Janey got up from the sofa when she was finished reading and went to stand by the window. She looked out at Chapel Square where the last light of the day was leaking away. Shadows thickened in doorways and clung to the walls. She shivered, looking at them, remembering the shadows in the story she'd just finished reading, remembering what Peter Goninan had told her and Clare about shadows and John Madden.

He can see through them, hear through them, speak through them . . .

Perhaps even move through them.

Was he out there in those shadows? Watching? Waiting?

"Did you finish?"

She turned from the window to see her grandfather standing in the door to the kitchen. The smell of frying fish lay heavy in the air and her stomach rumbled. She hadn't even thought of eating a moment ago, but now she was starving.

"I finished it," she said.

On the sofa Felix was just closing the book. Clare was sitting beside him, head leaning back, eyes closed. She'd finished that last page before either one of them.

"Was there something . . . wrong about it?" the Gaffer asked.

Janey shrugged. She was feeling unaccountably irritable all of a sudden, but she was determined not to take it out on either her grandfather or her friends.

Good practice for the new and improved Janey Little, she thought. Just saying Madden let them live that long.

"It just didn't end like I was expecting it to," she said.

Clare opened her eyes. "How did it end?"

"I'm not sure. I mean, I know how it ended, I'm just not sure what it means. I need a bit of time to suss it all out."

"I know what you mean," Felix said.

"I feel like doom's just hanging over our heads," Janey went on. "It's like no matter what we do, we're going to do the wrong thing."

"What you have," Clare said, "is an attitude problem."

Janey scowled at her, forcibly reminding herself not to come back with some sharp-tongued retort.

"And just what is that supposed to mean?" she asked.

Despite her good intentions, there was still a bit of an edge to her voice.

Clare smiled to take the sting from her words. "It's just that if you expect things to go wrong, they usually will."

"*I* didn't bring this all down on us," Janey protested. "You can blame Bill Dunthorn for that. I only found the book after *he* wrote it." She frowned as she said that. "Or whatever he did to make it."

"That's not what I meant."

Janey took a moment to answer, then sighed.

"I know," she said. "But it's hard feeling positive when everything feels so bleak. I expect this Madden bloke to come bursting through the door with a gang of thugs any minute."

"You've been watching too many American movies," Clare said.

"I suppose. But I swear, if one more thing goes wrong, I'm going to do more than scream. I'm going to bash someone. I really am."

So much for the new and improved Janey Little, she thought.

"Remind me to keep out of her way," Felix said to Clare in a loud stage whisper.

"She's a frightful bully, isn't she just?" Clare replied in a similar voice.

Janey shook her head and couldn't help a smile. It felt good.

"All right," she said. "But you have been warned."

Felix and Clare started shaking with mock fear until Janey started to laugh. She collapsed into the Gaffer's reading chair, unable to stand.

"Feel any better?" Clare asked when Janey's laughter had finally subsided.

Janey nodded. "Much."

"Dinner's ready," the Gaffer said.

"I could eat a horse," Felix said as he got up from the couch to follow the Gaffer into the kitchen.

"You are a horse," Clare told him.

"Would that make me a cannibal, then?"

"Don't know. Aren't horses vegetarian?"

Felix put two fingers on either side of his mouth and assumed a very poor Boris Karloff imitation.

"Not vher vhe come from, mine dear."

Clare made a cross with her own fingers and brandished it fiercely in his face whereupon Felix began to moan.

They were being silly, Janey thought, and it felt good. It was just like old times. She could almost forget all the mad things that had been going on, not to mention the perplexing end to the book. . . . Unfortunately, none of their problems were going to go away as easily as her irritable mood just had.

"So do you still want to go to the Men-an-Tol?" Felix asked a little later while they were still eating.

"More than ever," Janey said.

Felix nodded. "It's worth a try, I suppose. But I wouldn't hold my breath expecting that we really are going to call up some magical world full of piskies and the like."

"I know."

If she did that, she'd soon turn blue and asphyxiate. But she knew she had to try.

"Before we go," Felix went on, "we should wrap the book in plastic. That way we can still hide it somewhere out in the fields."

"Won't Madden just track it down?" Clare asked.

"Well, we've all finished reading it now, haven't we? Didn't your friend say that that would close off its magic?"

Both Janey and Clare nodded.

"The last time odd things occurred because of that book," the Gaffer said, "the effects remained for some time afterward."

"Doesn't change anything," Felix said, "because here's what we're going to do. We'll hide the book as best we can, then when we get back here, we'll call Lena Grant and tell her that we'll give it to her for a price."

Janey's brow furrowed.

"But—" Clare began.

"No, hear me out. We'll arrange to meet at a certain place—you can figure out where, Janey, but someplace fairly public would be best. . . ." His voice trailed off.

"And then what, my robin?" the Gaffer asked.

Felix looked around the table at each of them.

"I don't know," he said finally. "I haven't worked it all out. We want them to incriminate themselves, but I can't figure out how we'll do that."

"They won't do anything in a public place," Clare said. "They've already proved that they're too smart for that."

"But hiding the book's a good start," Janey said.

She laid down her utensils, her meal done. She'd been so hungry that she hadn't even been aware that she'd polished off everything on her plate until she was done. She looked down at it ruefully.

"I'm sorry, Gramps," she said. "I didn't taste a thing."

"Understandable, my treasure."

"We should go," Janey said.

"I'm too old for that kind of a trek," the Gaffer said.

"But will you be safe here by yourself?" Janey asked.

"They won't do anything in the middle of the village when everyone's still awake," her grandfather replied.

"And we'll be back soon," Felix said.

"Should we call Dinny?" Janey asked. "He did ask us to."

Felix shook his head. "And when he asks *why* we're going out to the Men-an-Tol? We'll call him when we get back."

"But I'm coming," Clare announced. "I promise I won't slow you down."

"That's all right," Janey said. "I know the farmer there—we can drive most of the way up his track."

They stood up from the table.

"Leave the dishes," the Gaffer said as Felix started to clear the table. "It'll give me something to do while I'm waiting for you."

"If you're sure . . . ?"

The doorbell rang, halting any further conversation. With the day they'd just had, no one wanted to answer it.

"It's more bad news," Janey said. "I can feel it in my bones. Why don't we just duck out the back and ignore it?"

"That's brave," Clare said, trying to make light of the nervousness that she was feeling as much as Janey was.

"Well, you go answer it then."

"I'll get it," Felix said.

2.

John Madden's spirit traced the pattern of the countryside surrounding Penzance like a cloud of birds.

He was a sharp-eyed kestrel, hovering high in the still air, missing nothing of what went below. A hook-beaked fulmar petrel that stalked the strand line along the coast. A long-legged curlew wading in boggy moorland. A stonechat in the furze, hopping closer to where two old men sat on a stone wall with their cloth caps and gum boots, gossiping as they rested. A jackdaw catching a vagrant breeze above a reservoir.

His spirit soared high, sailed low, and the patchwork countryside was laid bare to his view. He traced ley lines, rediscovered old secret places, marked new ones: stone crosses and standing stones; barrow mounds and old battlefields; smugglers' caves and deserted tin mines; pools where salmon wisdom lay dreaming and graves where old spirits stirred at his passing.

And central to it all, like the hub of a spider's web from which its emanations spread out in patterning threads, he was always aware of William Dunthorn's secret key, thrumming to its own rhythm, a rhythm that twinned and was yet apart from the heartbeat of the land. A hidden wisdom that whispered and promised and had lain central to his thoughts for longer than he cared to remember.

Soon to be his.

Soon to—

He started and opened his eyes.

"What is it?" Grant asked.

Madden lifted a hand for silence as he concentrated.

The gate that Dunthorn's key had opened was closing, withdrawing. It was recalling its secrets—all the untutored enchantments to which it was heir—and locking the door on them once more.

It wasn't possible.

The Littles should have had no knowledge of what it was that they held. They could open it—for the door to such secrets could easily be opened by accident. But they should have no understanding as to how to close it once more.

Yet it *was* closing.

Senses stretched taut, he could already feel its presence fading.

The process was slow. Residual traces would remain for weeks in the area. But the gate itself that the key unlocked was closing. When it was shut, he would be returned to the same moment of frustration as he had been some thirty-five years ago.

That he wouldn't allow. Before he let Dunthorn's secret slip away from him again, he would risk a tide of blood to acquire it.

He turned to Grant.

"I need a car," he said.

Grant nodded and glanced at Gazo who had laid aside his magazine and was looking at them.

"I don't know what I can find at this time of day on a Sunday," he said, "but I'll see what I can do."

He stood up and headed for the door, pausing when Madden called after him.

"I don't care how you get it, or who you get it from, but I'll pay well for its use. Perhaps the clerk at the desk can provide us with something."

Gazo nodded. "I'll get right on it."

"Where are we going?" Grant asked when the door closed behind him.

"Not we," Madden said. "Only I."

"But—"

"I appreciate your wanting to help, but this is something I must do on my own, Rollie. I'm afraid that there will be a price paid for what must be done; a price paid inside"—he touched a closed fist to his chest, just above his heart—"and you are still not far enough along the Way to disperse the inevitable effects that will result from tonight's work."

It must be *mine,* Madden thought. He'd learned the lesson that Michael's treachery had taught him. First it must belong to him alone. If there were aspects he could share with others of the Order, tidbits he could pass out to those he favoured, he would do so. But first it must belong to him. Heart and soul.

"What about Bett?" Lena asked. "What do we do if he comes back?"

"There's no more time to wait for Michael."

"But if he *does* come back?" Lena pressed.

"Have your man Gazo restrain him. But I don't think we will be seeing Michael here tonight. I can sense his hand in this."

Grant shook his head. "I don't understand. In what?"

"The Littles have found a way to undo the spell that woke Dunthorn's secret. It's fading away again."

"But—"

Enough, Madden thought.

Though he rarely used the influence of his will in such an undisguised manner with members of the Order, his patience had run out. Time was speeding by, almost out of control—time he could not afford to waste with explanations.

He locked gazes with them—first Grant, then his daughter.

You will do as I tell you, he told them. *There will be no further discussion.*

When he let them go, Grant squeezed his eyes shut and rubbed at his temples.

"Maybe it's best you go on alone," Grant said. "I've got a migraine coming on."

"Do you want me to get you something for it?" Lena asked, all her concern now focused on her father.

Grant shook his head. "I think I'll just go back to my room and lie down for a while."

Madden and Grant had worked in such close proximity for so long, with Madden constantly influencing him, that Grant didn't have a chance to fight the older man's will. Grant would never even begin to suspect how he had just been manipulated. Madden's control over his colleague was absolute, though he was usually far more judicious in his display of it.

The daughter was another matter. For all the years he had known her, she was still an unknown quantity that Madden suspected had far more natural affinity for the Order's teachings than anyone suspected. She might present a problem.

Madden could see questions lying there behind her eyes, but either the force of his will was holding strong for the moment, or she was wise enough to keep silent. That would have to do for now. If she did remember this incident and raised a fuss about it later, he would deal with her at that time.

But for the present moment ... He caught her gaze again and locked his will to hers. Knowing her preoccupation with the pleasures of the body, it was a simple matter to influence her, and then Gazo when he returned with word of the car that he'd found, to busy themselves once he was gone.

The questions faded in her eyes, and he smiled. He had set the desire so firmly upon them that they might well be at it before her father even had a chance to leave the room.

Madden stopped in his own room long enough to put on an overcoat. When he stepped outside the hotel a few minutes later, the car was right where Gazo had promised it would be. It was a small red Fiesta—smaller than Madden would have preferred, but beggars couldn't be choosers, he told himself, and considering the narrow back roads and lanes of this area, it was probably the most appropriate vehicle Gazo could have acquired for him.

He had a few awkward moments, getting behind the wheel on what felt like the wrong side of the car for him, but he adjusted almost immediately and was soon on his way along Penzance's seafront, heading for Mousehole.

3.

Felix opened the door to a pair of strange faces. One belonged to a well-dressed woman, the other to a hulking man in a cheap suit who for some reason reminded Felix of a bodyguard. It was something about the careful way the man held himself. He stood a bit behind the woman and off to one side, measuring Felix with as watchful a gaze as Felix was studying him.

The woman was holding an envelope in her hand. She seemed calm, but her fingers were nervously fidgeting with the envelope.

"Can I help you?" Felix asked.

But then the Gaffer and the others were there. Janey stood at her grandfather's shoulder and peered at the woman, struck by her familiarity. She struggled to place the face.

"Hello, Tom," the woman said to the Gaffer. "It's been a long time, hasn't it?" She turned her attention to Janey. "And you must be Jane. You've grown."

The accent was American. The clothing, the fresh face with just a touch of makeup, was nothing like what Janey remembered from her dream, but then that had been a dream. Not real.

But this didn't feel real either.

"Mother . . . ?" she said.

The Gaffer stood stiffly at her side, his anger a palpable presence that seemed to spark from him.

"You . . ." he tried. He could barely speak, he was so enraged. "You dare. . . ."

Felix moved to one side so that the Littles could directly confront their visitor. He and Clare exchanged worried looks. Clare's hand crept to Janey's who clasped it with a grip so tight it hurt.

"I want to talk to you," the woman said.

The Gaffer pointed a stiff finger to the street beyond his garden gate.

"Get away from this house!" he demanded. "Take your whorish—"

"Now wait a minute," the woman's companion began.

He took a step forward, pausing when Felix straightened up from the doorjamb where he'd been leaning. The stranger held his hands out in front of him, palms outward.

"We don't want any trouble," he said. "We just want to talk to you for a minute, Mr. Little, and then we'll be on our way."

"I've nothing to say to the likes of her," the Gaffer told him. "Nor to you, if you're her friend."

Janey could only stare at the woman. She'd always wondered how she'd feel if she ever met her mother. A hundred scenarios had gone through her mind—her mother would come back to Penzance for a holiday and they would run into each other by chance on Market Jew Street, or they would meet at one of Janey's American gigs, her mother coming to listen to her talented daughter whose career she had been following with pride from afar. Or maybe on a plane, or on a bus. On a crowded city street somewhere. Always a chance meeting. Always they would find they had so much in common. . . .

Never like in last night's dream.

But the sentiment would be the same. Her mother would turn to her and whisper softly, with tears welling in her eyes, *Forgive me.*

Janey laid a hand on the Gaffer's arm. "Wait a minute, Gramps. Can't we see what they want?"

She drank in her mother's presence, memorizing her features. They had the same nose, the same cheekbones. Her mother's carriage was different—smaller bones probably—but they had the same peaches and cream complexion. The same long fingers.

"Thank you, Jane," her mother said. "May we come in?"

"We can hear you well enough from where you are," the Gaffer said stiffly, the anger in his voice almost raw.

Janey started to say, oh, let her come in, but the words died unsaid at what she heard next.

"It's about Paul's will," her mother said.

Janey thought of the man who had attacked Clare. Of her canceled tour. Of how the Boyds' farm was being taken from them. Of the woman who had drugged Felix. . . .

Forgive me.

Her mother wasn't here to be forgiven. She wasn't here to return to the fold.

"It seems Paul never made a new will after the divorce," her mother was saying. "My lawyer tells me that . . ."

Janey couldn't concentrate on what was being said. All she knew was that her mother was here because John Madden had sent her.

She could feel the Gaffer's anger deflating—turning to despair as her mother spoke of Paul Little as though his only legacy was nothing more than a commodity. There was no room for memory, for the warmth and kindness that had been so much a part of her father. Didn't her mother understand how much she and Gramps had *cared* for him?

"Naturally, it would be more convenient for us all to settle out of court, but we're quite prepared . . ."

How could her mother be doing this? Didn't she see what it was doing to Gramps? What kind of a hold did Madden have on her? Didn't she have a bloody heart?

Would a compassionate woman have left the way she did?

"Get out of here," Janey found herself saying.

Her mother turned her gaze from the Gaffer to Janey. "I don't think you really know what—"

"Don't talk to me like I'm a child," Janey said.

The new and improved Janey dissolved under a wave of anger that ran far deeper than the Gaffer's.

"But—" her mother started.

"You just tell Madden that he's not getting it," she said. "I don't care *what* he does, I'll destroy it before I'd ever let him get his hands on it."

"Now don't go off half cocked," the man who accompanied her mother began.

"Shut your gob," Janey told him.

"We don't know any Madden," her mother said.

"Oh, really? You don't know John Madden—the old bugger who sits around in an office somewhere getting a kick out of thinking up new ways to ruin people's lives? Too bad. I guess you can't pass the message on to him that we know what the secret is and we know how to destroy it. So why don't you just piss off."

She gave Felix a little push to get him out of the way and started to close the door.

"All right!" her mother cried, putting her own hand up to stop the door. "I'll admit we're here to get whatever it is that Dunthorn left you, but we're not working for any John Madden."

"You *aren't*?" Janey said in a sweet voice that bore a dangerous underpinning edge to it. "Then who are you working for?"

"I can't tell you."

"Too bad."

She started to push against the door again. She wanted it closed. She wanted the woman out of her life, just as she'd been for most of it. She wanted her to have never come, because if it was possible, she felt worse now than she had before. And poor Gramps. . . .

Felix started forward to put an end to the shoving match that had developed between Janey and her mother when Janey suddenly shouted: "I hope you rot in hell!"

The vehemence in her voice startled her mother. With the slight ease of her pressure on the outside of the door, Janey put all her weight behind her own side and slammed it shut. She had time to lock it before she turned and almost fell into the Gaffer's arms, tears streaming down her cheeks.

Felix started to reach for her, then turned towards the door. Clare caught his hand before he could unlock it and step outside. He started to shake her off.

"Don't," she said. "It'll only make it worse."

"But—"

"It's not worth it, Felix."

Felix turned to where the Gaffer was trying to comfort Janey. The old man's eyes were shiny.

"How . . . how can she be my mother?" Janey wept against her grandfather's shoulder. "How can she be so awful? I don't ever want to be like her."

"You aren't, my love," the Gaffer said, stroking her hair. "You're your father's daughter and as fine a young woman as I've ever known. Your father would have been proud of you."

"But she . . . she . . . How could she . . . ?"

"It's that man's doing—your John Madden. I'm sure he paid her well."

Janey finally stood back. She wiped at her eyes with the backs of her hands. Felix got a box of tissues from the kitchen and brought them back to the front door where he handed her one. She blew her nose and dabbed at her cheeks. She took a long ragged breath, slowly let it out.

She felt worse than awful.

"But *why* would he pay her to do it?" she asked. "What was the point?"

"To make you feel like this," Clare said.

Felix pulled back the lace from the window in the door and looked out.

"They're gone," he said.

Janey sniffled and blew her nose again.

"And we have to go, too," she said. "Before something else happens. I can't bear any more."

Felix nodded, then turned to the Gaffer. "You'll have to come with us now, Tom. There's no telling what they'll do."

"They're not chasing me out of my own home," the Gaffer said.

"Will you at least call someone to stay with you while we're gone?"

"I don't need baby-sitting."

"Please?" Janey put in.

The Gaffer sighed. "All right. I'll ring up Dinny. But don't you wait for him to come. You just go on and do what you can with the book."

"But—"

"I won't budge in this, my robin. I'll be fine."

Janey looked to Felix for help, but he only shook his head.

"We don't have much time," Clare said. "The moon will be rising soon."

"Oh, Gramps. . . ."

The Gaffer gave her a hug. "Go on then, my gold. No one will be bothering me here."

He went to the phone as he spoke and dialed the Boyds' number.

Full of misgivings, Janey collected the Dunthorn book that they'd wrapped, first in a plastic bag, then in a waterproof oil-skin satchel. She waited until the Gaffer had finished his call, refusing to leave until she could at least be sure that Dinny was going to be staying with him.

"There, my treasure," the Gaffer said as he got off the phone. He tried, but didn't quite manage, a smile. "It's all arranged."

Janey could see that her grandfather felt about as much like smiling as she did, but she loved him for trying.

"We should go," Clare said.

Janey nodded. "I love you, Gramps," she said.

"I love you, too," he told her.

Blinking back new tears, Janey reached for the tissue box again. It was sitting on the back of the sofa, beside her purse. She blew her nose, then stuffed more tissues into her purse. Her Eagle tin whistle, the kind that came in two parts so that it was easy to carry around, was in the way. She started to take it out, then just stuffed the tissues around it, and hung her purse from her shoulder.

She gave the Gaffer one last look. "Don't let anyone in," she said, "unless you're sure it's Dinny. And if it's not, if *anything* happens, promise me you'll ring the police straightway."

"I will."

Plainly unhappy at leaving him behind, she finally let Felix and Clare hurry her out to the car. The little Robin started first time around and moments later they were chugging up the hill to Paul.

4.

"Well, that's that," Connie said after a moment's stunned silence.

She and Dennison stared at the door that had been slammed in their faces. Connie couldn't help shivering as she remembered the look on her daughter's face just before the door closed.

I hope you rot in hell.

Connie had been cursed before, but never with such conviction. Coming from her own flesh and blood seemed to lend more weight to it. She suppressed another shiver.

"I guess I blew it," she said, turning to her companion.

And she felt like shit for trying.

Think of that ten grand, she told herself. Bett's still going to pay up. All she'd lost was her shot at the bonus.

And her self-respect.

"I don't think so," Dennison said.

Connie just shook her head. "Where were you when all this was going on? Didn't you see the look she gave me?"

"But that's exactly what Mr. Bett hired you to do—shake them up. Put them even more off their stride."

"So how come I feel so bad?"

Dennison gave her a considering look, then shrugged. "I didn't say what you did was right—I just said you'd done what Mr. Bett hired you to do."

"Thanks for caring."

Christ, she thought as soon as she said it. Like she should talk about caring after what she'd just done.

I hope you rot in hell.

She probably would. And living as she had for the better part of her life, she knew just who'd be keeping her company down there. All the sleazebags and lowlifes and losers.

Dennison took her arm and steered her out of the Littles' tiny yard.

"Let's see if we can find a phone booth and call ourselves a cab," he said.

Connie shot a lingering glance at the Gaffer's house and suppressed a sudden desire to go back and apologize, then she shook her head.

Like they'd even listen.

As though even if she'd known exactly how she'd be feeling right this moment when Bett had first asked her, she wouldn't still go right ahead and do it all the same.

She knew herself too well. She needed that money. She needed whatever she could get.

"Connie?" Dennison said.

She turned from the house and let him lead her back down to the harbourfront.

5.

It was Lena's sprained ankle that saved her.

She had the faint buzz of a headache in the back of her head, but it wasn't enough to stop the wave of pure animal hunger that had her shivering every time she looked at Gazo. As soon as Madden left she could barely hold on for her father to leave the room before she started to peel off her clothes.

Her jacket dropped to the floor, quickly followed by her skirt. A glance at Gazo showed her that he already had his pants off, his penis standing at stiff attention as he crossed the room towards her. She fumbled with the buttons on her blouse in her hurry to get it off but then Gazo was standing in front of her. He tore it open, popped buttons spraying across the room.

Pushing her bra up from her breasts, he pressed his face in between them and started backing her towards the bed. Lena could hear herself making small moaning sounds in the back of her throat. She reached down and grabbed his penis, wanting it inside her, wanting—

Her ankle twisted badly as Gazo backed her up—the sudden sharp pain momentarily clearing her mind.

"Wha—"

Gazo pushed her back onto the bed. His hands were all over her.

Her ankle felt like it was on fire.

She tried to push him aside.

He had his penis in his hand and was roughly pushing its head against her vagina.

That hurt too. Her need for him had fled and she wasn't wet enough. It felt like he was trying to stick a roll of sandpaper up inside her.

"Stop it," she said, trying to wriggle out from under him.

But he was too big for her. His weight alone was enough to keep her pinned to the bed, never mind his superior strength.

Panic set in.

"Stop it!"

She drummed her fists against his back, but that just seemed to excite him more. And then he was inside her and she shrieked from the agony. Her arms flailed. One hand brushed up against the lamp on the night table beside the bed. Her fingers grabbed hold of it and smashed the lamp alongside his head.

He stiffened, pulling partway out of her.

She hit him again. This time the lamp broke.

He rolled from on top of her to lie on the bed, curled up now, hands clutching his head.

Lena backed up against the headboard, still clutching what remained of the lamp. Her breathing came in short, ragged gasps. Pain moved in waves from the hollow in between her legs and her ankle. She lifted the broken base of the lamp as Gazo straightened up and turned his face towards her.

"Don't touch me!"

But his eyes were different. The blow to his head had cleared his mind as well. He sat up, looking shocked and confused, but no longer dangerous.

"What . . ." he began. He shook his head and winced at the pain. "What the hell . . . happened?"

Lena started to shake her head as well. How should she know? One moment they were all sitting around in the room and everything was normal. The next . . .

She remembered Madden's eyes.

The low buzz of a headache sharpened in the back of her head to join the rest of the pain.

And then she knew.

"Madden," she said.

"What?"

"Madden—he did this to us."

Gazo just looked more confused.

"His will's that strong," Lena said.

A dull anger was building up inside her. He'd used her and Gazo like they were his sheep. She thought of her father's sudden migraine. That had been Madden's doing as well. If it suited his purposes, he'd use even his most trusted colleague as though he were nothing more than a servant—less than a servant. Servants at least got paid. It was a job, for them. They *knew* what it entailed before they ever hired on.

But this. . . .

When she thought of all of Daddy's migraines, she realized that they must have come from exactly this kind of a situation. Madden forcing his will on Daddy. Who did Madden think he was, playing around with their heads like this? With *her* head.

Lena knew exactly what he was. A monster disguised as an old man. But a very dangerous old man.

"What do you mean his will?" Gazo asked.

Lena looked up at him.

Of course, she thought. He wouldn't know. He wasn't an initiate.

He was part of Daddy's security force. He knew all about the cut-throat practices of the business world, stood in as a bodyguard some-times, but he knew nothing of what the Order really stood for. That secret wasn't trusted to outsiders. If Gazo knew about it at all, he would simply think of it as some kind of an exclusive country club, though what he'd thought of some of the conversations he'd over-heard—like when Madden and Daddy were discussing this thing of Dunthorn's—Lena didn't know.

Maybe it was time he learned, then. Time everyone learned.

"He got inside our heads," she said. "Got in there and manipu-lated our thoughts so that we'd do whatever he wanted."

"You mean . . . this . . . ?"

Gazo indicated their state of undress.

Lena nodded.

"He hypnotized us?"

"That's one way of putting it."

Gazo shook his head slowly.

"I don't know," he said. He looked around the room at where their clothing lay scattered on the floor. "Jesus, I'm sorry, Lena. I . . ."

He got up and collected her skirt, jacket, and what remained of her blouse. Passing them to her, he went to put his pants on. Lena dressed as best she could. Her ankle screamed when she was slipping her skirt on. She pulled her bra down. With the buttons torn off her blouse, all she could do was pull it closed. She put her jacket on overtop and buttoned it up.

Being dressed helped—but not enough. When she thought of what Madden had done to them, how he had manipulated them . . .

Suddenly an intense feeling of revulsion came over her.

Felix.

My God. When Felix thought of her . . .

Knowing how she now felt about Madden, she realized that Felix must really hate her. And there was nothing she could do to make it up to him. It wasn't the kind of thing that could be forgiven, that you could make better, because the memory of it was always going to be there, sitting in the back of your head just like this headache was sitting in the back of her own mind.

He would never forgive her.

She didn't deserve to be forgiven.

But she could warn him. About Madden and Bett and the kind of power they had behind them. Not just their wealth and influence, but this other thing. The ability to crawl right inside your head and manipulate your thoughts.

She'd never dreamed that the Order's tenets concerning the power of the will could be taken so literally. She'd always thought of it as a kind of psychological edge. Not a physical reality.

It was like magic.

"Maybe I'd better go," Gazo said.

She looked up to find him watching her. His features were guarded, embarrassed.

"It wasn't your fault," she said. "Madden *made* you do it."

"Maybe. But maybe I . . . maybe I've always been . . . interested in you. In that way. Not forcing myself on you," he added quickly. "But, you know. Attracted to you."

"There's no law against being attracted to someone," Lena said.

"Yeah, but I'm supposed to be working for you. Your father hired me to protect you. Instead—"

"Read my lips," Lena said firmly, "I'm telling you it wasn't your fault."

"Yeah, but—"

"Maybe I've thought that way about you, too. Are we supposed to feel bad every time we see someone that turns us on a little?"

"I suppose not."

Lena smiled wearily. "Could you bring the phone over? I need to make a call."

She had the operator connect her with the Little household. A man's voice answered, but it wasn't Felix. It was an older man— probably Janey Little's grandfather.

"May I speak to Felix?" she asked him.

"He's just stepped out."

Tom Little's voice was heavy with suspicion. Must be the American accent, Lena thought. She couldn't really blame him. With all that had been going on lately, he wouldn't be feeling too kindly towards Americans at the moment.

"Can you tell me where he's gone?" she asked.

"He didn't say."

"It's very important. When will he be back?"

"He didn't say."

Wonderful. Tom Little's voice sounded like a recording.

"Could I leave a message then? Would you tell him that—"

Tell him what? That Lena Grant called? That would certainly make Felix eager to get back to her.

"Yes?" Tom Little prompted her.

"Never mind. I'm sorry to have bothered you."

She hung up.

"What were you just trying to do?" Gazo asked her.

She set the phone aside and gave him a considering look. "Warn Felix about Madden."

"He wasn't in?"

"No. That was Tom Little I was talking to."

"So why didn't you just warn him?"

Lena sighed. "I didn't think he'd listen to me. Felix might. I'm sure he hates me, but I think he'd still listen. Especially about something that might hurt Janey."

"Do you want to drive over and wait for him?" Gazo asked.

"I don't think so. I think we should tell Daddy about what Madden's been doing to him."

"I'm still not sure about that myself," Gazo said. "This hypnotizing business . . . I thought they had to, you know, move a watch back and forth in front of you until you fell asleep—or something along those lines. I've never heard of someone being able to do it just"—he snapped his fingers—"like that. It's like . . . I don't know . . . like . . ."

"Magic."

Gazo smiled. "Yeah, right."

"It takes a leap of faith," Lena told him, "but that's about the best description I can come up with."

"Magic."

Lena nodded. "Would you help me up? I want to go talk to Daddy."

"He's going to be angry when he finds out."

"I hope so," Lena said.

6.

Bett arrived at his vantage point behind the wall fronting the Methodist Chapel a little later than he had planned. He'd had a lot to take care of and it all took longer than he'd thought it would. The whole damn country seemed to close up on a Sunday.

He settled down where he could see the house easily and tuned in his radio transmitter just in time to hear the Little woman and her friends saying good-bye to the old man. He removed his earplug when they came outside so he could hear what they were saying.

"How far is the Men-an-Tol?" Gavin was saying.

"Just a little ways past Madron," the Mabley woman replied. "It won't take us that long to get there."

Gavin said something else that Bett couldn't hear over the sound of them opening their car doors.

"I doubt we'll get lost," the Mabley woman said. "There's a footpath that goes all the way from the track. Didn't Janey ever take you out there?"

"Yeah, but not at night."

The doors closed and the Little woman started up the car, effectively muting any further conversation that Bett might have been able to overhear.

Maybe he should have had Dennison wire the cars, too, he thought.

He ducked down out of sight as the car's headbeams washed over the chapel's low wall, lighting up the side of the chapel itself with a bright glare. He waited until the car had passed him and was going up Mousehole Lane to Paul before lifting his head again. He saw the Reliant's taillights go up the hill then disappear as the car went around a corner.

The Men-an-Tol, Bett thought. That was one of those stoneworks that Madden was so keen on. Now why the hell would they be going out there at this time of night?

He looked back at the house.

Didn't matter. He needed only one of them—the old man or his granddaughter. Made no never mind which of them he got. The woman would have been fun, but a man screamed just as shrilly as a woman if you knew how to coax it out of him.

He stowed away his earplugs and the radio receiver in the knapsack that hung from his shoulder by one strap and started to rise, only to be forced to duck down again as another set of headbeams hit the wall. These came from a small red Fiesta that rolled up from the harbour. It stopped in front of the Little house, its engine idling, the headlights no longer aimed at the chapel. With the cover of darkness, Bett peered above the wall. When he dropped back down behind the wall this time, it was with a curse on his lips.

Madden was in that car.

Bett had been hoping to get the night's work done without Madden's interference, but he'd prepared to deal with his mentor if the need arose.

He looked above the wall again to see Madden just sitting there in his car, eyes closed. When Madden lifted his head suddenly, Bett was sure that his mentor had spotted him, but Madden wasn't looking in his direction. Instead, Madden gazed up the hill to where Janey Little and her friends had driven off. Putting his car into gear, Madden drove off in the same direction.

Bett waited until the Fiesta's taillights had disappeared around the same corner that the Littles' car had before he stood up and brushed himself off.

Looked like Madden was walking on the edge tonight as well, he thought. Got himself locked onto Janey Little's wavelength and he wasn't going to let go.

Bett wasn't happy with the complications this was going to bring to his own carefully orchestrated plans.

He jumped down to the street and crossed over, slipping in through the hedge behind the Littles' house so that he was approaching the building from its own tiny backyard. He could see Tom Little in the kitchen, cleaning up dishes.

That made it nice and easy.

He pulled a gun from his knapsack, then slipped the loose strap over his other shoulder so that the knapsack was hanging against his back.

He didn't have to do this himself. He could have hired someone to pick up the old man or his granddaughter for him. But the more people you brought into this kind of thing, the more problems you made for yourself. Besides, he *liked* the look of shock that came over a victim's face when they knew they were screwed.

It sharpened the edge and brought everything into focus.

He didn't waste time pussyfooting around. He just kicked in the door and leveled the gun at the old man. The look on Tom Little's face was everything he could have hoped for.

"Hi there, pops," he said. "Mind if I use your phone?"

The old man was holding a pot and looked like he was ready to throw it.

Bett shook his head. "Uh-uh. That'd be a bad move. Just put it down."

"I don't have what you're looking for," the old man said.

"Maybe, maybe not. But you're going to tell me where I can find it."

The old man's face just shut in on itself.

Bett smiled. Like the old geezer wasn't going to tell him anything Bett wanted him to. Not now, maybe. Not here, for sure. Bett was saving that bit of fun for when they had a bit more privacy. For when the old man could scream his head off and nobody would interrupt them.

And he was going to scream. No question of that.

"The phone," he repeated.

He stepped in close, the gun never wavering in his hand. Giving the old man a rough shove, Bett spun him around and walked him into the living room where he spotted the telephone. He sat the old man down in a chair.

"This won't take long," he assured Little as he dialed.

Grimes completed the connection on the other end of the line half-way through the first ring.

"Yeah?"

"The job's on," Bett told him. "Madden's driving a red Fiesta." He gave him the license plate number. "Last time I saw him he was driving up to the Men-an-Tol stone."

"What the hell's that?"

"Some kind of old rock stuck in a field somewhere."

"I need more than that."

"It's near Madron," Bett said, remembering what the Mabley woman had told Gavin earlier.

"Jesus, Bett. Why don't you make it a little easier?"

"Would if I could. There's some topographical maps in the glove compartment of the rental car I got you. Look it up on one of them. I'm kind of busy right now."

"You're a real sweetheart, Bett. If I didn't want Madden this bad, I'd just—"

Bett hung up, cutting him off. He took a folded piece of paper from his pocket and laid it on the mantel where it could be easily seen as soon as someone entered the room.

"Okay," he told the old man. "Time to get our show on the road. On your feet."

When Tom Little refused to budge, Bett just sighed. He stepped over to the chair and, holding the gun against the old man's stomach, hauled him to his feet and shoved him back towards the kitchen.

"We're going to have some fun, you and me," Bett told him as he steered him into the yard, back through the hedge, then down the lane to where Bett's own rental car was parked.

He walked close to the old man, shielding his weapon from the chance view of anyone looking out a window. When they reached the car, he opened the passenger's door and pushed Little inside.

"Scoot all the way over," he said. "You're driving. And don't think of playing any games on the road. You might think you're feeling real brave and decide to kill us both in a crash, but if something happens to me . . . well, I'm not alone in this deal. Be a shame if my friends had to take it out on your granddaughter. . . ."

"I won't do anything foolish," the old man said.

Bett smiled. "That's what I like to hear."

But the possibility still hung there between them, and Bett relished it.

It made the edge he was walking all that much sharper.

7.

"What if there really *are* two different groups after the book?" Clare asked from the back seat of the Reliant Robin.

Janey and Felix were sitting in the front, Janey actually driving carefully for a change. They entered Newlyn from a back road, turning left at the A3077 that they followed until it connected with the A3071 that would take them northwest to Tremethick Cross. There they turned right, heading north to Madron. They passed the National Trust gardens of Tregwaiton House on their left, the Boscathnoe Reservoir on their right, before they reached the village where they made another left onto the B3312.

"Doesn't make any difference for what we're doing now," Felix said.

Clare nodded. "I'd just like to know."

"Mr. Goninan didn't say anything about another group of people," Janey said.

"Doesn't mean there isn't," Clare said.

"I suppose."

The road they were on now would take them all the way to the village of Trevowhan if they kept following it. A little farther past the village and they would be at the Morvah cliffs where, far below, the Atlantic washed against the tiny islands of Manakas and Wolf

Rocks. They'd often picnicked on those cliffs in the years before Janey and Felix broke up—sometimes just the three of them, other times with Dinny and his sister Bridget joining them.

There was good music at those picnics—little sessions with the sound of the wind and the waves adding their own counterpointing rhythms to the sounds of fiddle and accordion, whistle, flute, and the two sets of pipes, Northumbrian and Uillean, that Janey and Dinny invariably brought. Janey was half inclined to go there now and never mind all the mad things that had come along to turn their lives topsy-turvy. But when they reached the Men-an-Tol print studio, housed in the old Bosullow schoolhouse, she dutifully turned the little Reliant up the dirt track that would take them across Bosullow Common and most of the distance to the Men-an-Tol itself.

The holed stone wasn't the only stonework in this area—just the most famous. It was the largest tolmen in the British Isles, which often surprised visitors who were expecting something along the scale of Stonehenge. Instead, what they got for their twenty-minute walk from the B3312 was a round wheel of a stone with a large hole in its center, two short menhir on either side of the hole, with a third stone lying flat on the ground beside the easternmost longstone. The hole in the tolmen was large enough for a grown man to crawl through, although someone with shoulders as broad as Felix's might have some trouble.

Besides the Men-an-Tol, there were only two other major stoneworks nearby: the Boskednan, or Nine Maidens, stone circle to the east, and an inscribed stone known as the Men Scryfu to the north. But the area was riddled with smaller stoneworks, both ancient and more modern. A little farther north of the Men Scryfu was a point called the Four Parishes, a large slab of rock bearing an incised cross-hole where one could stand heel and toe with the parishes of Gulval, Madron, Morvah, and Zennor. There were also any number of cairns and crosses, solitary stones and hut circles, tumuli and all the remnants of the old tin mines: shafts, pits, and the disused mines themselves.

Janey stopped the car when the track finally gave out and they could go no farther. They all got out, Felix rooting about in the glove compartment for the flashlight that he knew Janey kept there. The night was quiet, the moon still below the horizon, but they could see its glow. As their eyes adjusted to the dark, Felix thrust the flashlight into his pocket in case they needed it later.

"We should get moving," he said.

"Just a minute," Janey said.

She was looking back down the track towards the Coronation House farm that lay on the other side of a privet hedge that they had passed earlier.

"We don't have long," Felix reminded her.

"She knows," Clare said. "She's just waiting for Kempy."

"Who?"

"You'll see."

Janey put her fingers to her lips and let a shrill whistle sound out across the land. A few moments later they all heard an answering bark.

"Kempy?" Felix asked.

Clare nodded.

Kempy was a mad border collie that invariably followed any visitor on their walk to the Men-an-Tol. His biggest thrill was to have stones tossed for him that he would then fetch and bring back to lay at the thrower's feet, a lunatic grin on his face as he barked for the game to begin again.

Janey had always loved the name of the moorland here—the Ding-Dong Moors. It was an old name, and she knew that the inspiration for it couldn't have been taken from Kempy, but she couldn't help but believe that if it hadn't been named for Kempy's antics, then one of the border collie's forebears had had that dubious honour of being responsible for it, which was "Almost the same difference," as Chalkie liked to say.

The name actually came from the bottle or bell mines from which the ancient Romans had excavated rich lodes of ore, particularly from the one known as the Ding-Dong Mine on the eastern edge of the moor where, during the last century, a loud bell was rung to summon the miners to work.

Kempy himself came charging up just then. Janey bent down to accept an enthusiastic faceful of licks before she finally stood up.

"Want to go for a walk, Kempy?" she asked.

The dog barked happily. He went and danced about Felix, sniffing at him, tail wagging, then tried to stick his head up Clare's skirt. She pushed him away with a laugh.

"Pervert," she muttered.

Janey threw a stone that rattled off farther down the narrowing track when it landed. Kempy raced after it, charging through the darkness, leaving the others to follow at a slower pace. About fifty yards on they came to a stile on their right that took them directly onto the moor. From there a path led off through the thick gorse, ling, and bell heather to the holed stone.

8.

Madden had no trouble tracking the artifact that was Dunthorn's secret—and it was an artifact, he had decided by now. A talisman of some sort. He could almost see it. It occupied space, had physical weight. All he lacked now was an understanding of its actual shape.

But although he could track the artifact as Janey Little ferried it across the countryside, his unfamiliarity with the area itself slowed him down. He knew exactly where the object was at all times, but found himself going down too many dead ends where he had to back up and start again, or following narrow lanes that, after leading him in the correct direction for a time, unaccountably veered off, taking him out of his way.

When he eventually reached the Men-an-Tol print studio, the moon was already rising. He turned up the lane, following it until he reached a Reliant Robin that had been parked there ahead of him. He pulled in behind what he assumed was Janey Little's car and stepped out onto the lane. Closing his eyes, he turned slowly in one spot until he had the object's position fixed once more.

He was about to start off down the narrowing track when he heard a call from the direction of the Coronation House farm he had passed earlier. He turned to see the beam of a flashlight bobbing along the dirt. The man following it was short and stout. He had a Cornishman's round face, wellie boots on his feet, a rain slicker, and the unavoidable cloth cap on his head.

"You there," the farmer called out as he approached. "What do you think you're doing?"

"Parking my car."

The farmer shook his head. "Not allowed. This is private land. You'll have to move it."

"But this other vehicle . . . ?"

"That belongs to a friend of mine—she can park there anytime she likes—but you'll have to park back at the road."

Madden had no patience for this sort of nonsense—not now, not when he was so close. He locked gazes with the farmer, his annoyance making him use far more force than was necessary. The man staggered back, clutching at his head with one hand. The beam of his flashlight pointed skyward, weaving back and forth as the man fought for balance against the fierce, sharp fire that was hammering behind his eyes.

"You don't mind if I park my car here, do you?" Madden asked.

The farmer shook his head slowly. He didn't glance at Madden; he simply pressed his hands against his temples in a vain hope to alleviate the pain.

"Perhaps you should lie down—get to bed a little early tonight," Madden suggested. "You appear as though you could use the extra hours of sleep."

"Think I will," the farmer said.

His voice was dull with pain.

A dim-witted sheep, Madden thought as he watched the farmer walk slowly back the way he'd come. That was all the man was. That was all any of them were—the world teemed with them.

He sighed, flexed his fingers, then turned to look across the dark moorland once more.

He concentrated for a moment, marking the location of Dunthorn's artifact, then set off along the narrowing track that he'd been about to follow before the farmer had interrupted him. He knew this area. He could even guess, when he reached the stile that would let him out onto the moor, where Janey Little and her friends were going.

To the Men-an-Tol.

What he couldn't comprehend was why.

And that troubled him more than he would care to admit to anyone—including himself.

9.

The moon was peeping over the horizon when Janey and the others finally reached the Men-an-Tol. As always happened when she found herself in an ancient site such as this, she couldn't help but shiver with its sense of mystery—no matter how small or insignificant the stonework might be, no matter if it was out on a moor like this, or stuck in a farmer's field with cows placidly chewing their cuds around it.

The moor around this tolmen was one of her favorite spots—and it had obviously been one of William Dunthorn's as well, considering how much it had played a part in his writing, not only its significant role in *The Little Country,* but also in a number of articles he'd written for various journals. She'd often brought her pipes up here, enjoying the mood that their music woke in her when it mingled with the antiquity of the place. She smiled as she remembered the face of more than one tourist who'd followed the sound of her music to the stone. She was never sure if they were disappointed or relieved to find that it was only her toodling tunes by the tolmen and not some faerie piper.

"Well," she said.

She looked at Felix and Clare who were both waiting for her to make the first move. Kempy lay at the edge of cleared ground that surrounded the stone, smack dab in the middle of where the path from the lane joined it. His tongue lolled from his mouth and she couldn't shake the feeling that he was grinning at her.

If he was, she knew why.

The tingly feelings she got from places like this, that sense of old mysteries lying thick in the air just waiting to be called up, that was one thing. What had brought them tonight . . .

"I feel kind of dumb," she said.

"You have to give it a try," Felix said.

"I know. It's just . . ."

She sighed, taking the satchel with the book in it from her shoulder.

"Is there anything we should do?" Clare asked.

Janey smiled. "I don't even know what *I'm* supposed to do."

But she did. Hadn't Dunthorn told her, his counsel crossing the boundary of the years by way of the book? Maybe it was her story that she'd read in *The Little Country,* her phrasing, her voice, but it was still Bill Dunthorn speaking to her.

Nine times through the hole at moonrise.

"Better get to it," Felix said.

Janey nodded and walked over to the stone. "Give me a hand?"

He stepped over to the opposite side of the hole. She looked at him through the gap in the stone, still feeling foolish. He smiled reassuringly.

"Here goes nothing," she said.

She passed the satchel through to him. He took it and handed it back to her. She put it through the hole again.

That was twice.

And she felt more than dumb: She felt downright harebrained. But she kept passing the satchel through, counting off the times softly under her breath.

Six.

What if there really *was* another world on the other side of the stone? Who would end up guarding the book, then? Some little pointy-eared piskie?

The whole situation was mad. But the book itself—there *was* a magic in it. They'd proved that, because they'd each read a different story in it.

Seven.

She paused as she got the satchel back from Felix, thinking she'd heard something. She cocked her head, listening. The sensation grew in her that something was approaching. She felt it, not in the rational part of her mind, but in the intuitive side: an odd, inexpressible feeling that crept into the marrow of her bones and resonated there.

A sound.

She remembered what had happened in the Dunthorn book and then, as though that memory was a catalyst, she recognized what it was that she heard.

A faint trace of music, distant and eerie.

And familiar.

It was the same music that she'd heard coming from the book. . . .

She looked at Felix, wanting to ask if he heard it too, but she didn't need to ask. She could tell by the look on his face that it wasn't just her imagination. There was a look of wonder in his eyes, a slight loosening of his jaw.

It had to be real, because he was hearing it as well.

She passed the satchel through again.

Eight, she counted to herself.

And now she could pick out individual instruments: whistle and pipes; the clear ring of harp strings and the long, slow notes of a bow drawn across a fiddle's strings; the soft rhythm of a drumbeat—

Dhumm-dum. Dhumm-dum.

—that seemed to twin her own heartbeat.

And there, in the center of the Men-an-Tol's hole, a pinprick of light. A faint glow. A glimmering.

Her breath caught in her throat and she found it impossible to take another. She was numbed with awe.

It's real, she thought. There was a real magic here. . . .

Beyond the tolmen, mists were rising from the moorland. Slowly Janey took the satchel that held the Dunthorn book and passed it through the hole for the last time.

Nine.

Light flared, blinding her. The music rose to a crescendo. Janey let the satchel go. The flare died down, fading on the last strains of the music that seemed to be moving away, over one hill, over another, until it was gone. The silence around the stone lay heavy and deep, sweet with wonder.

When Janey could see again, she found Felix looking at her through the Men-an-Tol's hole. His hands were empty.

"The—the book . . . ?" he asked haltingly.

"Gone," Janey said.

Her heart sang. She could still hear the music—the memory of it— inside her, its rhythm still twinning her heartbeat. She fumbled in her purse for the tin whistle that she'd brought with her, her fingers trembling as she put the two parts together and then brought the mouthpiece up to her lips.

"It was unbelievable," she heard Felix say.

His voice seemed to come from a great distance. Clare was kneeling on the grass beside her, one hand reaching out to touch the stone. Janey felt aware of everything and nothing in that moment. She started to blow into the whistle, wanting to capture that music, or at least what she could of it, before the memory was completely gone, but then Kempy barked, and the moment of wonder came thundering down in a crash.

She turned to look at the path leading up to the stone. Kempy was backing up into the clearing, still barking. Standing there on the path was a tall figure; an angry figure. His eyes seemed to glow with his rage. They were red coals that caught the moonlight and took it inside them, swallowing it.

"What have you *done*?" he cried.

The voice was like ice, promising pain. Power crackled in the air around the man. He shot a gaze at the dog and Kempy abruptly stopped barking. Whining, the dog crawled on its belly away from the dark figure.

It didn't take much insight for Janey to realize that they were finally face-to-face with John Madden.

10.

Grimes was in a foul mood by the time he finally pulled up across from the Men-an-Tol print studio on the B3312. He looked at the darkened building, then over to the signpost on the other side of the road that indicated the beginning of a public footpath to the Men-an-Tol.

It had taken him longer than he'd expected to get here. The maps that Bett had left in the glove compartment of the rental car had been more than adequate. It was matching them up to the often unmarked roads that had been a bitch. Especially at night.

He looked past the signpost, off into the darkened moorland. So how far was this stone anyway?

Turning on the interior light, he pulled the map up from the seat beside him and spread it out across the steering wheel.

Not too far. Close enough so that he could leave the car here and walk up. That'd save the sound of the engine carrying across the moor.

He didn't want to give Madden any more of a warning than he could possibly help. When he thought of the man's eyes—

His missing hand started to ache again.

Uh-uh, he thought. This time it ends differently.

He parked his car over in the small lot near the print studio and crossed back over to the lane that led up to the Men-an-Tol. Removing his .38 from his pocket, where the cloth might snag against its trigger if he had to get it out quickly, he thrust it into his belt, under his jacket. Then he started up the lane.

He walked at a steady clip, reaching a pair of parked cars in under fifteen minutes.

Bingo. One red Fiesta.

Thank you, Bett. I owe you one.

The other vehicle was one of those weird three-wheeled Reliants. He wouldn't ride in one of those if you paid him to. Damn thing looked like it'd tip over the first time it went around a sharp curve.

He studied the surrounding landscape, trying to decide where Madden and the owner of the other car might have gone, then figured he'd just stay put. Wandering out on those moors, who knew where the hell he'd end up? Getting lost he didn't need—not when he was this close. Sooner or later Madden would be coming back for his car. He'd just wait here for him.

Grimes stepped over into the deeper shadows of the hedgerow on the west side of the lane and leaned up against a stone. He slowed his breathing, relaxing until a deep calm settled over him. It was a simple hunter's trick. You just melted into the background—*became* a part of the background. Until you made your move.

For this kind of a thing, all you needed was patience.

And Grimes had that in spades.

11.

Dinny Boyd arrived at the Gaffer's house to find no one home. The front door was locked, and though he rang the bell a number of times, there was no reply. His pulse quickened as he tried peering in through the lace-curtained window above the door, but he couldn't make out very much.

It wasn't like Tom Little to say one thing, then do another. If the Gaffer planned to meet a body somewhere, then he would be there for that meeting.

Unless he'd run into trouble.

There was something decidedly odd going on—Dinny had no doubt about that. This business with the farm and then the things that Janey had told him earlier this afternoon . . .

He went around back, his pulse quickening still more as he took in the state of the kitchen door.

Someone had broken in.

He stepped nervously inside, stilling his first impulse to call out.

What if whoever had done this was still inside?

There were dirty dishes piled up near the sink. Taking a bread knife from where it lay on the counter, he moved cautiously into the living room. A thorough search of the house let him know that he was alone in it.

Janey, Clare, and Felix were gone.

And so was the Gaffer.

Then the phone rang.

Dinny went back into the living room.

That'd be one of them ringing up to explain matters, he thought as he picked up the receiver. But he couldn't still the prickle of uneasiness that had lodged in between his shoulder blades—an uneasiness that only increased when he answered the phone.

"Hello?"

"Who's this?" an unfamiliar voice asked. The accent wasn't quite American.

"Dinny Boyd."

"Sorry. Wrong number."

The line went dead.

Dinny slowly cradled the receiver. He looked around the room again, searching for some clue as to what was up. His gaze settled on a piece of folded paper that was propped up on the mantel. He crossed the room, read the note, then returned to the phone.

"Dad?" he said when the connection was made. "I think you'd better meet me at the Gaffer's."

"What's the matter, then, Dinny?"

"I'll explain when you get here. Bring Sean or Uncle Pat with you, just don't leave Mum and Bridget alone."

He went to the front door and unlocked it, standing on the Gaffer's small stoop while he waited for his father to come. The early evening lay quietly upon the village, giving no indication of the danger Dinny could feel closing in on him, his family, and his friends.

Kick the World Before You

I seem to be a verb.

—attributed to
BUCKMINSTER FULLER

Bodbury seemed a strange and furious place to Jodi when the Widow's fetch carried her through it.

The wind howled and leapt through the narrow streets in a hundred different directions at once, whirling and spinning like a mad pack of dervishes. It crept in between the glass panes and metal frames of the gaslit street lamps, blowing out the flames, making the dark streets darker still. Litter danced and tumbled in its wake. Shutters rattled. Red clay shingles were torn from the rooftops to shatter on the cobblestones. Windows were blown open, curtains billowing inward until the owners of the houses had a chance to shut them again.

The fetch chittered happily to itself as it scampered down the steep streets towards the harbour, careening from side to side to keep its balance as the wind buffeted it. The creature seemed utterly in its element, its fearsome mouth split from ear to ear in a grin as it ran.

When they reached Peter Street, Jodi shrieked as loud as she could in the hope that she'd been wrong about those new longstones out on the moor near the Men-an-Tol. Surely they weren't her friends, enchanted by the Widow the way that legend told that the wicked young women who danced on a Sunday had been changed into the Merry Maidens or Boskednan stone circles in times long past and gone.

The fetch paused to look up as the window to Denzil's loft rattled and then flew open. Jodi's heart lifted high with hope at the thought of rescue, then plummeted again when she saw it was only Ollie, peering curiously out into the stormy night from the windowsill. Denzil's monkey clung to the curtains as the wind tried to blow him from his perch. Jodi opened her mouth to call again, but then Windle hissed and she realized that while Ollie could easily swing down from the upper story to the street, she doubted that he was any match for the Widow's fetch.

She kept silent, allowing the fetch to bear her off down to the harbour. Ollie remained behind on the windowsill, playing tug-of-war with the wind as he tried to close the window once more. The last view Jodi had of the monkey, before the fetch bore her around a corner, was of him hanging from the window as it was swept back and forth by the battering wind.

Now they were nearing the waterfront. The waves lashed up against the shore, spraying in enormous white spumes as they struck the wood and stone of the piers. By New Dock, fishermen were struggling with their luggers and boats—to little avail. Jodi saw that some of the boats were already wrecked; others were breaking free to smash against the stone quay.

And then there was the Widow.

She stood well back from the washing spray of the seawater, a tall forbidding figure in a dark mantle with eyes that seemed to glow with their own inner light. On either side of her, shadowy sloch capered and flittered in the wind. Between where she stood and the wild sea itself were rank upon rank of drowned men—corpses dragged up from their sea graves to serve her. They paid no mind to the battering waves that lashed them. Seawater streamed from their limp hair, their tattered rags and the seaweed that clung to their limbs.

It was all some horrible nightmare, Jodi prayed. Please let that be what this was. Don't let it be real.

But the grip of the fetch's bony fingers was too solid to be a dream; the storm too wild. The Widow too imposing. The sloch and sea dead . . .

Yammering happily to itself in its high grating voice, Windle bore her forward and presented her to the Widow. Jodi shivered as the Widow's cold fingers closed around her and took her from Windle's grip. She lifted Jodi to the level of her eyes.

The fires in them burned like hot coals and Jodi remembered Edern's warning.

Don't look into her eyes.

The memory came too late. Jodi tried to look away, to block the crackle of power that leapt from the Widow's gaze into her own eyes, but the Widow's witcheries tore down the feeble walls Jodi tried to raise and easily entered her mind.

The fingers squeezed painfully, rubbing Jodi's ribs against one another. It was growing impossible to breathe.

No, Jodi realized mournfully. It wasn't a dream.

It was all too real.

The Widow's witcheries stirred about in Jodi's mind as though they were a ladle, her mind a cauldron. Jodi's memories churned and roiled in confusion until, as though from a great distance, she heard a vague rhythmic sound.

Dhumm-dum.

"You've led me a pretty chase," the Widow was saying, "but now you're mine, you miserable little wretch."

Her eyes glittered with promises of the torments she had in store for her diminutive captive.

But Jodi was beyond fear now. The Widow's witcheries had called up a trace of that sense of unity that Jodi had shared with the Barrow World, a sliver of memory that had still remained lodged inside her. It echoed to her heartbeat—

Dhumm-dum. Dhumm-dum.

—and distanced her from the moment at hand. It took her past her terror into a place where a numbness spread throughout her limbs, separating her from her body and the pain that the Widow was inflicting upon it until she could look on what was happening to her and the town with the dispassionate gaze of a simple observer.

She was still aware of her danger, still afraid. But the part of her that was an observer was now able to consider the situation from a more objective point of view. She took in the fury of the storm that the Widow had called down. The monstrous creatures . . .

Yesterday the Widow had been hard put to raise a few miniature shambling sloch and send them after one clockwork man and Jodi herself. And failed. But today . . . today her sloch were tall and moved like quicksilver, the sea dead answered her call, and she seemed to rule the elements.

How had she become so powerful?

"I want the secret," the Widow went on. "You will give me the secret to the Barrow World."

Jodi merely looked at her, thinking, what secret? It lay all around them, separated only by an invisible boundary of onion-layered thickness. With her sympathy to the Barrow World still thrumming powerfully inside her—

Dhumm-dum.

—Jodi could almost see that otherworld superimposed over the storm-wracked view in front of her. It was that close.

"Each time you refuse," the Widow said, "I'll pluck a limb from your body. I'll keep you alive until you're nothing more than a bodiless head, pleading for death. And don't think you can trick me. I can smell the stink of a lie."

The pressure of the Widow's witcheries in Jodi's mind was like a dull, throbbing headache.

"Lie . . . ?" Jodi asked.

Her voice was still hoarse from when she'd cried for help on the mad journey from the Men-an-Tol to Bodbury in the fetch's grip.

Lie, she thought dreamily. She would like to lie down if she could.

For everything had become increasingly bewildering. It was as though she were here, but not here. Viewing a droll from the safe anonymity of an audience, rather than from the stage itself. The world about her was now a surreal blending of two worlds—on one hand, the storm-tossed bay at Bodbury's harbour; on the other, the clear, still water of the Barrow World.

The night here with its thunder and shocks of lightning set against the Barrow World's bright blue skies. The Widow, her monstrous sea dead and sloch and the struggling fishermen compared to a strange array of the Barrow World's creatures who had gathered near the shore of their own world—mermaids and piskies; a man with a raven's head, another with a stag's antlers sprouting from his brow; creatures that appeared to be small trees that had pulled their roots from the ground and gone walking; a woman with a round face like the moon, whose hair was green, whose eyes were golden, whose hips disappeared into the shoulders of a grey-backed horse so that the two disparate segments were a part of the same body. . . .

In this world, the Widow and her creatures threatened; in that world, the folk were listening to that music—

Dhumm-dum. Dhumm-dum.

—that echoed inside Jodi.

"You *will* tell me," the Widow said.

Her voice seemed to come from very far away—a vague murmuring sound against the deep richness of the first music.

"Tell you . . . ?" Jodi asked dreamily.

She saw that Bodbury's fishermen had given up their struggle with the sea and were gaping openmouthed at the Widow and her creatures. One or two, more attuned to secrets and hidden things than their fellows, were pointing at cottages and buildings that flickered, were replaced by the green swards of the Barrow World, only to blur and disappear again.

Dhumm-dum.

And now Jodi saw more than a blurring blend of the two worlds. She saw the past and present mingled: Old Bodbury mixed with the new. All was changed—the same but different. There were fewer buildings in the town, there were more. New Dock existed; it was gone as though it had never been. The ruin of the Old Quay appeared as it had been in its former heyday; echo of her heartbeat, the drum of her pulse, the heartbeat of the town, of the bay, or the moorland that lay beyond. . . .

Dhumm-dum.

Jodi felt herself expanding to become a part of it all, of both worlds, of the past and of the present, drifting further and further away from the moment at hand, from its danger, from the Widow and her creatures. . . .

Dhumm-dum.

The Widow shook Jodi until her teeth were rattling in her head.

"*Tell* me!" the Widow cried.

The shaking brought Jodi somewhat back to earth. She stared deep into the fires that lay at the back of the Widow's eyes and was surprised to find that all her fear of the woman had gone. The pressure of the Widow's witcheries was gone from her mind.

"I can't tell you," she said.

The Widow's eyes glittered dangerously.

"I can only show you . . ." Jodi said.

Something sparked between their locked gazes—a fire more ancient than anger.

And then the Widow was drawn into seeing the world as Jodi perceived it; hearing the heartbeat rhythm:

Dhumm-dum.

Two worlds flickering between each other, past and present mingling.

In one moment she knew all that Jodi had ever been. And Jodi knew her. Jodi met Hedra Scorce—the girl the Widow had been before she'd lost her innocence, before she'd changed. Jodi saw Hedra's life unfold, heard the whisper of the shadows that had turned the Widow from what she'd been into who she was now.

Those awful shadows who approached so eagerly now. Not the capering figures of the sloch that surrounded the Widow, but older shadows: the dark voices that whispered to every man's and woman's heart, that fed on jealousy and anger and hatred.

"I'm so sorry," Jodi said.

And she was. Tears welled in her eyes and spilled down her cheeks.

"No," the Widow said in a small voice.

The winds had died. Above, the sky was still dark with clouds, but the lightning had ceased, the thunder was silenced, the rain still held back.

The sea dead shambled back towards the sea. The capering oversized sloch that the Widow had made from bog and shadow and parts of herself collapsed in upon themselves into heaps of putrefied mud and rotting vegetation.

The Widow fell to her knees.

Dark things crept from the sides of the buildings and walls where the night lay thickest. Old shadows. Evil things.

A witch cannot cry, Jodi thought. And she knew why. Tears, with their salt content, were anathema to them. It made sense that a witch would lay a spell on herself, some form of a defense mechanism to ensure that she physically *could not* weep.

But the Widow was no longer just herself now. A part of her was Jodi Shepherd; a part of her was Hedra Scorce, the innocent child that she had once been. That part of her wept at the knowledge of what she had become.

Tears welled in her eyes, blinding her. They ran like lava down her cheeks, stripping the skin to the bone. Her flesh smoldered and filled the air with an awful reek. On her knees, the Widow bowed her head until her brow rested against the cobblestones. The muscles of her hands went limp and Jodi slipped free.

Jodi backed away from the Widow, but couldn't go far. The old shadows that had ringed the Widow completely blocked her escape. They whispered and snickered among themselves. Their greedy eyes drank in the Widow's pain, her defeat. Forgotten for now was the Barrow World and its secret gate. Sweeter by far was the immediate moment.

The Widow whimpered. Her fetch stroked at her hair and made mewling sounds.

The tears continued to burn from the Widow's eyes. Her skin smoked. She opened her mouth to scream, but the tears ran down her throat and only smoke issued forth. Her throat worked involuntarily and now she burned from the inside as well as the out.

The shadows tittered.

"Fight them!" Jodi cried.

She didn't think it at all odd that her sympathy lay now with her former enemy, for when the first music had taken her through the Widow's history, Jodi had understood that the blame lay not wholly with the Widow herself. The Widow had been weak, she had listened to the evil whispering of the shadows and allowed her own disappointment and sorrow to blind her to the wrongness of what she did, but it was the shadows themselves that were the real enemy.

Their incessant whispering.

How they trapped those whose despair and weakness left them susceptible to the endless chattering of their voices.

And their false promises. . . .

Jodi could hear them as she stood there watching the Widow die; their whispering battered against her mind. It crept in under her thoughts, tempting her with a dark power. No longer need she be victim to any other, they told her. Hers would be the mastery. Hers the control. Let others beware *her*. . . .

But Jodi could ignore their voices. She could push them aside. Not because she was stronger than the Widow had been when her name was still Hedra Scorce, and not because she was necessarily a better person, but because she had the first music thrumming inside her.

Dhumm-dum. Dhumm-dum.

Its rhythm showed the whispers to be the lies they were. In its harmony there was no room for their untruth. They brought only pain and suffering while the first music healed.

"Listen to it," Jodi told the Widow.

She knew the Widow could hear the music—it was there inside her the same way that the Widow's memories were in Jodi.

"Let the music heal you," she added.

The Widow lifted her head to look in Jodi's direction. Her ruined features made Jodi's stomach churn. Bone showed through the flesh. Skin hung in tattered strips from cheeks and chin. The blind eyes fixed sightlessly on her.

For one moment Jodi saw another face there—that of Hedra Scorce, the sweet and gentle face of an innocent child—then the ruined mask returned.

"It . . . is . . . too . . . late . . ." the Widow said.

Her voice was a rasping croak. More tears streamed from her eyes as she spoke, burning their way through her flesh.

"Try!" Jodi cried. "Oh, please try!"

"I . . . can't. . . ."

The shadows tittered with great good humour as the Widow collapsed on the cobblestones again. Smoke wreathed from her flesh. Her fetch howled and threw itself upon her as an unearthly blue-green fire flared up, consuming them both.

Jodi stared horrified, unable to turn away. She watched until the flames died away and all that remained of the Widow and her fetch was an untidy heap of her empty clothes. All else was gone—flesh, skin, and bones.

With the Widow gone, the shadows turned their full attention on Jodi, but she barely heard them. She stumbled forward, and fumbled about the Widow's mantle until she came upon the buttons that were sewn there. Unerringly, steered by the rhythm of the first music that still rang inside her, she reached for the button that was her own.

When she touched it, a fiery pain flared through her body. She dropped to her knees, blinded by its raw fury. She couldn't breathe, couldn't think. All she knew was that unending hurt that seemed to go on and on forever.

It was a very long time before she could finally lift her head again.

She found herself crouched upon the Widow's empty clothes. The first music was gone, though she could still hear its echoes. The shadows were fled, back into their dark corners, though she could still hear them, too, as a faint annoying bee-buzz in the back of her head.

She sat up slowly.

"Do you need some help there, girl?" a voice asked.

She looked up to find a burly fisherman offering her his hand. He was so matter-of-fact, so plainly here and now, of this world, that Jodi could only look at him with confusion. Others stood nearby and she heard snatches of their conversation.

"Strange wind, no doubt o't."

"Come like a tempest, gone as quick."

"Well, now, autumn's the time for odd weather."

"My old granddad had a tale about a night like this. . . ."

They didn't remember anything about the Widow or her creatures, Jodi realized. Nor the strange shifting between the worlds. Nor the ghosts of times past and people long dead who had flickered to life all around them.

"Up you come then," the fisherman said as he gave her a hand up. "Were you hurt at all by the wind?"

Jodi shook her head.

"Well, you've dropped your laundry," the fisherman said. "Basket's long blown away, but you could wrap it up in this mantle."

Jodi let him bundle up the Widow's clothes and hand them to her.

"Do you need some help finding your way home?" he asked.

"No. I . . . thank you."

"You look like you've taken a chill," the fisherman said. "Best get yourself home for a cup of something hot."

Jodi nodded. "I . . . will."

She found a faint smile to give him and walked unsteadily off, not really sure where she was going until she was up at the top of Mabe Hill, above the town, standing near the ruins of the Creak-a-vose. She let the bundle she was carrying drop to the ground and sat on a nearby stone.

She lifted her hands up to her eyes and studied them carefully, comparing their size to the dried blackberries on a bush beside the stone.

She was her own size again.

Unless . . .

Oh raw we. Had she ever been a Small in the first place? Perhaps she'd gotten herself a thump on the head in the middle of this odd storm and only dreamed the whole affair?

No, she thought. It had all seemed far more real than a dream. And if she listened hard, she could hear the faint rhythm of the first music, still twinning her heartbeat, but it was a far and distant sound now.

It had all happened. She was sure of that. Only something was making her forget—just as the fishermen on the waterfront had already forgotten.

Well, she *wouldn't* forget. That was the promise she'd made to Edern, wasn't it? To wake the first music in her own world, to bring the two worlds closer together again. But how was she supposed to do that when people could stare something magical straight in the face—as the fishermen had done—and then simply turn away from it as though it had never happened?

The thought of it just made her feel depressed.

But at least she was her own size again. And the Widow wasn't a threat anymore.

That didn't make her feel any better. It was a relief to feel like herself again and know that she was safe from the Widow, but she got no pleasure from having defeated the old woman. It seemed to her that the only winners were those whispering shadows. If they fed on pain and despair, then they had fed well on the Widow tonight.

Jodi sighed.

She looked down at the bundle of clothes. Reaching down, she unwrapped the bundle until she could shake the mantle free from the rest of the clothes. Sewn there, on the inside of it where that piece of her had been sewn, were a double handful of buttons. She touched one and the image of one of the Tatters children rose in her mind. Another, and she saw Henkie Whale.

She thought of the new set of longstones out by the Men-an-Tol.

Magic *was* real, she reassured herself yet again.

The good with the bad. Which meant one really did have to beware of the whispering in the shadows. But there was the first music—

Dhumm-dum.

Just thinking of it made it seem closer. Where she'd felt a bit of a chill thinking of what watched from the shadows, now a comfortable glow started up in the center of her chest and spread out to enclose her in a soft cocoon of warmth.

The one helped to balance the other, she supposed.

Standing up, she slung the Widow's mantle over her shoulder and set off across the moorland to where her friends stood like so many stones in the gorse, waiting to be rescued.

The Eagle's Whistle

The thing to remember, is that artists are magical beings. They're the only people other than the gods who can grant immortality.

—MATT RUFF, from *Fool on the Hill*

Felix smiled as Janey pulled her whistle from her purse and put its two pieces together. The sheer beauty of the music that seemed to rise up from all around them had his fingers itching for an instrument as well.

Capture the magic, he thought, watching Janey bring the whistle to her lips. For it *was* magic.

He looked at his hands, then at the hole in the stone where the satchel had disappeared in a flare of light. If he hadn't seen it with his own two eyes . . .

His heart was singing. There was a foolish grin on his face and he didn't care who saw it. The world had changed, in one moment, into a place of infinite possibilities. Every wonder was possible. Every mystery could be revealed.

On the back of that music . . .

And then it all came crashing down with John Madden's appearance.

Music fled: and with it, the wonder. The magic.

For a long moment Felix could only stare at Madden and curse his intrusion. He was only barely aware of the glow in the man's eyes, of the way the border collie fled their eerie gaze. He rose to his feet, anger tightening the muscles of his shoulders until his own gaze locked with Madden's.

He thought he was falling.

Madden's gaze swallowed him whole and then the ground opened up underfoot and he was plummeting some unguessed distance, stomach lurching at the speed of his descent, head dizzy, muscles all gone weak.

It's just a trick, he told himself. The man's just putting the evil eye on you—like he did the dog.

But then all logic fled. He was caught in the sudden flare of a spotlight and he was no longer falling. He was seated on a stool, on a stage. His box was on his knee; before him an ocean of faces.

Im-impossible. . . .

But he could feel the hard wood of the stool under his buttocks, the familiar weight of his accordion, the sweat that broke out over his face under the onslaught of that piercing spotlight. The audience was vast. He couldn't make out individual faces—just a presence in the darkness beyond the stage. An animal crouching, waiting for him—

To play.

His hands shook. Gone was all memory of how he'd come to be here, or any question of where here was. There was only the feral presence of the audience and his own panic—a gibbering, howling panic that settled on him like a too familiar nightmare. There was a dull pressure on his chest. He felt feverish and sweaty cold. The restless noises from the audience as they stirred impatiently in their seats faded away in one moment, became overly bright in the next.

His chest was tight now, heart speeding up, its beat ragged. Simply breathing was a labour. The restless sound of the audience pressed in on him, beating at his ears in a shrill cacophony of overly loud coughs, fabric rustlings, foot tappings.

Snickering.

They know, he thought. They know I can't. . . .

A stifled chuckle to the left—a stagehand, with his hand up against his mouth, the taunting laughter still bubbling in his eyes.

Felix shook his head numbly. His voice was trapped in his throat. He spoke with his eyes.

Please. I . . .

A great big bloke like you, a mocking voice whispered in the back of his mind. *Where's your courage?*

I . . .

Play or die, that voice whispered.

No. I . . .

His legs trembled uncontrollably. His box would have tumbled from his knee were it not for the death's grip his hands had on its straps.

Play.

The laughter was spreading through the audience and he could feel his soul curling up inside himself into a fetal position, thumb in its mouth. . . .

Play—

I c-can't. . . .

—or die.

He was bent over his box, sweaty brow pressed against the cool surface of its plastic casing. He wrapped his arms around it, hugging it to his chest.

The laughter grew into a wave of ridicule, wailing inside his head, shrieking behind his eyes. His heart was hammering an explosive tattoo. Sharp, whining pains pierced his chest. His bowels grew loose.

Play—

The laughter was like thunder. He moaned, trying to shape words, if only in his mind.

I . . .

—or die.

Thousands of heads tilted back, roaring at his discomfort, their laughter thick with derision as they pointed their fingers at him. Individuals all melded together into a lumbering beast, galvanized by his panic, drinking in his terror like greedy vampires.

I . . . can't. . . .

It's show time, kid, that awful voice inside him mocked. *Time to play or—*

He'd just have to—

—die.

2.

Charlie Boyd took the note from his son's hands when he arrived at the Gaffer's house. He'd come alone, leaving Sean and his brother at home with Molly and Bridget. He took out a pair of glasses and settled them on the bridge of his nose, his face growing grimmer with each terse line he read:

Dear survivor,

Here's the game plan. You got something I want and I got something you want. We do a straight exchange. No muss, no fuss. And no cops. Screw up, and what I got comes back in pieces. And then I'm coming after you. Hang loose now. You'll be hearing from me real soon.

When he had read it through a second time, Charlie laid the note down on the table by the door. He put away his glasses.

"Where did you find it?" he asked.

"On the mantel."

"And the Gaffer?"

"There was no sign of him, Dad. Just the back door—broken in."

"And someone rang up?"

Dinny nodded. "A wrong number. The accent was American—or close enough to it to make no difference."

"It was an American that rang us up earlier," Charlie said thoughtfully.

"It must be the same man."

"So it would seem."

"What do we do now, Dad?"

Charlie sighed. "We've no choice," he said. "We have to ring up the police."

"But the note said—" Dinny began.

"I know what the note said, son. But what can we do? I'm not bloody John Steed."

"It's just that . . . if something happens to the Gaffer because of what we've done . . ." Dinny turned pained eyes to his father. "How could we face Janey?"

"Where *is* Janey?"

"Gone off somewhere with Felix and Clare."

Charlie glanced at his wristwatch.

"We can't wait for them to come back," he said. "We have to turn this over to the professionals, son. We'll tell them what Janey told you—about this Madden man and all—and let them deal with it."

Dinny nodded glumly. His father crossed the room to where the phone stood. He had no sooner put his hand on the receiver than the phone rang, its sudden jangle startling them both.

3.

Clare leaned on her cane and almost didn't feel the need of its support. The music that washed around the Men-an-Tol made her want to throw it away and dance—really dance, with complete freedom, with utter abandon. With the liquid movement of a ballerina, or the animated spontaneity of a modern jazz artist, not the laggard shuffle of a slow dance that was the best she could manage.

As it was, she swayed where she stood, marveling at the magic. Of the music. Of the flare of light that had swallowed Dunthorn's book. Of the sheer wonder of it all.

She grinned when Janey took her whistle from her purse and wished she'd thought to bring along one of her own. But then she'd never be able to come close to capturing this magic. Not like Janey could.

So she just closed her eyes, her body moving in an easy swinging rhythm, back and forth in one spot, letting the wonder wash through her—

Until a sudden coldness bit into her with the force of a knife thrust and everything changed.

She turned to see John Madden standing at the end of the path, his eyes glowing. Kempy fled his gaze, whimpering. Janey's music faltered before it even had a chance to really begin. Felix rose from the other side of the stone. He took two steps towards Madden, then crumpled to the ground, moaning and curling up into a fetal position.

Clare took a half step towards him. "Felix, what . . . ?"

But then she made the mistake of looking into Madden's glowing eyes herself. His gaze locked on to hers and then she was falling too, just like Felix had. She sprawled onto the ground, but she couldn't move. Though it had been years since she'd known this feeling—that emptiness in her legs where there should be feeling—she could never forget it.

That lack of feeling was there now. Her nerves were dead, muscles unresponsive. Corpse limbs attached to her body.

Madden had paralyzed her, but not just her legs.

"Nuh . . . no . . ." she moaned, her voice no more than a whimper.

Oh, no. Not just her legs, but her whole body. Paralyzed from the neck down. With that one fiery glare from his eyes, he'd turned her . . . not back into a paraplegic.

No. That was too simple a horror.

Instead he gave her her worst fear: He'd made her a quadriplegic.

And that she couldn't bear. That was *all* possible control stolen from her. Better to take her life. Better to just die now than to try to live with this horror.

Because she couldn't.

She'd been strong. All her life she'd had to be strong. But she wasn't this strong. Nobody could be this strong. Nobody could go through all she'd had to go through, recover as much as she had, and then have it taken away like this.

"Puh-please. . . ."

All she could do was turn her head towards him, begging him. Her body was some monstrous mound of dead flesh, attached to her only by flesh and bone. There was no connection with meaning. No nerve. No muscle. There was nothing there.

She couldn't live with it.

"Nuh-not . . . this. . . ."

But he was already turning his attention away and looking towards Janey.

4.

Bett grinned at his captive. They were hidden from sight and from hearing both at the bottom of one of the silos of the bay side of the quarry that lay almost midway between Mousehole and Newlyn. Apparently they still used these old silos to ship the stone out to Germany and the like. But they didn't use them at night; they certainly weren't using them tonight. Bett had made sure of that.

And all he needed it for was the one night.

He'd tied the old man to a chair that he'd brought along for that purpose and now it was just the two of them, here on the edge. Walking the thin line.

"It's you and me, old man," he said.

He'd tried to impose his will on his captive, without success. He had to give the old man credit. Tom Little proved to have far more resistance to Bett's mesmerizing than Bett had ever imagined he would. But it didn't matter. It would just take a little longer, that was all.

And they had all night.

"Be a shame if I got hold of that cute little granddaughter of yours," Bett said. "She already likes me—I can tell. Thinks I'm her step up to the big time."

"You . . . you're the reporter?"

Bett laughed. "In the flesh. To tell you the truth, I was hoping to grab her instead of you. I figure she'd squeal quicker and I do like to hear them squeal."

The Gaffer spat at him, but that only made Bett laugh louder.

"Now here's the game," Bett said. "We're going to make one more call to your sweet little granddaughter. She comes across with the goods, we're all going to leave this place as friends. But if she doesn't . . ."

He patted one of the three jerricans of gasoline that he had sitting beside him on the loose stones.

"If she doesn't, you and I are going to have ourselves a weenie roast, old man."

"You—"

"And then I'll *still* go after her."

"If I—"

"Yeah, yeah. If you were free. If I faced you like a man. Grow up, you old jerk. That's not the way the game goes. Uh-uh," he added as the Gaffer opened his mouth again. "Time to make our little phone call."

He took the portable phone from the knapsack that lay beside the jerricans and punched up the number for the house on Duck Street.

"There," he said. "It's ringing. Scream all you want now. It's just going to add to the . . . validity of the call."

He smiled at the tight line that the Gaffer's lips made.

"Who's this?" he said into the receiver when the connection was made.

"Charlie Boyd," came the reply.

"Wrong answer," Bett said.

He hung up and put away the phone. With an exaggerated sigh, he rose to his feet and shook his head.

"Gee, I'm real sorry about this, old-timer. But the ball's really in your court now."

He unscrewed the top of the jerrican and stepped over to the chair, pouring the gasoline over one of the Gaffer's legs. With a show of great care, he took the can back across the small space and put it next to the others, then returned to stand in front of his captive.

"Anything you want to tell me?" he asked as he pulled a lighter from his pocket.

The Gaffer's eyes were round with fear, but he shook his head.

Bett sighed again. The old coot had balls. No doubt about that.

He really wished that he did have the girl instead. There's no way she'd've lasted out fifteen minutes of this. Splash a little gas on her face and explain how pretty she was going to look when the fire got to her skin. . . .

Guys always had to prove how tough they were—even an old bird like this one here.

"You're not being brave," he told the Gaffer as he flicked the lighter into life. "You're just being stupid."

The Gaffer's gaze locked on the light's flame. Bett could see the whole world narrowing in for the old man, focusing on that one spot of flickering light.

He brought the flame close to the gas-soaked pant leg, laughing when the Gaffer shut his eyes and flinched. Bett snapped the lighter shut.

"Hey, but we're having fun—right?" he said when the Gaffer's eyes opened to glare at him.

Bett fed on his captive's fear, drinking it in.

"Okay," he said. "This time it's for real."

He opened the lighter again, spun its steel wheel against the flint. The flame leapt up from the wick, an inch and a half high.

5.

Janey had a forewarning that neither of her companions did.

Her version of the Dunthorn novel had predicted this very situation, from the magic of the Men-an-Tol through to Madden's arrival. Not perfectly—the details were different. But all the same, she could almost smell the stink of a bog in the air . . . could almost see the Widow's sloch, twisting and writhing on the moorland behind the intruder's tall figure.

The whistle tune faltered on her lips, fell still.

She saw Felix go down—curling up into a ball like a threatened hedgehog—rapidly followed by Clare who looked as though all her muscles had just turned to jelly on her. She started to take a step towards them, but then Madden's eerie gaze was turning on her. The magnetic intensity of his will bore down on her, sending a knife-blade chill up her spine, turning her heart to stone, until she heard a small voice, coming to her as if from far away, from a dream.

Don't look in his eyes. Don't listen to what he says.

And she remembered the little man in the Dunthorn book. The Small. . . .

Before Madden's magnetic gaze could lock fully on her will, she managed to turn her head away and lift the whistle up to her lips again.

She'd never been that fond of this particular Eagle brand tin whistle; she'd bought it on a whim, for the way it came apart in two pieces, which made it easy to tote about in a pocket or purse, rather than for its tone. It was fine in the lower register, but the upper one always sounded as though the instrument was being overblown, no matter how much she controlled her breath. It was hard enough to control its tone, little say play a tune.

But at the moment what was important was that it *did* play a tune, no matter how faulty the upper register notes sounded. All she needed was its music. It wouldn't have the magic of that other music—the first music, she thought, naming it as the characters had named it in the Dunthorn book—but so long as it kept her from hearing Madden, from looking into his eyes, it would be magic enough.

She started up a version of "The Foxhunter's Jig"—a slip jig in 9/8 that rang out far jauntier than she was feeling at the moment. She leaned into the long B notes in the second part, wishing she had her pipes with her so that she could really bend the note, and then realized it was working.

Madden's presence was a buzz that lay behind the music. He spoke, but she couldn't hear what he was saying, and so long as she didn't look into his eyes. . . .

The tune faltered as it skirted into the high notes of the third part. It was partly the whistle's fault—making her overblow the notes—but all the blame couldn't be laid on the instrument.

There was Madden.

She couldn't hear him. She refused to look at him. But she could feel him approaching her. His presence was a dark shadow in her mind—an ugly buzz. It set up a discordance—not only in the music, but in the night itself. Because she could feel him, drawing nearer, step by step.

And she didn't know what she was going to do.

She fumbled the run in the fourth part of the tune that took it back into the lower register. And heard—

"—at me. You *will* look—"

She centered all her attention on the music, circling around the stone, away from his approaching presence. But there was a crack in her concentration now. A hole in the music.

She could feel his eyes boring through it.

She tried to imagine sheet music in front of her.

The eyes burned through it.

She switched to a faster 4/4 tempo, same tune title, but a different tune. "The Foxhunter's Reel."

His eyes were the hounds and she was the fox; his will was the hunter's gun, its muzzle bearing down on her.

The tune grew ragged and she began to flub notes.

She could hear his voice again—a wordless sound that prodded and pushed at her. Her fingers faltered on the whistle's finger holes. The tune came tumbling to a halt.

Her gaze locked on Felix, lying almost at her feet, still curled up in a fetal position. Clare was lying like a dead fish a little farther away. Vaguely, in the back of her mind, she could hear Kempy whimpering, but she had no idea as to where the border collie had hidden himself.

She still couldn't hear what Madden was saying, but the tone of his voice was slowly turning her face towards him, his eyes drawing her gaze to them like a shark snagged on a mackerel-baited hook and hauled towards the sharking boat.

The mouthpiece of the whistle was still at her lips, but she couldn't seem to draw the breath needed to blow it awake again. Her throat was dry, raspy as sandpaper.

She could run. Off across the moor, into the darkness. He'd never catch her because she had to be faster on her feet than he could ever be, and fear would fuel her.

But Felix—and Clare—she couldn't leave them.

She bowed her head and looked at the ground as her traitorous body turned completely around and faced Madden. She refused to look up.

Think, she told herself. What happened in the book?

So much of what had befallen in its storyline was happening to her now that there had to be a clue in it. But the Small's voice was silent.

Salt, she thought. They'd used salt.

But she didn't have any, and whatever paranormal powers Madden had, she doubted very much that salt would do anything to stop them.

Her head was slowly lifting.

Tears, she remembered then. The music had been called up and the witch's own tears killed her. But that was back to salt again and she wasn't sharing Madden's memories. Neither could she call up the music. That needed calm, a relaxed mind. A twinning of her heartbeat to the music's ancient rhythm—

Dhumm-dum. Dhumm-dum.

—only her heart was jackhammering the blood through her veins. Quick tempo. No old slow dance tune this, but some mad Eurobeat rhythm.

Slow down, she told herself.

She forced her foot to tap on the packed earth around the Men-an-Tol.

Pat-pat. Pat-pat.

That was almost the beat. A simple rhythm—deceptively simple, because now that she was starting to get it, she couldn't understand how she might ever have forgotten it. Was it the Small from the Dunthorn book or Peter Goninan who had said . . . something about . . .

The magics of the world are far simpler than we make them out to be.

She could hear the voice in her head. And with it, a hint of music. *That* music. Thrumming to its hoofbeat rhythm.

Dhumm-dum. Dhumm-dum.

It put a brake to the jackhammering of her heart, slowing her pulse until it was beginning to twin the music's own stately rhythm. But it came far too late.

Her head had been lifting higher all the time until she was looking at Madden's chin, the thin frown of his lips, the hawk's nose. . . . Every detail, every tiny hair, every pore of his skin, stood out in sharp clarity—never mind the darkness. She could almost see below the skin, to the blood moving through his veins and arteries below it, the pull of his muscles as his jaw worked, the fiery webwork of his nerves. . . .

The heartbeat rhythm of the first music steadied inside her. The strains of its melody were whispering in the distance. It lay just over that gentle sweep of land on the Men-an-Tol's moor. Just around that corner of her mind. Coming from the deep well of magic that was the Barrow World, into this Iron World where its enchantment was almost forgotten.

She tried to shut her eyes, to let the magic fill her, but her lids wouldn't close. It was as though they'd been locked open.

And then Madden's gaze connected with her own and her head filled with a babble of voices that drowned out the music.

Tell me, tell me, tell me....

What have you done....

Tell me....

Give me the secret....

TELL ME.

Madden's voice ringing in her head multiplied a hundredfold into a deafening jabber. Amplified and ringing. Drilling through her mind. Pulling her into him.

Tell me, tell me....

She tried to fight him, but it was like trying to stem a storm on the bay with a sieve. The waves of his voice lashed against her mind with a gale force—raging, demanding. Allowing her not a moment's respite.

She dropped to her knees, never feeling the jarring impact with the ground. Her head tilted up, gaze still trapped, still locked on his. The music was lost now, somewhere under the roar of his thundering voice as it stormed through her. And with it hope.

All that remained of herself was a tiny core of being, crouched in a corner of her mind. Hidden, as Madden's will smashed through her feeble defenses. Buried in those few memories that Madden had not yet overturned in his raging search, secreted away as Dunthorn's riddle had been hidden from him for all those years. But not for long.

She knew it couldn't last.

So she let herself go. Let herself fall into him, as the heroine of the Dunthorn book had let herself become a part of the witch that was tormenting her. And found....

Not his life, laid out before her in all its layers of memory as the witch's had been for Jodi, but the world as Madden perceived it through his heightened senses. She became a part of how he connected to the ancient heartbeat of the land, and saw how the web-work of the land's secrets and mysteries shaped a pattern, even in its apparent confusion; how it created a harmony despite its differences—*because* of the differences.

Floating there, a disembodied spirit trapped in another's mind, she finally understood what Peter Goninan had meant about the discrepancy between being asleep and awake. If this . . . if this was how it felt to *almost* be awake . . . a wide-awake equivalent of that moment that lies between sleep and waking when anything was possible. . . .

What more can you want? she asked her captor.

The secret, Madden demanded. *Dunthorn's secret.*

But you already have it, she said.

For she saw what he did not, that for all his manipulations and self-interest, he was ignoring the real truth to this mysterious patterning that underlay the world. It was the sheet music to the first music, there to be read for any who could perceive it.

Listen, she said.

To what?

It was unbelievable, Janey thought. Madden was tuned in to the existence of the hidden meaning that resonated to the first music, had been for years, but he couldn't hear it. He took bits and pieces and used them to override other people's wills, to give himself power, but he never once saw it for what it was, never guessed, never heard—

The music.

So she called it up.

Dhumm-dum. Dhumm-dum.

The deep bass rhythm boomed like ancient thunder on the first day of the world. Harp strings plucked an ethereal counterpoint against a skirling wash of fiddles and flutes and whistles. And there, taking the melody and imbuing it with a power that Janey could never have duplicated, was a set of pipes; drones, deep and rumbling, like the speech of mountains, stone grinding against stone, rock faces speaking from the sides of time-rounded hills; the chanter wailing like all the winds of the world blown through its bore with perfect control—the melody both bitter and sweet, quick tempo and slow air, all music distilled into one flawless sound.

She had no fear of giving the first music to Madden for she knew that no matter how he might have manipulated the bits and pieces of it that he'd borrowed or stolen over the years, it was impossible for any one being to control. It required the joint accord of every being, of every single part of the world.

Perhaps of worlds.

Like the world that lay through the hole in the Men-an-Tol.

Loosing the music inside Madden was like waking magic in the Barrow World. The music ran wildly through him. The more he fought it, the stronger it grew, unbalancing him.

But Janey, by letting it simply flow through her, by accepting it, and, rather than attempting to control it, by merely welcoming it, she shivered with the gift of its beauty.

At first she floated there in Madden's mind and remained unaffected by the storm that he fought. But after a time, she visualized herself in her own body and went walking through the dark corridors of shifting shadows that was Madden's mind. In the rooms that led off from the corridors—which were pockets of memory or thought, she realized—she came upon knots and dark, twisting patterns that she loosened and set free.

In one such pocket, she found Kempy's spirit. The border collie was trapped in a dream. Men surrounded him and whenever he tried to move, to break free of their circle, the men's booted feet would lash out at him, driving him back into the center again.

Janey slipped in between the ghost figures of the men and lifted the dog in her arms. When she turned to leave the circle, the men had vanished and there was only the moor surrounding them. She set Kempy down.

"Go on," she said.

But the dog merely pushed his head against her leg and followed her as she went on down the corridor.

And found Clare.

Her friend lay in an absolutely featureless place, sprawled on the floor, limbs splayed out around her. She looked as though she were dead. But her gaze tracked Janey's movement as Janey stepped closer and then crouched down by her head. Janey stroked Clare's head, brushing the hair from her brow.

"What's the matter, Clare?" she asked.

"I—I can't move. Not just my . . . legs. But nothing. Only—only my head. . . ."

The ancient wisdom of the first music still sang through Madden's mind, still filled Janey.

"It's not true," she said. "Madden's just making you think it is."

Clare blinked back tears. "I can't *move*!"

Janey continued to stroke Clare's hair, her touch tender.

"Listen," she said. "Listen to the music."

"I can't. . . ."

"Listen," Janey repeated, softly but insistently.

Then, as Clare finally heard the ancient strains, Janey helped her friend to her feet. Clare wasn't even aware of what she was doing until she was standing beside Janey.

Clare moved her hands in front of her eyes, touched her upper arms, hugged herself.

"I . . ."

But words failed her.

Janey smiled at her and put an arm around her shoulder for support.

"Come on," she said. "We've still got to find Felix."

They came upon him, sitting alone on a vast stage, an enormous audience jeering at him and throwing beer cans and rotting fruit at where he huddled on his chair, arms wrapped around his accordion. Kempy growled at the audience as the three of them picked their way through the litter on the stage, but that only made the audience laugh more.

Janey handed Clare her whistle.

"Play a tune," she said. "Something simple. Something old."

Clare looked at the audience, her eyes blinded by the spotlight. Her gaze turned back to Felix and in that moment Janey saw Clare's love for him reflected. A deep, hopeless love.

"But . . ." Clare began.

The first music stirred its wisdom inside Janey.

"I'm sorry," she said. "I never knew. But he loves you, too, Clare. Not in the same way, but . . ."

Even the first music's wisdom failed here.

Clare blinked back tears and nodded slowly. "I know."

She brought the whistle to her lips and began "The Trip to Sligo," a jig that was one of Felix's favorites. Its bouncing rhythm was almost lost as the audience ridiculed her. Clare faltered on the tune. The whistle, with its faulty upper register, didn't make it any easier. But Janey nodded encouragingly to Clare as she bent down beside Felix.

So Clare played on.

The tune changed on her as she kept at it. Her playing grew more assured as the first music took hold of her instrument and sang through it.

Janey pressed her lips close to Felix's ears and began to murmur soothingly. She pried his hands away from his instrument, took them in her own. She told him what strong hands they were, how she loved their gentleness when he touched her. He was better than the whole audience combined, she said, and reminded him that the music was important for how he wanted to play it, not how others wanted to hear it. She assured him she didn't care if he never played on even the smallest stage, just so they could be together. Just so that they couldn't lose what they'd so recently regained.

"Listen," she said. "Listen to Clare play."

She laid her arm around his shoulder and pulled him in close to her. He trembled—a feverish shiver that ran through his entire body.

"J-Janey . . . ?" he murmured.

"I'm here."

"They . . . they . . . I can't. . . ."

"This is all a lie," she said. "There's no stage. No audience. It's just Madden."

As she spoke the sound of the audience was finally overwhelmed by the music. Clare stood straight and tall, her fingers dancing on the small whistle. Janey had never heard the instrument sound so good. She'd never heard Clare play so well. She took her arm from around Felix's shoulder. Picking up his accordion, she took it from his lap and set it down on the floor. Then she tucked her hand in the crook of his arm and gave him a gentle tug.

"Come on," she said. "We're going to leave this place."

Felix finally lifted his head.

"*Why* does this happen to me?" he asked.

"I don't know, Felix. It doesn't matter. This isn't real."

He shook his head. "It's just as real as what . . . as what happens to me anytime I get on a stage."

"But this time it's just Madden's doing. Let's go, Felix. These people don't matter."

She nodded towards the audience who sat utterly silent now—so still that in the darkness beyond the spotlight they might just as well not have existed at all.

"I could play that music," Felix said. "Any other place. On ship, at a session, on a bloody street corner. . . . Why can't I play it *here*?"

"I don't know," Janey said. "It really doesn't matter."

"It does matter," Felix said.

He disengaged his arm from her grip and picked up his box.

Janey started to protest, to tell him he shouldn't try again, but she stopped herself. She knew he could do it. There was just something inside him that blocked him. Trying again now might make things worse, but she knew she couldn't stop him from the attempt. Maybe the first music would help him. Maybe nothing would change. It seemed an awful lot to expect that a lifetime's fear could be dissolved in just a few moments like this. Whatever the root of his problem was, it had to be far more complex than what a few bars of music could cure.

But then she remembered: *The magics of the world are far simpler than we make them out to be.*

"I love you, Felix," she said as he strapped on his box.

She stepped back from his chair. He lifted his head, stared into the spotlight's glare, trying to look past it to the darkness beyond. He's trying to focus on just one person, Janey realized. Trying to convince himself that he was playing just for that one person, that there's no one else out there.

She'd done the same thing herself when she first got stage jitters at the beginning of her career.

He put his left hand through the wrist strap near the accompaniment buttons, rested his left hand lightly on the fingerboard. Thumbing down the air release button, he stretched out the bellows.

Oh, do it, Janey wished.

But he couldn't play. Sweat broke out on his already glistening face. His hands started to shake. He tried to play along with Clare, but the notes came out in a discordant jumble. They were all wrong.

Janey couldn't bear to watch it happen to him again.

Before the audience could react, before he froze up completely once more, she stepped in behind his chair and pressed her chest in close to its rungs. She put her arms around him.

"Listen," she breathed in his ear. "To the music. To what Clare's playing."

"I . . ."

"Don't try to play. Just listen. Let the music fill you. Close your eyes. You're not here. You're not anywhere. There's just the music. Feel the rhythm—it's the same as your heartbeat. The tune's as simple as breathing."

She stroked his temples.

"Who cares about who's listening?" she said. "It's the music that's important. And this music . . ."

"This . . . music . . ." he repeated slowly.

"It's magic."

Haltingly, he worked the bellows and played a simple two-note chord with his right hand on the melody buttons. Incomplete as it was, it didn't matter if the tune Clare was playing was in a minor or a major key. The partial chord fit.

"That's it," Janey encouraged him as he drew the chord out, shifted to another as the tune required it.

He fumbled the next chord change, but caught it quickly.

"Magic," Janey whispered.

"Magic," he said, repeating the word as though it were a talisman.

The next change went more smoothly. As did the next. He added some accompanying notes to fill in the space between the chords. Janey could feel the tension in his shoulders. His muscles were locked tight as braided wire. She kneaded them, feeling them loosen as much from her ministrations as from his growing confidence.

He was playing along with the melody now—tentatively, catching two notes in three the way one might play at a session when the tune was unfamiliar and you were learning it as you went along with the rest of the musicians, letting them carry the bulk of the melody while you were still picking it up.

Felix straightened in his chair. His box began to bounce on his knee as he tapped his foot. The notes came more quickly, the music changing, catching up both accordion and whistle and pulling them along into the brisk 4/4 measures of a high lilting tune.

Janey recognized the tune, and smiled. It was "Miss McLeod's Reel," but both she and Felix knew it as "The May Day." A spring tune, to call in the summer, like the old "Hal-an-Tow" song. A promise of new beginnings. Of the wheel turning, the cycle of the year beginning anew.

And the first music was a part of it—as it was a part of all tunes. It sang a counterpointing harmony of wonders and wisdoms . . . and magic.

Of hope found.

Music was immortal—but it needed the players to keep it alive. Just as the world itself needed those who walked it to keep its heartbeat singing.

Someone whistled in the audience. A few people near the front began to clap along. By the time the three-part reel came 'round to the first part again, the whole audience was clapping in time to its infectious rhythm.

When the tune ended, they broke into a thunderous applause. The spotlight dimmed. Janey looked out over Felix's shoulder to see the thousands of cheerful faces and she hugged Felix proudly.

"I . . ." he began.

"You did it," Janey said.

He set the accordion down and turned to grin at her. He got up from his chair and lifted her to her feet to return her hug. Behind him, the applause was dying down.

No, Janey realized, it was fading. As was the stage. There was just her and Felix here now. Clare stood nearby, the Eagle whistle in her hand, Kempy sitting at her feet. She felt Felix's body grow insubstantial in her arms. Clare and Kempy fading. Felix fading. And she was—

She opened her eyes to find herself kneeling in the dirt by the Men-an-Tol. The silence, after the constant presence of the first music inside her, after the thunderous applause in the concert hall, seemed almost deafening. She lifted a hand, touched her shoulder, ran the hand down her arm.

Had any of it been real?

But then she saw John Madden, hunched on his knees by the tolmen, face pressed against the stone, one hand reaching through its hole and dangling limply out the other end. She turned to find Felix sitting up, staring around himself in confusion. And Clare—Clare was now holding the tin whistle that Janey had had in her own hand before Madden took her into his mind.

Impossible as it seemed, it had to have been real.

"What—what happened?" Clare said. "I was having the most horrible dream, but then it turned . . . all golden. . . ."

"We won," Janey said.

She collected her purse from where it lay in the dirt in front of her and got to her feet.

"We hid the book so it can't ever be found," she went on, "and though Madden tried to use his mind powers on us, they didn't take hold. We proved we're stronger than him."

Except there was still her canceled tour. And the Boyds' farm. And—

No, she told herself. Don't think about any of that right now. Hang on to the victory and face the rest of it when it comes.

Clare and Felix were looking at Madden, but the man never stirred from beside the stone.

"Is he . . . dead?" Clare asked.

"I don't know," Janey said.

She gave Kempy a pat as he came out of the nearby gorse where he'd been hiding and pressed his face anxiously against her leg.

"And I really don't care," she added.

"But we can't just leave him here. . . ."

"Why not?" Felix said. "We don't owe him anything."

He was remembering what Madden had done to him, Janey thought.

She moved closer to Clare and took her arm.

"Let's just go home," she said.

"We really did beat him, didn't we?" Clare said as she let herself be led away.

"We beat him." Janey said.

"Together," Felix added.

Janey nodded. "Together," she agreed. "The three of us—all right, four," she added as Kempy pushed against her leg again. "The four of us and the music."

"The music," Felix and Clare breathed in unison, remembering.

None of them spoke again as they followed the path back to where they had left Janey's car.

6.

Madden couldn't move. He leaned against the Men-an-Tol, face pressed against its rough surface, one arm still hanging through its hole. The world had closed in on him. He tried to shut off his mind, but the secret—

Dunthorn's secret that the Little woman had so casually handed over to him—

That damned music—

It fed back through his mind, overloading his mind's ability to process the information. He was aware of everything. Every sound, scent, sight, taste, emotion that existed in the world and beyond it was flooding into his mind.

He could no more control the vast torrent of input than a man could cease to breathe and still live.

He was aware of it *all*.

From molten rock flowing deep under the earth's crust to a whisper of conversation halfway around the world.

From the sugar-heavy cereal that some snotty-nosed child was consuming in a suburb of Chicago to the fall of a tree in a Brazilian rain forest.

From a deep-space panorama of uncharted stars, far beyond the scope of earth's most powerful telescope, to a bug crawling along a water-logged wooden post on a Cambodian riverbank.

From a high Himalayan wind to the brain-dead mind of a drunken man lying in a Melbourne alley.

It was the detail, the vast wealth of unfocused detail, flooding him.

From the lumbering tread of a Kenyan elephant to the whine of a mosquito in a Florida everglade.

From a marital dispute in one of the stately houses near his home in Victoria to the ear-piercing shriek of a heavy metal band in a small London club.

From the vast sweep of the empty silent spaces between the stars to—

He caught that tiny fragment of input and held to it.

Be calm, he told himself. Be calm. Still your mind. Hold that silence.

He wanted to scream.

Hold the silence. Let it spread. Here and here, and over there. . . .

Slowly he regained control of his ability to focus and channel external stimuli. When he could finally rise, he looked out across the moor and almost laughed.

He had been a fool.

It was true. Dunthorn had unlocked a gateway to unlimited power, but of what use was it when it couldn't be controlled? When all one could do was apportion small parts of it to one's needs—as he had been doing all along?

But the Little woman—why hadn't *she* been affected? How had *she*, untutored as she was, learned to deal so easily with it?

There had to be more to it than what he had taken from her mind: a book in which each person created their own story; a gateway through the hole in the tolmen to another world; tiny people the size of mice. . . .

These were fairy tales.

But if they were real? Dunthorn had to have had some reason to let himself die before allowing his book to fall into Madden's hands. And this Janey Little . . .

He knew he had to leave that puzzle for another day. Tonight he could barely keep his balance leaning on the tolmen. Tonight it was enough that he had survived to learn the lesson.

But the waste. All those years, searching for Dunthorn's secret, following his own arcane paths, only to find that what he sought couldn't be had. To find that it was merely the harmonic vibration to which every element of the universe vibrated.

Such a simple skein of knowledge. A high school student knew as much. That student couldn't control it any more than Madden himself could, but at least he *knew*.

Madden shook his head.

The waste.

He was too old now to begin anew. And with Michael turned against him, he no longer even had an heir to whom he might leave the heritage of this knowledge that he had so painfully acquired tonight.

And the real irony was that by forcing his hand as he had, he was now left in a position where he was unable to even utilize those strengths that he had gained on his own. He couldn't open his mind, couldn't let down his defenses for a moment, without having the flood of the world come rushing back in. He had to fare deaf, dumb, and blind through the world, along with all the other sheep.

He thrust his hands deep into his pockets and slowly made his way back along the path that led from the Men-an-Tol to the lane where he'd left his car.

He had to find a way to regain what he had lost. The Little woman would be of no help. Dunthorn was dead. But there was Peter Goninan. He seemed, from what he'd taken from Janey Little's mind, to know far more than Madden had ever supposed he did. Like Little's grandfather, Madden had never even realized that Goninan and Dunthorn had been such close friends.

He would speak to Goninan. But without his power to *make* Goninan tell him what he needed, he would be reduced to accepting only those tidbits that Goninan deigned to hand him. . . .

Madden sighed.

The simple truth was, he could plan and scheme all he wanted, but it changed nothing. He had opened a door that must not be opened—not as *he* had opened it—and like all the other feckless meddlers in the history of those who studied the hermetic secrets, now he, too, had to pay the price. The devil would be getting his due.

Madden didn't believe in either a benevolent deity, or his evil opposite.

But he believed in Hell.

Hell was knowing that he would be spending the remainder of his life as much a sheep as the rest of those who inhabited this sorry world.

No, it was worse than that. They slept, never knowing that they slept.

But he knew. He had been awake, and now must sleep.

It was that or go mad.

7.

Ted Grimes straightened up by the hedgerow where he was standing when he heard the voices coming down the lane. He marked them— three voices and not one belonged to his quarry. Unless Madden was keeping silent, he wasn't with them.

But there was a dog.

Invisibility was another hunter's trick Grimes knew well. It was easy with people and most animals. You just stayed still. You never looked at them—some sixth sense warned them when they were being watched. You just melted into the background and *belonged* there.

He wasn't so sure how that was going to go over with the dog. But at least the wind was blowing from their direction. If he didn't move, didn't look at them . . .

"I still don't think we should have just left him there," a woman was saying.

"Would you want to touch him?" another woman's voice asked. "Not likely."

Grimes almost gave himself away. They were talking about Madden. If something had happened to Madden, if they'd taken away his revenge, he'd hunt them down one by one. . . .

Standing out here in the dark as long as he had, his night vision was about as perfect as it was going to get. There was enough moonlight that he could easily make them out now, studying them from the corner of his eye. Indirectly. Not making waves. Not even breathing.

There was a woman with a cane, being supported by a shorter woman. The man was big—a broad-shouldered, hefty sucker. And the dog. . . .

The dog never even looked in his direction.

Stupid mutt.

"I feel like letting the air out of his tires," the man said.

"Why bother?" the shorter woman said. "We've already let the air out of *him*."

"What really happened, Janey?" the woman with the cane asked.

Yeah, Grimes thought. What happened?

But Janey's reply was muffled by the opening of the car door.

They all got into the little three-wheeled job, including the dog. The car's muffler coughed twice, then the engine caught and the quiet moor was suddenly awash with the intrusive rumble of its motor. Grimes closed his eyes when the headbeams came on, not wanting to lose his night sight.

He tracked them with his ears, listening to them head back down the lane towards the road. When they paused halfway there, he looked down the road after them to see that they were only letting the dog out at that farmhouse he'd passed earlier. They pulled away again, going on until they were out of sight, though he could still hear the car's engine as they drove on down to the road.

When they reached the end of the lane and turned onto the road, Grimes looked back up the way they'd come from the moor.

I'll give you ten more minutes, Madden, he thought. And then I'm coming to look for you.

He didn't bother worrying about what he'd just heard, didn't think at all. Madden would come, or he'd go find him. It was that simple. He just let himself sink back into the invisibility of the night.

Ten minutes hadn't quite gone by when he heard footsteps coming from the direction of the stile that led onto the moor.

He was careful now, far more careful than he'd been when the other three had been approaching.

His missing hand ached, reminding him of just how much Madden was capable. One look in that sucker's hoodoo eyes, even in the dark, and it was game over. No way Grimes was letting that happen to him again.

He gave Madden all the time he needed to make his slow way down the path, not moving until he was opening his car door. And then Grimes drifted across the space between them like a ghost— swift and silent. He had his right arm around Madden's neck, the prosthetic digging into the old man's flesh, and slammed him up against the side of the car before Madden could have possibly guessed he was there. His left hand rose and brought the muzzle of his .38 up to Madden's temple.

"Hello, John," he said. "Remember me?"

He felt Madden stiffen.

"You . . . you're Sandoe's man."

"Yeah, and whoever you sent after him took care of old Phil just fine. I appreciated not having to pay back my advance for screwing up. But I didn't"—he shoved the prosthetic harder against Madden's skin—"appreciate *this*."

"What do you want?"

His coolness enraged Grimes and it took all his willpower to not just pull the trigger right then and there.

"I know you like games, John—like the one where you made me cut off my own hand. Well, I've got a game for you now that goes by the name of Russian roulette. Feel like playing?"

"It doesn't matter."

What the hell did he mean, it doesn't matter? Did the sucker think he had some ace up his sleeve? Did Madden think he was going to turn him around and let him have a chance to use those hoodoo eyes of his? Maybe Madden figured he was going to just hand the gun over and let Madden pull the trigger himself.

Hang loose, Grimes told himself. You've got the advantage. He's just trying to spook you.

And doing a damn good job of it, too.

"This gun's got six chambers," Grimes went on, his voice only slightly betraying his nervousness, "but only one of them's got a bullet in it. I gave her a little spin after I loaded her up earlier tonight, so even I don't know which one it's in."

"Fine."

"You just might be dying right here," Grimes said.

Come on, he thought. Give me a reaction.

"It doesn't matter," Madden said again.

Screw this, Grimes thought.

He pulled the trigger. Madden bucked in his arms. The bullet made a small hole in the old man's left temple and took out most of the right one on its way out.

Grimes stepped back and let the body fall. Then he fired again, emptying the gun into Madden's body.

"About that one bullet," he said to the corpse, "I lied."

He stared down at the corpse and heard only a whispering echo of the old man's voice.

It doesn't matter.

He's dead, Grimes told himself. You said you'd get him for what he'd done and you kept your word.

But he didn't feel anything.

It doesn't matter.

Only an empty feeling inside.

Two years of waiting for this day, of imagining how it was going to go, coming up with a hundred different scenarios until Bett finally got in touch with him and told him to be patient, he'd deliver Madden to him, no problem. So he'd been patient. Waiting for Bett to come through.

And Bett had come through.

It doesn't matter.

And now here he was. The sucker was dead and all he felt was zip. Nada.

There had to be more.

He wiped down the gun and stuck it in Madden's hand.

Suicide, he thought with a smile. Maybe the local yokels will actually believe it, too.

He straightened up, still waiting for that sense of accomplishment to hit him, but the emptiness just sat there inside him.

It doesn't matter.

It was like the sucker had wanted to die. Like he hadn't cared. . . .

It doesn't matter.

Grimes's missing hand still ached. There was no relief of the burning need inside him.

Bastard won, he thought as he trudged off down the lane towards his own car.

I kill him and he still comes up on top.

It doesn't matter.

Because he'd wanted to die.

Grimes paused to look back, his prosthetic hand held against his chest, its ache deepening.

Go figure it, he thought.

He continued on down the lane.

The Touchstone

A church is a stone tooth in the jawbone of the ground. That's why the cold bites. The toothache of antiquity, the twinges of time. A church gets you ready for your coffin.

—IAN WATSON, from "The Mole Field,"
The Magazine of Fantasy and Science Fiction, December 1988

Somehow Jodi wasn't surprised at how quickly the memory of the Widow's magics faded from her friends' minds. She'd already had some forewarning with the fisherman down at the waterfront the night of the storm, and while it took longer for Denzil and the others to forget, in the end it was less than a week, all told, before their memories were gone as well.

That Denzil put it so easily from his mind was the least surprising. His thoughts worked along such logical byways that any twisty path that might lead to something out of the ordinary was immediately suspect. She had expected more from Taupin, but he was less inclined to whimsy now than he had been before the whole affair began. And while she didn't know Lizzie well enough to form much of an opinion as to how she might react, Jodi was amazed that Henkie Whale—who, after all, kept the body of his dead friend somewhere in the catacombs under his warehouse and was known to talk to that corpse—should also be able to forget so easily.

The Tatters children still talked about it—but they spoke of it as though it were a story that they had heard, not as something that had happened to them personally. Only Ratty Friggens—whom the Widow's button charm had called back from the air itself, rather than from a longstone like the others—still seemed affected by his ordeal, but he wouldn't speak of it. When he was about at all, it was with a haunted look in his eyes; mostly he kept to himself.

As time passed, Jodi found it increasingly difficult to remember it all herself. Details kept shifting in her mind, fading out, getting tangled up with bits of fairy tales that she'd heard as a child, until there were times when she doubted much of it herself.

For even the music had left her. She remembered the *fact* of it; she just couldn't call it back up. When she listened to her heartbeat, all she heard was the *thump-thump* in her chest. There was no answering rhythm, no twinning of her pulse with that ancient rhythm.

She didn't see much of Taupin in those days. His wanderings took him farther afield from Bodbury than usual—and for longer periods of time. Neither Henkie nor Lizzie seemed to do more than vaguely recognize her when she passed one of them on the streets, and the Tatters children were strangely quiet around her. Denzil, when she tried talking about it with him, had less patience than ever for what he termed "Complete and utter nonsense. If you keep filling up your head with such tomfoolery, soon you won't have a speck of room left for common sense, you."

Jodi took to wandering the streets of Bodbury at all hours of the day and night, searching for something that grew more vague in her mind with every passing day. She often found herself standing outside the Widow Pender's cottage that was boarded up and presented the only mystery that the people of Bodbury had the inclination to gossip about.

Where had she gone? What had become of her?

They had a hundred theories, each more preposterous than the next, but not one came close to what had actually taken place.

Only Jodi knew, but no one wanted to listen to her.

So she would stand there in front of the cottage, remembering her and Edern's descent from the windowsill and their mad ride through the town, dangling from Ansum's collar. She no longer worried about what had been real, and what not. She just appreciated the memories she still had, for day by day they became less defined, so vague that at times she felt like one of the Tatters children, remembering a story rather than something that had actually happened to her.

The boarded-up windows of the cottage depressed her—they reminded her too much of the boarded-up minds of her friends and the way her own mind was being boarded up. It was as though she'd spent her whole life half asleep and had woken for just a moment before drifting off again, her memories fading like dreams in the morning light.

The Widow's cottage was the best place to bring those memories all clearly to mind again—or at least as clearly as she could recall them. She would stand there, remembering and thinking. Of being a Small. Of Edern and the Barrow World and the first music. Of the Widow and how the poor choices she had made had created such a ruin of her life.

Jodi would always turn away then, feeling sorry for the Widow and pretending that she didn't hear a whispering in the shadows along the garden hedge and close in to the walls of the deserted cottage itself. She would see the Widow's ruined features, the innocent child that the old woman had been superimposed on her features for just a moment before she died, and tears would well in Jodi's eyes.

She wondered sometimes how she could be so sympathetic towards someone as evil as the Widow had been, and yet have so little patience for her own friends. She knew it wasn't their fault that they forgot. It was this world that they lived in that made magic fade and logic rise to the fore; just as logic was absent from the Barrow World. But she couldn't help but be angry with them.

It wasn't as though they hadn't *seen* the magic with their own eyes. It wasn't as though they hadn't been enchanted themselves. . . .

One day, after a particularly frustrating morning spent arguing with Denzil, she found herself walking up Mabe Hill to where the ruins of Creak-a-vose lay in a jumble of stone under the afternoon sky. The Widow's clothes were no longer where she'd dropped them after taking the mantle with its buttons that she'd needed that night; someone had stuffed them—dress, stockings, and all—into the hedgerow where they were now grey with dust. She stood and looked at them for a long moment, then went into the old ruined church and sat down on a fallen pillar.

She felt depressed. She'd been moping about for days now and she knew the real reason. It wasn't anything to do with how everyone else was forgetting the magic, nor even how she herself was losing her own memories of it, thread by tattered thread.

It was the promise she'd made to Edern Gee about the first music—about keeping it alive in this world so that both it and the Barrow World would grow closer together again.

She'd defeated the Widow, rescued both herself and her friends, but the most important thing was still undone. In the great scheme of things, in her memories of the music that she could still recall, she remembered what was lost with the music. Not just magic, or wonder, or mystery. But the perfect symmetry of the land itself that was slowly unraveling as the worlds drew further and further apart. If she closed her eyes, she could remember the feeling—

Species extinct.

Hopes extinguished.

Heartlands ravaged.

Waste and barren lands lying both in the world and in the hearts of its inhabitants.

—but she could no longer *feel* it.

Edern would just have to find someone else, she thought. He'd have to go into somebody else's dreams.

But what if he couldn't? What if she'd been his last chance?

Thinking that just made her feel worse.

I'm where I should be, she thought. In a ruined church with a barrow underneath it. A forsaken place of worship built up on the bones of those long dead. A place where hopes die.

She sank lower and lower into her depression. She looked around herself and everything had a dull pallor about it, as though someone had draped the gauze of a corpse shroud over her head and she was only able to see through its dimming fabric. There was such an utter pointlessness to everything, she realized.

The first music? Better to call it the lost music: the forever lost music.

And what if she did find it again? Of what use would it be? Who would hear it—who would even remember it long enough for it to do any good? If she, caught up in its thundering measures as she had been in the Barrow World, living and breathing its rhythm and the power of its cadences . . . if she could forget *that,* if it had changed inside her from something she felt and *knew* to something she could only vaguely recall, the way she could remember the first time she met Denzil's menagerie, but not how she *felt* at that moment, then how could she expect anyone else to remember it? All she'd be able to call up would be some faint echo.

And what good could that possibly do?

She'd had the chance to do something important with her life—

just like she'd always wanted. To do something that had real *meaning*. And she'd let it slip away.

Lost.

Like the music.

It was so frustrating, to remember but not *remember*. She could call up the logic of what she'd experienced, but not the emotion of it. It was like the proverbial word on the tip of one's tongue—so close, but it might as well be a thousand miles away.

If only . . .

She lifted her head, hearing a sound. Her heart lifted for a moment, thinking that the music had returned, but it wasn't that. Nor was it the wind. It was more a soft, snickering whisper of dark laughter coming from the shadows. . . .

She looked at those places where the shadows lay deepest.

"Go ahead," she told them. "You might as well laugh. After all, you've won. . . ."

Won, won, won. . . .

The echoes mocked her.

And then she stopped to think about what she had just said. The shadows had won. Won what?

It wasn't the shadows that were at fault here—as they had been with the Widow—but her own self. The shadows didn't mock her because they'd won, but because she'd simply given up.

The insight shivered through her.

She stood up from where she'd been sitting and walked out of the gloom inside the ruined church's walls to stand in the sunshine outside. The step she took, from shadow to light, was like a switch being thrown in her head. She looked around herself, *truly* looked around and wondered how she could have let herself sink into such a morbid mood.

No matter which way she turned, everything looked marvelous. The hedgerows, the moorland behind them, the rooftops of the town, the old ruins of Creak-a-vose . . . they all had a crystalline clarity about them that simply took her breath away. Why did men worship in churches, locking themselves away in the dark, when the world lay beyond its doors in all its real glory?

Bother and damn. The only pointlessness at work here was her own moping about. So what if Denzil and the others didn't remember anymore. She still did, didn't she? Not everything, but enough to keep it alive.

She couldn't change the world all at once. But she could change a bit of it—her bit, at least. It might not be much, but something was better than nothing.

It seemed so childishly simple. She could almost hear Edern's voice.

The magics of the world are far simpler than we make them out to be.

The music wasn't lost. How could it be lost when it was there inside her all the time? She hadn't discovered it in the Barrow World, she had *rediscovered* it.

"Thank you!" she called to the shadows that lay inside the ruins.

There was no response from them as she slipped through a hedge and headed off across the moor towards the Men-an-Tol, but then she probably wouldn't have heard it if there had been a response. Her heart was bubbling over, too full with the simple joy of being alive. She couldn't have begun to explain to anyone how it was that she could be so depressed one moment, and so alive in the next. She only knew, as she skipped through the yellow-flowering gorse, that she'd been walking through the past days like one deaf, dumb, and blind.

But she could finally hear again—the rustle of her trousers against the gorse, the skip of her step on the ground, the distant sound of a birdsong, the breath of the wind as it rattled dried ferns, one against the other; she could sing—wildly off-key, but full of enthusiasm as she made up her own words and her own melody to propel her along her way; and she could see—the rolling sea of yellow and green gorse, brown ferns and the dusty-rose blooms of the heather.

When she finally reached the tolmen, she was out of breath and giddy. She collapsed on the ground beside the holed stone, and lolled back against it to stare up at the sky where a kestrel was silhouetted against a dusting of white cloud, islanded in a surrounding ocean of blue.

"Hello, up there!" she called, waving up at the bird.

And didn't it seem to dip its wings—just for a moment there—in response, or was it only her imagination?

She didn't care. Wasn't that half of what life was all about—imagining possibilities and then following through on them? And what she was going to imagine—what she was going to *do*—was make the Men-an-Tol sing. Out here, on the moor. It would sing and never stop singing, and whoever came by would hear that music and take it away with them. The wind itself would carry it to other lands until one day the whole of the Iron World would hear and recall that music.

The first music.

She got up from where she was sitting and clambered up onto the stone, straddling it so that her stomach was pressed against it, her elbows in front, propping up her head, her legs dangling down either side. She lay very still then, quieting her mind—

Think of nothing. Don't *think at all.*

—trying to soak up the ancient stillness that was hidden deep in the stone below her, a stillness that was like—

an old dance

—focusing on her heartbeat, on its rhythm, on how the blood that moved through her twinned that—

hidden music

—until she was drifting in that state between sleep and wakefulness when all things are possible.

And then she heard it.

Dhumm-dum. Dhumm-dum.

A distant, far-off sound like a hoofbeat. Coming closer. And she was floating, floating away. . . .

Edern's features drifted up in her mind. He was in the Barrow World, a look of worry making him frown.

"What are you doing?" he asked.

"Dreaming," she said. "Dreaming magic."

Dhumm-dum. Dhumm-dum.

His worry deepened into alarm.

"You won't ever be the same again," he warned.

"I know. But the music will go on."

"The Barrow World will be closed to you as well—because of your Iron World blood."

"I know."

Dhumm-dum.

"I'll become the music," she added, "and I'll never let it fade again."

He shook his head. "That's too steep a price—"

"I won't die," Jodi interrupted him. "I'll go on forever."

"But changed," he said.

"But changed," she agreed.

"I didn't mean for you to do this."

Dhumm-dum.

"*I* chose to do this," Jodi told him.

"But—"

Dhumm-dum. Dhumm-dum.

The music was taking her away now. Parts of her dissolved to fuel it. It sang with her voice now—not the off-key voice with which she normally tried to sing songs, but with the pure, clear tones that lay inside her, echoing her heartbeat. She felt as though she were unraveling into the Men-an-Tol, becoming part of it. She followed the roots of its mystery as they spread away from the center of the hole in its stone, deep into the heartbeat of the land. The wind carried her across the moorland, through forest and over Bodbury to the sea.

"Good-bye, Edern," she said. "Remember me."

"How could I forget?" he asked as the crack between the worlds faded and he could see her no more.

But the music went on, echoing and echoing forever, through the Barrow World and beyond. And this time it raised no tempests. It soothed the land, bringing the gift of logic to his world just as it brought the gift of magic to hers.

Sustaining the Mystery, so that it echoed and echoed, on into forever.

2.

Denzil couldn't concentrate that afternoon. He kept thinking of Jodi and the pointless argument that had sent her storming out of his loft earlier that day. The animals had been restless ever since she'd gone and that restlessness translated into a nagging feeling inside himself that he could no longer ignore.

Finally he set his work aside.

He'd been too harsh, he realized. She was still young and wasn't youth allowed its fancies? Who was he to rein in her sense of wonder? The world itself would do that to her all too soon on its own. And then she might discover that there was a different kind of wonder in the world—not magic like in fairy tales, but a magic all the same. For what were the wonders of nature, but a magic?

But she had to come to that realization herself. And until she did, what sort of a friend was he proving to be by constantly pointing out the errors of her thinking? There came a point when helpfulness merely became a kind of fussing criticism that would do neither of them any good.

"Come along then, you," he told Ollie as he put on his coat and hat.

The monkey jumped from the back of the chair where he had been mournfully plucking at a bit of loose stuffing and crawled in under Denzil's jacket.

"We'll see if we can't find her," he added.

But once he was on the street below, he was at a loss as to where to begin. That odd nagging sensation returned, but this time it was a feeling of his having done this all before.

There was a dream he'd had—one he should never have shared with Jodi because all she did now was talk was of it—of when the Widow Pender had turned her into a Small and how they'd all gone to the old tolmen out on the moorland behind the town. . . .

The certainty came to him then that that was where she had gone.

Grumbling a little to himself, he set off up Mabe Hill. When he reached the moors beyond the old ruins of Creak-a-vose, Ollie grew increasingly restless where he was tucked away under Denzil's jacket.

"Stop your fussing, you," Denzil told him, but he was beginning to feel a little light-headed himself just then.

There was the sense of a storm approaching in the air, yet that was patently impossible, for the sky was clear as could be except for a small desultory smear of ragged clouds to the west. Ollie pushed himself out from under Denzil's jacket and sat up on his shoulder, chattering urgently, tugging at Denzil's hair as though to make him hurry. There was a sound in the air, an odd sort of thrumming like a drum playing a heartbeat tempo over a wash of wind that was almost like music.

And Denzil thought he could recognize a melody in it—it was one he remembered from when he was a boy, an old tune that his father used to sing. It had always been Denzil's favorite song. Today it filled him with foreboding.

He stepped up his pace, feeling that same urgency as Ollie obviously did—an insistent need to reach the Men-an-Tol as quickly as he could.

When he got there, he wished he'd never come.

Ollie shrieked and bounded from his shoulder to scamper across the last few yards separating them from the holed stone. He bounded up to the top of the stone and turned a mournful eye to Denzil.

"Oh, Jodi," Denzil said. "What have you done?"

Ollie plucked at the clothing that lay there on top of the stone, pushing his face against the all-too-familiar shirt and trousers that Jodi had been wearing when she'd stormed off earlier that day. Her jacket lay on the ground beside the stone. One shoe on either side of it. But of her there was no trace.

The monkey whimpered, holding out the shirt to Denzil, but he was frozen where he stood, listening to the music.

Remembering.

A mad time: a night, a day, and then another night—of magic. Of Smalls and reanimated corpses. Of witches and stone.

Especially stone.

A longstone.

He had *been* a longstone, enchanted by the Widow. . . .

"Oh, Jodi," he said again, his voice a bare mumble.

The unearthly music sang all around him now and he swayed in time to its rhythm, tears blurring his sight. He could hear Jodi in that music, knew that she'd sacrificed herself to wake it.

It's got to be heard, she'd tried to explain to him more than once in the past week or so. *Without the music, both worlds are doomed.*

He'd told her that was nonsense. There was no Barrow World.

Can't you remember anything *about what happened?* she had shouted. *How can you be so blind?*

"I'm not blind," he had replied. "I can see how the world is perfectly well, you."

All you see is the world the way a sleepwalker would, she had replied this morning in the latest installment of their ongoing argument.

And then she'd stormed out, leaving only the echo of her words behind.

The way a sleepwalker would.

The tears streamed down his cheeks. He didn't know how she had done it, but she had *become* the music. To prove it was real. To him. To all the rest of the sleepwalkers. . . .

A hand fell on his shoulder, but he never started. He only turned slowly to find Taupin standing beside him.

"She . . . she's gone," Denzil said. "Into the music."

Taupin's eyes were shiny as well. He nodded slowly.

"I know," he said. "I was . . . walking nearby . . . thinking. And then I heard it. And remembered. . . ."

"I was wrong," Denzil said. "I treated her poorly—without respect. But it seemed so mad, what she was saying . . ."

"I treated her worse," Taupin said. "I always knew, but somehow . . . somehow I forgot. . . ."

"And now it's too late. She's gone."

Taupin laid his arm across Denzil's slumped shoulders.

"Into the music," he said softly.

His voice was filled with wonder, with sorrow.

Into the music, Denzil repeated to himself.

They stood and listened, arms around each other for comfort, as the sound washed over them. It reverberated in the marrow of their bones, sung high and sweet, heartbreakingly mournful, quick as a jig, slow as the saddest air. Their hearts swelled with its beauty, its mystery. With all it revealed, and all that it hid.

They couldn't move, couldn't speak. They could only hold on to each other and stare at the holed stone with its scattering of clothing that lay upon it.

They could only listen.

And then slowly the music faded, faded to a soft murmur that became the wind breathing through the hole in the Men-an-Tol. A wind that still held an echo of that music, but allowed them to move once more, to stir and sadly sigh.

Finally Denzil could lift a sleeve and wipe at the tears that spilled from his eyes. He looked at the stone where Ollie sat clutching Jodi's shirt. The monkey's thin little arms pulled the fabric close to his chest and rocked sadly back and forth. Denzil moved forward to collect the rest of Jodi's clothes from where they lay.

Then suddenly Ollie peered over the side of the Men-an-Tol that was hidden from Denzil's and Taupin's view. He tossed aside the shirt and jumped off the stone, landing on its far side with an excited chatter.

"Jodi . . . ?" Denzil asked.

His heart leapt as he rounded the stone, dropping when he saw no sign of her there. But Ollie had something in his hand. It looked like a little pink mouse that was squealing and flailing its limbs about. . . .

But a mouse never had limbs like that, Denzil thought. Nor a shock of blond hair. And now he could make out what the little creature was saying.

"Put me down. Put me *down*!"

He knelt down quickly and pried Ollie's paw open. A tiny nude Jodi Shepherd spilled out onto his palm. She immediately covered herself up with her hands. Denzil turned away, blushing, until Taupin shook the lint from a handkerchief that he pulled from one of his voluminous pockets and offered it to the diminutive Jodi. Denzil looked back at her, once she'd wrapped herself up in it.

"*Now* do you believe me?" she asked in her high piping voice.

Denzil nodded slowly. "What . . . what happened to you? I thought the Widow was dead."

"So you *do* remember."

"Ever since I heard the music," Denzil said.

"Well, the Widow is dead," she told him.

"Then how . . . ?"

"Did I get this way?" Jodi said. "I gave up part of myself to make the music live. All that's left of me now is a Small."

"But . . . that is, can you . . . ?"

She shook her head. "I can't change back. It's not like when the Widow shrank me down. She kept that other part of me in her cloak. But I've given it away."

"To the music," Taupin said.

Jodi smiled. "To the music," she agreed.

"But what will we *do* with you?" Denzil asked.

"Take me home, I hope. Otherwise I'll have a very long walk ahead of me."

Ollie put a paw tentatively out towards her and she gave it a playful whack.

"But don't you dare think of exhibiting me at some scientific meeting," she warned.

"Or worse," Taupin added with a grin, "a circus."

Jodi proved her new maturity by sticking her tongue out at him.

"We can't tell people," she said. "Not about me—just about the stone. Everyone should come and listen to the music in the stone."

"But your aunt," Denzil began.

"Oh, we can tell *some* people, of course," she allowed. "We'll just have to be careful as to who."

Denzil could only shake his head.

"Just think how much I can help you with your experiments now," Jodi said. "Or I can go traveling about in Taupin's pocket. There's hundreds of things I can do."

"You're daft, you," Denzil said as they set off back across the moor towards Bodbury. "How could you do such a thing to your-self?"

"Listen," Jodi said, pointing back towards the stone.

Denzil and Taupin paused and turned back, doing as she'd asked. They found that they could still hear the wind in the stone. And borne on it was an echo of the first music—just a whisper, it was true, just a hint, but enough. Enough for the wind to carry, away across the moor and perhaps, in time, across the world.

"Don't you think that's worth it?" Jodi asked.

Both Denzil and Taupin nodded.

"Just don't let them build a church around it or something," Jodi said. "It needs to be free to work its magic."

Some Say the Devil Is Dead

Gods that are dead are simply those that no longer speak to the science or the moral order of the day . . . every god that is dead can be conjured again to life.

—JOSEPH CAMPBELL, from *The Way of the Animal Powers*

Charlie Boyd cradled the receiver and turned to his son.

"That was himself," he said.

"The same man that rang us up at the farm this afternoon?" Dinny asked.

Charlie nodded. "Considering what he had to say to me, I wouldn't soon forget that voice."

"What did he say?"

Charlie told him.

"What does he mean by 'wrong answer,' do you think?" Dinny asked.

"That it's time for us to ring up the constable," Charlie said.

"But the note said—"

"I know, son. It's not a decision I care to make. But Janey's not here and it has to be made."

Dinny sighed and went over to the front door as his father called the police. He looked out at the night. Chapel Place was quiet, except for a cat that was sitting in the middle of the street, washing its face. The windows of the cottages that lined the narrow street cast squares of light out onto the pavement—there the soft yellow glow of a reading lamp, a little farther down the blue-white flickering of a telly.

To all intents and purposes, it was merely another peaceful night in Mousehole. Life went on. Except somewhere out in that same night a madman had taken their friend hostage.

Dinny shook his head. This was a situation one might expect in Northern Ireland or the Middle East. Not here, not in Mousehole.

His father joined him at the door after he'd made his call and laid a hand on his shoulder. He seemed about to speak, but then sighed as Dinny had. They just stood there, waiting. Trying not to think of the Gaffer or what they must tell Janey.

Dinny felt his heart sink as he saw a familiar set of headbeams come down the steep hill from Paul. Moments later, Janey had parked her Reliant Robin beside the Gaffer's yellow delivery wagon.

"I think our troubles are all over," Janey said as she got out of the little car.

She had a cheerful bounce to her step that faltered as she took in the Boyds' glum faces.

"What's wrong?" she said. "Gramps . . . ?"

"It's not good," Charlie said.

But before he could explain, the local constable arrived. The policeman stopped Charlie before he could get too far into his tale to call the assistant chief at the subdivision station in Penzance to send for more help. When he finished his call, he turned back to Charlie.

"All right," he said. "Let's take it from the beginning again, shall we?"

2.

The Gaffer had been in tight situations before—during the war, of course, and too many times out on the bay when gales drove the sea against the cliffs, and sometimes boats with them. He didn't consider himself a particularly brave man. He just did what needed doing, when it needed doing. When the Penlee Lifeboat, the *Solomon Browne*, went down in '81, attempting to save the crew of the *Union Star* that had run up on the Boscawen Cliffs, he'd been out there with the rest of the men of the village, not considering the danger nor whether he was brave or a coward, simply doing what needed to be done.

If he had ever been brave, it was carrying on after the deaths of

Addie and his son. That took more courage than he'd needed on either the beaches of Dunkirk or Mount's Bay. Janey had seen him through that time. And it was only by thinking of Janey that he could face his present straits.

For her sake, he must hold out. Because the longer his captor was busy with him, the longer it would be before he could turn his attention to her. By that time, he hoped that she would have had the good common sense to ring up the police.

They would protect her.

But until then, he needed to buy time and the coin was dear.

The reek of petrol was strong in the air. His pant leg was soaked with the fluid. His arms ached from the rough way that he'd been tied to the chair. By the light of the electric lamp that the American had brought with him, he could see the strange gleam in the man's pale eyes as he brought the lighter forward a second time.

They were not the eyes of a sane man. They were the eyes of a man who took pleasure in pain—another's pain. Pain that he inflicted upon them.

The Gaffer couldn't hold back a cry as the gas on his pant leg burst into flame. The gas ignited with a *whoof* of blue fire, the heat searing his eyebrows and hair as he whipped his head back. He pulled at his bonds, arching his back against the chair for leverage, but the ropes binding his arms and legs allowed him to do no more than feebly jerk against their tethering. There was a sudden cloud of black smoke and the stink of charred fabric and burnt hair. He could feel the heat on his leg. The skin blistering—

Bett threw a blanket onto his leg, suffocating the flames.

But the pain was still there.

And the promise of more to come lay in Bett's eyes.

With a sense of shame, the Gaffer realized that his bladder had emptied, soaking his pants. Sweat glistened on his brow. His shirt clung damply to his back. His fear sent a fever heat through his limbs, but it was also like ice, tightening in a cold grip on his chest.

He trembled uncontrollably from the hot and cold flashes.

He blinked sweat from his eyes, not wanting to look at his captor, but unable to look away.

And the fear continued to compound—not simply for himself. Mostly it was for Janey. For what this madman would do to her.

And he *would* go after her. No matter what happened here tonight, Bett would go after Janey next.

The Gaffer couldn't bear the thought of it. If he went after her too soon, before she'd had a chance to call the police . . .

"I tell you, we don't have it anymore," he tried once more.

Bett shrugged. "Maybe, maybe not. But you know where it is."

"It—"

But the Gaffer had to close his mouth as Bett upended a jerrican above his head and the gasoline poured all over him. It burned at his eyes. The fumes made him choke and his stomach twisted with nausea. He shivered with a sudden chill as a waft of cool air blew up against his wet clothes.

Bett tossed the empty jerrican aside and fetched another. He unscrewed its cap, then paused as the sound of a siren went screaming by, out on the Newlyn Road to Mousehole. He looked at the Gaffer and slowly shook his head.

"Someone's doing what they're not supposed to," he said.

"What—what do you mean?"

The Gaffer stumbled over his words, trying to hide the relief he felt. At least Janey would be safe.

"I said no cops," Bett said. "But people never listen, do they? It's just like you, old man. I'm giving you a choice, but do you hear me?"

"I . . ."

"You know what I think? I think you *want* to burn."

Please God, the Gaffer thought. If I have to die in such a way, then let me at least take this madman with me.

He pulled against his bonds again, but the knots held too firmly.

Bett laughed. He set the second jerrican down.

"I think you're juiced up enough for what I've got in mind," he said.

He stepped over to where the Gaffer struggled helplessly in his bonds.

"How long do you think you'll last? Will the pain get you first—maybe make your old ticker kick out? Or do you think it'll be from sucking those flames into your lungs?"

He took the lighter out of his pocket.

"Only one thing's going to save you and that pretty little granddaughter of yours," he said. "You've got to tell me—"

There was a sudden boom. The Gaffer flinched, closing his eyes to the roar of the gas igniting.

But there was no increase in his pain.

No heat.

He opened his eyes to see that the lighter had fallen from Bett's hand. Bett himself was lying in the loose stones, clutching his leg. Blood seeped out from between his fingers. He was looking up at the top of the ladder that leaned against the stone wall of the silo.

"Y-you . . ." Bett said through clenched teeth.

The Gaffer followed Bett's gaze with his own. The poor light cast by the electric lamp made it difficult for him to identify the man standing up there. The stranger was a big man, pale-skinned and wild-haired. A rude, bloodied bandage was wrapped around one shoulder, the arm held in close to his chest, the hand tucked into his belt. The other held a gun.

"You're . . . dead," Bett said.

Awkwardly, the man started down the ladder. He came down, facing outward, leaning back against the wood frame. The gun centered on Bett, but wavering.

It was Davie Rowe, the Gaffer realized as the man came farther down into the light. He appeared to be on his last legs. What had Bett said about his being dea—

Bett reached into his pocket and Davie fired again. Bett howled as the bullet tore into his other leg.

The shot's report boomed and echoed, louder still now that Davie had descended deeper into the silo's confines.

"Followed . . . you . . ." Davie said to Bett. "You're in my . . . head . . . can't get you . . . out. . . ."

His speech was slurred and it was obvious to the Gaffer that he was in a great deal of pain. Davie winced as he made it down the last few rungs, then leaned weakly against the ladder for support once he reached the bottom. He turned slowly to the Gaffer.

"I . . . I'll have you . . . free in . . . in no time . . . Mr. . . . Litt—"

He shouldn't have looked away.

The sound of the gunshot was like a thunderclap.

The bullet hit Davie high in the chest and smashed him back against the ladder. A second shot spun him away from its support, but though he lurched, he didn't fall.

Bett had pulled his own revolver from his pocket. His features were twisted with pain, his eyes livid with anger, mad lights dancing in their pale depths. He fired a third time.

"Die, damn you!" he cried.

He lay on the ground, propped up on an elbow. Both legs were useless, blood pumping from their wounds to spread in a widening dark stain over his pants. His third shot took Davie straight in the chest, but still the man didn't fall.

"Why won't you die?" Bett screamed.

"C-can't . . ." Davie mumbled.

His chest was a ruin. Blood seeped from the corners of his mouth where he'd bitten down on his tongue. He staggered one step, another, moving towards Bett, the gun raising slowly in his hands. The Gaffer couldn't understand how Davie could still be on his feet, little say moving, but mobile he was. Before Bett could fire a fourth time, Davie's gun bucked in his hand. A hole appeared beside Bett's nose where the bullet went in and then the back of his head exploded outward.

Davie simply stared at him, swaying there on his feet.

"E-every . . . dog . . ." he said, choking on blood as he tried to shape the words. "Has his . . ."

He emptied his weapon into the body. The corpse twitched as each bullet struck, but it was only from the impact of the bullets. Bett had died from that shot in the head.

"My . . . day now . . ." Davie mumbled.

He continued to pull the trigger of his weapon, long after his ammunition was spent. The Gaffer's ears rang with painful echoes, but he could still hear the dry click of the gun's hammer until Davie finally dropped the weapon onto the loose stones.

He moved towards the Gaffer, fumbling a clasp knife from his pocket. He dropped to his knees when he reached the chair, his upper torso falling across the Gaffer's lap. Slowly his hand brought up the knife, but he didn't have the strength to cut the ropes. He coughed up blood. His body shook with violent tremors against the Gaffer's legs.

"Always . . . wanted . . ." he began.

And then he died.

It took the Gaffer a long time to move Davie's body from his lap. His every movement woke flares of pain in his burnt leg, but he put the pain aside as best he could. He pushed with his feet against the loose stone until the chair was finally shoved back far enough for the corpse's weight to do the rest of the work.

The Gaffer tipped the chair over then, wincing at the pain as his shoulder hit the stones. The seared nerve ends in his legs screamed. For long moments all the Gaffer could do was lie there, choking on the gas fumes. Then slowly he pushed the chair around, infinitesimal inch by inch until eventually his hand closed on the clasp knife. It was another age before he got it open, longer still to saw through the ropes.

When he was finally free, he didn't climb out of the silo. He crawled to where Davie Rowe lay and cradled the man's head on his unhurt leg, gently stroking the hair from Davie's brow.

"I'll tell them, my robin," he said. "Be sure, I'll tell them all you were a good man."

He was still holding the body when the police arrived.

3.

Peter Goninan was the only person to whom Janey told the whole story.

The days following that Sunday night were miserable. Janey and the others spent hour upon hour being questioned by the police—the local constables, the C.I.D., and even Scotland Yard. They were interviewed separately and had to repeat their stories over and over, ad nauseam. At one point, because he was unemployed, a foreigner, and the only suspect with a reasonable motive, the police were set to arrest Felix for Madden's murder, but a sergeant of the Devon and Cornwall Constabulary—a nephew of Chalkie's who knew Felix from when he'd stayed in Mousehole before—interceded on his behalf. They finally let Felix go and eventually left them all in peace. Madden's murder remained unsolved.

The Gaffer only had to spend a half day in the hospital—his burns, while painful, were mostly superficial. If Bett had waited only a few seconds more before dousing the fire . . . But none of them wanted to even think about that.

The threat against the Boyds' farm never fully materialized; nor did the one against Clare's job at the bookstore. Janey's tour was as mysteriously restored as it had been canceled, but she had it postponed. She could no more face a gig at that point than she could bear dealing with even one more of the crowd of Fleet Street vultures who descended on the village and pried into their lives with such obvious relish.

It was a week after the night of the murders when she, Felix, and Clare drove out to the Goninan farm. Janey still felt she needed some explanation as to exactly what had occurred and she could think of no one else to turn to.

As it was, Goninan was expecting them. A considerably less sulky Helen ushered them into the little cottage and, with Felix's help, saw about readying tea for them all.

"Was it real?" Janey asked when she finished relating what had happened by the Men-an-Tol.

"It depends on what you mean by real," Goninan replied.

"No, I'm serious. He just hypnotized us all—out there by the stone. Didn't he?"

Goninan smiled. "Aleister Crowley defined magic as 'the science and art of causing change to occur in conformity with the will.' "

A moment's silence followed as they all waited for him to expand upon his statement, but Goninan merely sipped at his tea.

"Are you saying it *did* happen?" Felix asked at last.

Goninan shook his head. "I wasn't there, so I can't tell you what did or didn't happen. All I can tell you is that Madden—like Crowley whom he so admired, and many others besides—*were* great magicians. They could work what we can only perceive of as miracles."

"And you . . . ?" Janey asked.

"I'm not a great magician."

"Why are they all evil?" Clare wanted to know.

"But they're not," Goninan said. "There are a great many magicians who have worked only for the good of the world and its people. Men such as Gurdjieff, whom we spoke of before, and Ouspensky. Rudolf Steiner . . . the Native American, Rolling Thunder . . . or Spyros Sathi, the Cypriot better known as Daskalos. They do only good work. They seek to lift mankind's spirit to a higher destiny. And they accept no reward for what they do."

Clare shook her head. "Those aren't magicians—they're philosophers."

"The best magicians are, for it's not the magic that draws them to their studies, but their need to understand the world and their own place in it. That is where they differ from men like Madden. Madden thought only of himself—worked only *for* himself. So his downfall, like that of so many other great magicians who have been led astray, was his egoism. He couldn't conceive of a normal man or woman being his peer, and for that reason underestimated those he thought of as 'sheep.' "

"It seems awfully tidy," Janey said, "the way everything worked out in the end."

"That's the beauty of magic," Goninan said. "It thrives on coin-

cidence and synchronicities. That's the way the world's subconscious—what Jung called the racial memory—tries to wake us from
our sleep. It teaches men like Madden that there is a harmonic balance, and it teaches the untutored—in this case, yourselves—that
there is more to life than the gloom most people feel boxes them in."

"But then why does it fade?" Janey wanted to know. "Why can't
we have real proof? I've got nothing—just little bits of memory and
mist, and I'm even losing them. Everything's starting to feel like it
was only a part of a dream. If magic's here to teach us something,
why does it fade?"

"It doesn't," Goninan said. "Your interest in it does. This is a
practical world we live in—or I should say, we have *made* it a practical world. It leaves little room for ancient wonders or magical phenomena. We're so busy with the practical day-to-day aspects of our
lives that we don't have time to pay attention to whatever else might
be around us as well.

"Yet if you immerse yourself in their study . . . The more time you
spend in that sort of an atmosphere and with such beliefs, the more
you yourself will become subject to unusual experiences and encoun-
ters. If you keep your distance, then the phenomena will do the same
and eventually fade.

"It will still exist—it just won't exist for you."

"It all sounds kind of . . . spacy," Janey said with an apologetic
smile.

Goninan laughed. "I suppose it does. To tell you the truth, in some
ways, magic is irrelevant. As are our concerns over life after death,
spiritualism . . . all that sort of thing. What is important is that we
utilize our potential as human beings—and we have *great* potential—
to the utmost of our abilities."

"To be awake," Janey said.

Goninan nodded. "And then you will discover—truly *comprehend*—that *everything* is connected. The past, the present, the future.
Ourselves as individuals, and the world in which we live. This life
and whatever lies beyond it when we leave it. There is no end to our
potential.

"The trouble is we tend to concentrate on what we don't have,
rather than on what we do. We must learn to recognize what we
already possess to its fullest potential."

"That sounds like Buddhism," Clare said.

Goninan smiled. "Everything is connected," he repeated. "I think it was Colin Wilson who pointed out that we accept the present moment as if it were complete in itself. But the present moment is always incomplete and the most basic achievement of our minds is in completing it. In making all the connections.

"If you don't want the magic to fade, then learn to wake up and stay awake."

"But *how* do you do that?" Janey asked.

Goninan swept a hand around his cluttered cottage, taking in the tangle of bookcases, stuffed birds, and display cases with the gesture.

"You might try watching birds," he said.

4.

They hadn't been back at the house on Duck Street for more than an hour before the doorbell rang. With everyone sitting about in the kitchen having the second tea of the afternoon—this one provided by the Gaffer, complete with thick clotted cream and homemade scones and blackberry jam—they took a quick vote as to who would answer the door and Janey lost. She was smiling good-humouredly as she opened the door, but scowled when she saw who was standing there on the stoop.

"You," she said.

Lena Grant nodded. "I don't expect a welcome," she said.

"That's good."

The new and improved Janey was having a hard time remaining civil, little say friendly. She wanted to slam the door in the woman's face, but she kept a rein on her temper. It wasn't easy.

"What do you want?" she asked.

"To apologize."

Janey couldn't help but laugh. The sound was harsh even to her own ears.

"There's nothing you can say to make up for what you've done," she said after a moment.

"I know."

That gave Janey pause. She gave Lena a long considering look. There was something subdued about the woman that didn't at all fit in with Janey's mental image of her.

"Then what do you want?" Her voice was softer now. Still not friendly, but the new and improved Janey was at least trying to listen.

"I told you, just to say I'm sorry. It's not enough to say I didn't know what I was doing. I did. I just didn't think about it. I'm going to change myself and I just wanted to . . . thank you, I suppose."

Janey blinked with surprise.

"Thank me?"

"You and Felix—for showing me how people *can* conduct their lives."

"You're the one who fixed things—aren't you?" Janey asked. "The tour, the Boyds' farm . . . ?"

Lena nodded. "When we woke up, really *woke up*—"

Janey heard Peter Goninan's voice in her mind.

Learn to wake up and stay awake.

"—to what Madden was doing, not just to us, but to everyone around him, and then what we in turn were doing to those around us. . . . Let's just say that Daddy and I are going to make sure that there's some changes."

"In the Order?" Janey asked.

Lena shook her head. "You can't change something like that—not from inside. It just sucks you in. We've left the Order. Now we're going to do what we can to discredit it and its influences."

"I don't envy you," Janey said.

She saw in Lena's eyes that she read a double meaning into that simple statement.

"Felix," Lena began. "He . . . would you apologize to him for me?"

Janey relented. She couldn't help herself.

"He doesn't know what you did," she said. "Just that you—you drugged him."

"Why didn't you tell him?"

"For his sake at first," Janey said. "And now . . . there's really no point to it, is there?"

"Who's at the door?" Felix called from inside.

Janey studied Lena for a long moment, then she sighed.

"You might as well come in," she said. "I can't pretend I'll be your friend, but if you want to say you're sorry to him . . ."

Lena shook her head. "I couldn't face him," she said. "I can hardly . . . face you."

She took a business card from her pocket and pressed it into Janey's hand.

"If I can ever help you," she said, "with *anything* at all, just call me."

She turned and walked away then, just as Felix came to join Janey at the door. Her step showed only a slight trace of a limp now.

"Janey . . ." he began, then he saw Lena's retreating figure. "Is that . . . ?"

"Lena Grant," Janey agreed.

Felix's eyes narrowed, but Janey just gave him a tug and steered him back inside.

"She came by to say she was sorry," she said.

"Sorry?" Felix said. "How can she expect us to believe that?"

"She didn't."

Janey looked at the business card again, then stuck it in the back pocket of her jeans.

"But I think she really meant it," she said as she closed the door.

Coda

All things are known, but most things are forgotten.
It takes a special magic to remember them.

—ROBERT HOLDSTOCK,
from *Lavondyss*

The road that will take us forward is also the road
that will take us inward.

—COLIN WILSON,
from *Beyond the Occult*

Absurd Good News

His playing, to me, seemed to typify the wild hills and moorland.

—BILL CHARLTON, founder of the Northumbrian Gathering,
referring to Billy Pigg

I **wonder** what happened to them after that," Jodi said as Denzil closed the book.

She was sitting on the windowsill, comfortably ensconced in a tiny beanbag chair that Denzil had made for her at the height of the sudden enthusiasm for miniature furniture that had taken hold of him in the first few weeks since the mouse-sized Jodi had come to live in his loft. His worktable was littered with more half-finished pieces, while all about the loft his handiwork made life easier for Jodi's diminutive size.

He'd taken a wooden crate and built a private bedroom for her that was now set on a lower shelf on one of the bookcases. A multitude of ladders provided her access to various tabletops and the windowsill and he was currently at work on an elevator device that would allow her to come and go from the loft at her pleasure, though he worried constantly under his breath about her being out on the streets alone. He was afraid of some normal-sized person stepping on her—not to mention Bodbury's all-too-many cats.

As it was, when she went outside now, it was in the pocket of one of the Tatters children, or with either Denzil or Taupin. Her days were full, filled with such excursions, or in helping Denzil with his work; she had the eye and size for the most painstakingly tiny craftsmanship—although not, much to Denzil's dismay, the proper enthusiasm. What she liked best was lolling about in the evenings and having Denzil read to her as he had done tonight.

The book they'd just finished was an old leather-bound volume that Taupin had found out on the moors near the Men-an-tol and subsequently presented to Denzil and Jodi since they were, as he put it, "the only ones he knew who would fully appreciate its preposterous conceits."

And then he had winked.

"I hope they lived happily ever after," Jodi said.

"Maybe some of them did."

"Taupin says that the stories go on forever, whether we're a part of them or not. They have their own lives. When we open a book, it freezes the tale—but only for so long as we're reading it."

Denzil hrumphed. He and the hedgerow philosopher continued to have their long—and to Jodi, pointless—arguments; only now they centered around the particulars and specifics of certain aspects of folkloric wonders and their properties rather than the reality of magic itself.

Two nights ago, which was the last time Taupin had been over, they'd gone on for hours about whether or not whiskey was an actual cure, or if calling it "the water of life" was merely symbolic of the altered state of mind into which the alcohol led the tippler.

"The pair of you are like two peas in one pod," Jodi told him. "I don't know which one's worse than the other."

"Watch it, you, or I'll put you in a jar."

Jodi smiled, then cocked her ear to the open window.

"Listen," she said. "There it is again. Can you hear it?"

"I hear something. . . ."

But what was vague for him was clear as crystal to her. The wind was bringing a strain of the first music down from the moorland near the Men-an-Tol. In its measures, lifting high above the rest of the ethereal instruments, was the lilting voice of a set of small pipes, humming like a bird's chorus against the bee-buzz of their drones.

"I wonder if Taupin managed to remember to take it to the stone yet," Jodi said.

Denzil knew just what she spoke of—she'd talked of little since they'd finished making the small tin brooch that was a perfect replica of the cover of the book that Taupin had found by the stone.

"Brengy does what he says he'll do," he admitted. Ollie was curled up on his lap, fast asleep. He scratched the little monkey between the ears. "He may forget for a week or two, but eventually he gets done everything he said he would."

"I wonder what she'll think when she gets it," Jodi said.

"Maybe she'll write a book to tell you," Denzil said.

Jodi smiled. "Maybe she'll write a tune, instead."

Outside the window, where the night lay thick on Bodbury's narrow streets, the wind continued to bring a fey music down from the hills and take it through the narrow streets of the town and out to sea. In its measures were the steps of an old dance—the whisper of a mystery, echoing and echoing, across the moors, across the sea, hill to hill and wave to wave, on into forever.

Contentment Is Wealth

I met you long ago, but you couldn't have known,
for you weren't there. Only your ghost.
The ghost that slid out of one of your books and met me. . . .

—JACK DANN, from *"Night Meetings"*

A year later Janey Little stood again on the moor by the Men-an-Tol, the small box in which she carried her Northumbrian pipes tucked under her arm. She often came out here, sometimes at night, sometimes during the day; sometimes with Felix, sometimes alone. She'd sit nearby the stone and play her whistle, trying to clear her mind, trying to remember. Tonight, on its first anniversary, she looked at the tolmen and regretted more than ever her inability to recall that night with the clarity and detail she tried to recapture every time she found herself here.

But it remained obscure. She could remember John Madden and all he had put them through. She could remember what her grandfather had told her about his ordeal with Michael Bett and poor Davie Rowe. But the magic and the music . . . Memories of them stayed vague and distant. Especially those of the music.

It was just like it had happened in the Dunthorn book—in *her* version of what lay between its boards.

No one remembered, not really. It had all taken on a dreamlike quality for them as the months went by and one by one the various aspects of the sheer *wonder* of what had taken place were forgotten. Except by her.

Sometimes she'd take out that photo of her grandmother and stare at the Small perched on the arm of her chair. It *was* a little man—she'd swear to that, and he was playing a fiddle—or at least it had been that night when they'd first come across it. But all too often these days it looked like just a smudge of light.

There was a session at the Boyds' farm tonight—in honour of her and Felix's return from a fall tour of California. Felix didn't play on stage yet—except for adding a bit of rhythm on the crowdy crawn towards the end of an evening. Mostly he worked the soundboard— and Janey knew she'd never sounded as good as with him on it— and played at the sessions afterward.

But he was getting closer. She could tell. If he didn't get up with his box this next tour they already had booked, then it'd be the one afterward. She could be patient—the new and improved Janey Little still holding firm to all her resolutions.

And he had played on almost every track of her third album—so much so that the only real argument they'd had this past year was in her wanting him to share the billing for the album, while he refused, saying that people would then expect him to be playing up there on stage with her on subsequent tours. He'd much rather just be listed in the credits with the other guest musicians, like Clare and Dinny and the other regulars of the sessions that had sat in on a tune or two. The new and improved Janey hadn't pushed him after he brought that up.

The album had done well—racking up pleasant sales both domestically and abroad, where they sold it off the stage in between sets and after the shows. They'd called it *The Little Country,* naturally enough. A reviewer in *Folk Roots* magazine opined that the title came from her surname, or from the "little country" that Cornwall might seem to some, but only those who had been involved with the Dunthorn book knew the real origin and they kept it a secret.

There had only been one other major change in Janey's life over the past year: her mother had begun to write to her. Janey had ignored the first letter, complete with its muddle of confused apologies—after all, what did she owe the woman? But the correspondence continued to arrive, once a month. There was never a reprimand for her not replying to them, hidden there in her mother's untidy script. They were merely gossipy letters, talking about the changes in her mother's life. How she'd moved from New York. How she'd finally become involved in repertory theatre in New England as she'd always wanted to. How she was poor, but finally happy. How she'd bought all of Janey's albums and was so very proud of her.

The close of each was a flourishing, "Your loving mother, Connie."

That afternoon Janey had finally sat down and written back. She sealed the envelope and took it up to the post office for a stamp just before tea. As she sent the letter off on its way, a weight that she hadn't been aware she was carrying slipped from her shoulders.

She'd felt a little light-headed and that was when she'd decided to come up to the Men-an-Tol tonight before the session.

By herself.

At moonrise.

With her pipes.

Kempy had been delirious to see her again, bounding about with great good enthusiasm. He lay now near the tolmen, tongue lolling, as he watched her fuss with her pipes. Opening their carrying box, she took them out and put them together, bellows attached to the air bag by one tube, chanter by another. But before she blew them up, she lay them down on the lid of their case and, giving Kempy a small embarrassed smile, walked over to the stone.

The moon was just rising.

She looked about the dark moor. Satisfied that there was no one watching her except for the border collie who was half mad himself anyway, she squeezed through the hole in the stone. Walking around, she went through again. And again. Nine times, all told.

She wasn't trying to find her own way into that otherworld. She just wanted to *see* it. To know that it was real.

But the mist never rose from the surrounding moorland. There was no flare of light.

No music.

Just the quiet of the night. The stars glimmering high above in a sky that was surprisingly clear for this time of night. The moon steadily rising.

She had to laugh at herself for even trying. Standing on the far side of the Men-an-Tol after her ninth passage through its rounded hole, she brushed the stone dust from her jacket.

That was desperation for you, she thought.

She was disappointed with her failure, but not surprised by it. After all, if the magic could be so simply called up, why then anybody could simply waltz up to the stone and prove that there was such a thing. And as Peter Goninan had told her, the magic was more secret than that.

It was—

She paused as her fingers touched an unfamiliar object pinned to her jacket. Fumbling in her pocket, she took out the torch that she'd brought from the car with her and shone its light onto her chest.

There was a brooch pinned to the fabric that hadn't been there when she'd left the house earlier this evening. She touched it with wondering fingers. It seemed to be made of heavy tin—like the hefty little souvenir cottages and lighthouses that used to be on sale in Penzance and the village two summers ago. It was the shape of a book and the design of its cover . . .

She traced the words of its title with a finger, wonder growing in her mind.

The Little Country.

An eerie warmth spread through her. Looking at the stone, she half imagined she saw a man sitting there on the top of the Men-an-Tol, swinging his legs so that his heels tapped against the stone. And she recognized him. William Dunthorn. Not as she knew him from her grandfather's old photos, but the way he'd look if he'd lived to this day. Smiling at her, mysteries brimming in his penetrating gaze.

She blinked, and the image was gone—but not the warmth. Nor the memory of him sitting there on the stone.

And not the brooch.

She flicked off the torch and picked up her pipes. She buckled on the bellows and arranged the small drones so that they lay across her left forearm. Then she blew up the air bag with a squeezing motion of her elbow. The drones hummed their quiet buzz. Inspired, she woke a new tune from the chanter, composed on the spot. For its title, she took that feeling of two Billys' worth of Bully that was singing through her veins, following the deep rhythm of her heartbeat—

Dhumm-dum. Dhumm-dum.

—that seemed to echo in the ground underfoot and off, away, across the moor.

She felt as dizzy as though she'd just received some absurd good news and needed to shout it out to the world in a tune.

A simple bit of a jig that was an echo of the first music. In its measures were the steps of an old dance—the whisper of a mystery, echoing and echoing, across the moors, across the sea, hill to hill and wave to wave, on into forever.

• • •

The session at the Boyds' that night was a rousing success, so much so that friends of theirs claimed to have heard the music spilling out of the Boyds' kitchen from as far away as St. Ives and Land's End.

But Janey knew what music it was that they'd really heard.

It had been an echo of the first music, she had explained to Felix and Clare the next day.

The music of the Little Country that every person had hidden away inside them.

Appendix I:
A Selection of
Janey Little's Tunes

The following tunes were written on the fiddle, but have proved admirably suitable for a wide variety of instruments. All tunes are copyright © 1991 by Charles de Lint; all rights reserved.

ABSURD GOOD NEWS

ALL OF A MONDAY NIGHT

BILLY'S OWN JIG

FELIX GAVIN'S REEL

THE GAFFER'S MOUZEL

THE GIRLS OF EDMONTON

HER TWO CHAIRS

JOHN WOOD'S MAZURKA

THE MEIKLEJOHN JIG

THE MEN-AN-TOL WALTZ

THE NEW TASSELED SHOES

THE NINE BLIND HARPERS

SHE'S TOO FAST FOR ME

STARGAZY PIE

THE STONESS BARN

THE TINKER'S BLACK KETTLE

Appendix II:
A Brief Glossary of
Unfamiliar Terms